STATE OF GRACE

Bob Benner

A Novel By

BOB BENNER

First Edition

Additional copies available from BobBennerBooks.com

A few points of note:

The government of Papua New Guinea (PNG) fought a civil war with the Bougainville Revolutionary Army (BRA) from 1988-1998. There were more than 10,000 fatalities in that period, and 30,000 casualties. There was a cease fire in place when I visited, but it was a sad and unstable business.

Fr. Eduardo Armenta arranged for my lodging in Port Moresby at the Franciscan Seminary. He provided a commentary on Moresby, and a guided tour, courtesy of one very gentle seminarian, Francis, who is called Vilapaia in his native home. Francis did the translations that occur in this work. I am very grateful to Brother Francis who is, by now, an ordained priest serving the people of PNG.

The cease fire is tenuous, but still exists according to Fr. Hendry Saris of Buka Island. I have used Fr. Saris in this work, with permission, setting him in his parish and surroundings, but inserting my fictional character into his life for a few brief days. Fr. Hendry visited my home during the Thanksgiving weekend 2001 and provided much information about his mission place in the world. One year later he sent me the most amazingly detailed map of Bougainville, which he rolled up in a piece of PVC pipe and sealed at both ends. Without his help I would never have been able to write this work in detail.

There are many "out there" on station, who serve their fellow man with quiet determination, despite the difficult conditions that exist, and do it with a serenity that defies explanation. Their confidence and peace of mind can only come from the God they love and serve. It was a privilege for me to meet and spend time with each one:

Thanks to Fr. Joseph Klouwen who encouraged me to come visit Honiara, Guadalcanal. Fr. Joe gave me many rides between the city and his provincial house at Tanagai. Tanagai was "no man's land" in the war of 2000. The civil war was a coup d'etat orchestrated by the Malaitans, who decided to rearrange the government and melt the government buildings in the process. Tanagai is a suburb of Honiara, the capitol. It is hundred yards of beautiful ocean frontage, facing out across Iron Bottom Sound, from which Savo Island can be seen in the distance.

Fr. Norman Arkwright is the pastor of St. Marys Church in Tanagai. Norman took me into the city and showed me the Memorial, which was appropriately dedicated in 1992 – the Fiftieth Anniversary of the Battle for Guadalcanal. It is one of the more spectacular memorials of the 2nd World War, and sits high up overlooking Bloody Ridge, Henderson Field, and other terrible places in history. It also provides a fantastic view of the Sound, with bronze depictions of the many land and sea actions that occurred there in mid to late 1942. Father also arranged for me to fly from Guadalcanal to Vangunu, catch a canoe ride up to New Georgia, and meet some of the men described in that part of the story.

Fr. David Galvin, an Irishman from Boston, also is stationed on Makira, once known as San Cristobal. Fr. David came to visit us in St. Louis in 2003, and Patty and I had the opportunity to introduce him to many of our friends one evening. David has been helpful and encouraging with my research on Fr. Albert Lebel, who is one of the main characters in *Kennedy & Lebel*, not yet finished.

I am indebted to Frank Iputu, Scotty Naisi, Mason Liangua, and especially Peter Lolo for their help in getting me around in the islands by canoe – and for their hospitality, friendship, wonderful stories, and for food and lodging in a strange and beautiful part of the world.

Thomas Eagleton is the former United States Senator from Missouri. I do not know the man, although I voted for him many times. He is reputed to be *a veri good man*. He is a well known St. Louisan.

Nancy Kassabaum visited the islands, according to Peter Lolo.

Hoyt Wilhelm introduced me to Beachnut tobacco and he really did teach me to throw a knuckleball in 1959.

I am indebted to my unpaid readers and mostly *unwilling* critics:

Mary Cockerell
Cissy Hacking
Sharon Neuner
Joan Zell

And to Patty, a *most willing critic:* I gave her the manuscript on Valentines Day last, put it in a gaudy red bag with red rope handles, and included two red-ink pens. She called to say she was out of ink shortly after. At the time I was away in Gulf Shores working on another book. Patty Benner is the Katherines & Maggies of my life. I have loved only once, but I have loved extravagantly.

Ye Old Standard Disclaimer

When I was a little boy I had an imaginary friend. Whenever I went to see my grandmother she would ask me to tell her a story about him and I would drift off on a wild tale about another 7 year old, making it as good as I could and when I was done she would say, "Oh boy, that was a real whopper."

Most of us like to tell a story, and some of us like to embellish a little in the telling. I guess e*mbellishing* is a polite word for lying. I'll admit I can embellish with the best. Writing is another way of *embellishing;* telling a "good" story, telling an outrageous tale, going off on a tangent, and not having to worry about getting caught in a lie. Maybe it's legalized lying? Matter of fact, you have to worry more about being accused of telling the truth! This book is a work of fiction set in my home town and some of the places I've visited. It draws on my hobbies, the experiences of my past, trips taken to do research, and the simple process of living, to create a story about the fictional people who people this work. It is a *whopper* of nearly 600 pages…*and it is all a big lie.* I made it up.

Recently I saw two specials on Television. The subjects were Charles Dickens and Rod Serling – about how both borrowed from their times and from the culture they inhabited. Their stories were based on people they had known, or lived amidst, how they had copied their manners and used them as a basis for the characters of their fiction. I don't know how else you could possibly write, or what you could write unless you fictionalized and characterized the people that people your life.

I like to write. I wrote my first novel thirty years ago…in long hand. I wrote some short stories about the same time, some of which I published. There was no money in writing and I had a family to feed, but I enjoyed it so much I decided to write this novel, save it, and read it later just to hear how it sounded. Somehow, amidst much challenge and confusion, it has become a published work. Amazing! It was such a "blue sky" idea in January of 2001.

Hemingway maintained, *you can leave it out if you know it, but if you leave it out and you don't know it, the reader will know you don't know it.* With this in mind, I went out and visited the people and places in this book, got first hand experience with both. Many of the people I met in the islands appear in this book, and I want to thank them. They made it possible for me to get deep into the island culture of Vangunu and New Georgia, where I slept under a thatched roof and listened to the plants brush the walls of the hut, and smelled the heavenly odor of frangipani. I looked at the starlit sky below the equator each night, got caught in the terrifying surf of the Solomon Sea, and experienced the tragic poverty of Papua New Guinea.

I also prayed with the Franciscans and the Marists in Port Moresby and on Guadalcanal. It was an experience and an inspiration. I still get letters from Michi and Seghe, and emails from Buka and Guadalcanal, Makira, Lae and Madang, where today is tomorrow. I also prayed with the Benedictines of

St. Marys Abbey, and the brothers keep me informed about the goings on up in Richardton, North Dakota.

I had a partner once, like the *Ned* in my book. He also *is a veri good man,* and a very big one. He can coin a phrase, and often a wonderfully appropriate metaphor. We spent a lot of time eating lunch together over the years too. Like partners the world over, we had to overcome a lot of adversity. But there all similarity with *Ned Grant* ends. My partner is well read, literate, articulate, and also happily married, has been for nearly fifty years. He's a faithful and wonderfully loyal man. I couldn't have done any better and I'm glad I shared his friendship all the years we were in business.

This work has been copy-edited only, checked for mistakes in punctuation and spelling. What it really lacks is criticism. I don't have an editor. Nobody is interested in editing an unpublished author, so it has not been properly edited for content, chronology, etc. Any mistakes are my own, and I apologize for them in advance.

And, by the way, I want to thank you, for taking the time to read this book!

Bob Benner,
October 9, 2004
Lafleche, Saskatchewan

In memoriam:

Lt. John W. Grutsch, Jr.
Jim Anthony
Gene Pisani
Johnny Benner
Tom Hattrich

In this life, if we are lucky, we're touched by others who make living worthwhile, who make it special. I've been blessed to know some fine people who have taught me simple lessons, or who have simply added to the quality of my life, some of them in an immeasurable way. This book is dedicated to their memory, and they are listed above in the order in which they left.

Hellroaring

Coming over the ledge, Bakewell hit a flat spot and stopped behind a boulder, bent, hands on knees, gulping for oxygen, mouth open wide. He tried not to gasp, tried not to make any breathing sound. He waited, exhausted, sucked the thin air through his throat like an antelope at full gallop. His pulse pounding, he fingered his carotid artery and counted out of habit. *Twenty in ten seconds: a hundred and twenty. Not bad.* It had been much higher, especially at this altitude. He moved up against the boulder, pulled his hat off and, pressing his face to weathered rock, slowly looked around and up.

There, knew it. He wanted to shout. It was only the second time he'd seen him this close. He appeared older each time Bakewell got a closer look, but he wasn't showing any sign of strain in the altitude. The old man was still upwind, the ground between too exposed. He turned, absently looking over his shoulder back down the steep slope. Bakewell wondered if he knew he was being pursued. *No, not likely. You'd be long gone by now.* He was glad the old man seemed indifferent. There was no way to close the gap until he moved on over the top. Bakewell didn't want to chance trying to look through the glasses with the sun so low. He pulled back, giving up his field of view reluctantly, looked across at the talus field instead. It sloped up the hill to the north, paralleling the trail the old man had chosen. The talus was huge, man-sized. Bakewell knew he couldn't traverse it in a flanking move. He waited half an hour getting his pulse under control; gradually accumulating the blessed oxygen he needed, recovering one more time. When his breathing returned to normal he caught the smell of conifers again. He loved the clean smell of the conifers, always associated their smell with wilderness, with adventure, even danger. He peeked around the boulder several times not wanting to break contact. The old man finally looked back down toward him, his attitude cautious still, a habit of a lifetime. He turned and went up over the top and was gone.

Damn, I want to come on after you, just can't risk it. Bakewell knew if he guessed wrong and exposed himself it would be over. The old man would nail him. He had to wait. He came out from behind the boulder and marked the spot where the old man had stood in order to step it off later, guessed it was about 175 yards, sat on a flat chunk of talus the size of an end table and dropped his backpack, pulling his water bottle from an open sleeve. It was a syrup bottle: Aunt Jemima. He squeezed some into his mouth and thought about the uphill shot. *Should have killed him from right here. It was no shot at all.* He leaned back and sprayed water into his mouth again, pulled a small nasal sprayer from his breast pocket, pointed it upward and squeezed. A cloud of blue chalk dust went up and quickly dissipated down the hill. *Still got the wind.* He shouldered his pack, picked up the rifle and started up the hill, counting his steps as he went. When he got to the spot where the old man had stopped he was already out of breath: *a hundred and sixty seven yards.* He was pleased with his guess. *Only off 5 percent!* He had become very good at the guessing, the estimating of distances.

He bent down and looked at the old man's tracks, happy he recognized them as the ones he'd seen yesterday morning. He went on up, bending low as he neared the top, sank to his knees and crawled the last twenty feet. One knee of his corduroys was worn through and his Duofolds showed. The long underwear was beginning to tear through the knee also. At the top he found a place where he could crawl between two rocks. Pulling off the western hat again, he eased through and looked anxiously over the ridge. The opposite side dropped off steeply. His glasses tended to fog when his body heat came up from the neck of his open shirt. He stared down the slope, waiting for it to come into focus, knowing any movement would draw his attention. After a minute, he pulled the binoculars from his vest and brought the 7X lenses up. A single weathered juniper at the bottom caught his attention and, when he brought it into focus he saw movement just above it. The old man looked older through the glasses, especially from behind. He was moving again. He lacked the coordination he'd had in his youth and appeared to limp slightly before he broke into another run.

Damn! Where does he get it? It was a short burst. He slowed to a trot within thirty yards, picking his way carefully as he went over the next rise. Beyond the rise, Montana appeared in the distance: vast, enormous. Bakewell had flown the area in a Super Cub years before. It was breathtaking, hugely beautiful to an aviator, but overwhelming for a foot soldier. He'd been up in these same rocks many times over the years, but never above the tree line so long, never so low on oxygen for so long. He tried to do everything with minimal motion and effort. He waited again, remembering to pass the time. If his movements were minimal, his thinking was in shorthand. He tried to keep everything lean, hoping it would preserve energy, preserve oxygen. *Must be Thursday...left the trail Sunday evening, camped next to Hellroaring Creek. I've only got two days food at the tent...enough with me to last another day...running out of time.*

Chalking wind again, he decided to make one final burst to close the gap; daylight wasted quickly late in the afternoon. He removed the noisy down vest, loaded up again and started down the hill as fast as he dared on legs rubbery from exertion. It was a gamble he had to take. He tried not to think what would happen if he fell. At the bottom, Bakewell dropped his pack and started to run in earnest, a controlled, methodical pace that wasn't as tricky on the flatter ground. He went up the other side, jumping small boulders on the way. He was on the top of a ridge mostly, on the lee side, hopefully opposite the old man; he could see far ahead. He alternated after a hundred yards, running in spurts then walking to get some extra oxygen into his blood before running again. He was about done; this would have to be the day, there would be no other chance after today. The sense of urgency was compelling, despite his exhaustion. It took another thirty minutes before he located him. This time he really *had* closed the gap; better still, the wind had quieted as it usually did late in the day. There was only a zephyr across his sweat soaked neck when he stopped behind another rock and watched. He was up there above again, *always above.* Bakewell's pulse was racing. He didn't need to check it with his finger, could hear it coming up out of his throat, making a popping sound. He counted thirty pops in ten seconds. *One eighty!* He was in trouble. He couldn't go much farther. He bent over, steadying himself against the little rifle, so gassed he couldn't close his mouth to swallow; saliva dripped to the ground as he sucked for oxygen. He was desperate for oxygen.

He forced himself to wait another five minutes to get control. *Late now, he's got to be down; got to be down, got to stop this time.* He opened the bolt and chambered a round, ninety-five grains in the hollow-pointed bullet protruding from the case as it slid into the barrel. He knew the ballistic coefficient, knew the weight, how many grains of powder were inside, even the type of primer. He'd put it together himself, hundreds just like it, knew the trajectory over level ground, the effect gravity had on it all the way out to 300 yards.

One shot, no seconds. Be less than forty yards...if he's where he's supposed to be. He's camped for the night. Slow down. Go slow...can't go too slow now...he's not going to move again, not this evening. Bakewell kept the refrain going as he made his way around the hillside in a final flanking move.

As he came up the backside, the east side of the knoll, he found the hillside covered with yellowing grass. It was damp, perfect for stalking, so quiet, the wind so light, he could hear the grass up ahead brushing against the rocks. Twenty yards from the top he had to get down and crawl. It was wetter than he expected. He didn't want to get wet this late in the day. He knew he would be spending the night up high, away from the warmth of his bag and the tent. *Must have been a shower up here...day's been too warm for the ground to be wet.* He kept up a continuous mental chatter to calm his nerves, to focus, to stay sharp. His pulse rate was still rolling, but had settled down enough that he could have closed his mouth and breathed through his nose. He removed the hat, pushing it away in the tall grass, crawled on slowly, making the final ascent inches at a time. He looked over the top.

The old man was right where he was supposed to be, not more than ten yards from the last fix, but he'd settled between the boulders facing down hill. *Finally, a break.* Normally he would watch the terrain above and leave his sense of smell to determine what might threaten below. The only shot was a headshot from above and behind. Bakewell pulled the rifle up, trying not to rub it against anything. It took forever. When he placed it against his shoulder, he reached over the top of the bolt and turned the power down to 2X and pressed the stock to his cheek. *Don't rush...not after all this... Quiet...Breathe slow...* He slipped the safety forward, made a sniffing noise, long and slow, just loud enough for the old man to hear. He came off the ground startled, Bakewell knew he would, looking back up the hill; his big eyes bulging with the effort. Bakewell put the bullet behind his right shoulder. The noise shattered the quiet and reverberated down the hill and across the valley. The old ram bolted down the hill, his footfalls almost in sync with the reverberations before disappearing through the cascading echoes down toward the hillside below.

Bakewell scrambled to his feet, trying to watch him go, but the boulder-strewn hillside made it impossible. The shot had charged the air, stirred everything, including a breeze that came across the mountaintop. He was too pumped to notice the chilling effect the breeze had on his wet clothes, but the wind made him think of the gear he'd left behind. He cleared the bolt and left the rifle to mark the place and started back at a steady jog. He felt like he could run all night. It only took ten minutes going down hill to retrace his route and gather his pack and vest where he'd left them. He started back at a fast walk. He was wet, but warm from exertion. As he crested the hill where the kill had taken place and recovered his rifle, he realized he was at one of the highest points in the range. He didn't think he had ever been so high, physically or mentally, for so long. The adrenaline was still coursing. The wind came on again and this time he felt its chilling effect on wet pants and the sweat soaked shirt. He put the vest back on and slowly picked his way down the rock-strewn slope, aware of the danger of moving down hill on tired legs in such demanding country. He was flushed with excitement, but distrusted the strength remaining in his legs.

The old man was a hundred yards down the hill, sprawled on his right side, head below his body. The exit wound was small, through the left side of his chest. The speed of the bullet had caused it to pass through with little expansion, but there would be massive damage in the lungs and probably the heart if he had called his shot. The last memory he had of the old ram as he came off the ground was the rheumy look in his eye and the flaccid musculature along his shoulder and flank. He guessed he was in his last year – probably the reason he was alone. He passed his gaze over the entire body, noticing the scars on his flank and leg front and the worn hooves. Finally, he looked at the great horn. He was full curl and then some, with tips broomed back behind his eyes to keep his peripheral vision. The tips of his immense horns were nicked and flaking. He tried to count the rings. *Thirteen maybe*? It was hard to tell with the first and last rings.

He went down on one knee and spoke reverently to the dead animal. "I know I'm rationalizing, but you would have died up here in another year. I took you at the right time." He looked out across the huge valley and smelled the conifers, an updraft from below bringing their exhilarating odor. He took a long deep breath. It was a fantastic smell in a place too fantastic to describe. He looked down at the old giant. "You will have your place in my home. People who understand these things will marvel at your scarred head and horns." He ran his hand over the warm, rough coat. "No one will ever hang anything on you as long as I'm alive, and you will be esteemed by those who know us both." He tried to raise the huge head, but was only able to move it sideways with one hand. "I want you to understand how honored I am to be here and to have taken you, especially so high and so close."

It had been 80 degrees and dry under a cloudless blue sky when he started the race across the Absarokas; now the zipper-pull thermometer attached to his vest was dropping past fifty as the sun fell off the continent. He shivered as he placed his gear on the ground next to the ram and pulled the little knife from its sheath. Pausing before the butchering started, he looked around and found a rock a short distance away, placed his camera at a slight angle on the rock, tried to sight through it, struggling with the hated bifocals. When he was satisfied with the angle, he went back to the ram and struggled to move him around for the pose. He closed his jaw, careful to make sure there was no tongue dangling and no blood. When all was ready, he set the timer on the old camera, went back and sat next to the ram and waited for the shutter to snap.

The incision started at the base of the chest, up behind the shoulders to the top of the withers. Bakewell made another from the back of his head below the crown, down to the withers. He put his leather gloves on and began to pull on the thick hide, separating it from a heavy coat of white fat that clung to the muscled neck, until the entire cape was gathered behind the ears and the base of the throat. He cut the ram's head reluctantly from his torso with his knife and a small folding saw and was amazed by the weight when it fell free. He wrapped the caped head tightly with fishing line and bound it to the empty frame of his pack. Then he eviscerated the animal, caped and quartered it, working fast in the dying light. While he worked a gloomy overcast settled in around them, so low he felt like he could reach out and touch it. By the time he finished, it was dark. He was afraid it might rain.

They were far above the timberline, not even a camp robber for company. Bakewell missed the camp robbers, their brazen antics, plucky disposition, their opportunistic behavior, but there was nothing for them this high: no seeds, no leftovers. The larger predators, making a living down below, wouldn't come so far up to find a meal either. He made provisions for a camp in the rocks next to the dead animal. In a day or two the gut pile would attract lots of attention but not the first night.

There was a small alluvial, fanning out below the site that pointed down toward the timber. He walked down a quarter of a mile to find wood large enough to burn. After hauling it back up the hill, he cleared a place in the rocks and built a small fire. He needed more wood for the long night ahead, but was too tired to make another trip. There was no starlight. It was very dark. It would be a cold, lonely vigil, and a long one. After the fire was going well, the base full of glowing embers, he cut a piece of back strap and put it on a small stick, which broke as soon as he lifted it over the fire. He was tired, not thinking clearly, the flimsy stick a good indicator. He had learned to watch for the little signs, indications of fatigue that forewarned, cautioned him his mind was unreliable. He took two thin, flat rocks, dusted them off and put them in the middle of the fire and waited for them to heat in the coals. When the flame was gone he placed the meat on one rock and covered it with the other, letting it roast in the small fire, turning it occasionally with the folding saw, not wanting to expose his knife to the heat. The knife was a small drop-point. His rifle was small caliber. Everything he brought into the high country was small with the exception of his camera. He didn't trust the newer ones and this one had served him for thirty years.

He had a pair of down booties in his pack and one down mitten, the other having disappeared years ago. He removed his boots and placed them between his legs then removed his sweat soaked socks, laying them over a rock near the fire. He rubbed his feet vigorously until they were dry and coming to life again then put his feet in the booties, hoping they would warm. He took his down coat, taped tightly inside the pack, unwrapped it, placed it over his shoulders and draped a small space blanket over them both, covered his head with an old woolen watch cap, folded the down vest and put it under his butt, wondering how long it would hold the heat. He surveyed the scene around and below. There was a time once when he would have felt he was in a bad predicament. Now he was satisfied: knew he had prepared for this night, had been preparing for it for years. He could smell the meat about the time it began to sizzle and waited just a little longer before he cut it into strips, holding it against the rock with the saw. He had learned to eat wild game as rare as he ate good beef. In his haste to eat, he burnt his mouth and laughed at his folly, and at his amazing good fortune, and the daunting prospect of spending a night on the mountain if the weather turned bad. The weather worries were nagging, but offset by preparation, tempered by confidence; he would get through. *Just have to grit it out, not mind the cold too much.* His mood alternated between exhilaration and semi-dread. Everybody liked to be warm, especially at night; he wouldn't be warm again until tomorrow, a long time off: *hunting and comfort, exhilaration and fear, fantastic vistas and hard rocky surfaces, wildlife and weather: the dichotomies of an outdoorsman.* He was totally exhausted.

About ten, his luck changed; the sky cleared and filled with more stars than he ever remember seeing before. It was a special time, a time of tranquil immersion, and he got caught up in the heavenly show above. *It's easy to have faith in God in a place like this.* He wanted to think the ram's spirit was there to experience it too. *You've done this before haven't you, old man? A spectacular night like this is just another night on top of the world for an old boss like you. Don't mind me; I'll appreciate it for both of us.*

Bakewell looked at his hands, barely visible in the starlight, showing abuse. They had been working hard in the harsh environment. He put his only mitten on one and tucked the other inside his shirt. It was getting cold; promised to be a miserable night. After the wood ran out an isolation he hadn't felt in years settled around him. He began to pray, prayed for a long time: for his children; for Brenny, gone to Viet Nam; for his parents; and for Katherine, especially for Katherine. She had died two years before, almost to the day. The hunt was the first he had taken since her death. The pain wasn't as sharp after the first six months, those terrible months of depression when he stopped functioning. Eventually he began again; it got better, but the pain never would go away. Sometimes he even welcomed it, welcomed the opportunity to share with her again, holding one of her photographs, wondering. Bakewell talked to Katherine often; it had become a way of life.

***

I never stopped worrying about losing you, not in all the early years, never could I let go of the fear. It was always there, under the surface, only a moment away when you were just a young bride, a beautiful girl with a golden tan, sun streaks in your long hair; not once could I stop worrying, let go of the fear. When you became a young mother, eyes radiant with happiness, breasts still wet from nursing my little boys, when they stopped suckling, tiny mouths open, asleep in your arms...I remember you giving them to me, trusting me with your treasure, our treasure; the smell of them and of you still so sweet; the pride of having them, having you, as I watched you cross the room – wondering what my life would be like, our lives would be like, without you.

I used to watch you in the driveway, up-righting Tyke Bikes, guiding baby hands to handle-bars, stretching short legs to peddles on Big Wheels, preventing crashes, intervening between maniacal little drivers – wild-eyed and frenetic – with your long lovely legs; calves flexing, thighs rippling, so lovely, so muscled, and always sun-tanned.

Sleigh riding in the park, pulling cherry little noses up hill after hill, guiding them down subtly, to delightful shouts of joy, their faces and yours blissful, voices filled with elation, rising and falling over bump after bump. So ebullient, so happy, so filled with delight; you were our source of happiness. You made us so happy...the thought of losing you made my mind cringe with fear, my soul with horror and fright.

You were our mommy, so amazing, so skilled and so competent; making things work; so responsible, so reliable, so trustworthy – and we gave you all ours in return. You made life go according to God's will. How could we live without you? Where would we go? What would we do?

When they were grade-schoolers you volunteered for everything: room mother, helper, gym decorator, other-mother motivator, sign-painter, crossing guard. It made me wonder how they would get along without you too. I watched you as you watched our babies, growing, performing and singing, making drawings and costumes. You were always such a big subject, overwhelming us all. How I loved to take you in; to take you, us, for granted, convince myself you would outlive me, would always be there. Then would come that terrible, dreaded feeling, a longing, a yearning, painful, desperate; wondering what it would be like, my life, our life, without you. The thought made me weak, brought fear, nausea. It used to roll over me, a dark, disorienting, black wetness, penetrating me, deleting me.

When they finally grew up I lost my concern briefly, began to think you were like the rest of us; thought maybe you would endure. We began aging together, remember? You began to wrinkle, delicate little lines about your eyes and mouth; the backs of your hands started to freckle. You said sometimes your neck hurt when sleeping. I heard you protest little aches as you climbed the stairs in the evenings; just little things, but I'd not heard them before. You developed a heel spur that made you hobble to the bathroom mornings one summer. You got tennis elbow the year Nancy went off to college. I finally began to think of you as mortal, as normal. I let my guard down. I stopped worrying about you, about losing you, for just a little while. I lost my edge and then...

And then you were gone. And I wasn't ready for it, no longer prepared. We weren't prepared, none of us. After you were gone, I learned both Andy and Nancy had shared my fear. They always believed you were too good a mom, too good a person to be true. They said they worried, wondered if they would be able to keep you, feared they might lose you too.

That night on the deck, after you left us, after they took you away, before the wake, before people started coming, we were alone, had a quiet time and talked. We each admitted to the others we had loved you the most, loved you more than we loved each other. It made us feel guilty all of our lives. But we each saw something vulnerable in you: there was something about you, even though you were always the most capable, more capable, more competent, more responsible than the rest of us. It made us realize we had no cause for guilt. You were a special gift. We each got a part, some more than others. I guess I got the best part, although the children would argue that. I felt like I got your heart. I know you got mine. I think you took it with you. There's only an empty place here now – and it hurts. Sometimes it hurts so much I want to stop breathing. Sometimes I want you to make it stop beating.

I just let my guard down; I stopped worrying about you, and I am so sorry. I feel like I let you down, let us all down. I lost my edge. I didn't mean to. I always wanted to be ready, wanted to watch out, to keep on worrying, protecting, keep the vigil; fearing if I stopped, something terrible might happen to you. I just lost the edge for a little while, just let my guard down. I just...

He prayed for their immortal souls, his own too, using prayers he learned in childhood; words coming softly, a barely audible sound, sharing them with the ram and the awesome stellar display. He went through his inventory of remembered prayers twice and five decades of the rosary, saying the words slowly, trying to put meaning into each prayer. He allowed time for spiritual adlibbing, time for straight talk with God and with his brother. He never talked to his mother or father or any of the others. He wondered about old friends who were gone, wondered about the crossing-over part, crossing over to that somewhere he never stopped wondering about. Lastly he prayed to his Creator, always sobering. Bakewell was afraid of God Almighty, thought of him as an Old Testament God. Jesus was the Redeemer, the Holy Spirit the Advocate, but God Himself he feared was a vengeful God. The praying usually made him fall asleep, almost always worked, especially the second time around; but he couldn't fall asleep. He was bone weary, weak with exhaustion, wished for sleep. He hunkered down, pulling the coat over his head for additional warmth, avoided looking at the stars, waited for the deep chill to set in.

Reveille

He woke about five thirty for the last time, not sure he'd ever really slept, no longer able to remain still, painfully stiff, but needing to move. He found his world inside a cloud, visibility less than twenty yards. *How in hell am I going to find my way?* He badly wanted to start a fire, to eat and drink something hot, but there was no wood. Finding his way back to base camp was no problem; trying to find the spike camp he'd left yesterday would be nearly impossible. His body, cement like, needed to move. He put the nearly frozen boots back on, panting with effort, his aching feet protesting the cold stiffness of the hard leather. He pulled his survival gear together around him and packed it tightly. He could barely straighten up, his legs and back stiff, unbelievably sore. When he made it to his feet, his legs were like distended members, not part of his body. He knew he would warm soon enough from exertion; finding water would be no problem – he would probably hear it before he saw it – but *finding the trail* in fog was another matter. He dropped to his knees, checked the wiring on his pack frame, then stood and surveyed the site.

My survival site. He took a picture in the gray light, wondering if it would turn out. He rocked back and forth on aching legs, waiting for the pain to subside. He tried to do a knee bend, nearly fell, and gasped in pain. *Going to have to be careful starting out. Downhill's always more dangerous.* He thought he remembered some howling during the night, tried to remember the sounds: *coyotes for sure, wolves, maybe?* Last night had all melded together. After the stellar display the clouds had eventually rolled back in and the animal noises had stopped.

He looped the pack behind his shoulders and gathered rifle and binoculars and started down the steep slope, each step an awkward stumble and a painful jolt. After ten minutes he began to loosen up, regain coordination. He found a trickle in the rocks and filled his syrup bottle half full, put a tablet in and placed the bottle inside his coat. He shook it occasionally as he made his way down, watching for familiar sights, for footprints. He was tracking himself now – in reverse. The water and the last of his gorp got him going about the time a breeze came up, and the fog lifted enough to see across a little valley several hundred yards. The wind would dissipate the fog, and his spirits lifted with the ceiling. Finding his way easily now, he made good time. When he got back to the spike camp, he rolled his tent and bag up and put them in the pack. Then he re-strapped the trophy on the top, putting the weight up high between his shoulders where he could control it. It was a long exhausting walk down, one treacherous hillside after another, with small rises separating each one.

He made it to the meadow south of the ranger station right after noon and dumped everything on the ground next to the tent. He examined his camp quickly for disturbance, relieved to see everything in place. Then he started the burner and placed a quart of water on top and went to look for his horses. They were up the valley near the Forest Ranger buildings, grazing in the long yellow grass, looking for fresh green shoots. The meadow was full of seeps, swamp-like in places. When he closed the distance, they recognized him and started an ungainly hop toward him. They would be expecting food. He snapped a lead rope to each halter and bent down and released one side of each hobble, freeing them to walk back to camp. Near the tent he re-hobbled each horse, took the collapsible bag, and went down to Hellroaring Creek to fill the bag half full with fresher water. The valley and ranger station were named for the wildly cascading watershed. He let the mare, the more aggressive horse, drink first, gave water to the second horse and, before a scuffle could break out, poured a can full of oats into a feed bag and looped it over the mare's head. He did the same for the gelding.

"Don't get a belly ache. We've got a long walk out tomorrow."

He went back to the tent and collapsed inside on the soft inflated mattress, listening to the sound of horses chewing, bugs buzzing and water beginning to boil. He ate a hot meal of chicken stock and rice with chunks of chicken he'd dried himself the month before. It was the same meal he had eaten four times in the last six days. He drank two mugs of tea, heavily laced with honey and treated himself to a half hour nap. He had to make another trip back to recover the ram or he would be in the mountains another day and he didn't have enough provisions. If the weather turned, he could get trapped for an indefinite time. He wished he could take both horses, riding beat walking, but some of the country was so treacherous he could only handle one horse. He would take him up and leave him below the kill site at the little dip where he had left his gear the night before then bring the quarters down to the horse. He loaded the gelding with panniers and belted them tightly. He would rather take the tough, sure-footed little mare, but knew she would never stand for the awkward weight of the panniers. Just before he set out, he placed the trophy inside the tent and got a small plastic bottle from his gear and opened it. It contained several small rags soaked in diesel fuel. He placed them around the tent, hoping a bear would find the odor so offensive he wouldn't bother looking inside.

Going up was hard on his cardiovascular engine. His legs were begging for rest. His body couldn't get enough oxygen, burned oxygen like an old motor burned oil – he was about four quarts low. The risk of falling was less going up; the difficulty three times harder. He made his way back up to the kill site without any weapon, moving quietly. *You're hiking not hunting. You're supposed to make noise; scare the bad guys off; no damned place for a hiker.* He wondered what he might find this late in the day as he approached the site from below where he'd gathered wood last night.

He was lightheaded, stopped, leaned against a rough-barked dwarf pine. His thighs and arms were shaking in comedic unison as he tried to glass the hill. What he saw caused an involuntary convulsing. There was a mountain lion, yellow in the sunlight, all sinew and muscle, magnified in the lenses. The cat crouched low, with shoulder blades protruding, looking spooked, taut, alarmed, just above the kill, perched on a rock. Bakewell wondered if it was a male, unable to make the distinction. He wished he had his rifle. The wind was coming around the hill toward him; he could feel it on his face. He was mesmerized by the predator, couldn't believe he had taken him by surprise. He was almost certain the cat would bolt if he showed himself. He looked like he was about to launch any second. Predators had a habit of finding an easy meal; even the most efficient killers would take an easy meal. He had been more worried about approaching the dead ram a day later than he had been of spending the night with him. A bear would stay with a carcass, would be hard to dislodge from a kill that could feed him for days. He'd seen a big cinnamon bear sleeping on an elk carcass on the bank of the Gardiner River years before, sleeping while fifty people gawked and commotioned from across the river. He dreaded a bear, never anticipated a lion. He thought about yelling to chase the lion off, decided to experiment instead; wanting to see the animal spook, and to know when he left, and what direction he would take when he scented *man.* It was late, there wasn't much time and he was tired, but the cat was special, a one in a thousand, a moment he couldn't let pass. A mountain lion was the single most exceptional wildlife sighting. He waited, resting.

Bakewell had always been afraid of bears; they were about the only thing he really feared in the mountains. The rest of the creatures were mostly harmless if left alone. The cat seemed to calm down. He decided to throw something to the off side that smelled human. He pulled off his boot and removed his heavy wool sock and put one of the little rocks littering the ground in the sock to make a sling. *Kind David.* Dropping low behind the tree he swung the sock around several times to get the hang of it. Then he dropped off the hill a few yards and spotted a place in the rocks about thirty feet from the lion and aimed for it. He swung the sling again and let it go. It arced up over the terrain, and before it landed he was back to his original vantage, watching the lion. The cat was looking toward the sock before it landed. When he heard the sound he was up again, body taut. He seemed to flatten out on the rock then to move laterally away, through the air, without jumping, effortless, with a mysterious speed, coming from a hidden place, moving in slow motion, like a great fish moving through the water; then he was gone. Bakewell didn't remember hearing a sound, even though he was close enough to hear the sock hit the ground.

You are a silent killer all right, he shivered, realizing how impossible it would be to know when such a creature was stalking him. It was a special moment, another gift from the mountains and the God who made them.

The ram was where he'd left him: four quarters and a large cape draped inverted over one of the bigger rocks, showing cracks from dehydration in the afternoon sun. The lion hadn't touched it. He boned out each quarter, looking over his shoulder as he did, wondering, doubting the cat would be back, still... He lifted a larger rump quarter and started back down. Each trip took ten minutes and there was one for each quarter and one for the cape. He would leave nothing behind but the gut pile, also drying, cracking in the sunlight. He left the cape open, not wanting to roll it up. It was still gooey and wet in places and unwieldy. Hauling it down he stepped on part of it and pitched end over end down fifteen feet of steep, hard, unforgiving terrain. He cracked his elbow and the back of his head hard enough to leave him unsure he was conscious. He stayed still, counting his parts physically, abusing himself mentally. *Slow down! There's no hurry! Not in this country! You can't get in a hurry up here!* He cursed aloud. Bakewell rarely cursed.

When he got back to the gelding, he wrapped the quarters tightly and put them in the panniers one at a time to keep the weight distributed, trying not to spook the wary horse.

"You're about as far from home as you're likely to get buddy, so just enjoy the day and this marvelous view." He stroked the horse gently as he talked, and he talked to him each time he added to his load. They made their way down in the setting sun, Bakewell speaking soothing words, encouraging the horse, who grunted with each step and stopped several times to assay the rocky terrain before moving on, going slowly in the steeper parts, almost loping across the flatter meadows. Bakewell hung tightly to the halter each time they crossed a meadow, knowing he would be in a fix if he lost hold.

They beat the sunset by fifteen minutes, arriving at the meadow camp just as a rainsquall moved in. Bakewell unloaded the gelding and gave him some additional oats, while the cold rain pelted him. By the time the meat was unloaded and the horse was hobbled, he was soaked. He wanted to pull off his clothes and dive into the dry tent, but he had one more important chore. He retrieved the trophy and took a long piece of nylon rope and tied it to the top of the bag containing the ram's huge head. He tied his folding saw to the other end and threw it over a branch high above. It took three attempts before he succeeded. He pulled the trophy up close to the branch, leaving it about 12 feet above the ground, tied the end off to the base of a second tree and inspected it in the last light. The rain had nearly stopped. Satisfied, he took off his clothes, stripped to his socks, left everything in a pile, knowing it would never dry before morning. He opened the tent, toweled off, and crawled naked inside the down bag. It took a few minutes to warm up, helped by his racing pulse, which raced as much with the excitement of knowing he had done well as from the day's staggering exertion.

He prayed for a long time, thanking God over and over for his safety and success, prayed for more of both the next day. He thanked Him for the sheep, the hunt, the weather, the horses, his children, his life, his faith, his soul. When the exhilaration finally wore off he prayed for Katherine and fell into an exhausted sleep.

***

The temperature inside the small tent woke him the final morning. Bakewell had overslept. The sun was high, baking the plastic fabric. He took his time, reviving slowly, knowing the worst part was over. Normally he'd awake in the dark, roll over and heat water on the burner outside the tent flap within reach of the sleeping bag. But it was hot; he needed to get out and stretch his aching body. His six foot frame had supported 190 pounds nicely most of his life, but he was carrying another twenty-five. When he first got to Hellroaring, he felt primed and ready to go, had logged miles jogging in the months before, but the mountains required a different fitness: an attitude of endurance, sure-footedness, resolve and a determination to push on.

He watered and fed each horse and loaded the panniers carefully, making sure the gelding was ready, all points were secure. He saddled the mare and put his personal gear in her saddlebags, pulled himself stiffly up, found his stirrups and tugged at the reluctant gelding. The horses were full of energy, tossing heads, blowing, anticipating the return to better pasture. They knew the return trail well; it was part of the drill. By the time they topped out west of Bull Mountain things settled into a normal routine, and travel became the monotonous task it always is for those doing the work.

Out in the sunlight, free of the thick forest Bakewell, was soon somnambulant in the warmth and struggled to stay awake. The midsection of the return trip, where they crossed the steep talus field was the tricky part; he ran into a group of elk hunters coming in the opposite direction across the dangerous trail. The talus was big and the trail only a few feet wide. There were ten of them and two of him, so Bakewell pulled up to get above the trail and wait for them to pass. The group was mostly first time elk hunters, scabbards mounted the wrong way, stocks of expensive rifles protruding, waiting to hang up on a pine branch. *Probably Weatherby's*. The passage was always scary. If somebody lost control of a horse, and he had seen it happen, trouble started and injury was inevitable. It was nearly vertical above and below. The talus was large and angular; it seldom moved, was hell to move through. Bakewell prayed his horses wouldn't shy, and no one else's would either. His prayers were answered when the last rider, looking out of place and uncomfortable, passed a few yards below him. The hunter, obviously new to the country, pulled his lowered head down inside his jacket collar, sheepishly. Bakewell remembered the feeling, had been there twenty years before.

Once he was able to ease his horses back down on the trail the rest of the trip was idyllic, filled with spectacular vistas and panoramic views. He could see the Tetons down south of the Park. He made Crevice about one and got down from the mare slowly, on shaky, cramped legs. He put the horses in the small corral after unloading them, leaving the tack on the rail, and, after putting the gear in the back of the pickup, he unwrapped the trophy and laid it on the tailgate. Retrieving a box of fine granulated salt from the cab, he began to salt the eyes and lips of the ram, poured quite a bit down inside the ears. He was preparing to leave when his man showed up, roaring into the compound and skidding to a stop. Bakewell retrieved his checkbook. The outfitter walked from the cloud of dissipating dust, whistled slowly as he came up to the ram. He swore softly and looked at Bakewell.

"Gee God, man! I haven't seen a ram that big in years. Not in years. Criminoly, that's one big, son of a bitch of a bighorn." He looked at Bakewell expectantly.

"This check is for a couple of hundred more, George," Bakewell said. He held the check out and George took it without hesitation. "The horses did very well. Had a little trouble in the talus field, ran into a long pack train, but they behaved just fine. That big guy was a sure footed dude; he did great coming down from Oregon Mountain."

"You did pretty good yourself," the lanky outfitter said, waiting for an explanation.

"If I was still a horse owner I'd try to buy your mare," Bakewell nodded toward the corral. "She's plucky as hell, but she's predictable. She never makes a dumb move. That's important up here." He brushed the salt from his hands and put the container back in the cab. "You don't want to let go of her as long as you're in this business, George." Bakewell rolled up the trophy. When he lifted it, he groaned, pretending to strain under the weight. He put it in the front seat with the rifle and his down bag; the most valuable possessions rode up front.

"There ought to be a hell of a tale about that ram, Mr. Bakewell. A lot of boys would like to know where you found him."

"Andy," Bakewell smiled contentedly, thought *I bet they would,* stretched his sore neck and back. "You look for ten years, George. One day he shows up." The outfitter waited for more. Bakewell, always reticent, didn't expand.

"Son of a bitch," George said, pulling a greasy ball cap, scratching his head. "I need a story, here Mr. Bakewell. That's all you're gonna say? That's it? The whole story?"

"That's how you do it." Bakewell said, understating each word. He walked around the pickup and shook the wrangler's hand. Bakewell was naturally quiet, but he was a man's man, lived in a man's world. His body language conveyed sincerity. "Thank you," he said, squeezing George's hand tightly, patting his arm in gratitude. "I would still be up there without your horses." He walked to the door and opened the cab.

"Well, what the fuck, let's do it again next year, Mr. Bakewell." George clapped his hands, "All right, then!" He was very animated.

Bakewell chuckled, said, "You know the rules, not for seven more years. I'm already too old for these hills. In seven more years they'd have to put a handicap ramp up here for me."

"Man," George sounded out of breath. "How long did you have to track him?"

"About seven years." Bakewell smiled, amused at George's dilemma. He wondered what the story would be down in town. He got in and turned the key, pleased the old pickup started on the first try. He rolled the window down and waited for the truck to warm up, checked the gauges. Once satisfied, he put the truck in reverse, nodded to George, turned away from the collection of ponderosa buildings they called Crevice City, and started down the steep gravel road that switched back on itself repeatedly before hitting the main road to Gardiner.

Gardiner

Montana's Fish and Game had the same bean counters that populated every bureaucracy, rule followers who lived compliant, deferential lives, scrutinizing the nuances of the law, looking for a petty violator, interpreting "the book," then reinterpreting the annual changes. "The bastards er everwhere!" Ned often complained. Ned, Bakewell's colorful business partner, hated bureaucrats. "Sons a bitches don't question nuthin, find safety hidin out, followin orders, always avoidin makin decisions, can't never lead, take a chance, always wantin a pressa-ment…"

"Precedent?"

"Whatever, them rotten fuckin seducers (Bakewell once called them Sadducees), rev-lin in them rules like they was the tablets Moses brung down from the mountain."

Ned was right. Wildlife policy was a never-ending flux of new information, ever evolving procedures and practices reconsidered, especially during the years Bakewell had hunted the high country. Ned likened the bean counters to the Third Reich cattle: "followin a bunch a turrabul orders."

They spoiled it for everybody, especially those guided by real motives, by a desire to apply logic to their jobs, to make decisions. Montana's bureaucrats were offset by an indefatigable group of good people, tough individualists, common sense pragmatists, who did the real work: their energy, research and writings eventually prevailed, kept logic flowing, a logic that lead to progress. Gardiner had both types.

Bakewell stopped at the Pump Handle first, got a coke and a bag of chips and filled the tank. The coke tasted wonderful and he bought a second and drove down to the lot next to the Park. The quickest way to check an animal in at Gardiner was to pull up across the street from the Towne Café in the shadow of the Park Entrance and drop the tailgate. When he got there he unrolled the trophy and put it on the tailgate. A crowd formed almost on queue and questions were asked, answers actually given, by the onlookers. Bakewell pretended to be an onlooker, enjoyed the attention the ram got, attention he deserved. *Let him have it; he paid the price.* Within minutes there were thirty people around the truck. The Fish and Game showed up, looking to identify the hunter. Bakewell moved in and offered his license.

A heavyset man took the license, read it carefully, making notes on a clipboard. Bakewell produced the additional license required and his own driver's license. The man made several additional notes and held onto all three. A second man, shorter in stature, who Bakewell recognized from previous years, appeared and took a quick look at the license and put out his hand. "Mr. Bakewell, right?"

"Right," Bakewell shook his hand.

"You've had some success here, sir." He looked at the ram's great horns and shook his head. He counted the rings. "Thirteen?"

"I think so. You boys are the experts. I'd appreciate your count. You could measure the bases too."

"Well, that's a little out of my league," the smaller man said shyly.

"It doesn't matter, they're big enough."

"I'd say…"

The heavyset man turned and asked him how he managed to bring such a ram off the mountain only three days after opening day. He also wanted to know how close to the Park line the ram was, his implication obvious.

Bakewell said, "You start by getting up here three days early. You need some luck." The man still held his licenses. Bakewell looked at the nametag pinned to his shirt, asked if he had a card, took a small notebook from his pocket, wrote the man's name down. The slighter man took the licenses, looked them over and gave them back to Bakewell.

"We'll need some information on the kill site," the big guy said.

"No problem." Bakewell handed his topo to the shorter man. It was worn and wrinkled by use, with years of notations. It was covered with clear tape in places where he had made his notes and at most of the creases. He took a pen from his pocket and turned to preclude the bigger man and most of the crowd. He spoke in a low voice to the smaller man. "I found him here on the 22nd and followed him that day and the next. I shot him here on the evening of the 23rd. Spent the night up there with him and brought him back down to the ranger station yesterday."

"Did you check in with them up there?"

"There was no one around that I saw. Was that required?"

"Well, technically you need to show the animal to the first available official. It would be just good policy when you're bringing an animal like this out to present it at the ranger station."

"Well, if they were up there they were keeping to themselves." He put his licenses away. "I was in a hurry to get down here and report in before the season closed."

"Well this old giant closes the season in Area 500," the bigger man interrupted.

"Good. I'm glad I finally got to be the one." Bakewell let the edge in his voice come through. He turned to the bigger man. "Why is it when somebody brings a trophy down here he feels like a criminal?"

The bean counter waited for the smaller man to answer. "You know the answer to that one, sir. You've been hunting up here before, many times I believe?" He spoke agreeably.

"Twenty years, on and off."

"Well, you are pretty close to the Park line in that country," he tapped the map.

"After twenty years I know where the Park line is."

"You'll need to show us the kill site." The heavyset man said.

"No problem. I marked it right there."

"You'll need to take someone up there."

"Not unless you've got a helicopter and you're ready to go now. It's there on the map," he turned to the smaller man. "The gut piles your evidence. You have my name and tag number. You will know where to find me if there's a problem. If I'm not under arrest I have a plane to catch."

There was a pause. Several onlookers shuffled. There was a general murmuring of agreement. The Fish and Game wasn't popular with the locals, despite the Herculean effort they made on behalf of both game and hunting community. Bakewell attributed it to the bean counters.

"No, everything's in order here," the smaller man said. "I'd like to talk to you for a few minutes. I would appreciate your input."

"Sure," Bakewell recognized an ally, sensed a friendship, wondered why he hadn't made more effort with the man before. It could have been oversight, but, until today, he was just another dude, another hunter who came up every year. *Now all the sudden I'm "experienced", the guy who brought the trophy down, somebody to take seriously.* While they all watched, Bakewell put the trophy in the cab and locked the door.

"You got a few minutes to watch after the truck for me?" Bakewell asked the bean counter. He nodded and Bakewell turned to the other man. "How about we go over to the café and talk there?" The heavyset man said he would remain with the truck, making it sound like official government business.

There were many fine sheep on display inside the Cafe. Bakewell ordered a hamburger and the agent agreed to join him. "Is my trophy going to be all right out there?"

The agent assured him it would. They relaxed and talked about sheep, sheep populations, diseases, trends, the books on sheep they had read – both men impressed with the other's knowledge. Bakewell paid for lunch over the agent's protest. "Where have you been all my sheep hunting life?" He asked as they came out into the sunlight.

The agent chuckled, "I have a suspicion we could have been friends. I remember seeing you up here many times over the years."

Bakewell nodded. "I wish we could have hooked up together ten years ago. I could have used the help."

"And I could have used yours. Not everybody that comes up here is so knowledgeable. You could have been a great resource for us. We could have used a man with an airplane, someone who knew the country and came every year."

Bakewell laughed at the irony. "We would have been a match."

"You're right. It's not that easy to find hunters with your background.

You have learned a lot up there on your own; a lot of it would probably be of value to us."

Bakewell nodded, appreciating a compliment coming from someone who had dedicated a lifetime to management of the animals and the country they both loved.

"Well, maybe next year we can make plans to talk ahead of time. Will you being returning for elk, or a mule deer perhaps? We could hook up for some mountain time together?"

"I would like that, I really would, but this caps off a long couple of decades for me."

"I'm sorry to hear that," the agent said. "I hope you change your mind." He gave Bakewell his email address and they shook hands and parted by the truck. Bakewell took the pickup over the bridge across the Yellowstone River out to the airport.

***

He loaded his gear into the baggage compartment, snapping the tight latch on the door. The Commander was nearly new, most of the latches and switches made a sharp, crisp sound that only a seasoned aviator could appreciate. An older man, bent at the waist, legs bowed from years in the saddle, came up the hill from behind. He nodded at the tight sound of the latch.

"I filled the truck with gas." Bakewell said.

"There's a rumor goin round town somebody took a nice ram off a hill east of Hellroarin Creek, said he was forty-two plus." The old man pronounced creek "krick," in the fashion of westerners.

Bakewell took the trophy from the seat and unrolled the caped head and spread it out on the gravel. While the older man inspected his trophy, he walked around and checked the filler cap in each tank again then, shaking his head in disgust, went back and opened the baggage compartment again and got a fuel strainer. "You get in a hurry around these things and sure enough you forget something."

"Yeah, and end up pissing yourself up there once it's too late," the man said. "I get the feeling you're anxious to get on back home, Andy. I thought you'd want to go have a couple of beers over at the Mine Shaft, maybe get a hard earned night's sleep." Bakewell didn't respond, only smiled, a habit of a lifetime, let his body language do his communicating. "You see any grizzlies?"

The comment evoked embarrassment and drew some conversation. "The credit you give me for nerve is undeserved, Sid. You've been up there more than any man I know."

"Alone up there takes some nerve, Andy."

"You mountain boys do more amazing things in these hills than I could ever dream of."

"Not me, not anymore anyway. Bears scare the shit out of me. Now we got wolves to worry about, not to mention the lions they've been bringin down the last few years."

"Well, we're not supposed to worry about the wolves," Bakewell said, breathing hard as he came out from under the wing. "And the cats were always up there. I saw my first one, by the way." He put the strainer bottle away after checking each tank and closed the latch with another crisp snap that made them both smile.

Sid nodded knowingly, didn't doubt Bakewell had seen a lion, despite the rareness of such an occurrence. "Damn, I can't remember the last time I saw a decent plane on this ramp, unless it was a sharp looking Super Cub."

"It's not that new, but it sure is more than anything I ever dreamed of flying." Bakewell turned and looked at the faded windsock that favored runway 28. "Thanks for the wind. I'll just go straight down Two-Eight and follow the river out." He held his hand out; the old man shook it. Although stiff with age, he still had an easy Montana grace, the same coordination Bakewell remembered from years before. "I know you've been hanging out here and I appreciate it, Sid."

"The moon's been nearly full and the weather's been real good," Sid answered. "I don't have much excuse to sleep out anymore. It's a nice airplane."

Bakewell threw a greasy paper towel into the trash drum and walked back to the trophy. Sid had already rolled it and packed it in the plastic bag. Bakewell picked it up, put it in the copilot seat, and came back to the old man. "I know better than to offer you any money; we've been down that road, but if you go into town there's a certificate for the Stetson of your choice waiting at the fancy joint the tourists all love. If you don't go and pick one out, that little gal will buy one for her kid, or the guy that owns the place will pocket the money." He started back to the plane. "Go treat yourself to a Go-to-Meeting hat, and save that greasy thing for cowboyin."

"My cowboyin days are pretty much over, you know."

"More reason to get a decent hat with some texture to brush," Bakewell said over his shoulder.

"Well, I guess I better go over before the sum bitch tells me he sold the last one."

"That little gal said she'd hold onto a selection of those creased jobs you favor."

Bakewell paused, allowing himself a sentimental moment, knowing he would never see the old man again. He had always liked him, even in his rougher days, when they met over drinks at the bar in the Mine Shaft back in '85. "You've been a good friend, Sid, a good friend to me for years; I appreciate it,"

"Thanks," Sid said, added self-consciously, "Well, okay then, see you again next year, Mr. Bakewell?"

"Andy."

"Andy, sure," he nodded and gave him a creased, leathery smile, taking in Bakewell's jaded condition with an experienced eye.

"I don't think so, Sid. Not next year. This was my last time above the Park," Bakewell sighed, hurting, rubbing his ribs. "But I sure have some great memories for my old age." He looked back over his shoulder, "And I'll always remember the first time you took me across the trail to Hellroaring. I was a dude if ever you met one, wasn't I?"

"You did pretty good," Sid said, removing his ancient western hat. "Not many flatlanders that go into that country ever go back, especially by themselves. Shit, ninety percent of the locals here never been *up there* by themselves." Sid looked off to the northeast toward the ridgeline above Yellowstone, remembering years of travel in the Absarokas. Bakewell was embarrassed, turned and ran his hand over the static port. He stepped up on the wing before the old man saw his face color.

"I hate to think this is the last time we might meet," Sid called. He watched Bakewell lose his balance opening the cockpit door, nearly fall off the wing. Sid knew the younger man was exhausted, knew his legs were about gone, knew the toll the "Absorkies" extracted from any man, young or old. He walked out to the end of the wing so Bakewell could see him after he got into the cockpit and waved one last time. When Bakewell waved back, Sid pointed his finger at him and pulled an imaginary trigger, feigning a recoil, gave Bakewell a two-fingered salute.

Bakewell went through the preflight carefully before starting the engine. He didn't want the prop spinning any longer than necessary over the gravel ramp. He called "Clear!" and started the engine and let the prop pull the plane out onto the runway as soon as it caught. He did the run up at the east end in the grass away from the loose gravel and went through the D'FAT CIGARS acronym several times, checking, rechecking, waiting for the oil temperature to creep up into the green. As soon as the engine was warm enough, he turned it around and centered the plane on the runway, and, looking over to the old cowboy, gave him a farewell nod and a catapult pilot's salute, advanced the throttle and opened the mike.

"Gardiner traffic, Commander One-One-Three-Alpha-Poppa, departing runway Two Eight, Gardiner. We'll be heading down the river after lift off."

He held the attitude nose high and trimmed the plane hard aft for a short take off run. At full power and going downhill he used about nine hundred feet of the runway before he was airborne. He pushed the nose over and leveled off twenty feet above the field, retracted the gear and flew down the runway letting the airspeed build. When he reached the very end he hauled back on the yoke and watched the VSI peg out as the plane gulped altitude. At 7500 feet he cleaned up the airplane and leveled off, following the Yellowstone River west down the valley then north up past Tom Miner and a place called Ramshorn Peak. He had hunted both places with his oldest son in '87, the year before he got together with Sid. He would miss the country. It had become familiar over the years. He'd climbed it almost every September. The only years he'd missed were the last two, after Katherine died.

After he was clear of the Absoroka Range he called Billings Flight Watch to get the weather. When he was satisfied with the forecast and the winds aloft, he put an IFR flight plan on file with Billings, opening it later south of Billings, and was cleared direct to Rapid City. Level at eleven thousand feet he turned the oxygen bottle on and put the mask to his face. He programmed the GPS, engaged the autopilot, and let the computers fly him east across the northern end of the Absoroka Beartooth Wilderness. The Absoroka Plateau was the largest plateau above ten thousand feet in North America. With his feet on the floor, he leaned back in the seat and relaxed for the first time since he started the stalk on the ram four days before. He was careful to monitor the gauges – a vigilance caused by years of solo flying – but allowed himself to relax and settle into a soft reverie, filled with satisfaction as he thought about all the years he had put into the pursuit of the ram. He put his hand on the trophy in the copilot's seat and wondered if he hadn't seen the ram up on Deckard Flats about ten years before when he was just a little guy.

"Thank you," he said, moving the plastic bag enough to touch the heavy horns. "You were a tough chase. We both know I had to have the luck to find you over there." He looked across the right wing at the awesome peaks, some partially covered in early September snow. They filled the southern horizon. "From now on you'll be warm and safe; no more sleet filled wind in your eyes; no more wondering where the next patch of grass will be. Your fighting days were over last year. That's why you were all by yourself. There's another big buster over there. He probably kicked your butt a couple of months ago, probably addled what was left of your old brains. I got you just in time."

Bakewell smiled at the thought of sitting in his den, growing old with the ram there above him, looking grim but satisfied. They would keep each other company in the time ahead.

He looked at the Bighorn Canyon ahead in the distance; the west facing walls of the canyon were painted with the shadows of jagged ridges. There was a slight bump as a gust of wind came off the mountains behind. The air was quiet for the most part, cooling late in the day. The setting sun usually quieted the thermal lifting and the chafing wind, typical of mountain flying. He was glad it was late and the sun was behind him and the air was cooling. It would be a peaceful ride to Rapid. He was ready for a less arduous lifestyle. He said a brief prayer, spoke to his brother, mostly thought about Katherine, did it dozens of times each day. After a while, he shook free from his reverie and turned his head slowly from side to side, stretching his sore neck, and whistled softly.

"Amazing. You killed this monster of a bighorn. Now all you have to do is take him home and give him a room of his own in that empty barn of a house you live in." He shook his head again in disbelief. "Amazing!"

Going East

"Rapid City Approach, Commander One One Three Alpha Poppa with you at eleven." He was crossing the Black Hills about ten miles west of Mt. Rushmore.

"Commander One One Three Alpha Poppa, Rapid Approach. Turn right to one-two-zero and descend to and maintain niner thousand for vectors to the ILS runway three-two."

"Right to one-two-zero, tradin eleven for nine." After a few minutes there was a soft-voiced query from the controller. "How's the visibility up there?"

"Hard to tell, I think I'm getting about fifty per cent ground viz, but there's not much reference."

"That's why they're called *the Black Hills*," the controller chuckled. "They tell me it's clear south of the field. Appears you might get a visual; the last guy in got one. You'll have to let me know."

"That'll work." Controllers sometimes liked to talk on slow nights, probably to stay awake. This one would provide extra help. Bakewell was fatigued beyond describing, very grateful for any extra help. He set up the Horizontal Situation Indicator and identified the localizer. The GPS showed him eastbound, doing 182 knots, downhill. The Vertical Speed Indicator indicated 500 feet per minute. Leveling out at nine he picked up more lights for ground reference, still few and far between. Population was grouped in the Black Hills; lights came in clusters or not at all. Rapid cleared him to 7000' and turned him northeast then north for a thirty degree intercept.

"Commander One One Three Alpha Poppa, you're cleared for the ILS THREE TWO. Maintain six thousand feet until established."

He read back the clearance, couldn't see the field and stayed with his gauges, using the heading bug on the autopilot for direction. When he got the localizer he turned 320 degrees, and once established, started down the glide slope, still looking for the runway. An Instrument Landing System took much of the stress out of landing in weather. He was in and out of cumulus until he finally broke out at 1700 feet above the ground to see runway 32, well lighted, beautiful, welcoming.

"Commander Three Alpha Poppa has the field in sight."

"Three Alpha Poppa, roger. Contact Rapid tower on 118.7. Have a pleasant night."

Tower cleared him to land, said, "Stay with me" after he rolled out. He turned off the active and asked for directions to the nearest service and got the standard non-commercial-multiple-choice-response, since the controller couldn't favor a service provider. *"Jetstream closed at eight. West Jet is open 24 hours."* Bakewell taxied to West Jet and shut down.

When he got out of the plane, he smelled the conifers on a trailing wind out of the northwest. *Last real smell of the mountains.* He doubted he would ever smell them again. There was some moonlight coming off the north end of the field through the broken cloud cover. It was very tranquil. He was alone on the dark ramp, wondering if he was the last plane in for the night when he heard the motor of the line service truck.

"How ya doin?" a young man asked. He spoke with a drawl.

"Pretty good. I need fuel in both tanks; top them off; and can you tell me how I could get a ride into Rapid?"

"If ya can wait on me to fill ya up, I'll take ya. I get off in another few minutes and ama headed thatta way."

Bakewell nodded gratefully. He tied the plane down while the fueling took place, tossed his overnight bag to the tarmac, took the plane cover from the cargo hold, and carefully locked the Commander. He put the cover over the entire cockpit section, covering windows, doors and cargo hatch, and crawled underneath and Velcro-ed the straps tightly. It was the first time he had ever used the cover. By the time he was finished the driver returned with his own car, and Bakewell put his bag in the back seat.

"Where you wanna go in Rapid?"

"The Alex Johnson." They drove into town chatting about airplanes and hunting. The attendant was in the Air Force, working part time to earn tuition money, due for discharge in a few months. He dropped Bakewell at the old hotel. The Alex was one of the West's great dining places. Bakewell checked in then took his room key and bag and went straight into the dark, carpeted dining room. He ordered an Absolut, and when the waitress brought the drink he ordered salad and roast bison with a glass of merlot.

When she left he enjoyed the peace of the softly lit, quiet dining room, rotating the cold glass in his hands. He had a great affection for The Alex. It was often a first stop when heading east, always made him feel safe, closer to home. He was glad to be away from the stress of airplanes and mountains and survival. He turned the cold glass in his swollen hands and let the fatigue overtake him. In the warmth of the room in a soft cushioned chair, he stared absently into the glass, feeling his wind-dried eyes begin to water. He'd been running on willpower ever since he left Crevice City. The wonder and awe of what he had accomplished in past days overtook him.

For a hunter, a bighorn is the ultimate quest. Bakewell had been in love with the idea of taking one since he read his first Jack O'Connor story years before. He was running out of time. He was just 28 the year he talked Katherine into letting him make his first attempt. That was above Cooke City at the northeast end of the Park. After years of effort in the 10,000' altitude, he finally accomplished what he had only dreamt about. He felt the emotion welling up; his shoulders began to shake. He dropped his head, closed his eyes and waited, wanting to be in harmony with the room, in harmony with Katherine, who was missing, yet everywhere – just across the room where they sat the last time they had come. Not far away was the table they had been seated at one August evening so long ago. That was the first year he brought her to Montana for a fishing trip. They had drunk too much wine, spent the night making love, and slept late before the long ride home. He hoped he wouldn't be staying in the same room.

He ate the salad quickly and when the waitress returned with his second drink he asked for another salad. He had been living on meat and carbohydrates. He ate the meal slowly, enjoying each bite, sipping the wine between tender mouthfuls. The food made him think of other wonderful dinners they had enjoyed together. They came one year when the boys were in grade school to visit the park and camp in Ennis – that was the year they left Nancy with grandparents

Bakewell missed his wife. There were no words to describe it. The memory of her, his memory of her, gradually becoming a private thing, a secretive affair, a way he learned to deal with his loss, to appreciate her without self-pity. She was in a special place, both in his world and beyond: in paradise, which she never doubted, and in his heart, where he kept her constantly, talked to her, sometimes ruefully, sometimes whimsically. Their marriage had been an amazingly short few decades of excitement, joy, occasional exasperation, but mostly simple, blissful contentment in which they relied upon each other for support, for happiness, for energy, for stamina, for oxygen. It had also been filled with mischief; Katherine often wildly unpredictable, full of devilment and outrageous pranks. It had been emotional, physical, spiritual, lustful, and intellectually challenging, although he was no match for her intellect or her wit. Mostly it had been unbelievable happiness.

When the meal was finished he ordered a glass of warmed port and lingered in the dining room, watching them clean up, preparing to close. One of the waiters finally gave him a questioning look, he nodded and the young woman appeared with his check. He paid and went upstairs to his room, taking the ancient staircase deliberately, wanting to push himself one more time, wondering if it was the stiffness in his legs or the liquor that made him wobble down the hall, bumping the wall as he went. Before he went to sleep he decided to call Nancy and tell her he was out of the mountains, back on flat ground. She would be worried.

"If you called, I'm supposed to ask if you got one?"

"I got one; I got a real nice one."

"Should I tell my brother?"

"Sure."

"Is there a story behind this one, Dad?"

"Not really."

"Did you try and fall off another mountain? Try to break your neck, almost kill yourself again?"

"No," he spoke through a compulsory laugh. "It's a simple tale of mindless obsession; you know your father."

"No broken bones?"

"Nothing exciting, just a lot of walking and camping; eating the same thing; sleeping on top of the world."

"And no grizzly bears?"

"No grizzly bears. I'm fading away here now that I've laid down, kid." He reached up for the light. "I just finished a big meal and drank way too much. See you tomorrow. Olive."

"Olive-you, dad, I'm glad you're safe."

"Tell my grandbabies Old Pop says 'olive'."

Des Peres

The trip across mid-continent was uneventful; Bakewell left Rapid early and caught the leading edge of a high pressure ridge, like a surfer running a wave. He stopped outside Omaha for fuel and was back in the air half an hour later, humming on toward St. Louis. The ceiling and visibility were unlimited, so he decided to go outside the IFR system, airplane and thoughts resting on autopilot, using "radar following" for traffic advisories. He was exhausted, adrenaline spent, not sharp enough to be flying in anything but the best weather, using the computers to insure his safety. He programmed the GPS direct to Spirit of St. Louis, and while the autopilot did the driving, he rested the computer between his ears. When the wind dropped off east of Columbia; he had outrun the high-pressure system and was back to 155 knots ground speed coming into St. Louis.

"Spirit tower, Commander One One Three Alpha Poppa over Lake St. Louis with information Lima, for Eight Right."

"Commander One One Three Alpha Poppa, Spirit Tower, make traffic for a straight in Eight Right. You'll be number two following a Citation on a three mile final."

He turned south to pick up the localizer and flew it down the extended centerline of the runway. The only one talking to the tower after the Citation landed, he was surprised by the lack of traffic on a Saturday afternoon.

"Commander Three Alpha Poppa, clear to land Eight Right."

"Clear to land Eight Right. Where is everybody?"

"Don't know," was the friendly reply. Bakewell loved Spirit, loved the radar environment, precision approaches, people in the tower, even the ground personnel. It was one of America's great commuter airports. He rolled out at Alpha 5 and requested permission to taxi to his hangar. When he contacted the ground controller the voice on the other end said, "Is that you Andy?"

"It's me Bobby."

"Where you been? Haven't heard you in a while."

"Montana."

"Montana, *wow!*" Then the controller broke off to handle an IFR departure.

While they fueled the plane he transferred his gear, taking care with the ram, placing it on the front seat again. The ground crewman was fascinated with the trophy.

Driving home he enjoyed the same clear weather that had followed him across the continent. It was in the 80's, still summertime in late September. The humidity was up, so was the heat index; he was sweaty after the equipment exchange and needed the air-conditioner. *Hard to believe I was so cold 3 nights ago*. The trees hadn't begun to turn in the river bottom or along the ridge south of the airport. It could have been July.

His grass needed cutting and his dogs were jubilant and he opened the gate. He played with each dog separately, emptied the feeder and refilled it, did the same with the water bucket, while they frolicked between his legs, licking his face each time he bent down. He took his gear into the shade of the garage and began to unpack, taking care to inventory each item before putting it up on the shelves he'd made for Katherine years before.

The mailbox was empty; Nancy had already been by. He got the cordless phone, a pad and pencil and went out on the deck to listen to his messages. Several were business, two from friends, needling him about being gone; one call was from Maggie Walker.

The longest message was from Michael, his youngest son, still in Montana. He had hoped to get together with Michael, was disappointed they hadn't made connections, but once he killed the ram he gave no thought to going further west. He listed each call, scratching them as he went; only three needed a response. He replayed the message from Michael twice, partly for content, mostly to hear the sound of his voice.

Dad, I know you're going to get this after you get home and I'm sorry. I had another cancellation on Thursday so I was free – some bozo had to have an operation. It's always an operation with these rich guys. Guess they want their deposit back. Why do they think we ask for a deposit? Anyway, shit, we missed a great chance to fish together or just do something! The water's too warm and the fishing isn't much except late in the day. Hope you got into some cooler weather up there. I know you did. Don't be too disappointed about the sheep. It ain't easy Pop; if it was, everybody would be up there. Damn, wish we could have met up. I miss you Dad. Love you Pop. Next week.

He sat back and called the neighbor kid hired to check on his dogs. The older dog rested under his chair, conserving energy, while the puppy patrolled the yard, stalking doves in the lower branches of his pine trees. The kid showed quickly, coming round to the back yard. They shook hands and Bakewell got an update on how many surreptitious visits the divorcee across the street had had. The kid's mother was the neighborhood gossip. Her insatiable appetite for would-be scandal had gotten to the point where no one paid attention any longer. Katherine said the neighbors had learned to leave her many character assassinations "unembalmed;" said, "Time would corrupt them if they were left unacknowledged."

"My dad said if he were you he'd think about drilling her himself." The kid said cheekily. He was a bold case, standing in front of the table, legs astride, a lot like his old man. Bakewell was offended by his impudence, but knew the kid couldn't help it. The heavier genes floated to the bottom, always favored the lower side. Still, he was annoying. He stared at the boy until he dropped his head sheepishly and looked at the deck.

"It's Saturday, Buzz. You and your dad ought to be thinking about evening Mass, not the neighbor's wife." He handed him a fifty-dollar bill.

When the teenager left, Bakewell stared down the hill, through the grove of shortleaf pines to the pool on the other side. It needed to be cleaned and covered for the winter. He could tell by the arrangement of the deck furniture it had been used while he was gone. He hoped it was family and not pool hoppers. He worried about the liability of having the pool now that there was no one around. He built the pool during the peak of his comeback years, which coincided with the end of the big tuition bills. It was Katherine's idea, design and creation. Once the grandchildren started coming she had to have a pool. Bakewell thought it was a little late in life for a pool, but acceded, like he almost always did.

She was boss when it came to home and family, had spent hours there with a happy contractor who never tired of making changes as she perfected it. It took three months to build. "My god Lew, we could have built a house in the same time," he'd protested. But it ultimately came together in a spectacular free-formed creation, surrounded at the uphill end by boulders, water cascading down them, into the deep tank, surrounded by a flagstone deck, interspersed with small planters brimming with dwarf bushes and flowering plants – the whole affair, softly under lit, with the sound of moving water, creating a burbling, mood enhancing effect each evening at dusk. Katherine called it an, "outdoor entertainment center." They used it day and night that first year. There were parties or "drop-ins" nearly every night: friends, family and neighbors. Bakewell thought the pool cost was nothing compared to the entertainment expense.

The following year Katherine had gotten sick, and it was more like a convent courtyard, giving way to somberness and sobriety, and, eventually, as summer wore on, becoming a place of near reverence as family and friends flocked to her side. Katherine had insisted on being out there under an umbrella during the day, and on the deck in the evenings until the very end. She loved her yard, her garden, the sound of water running by the pool and the sound of her grandchildren. Her friends couldn't leave her alone. They planted and trimmed, pulled weeds and fertilized, brought food and small gifts, couldn't spend enough time looking after anything that needed attention. At first the husbands came too, dropped in after work, and the atmosphere of the previous summer continued; but by the end of July it was mostly grief stricken women, visiting, watching her slowly die, hugging each other tearfully out on the driveway at shift change.

Bakewell had never been hugged so many times as that summer her life came to a slow, withering conclusion. His grief was just bearable, but the affect her death had on his children was a source of pain so excruciating he thought he might lose his mind as he watched them watch her die one slow day at a time. The kids tried to keep their spirits up in her presence, but they were immobilized when they left her side, or when she absented herself for medical needs. It was a scene inexorably revisited, day after day, and watching their suffering was the one time Bakewell's faith was truly tested. Michael had been the tenderest spirit, appeared to suffer most – his mother's dying incomprehensible initially, the boy nearly inconsolable.

Bakewell thought he would never reconcile himself to losing her, or to watching his kids experience the terror of losing their mother. Each of his three children was as wasted emotionally as Katherine was physically when her life finally ended. His daughter had been the stabilizing force of his life, her diminutive stature belying a spirit and resolve he thought only Katherine herself capable of.

Now as he watched the puppy point, creep, come to a final, beautiful point before the dove flushed from the bush, he pondered the greatest loss of his life one more time. Earlier he'd observed his dogs rejoice at his return; they gave a trust and devotion so complete, dependent on him for life and nourishment. He envied such unconditional trust. Katherine had that kind of trust. Her life had been rich in grace and the trust that accompanies it. Bakewell longed for the ability to trust God as totally as Katherine had, as unconditionally as his dogs trusted him. But he was jaded, a spiritual part of him had wasted away with her. He recognized her illness and her death as a trial of his faith, but feared it had dulled it instead. He prayed just as fervently, but there was doubt now, God had confused him with his wife's death. He prayed through an ever thickening cynicism, trying to find the loving hand of God, the one he'd been taught to look for, to trust in, to believe in. His prayer life was enshrouded in the emotional humidity left behind by so many tears.

Bakewell was a private man who trusted himself exclusively for his needs and he never let his despondency become morbid self-pity. He kept to himself when he could, preferring his loneliness to all the commotion that accompanied well-meaning friends. His loneliness always came over him the same way: like a warm soft swelling of surf that drenched without leaving a chill. He loved Katherine's memory, bathed himself in it, and he had loved her totally and with fidelity. Once he made the decision to settle down, he became, "totally and completely addicted to marriage," a line he directed to his children, often accompanied it with another: "We're like the Canada geese, we take our time, we choose, we mate for life."

He and Katherine both hoped their children would pay heed. They had seen the debilitating effects of divorce and the carnage it left behind.

Bakewell

After four years on an aircraft carrier Bakewell had been loosed on a university campus, a veteran in the middle of thousands of coeds, free from home and new to adulthood. Among them he had all the vices, was fraught with hormones and a GI's desire to know the flesh. He would later regret much of his behavior. The university had been his worst period, his "wanton period" – years of European liberty hadn't been as carnal. He played hard, but he studied hard too, obsessed with the idea of getting a diploma. He would be the first in his family to graduate from college.

After four years of intellectual bottom-feeding in a steel bachelors' quarters, an eternity of limiting conversation, restricted to anatomy, always pornographic, Bakewell was determined to learn the language of higher education, determined to enrichen his vocabulary. Surrounded by derisive peers and a mentality that held education in contempt, he pined for solitude and a place to read in peace, and he read everything from old newspapers to the torn and wrinkled avalanche of magazines that hit the ship with each mail call.

Early on he became obsessed with the learning of words, became an amateur philologist, beginning his preparation for college long before he was discharged. Bakewell loved each new word, practiced covert pronunciations in secret, occasionally conversing with one of his superiors in Officers' Country. He tried to add new words to his vocabulary daily. His most prized text was a woefully inadequate dictionary purchased before the ship left Mayport, Florida.

While his vocabulary more than measured up in his first year of college, he was unsure of his position, even his right to be on a college campus, was uncomfortable and often embarrassed. But his shyness attracted friends, his dogged resolve and sincerity became the trademarks of a developing personality. He was quiet, honest, sincere, and occasionally a little too candid.

In high school he'd been a disciplinary problem, directionless, adrift and unproductive. He'd been a loner without discipline but loved team sports, especially loved the structure of baseball and football. The guys he played against, the ones he admired and tried to emulate were always the disciplined ones, the team guys who had less talent but worked hardest. What discipline Bakewell had at the time, he'd learned playing ball. He was a determined student of both games and a hard worker. But the unrepressed anger that characterized his youth ruled out any possibility of righting himself before military service. His early life had been spent on self destruction, until, expelled late in his senior year, he joined the navy and found his own special tutor: heavy handed, threatening, and cruelly enforced. It quickly forged him into a responsible, competent, and even more independent man. It also ended up funding his education.

Navy boot camp didn't *teach* discipline, it *lived* discipline – a shocking new kind. The structure of military discipline changed Bakewell's perception of authority, of how things were done and he regretted his mistake the day he arrived at boot camp. Fortunately, millions made the same mistake, or were drafted into making it, and quickly got the new version of authority, while they learned how to defend their country. Uncle Sam did the parenting where parenting had failed, redirected lives, produced focus, taught skills and made demands that were enforced. Instant obedience became a way of life. Boot Camp was a 24-hour a day experience that taught how teeth were to be brushed, clothes washed, a body bathed, a face shaved, even how to chew and swallow food. It was a relentless, comical dehumanizing of young men, who took showers together, thirty at a time, in a room 15' square. He also learned a shared commodal intimacy, with fifteen others in a "head" that featured toilets without partitions. Boot camp accommodations were almost classy compared to shipboard facilities, which featured a metal compartment, where fifteen guys shared 2 showers, 2 sinks and 4 toilets – the toilets 2 to a side, facing forward, kneecap to kneecap, where one man had to lean back when the other leaned forward.

Time at the Recruit Training Center, with the exception of one serenely insulated hour each week when they were allowed to spend time worshiping whatever God they professed to adore, belonged to their maniacal keepers. *Every* man went to church on Sunday, if for no other reason than to gain a brief hour's respite, finding peace and some temporary humanizing status in His Presence. It worked. Bakewell was a perfect subject. He adjusted to their attitudes and methods, was malleable and acquiescent, and determined to stay out of trouble. He took them seriously and wanted no part of "military justice." He also recognized they were improving his character, his attitude and his appearance, although they tried to kill him in the process. The navy expiated his aimlessness. He knuckled under, had no desire to test the threat of force, got along.

Years later his partner Ned phrased it best over drinks at Rick's one night: "No rehab clinic or psycho barn ever did so much for the fuckin youth of America as a good-ol-boy drill instructor. Them rotten-mean sons-a-bitches straightened out more dumb shit kids than Dr. Spock or Charlie Darwin ever coulda thoughta." Ned didn't know a psychologist from an evolutionist, but he was a gifted, streetwise analyzer of people. "Them motherfuckers purified generations of dip shits, like you and me, Andy; even in the years they didn't have no wars to help 'em out doin it."

Bakewell had surrendered himself to an authoritarian rule that relished conforming the non-conformant. Humiliation, degradation and intimidation were the methodology of militarism. Surrounded by screw-ups and misfits, and the violence that characterized them, and living in such tight confinement, was an eternity. His passion for education started before he left the Recruit Training Center. It was a passion that didn't sit well with shipmates. Reading anything other than a "fuckbook" made the reader a target of derision. Fortunately his size kept him out of most skirmishes – the only two requiring his participation were monumental and memorable – one taking place over most of the forward chain locker, setting a record for endurance, to the dazed appreciation of shipmates, before a fascinated and fluttery-voiced OD made his presence known, and someone mercifully shouted "ATTENTION ON DECK!"

There were no repercussions since the Officer of the Day, a product of Princeton academia, like the crowd in attendance, was appalled by the tenacity of the combatants, who remained contemptuously indifferent to each other afterward, and smart enough not to reengage.

The University was a singular challenge and Bakewell struggled to pass his first semester before hitting his stride. When he began college he didn't know the difference between a participle and a gerund, calculus and algebra, a psyche or a psycho (although he'd experienced both).

If his social life was spirited – he made his way through an alluring string of coeds, who found his background and alleged experience glamorous, and included a thirty-something Teaching Assistant who taught American Literature – his academic life was daunting. Bakewell loved higher math, but hated public speaking. He was disconcerted by the size of the student body; intimidated by instructors who used humiliation to cover their own insecurities; awed by the very buildings he entered to attend class. He came home that first summer drained, wanting to escape books, looking for mental rest and a chance to play baseball on weekends and softball on weeknights.

A dark episode during his last Mediterranean cruise had left him flush and independent, funded his education, and left enough money to afford a summer long hiatus, ball playing for the saloons and beering in them.

***

The hunt in Montana had been his swan song. He would never go back, had mixed emotions about the ram, had only wanted to get away one more time. He didn't really expect to see a big ram, and never expected to shoot one. Montana was an annual escape he had missed the previous two years. The Absorkies were his special place, the place where he could appreciate the beauty of the high country, the smell of the wilderness; a place to focus on survival and use skills acquired over years of experience; a place that fulfilled a longing to be away from things civilized, in a big, wide, deep, open, daunting world, where money, power and influence didn't count. The ram was his legacy to himself, something for his sons to remember him by, and once the stalk began he was consumed by it. Once the old ram showed himself it became an obsession to take him while he was still magnificent, a chance to bring him home where he would be revered and protected from the withering process Katherine had endured.

Bakewell had to think on that: would a bone picking natural decomposition, a process so crystal clear, so minimal, in a spectacular location, be the one really pure way to disintegrate without the anguished fuss, the expense and the macabre ordeal of wake and funeral? The answer, of course, was no; there had to be closure. People had a right to offer sympathy, to express condolence, to perform little kindnesses. Everyone needed that last chance to come to grips, to say goodbye.

Bakewell believed he was doing many things in his life for the last time, felt like he was going through the motions. He had the feeling he was repeating a year in his life, and it would be the last. He couldn't explain it; he just felt like he was winding down.

He had accomplished most of what he set out to do: married beyond expectation, fathered two solid citizens – one a husband and father like himself, the other living his dream in the high country. And he had one very special, beguiling daughter. He had served his country, community, Church – even the local government briefly. Some of his successes came slower than others, and he took consolation in the biographies of men who succeeded late in life: Grant and Sherman; men who continued to grow throughout their lives without flaming out: the Holy Father, Lincoln; and men who had to wait for recognition, like Harry Truman, who was long into his life before reaching his place in history.

He counted only his children and his marriage as the successes of his life. Business had been a never-ending hassle; he got little pleasure from it, could point to too many failures, his self-critical nature attentive to the failures, always there to offset any satisfaction success might offer. He feared his faith might end up being his greatest failure. He had been faithful to his marriage and to the sacraments all his married life but, right at the end, the worst possible time, he feared he might lose Hope, give up on Final Perseverance – two spiritual accouterments necessary for that final embarkation. His timing had always been off, but that one, *Merciful God!* It would be the penultimate in bad timing. Still, the dendrites of his emotional fingertips were cauterized by his loss. He could only hope God *would* be merciful – the thought of dying in a *non* state of grace was too appalling, too horrifying.

Still, he *was* losing faith and it terrified him to think his faith might fail at the critical moment. He desperately wanted to be willing to die when the time came, never stopped worrying about it, and never had anything approximating Katherine's confidence about death. It haunted him, his doubt. They were both raised in the faith, Parochial school, Catholic high school, but where Katherine never doubted, Bakewell lived in doubt; where her faith had been total and complete, his was unreliable and confused. Bakewell never stopped worrying about his soul, and, like many guilt-ridden people, became a daily communicant, prayed often, attended the Carmelite Monastery, belonged to their Legion of One Thousand, spending hours in Eucharistic Adoration. Yet none of it gave him the assurance he needed to know he would find life everlasting, though he never doubted Katherine had found hers.

Katherine

Mizzou tested over the long Memorial Day weekend. As soon as Bakewell had taken the last final he headed home. The Wednesday after the holiday weekend he came home to find Katherine Durham "tooling around" in a '55 T-bird; she was 20 years old, "all grown up." Katherine was years younger than Bakewell, but he had known of her most of his life. They attended the same Catholic Church. The Durham's lived in an upscale part of Webster Groves, not quite walking distance from his home. When he joined the navy Katherine was in grade school; when he got discharged she was still in high school. The winter he turned 25, she was in that recognizable car, fully bloomed, and to a mind jaded by the military, the embodiment of purity.

Katherine was happy, full of witty conversation. She had a natural ease, an irrepressible confidence, which Bakewell couldn't have identified at the time, but later came to envy. She had beautiful eyes, a job as lifeguard at the Swim Club, a fantastic suntan, thick lovely hair, streaked with chlorine and sunshine, white teeth contrasting with her incredible tan, a beautiful smile that lit up everything around her, and made her seem even younger. It took two weeks of saying hello and making small talk, and two months of dating and discovering to bring him down. His callow arrogance replaced with virtuous enthusiasm, his contemptible indifference with honorable intentions, his smug self-importance with tender attentiveness that bordered on devotion. He was crazy about her, loved to hold her, to kiss her, but wouldn't dare take advantage of her, fearing God's wrath, a bolt of lightening, like the one that de-horsed Saul of Tarsus.

To the seething objection of her medical doctor father – whose ego Bakewell compared to the size of Canada – they were married the following spring in a bizarre sacramental and social fanfare that only happens when poverty marries wealth. The wedding was a cross section of blue collars and starched collars, cubic zirconium and sparkling diamonds, penny loafers and Bostonians; where cracked and calloused hands shook the soft, manicured hands of ladies and professional gentlemen from an upper middle class that insisted on an education provided by the Benedictines or the Jesuits for young gentlemen, and the Academies of St. Joseph or the Visitation, for young ladies.

***

Katherine never feared death – her Catholicism stood the test, steadfast, unwavering, while her body withered and her energy ebbed –welcomed it instead, told her husband and her children she looked forward to it, to escaping her debilitation. Only the sadness and sense of loss her death would bring worried her. She was confident of salvation, expected it, never doubted her next life would be an eternity of happiness, and said many times that summer she hated leaving her "babies" (children and grandchildren), but she was certain they would all be together in eternity. She never worried about things that were beyond her control; by the end of summer her health was beyond anyone's control. Characteristically she turned to other concerns and concerned herself with details of what was to be done after she was gone. She helped plan her funeral, directed the conferring of proceeds from an insurance policy: the kids, a small allotment to a needy classmate, even told them where her clothes and jewelry should end up. Her things were to be given to a list of people, but only after Nancy decided what she could part with.

Bakewell understood Katherine's confidence. It was a pleasing source of consolation at the end. She had lived a wonderful life, filled with concern for friends and neighbors (neighbors being anyone who wasn't a close friend). She would do anything for anyone. In their early years the strength of her character and her charity had amazed him. She was a friend and favorite of everyone, an especial darling of their older neighbors, who adored her zest for living and for raising her children. They loved her fun loving, prank-filled enthusiasm for everyday life. Those early neighborhood years made for countless stories, and were a source of wet-eyed emotion as they reminisced the night of Nancy's wedding reception.

At first it was the little things Bakewell took for granted, failed to notice, later came to respect. She was never critical, never participated in gossip, never gave scandal, always looked for the goodness in people. If there was a scandal, she found something positive to say about the victim. As she matured and tackled bigger tasks, her reputation and her charity took on a greater dimension. Everyone who knew her or knew of her recognized the strength in her character. As their circle of friends expanded, her popularity exploded. Bakewell honestly thought her friends weren't countable, would nod unconsciously as he remembered the way her reputation grew to a proportion unimaginable in their youth. She was his greatest accomplishment, his singular quest. She was also one of his greatest business assets. She could dazzle a customer – more important, a customer's wife – captivate them with her down to earth modesty and charm. The consequence of such socializing resulted in long profitable relationships.

Bakewell winced at the memory of their early life together. He had been inconsiderate and inattentive at times, usually when preoccupied with his business. Nothing pained him more than remembering how he had resented her charity. Charity is about inconvenience, including inconvenience for the practicer's family. And Katherine's charity *was inconvenient*. People took advantage. He complained he was too often alone with the kids while she was on a "mercy mission." Troubled friends, family, divorcees and people in all kinds of need called on her for help. In time he came to recognize her charity for the virtue it was. In the early years he thought her charity was done for her own gratification – for praise and adulation. Eventually he learned she did do it for her own gratification, but never for praise or adulation. Given time he learned to appreciate her amazing goodness. It grieved him to think how long it had taken him to grasp it.

Bakewell loved to observe his wife, especially with others, and there were always others. If she loved a few friends, she loved having lots of friends even more. Their house was always crowded. Her girlfriends found any excuse to drop by. Bakewell admitted later, he felt threatened by their determined attention. He *was* jealous. They took a lot of "Katherine time." It was an adjustment made easier as the years passed, and his appreciation of her grew. "Katherine doesn't make friends, she makes disciples," he said to a neighbor one evening when they were under the influence. Years later the woman candidly admitted she had become a disciple. The number who kept vigil in his yard was proof enough.

The one bone of contention they were never able to reconcile was the telephone. "Telephone Wars" he called it. Katherine was devoted to the phone, once injured herself racing to answer it. Bakewell was a contractor, made his living on the phone, had one on his hip as soon as they went cellular, but hated the phone in his home. The phone never rang for him, unless it was trouble. Nobody called him at home. His cell phone was his only phone. He hated the constant interruptions the phone represented, and *always* at dinnertime. The phone forced him to share her with everyone. Quiet evenings on their deck were often evenings listening to her talk on the phone. He was more jealous of the phone than any inebriated admirer she might attract.

After the kids were old enough to leave in the evenings, he often took it off the hook. "Hey," she would say, "Someone's left the phone off the hook!" and they would all check in, an electronic traffic jam that might last until bedtime. About the phone she made one concession: if it rang earlier in the evening, as in *too early for a crisis* – with teenagers, crises most often came late at night – and circumstances conspired to put them in a no-turning-back intimacy – she would let it ring; but only after several brief wrestling matches, urgent grapplings where he overpowered her, refused to give her up, convincing her in the process. Later, in a pleasant afterglow and to an appeased husband, Katherine admitted, not answering it had been more gratifying than finding out *who the hell was on the other end.*

Bakewell never got over his resentment of the phone, even at the very end *when it finally did stop ringing*. It was then she *needed* to talk to someone. But by then people were afraid to call and for the first time in his life he really had her all to himself.

"My God, how I long for eternity," she sighed faintly one evening while they gazed at the stars. It was just the two of them, alone; almost his final memory of her in life – the one he chose to hold onto the hardest – the one he used to block the bad memories of the last days.

At the beginning of the funeral service, the priest who had performed their marriage ceremony years before stopped them in the vestibule. "This is where Katherine first entered the church," he said. "This is a homecoming in the truest sense of our faith. It is from here she first entered the Church for Baptism, and it is from here where she returns today, here in this Church, where family and friends come to bring her before the altar and celebrate the Holy Sacrifice of the Mass in her burial liturgy; from here we take her on to her final resting place, although we know she is already with God, even now as we celebrate this difficult service."

At that moment Bakewell began to shake inside, knew if the shaking got out of him he might lose control. It terrified him. It wasn't the fear of making a fool of himself as much as the thought of interrupting at such a poignant and necessary time. Nancy recognized his dilemma and left her husband and took his hand and squeezed it every bit as hard as Ned might have. He was able to get through, barely.

The second reading was from St. Paul's classic digression on Charity, and after the homily each of his children told a poignant story about their mother, while hands wrung, groped, clutched, shoulders heaved, and people wept into damp cloths, and wiped swollen eyes in an agonizingly beautiful service.

Bakewell told Nancy he couldn't speak that morning and Nancy, horrified, cried, "My God, Daddy! Nobody would expect you to. Everyone in the church will be dying for you, for themselves too. They would never expect you to find your voice at such an unbearable time. Their own hearts will be breaking if they haven't already. Give yourself a break. You were the best thing that ever happened to her. They all know that. Mom knew that. They love you. They're proud of you and sorry for your loss. They want to console you. They don't expect you to speak to them."

She was right. He hadn't been thinking clearly, wondered if he was capable of it at the time. They wrote a brief note of remembrance together, Nancy helping her father remember happier times. She read it at Mass just before the service ended. The last line was simple: *She held onto Hope, persevered to the end; she lived a life of Charity, loved charity, was addicted to charity; and she died in Faith, complete and pure, without ever asking why.*

A big part of Bakewell died with her. He never cried or made a fuss during her illness, and, although he almost gave way there in the vestibule, he was able to hold together. Father had said that mourning was for the living; there was no doubting that: the dead moved on to a better place, left pain and sorrow behind. For Bakewell there was no cure, only an hour-by-hour enduring. No place to go, nowhere to turn, no solace; just a one-long-day-after-another kind of dealing with it. He hoped it wasn't the same for his children. They held onto each other, but, while the children and grandchildren were willing to, happy to, looked forward to, talking about her, most tried to avoid the subject, not knowing how to deal with it. And they had their own grief to deal with. He expected nothing from them, knew he had their prayers and best wishes. It took three of her closest friends four days to send answers for all the Mass cards, enrollments, spiritual gifts and beautifully scripted letters that flowed on for weeks. They had done all they could. In the end it was just the simple passing of time. There was nothing else.

Bakewell prayed throughout the long bitter ordeal and just as hard after she was gone. After she left, he was devoted to his children, wanted to be a better role model, determined to leave something of himself, something worthwhile behind. The only other thing that mattered was Ned.

For Ned he had a peculiarly equal, yet totally different kind of loyalty. Bakewell was devoted to Ned.

Nancy

Bakewell settled back into the heavy wrought iron chair, tipping it slightly, knowing Katherine would have scolded him for doing it. Drained from hours of flying and days in the wilderness, free of hostile environs, he let go, closed his eyes, remembering the previous week with contentment. When he opened them again, there was movement to his right. He turned to see his granddaughter, carrying a small plastic container, making careful progress up the steps, holding to the railing with her right hand, focused on the task of delivering her prize. Her mother and baby brother followed at a distance, offering words of encouragement. She approached him shyly, barely raising her eyes, "We brought you some dinner, Old Pop."

"We thought you might be hungry so we brought dinner," Nancy called from the yard. She had the rest of his dinner in one arm and a ten month old in the other.

He stood and took the larger plate from her, placed it on the table then took his grandson, giving his daughter a kiss at the same time. He put the baby down, made sure he had something to grasp and singled out his granddaughter, making sure she got his attention first, gave her the expected hugs and kisses, turned her quickly loose, remembering Katherine's admonition, "Don't force yourself on them." It had become a reflex now. Leaning over the little girl he whispered in her ear, asked half a dozen questions about her toys, day care, friends, getting "nothing" and "huh uh" for an answer each time. When she wandered across the deck he turned his attention to his grandson, picking the little boy up from where he held to the leg of a chair.

"Whoa, buddy, you're getting to be a big man," Bakewell groaned, lifting him high, avoiding the string of drool that fell from his wet chin.

"Welcome home, Dad. You look like you've been in a fight…in the desert." Nancy hugged her father affectionately, kissed his cheek from behind while he played with his grandson.

"Montana's the best place in the world to get a tan."

"What happened to your face?"

"Just the usual nicks and scratches."

"You sure you didn't have a bear?"

Bakewell laughed, "I would have been home a lot sooner if I'd had a bear. Where's my son in law?"

"Mizzou," Nancy said. "Big game, they're on television. He should be home in another two hours. It's already over." Nancy and her husband were Missouri Tigers, like their fathers before them.

"Losing?"

"Yeah, overmatched, Ohio State."

"Pity. When we had Onofrio we whipped the hell out of those guys, kicked Ohio State's butt on national TV, prime time, Saturday night."

"The good old days," Nancy had heard it before.

"We were a contender. Sugar Bowls, played in the first Liberty Bowl, you know? Hell the Liberty Bowl was chump change; we played in three Orange Bowls."

"You sound like Ned."

"It's the truth."

"I know. Now we're a basketball school."

Bakewell shook his head. He didn't care much for basketball. Nancy sat and looked out at the pool, while he held his grandson who gummed the phone wetly. "Been swimming?"

"Yes, the weather's been wonderful. We spent all weekend out there last week."

"I see we're having fall-needle-drop, I better put the cover on soon or we'll burn up the pump." He put his grandson down and held onto him as he balanced unsteadily. "He's not walking yet?"

"Close, maybe another two weeks," she said, watching her infant son. "He's almost there." The baby grabbed for her chair and began to work his way around, while his sister scraped her way across the deck on a faded plastic tricycle that had spent the winter outside and hadn't weathered well.

"How we doing at work?"

"Good. Everybody's working; we need more guys. The big boss's been grumpy all week. Something is really bothering him."

"When I'm gone Ned gets edgy. It always happens."

"Well he's plenty edgy. He's bitching at everybody."

"Ned's harmless, you know he doesn't mean it."

"I know. He'll be okay when you get back Monday."

"How are things with you?"

"Good. The new babysitter's great. Julie loves school. Everybody's healthy."

"How's your biggest brother doing?"

"Andy's good, I think. I haven't seen much of him. I talked to Karen twice. The baby should be here right before Christmas. I don't know how we're gonna handle that though, but they're all fine."

They stared across the yard. "I need to cut my grass. Need to do something about the whole damned yard. I ought to hire a gardener."

"Right. I can see that, the way you love to cut grass, you'd be telling the poor guy what to do."

"Well, if he was smart he'd come when I was at work." Bakewell sighed, "Truthfully, I should sell this house and move."

"No! You need to be here," Nancy said emphatically; changing to a softer tone added, "By the way, the little people want to get together for a barbeque tomorrow, if it's okay?"

"Here?"

"Of course *here*; this is the place, especially in summer." She passed the toddler behind her, taking his hand again as he went around her chair. "Mom would want us to be here. We need to hold onto as much of her as we can." She looked away emotionally.

"Well, I'll clean the skimmers and the filters."

"No, don't bother. It's shady late in the day now. We're all swum out anyway. Tom and Andy can help you get it closed tomorrow."

He looked at the sad state of his yard: Katherine's once lovely garden. It was mostly wildflowers and perennials that bloomed at different times from April to October and required a lot of pruning and weed pulling. His daughter and daughter-in-law had tried to keep up with it, but small children and a home of their own made it impossible. He managed to keep it up early in the year for two springs but lost interest long before July. After that it gradually degraded.

Julie got stuck trying to ride the little toy up the steps and cried in frustration. Nancy helped her absently, a young mother action that looked easier than it was. Julie recovered her dignity and rolled on.

"I should move out of here, give the place to you or your brother."

"No Dad, you need to be here. You're too young to move yet." Nancy was silent, knowing her father wouldn't add much to the conversation. She was pensive. "You just need company."

Bakewell looked at his daughter, surprised, amused. Her mother had been the consummate matchmaker. "Are we talking a mate?"

She returned the smile. It was her mother's smile. "Speaking of which," she nodded for emphasis, "Mrs. Walker called me while you were out of town. *Twice*." Nancy raised her eyebrows. "She sounded mad. She said you never tell her where you're going. 'Always off in that damned plane somewhere.'" Nancy enjoyed herself. She moved a large gardenia plant so Julie could pass, speaking over her shoulder. "I think she's after you Dad."

"She would be a catch," Bakewell mused.

"You're not kidding. She dresses like a million and she looks great for her age."

"For her age."

"Hey, I'm not being critical. She's very attractive."

"You need a million to dress like Mrs. Walker." He nodded, agreeing with Nancy's assessment of Maggie Walker.

"Do you call her Mrs. Walker?" Nancy laughed.

"No."

"Was she a friend of Mom's too, did they know each other?"

"No." Bakewell picked his grandson up, cuddled him affectionately.

"So how many times have you been out with her?"

"Four." He sighed. "She's invited me to her club several times, but I really don't want to go."

Nancy nodded, laughing like she was in the know, enjoying the idea of her father having a suitor. "You really don't want to go?"

"I really don't, I probably know as many people at Algonquin as she does." He bent down and put his grandson on the deck, holding his hand as he made it across to his mother's chair. He was a beautiful little boy; Bakewell doted on him like a grandfather was supposed to. When he sat back in his chair he said, "I hate to be rude. I know it means something to her. Her family was there for years and now that she's back in town, they've let her rejoin. I'm sure she's thrilled to be there again."

"She wants to show you off, Dad!"

"Yeah, 'meet the old timer,'" he said, rubbing his week old growth of beard. It was mottled now, turning gray. "She could tell them she brought me out for the day…from the home."

Nancy laughed dutifully at his weak humor. Bakewell loved the sound of her laughter.

"Come on Dad. She's after you. She picked you out. Go for it!"

"I'm still in love with your mother, Nancy. I don't think I could ever let her go." He yawned, leaned back in his chair and sighed. After several minutes, he got up and went into the kitchen and brought back two bottles of beer.

Nancy held up her hand, "Yuk, too rich for me." Bakewell's taste in beer ran to heavy ales. He opened one bottle with the cap of the other, a trick he learned long before screw tops were invented then rubbed his arthritic hands. He ached from head to foot.

"Dad, please, don't misunderstand; I mean no disrespect, but I think it's fine if you get involved with her, and I know my brothers feel the same way. Just sort of date her on a casual basis, maybe?"

"No. She's a nice looking woman, but she's not my type."

"She's your type Dad. She's a lady, just like Mom."

"Mm. You're sure about that? She could be a vamp for all you know?"

Nancy laughed at the term. Her father was always using old-fashioned expressions. "You can tell with her. She's got the look. I mean she *doesn't have the look*."

"What look is that?"

"She's the type that can sit in a place like Rick's, alone, and none of the bozos at the bar would ever think of bothering her."

"Oh, they'd think about it all right."

"Well, they might think about it, but they wouldn't do it, Dad."

Bakewell was amused by the thought. "Mrs. Walker tends to draw men, Nancy. A lot of moths have burnt their wings around that flame."

"They wouldn't bother her Dad. They never bothered Mom and you made her wait at Rick's lots of times. She used to get furious with you for being late."

"You're right. Funny thing, your mom probably would have liked to be bothered. She could talk to anyone; she would never have been rude, no matter how obnoxious they were."

Nancy nodded, pursing her lips as she did. Her mother would tolerate anyone, including fools. But she was sure none of the malingerers at Rick's had ever approached her. The subject actually came up once with Dolly, the cocktail waitress. Dolly had been the one to first use "the look" expression. "Honey, none of these shits would dare approach your mom," she had said with contempt. "She's doesn't have *the look.*"

Bakewell stretched slowly, turning his head back and forth and rubbed his hands together again, holding them back over his head. "I've known Maggie Walker since she was nineteen. She's the most formidable woman, girl then, I ever knew, and that covers a few. To be perfectly honest, I'm a little afraid of her."

"You're not afraid of anyone. Not my dad," Nancy said, picking up the baby. It never ceased to amaze him, the power of parenting, the imprinting that went on and on. "It's okay, Dad; we've talked about it, Michael, Andy and I. We don't want you to be so alone. Really, you need to find someone. Mom would want you to do it. She would do it in your place."

"Your mother had more energy than me. That kind of stuff takes a lot of energy. When I get home, all I want is a beer and a book. I fall asleep in my chair, sleep half the damned evening, have to wake up to go to bed."

"It's not energy Dad. You're in great shape. You can still do stuff with Michael and Andy. I see you playing ball here in the yard with the boys whenever we're together, especially when Michael comes home. I think you're just a little depressed."

Bakewell offered no argument. He didn't know. Depression was a possibility. He had been very depressed the first months after his wife's death. They sat and watched the children and spoke gently of the past. There were years of memories there in the yard before them. After several minutes Nancy said, "Call her, Dad."

"Who?"

"Mrs. Walker. Don't be dumb."

"You're mother said I came by it naturally."

"She was only teasing."

"Nancy, I can't start chasing women at my age. Besides, what would I do if I caught one? Sex outside marriage is still a sin."

"Dad!"

"Well it is. It was a sin when Moses led the Israelites out of Egypt, and when Charlemagne signed the Magna Carta. It was a sin during the Renaissance and the French Revolution. It will be a sin five centuries from now."

"I'm not suggesting anything immoral." Nancy had heard the speech before.

"You can't reinvent morality," Bakewell said, determined to finish the discourse. "It isn't subject to interpretation, you know. It's not what these television nitwits say it is. It's what it always was. It doesn't change."

"Dad, please, you're preaching to the choir."

"I'm right about this. I know I am."

"I can't talk about sex with my own father." Nancy spread her hands wide.

"Good. We won't have this conversation again. It's too bizarre anyway."

"Agreed," she stared at him with an amused expression, knowing she would hear it again and again. Nancy leaned back in her chair, gathering him in. After a long minute she tilted her head back further and added wickedly, "But call Mrs. Walker anyway. You don't have to boink her."

"Oh my God," Bakewell said. He looked away, across his yard, frustrated, embarrassed.

There would be no more conversation on the subject. Nancy watched her father, not sure if she had crossed a line. He needed a haircut. He had cuts and abrasions on his face, arms and hands. He looked very tired. He was getting old. She knew it was inevitable, but she hated to be reminded, hated to see it. Her mother's death had aged him. She hadn't noticed it at the time, only that he seemed bent at the shoulders, but now she could see the added gray in his hair, especially his beard. Bakewell didn't notice her attention, lost in his own thoughts as he gazed across the long yard.

Nancy got up and handed him the baby and took the food she brought into the kitchen and put it in the refrigerator. When she came back outside, she leaned over him from behind and put her arms around his neck. She gave her father and her infant son both a kiss then gave her father a strong hug. She also gave him instructions on how to warm the food, as her mother would have done. When she started to leave Bakewell gave her the baby and quickly scooped up his granddaughter and smothered her with unwanted affection. Julie tried to get away but Bakewell was intent. He loved to hug and kiss his only granddaughter. Julie struggled. "Old Pop, Old Pop, I love you, I love you, but stop it, please."

Nancy laughed loudly, couldn't help it. She had said the very same words to her daddy when she was about Julie's age, when he would pin her to the floor and smother her with kisses. Julie tried to wriggle away and Bakewell quit kissing her and spoke softly instead, whispering secrets in her ear. She was indifferent. He told her she was the prettiest little girl in all of St. Louis, bragged on what a wonder she was. He called her Juliet, which she loved; gradually she accepted his affection. She liked when her grandfather whispered in her ear. She paid no attention to what he said, but enjoyed the idea of having secrets. She had been carefully schooled on how to love her grandfather, how to return his affection, ever since her grandmother had died. Bakewell carried her out to the car.

When Nancy put them in the car he got another hug from his daughter before she went around and got into the van. He stood on the hot pavement in his bare feet and watched them back out of the drive. The pavement felt good under his bruised feet. As they drove down the street Julie waved back and blew him an imaginary kiss. When they were gone Bakewell went back into the shade of the garage, opened the bag and unwrapped the ram's head and carried it out into the sunlight where he could see it better. He examined it carefully to make sure the soft tissue was drying properly. After he put it back in the shade of the garage he called the taxidermist and told him about his success. The voice on the other end was excited. He hadn't done a bighorn in a long time. He told Bakewell he had to leave his shop, but would meet him back there in the morning. Missouri's big game season hadn't opened yet. The taxidermist only had a few animals coming down from Alaska and Canada – mostly Caribou.

Manchester Road

O my Jesus, through the Immaculate Heart of Your Mother Mary... Bakewell prayed on his way to work. It took twenty-five minutes to get home in the evening, but only fifteen going the other way in the early morning, enough time to reflect and pray in the trafficless predawn darkness. The praying originated with a money crisis in the 80's, had continued, increasing in fervor through years of exacting struggle as he and Ned turned their economic fortunes around, reaching a fevered pitch when Katherine got sick. Bakewell tended toward repetition, using the same verses, the same prayers he'd learned in childhood.

He loved and hated the familiar drive because his daily commute took him east and west on a road he'd traveled his entire life. Like a rural resident taking the same gravel road to the same paved highway, crossing the same bridge over the same stream in order to reach the same town, he made his way. Manchester Road ran east/west through the sprawling west county of St. Louis.

St. Louis didn't count the county's population with the city's the way Los Angeles did, and for that reason the population had been dwindling for years even though the suburban sprawl surrounding the city continued to grow, running from Wentzville in Missouri, thirty-five miles west of the Gateway Arch, to Belleville in Illinois another twenty-five miles to the east. Flying over the area, shooting approaches at the satellite airports, Bakewell observed the exponential spread of habitation that was St. Louis, a sixty-mile metropolis, home to millions of people.

He almost couldn't remember a day that didn't start with Manchester Road. With the exception of his time in service and away at the University, he had never lived more than two blocks from Manchester. The road provided a common thread in the tattered and ragged tapestry of his life, a life that seemed long and much too narrow in retrospect. He was born a year after the war ended and lived his early childhood in Rock Hill, then only a village dissected by Manchester Road. Later the family moved to Brentwood. The house in Rock Hill was not a full block south of Manchester, the home in Brentwood a block north.

In Brentwood they had lived a bleak existence after his father surrendered to his wartime injuries. His mother had struggled to find closure with that heartbreak which followed too soon after the tragedy of losing her brothers on Day 1 of the Second World War. The responsibility of raising children in a male dominated world was an uphill battle for a woman in the 50's. Bakewell often thought of his mother's life as stream – a steep, narrow, fast moving stream, water shallow, rough and turbulent, with a seemingly endless number of little gravel bars that caused her to scrape bottom. It didn't take much to upset her fragile psyche. When that happened she went into tearful rages about life's injustice that often left her huddled in the corner of the couch, chain-smoking and despondent. Her emotion was a trial for the two Bakewell boys, and both developed an aversion to feminine emotion long before they were teenagers.

She lived with her parents after the birth of Bakewell's older brother. That was in 1942. She lived without her aviator husband for more than three years before the navy sent him home from the Pacific, broken, trying to navigate and not vegetate, as he put up the good fight in and out of the Veteran's Hospital. Bakewell was six the year his father died, his brother Brenden was ten.

The stream had calmer waters, where the current slowed to a crawl and the pace of life settled. Katherine and her grandchildren were the joys of Mrs. Bakewell's life. She loved Katherine and loved her grandchildren as life gradually settled down and she was able to devote her time to what assistance Katherine required. The last decade of her life was probably bettered only by the decade she and Charlie shared from high school to the middle of the war. She died two years before her daughter-in-law, content in life and with her place in the lives of her grandchildren. Content being a relative term, since Mrs. Bakewell was never reluctant to complain, and, with the possible exception of her daughter-in-law, never missed an opportunity to point out anyone's shortcomings. If suffering without complaining was the way to heaven, Bakewell thought his mother was in for a rough trip. If suffering by itself was the way to get there, he was sure she had found peace at last; the stream had slowed, flowed into what he hoped was a verdant delta of happiness where the grass blew gently yellow in a golden sunset of Eternal Light.

Bakewell's mother was Scandinavian, a large, attractive woman, born a Rasmussen, the oldest of three children. She lost both her brothers when the Arizona went down on December 7th – a day that would "live in infamy" in ways uncountable for the Rasmussens. Her immigrant father, a domineering man from a family of seamen, who had never been to sea himself (he made his living on the levee, a purser for a consortium of barge lines, not far from the site of the Gateway Arch), died shortly after the war, inconsolable and incommunicative. The old man passed away in his sleep when Bakewell was two.

Somewhere in his house was a scrapbook – Charlie's wartime career – sent on by sympathetic squadron mates as a gift to remind him of his glory days. Bakewell paid little attention to the musty collection, but it became the anthem book of his brother Brenden's young life. It was Brenden's most treasured possession. Brenden had lived in awe of the war, in awe of their father's contribution. Their father flew the famous P-38 Lightning, had participated in aerial combat, shot down something called a "Kate" and ditched a plane off the south end of a strip in New Georgia in 1943. Charlie

Bakewell's wartime career was the highlight of his short life. But Bakewell's memories of his father were vague, nothing compared to the memories Brenden cherished. Brenny had fallen in love with his father's wildly exciting stories of the war in the Pacific. Bakewell remembered the funny smell of the tattered scrapbook, which tended to fall apart when opened, and was full of age-browning photographs of young men leaning against airplanes with two propellers and big perforated cannons pointing from the snout of the fuselage. Brenny loved the war, loved his father's participation, loved the fact that he had been involved. Brenden would become a warrior.

The difference in the Bakewell boys' age coincided with their father's wartime absence, and because of the difference in age, Bakewell lived in awe of his older brother, who looked out for him and helped raise him with a youthful bravado as he tried to substitute for the father neither boy got to enjoy. They were soul mates as they shared their joint adversity; their lives constantly interrupted by the chaos of an overwrought mother, who often went over the edge. It left them forever apprehensive, tentative and confused by women in general, and gave both boys a nervous aversion to the feminine condition. Their childhood had been a pounding surf of tidal highs and lows, intense, strained, acute, always emotional, even at low tide.

At sixteen Brenny left to join the Marine Corps but was soon returned by an understanding man in dress greens who ended up staying for dinner and spent the evening on the front porch talking with "the widow Bakewell." At eighteen, unwilling to forgive the Marine Corps, and as soon as graduation was over, Brenny joined the army. Later, like his idolized brother, anxious to get away from the emotion of his childhood and find a life among men, when school was no longer an option, Bakewell opted for departure, taking a sweat soaked train to San Diego under a blistering September sun. Brenden may have been his idol, but Bakewell was no warrior. He hated every day of what he thought of as his "military captivity." Four years later he got an "early out," August 2nd – forty-seven months after enlisting. It was a date Bakewell had secretly celebrated as his birthday ever since.

During college he stayed at his mother's house each summer, thinking of it as "transient housing" while he pursued an education. His final year of college he moved to the married student housing, a section commonly referred to as "fertile valley," where he and Katherine mixed tradition with slang and conceived their first child, his oldest son and namesake. Then it was back to St. Louis and a little house not far from Manchester Road.

In the mid 80's, with Nancy and Michael still in grade school, they moved for the last time to Des Peres, again only a long fly ball from Manchester, where they could hear angry cars at the intersection on rare, pre-storm nights, when the wind was out of the northeast.

As he passed the abandoned Lincoln/Mercury dealership in Rock

Hill, an empty building in a crack filled parking lot, he remembered the grove of giant oak trees that once stood sentry there. The trees formed a canopy over a gravel lane that led to an old farmhouse and barn. It had been a blacksmithy and he remembered walking down the lane with a playmate one summer where they found a short, swarthy man named Bierman, lifting a piece of glowing steel. He placed it on an anvil and swung a great hammer with huge forearms, arcing it high as he brought it down on the hot steel. Sparks flew and the sound rang out, and they had backed away worried. The man was big voiced, dark-visaged and had a stern, intimidating demeanor. When he saw fear in their faces he filled the barn with great peels of laughter that chased them up the driveway never to return.

Passing the street of his childhood home, he vaguely remembered a man with a horse drawn wagon who came through the neighborhood to sharpen knives, mower blades, and old scythes – still a common yard tool after the war. Looking up the hill, he also remembered an ancient truck the kids recognized by the sound of the engine shifting gears as it climbed their hill. The truck delivered block ice to the only home on Plainfield still using an "ice box." The driver, another big man, placed a leather apron over his shoulder, before grabbing the block with a pair of tongs. He would heave it up on the leather apron and carry it down the sidewalk while the neighborhood kids stared in amusement – their parents ridiculed the neighbor for still having an ice box, even though everybody still referred to their own refrigerator as "ice box" at the time.

Just ahead, he crossed a narrow creek where it flowed under Manchester. He'd once planned to navigate the creek to River Des Peres then on to the Mississippi, in a little wooden crate he tried to convert to a boat by filling the cracks with tar from roofing shingles. He found the shingles on a nearby construction site, and painstakingly melted the tar, dripping it into the cracks with box after box of wooden matches. He was eight that year. Brenden had taken up hardball with the Khoury Leagues and was gone most of the summer…

Blacksmiths, icemen, horse drawn wagons...now space shuttles, Microsoft and cell phones – my life has spanned an epoch.

***

"Trudy, what day is it?" Bakewell asked as he came through the door.

"Well hello to you too, honey…and welcome back. It's Monday?" Trudy was always early, an unwed mother with a daughter problem, she had trouble sleeping. It didn't surprise him to find her there at six. "What in the name of Pete happened to you?"

His scrapes and scratches were scabbing now, enflamed, in purple contrast to his tanned skin. "I'm fine. You keeping them on the ball?"

"You know it, skipper." He liked her more for her attitude than her considerable skill. He looked at the pile of mail in his box, thought about going through it, grabbed the stack instead and walked to his office.

"Can I get you some coffee?"

"I get my own coffee."

"Just thought I'd ask." She had a tendency to mother him since Katherine died.

"Anybody asks you to get their coffee, give them their check," he called over his shoulder. He and Ned tried to act tough around the women in the office, seeking protection behind the façade. The women in their lives got whatever they wanted, so they wanted to keep them at a distance. He dumped the mail on the floor next to his desk, where he would have to step over it. His attention deficiency redefined forgetful, everyone in the office aware of it; they returned keys, coffee cups and folders regularly.

He turned his computer on, logged in, and while he waited for the investment page to appear, made himself a cup of coffee. Overhearing a profane exchange outside the door, he confronted the guilty parties. "There's a lady right behind this wall," he said, tapping for emphasis. The men dropped their heads. Surrounded by profanity for decades, Bakewell, like Ned, had three rules about language: never in front of women, never in front of his children, and keep it simple, with words about action and anatomy. Bakewell never took the Lord's name in vain.

When he returned, the computer screen was lit and he hit "Watch List" and waited. There was a presence behind him, a giant standing in the doorway.

"Hello Ned."

"Well, was you sneaky and stealthy or was you full of dumb luck?"

"You don't look good."

"How's it goin, bub," his partner said, still filling the doorway. "The kids said you got one. Damn! After all these years, you finally got one, huh?" Ned was a bear, whose sloping shoulders almost touched the doorway. Bakewell had known him for years, had worked for Ned when he first started, a fact Ned never let him forget. Ned loved to tell people he'd, "Taught Andy ever-thin he knowed."

"Geez, after all these years, you must be proud as hell, huh?" It was a question. Ned often talked in questions, but parsed his answers, kept them to simple sentences when he was sober.

"It was a thrill, Ned. I never expected to get a shot, certainly not a shot at the one I killed. I was your 'blind hog, finding an acorn.'" Ned nodded, smiled, satisfied. "I'm not sure; maybe things even out in the end." Bakewell slid his chair back from the desk and leaned far back against the soft leather, taking the pressure off his back. "You're worrying me with that distant look. You look like the bearer of bad news."

"I was worried about ya is all, Andy. I always worry about ya when you're in that piss-ass little plane, especially when yer up in them mountains fuckin with the wildlife." Ned kept his voice low so Trudy wouldn't hear the language. They were a pair of 19th Century men, a couple of dinosaurs, proud of it.

"I'm more worried about the look of you right now. Give it to me straight."

Ned closed the door and sat down heavily, filling the large upholstered chair. He looked directly at Bakewell. Ned always made penetrating eye contact. "We lost."

There was a stunned silence. Neither man spoke as Ned watched Bakewell's reaction. It wasn't long coming; Bakewell nearly shouted. "Aw shit, come on! How could we lose?"

"We lost. It's over. The lawyer's aw-ready looking to get paid. I guess they're scared they ain't, want to be first in line."

"How?"

"Judge…it was all her, didn't have a clue. A big fat one, inner city. Thinks ever-body owns a business is loaded." Ned rubbed his brow with the large fingers of his right hand. "She was real impressed with the slick dick doin the defendin. Guy just happened to be black too. Prolly her nephew."

"Our guys said it was in the bag – a no brainer. They said we didn't have anything to worry about. They told me to take my trip. Where were our slick dicks?" Ned didn't respond. Bakewell pushed his chair back. "Shit. We couldn't lose? What the…." His voice trailed off. "Shit!"

Ned slumped further in the chair; neither man spoke.

"When?"

"Last Tuesday, I think. Days run together at my age."

"Well fuck!" Bakewell looked around in disgust. "Shit-fuck-shit," he said quietly. Then he got louder. "Fuck! What the fuck! Where's the fucking justice? It was as plain as black and white. Where's the fucking law when you need it? What the fuck does an honest man have to do to ever, ever, ever get some fucking justice in the fucked up world of fucked up lawyers?" He knocked the calculator off his desk; it banged against the wall. After it settled the room grew quiet, both men devastated by the enormity of the loss, the silence interrupted only by street sounds.

"That's the most 'shits & fucks' I ever heard out of you, Andy."

"What are we gonna do, Ned? *What the fuck* are we gonna do?"

He and Ned had built a strong company from the rubble of an early disaster, had made a huge come back. They were proud of their success, bragged about it. They'd paid their debts and gotten back to the top of the industry, were only too happy to tell the world how they had done it. They were a success story. Everybody loved a success story, especially creditors. They never dreamed the world of corporate raiders would bother with them –

that was Wall Street stuff. When the Eastern crowd showed up with an agenda for consolidation, they quickly singled them out, the obvious and first choice. Neither saw it coming. It was swift and cruel. The raiders were fools, with money to invest. They were going to "reinvent the wheel" in a tough industry – without local connections or clientele. It was ill conceived. They went bust in a few years. Bakewell he and Ned were cleaned out, left with the building, the equipment and a skeleton force to run it. Everyone left with a blue sky offer to double their salaries – offers qualified with incentive clauses, proposed bonuses and wild promises. Everyone was sure they would get rich. Men he and Ned had invested years in, some with twenty years seniority, left to follow fellow workers in confused panic. The promises never eventuated and the venture failed. Everyone lost their job and the big hitters pulled out and left town; they also left a wake of debt, a lot in unpaid salaries. A few of the old employees came back, but only a trickle. Most were too ashamed to return.

"Our new hire loses close to a hunnert grand and now this," Ned said in disgust. "College boy, why we hired that fuck I'll never know."

Bakewell had heard the complaint often. Ned wasn't a fan of education, and no fan of engineers, had come up the hard way, believed in street education, and hard earned experience. He said Bakewell was the only engineer he knew "could walk and talk at the same time."

"What's the bottom line?"

"That's kinda your department."

"Don't bullshit me, Ned. You have the numbers in your head."

"After legal fees, court costs, miscellaneous expenses…" Ned turned a huge palm up and thought for a moment. "Close to two hundred grand, not to mention all the time I spent – wasted really with it. That prolly cost us another hunnert grand."

"We built that sewer to spec, Ned. We followed the drawing, did everything per the code."

"It's not our work, Andy. It's the tie-in."

"The tie in wasn't part of our scope. How could we know it was bogus? Everything we did was per the sewer district's specs."

"The way they see it they paid fer sewers that would work and the tie-in won't take the water. They ain't gonna pay fer no work that ain't workin, so somebody's gotta take the fall. When the fingerpointin started, them political fucks pointed at us and we didn't have enough fingers to point back with. The judge didn't never want to know our side." Ned paused for breath.

They had done the job for a general contractor who had a big home in the city in one of the few high rent districts. He was an egomaniac, full of himself, contemptible of anyone who wouldn't kiss his ring. According to Ned, he sold them out as soon as he saw the direction the court was headed. He was a ruthless, arrogant type, a type that made them both want to find another life.

"There's no fuckin fun anymore, Andy. Only thing's left is the misery. It's all about confrontation, about who's at fault ever time a job don't go perfect."

Bakewell couldn't agree more. Both men were tired, disgusted with the trend business had taken. They had stayed too long and they were suffering from burn out. It was a game for younger people.

"And that sonufabitch…" Ned began again, "One of your Catholic buddies. That prick'd sell anybody down the drain fer another award. Always been in it fer himself and them awards. The Archdiocese'll prolly give him another plaque." Ned stood, hitched his sagging pants and walked across the room. "And them engineers, them so called experts; finger pointin fucks, so tight with their inspector pals. They switched sides so fast I never seen em leave. Next thing I know'd I was sittin all alone. If I didn't have them lawyers next to me, I woulda been speechless with nobody to talk to." Ned paused, low on oxygen. "Those city inspector boys prolly went to the same school with the judge. And them dipshit engineers, them stargazers, spend a fortune entertainin them politicals."

Bakewell was numb, slumping in his chair. "What are we gonna do, Ned?"

"We're done, Andy. We can work till the end of the year then shut 'er down. This year's pretty much done. October, November maybe, if we're lucky, then it's over. Nothin left to do. It's all overhead after that. Nothin comin in, ever-thin goin out."

The phone beeped. "Yes?"

"You've got a call on line one, Andy."

"No calls right now."

"Nooo problem," Trudy said brightly. "I'll take a message."

Ned adjusted his watch. It had an expandable band that was permanently stretched around his enormous wrist. Ned leaned his head against the wall and sighed deeply. "Shit, I been here thirty years almost. Ever-thin I got is right here. Ever-thin I worked for my whole life's right here in this building. Now it ain't worth shit."

Bakewell waited for him to go on, trying to think. He was organized, the engineer in him, systematic, analytical. He was attention deficient, but his logical mind had always been his hallmark. "How much do you figure we're down, total?"

"Over six hunnert grand." Ned spoke to the ceiling.

The room was silent. Neither man spoke for a long time. A truck crossed the bridge outside. A voice called to someone. The only thing missing was a ticking clock. A death was taking place and they both knew it.

"So this is what it sounds like." Ned stared at him blankly. "I was expecting a sound, a gurgling, maybe a death rattle… although I don't know what a death rattle sounds like."

"Shit," Ned made another long sigh; it came from way down. "Shit." He put his enormous hands on his knees and looked at them pensively. "I shoulda stuck to a life of crime. I was a pretty good thief once. I prolly woulda done a little time, nothing big, I woulda been okay."

Bakewell went to the window and looked through the blinds then moved closer, sat across from Ned, leaned forward and spoke in a soft voice. "I've never thought like this before, Ned, never talked like this before, never considered the words even, but I have to ask. How much are we on the hook for? Personally?"

Ned was ready for the question. "The bank's got first pick; we're persunully liable for about eight hundred and fifty grand. Counting the building and some equipment loans, it's pushing a million, four. We're not on the hook, persunully, for nothin else. You don't want to hear this Andy, but there's a little that somebody's gonna get burned for."

"How much?"

"A few hunnert gran, maybe two."

Both men were sickened by the thought of not being able to pay someone. It had happened to them many times. They'd been stiffed more times than either could remember. There was no way to put a figure to it, but they had never stiffed anyone, never thought a time would come when they might not pay someone.

"You sound awfully knowledgeable," Bakewell said distastefully.

"I went and seen a bankruptcy lawyer the day after we lost."

There was another long silence; Bakewell tried to regroup.

"Okay, we've got equity in the building."

"Yeah, and we still got the steel."

"Another half million."

"At least."

"So we finish the year, making enough to cover the current overhead and we're down $650,000 when we close the doors?"

"You forgot the loss we've been carrying forward. That's another $300 grand."

Bakewell wasn't thinking clearly, still exhausted from the trip. It would take several days before his acuity got up to speed.

"It's about $475 thou apiece, it you want an exact number."

"My God, Ned, three years ago we were millionaires. Where did it go?"

"Losses, Andy. We been losin hunnerts a gran a year since we got raided. And with a dumb fuck accountant we never really felt it comin 'til the rug got pulled from under us, and then it was too late to duck. It's just a real kick in the balls, is all. We been fucked by a lady judge and a bunch a pussy willow lawyers and politicians."

"That's not going to leave you much."

"Or you. I can walk with my profit sharing. They can't touch that. Ever-thin I got I own, only got one car that ain't paid for. You're in deep shit, Andy. Your property's in your name. I give all mine to my daughter years ago. You ain't gonna have nothin left."

Bakewell put his head in his hands. Ned was right, but Bakewell didn't care about hiding from creditors. He wanted to pay them. He might have done his service with the navy, but he thought of himself as a Semper Fi marine when it came to a fight. He didn't know if he had the stuff; he'd never been tested, but he believed he would have done the right thing, sacrificed himself. He felt the same way about his subs and his suppliers. If he was going down, he didn't want to take anybody with him, wanted to fall on the grenade, take the hit, protect the other guys, pay his debts. It was about ego as much as integrity. He couldn't leave a trail of debts, couldn't leave anybody in his wake. He was relieved Katherine was gone. She wouldn't witness this, wouldn't see him go under, see him fail. His children and Ned were his only responsibility. He didn't care about himself any longer, was ready to check into a monastery, become a handyman or a janitor maybe. It was something he had been contemplating for a long time. But he had to take care of them first. Ned was probably more important. The kids were young, resilient; Ned was an old man now, out of gas and out of options.

Ned got up, started for the door, paused. "One thing, Andy. We gotta act good, like ever-thin's okay 'til the time comes. Nobody wants to be around no losers; nobody wants to work for no losers. We gotta hold onto our heads. Keep 'em up high where everybody can see em." He waited until Bakewell nodded in acknowledgement then left the room, closing the door behind. A closed door meant: DO NOT DISTURB. Ned knew the kid needed some time to work his way through the cruel reality of what confronted them.

Bakewell didn't move after he left, sick with fear, with knowing what was ahead: a nightmare of unpaid bills and unhappy people wanting money. They would come in two types: the sophisticated kind who had lawyers and went for the jugular, who could take his home, his possessions; and the other type, the kind, who wouldn't know how to deal with not being paid, who would resort to violence. Fifteen years before, during their rebuilding era, they'd had an altercation in the office and another out front of the building over unpaid bills. Bakewell had gotten blindsided during the second event, knocked unconscious by a little guy who hit him with a sack filled with something. Ned had waded in and run them off before he came to. The first altercation was even worse. Their secretary was confronted by a simple little guy who was out of cash and couldn't pay his bills. They had to wrestle the guy to the ground. It was ugly. Bakewell hated it, felt the guy's pain, and felt the sting of not being able to pay him. His poorer creditors would just be trying to get along. They wouldn't come looking for trouble, just wanted their money, and he wouldn't have it. He and Ned swore they would never get in that situation again, would always have plenty of cash laid away for working capital. They had done without to keep enough around in emergencies, now it was gone too. His stomach rolled, dreading what was to come: the ugliness, the tension, the stress. Dealing with the suits and their lawyers was one thing; not being able to pay the little guys was brutal.

The market hadn't opened yet but his computer screen showed the Dow and NASDAQ had plummeted the Friday before.

Brenden

Brenden Bakewell was a warrior. He grew up in a middle class, post-war neighborhood, where veterans abounded. Most of the neighbors had served in a world war. Mr. Chambers, across the street was a tail gunner with the 8th Air Force, had flown twenty missions over Germany. The man next door, a quiet, taciturn cigar smoker, had been a sergeant with the 1st Marines and fought in the South Pacific for more than two years. The man down the street drove a milk truck for the Pevely Dairy Company, left at 3AM each morning, but liked to join the summer evening chats, which often occurred on the Chambers' screened-in porch. Mr. Roach, the milkman, had fought on the Western Front in The Great War, had worked a machine gun, together with a second man, and told amazing stories about gun barrels melting from the heat of firing so many rounds, about how men actually died from the explosion of their own weapon. Brenden's first baseball coach had survived the Battle of the Bulge, another neighbor had been a prisoner of the brutal Japanese in Burma. Almost every kid in the neighborhood had a dad that had served in the war.

There was little talk of death when they got together after dinner. Mostly the men talked about the places they'd been sent, and the amazing variety of geography and people they'd encountered. They were all kids of the Great Depression, never dreamed of leaving Missouri, and ended up in North Africa, New Guinea, Sicily, Northern Europe, even Greece. Brenden loved the conversations, listened, wide-eyed, once asked how many men they had killed – a comment that brought a quiet reprimand and created a momentary pause in the conversation. They spoke of their different experiences and the times they'd had, good and bad. They also discussed the strategies that had succeeded – and failed – to win the war. Often they talked about men lost, for no good reason, because of the perceived incompetence of leadership. They spoke of MacArthur's vanity, the heavy load Eisenhower carried prior to D-Day, what a good man Joe Stillwell was, and where they were and what they were doing when President Roosevelt died.

Afterward the conversations turned to politics, especially 1949. It was an election year and they all chuckled in agreement, "the job was too big for Harry." Mr. Truman wasn't the revered leader he later became. In those days he was trying to measure up to his predecessor.

On colder evenings, Brenden would retrieve his father's wartime scrap book, the pictures already beginning to yellow and bend. The book had been sent on by squadron mates, who put it together after the war, when they heard about how bad Charlie was and what a tough time he was having. Charlie kept the scrapbook in a zippered case in the hall closet. Brenden would bring the book to his father, seated in a comfortable chair next to the large, stand-up radio with the tiny little dial; the one they listened to when they learned Mr. Truman had "lost" the election. Brenden would open the book and point to the planes and the men in the pictures and his father would get a faraway look and tell of the excitement of flying, tell his oldest son what it was like to fly a real airplane. He pronounced the word *aero-plane*, like the WWI veterans.

Charlie had learned to fly for free before the war, part of President Roosevelt's program to get kids interested in flying in the very likely event that they would go to war. He told stories about flying a tiny little yellow Cub over the city, of running out of gas because of quirky, untrustworthy gauges, of having to ditch in a corn field not five minutes from where they lived at the time. Because he was a pilot before he enlisted, Charlie was approved for flight training right out of basic, and where, after some early struggles, he moved on through three phases of advanced training. He flew P-40's for two years before moving on to fly the red hot, twin-engined Lightning, a reality that still brought a whistle of wonder and an amazed satisfaction. Charlie was wounded slightly when he took some ground fire on one of his sorties over the Central Solomons. The gear wouldn't come down and he made a belly up landing that left him unfit for duty for three weeks. That same year he dumped a plane near Bougainville and was picked up by islanders, eventually making his way back to duty via a submarine. His last incident involved a landing in the water just short of the runway in a place called New Georgia. Charlie loved reliving what he called the best part of his life, and made no bones about how much he enjoyed his flying days, his days of glory and success. That was before he was wounded the last time, when they found him in the jungle on New Ireland, busted up and beyond repair, and sent him stateside.

He talked with his hands, like aviators do, describing turns, banks, climbs and dives, and flying formation, and would describe to a wide-eyed little boy, the terrific increase in speed the twin engined plane achieved when the nose was pushed over, the sound inside the cockpit of a singing fuselage, the dizzying confusion of aerial combat.

Brenden loved the stories, but was disappointed his father had flown planes and not had the opportunity to kill Japs with a rifle or better, with his bare hands. He read the corny post war texts, the macho stuff, written by men who had been there and were anxious to tell their part as soon as they got home. Those books played down the misery and the gore, the horror that seared the individual memories of a generation of men who fought on every side. Brenden had a favorite book, *A Ribbon and A Star*, about the fight for Bougainville. His father thought it made light of the war's severity, but it had occurred on Bougainville, and Charlie had personal knowledge of Bougainville.

Brenny was a senior in high school when Bakewell was in the 8th grade, ready for his "second enlistment." This one would be successful. That was the year they talked their mother into letting Brenny drive the family's only car to the Meramec, where the two boys discovered a heavy wooden johnboat buried in flood debris after one of the spring floods. It was water-logged, a monster for two boys to handle, but they managed to right it, and Brenny, using a sapling he cut and trimmed, poled the boat, while his little brother bailed for all he was worth to keep it afloat. Later, when Brenden was home on leave, they would rent a canoe and float the streams comprising the scenic Ozark waterways. The best trips were in the fall, when the rivers were quiet and they could plan three days of over-nighting, sleeping under the stars on a gravel bar. By then Brenden had acquired some serious survival skills, had become the consummate volunteer, had an Airborne patch on his uniform and lots of training. Ultimately, he would end up with the Special Forces and wear a green beret. He did three tours in Viet Nam, the first one as an advisor, before America knew where Viet Nam was, or how to spell it. He started his last tour with two hash marks on his sleeve, a sergeant with nine years of service.

Brenden tried to teach his brother a variety of techniques during the peaceful midday lulls drifting the river. He'd learned stealth to the point of stalking wild things until he could touch them, grab an unsuspecting snake and dangle it just outside striking distance, before tossing it aside with contempt. Brenden thrived on the training, excelled at it, was later chosen to be an instructor.

Brenden could build a fire in the rain, without matches, identify edible plants, and edible foods in the forest, things that revolted Bakewell. Brenny tried to teach him hand to hand combat, throwing him down on the soft sand, pinning him, with one hand over his neck, a stick pointed at his throat. Bakewell was reluctant to learn the violent moves that could kill or maim. He was more of a straight on puncher, a hard hitting tackler, had no desire to break bones or tear someone's throat apart, but went along, his big brother intent on displaying his skills.

Bakewell loved the softer nights with a sky full of stars, Brenny preferred to rough it, looked forward to rainy nights and cold, blustery days, told his little brother he had to learn to tough it, to expect trouble, be prepared for it.

Brenden qualified for Special Forces during his second enlistment. That was the year he went to Viet Nam the first time as an advisor, and came home with dark stories of incidental combat, and the trouble brewing in the jungles of Southeast Asia. He was full of information about the new weapons and the ordinance they handled. He spoke with contempt about the small caliber rifle they carried, but said the explosives were "awesome beyond description." When he returned for his second tour in 1965, the war was raging, and he was wounded and shipped back to San Francisco for rest and rehabilitation. When he was back on his feet again, released for temporary re-assignment, he returned home long enough to spend two weeks with his little brother, who had arranged for a simultaneous leave from the navy. That was one year before Bakewell tasted the fearful anxiety of shooting a weapon at another human being.

They spent their two weeks together, in mid October, and they spent most of it away from home, from mom, hunting, fishing and floating, camping out, eating over an open fire, sharing stories of military service, ridiculing the stone-headed obstinacy of the chain-of-command that controlled their lives. By then Bakewell was pining for release and a second opportunity for education. Brenden said he was prepared to put up with "the bullshit," loved the career, anxious to return to duty and distinguish himself once again in the service of his country. Bakewell learned some valuable lessons on how to survive a harsh environment, his brother only too happy to explain. Those glorious weeks were the last the Bakewell boys would spend together.

Bakewell loved his brother more than any living person. Always bigger than life, Brenden was better than anyone. Brenden was friend, confidant, support group. Brenden was irreplaceable.

Predator Bitches

Through the long ordeal leading up to Katherine Bakewell's death, their home attracted a stream of friends and well wishers drawn by her magnetism, the simple force of her character. Her willingness to share herself was by then legendary, and they came hesitant, self-conscious, the conversation often stilted and embarrassed. Sometimes they brought husbands, with a wordless need to see her, or a need to comfort her and themselves in the process. They brought prayer cards, novenas, booklets on reconciliation, texts on death and dying, written by great seers of mortality. Katherine typically was first to break the tension, usually with humor, didn't seem to mind. She was glad to have them, happy with the gifts and happy for the company. Most of them had gained her friendship through some charitable activity. With the exception of her old classmates, most of her friends came to know her through some shared philanthropy. They filed by her chair, later her bedside, in a heartrending tribute of love and appreciation for the joy found in knowing her, and for the way she had touched their lives. Disciples to the last, they wanted to share a part of their lives with what remained of hers.

They had done auctions, bazaars, fundraisers of every type for church, school and community. In her fun loving, ebullient way Katherine brought life, joy, and plenty of nonsense to what otherwise would have been a mundane litany of donated time. In addition to the extended calendar of benevolence, Katherine loved to entertain. The pool had been the last hurrah, the concluding act in a lifetime of entertaining. It gave her a final opportunity. She didn't care who it was, as long as they would allow her to provide, to amuse and to engage in whimsical conversation. She was at her best, in her element, when she was up to mischief. Witty, quick with a retort, Katherine enjoyed all her friends, but especially loved the ones of like and nimble mind, was always more appreciative of the wackier types, willing to participate in a hoax, anything devious; the ones with a combustion to match her own; the ones who returned prank for prank until neither remembered who came up with the original trick that precipitated the string. Her humor could be insanely funny and she loved the ludicrous, but Katherine was no lightweight, a degree from the University of Cincinnati, obtained in three years and adorned with *cum laude*, framed in simple black plastic and buried amid children's memorabilia somewhere in the storage room, was proof enough.

Three friends in particular came almost daily the last weeks. They watched over her, careful not to patronize someone once so capable, attending to her anxiously, interrupting the hospice worker, who gracefully recognized their need and allowed them to interfere. Only during her most personal needs would they leave her, and then out of respect only, because they would have done anything for her. When she slept, which was often but intermittent, they prepared food and straightened up, and kept a steady stream of beverages flowing. Food came smartly prepared, sometimes from the kitchen, sometimes from a nearby restaurant, served on a tablecloth, accompanied by a fresh cloth napkin.

Most evenings, to escape the press, Bakewell absented himself to clean the pool, cut his grass, or mettle indifferently with his exuberant dogs – a new litter of puppies having recently departed the large kennel at the back of the property – one little tri-colored pup remaining behind with a now recovered mom, glad to be rid of their nuisance, happy to have a half grown playmate to romp with and bully around. The dogs stayed away from the pool, understood the ground rules, never wet or dropped on the deck surface. Bakewell vacuumed and trimmed, swept and watered and cleaned his way around the pool and yard each evening, keeping to himself, looking in on her whenever she was awake. The classmates kept an eye on him but left him to his grief, respected his privacy, interrupting only to bring something to eat or drink, most of which was returned partly consumed. Bakewell quickly learned liquor was out of the question in his time of grief.

Katherine had cautioned him about her oldest and dearest friends, referred to them as "the divorcees," and chided him about a sex life that was about to resume. He hated the teasing. The thought of it nearly broke his heart, but he was by then unwilling to take issue with her on anything. "You are a good man, Andy," she said many times when they were alone, "…a real sought after commodity in this world of broken homes," and he cringed in guiltless embarrassment. "They will come after you, you know," she said, her eyes filled with love, hoping only for the best in what might be ahead for him. The understanding in her eyes reached out like her fine hand, withered now, to touch and massage his heart until he thought his chest would split from the delicate, fractional pressure. When she spoke to him about her girlfriends he would look away, mostly to keep her from seeing the pain in his eyes. Her intents were pure; she was often under the influence of her medicine, or her pain, had no idea how her words tore at him.

Bakewell had been without sexual drive during her illness, unless she insisted. The last weeks they contented themselves to lie together in a queen-sized bed purchased years before. He'd suggested they buy a king at the time, but she told him she needed to be closer to him when she slept, told him she wanted to feel his warmth during the night. The bed had a luxurious pillow top mattress, covered with a down comforter in a soft cottony duvet that warmed to the touch, and which they preferred to lie on top of when they read or talked most evenings. Toward the end, they were satisfied to simply hold each other. Both needed holding and he found he needed her weak, delicate hug more than she needed his, her frail arms barely able to exert pressure against his still powerful frame. He held her tenderly for hours, his arm aching, not wanting to move, fearing he might wake her from her exhausted, near comatose sleeps, at the same time fearing he might lose her to those critically needed, deathly slumbers. Her lips were dry and cracking as she dehydrated. He would rub them tenderly with a balm, trying not to wake her, yet fearing she might never return as he did. He was thankful for the hormonal change. It was one less urgency in his unraveling life.

***

There was a brief moratorium the two weeks following her death, then the divorcees were back with purpose, in force, determined. It started with menial tasks. In addition to bringing food, they were continually cleaning up or cleaning out. The refrigerator got an overhaul, and a coat of spray-on wax. The pantry gained 40% of new space, everything neatly placed in a linear fashion that bordered on military. They went through his laundry and his drawers to the point of filing and folding his underwear and arranging his rack of seldom worn ties. Sweaters and sweatshirts he hadn't seen in months were squarely stacked, even arranged according to color.

Though food was one reason for their visits during her illness, it took on a new primacy after her death, ascending to the category of cuisine. It didn't come in quantity as before, when so many needed feeding. Now the meals were in intimate quantities, accompanied by bottles of fine wine. Bakewell was a BBQ guy who liked to throw it on the grill while he drank a beer, so they bought him a new BBQ grill and had it permanently placed in concrete out next to the pool. But the wine continued and eventually he learned to tolerate the sour varieties of white they almost always brought. Early on he didn't know what to do with the food, so he obtusely invited them to stay – the object of the exercise escaping him. Some evenings it was just one grieving, sympathetic divorcee, but most nights two or three. One was a friend from the University, the others friends from childhood. The university friend had been divorced for eight years, was still physically young by their maturing definition. She'd had several suitors, had known a little "action," but her conversations matched their own in wit, invective and sarcasm when it came to their late lost loves.

The first corroboration of Katherine's prediction was a change in the dress code. Blouses were lower cut, more revealing than the nondescript outfits they wore before, fabrics softer, clinging, more often to breasts than hips; hips were usually hidden under freshly starched shorts or summery slacks. Early on his grief, accompanied by a long familiarity with each of them, allowed for little more than a vacuous interest in their clustering and solicitous ways. He didn't pay much attention to their conversation. He was happy for the company. The second change was the language. They all loved the "F" word and used it indiscriminately. He had heard it many times so the word didn't embarrass him, but the new direction in their conversation did. Molly had been left by a high school sweetheart and husband of twenty-five years; he gave her four kids, "But I got the house, the mortgage, the grass and a thousand fucking things to do!" Her lament was greeted with a chorus of hoots and amen's.

They all complained about the endless repairs, the frustration of not having a man around, even though they derided men in a nonstop stream of vile and vitriol. The word for man ultimately became "penis": penis with a long accentuation on the E. "I need a penis in my life, if for no other reason than to handle the plumbing and the electrical," Paula mourned.

"Electrical is nothing; it's the carpentry. I can't do the *fucking* carpentry."

"You do need a *peeenis* for carpentry." Molly moaned.

"You need a penis for carpentry, for plumbing and for all that electrical shit," Tee added. A faded beauty queen, Tee deplored her humiliated fate after *the abandonment.* "I was homecoming queen for God's sake! What was he? A *fucking* bean counter!"

Bakewell had laughed longest, had known her husband all his life. They played ball together for years, more than once he had accused the former husband of being a bureaucrat. He was a sorely missed friend with a trophy wife now, a friend whose company Bakewell had once enjoyed on a bimonthly basis that coincided with the friend's bird-dogging years. By then the separation was imminent although Bakewell failed to see it coming. Most of their meetings took place an hour before Katherine arrived, and most of the time it was at Rick's – before Jocko "went surreptitious." Then they moved to a watering hole on Olive Street, but even then, Bakewell missed the point of meeting in a less conspicuous place. He remembered castigating his friend. "Jocko, you were a good shortstop and a pure hitter, but you sure turned into a bean counter…in a class of your own, peerless." Jocko was good-natured and Bakewell liked to needle him about having a life away from the beans. He had already taken Bakewell up on the challenge; Bakewell wouldn't learn about it for months.

"Well, he was always a bureaucrat, Tee."

"Yeah, a bureaucrat, bopping around with a kid half his age."

For Bakewell the wine and the rich diet were harmless and provided needed company. Most of his friends wanted to get together during the day, avoiding him in the evening. Late in September, while the weather was still balmy and the moon nearly full, matters got more serious as they got down to the business of which one was going to get him. With the outside air still room temperature, dinner was served by the pool and, after one bottle too many, slight but intended body contact became predictable. That night they actually got in the pool in a rowdy excess after Paula "stepped over the line," and blouses really clung to breasts in the warm night air as they misbehaved in the shallow water, making fun of each other, somehow managing to keep their hair dry. Hair was carefully coiffed, vibrant, always in fashion. There was constant talk of hair, breasts and thighs. They seemed to love one another's hair. They were mostly still proud of their breasts, but thighs, grown soft and large, were ridiculed, derided and wistfully remembered for their once tawny, tanned shape that had rippled with muscle tone. Even Paula, who had spent a fortune on cosmetic surgery, admitted there was little science could do for thighs.

That night, Tee, an especially voluptuous suitor, leaned across Bakewell, presenting a cavernous view as she served the food. Bakewell's eyes had met Molly's as Tee's sumptuous chest spilled before him.

"Hey, I see that! I know what you're doing!" Molly had nearly shouted. "No one wants to look at those artificial things."

"Yeah, those damned tennis balls made of silicone!" Paula added. "We see what you're up to!"

Tee, looking at her chest, smiled at Bakewell, saying, "Andy likes to look, don't you Andy?"

Discomfited, Bakewell looked for help.

"Andy, don't give her the pleasure. We see what you're up to, Tee!"

Tee and Molly had gone to school together, starting in first grade. Tee's real name, Theresa Thiessen, had earned the nickname "Tetee" almost as soon as they learned their letters. It was a nickname that followed her all her life, including to puberty where it became a brief liability when callow, insecure boys began to refer to her as "Titty" instead. Titty was a real misnomer, since her chest had been her biggest disappointment prior to her husband's defection. But Tee had corrected the problem as soon as medical science and a prosperous husband provided. It was her medical endowment being revealed to Bakewell's enforced gaze. The implants had eventually solidified and hugging her, which he was frequently required to do, was like having two balls fitted between them – they were more like baseballs than tennis balls, but Bakewell left the sizing to her detractors.

Tee had been Katherine's special friend and maid of honor, and was warmly affectionate. Despite their solidification, the implants gave her a sumptuous upper level, and she had taken to wearing the most revealing tops. At the time he was leaning back in a heavy wrought iron chair and when she leaned into him he glanced at her exploding bust, only to look up and meet Molly's imperious gaze.

Molly was unusually sweet, very innocent and vulnerable to their mean criticism. She seldom took offense, countered only occasionally, but when she did it was with inspiration. Paula, like Tee, was quick and mean spirited, especially with Tee. Bakewell suspected Paula might have been mildly jealous of Tee's bust. According to the others, Paula had spent more trying to salvage her figure than their graduation class, and, even though she poked fun at Tee, she had had reconstructive surgery three different times – Bakewell never sure where the third operation was located. She tried every new treatment, which had gotten into "colonics" and had to be explained to Bakewell after she left early one evening. Tee was always the worst. She got out of hand as often as not after the second bottle of wine, and she was by far the most abusive about her ex.

Troubled by the way Tee railed on about the *rotten bastard* his old friend had become, Bakewell kept his council, recognizing a need for the cryptic, often macabre remarks, and their potty-mouthed language. Humor hid the pain, and, although he refused to join in, he knew his old friends had left a lot of pain when they went off with younger women. Bakewell was shy and self-deprecating about women, whom he never pretended to understand, had lived through the midlife crisis and wouldn't take credit for fidelity, thought he might have been more lucky than good, and sometimes actually wondered what would have happened to his long record of fidelity if a woman meeting their definition of bimbo had popped up in his life at the wrong time. Katherine also recognized the possibility and made that period their most sexually active.

It was the night they came to refer to as "the pool fiasco" that things finally simmered down. Paula had demurred when it came to the observable advances. She had been single the longest, had enjoyed a dating action the others had been without, seemed in less need. There was no urgency with Paula; she was less obvious, her advances were cautious, even furtive. They created the most tension. Bakewell's antiquated radar missed most of the invitations, but Paula's subtlety made him uncomfortable and she knew it and enjoyed it. She was also capable of some outrageously blunt comments. She had been a slender, leggy filly, like Katherine in her youth and on that night of redirection, had put her legs up on a wrought iron chair, displaying her still finely shaped calves and ankles, only inches from Bakewell's plate when she dropped the bomb that precipitated the jumping-in-the-pool episode.

Holding her wine glass between her fingers, rubbing the tip of the glass back and forth against her lower lip, eying him seductively, she said, "So Andy, what's the long term plan?" Bakewell responded with a sheepish smile and a shrug; wasn't sure where the question was going, but had an uneasy feeling and wished to direct her to another subject. "Aren't you getting horny about now, or do you have a little bunny hidden somewhere in your mysterious life?"

"There's no secret woman in my life, Paula. You girls are pretty much it."

"Well isn't it about time you started to have a little fun. Don't you want to have sex again?"

He'd laughed nervously, responded, "I think maybe I'm getting too old for that sort of thing."

"Bullshit. You need a woman in your life; don't BS me, Andy. Under that hairy chest there's a lonely heart that needs massaging just as much as that thing between your legs."

Although her femininity was getting harder around the middle-aged edges, Paula was still provocative, some nights right on the verge, others unapproachable, almost aloof. Bakewell figured it was part of the grand plan and accepted her presence, glad to have it actually, whatever her mood. "We'd be good together," she said, ended with, "Think about it," as the others returned.

He'd showed no surprise; instead gave her a simplistic smile and wink, which conveyed compassion in a "no thanks" way. Embarrassed but game, Paula recovered her pluck, and when the others arrived with more ice, she told them she had made a pass, claimed it as a defense, told them she was only getting on with "the seduction of Andy Bakewell," and accused them of the same. She was blasé and nonchalant and made it sound offhand.

"God, you are so *fucking* aggressive Paula," Tee said.

"Hey, I asked him if he wanted to fuck, so what?"

Shocked, Molly had looked to Bakewell whom she adored, and, recovering her poise, spoke with a direct sweetness, the remark that set them off. "Oh yes, do think about it, Andy; we all would love to have you."

"GOOD GOD!!" Tee whooped loudly and the conversation erupted in a storm of bitter laughter. Tee decided they all needed to get into the pool and "cool off." She pushed Molly into the shallow end, but before she could jump, Paula grabbed her arm and they went in together. Bakewell enjoyed the lunacy, relieved.

Later that night, after they finished an airy, tasteless dessert from a box of something only dieting women could stomach, they opted for the beach towels he offered and the warmth of coffee instead of more wine. It was still warm, but they were in wet clothes, and during a lull in the "men are bastards" conversation, a pair of Canada geese made their nightly crossing overhead, heading for the lake behind city hall. They were so low, the air passing through their feathered wings could be heard between honkings. Bakewell watched them go, and, in a moment of piercing candor, on his flagstone deck, next to Katherine's beautiful pool, admitted he missed his wife desperately, said that he appreciated their company and loved their friendship and loved having them come evenings and hated his loneliness, but he couldn't let go of her memory.

"She was my treasure. She was my life…and my mate…and I never thought…I don't know what I never thought…." His voice broke and he almost gave way as he spoke the words in a painful, choking, unashamedly sincere voice, directing them to the geese, mated for life, and to a rapidly ascending October moon that appeared just over the pines – the same moon that set the geese in motion. It was a poignant moment that froze them all, crystallized by his honesty and the purity of his profession. And there, next to the pool, in a breezeless, breathless moment of perfect but unintended timing broken only when one of his lady friends gasped, a second looked down at the deck and the other shuddered and cried softly, he joined *The Club…*

They suddenly remembered how much they all loved Katherine, loved her more than they could ever learn to love him. After that night they stopped worrying him with their advances and left off the pursuit, learned to enjoy his comfortable character for what it was not: a threat, a potential for trouble. Or for what it was not apt to be: a pawing, whining widower, looking for sexual gratification. Instead he took on an aura, and they changed from competitors to companions, compelled to get on with their lives and leave off with what they had been referring to as "the seduction of Andy Bakewell."

A few nights later the conversation got funnier still, and more roisterous, although Bakewell didn't think it possible. Sensing his sadness and near despair, they shifted gears and tried to entertain instead of entice. They still teased him boldly and they accused each other of disgraceful behavior. But after that evening things changed forever; the wine bottles came in magnum size afterward, and they began to enjoy eating and drinking again – their real calling in life – and ceased to starve themselves to lose weight for his benefit. The conversation got more ribald and sank to new levels as the level of the wine sank below the decal. The two who had lusted after him openly, Molly and Tee, decided to call a truce, made an Andy-is-off-limits pact. That same evening Paula offended Molly more than a little in what passed for normal, with a callow remark Bakewell thought only men capable of. Molly's retort had been to tell Paula to simmer down, suggest she needed a "raspberry enema," which caused him to choke up part of his wine. Molly picked her spots.

Breaking one of his many periods of spectator silence, he accused them of being bad. Taking his cue, Tee spoke up and said what had been unstated but understood all along. "Oh what the fuck, Andy, we're just a bunch of predator bitches. You know that."

Bakewell's Gift

The women in Bakewell's life, the ones who really cared for him, who envied Katherine his great devotion, loved to tease him about his reticence, to accuse him of having a problem with words, even though he knew some very big ones. Paula had first called him "conversationally challenged," coined the phrase one boisterous evening when they all still had husbands. It was true enough; still, he loved words, spent hours pursuing a grander vocabulary, although he never felt any need to use them.

As a young father, he did his acquiring in the bathtub, his sanctuary – Katherine called it "the library" – where he tried to escape a noisy family, until she learned to pick the lock and his academic hours ended by a picky-scratchy sound, before the door opened and a little person slipped through, diaperless – a happy-faced, naked little urchin came crossing the tiled floor. Bakewell would pick them up, sometime there were two, and put them in the tub between his legs to keep them from tipping over in eight inches of water, his hour of solitude forfeit. Later, after they moved west, they had a den with bookshelves and a reclining chair with a reading lamp. By then the kids were old enough to occupy themselves and he satisfied his interest next to the fireplace.

His vocabulary was always in evidence, and he would use words uniquely appropriate, fitting them in a sentence with a subtle facility. Gradually he became something of a resource. Over too many bottles of beer in a burger joint in West County, when they were all still in their thirties, Bakewell was the only one who could differentiate between discrete and discreet.

But his ability to really communicate was tactile, visceral, discreet (and not discrete!), non-threatening, and gentle for a powerful man. He had an ability to shake a hand, pat a back, or make a simple gesture that conveyed good will. He might have been "challenged," but he never lacked the ability to generate warmth with a smile or a nod, escorted by his trademark: "that creasy-eyed smile." He couldn't smile without the seamy lines around his eyes cracking, even as a young man.

He could put a hand on a shoulder and create calmness, diffuse a situation or quiet an altercation by gently taking someone's arm before confrontation erupted. He was a handler of little boys, and of grown men, and he could communicate his happiness, disappointment, dislike, even hostility without ever saying a word.

His grandbabies learned what his children had learned a generation before. Nancy pointed it out one Sunday afternoon. "Dad, Julie's been talking about you, again."

"I hope she's not giving away our secrets."

"What secrets?"

Bakewell looked at his granddaughter and winked, as Nancy continued. "She said, 'when Old Pop touches you, he makes you feel good.'"

Julie smiled at the moment, loving the idea they were talking about her.

"Way to go Juliet. The Old Man may have calluses on those paws, but he sure knows how to make you feel good," one of the boys agreed.

When his grandchildren became bored with their toys or just tired, they would find him, usually in his recliner, climb in his lap and curl up. Nancy often put her baby with her father at days end while she cleaned up. The baby never fussed when placed in his grandfather's care. A common site on Sundays was to see infant and grandfather asleep in the chair.

His strokes, pats, any type of physical contact, conveyed a trusting legitimacy. Women loved his touch, some more than others, something he was quick to pick up on, and made him careful who he placed his hands on, once it became apparent certain women favored his touch more than others.

Part of his appeal stemmed from an inherent tranquility, but the main ingredient was a peculiar sadness in his eyes, which seemed permanent, and was identified more subconsciously than consciously, a sadness that made him appear exposed, vulnerable. Bakewell's children had learned a hug from the old man was worth more than a compliment.

Katherine had been the second recipient of his tenderness, physically and emotionally, and without discussing it, (and that was never a possibility), or even thinking about it consciously, Bakewell was glad there had been one other before her. It had made a difference, made him honest, grateful, even virtuous in his appreciation of her. When they were together, his reservoir of passion and compassion was total, especially when they were intimate. He never took sex for granted, wanted her always to know he loved her deeply, wanted to be worthy of her. He was decent, considerate and very appreciative of what they shared, and exquisitely delicate with her.

Dis-words

The pending death of his company, following so closely after the death of his wife, left Bakewell in need of a complete makeover. The prospect of another enormous loss left him existing in part, almost unable to function. He could see no possible cure, and that was the most frustrating part. He could handle hardship in many forms, could suffer deprivation, endure physical pain, show determination in the face of adversity; he could deal with lots of intimidation, could make a resolve, set a course (and stay it); he could suffer misfortune that demanded redirection, adapt to the change, go forward with vigor, and with new purpose, but he wasn't an emotional sufferer.

He couldn't cope with a lack of fairness, hated injustice, or a cruel break, especially if caused by freak accident. Katherine's suffering and eventual death, coupled with the legal loss were way beyond his capacity for understanding or for enduring. He was too obsessive about justice, and when the bottom fell out, he was tapped out, wanted to get out, to get away, to find any kind of exit. He was defeated and he knew it.

Over the years he'd observed the way some people endured one tragedy after another, kept getting up, plugging on. Often they were people of small stature, folks he didn't normally associate with courage, and he was surprised to see them display so much, to show such ability to endure, to show a mental toughness that defied defining. Bakewell had learned years before (Thomas Aquinas?), that mercy and justice were inseparable. Justice without mercy was cruelty. Mercy without justice was disintegration. His psyche was far too fragile. He was a man's man, who dealt in the world of physical action, a defensive back, a reactor, a responder, but he could only respond to problems that were palpable, doable, handle-able.

The cumulative effect of his disasters took a quick toll. He was at the end of his rope, George Bailey at the bridge, freezing hands resting on steel girders, snow blowing in his eyes, wishing an angel would jump, call out for help. But it wasn't going to be that way, and he knew it wasn't, was reconciled to it: *There will be no angel in the water, just a demon standing behind you, one hand on your back, saying, "COME ON, YOU GUTLESS, SON OF A BITCH, JUMP, DO SOMETHING. GET ON WITH IT!"*

He was disillusioned, discouraged, disappointed, disheartened, disgusted, every dis-word that came to mind. His life was disintegrating. *Mercy without justice.*

***

Ned's office was across the hall from Bakewell's and Ned had been immersed in an unhappy who-to-pay conversation most of the morning.

"Ozzie, I hate ta jerk ya around bub, but I'm like a ole bitch dog in heat right now. I feel like I'm surrounded by a whole pack a sons a bitches with hard-ons. I just wanna say, 'go ahead, all you motherfuckers, line up and take a turn.'" Ned paused, catching his breath, listening, "I know, it's a fuckin shame, but it is the way it is and I can't find no money. I can't just make the stuff; they got laws against it. All's I can say is I'll get you paid when I can." Another pause, while Ned listened, tapping a giant finger on the desk, a staccato sound, like a light caliber weapon. "Yeah, I heard them rumors about what's bein said about me and Andy too. They are only stories about people bein told by people that's got nothun better to do than make up stories. I'll tell you this though, if me and Andy's goin out of business you're the last one in line that's not gonna get paid and you can take that to the bank." Ned hung up. Bakewell leaned against the door.

"What! You gonna add to the burden of my load too?" Bakewell moved into the room and slumped in a chair. "What?"

"I don't know. I get so depressed with all this..." Bakewell opened his hand, looked at the ceiling, at Ned. "I don't know what to do. I can't get motivated. I'm so damned myopic, I keep trying to apply logic to what's happened."

"We ain't got no time for oh-pics, mine or yours, you just gotta keep goin."

"I don't feel like I can make a difference."

"You just need to get hot. Have someone give you a big job we can make some money on. You'll be okay you start makin money; that's the key. All our problems is over we make money." Ned wanted to get back to what he was doing. He was at his best in a pinch; he'd been whirling the past few days, while Bakewell sunk deeper into depression.

"You know it would be so easy," Bakewell said, pointing to Ned's desk. "I could just take that shiny magnum you keep in your drawer there one night after everyone left, put it to my head and just lean back and pull the…"

"YOU'LL FUCKIN MISS!" Ned shouted, coming out of his chair, pointing. He was ready to come over the desk. "Don't you miss, you fuck! I know you! You'll flinch! You'll flinch right at the last second and only scramble up your brains all over. You'll end up in a wheelchair with the spit dribblin off your chin! You'll be no good to me or nobody else! Then we don't get the insurance! You ain't no good to nobody and I got to face the music without the insurance and I'm fucked!" Ned sat back down and opened his drawer, out of breath.

After all the years Ned could still surprise him. Bakewell sat, taking in partner and outburst. They looked at each other without speaking.

"Gee, Ned, I feel a lot better now…coming in here to talk to you…I don't know. You have a way of cheering me up."

"Ya, well if you're lookin for sympathy go look in the dictionary under S-I-M." Ned shuffled some papers.

Bakewell started to laugh, tears came to his eyes. Trudy came to the door looking alarmed. “Are we all okay in here?”

“We’re okay,” Bakewell said.

“He’s gone off his nut on me,” Ned said. He pulled the big handgun from the drawer.

Trudy gasped. Ned flicked the cylinder open and pressed the ejector, spilling cartridges over the desk. “Here,” he tossed the weapon to Bakewell, “buy yer own bullets. I ain’t payin for no suicide.”

“Yee gods, Ned! What are you doing with that thing in this office?”

“Go find somethin to do,” Ned said.

She put her hand to Bakewell’s shoulder. “You all right Andy?”

“I’m a lot better than I was Trudy; don’t mind us. We’re having a session for the weak-minded. You don’t belong in this group.”

“You’re telling me.” She went back down the hall.

“What a fuckin world,” Ned was still upset. “I can’t believe what we’re gonna be goin through the comin weeks. It makes me sick…”

There was another silence. Ned shuffled through the pile of unpaid bills. Bakewell got up, started to leave, paused. “Thanks for cheering me up. I never know when I might get a laugh out of you. I needed a good laugh.”

“Yeah, right. I’m a real riot.” Ned looked at his partner. “Andy we’re like two old fucks peein on a bonfire, only one of us ain’t got no water pressure, not with my *prostrate*. It’s hopeless; it’s outta control.”

“Prostate.”

“Whatever.”

“We’ll hang together until the end.” Bakewell said, paused, “One thing though, I want to cash out of my house and take the equity and toss it in the pot before we close up. It’ll take some serious money out of the shortfall. You won’t be in for nearly as much when we split up.”

“Yeah, like I’m gonna let you do that.”

“Let me do it. I don’t need a house anymore.”

“The fuck’s that mean?”

“I’m seriously thinking about joining the Benedictines.”

“What Benedictines?”

“It’s a religious order. They might need a live-in janitor or something. Give me a place in the country, peaceful maybe. Hopefully, I can do my praying with the monks. I think I might like it.”

“You’re losin it.”

“You’re probably right, but it has a nice feel to it, makes me want to try it.”

“Andy, we’re like a couple a marines that been in too many foxholes together. We been together too long, been through too much. We been lookin out for each other’s backs for so long we wouldn’t know how to live without each other. If you’re goin down, I’m goin with ya. Count on it. I ain’t lettin you go by yerself."

"It doesn't make sense for both of us to lose everything. You could move back to Maine, start a fishing lodge maybe."

"If I do, you'll be right there with me. You can pump gas while you say your beads."

Bakewell smiled, fingering the rosary in his pocket. "I'll let you go. I've got to collect some money."

"Yeah well, collect a million while yer at it."

Mrs. Walker

Katherine Bakewell died on the last day of summer, one month after Princess Diana; Joe Walker died late in August the next year in the midst of Mark McGuire's singular quest. Maggie Walker called Bakewell the following June, a few months after she moved back to St. Louis and reestablished herself in her hometown. He would always remember her opening line: "Andy, its Maggie, please don't hang up."

After mutual sympathies were exchanged, they talked for nearly an hour on subjects ranging far and wide, went over a short history of events that occurred over the years in a stilted and awkward conversation, punctuated by embarrassed pauses, which Maggie navigated with nervous laughter and references to minor flaws she remembered them having. She asked many questions, honestly wanting to know about Bakewell's life and marriage, his business and his children. She was especially interested in his only daughter, persisted in a line of questioning that made her sound like a spinster aunt. She asked what sorority Nancy had pledged, what she'd majored in, and how she had done in school. She eventually drew him out to a point where he found himself describing Nancy in detail, recounting her high school days, sorority life and the evening of her wedding. When she switched to his grandchildren, he talked too long on the subject with many references to Katherine. Maggie had always been an enthusiastic listener, but the depth of her interest surprised him.

He asked fewer questions, some about her recent life, mostly about what they once had in common: each other and her crazy mother. Somewhat hesitantly he asked about her life in Little Rock and the famous people she had known during her years in the fast lane. Her answers were less than forthcoming and he assumed it came from a sense of obligation, or maybe the responsibility of knowing people who had peopled the news for so long. She was forthcoming about her mother and candidly described their bizarre relationship, filling him in on her amazing end. Bakewell had struggled to maintain any kind of civility with her mother during the tumultuous relationship he experienced with the bitchy, acid witted, petite nineteen year old he had known as Maggie Leary.

Maggie's parents were divorced long before Bakewell entered the picture. Mrs. Leary had been something of a debutante, and, as far as he could learn, married Maggie's father after a brief courtship that Maggie described as "whiz bang." Bakewell had too much first hand experience with Mrs. Leary, but only met the old man on three occasions. Mr. Leary was a veteran of the Italian Campaign, was wounded there and later became a successful seller of valves and things used in the newly developing field of cryogenics. Mr. Leary was a gifted wordsmith, who crafted sales relationships and held them fast, obsessive with his clientele, whom he protected and guarded with passion.

Bakewell often rued the fact he hadn't had the opportunity to learn more about the art of selling and the development of relationships from the old man. Mr. Leary made lots of money and supported his estranged family in style. Upon his death, and to her great surprise and bitter disappointment, Mrs. Leary learned she had been provided for in only the necessities; his three children got the money. By the time Bakewell had married, the story around town was that neither of the Leary boys had a mortgage, they were spending their inheritance quickly; both liked to collect toys in the form of cars, boats and memberships. Maggie's only display of wealth was a little MG Classic and a wardrobe the envy of West County.

Mrs. Leary had rebelled at aging and fought the inexorable process to the end. When Bakewell first met her she was renowned for the eccentric, long dresses she wore, that were both a generation behind the times and made for a woman a generation younger. At fifty, during the sixties, she dressed in a fashion from the forties, pathetically attempting to look "thirty something." She wore her hair long, with bows pinned to the side or back and favored large buttons to go with large bows on her overly long, bright-colored dresses. She never wore pants or shorts. Bakewell had never seen her legs more than six inches above the ankle. In her more eccentric moments she was a combination of Baby Jane and Hepburn without the slacks. Occasionally she displayed a lighter, more whimsical nature, when she wasn't haranguing or tirading about city government.

During her tolerable moments she could be fascinating, almost enchanting, full of a disarming youthful charm that belied her less stable days. At times like that he understood what the old man had seen in her years before.

The house was a weird combination of late Victorian and blond modern, with a Baby Grand dominating the dining room, which she insisted on calling the parlor. The three-story Tudor was filled with bric-a-brac from the turn of the century, and Elvis era glitz, recently purchased on a trip to Florida, where she visited often, to the enormous relief of both neighbors and city fathers. She played classical music from old 78's on a ridiculously dated Victrola, often filling the neighborhood with a scratchy background of Beethoven, Schubert or Bach. She never used the air conditioner, although the old man had put in one of the first central units. She said it "dried the skin and ruined the lungs." Bakewell was impudent with her, which further strained the relationship, referred to her as "wacko" in Maggie's presence. Much later he suspected mild insanity. Mrs. Leary was opinionated, particularly "on the human condition," and on civic matters to the point of observable lunacy. So much so she made the municipal newspaper on a yearly basis. Once, a front page black & white featured her blocking the extension of their dead end street, mouth opened menacingly, fangs bared, waving a large placard condemning progress as an invasion of her privacy, which she pronounced "privisee," avenging the little guy. "Political eunuch" was a favored expression.

He was honestly saddened to learn she had died in a wheel chair she claimed she never needed, in a pink dress she had been wearing for consecutive days. Incontinent, haggard with dehydration – she'd come to alcohol late in life, or been a closet drinker long before, no one quite knew – her hair recently dyed an angry orange. She passed the final hours of a wretched, smelly week, under the expectant and not so watchful eye of a disillusioned young hospice worker anxious to move on, and not sure she wanted another case.

The conversation revealed a daughter filled with bittersweet memories of a mother who so impacted her life, the memory left a permanent facial tick. Maggie had spent weeks at a time visiting St. Louis to be with her, because her brothers adamantly refused to go near the "nutty bitch," alternating with periods when she refused to come home herself for just the same reason. The memories she relayed over the phone were mostly humorous. Her mother had been such a source of horror Bakewell suspected Maggie learned to block out the dark parts, trained herself to focus on the zany and the outrageous instead. Bakewell thought Joe Walker was as much savior as suitor when he finally settled down, proposed marriage and took her off to Little Rock.

Maggie had waylaid him with the phone call. He answered the kitchen phone and was tethered to a short cord that kept him standing nervously with no place to pace. He really didn't want to see her, but she had been so enthusiastic about resuming their friendship, he agreed to meet her "just to do something together." She left her unpublished phone number, signing off with, "Andy, I want you to promise me you will call, and soon?"

He called her back, reluctantly, in late June and they met for dinner at a small Italian restaurant bordering the southwest end of St. Louis' Hill section. It was a quiet summer evening, the longest day of the year and they enjoyed a long twilight of conversation and light food, talking across the table about friends and family and the impact of world events on their lives, as sunset faded to a clear starlit darkness. It had rained the day before and the air was clean and fresh, without the usual summer haze. They hadn't spoken in twenty years and concluded the last time they had talked Nixon was president. She remembered seeing him at "The Muny" one evening with a little girl about five. The last time he remembered seeing her was on TV in the background at a political celebration for Tom Eagleton.

Being together after so many years and so much history was a warm and pleasant surprise. Maggie was carefree, happy, the way Katherine had been on their "Friday night dates" after the children were grown. Maggie's voice was filled with delight and a genuine enthusiasm at seeing him again. She clearly enjoyed herself. He had been reluctant to call her, not knowing what to expect, fearing a long difficult evening, attempting conversation with a sophisticated woman who had left his world behind to move on the autobahn of wealth, politics and history. His life was discouragingly mundane compared to hers. He also dreaded trying to fence with her. Like Katherine, Maggie was quick, her wit sharp; unlike Katherine it could be painful. She had always concealed the vicious tip of her dueling foil under a soft, contradictingly beautiful smile that was accentuated by her deep blue eyes.

He was overmatched in a parry and thrust conversation, hoped it wouldn't come to that. Maggie had been very unpredictable, had always made him nervous. Where Katherine amused herself and their friends poking fun at his obtuse vulnerability – which she termed "dopey and lovable" – Maggie had displayed a merciless ability to ridicule his gaffs and subject him to ruthless humiliations. He could remember every one. He also would never forget she had left him feeling inadequate and totally discarded, had dominated and intimidated him by the end of their relationship.

He remembered the day he first saw her, stunning and expensively coifed, as she took her seat in the Business & Public Administration Building. His first impression, that she was unapproachable and unobtainable, had been nearly correct. He spent years wishing he had never obtained her, but she had been so overwhelming, so appealing to the GI in him, he couldn't help being drawn in. He also remembered it was she who first approached him. It took only a few weeks to learn of her formidable character, her impressive social skills. They both remembered she was the one who had grown tired of their amazing relationship.

"You have a west county prefix so I assume you're living somewhere out there with the high rent crowd?" He poured more Chianti in her glass.

"I'm living in a wonderful gated community off Conway Road. It's really lovely, and I want you to come to a dinner party soon."

Bakewell knew the exact place. It was the only gated community on Conway and it was wealthy to the point of extravagance, a minimum of 4000 square feet per unit. The homes were lavishly appointed, many had elegant pools in courtyards and the front gate was always attended. He had done some of the original construction ten years before.

They finished the dinner sharing a bananas foster and a cognac. Maggie insisted on the cognac. Bakewell agreed, though he hated the bland tastelessness of the scorching drink. He would never develop a taste for cognac, no matter how expensive. Maggie enjoyed it, threw the last ounce off right before the check came. She argued with him about the check, insisted on paying, saying it was her idea. They had spent more on drinks than food. She left cash for the waiter, not waiting for change.

In the parking lot Maggie turned, looked up at him, asked if they could go for a ride. "Please. It's still early. I haven't been in this part of town since we were teenagers."

"Since you were a teenager, I was the old guy, remember?"

"My older man, yes I remember. You were such a wonderful change of pace, such a darling man."

"I was never a darling man."

"You were. You just don't know. You were wonderful."

It was an expensive car with a hard leather interior much in fashion. "Where are we going?"

"Just wait and see."

They drove up Hampton Avenue, north through Forest Park and passed the famous open air theatre, taking their time. She put the windows down so they could hear the sounds of summer. After one loop around the heavily forested park, they returned to the Muny. "Andy, let's get out and walk inside for just a minute."

"Seriously?"

"Yes, let's."

He was tired and his knee was acting up again, a dull ache that had been with him since he fell at a trench excavation in the spring, but he was happy to get off the hard seat and into the night. She parked the car close by the Muny. The first act was over and some of the crowd had already left. The ambiance of The Muny was special, but the quality of the shows seldom matched the atmosphere, people often left during intermission, so there were places to park close by the entrance. They strolled together, avoiding any contact, across broken concrete streets, careful to avoid the worst places. When they came through the entrance, they made their way up the long Walk of Fame on the north side of the historic outdoor theatre, and when they reached the gate, a young usherette smiled and nodded for them to pass.

It was a beautiful evening. There had always been a magical quality to the park after dark, especially at The Muny. They walked up the steep incline and found a vantage where they could see the big wooden stage beneath giant oak trees. The theatre was still three quarters filled. They stayed twenty minutes, soaking up the atmosphere, which flooded them with youthful memories, leaving in time to miss the exiting crowd. As they walked back down the vast sidewalk, they caught up with one of Katherine's high school friends. She was studying the bronze plaques that honored the century's theatrical heavyweights. Maggie recognized her. Bakewell didn't remember her name. She was married to a fraternity guy he had known vaguely at Mizzou. Maggie and Katherine had a few friends in common. St. Louis was a small town. It was a classic mid-summer night's exchange.

"Maggie? Andy?"

"Marsha!" Maggie made it sound like she was delighted.

"Nice to see you again, it's been a long time!" Neither woman could think of anything to add. Bakewell hadn't broken stride. They kept moving. Maggie looked over her shoulder and waved. She took his hand and squeezed it. Neither spoke as they went back out around the small lake, where the old World's Fair gazebo stood on a tiny island, dilapidated and crumbling in the middle of a sad, muck filled pond.

When they crossed the wide boulevard, Maggie smiled up at him, pleased. "Mmm," she said, turning her head away. "Cat's out of the bag." He looked at her curiously. "We've been 'made.' Tongues will wag now, Andy Bakewell. You'll have a lot of explaining to do; been seen with *that bitch* Maggie Walker, at The Muny no less. Probably seen by hundreds, lurking out here in the darkness." She waved her hand. She was enjoying herself.

"It won't be that bad," he said matter of factly, "You're not a bitch, Maggie; don't say that," then, with good timing, added, "Not anymore, anyway."

She poked him on the arm and took it boldly, and they walked in silence, reflecting on what had been said. There was truth in jesting. It gave them something to think about. Years before they had spent a lot of time together in the Park, often meeting for lunch that first summer. She was only nineteen that year, the main reason her mother objected to him. Having raised a daughter, remembering her at nineteen, Bakewell could sympathize with Mrs. Leary so many years later.

They drove the wide boulevards of the Park from end to end with the windows down once again, the car filling with the smells of the forest and the sounds of a warm summer night. They were quiet, each reliving pleasant evenings from the past.

It had been a wonderful time, that first summer. Maggie was anxious to grow up, *fast;* he had been happy to oblige, had been half way around the world and back before he was twenty-two, was just what she was looking for. She was full of life, full of fun, but reckless…and she made him nervous. That was the best part – the fluttery feeling he got being around her. The getting-to-know-part had always been his favorite part. He was trying hard not to feel like he was rediscovering it.

Maggie had introduced him to people and places he didn't know existed that summer, guided him through a labyrinth of social functions with the finesse and skill of an older woman. It included country clubs, dinner parties, moonlit nights on lighted docks, and warm summer evenings driving fast, top down in the little MG, always ending at a place where they could dance. Dancing was mandatory for any beau of Maggie Leary's. Several parties were on fine boats from docks on expensive lake front properties a few hours from St. Louis. Bakewell was nervous and uneasy around Maggie's friends. They were all on their way to fine educations and futures of power and influence. He had just returned from four years of menial observance. Her social group represented an old echelon of class-conscious people who made the rules he was taught to follow, and he was socializing with them, on their own turf, and knew he was trespassing. That was the first summer they shared, the only summer they shared.

They concluded the first "date" at eleven-thirty, when she returned him to the restaurant with a promise, "We *will do this again*, and soon. You're entirely too, too much fun to be with Bakewell – such a conversationalist."

"You're making fun. It must be that bitch part you mentioned earlier."

"Stop." She looked hurt. "I didn't mean to tease you. No, I mean I didn't mean to offend you. I did mean to tease you. I apologize." She pouted. He had seen it many times. "I do apologize. Really, you are a darling man. I'm so glad we got together again."

"It wasn't that painful. Don't be so contrite."

"Please. I mean it. Call me. The ball is in your court." He smiled and shrugged, not knowing how to get around it, not wanting to get involved with her high-powered friends, whoever they were, knowing it wouldn't be pleasant. "Call me."

"Okay. Thanks for dinner." *The ball is in your court. How many times had he heard her say that*? Earlier she said she wanted to introduce him to her "friends," Bakewell wondered what that might mean and what notable people he would be compelled to spend a long uncomfortable evening with. He told her he would look forward to it, an inner voice saying, *no way.* He wondered whom *friends* might mean now.

"Call me," she said again, pulling away. He waved goodbye. "Like your wheels," she added in a jocular tone that came right out of the past, pointing out his muddy pick up. Only the company name was missing.

The Smell of Deet

The Bakewell's went to Montana the first year they were married. It was the year after Bakewell started with the utility company (Katherine loved to tell her girlfriends she had married a sewer contractor. When the uppity ones asked, she said impishly, "I've given my heart to a sanitary man.") They were getting established, adjusting to marriage and a regular income. They had health insurance, a new pickup truck and a gas card he could use for personal trips. Bakewell had made an immediate impact in his new role and things were looking good – a bonus was expected at years end. They were, to quote his ebullient bride, "deliriously happy."

He sold her on the idea of camping in the mountains over their first winter together. Night after night while they painted, wallpapered and sanded hardwood floors, he would describe his passage through the Rocky Mountains in a sleeper car, in one of the last passenger trains to cross the continent on his way to boot camp. The mountains had left a lasting impression and he read many fishing articles on the streams of the Rockies that first year. Using more words in an evening than she had heard him speak in a normal week, he described the mountains with a reverence and awe that would be with him the rest of his life. Katherine had never heard him speak so enthusiastically about anything and agreed, happy to go anywhere her husband wished to go. "Husband" was a novelty. She loved to say the word, part of a new lexicon, she would start a sentence with "my husband," or "my husband says," or "I'll have to ask my husband."

By prior agreement she wasn't supposed to fish – she had brought enough reading material for an ocean cruise – and Bakewell made sure she was warm and comfortable in an 18' camper while he fished the streams. He was careful to find the best camper package and made arrangements with a local in Bozeman long before they set out for the "Shining Mountains." He wasn't about to put his bride in a tent on the ground and queer the deal on the first trip. In his mind Bakewell had planned many trips to the mountains, never considered going without her. Their initial vacation had to be perfect. They spent cozy hours each night in the camper, including several afternoons under a heavy comforter her mother had insisted she take, waiting out unpredictable storms in the fickle mountain weather of early September. They were as high up as they could get the first few days, which may have exacerbated her condition. Katherine was two months pregnant, retching each morning at sunrise.

When she wasn't sick she would sit at the little dining table pantomiming a sailing motion, "Oh Andy, I didn't know about this part," then run to the porta-potty where she would vomit through the open door and protest claustrophobia between gagging fits. He would hold her, his arms around her hips, feeling her swelling tummy as she choked and moaned and protested her sickness. He wanted to be a part of anything and everything that concerned her. She recovered quickly, each bout usually ending after she choked down half a dozen saltines and a can of Coke. Thirty minutes later she was bounding out the trailer door, her color restored, wanting to see where they were and what surrounded them.

They changed locations each day, spending their first night at Greek Creek, where they could see the mountain starlight through the tall trees, enjoying the smell of conifers at the same time, and where Bakewell was able to fish briefly in the Gallatin River, testing a new rod and reel. He read from a book on fishing in Yellowstone each evening, and was anxious to get into the water each morning as soon as Katherine was sufficiently recovered. The second day they camped near Cooke City, and he fished the Lamar briefly, before an overnight storm turned it to chocolate milk. The third night they camped at Madison Junction, enjoying a slide show with thirty others in the campground put on by the park's rangers. The next morning Bakewell had them set up along the bank of the Madison not far from "the braids" on the road to West Yellowstone, where he finally got into some serious fishing, working the slicks below big boulders in midstream.

As soon as the camper was set up, he was chest deep in the Madison, intending to stay for most of the morning, despite the snowy weather, which left half an inch of wet snow on the drooping brim of his Stetson. The camper had every amenity and Katherine was recovering well when he left her. A little after eleven she came out of the trailer and shouted him back to shore. When he was within earshot she called, "Andy, I didn't drive all the way to Montana to sit in a trailer and read!"

"Women never bother men when they are fishing," he said gruffly over his shoulder, turning to return to midstream, but hesitating to see what she really wanted.

"I've decided I'm going to learn to fish, so I can see the scenery from out here. I'm tired of looking at it through a windshield, and I'm tired of this camper." Raising her voice for affect, she shouted, "I'm tired of living like a redneck!"

"It would take weeks to teach you how to fish with a fly rod!" He came closer to shore so not to shout.

"Then give me something simple I can cast."

"They don't allow bait-casting in the Park, and I'm not going to be seen with a woman throwing treble hooks to trout."

"Then teach me to fly cast!"

"It's not something you can learn in five minutes. It would take days, weeks." He started back out through the strong current, slipping on a submerged boulder and cracking his shin. "Shit!"

"What?"

"Nothing!"

"Andy, teach me, please! I promise I'll learn quickly!"

Bakewell hated to argue with his new wife, but he wanted to get back into the water where the fish had started to hit an ugly green nymph drifted around the boulders. It was his first real experience with western trout, and he had already caught one fish larger than anything he had hoped for. He was excited, wanted to get back to the pocket water behind the boulders. Katherine persisted from the shore. He tried a different tact and shouted "NO!" sternly and pretended to be preoccupied with a fly while he waited and watched, looking for the effect his words might have, hoping for submission.

Katherine was surprised by the gruffness of his response and for just a moment she relented, her mind seeking another course. He turned to go back to the big rocks again, riding high in the icy current, looking inviting.

"If you don't teach me then I'll…I'll just throw myself into the river and you'll lose me and the baby!" She knew it was lame; she was on new ground. He ignored her, and she shifted quickly to form. "Don't give me any of that arrogant, jackass behavior you love to use at work. I'm not going to put up with it!"

"You're not going to jump in the river," he said, adding, "Come on!" but with less emphasis. There was a momentary silence; he looked back at her again. Katherine was standing tall, a strident posture, head held high. She looked both angry and hurt by his outburst. He brushed the wet snow from his shoulders. The wool shirt was soaked but holding his body heat nicely. It was all too perfect. He wanted to fish, wished she would go back inside the camper. There was amusement in her plight, but he recognized the predicament in his own. His smile was weak, concerned. He hoped she couldn't see. It wouldn't take her long to retrench. "Come on, Lew, be reasonable."

"Don't give me any of that arrogant crap you dose out to those poor construction workers. I know you're just a big bluffer. You're just trying to be a pompous ass and you're doing a good job of it too!" Katherine stamped her foot silently in the grass frustrated. "If you don't teach me, I'm going…I'm going…up on the road and hitchhike into West Yellowstone."

"You're not going to hitchhike to West Yellowstone." His words were filled with concession but the lure of trout in big water was powerful. He held his ground.

"I will. And I'll take my shirt off too, to make sure I get a ride."

Bakewell, irritated with the spoiled little girl routine, tried to sound determined, almost belligerent, "Come on! Be reasonable!"

"I will!"

"You're not going to take your shirt off."

She was wearing one of his heavy sweatshirts; she had taken to wearing them around the camper in the mountain chill. Without hesitating she yanked it over her head, her swelling breasts jellied, firm, incredibly white, in stunning contrast to the rest of her tanned anatomy. She stared at him defiantly.

Bakewell, shocked, stumbled in the fast water and what he shouted Katherine wasn't sure she heard, but it was just as shocking, even if she hadn't heard it right. He made his way to shore, struggling in the heavy waders, trying not to lose his balance on the slippery rocks in the sweeping current. He fell just before reaching the bank, going down on all fours, Katherine laughed at his clumsiness, a look of triumph on her young face. She was a tall, striking figure in the yellowing grass. She covered her nakedness as he came up the steep bank, not sure what was coming next.

Bakewell grabbed her, pulling her to him backwards and wrapped her up in his arms, covering her protectively. "Never do that again!" he said furiously.

"Oh Andy, there's no one around."

"Never, never do that again," he repeated. "Never show yourself to another human being as long as you belong to me."

"As long as I belong to you?"

"Never!"

"You're really angry?" she was surprised. She thought he was about to cry, knew immediately he was covering his emotion with anger.

"I'm mad as hell. Don't ever do that again. You're my wife; no one should ever see your nakedness."

"No one saw me."

"Don't do that again." Bakewell was confused by his reaction to her behavior, not understanding his anger, not wanting to analyze it, anger was easier.

"You're such a silly boy." She looked up at the side of his face. "Such a *fogie*. Such a *young fogie*."

"Never do that again; nobody should ever see your naked chest but me." He pulled her close to him, cupping her breasts through the heavy cloth, holding her tightly. She wiggled and protested, saying her breasts were getting sensitive, but he held on, lessening his hold slightly, wanting to punish her, but fearing it might hurt. She reveled in his embrace and warmed to his touch as he softened his grip and gently began to open and close his hands about her. She loved him and loved the control she had over him. She could feel him calming and was glad. When he first came out of the river she didn't know what he was going to do. But she knew he loved her, was confident in him, and getting very used to his forthright avowals of devotion that grew stronger each month. No matter how quickly the macho, truculent behavior came on, no matter how much the petty displays of arrogance dismayed her, she was confident he would let go of the controlled fury he kept just underneath, that his irritation would change to gentleness; later there would be a tenderness in his lovemaking that both thrilled her and filled her with blissful contentment.

"Such a stodgy boy. Such a grumpus."

"I can't have your beauty coruscating from the bank of a river, even this famous river. I don't care *if it is only God's creatures* you're displaying yourself to."

"I don't think I've ever coruscated before. At least, not physically."

"Please don't do it again?"

"Coruscating. You and your big words, such a silly boy."

"It hurts me when you behave like that."

"Really?"

"Yes. Deeply."

"I didn't think it was a big deal."

"Where your body is concerned it's a big deal. It makes me queasy and weak in the knees."

She patted his forearm and looked across the Madison. "Oh Andy, how lovely." There was a pair of white trumpeter swans together in the fast current at midstream, elegantly graceful as they turned, without effort, never more than a few feet separating them, their long white necks in contrast to the black of their bills. "Do you think they're a couple?"

"It looks like a couple to me."

"No. Do you think they're related or are they lovers?"

He didn't answer, holding his own lover; they watched the swans drift with the current. They were to see the swans almost every year afterward and Katherine liked to think it was the same pair, tragically childless, Greek and eternal in their devotion and their fidelity.

They packed up afterward, Bakewell giving no further thought to the hungry trout feeding below the boulders. They spent the rest of the day in the car touring Yellowstone. Later Katherine teased her husband, enjoying his vulnerability, saying, "lots of boys have seen my chest. Some have touched it too," while his hands turned white at the knuckles where he held the wheel. She was learning to relish the power she had over someone so big and so powerful, but was also learning how fragile his psyche was, and how much he worried after her when she was intent on worrying him. He was typically silent when confronted with a dilemma. She gave up the game after he stared stoically through the glass as the wonders of the Firehole Canyon passed, refusing to emit any sound, refusing to engage her in conversation. As they were driving down from Old Faithful, along the lower Firehole, she softened the moment by telling him he was her "only lover" and her only love, and she intended to die in his arms. Quoting, she leaned over and whispered huskily into his ear, "Andy Bakewell, I'll love you 'til the day I die." And they were together again, Katherine taking his hand, kissing it, holding it to her chest as they talked reverently of the scenery they had seen that day on their drive out of the Park to West Yellowstone.

Late in the afternoon they relocated to Ennis and the campground at

Valley Garden, beginning a lifetime affair with Ennis, and with that big country that housed the Madison. It was very hot in the lower valley, the temperature often up into the 90's each afternoon. They fished the river "wet," wearing only tennis shoes and light clothing. Bakewell taught Katherine to cast a fly, waiting at 10 o'clock for the line to straighten, back to 2 o'clock before lowering the tip down so the fly settled on the water in a nearly straight line. They fished with big drys so she could see her fly on the water as it flowed past "the sweepers" hanging low on the bank. In the midday heat they walked down the river and flushed Huns, and Bakewell told her they needed a bird dog to hunt the gray partridge along the benches below the Spanish Peaks, and Katherine told him one baby in the family was enough. But he persisted, saying no puppy would divide the attention he held in expectant reserve for the baby that was coming. He told her he would settle for just one bird dog, and she had taken his hand and responded, "We'll see what kind of father you make first."

They stayed in Ennis for five days and for five glorious nights, where they sat out in collapsible chairs and watched the sunset across the mountains, witnessing perfect nights of stellar beauty so extravagant in number and clarity it made them wistfully wonder about the future and their happiness together. Surprised to find a gourmet restaurant in Ennis, they enjoyed a fine dinner one night where they discovered the taste of smoked trout, delicately furnished with thinly sliced onions and capers, the menu weighted with dishes neither of them had ever tasted. Bakewell opted for a big steak – his cardiovascular system ready for the onslaught of cholesterol. The waiter, older, balding and strangely out of place amid sagging Stetsons, calloused hands and cracked boots in the mountain hamlet, suggested a wine. Bakewell told him they were on a budget and ordered the cheapest glass of burgundy. The older man, taken by Katherine's vitality and fresh scrubbed look – complimented her large eyes, wet and luminously set in a bronzing Montana suntan – offered them a bottle of fine cabernet for the discounted price of $7 and they accepted, toasting their health, their happiness together and the new family they were starting.

Afterward they walked the broken sidewalks, taking in the sights and noisy barroom sounds that came out onto the street of a town turned out for the final weeks of the "end of season." The sun was still out at eight and the stores offered sales, spilling their wares over tables placed at the doorways. Bakewell bought Katherine a fishing vest, and carefully fitted it with scissors, nippers and forceps and a variety of drys. They bought hand lotion and lip balm at the tiny grocery store – Katherine's hands were dry and cracking in the low humidity – and they both had the seamy beginnings of cracked lips that were stiff and felt arousingly rough when they kissed.

They fished the braided stream above and below the campground; Bakewell patiently showed his wife how to pull down on the line with her left hand as she shot the rod back to 10 o'clock, waited for it to tighten, before casting it forward again. She advanced quickly to the point of getting the fly to a fishable place with a floatable presentation. Each time she lost a fly to the sweepers along the overhanging bank he would patiently tie another on, his big fingers having developed a dexterity over the years that Katherine admired as she waited childlike, eyes wide and bright, the water bifurcating about her hips, while she nodded understandingly in the bright sunlight, listening to his short discourse, her hair in a pony tail, or parted down the middle and pulled in Swedish braids that made her look even younger. He would dope the fly with floatant and hold it up for her inspection, and she would study it seriously, eyes wider still in appreciation, grateful for his attentiveness and the sincerity of his concern. Eventually he nodded a proud approval at one of her better casts and pronounced her "ready to fish" and went off down current.

He was anxious to learn the ways of trout, watched his neighbors in the campground as they rigged up and headed out each morning and evening, grilling them when he next saw them with questions about their luck and their methods, eventually honing in on one 70's plus gentleman who "fished with cane" and "only on top," and did both with disdain for the competition and a superior attitude. Bakewell scavenged much from their abbreviated conversations. On the 4th day the old man reluctantly suggested a technique.

"If you really want to help that pretty child catch a good fish, you should take her out on the river at sunset and watch for a hatch moving over the water near the runs just below the widest, shallowest riffles in the river." He gave Bakewell two caddis patterns, explaining how to match the hatch with size and color, then in an oh-what-the-hell afterthought, reached out and pulled a huge black Woolybugger from Bakewell's vest patch, adding, "If you want her to pull in one of those luggers, throw this monstrosity into the shallows after dark," turning away he looked back over his stooped shoulder and said, "Don't leave that child alone on the river after dark! I don't want to be responsible for another idiotic tyro catastrophe."

They fished that same evening at sunset, but gave up before dark because Katherine couldn't stand the swarming insects in her hair. The following night Bakewell, salivating to catch a big fish, doped his expectant bride with paternalistic pride, and bug spray from an aerosol can, spraying it on his fingers and carefully daubing it around her ears and neck and the back of her hands. He put his ball cap on her head backwards, havelocking her graceful neck before he zipped her into a plastic windbreaker and pronounced her bug-proof.

That was the night they caught a big, heavy sided brown cruising in a narrow run just below the widest part of the river, and Bakewell spent long minutes with cold hands in the dark water trying to revive the played out fish who had stripped the line and made the reel sing on two long runs before they were finally able to coax him to a place where they could beach him and unhook him. Afterward they shouted their success to the brilliant Montana sky, and to several deer watching wide-eyed and cautious in the willows close by. They nearly ran across the water, "home" to their campsite, later celebrated by slowly making love in the warm darkness of their camper, heads together brushing the rough curtain next to the half opened window that protected them from insects that bumped the screen, and from where they could hear the sounds of the willows moving in the breeze along the river and other campers in the clean chilly air, and smell the odors of campfires and the great conifer forests across the valley; sometimes eavesdropping on a guarded fireside conversation close by.

It was a velvety time of soft love, discovering the physical nuances of their intimacy, Katherine cautioning him again about the sensitivity in her breasts, but enjoying the tenderness of his dried and calloused hands. When he finally shuddered, complete and heavy, she felt the weight of him, his chest heaving against hers as he waited, never wanting to be done, to be finished with her, rather holding himself perfectly still, arcing, hips pressed tightly against hers, as if still reaching, still wanting. That was the night it happened the first time. The night she shuddered in return and gave herself up to the uncontrollable aching, not sure if it was ecstasy or agony, and he put the palm of his hand over her mouth to stifle her sound and held her very tightly, loving her trembling, convulsing body, loving her sounds, and when it was complete, he professed his love with such fealty, such profound ardor, she was so overwhelmed by it, and by his gratitude, she felt complete and whole and alive and more sure than ever before about her choice of husband and lover. It was perfect: a night to be remembered for a generation, *the night* Bakewell learned to forever associate the smell of Deet with Katherine's passion, with the warmth of her neck and ear caressing his, with lovemaking and Ennis and fishing the Madison.

***

Six months after Katherine's death, Bakewell left Ned with the company, saying he was going down to the beach for an indefinite stay. "Take all the time you want, bub," was Ned's only response. "St. Louis ain't goin nowhere before you get back and neither are we. You need to get away from your grief for awhile and find a place where you can get some peace of mind and rest your emotionalistic parts." Bakewell said he just wanted to find another routine. "I've did that myself before, earlier in my life, and in the past. After my wife went, I never knew if I was sorry or happy over her finding that other fuck; I just knew I was goin through a change in my life and needed a change in mine for myself."

Bakewell had heard the story before, knew it by heart, in and out of tense changes. He left the next morning, driving straight through the way Katherine liked to, stopping only for fuel. He rolled the windows down in Hattiesburg, enjoying the fecund smell the humidity added to the Deep South even in winter. He sped most of the way across the newly completed highway from Hattiesburg to Mobile; trying not to remember all the previous trips, glad for the changes. The new construction gave the trip a different appearance. The beach house was clean and very empty when he got in late that same night, the house soundless next to a dark surf, barely raising to foam and not making enough noise to hear through closed windows. He tossed his pack in the guest bedroom, avoiding the lofted bedroom hovering overhead, filled with memories of his physical marriage and some of the best emotions he had known in the past. Katherine loved the beach house and the sound of the surf pounding and the late night walks they took on evenings just like the one he had driven into.

He spent long hours walking next to the surf early in the morning, watching the sunrise. He went to Mass at eight, listened and prayed attentively. In the evenings he walked long into the darkness, often under an overcast sky that hung low and ominous over the deserted winter coast. He avoided the favored joints, so many places they had frequented for years, knowing they would haunt him always. He still went out to the State Park, a place he associated with no one in particular, a place he could go each day and spend hours rifling golf balls down a tree lined practice area, the practice peaceful now that he was out of anger, now that he had lost his aggression, now that he was no longer upset by his misses. Unburdened of so many things that had once weighed heavily, that had once set him off, the practicing was relaxed, structured and satisfying. By the end of the second week he was getting so much satisfaction out of the ball striking it became almost an obsession. His success amused him and the progress he made absorbed and engrossed him each afternoon. It was good to find something other than the airplane that could take his mind off his troubles. He didn't expect to find it on the practice range. In the years before, hitting golf balls had only created tension and anger.

The second week it turned unseasonably warm and an hour before sunset the no-see-ums were biting with force. Wanting to stay later each evening with nothing better to do and enjoying the time more, he sought relief the second night of the warm spell in a bottle of non-aerosol bug spray amid the gear he kept under the false floor of the truck bed. He pumped it over and around his head and neck, wiping some on his forearms and the back of his hands. He hit balls for an extra hour that last night at the beach – hit them solidly, with terrific force, got great satisfaction out of the simple purity of contact between clubhead and ball – finishing what he would remember as the best practice session of his life. When it was too dark to see them land, he walked over to the putting green and dropped half a dozen balls and chipped and putted better than he had in years thinking, *I may still be able to play this damned game.*

As the last light of day disappeared through the long needled pines, Bakewell bent to retrieve the golf balls he could no longer see rolling across the green and the full force of the smell of Deet hit him with a sudden, excruciating jolt and – *one more time* – he remembered Katherine and Ennis and the sound of the river running past on a calm and perfect September evening and, giving in totally to the emotion of knowing it was – *one more thing* – he would never, ever do with her again, fell to his knees on the wet grass, landing on his hands as the air rushed from him.

A Park Ranger, impatient to leave was the only witness. "Ya'll all right there, mister?" he asked, coming forward from the cart shack. Bakewell looked at the man in the brown park ranger's uniform. The uniform accelerated the memories of Yellowstone, Park Rangers and trips to Ennis, and they swept over him, making him groan, wanting to let it all out; to quit breathing; to just quit breathing and let it all be over; to let the pain and sense of loss go out of him forever.

"Ya'll need some help there?"

"No…no, I'm okay." Bakewell got up slowly, reaching his feet weakly, gathering up his things as he tried to gather himself. He steadied himself against the bulk of the golf bag. The emptiness of the quiet evening and the odor of pines surrounded him, consumed him with loneliness. He shouldered his golf bag and walked back out to his truck and sat down heavily in the seat and waited for the ranger to swing the closed gate open so he could pass. The drive back up to the intersection took all his effort, all his effort to steer the truck and hold his head erect. He stopped in the parking lot at Delschamps as soon as he crossed the intersection and waited for some energy, some kind of reason to have energy, to enter his body and give him the strength to move.

He sat there for a long time, before finally stirring. He went inside and bought a six-pack. He knew before he drank the beer it would only worsen his melancholy. He didn't really care, doubting there was a place more painful he could get to that would make him wish he were back to where he was before he drank the beer.

He drove down to the beach and sat on a wet sand dune between two low-rise resorts and stared at the emptiness of the gulf, the view below him, black and foreboding above the water and the horizon. It took some time before he realized he wasn't thinking, wasn't remembering or thinking of anything. Before Katherine died, he didn't think it possible to be conscious and think of nothing, but he was doing it, did it often, numbed to a non-consciousness as he stared ahead and thought of nothing for hours. He drank all six beers.

Later, seeking the lights and noise of friendlier confines, he drove down to Tacky Jacks. He'd never been there with Katherine. He ate on the outdoor deck, listening to the water lap at the pilings under the stars that had turned out again, not feeling the wetness or the cooling air around him. He had two more drinks, didn't wonder where the alcohol had gone, didn't care. When he finally left it was late, and he drove carefully down the inland waterway road. When he got to the intersection, he turned north, wanting to go out to the airport. Next to Ennis it was his favored place to stare at the night sky. The weather would be closing in soon.

It was quiet at the airport, with no planes in the pattern and nobody left around late at night. He knew it would be. He parked the truck and walked out onto the ramp where he often parked his own plane, kept on going down the taxiway to the end of the southbound runway before turning back again. The temperature and dew point were tied when he checked the AWOS recording on his cell phone. It wouldn't be long before fog formed; a serious headache was already forming when he got back to the ramp. He leaned back against a single-engined Piper, resting his head on the fuselage. The wet metal felt good against the back of his head. He rolled it back and forth to absorb the cooling moisture.

"Ought to chew your ass out for taking such an overdose," he said, talking to himself. He did it often. "Hell, I don't really give a damn, get as drunk as you want." He lost his balance and rocked awkwardly. The stars were still above but not as clear as before.

"Next to Ennis, this is the best place in my world to stargaze." There was no answer. He wasn't sure if he had spoken out loud. In his mental haze he wasn't sure about a lot of things. He was very inebriated. "Are you listening? Are you there…are you there somewhere just beyond my vision? Just outside my reach?" He could hear the slurring of his speech. "Can you hear me? …I love you. If you can hear me… I love you so much…I miss you so much…I am dying with it. *I am dying with the missing of you."*

There was no answer, no breeze, the silence infected with the sound of insects off in the dense cover that surrounded the airport. He had to urinate badly. He looked around, spoke to the space next to him. "We still have to do this here on earth." He said, hoping he wouldn't break the spiritual tension. "Please don't look if you're offended." He rocked as he spoke, pointing his stream far out so it wouldn't splash on his shoes, weaving as he did. A pack of coyotes began to cry at the end of runway 9 far in the distance.

He leaned back against the plane again, almost falling as he did and stared up at the sky for a long time, trying to recreate the mood. His neck hurt with the effort. There was a quote Father had used at Mass earlier that week. *... From a poem maybe? From someone famous, surely? 'S been running around in my head all week.* He was very drunk. He looked at the sky, trying to remember the words.

In a voice barely audible and hoarse with grief and doubt, he decided to quote from memory, satisfied he could do it, could still ask the question:

Is my gloom after all, the shade... of Thy hand outstretched, caressing?

The wet air formed little halos around each light in the sky and they tried to shimmer on through the thickening mist but it was too late. The fog continued to form and they were gone.

Charcoal House

In the weeks following their disaster they kept to a familiar pattern, days brutally long as both men tried to overcome their joint adversity, frustrated, knowing no amount of effort would overcome the debt. They needed a miracle and Bakewell prayed on dutifully, wondering at the minimal prospects his prayers might expect. They spoke regularly on radio and cell phone, but it was different; neither had the stomach for what was happening, for what was coming. Knowing they couldn't pay everyone sickened them, gnawed at their collective soul. They could point to dozens of times they'd been burnt – from a few hundred to huge chunks of money, when someone hid behind the expense of the law, or hid assets behind some outrageous nuance in the hapless, ineffective law.

"Fuckin law's for pimps and drug dealers," Ned said.

Bakewell nodded. The law was a joke. It had never protected them in their pursuit of wealth. They had learned to live with the lackless results, including a suit they actually won: seventy grand. Once the judge banged his gavel it was over – the loser never paid. The judge said they won, justice had been served. No money was forthcoming. They paid $9,500 in legal fees.

They still found time to meet for lunch in a city filled with fine restaurants. They covered most of it in a normal week, their work scattered from the Gateway Arch in every direction. When they wanted to drink they kept it to a few watering holes they'd frequented for years: The Charcoal House and Rick's mostly. Much of the time was spent in gloomy silence, some in solemn conversation, but they still managed to lift their spirits reminiscing. The good old days had been good.

***

After college Bakewell had taken his first full time job. It turned out to be his only job. The utility company, run by a generation of "Depression babies", put little value on education, but as time passed and the industry changed, they found they needed an engineer with a PE stamp. They put him out as a laborer to get *field experience*. Bakewell had wanted to plant his flag and make an impression; starting at the bottom was fine. A local beer tycoon, whose brewery helped make St. Louis famous, allegedly put his son to work on the docks. The son, a fourth generation baron ultimately became CEO and a fellow dockworker occupied the brewery's Presidential suite.

Bakewell worked hard in the field that first summer with a strapping foreman who eventually became superintendent. Years later Bakewell still referred to Ned as "the Soup". Their common bond was their company and football. Bakewell had played two years of varsity ball. Ned hadn't gone to high school. Not playing football was his biggest regret. He loved the game and knew the name of every Hall of Famer who'd played middle linebacker. "I woulda kicked the shit outta ever dazzley-legged, whippy-assed, little son of a bitch that ever touched the ball or thought he mighta seen a chance to make a *gold* against me." Ned bragged.

Bakewell soon learned to enjoy Ned's raconteur skills and his potent regard for time. Ned taught him *Lombardi time,* "Be ten minutes earlier than the clock. People who're late wasted our times and other peoples times too, as well as their money, and if they don't have no regard for it they ain't got none (money) and wasn't worth waitin for in the first place." But Ned later had to amend his policy, "After I missed a job 'cause a squirrelly-assed little stargazer, one of them sara-bul dopes was late for our meetin."

"Cerebral?"

"Whatever. After that I waited another ten minutes to the ten I was already early for before."

Ned loved to say Bakewell was "the only son-of-a-bitch-engineer smart enough to get outta the rain." It happened on a steamy July day when they were together at a boiler plant on the riverfront and it began raining hard. Bakewell had just started wearing glasses and couldn't see through the dripping, fogging lenses; had asked Ned cautiously, "What say we take a break and get out of the rain, boss man. The walls are caving in. We don't have enough shoring." Ned had to think about it; he was senior man. With an ingratiating smile Bakewell added, "It sure is getting cooler." The temperature had dropped 15 degrees. Ned made a big deal out of a college boy who knew enough to get out of the rain. He took Bakewell up on South Broadway to a lunch place with pool tables, telling him he would teach him how to "shoot stick." Bakewell never forgot the experience. There were two characters at the other table wearing what Ned called *prison tattoos*. Ned convinced them he needed their table, "'Cause this here one ain't level and the balls is all runnin uphill." The tattoos gave Bakewell a hard look before stepping aside.

"Them'r prison tattoos they got on their arms. You can tell 'cause they ain't got no other color than blue. Dumb fucks sit around stickin needles in theirselves."

When confronted with people from his past Ned resorted to the language of his youth, the stuff of truck stops, a seminal graffiti obtained from toilet walls; the language more odious than the commode nearby.

Ned "got sent down to the Louisiana Delta" country by an indigent mother when he was twelve, to Pecaniere, north of Lafayette, where he grew to formidable proportions in the bayous he called swamps, where cypress trees grew to immense size and the muddy playground gave him an opportunity to trap muskrats, catch shrimp and crabs, small alligators and crawfish, all fondly remembered table fare. Ned loved Cajun cooking, loved spicy sauces. He never learned the Cajun parlance, but picked up the dicier words from "a passel of big brothers and bigger cuz-ants," while being raised by a violent uncle, his father's brother, after his father went to prison for the last time. By the time Ned reached maturity and joined the Corps, his brothers had followed the old man to a variety of penitentiaries up north.

Ned liked to say, "I was alley-raised," sometimes referred to himself as, "A man of the street," although Bakewell suspected there were few alleys and Pecaniere's thoroughfares were probably more dirt than pavement in Ned's youth. Ned had great memories of his Delta youth, and that background coupled with his earthy witticisms made him a raconteur of wonderful stories, mostly told on himself. Ned never boasted and never exaggerated his role in the events of his often violent youth. It had been a hard and fascinating time, and he had enjoyed it to the fullest. It had fashioned him into a tough, honest and decent man.

"You were the rose that grew out of the manure pile."

"You ain't shittin." Ned was the only member of his family who held a steady job, paid his bills, and achieved a positive net worth.

Much of his youth was spent among blacks and the experience had been indelible.

"Where I growed up there was a lot of colored folks that had more than me. Hell, we looked up to the colored people when I was a kid." Ned had few prejudices, but used the epithets he'd been raised with, part of his vocabulary long after he came north. In his later years, as he graduated the ranks to salesman, later owner and salesman extraordinaire, he dropped the slurs. Ned was as good a listener as a storyteller. He was also determined to expand his own vocabulary, without bothering to master the pronunciations, and loved the limitless variety of words that filled Bakewell's sentences. Because he mutilated his words with incredibly creative metaphors, Bakewell never tired of fitting them in, knowing Ned would attempt later to weave them into his own stories, creating a crazy quiltwork of malapropos.

Ned learned salacious, "that filthy sal-a-shus shit on TV," and egregious, "lousy greegee-ous thievin bastards," and hundreds of others. During their luncheons Ned would sip his drinks, tossing out little pearls, like: "A pair of parallels," and, "a pointed triangle." Bakewell's favorite, was "I'm psychedelic," which Ned used when he meant clairvoyant.

Ned was shamelessly complimentary, especially around women. Sometimes his compliments amazed even Bakewell, who thought he'd heard them all. Ned was corny and way too obvious, but got away with much because his sincerity matched his size. They walked into an office full of middle-aged women one day and Ned blurted, "Geez, whaddaya gotta do to get a job in here, win a beauty contest?" Bakewell lowered his head embarrassed; the room lit up with giggles and appreciating smiles.

***

"It's humiliating. I've been robbed and made to look a fool. I feel like it's on the front page."

"Quit beatin up on yerself, you ain't done nothin wrong." Ned admonished. "You're like a little girl's been raped and left naked in the middle of the street feelin shameful. It ain't her fault the world's full of no good pieces a shit lookin to do turrable things."

"I feel like I've been raped alright."

"It ain't your fault. Stop torturin yerself."

"It's like having a knife in your back that's being removed slowly. You want the thing out. It's taking so long you can't bear the pain."

Ned patted massive forearms with huge digits, shook his head, hated to watch the kid's pain. He always saw Bakewell as a younger brother, a kid, and it made his own pain worse "You been through a lot, Andy. You had it all once: beautiful wife, kids, home at the lake. You had a beautiful life. I envied you; you was so full of confidence, had such a great lifestyle, country club membership, so many people lookin up atcha. Now you lost all your toys, yer life, yer money. Geez, God even took your wife. I don't see how you can pray so much the way God's humiliatin you. Sayin all them rosaries for what? Seems like the more you pray with them little sisters over there at the monastery the more shit comes rainin down on yer head."

"You've got your problems, Ned. I'm not the only one that's suffering."

"I ain't got no problems compared to you. I'm not crazy 'bout burnin people over money, but a lot of them fucks we can't pay has made bundles off us over the years. It ain't like we just went into business and then fucked ever-body outta money." Ned took a long pull on his drink and nodded to the waitress for another. "Besides, I can walk away. I don't need this town to make a life in when there's other places to fish. I could go all the way to New Zealand if I wanted. There's fish over there's never been caught." Ned spread his hands wide. "I watch it on them cable channels all the time."

Ned grew quiet again. Bakewell was dying inside, from mortification, from a sense of abandonment, a sense of loss, from just plain going broke. His life had been about accomplishment. He had managed to put marriage and family first, but sometimes just barely. He truly believed Katherine and the kids were his biggest success, but he loved his toys, his status in the industry, his position at the bank, the position he occupied in his little society. Ned understood better than anyone how Bakewell had equated success to money and material things before Katherine died, and he knew the kid didn't care about them now. It was a good thing; he'd lost all of them.

"I heard on the TV recently that *reason* was human but *intuition* was divine. I ain't no diviner than the next guy, but you're an engineer Andy, and you got a engineer's mind. Yer always tryin to apply reason to stuff; sometimes you just got to intuition it. You ain't got no intuition-ative powers."

"I keep going back to the knife thing. It's in my back, and it's coming out...slowly," Bakewell answered, ignoring the intuition thing. "You want the thing out, but it takes so long you can't stand the pain." Ned nodded in agreement. "Every week we hang in there we make a little bit more to pay off the debt, but it isn't enough. We'll never make enough."

They'd been having the same conversation for weeks. Bakewell put his head in his hands.

"Your ana-lodgy fits."

"Analogy," he spoke to the table.

"Whatever. You been talkin in ana-lodgies all our lives together. As long as I can remember you been talkin in em. You got me doin it to myself sometimes."

Bakewell was out of words, waited. They had been together so long he could almost read Ned's mind. Maybe he had a little intuition too.

Ned said their partnership was like a marriage without sex. "We know each other's thinkin and plannin before the other one knows he's gonna do it, or its gonna happen." The drink came and Ned took a sip, enjoyed the sting of vodka, "I'm not stupid, Andy, I know the knife's in there. I can feel it bein takin out a little each week that we have a good one, but it still hurts like hell. It sure as fuckin well hurts, and it ain't never comin all the way out, and the way its comin seems only to add to the pain of havin it come out at all."

"You want to close up? I'm about done. I don't think I can stand it much longer."

"No! Fuck no. We're gonna stick it out. It just pisses me off."

"I just wish it would end. It's humiliating and I'm tired of the fight."

"Yeah, well we stepped on our dicks a few times over the years, but this one wasn't our fault as much as them others. This one was about bein stold from and there ain't no way to prevent that. If the bastards are gonna get ya, there gonna get ya. The old man always preached that. It just never cost us so much as this time."

Bakewell believed he was the laughing stock of the industry. If he wasn't, he would be soon enough. The debt part was a repetition of the misery they'd been through years before; going through it a second time was too much. He couldn't understand why God wanted him to re-live the nightmare. They both swore after surviving the first one, they would never have a repeat; but it was back. Bakewell called it a recrudescence.

"It's pretty cruddy aw-right. I don't care what you call it – its bullshit! I just wisht I could kill somebody for it. Might make me feel better."

They had another big problem, a real estate problem. Bakewell blamed himself, rightly so. He had done a development in Grover, thirty miles west of their office. The guy set him up. After the sanitary work was done, before any streets went in, before any houses were built, the guy took off, leaving them with a lien against a dead company. Eventually they had taken over the property and the problems kept coming. Ned called it the "Grover Monster." They knew nothing about developing property, and had a bad piece of land to boot. The little cheat was five feet tall with reddish hair and a cowlick that stuck up on the back of his head. In a moment of despair Ned had said, "Geesus, Andy, we got outsmarted by Woody-fuckin-Woodpecker!" Two years passed and they hadn't sold a lot. Rates were high and the interest clock was ticking. It had been manageable when they were making money, but only added to their exasperation when the losses set in.

Bakewell cringed. Everywhere he looked there was debt. They'd killed themselves for years and had nothing. The first generation got it started, created a reputation, he and Ned had taken it to the next level. He hoped Nancy would end up with it, be his legatee. Before the lawsuit calamity and the raiding, he'd had enough money to walk away, had only stayed for his daughter and for her generation – the generation they now regarded with contempt, the generation without loyalty.

Bakewell had a favorite expression, "It's not how you start; its how you finish." They all heard it many times. In his younger, confident days, even with the Patton-like arrogance, he'd been a leader, a motivator, could be almost inspirational at times. After all the years and all the trying – thousands of hours of inspired effort, and more thousands of monotonous work, there was nothing left. *It wasn't how you started; it was how you finished.* He was finished.

Maggie

Bakewell adjusted to college life cautiously, his first tentative weeks a series of uncertain days, making his way through crowded corridors and across campus surrounded by thousands of students in a hot environment of politics and dissension. It was the year Martin Luther King and Robert Kennedy were assassinated, a year of riots and anger – and shouting.

The football season was underway. Saturday home games brought a welcome diversion, a mania of enthusiasm, where the booze flowed in the stadium and through the town, as it only can on a football weekend, consumed by a generation determined to show how fast they could put it away. Bakewell hated the juvenility of his younger classmates, had trouble blending in, their ridiculous brio made him feel like a marked man. He had a new student ID number that was two digits shorter than his serial number, but he felt like the longer one was tattooed to his forehead, even though he looked like a hundred other graduate students in unpressed khakis, strollers and a sweatshirt turned inside out. He was grateful to be "free at last," alone in his own apartment, without the hassle or the rancor of a barracks. The solitude seemed almost surreal at times.

He learned to take good notes, do the math assignment right after class, and spend his afternoons in the undergraduate library, euphemistically known as "the U-GLEE." Evenings were spent in the beer joints that populate every campus. The Italian Village was mandatory, although he didn't care for the hygiene. The Heidelberg and the Hofbrau House were more to his liking. He became a regular in both, enjoyed watching the mating rites of the Greek crowd as they got far into the 3.2 beer.

In his fourth semester he took an elective: *Introduction to Political Theory,* a course thick with men. It was supposed to be a survey course on the philosophy of everyone from Socrates to Hegel, with some Machiavelli and Jeremy Bentham thrown in, but it soon devolved into a heated debate over the Viet Nam war. Bakewell fell in with the hawks and bit his lip most days as his side was out-shouted. The professor, anal and acerbic, assigned seating alphabetically, which left Bakewell in the front, on the downhill side of an uphill struggle. At the time draft-dodgers were hanging on academia with the tenacity of Kudzu vine, and there were many graduate students in the class of fifty. He was outclassed by the intellectual level of his peers, some of whom had been there five years longer.

The professor had asked for a hand count of veterans the first week; Bakewell was in a minority of five. Still there were twenty others who defended the war, enough to make a confrontation, albeit lop-sided. Not so one argumentative, brassy young blond seated two rows over and three seats behind. She was beautiful, strikingly so, with lustrous eyes so deeply blue they had every male wondering what it would be like. She was careful about picking her fights, restricting her participation, weighing in only at the opportune moment. When she did she was incisive; her biting comments resonated with the contemporary anger. Bakewell hated being subjected to the spleen of draft-dodgers and teenyboppers. He didn't like the military he'd just left, but recognized the debt he'd paid his country and the service his service had provided in return. He was structured, organized and disciplined, and had a military appreciation for each.

It was hard to stay quiet in the verbal scrapping that ran half the class period, and, in a momentary indiscretion, he joined the fray, picking a fight with a scruffy, opinionated little guy in need of a haircut. He made the mistake of using the time worn sentiment of duty, honor, country: *If it was good enough for my parents' generation it was a good enough reason now.* Patriotism was the rallying cry of the hawks. The comment fell weakly and mostly on deaf ears. Because he had never spoken before, he was allowed a grudging moment to voice his opinion before the hisses and boos started. When the brassy blond took issue, the class quieted and Bakewell resorted to an old palliative.

"My father was shot down in the Solomon's during the last war."

"My father was wounded at Anzio," she shot back. "A World War doesn't justify fighting this war."

"It's called patriotism," he shouted over the exploding din.

"It's called stupidity," she responded with equal passion. "And it's ludicrous to think we should be fighting a war when our President is so unsure of our position he's unwilling to run for reelection. Why should anyone – *man or woman* – be expected to go and risk death or injury for our country when the country's not sure why it's in Viet Nam?"

It was curious the way the others shut up when she spoke – Bakewell supposed they were all secretly smitten – but there was a chorus of yeas and the usual out-of-control fracas ensued. He knew he had lost the argument, worse, lost face, and felt his own coloring in defeat. It was humiliating and left him in the uncomfortable situation of sitting in front of her, feeling her derisive contempt hot against his cheek. The misery was short-lived. His family got word the beginning of May that Brenden had been killed in Viet Nam. Brenny had died during the fiercest fighting at the tail end of the Tet Offensive. Bakewell was excused for a week of class, and when he approached his instructor after returning to school, was told he was doing B work and would receive a B in lieu of testing for finals. He got a similar response from two other instructors who wanted to be off campaigning for Eugene McCarthy on weekends. He took only two finals his last week.

They shipped Brenny's remains home two weeks later. The funeral was enormous, filling the church with classmates, family, friends, and a generation who'd fought World War II and came determined to show respect for a war hero. He was buried at Jefferson Barracks with full military honors.

The line of cars making the trip to the national cemetery stretched far down the new interstate highway. The brassy young woman showed up for the gravesite ceremony and the exquisitely painful playing of "taps." When it was over, she waited amidst a throng of mourners and approached Bakewell hesitantly, held out her hand and took his and gravely extended her sympathy. Bakewell had looked right through her, daggers in eyes, unmoved by her sincerity.

Weeks later, after an anguished period of loss and mourning and a terrible depression that kept him flat on his back, aching and immobile, he finally turned the corner and resumed life. When he did, he clearly remembered her appearance that sunny morning when his brother's remains were interred and, in the remembering, began to appreciate the situation she put herself in at such a difficult time. He also began to regret his behavior.

In late June, making his way through a round of summer parties, trying to get moving again, he came across her in a backyard overflowing with young people and a single guitar. It was a Pete Seeger war-protesting-sing-a-long that he had learned to tolerate. She was standing across the yard in a pink, sleeveless blouse, her sparkling blue eyes and striking hair illuminated next to a Japanese lantern. They were under a beautiful star filled night made fresher and clearer by a late afternoon thunderstorm. She was surrounded by admirers when she first spotted him. He quickly looked away then, aggravated by his insecurity, looked her way again, but she was gone. Moments later she came up behind him while he searched the yard for her. She put her hand on his arm and said, "My, my, if it isn't Andy Bakewell, as I live and breath," a not bad imitation of Scarlett O'Hara.

"I owe you an apology," were the very first words he ever spoke to her.

"Whatever for?" the act continued.

"For my behavior at the cemetery."

She softened quickly, continued to touch his arm. "How are you?"

"I'm okay. I'm doing okay."

"I *am sorry* about your brother, really." Lines of pain appeared around Bakewell's eyes and she didn't fail to notice. "How are your parents doing?"

"It's just my mom. My father died a long time ago."

"Yes. I saw her at the Mass. I wondered about your father."

"You were at the Mass?"

"Oh, you know, any excuse to go to Communion." It sounded flip and she quickly added, "I didn't mean that the way it sounded. I'm sorry. I wanted to be there."

"Really?"

"Yes. I wanted to show respect for an American hero," she sighed deeply as she pronounced the words. "We've been losing them at an alarming rate. I hate the damned war, but I'm not stupid. I know lots of boys go over there to do what they think is right. I'm sure your brother thought he was doing the right thing, *was doing the right thing,* following his conscience. That makes him a hero."

"I thought you were against the war."

"I am, but I can still feel your loss. You look like you've been in a lot of pain."

"Well, you're right about Brenny. He was a hero, mine anyway."

"I bet he was." She squeezed his arm affectionately. They didn't speak – Bakewell shy, intimidated, couldn't come up with anything; the girl with the blue eyes waiting, searching.

Finally she said, "Andy, I know your name, but you don't know mine."

"Margaret Leary," he said. "Introduction to Political Theory."

"Maggie," she put out her hand. He'd never shaken a girl's hand before. When he took it she folded it between both of hers. It made him nervous, but it felt wonderful.

"Andy Bakewell."

"Yes, I know, I think maybe the Bakewell's are famous now. Your brother's made them so," adding, "I never expected to see you in Clayton."

Bakewell laughed. "I didn't expect to see me in Clayton either. It's not exactly my kind of town."

"No, you look like the outdoorsy type," she said, amused.

He didn't know what to say. She asked him if he sang and he laughed. She said she didn't care for the anti-war music. People came and went as they made small talk. She was popular, and many took the opportunity to stop and talk to her, Bakewell ad-libbing his way through. They stayed together for another ten minutes before she said, "Would you like to go somewhere? Get away from this for awhile?"

He wanted to say *are you kidding,* nodded without responding instead. She pinched his shirt between her thumb and finger, a tiny delicate move, pulled him away from the group, turned and walked off into the darkness, knowing he would follow. Out front, in the street crowded with cars, she led him to her small sports car. Maggie stepped over the door into the seat, indicating he do the same. The car was parked under a street lamp; the steering wheel on the wrong side. She wore an expensive pair of leather sandals that barely covered her suntanned feet and a pair of the whitest shorts he'd ever seen. He noticed the cracked leather and entered through the door, not wanting to test it with his weight, almost fell into the low-slung sports car, bumping against her. She laughed softly, the sound coming from deep down in her throat, said, "Coordinated."

They left and were soon moving at a mad pace as she shifted gears, yanking and jerking them about, heading across town. They stopped at a RR crossing, waiting for the noisy train to pass and she said, "So you've done your time; you're all through now?" Bakewell only nodded. "A veteran of the war, discharged honorably I'm sure, and on your way through college, then what?"

"I missed the war. Most of my time was in the Med and the Caribbean. "

"The Med?"

"Mediterranean Sea."

She nodded. "A man of the world then. I'll bet you could tell some stories about all the little chickies you met in the navy." Bakewell couldn't come up with anything. "I'll bet you had some wild shore vacations, huh? Is that what they call it, shore vacation?"

"Liberty."

"Liberty. So how was it? How were the Mediterranean women?"

"Not as pretty as college girls."

"Thanks. Or were you talking about sorority girls?"

"No, you're right in there."

"Thanks again, *right in there*. Wow."

"You have better wheels."

"Are we talking about my legs or my car?"

"Both."

The train moved off; the crossing gate was raised. "Is conversation with you going to be this much work?"

"I've been away. I've been away from civilization for a long time. My familiarity with the opposite sex is limited."

"I'll bet. Tell me about the girls in the Mediterranean."

"No."

She made the same laughing sound again. It was sensual, "Tell me."

"No."

"Tell me. I'm dying to know."

"No!"

"Please?"

"They tend to be fast – working girls mostly."

"Were they expensive?"

"Aw, shit."

"You always had enough money?"

"Come on."

"I'm interested."

"Give me a break."

"It's interesting. You're worldly. You've been around."

"You're making fun of me."

"You didn't participate…with these working girls?"

"I don't want to talk about this."

She laughed.

"Stop, please."

"I'm not making fun; I want to know. Were you a bad boy?"

"Disgraceful, let's move on."

"We're moving," she laughed, enjoying herself as the car sped down Clayton Road, creating a welcome breeze.

They drove through Forest Park, site of the 1904 World's Fair, past the Art Museum and the Municipal Opera, where music could be heard in the soft night air. They went by the giant birdcage, built for the fair, a tradition with young people on summer nights. They stopped at the lighted fountain west of the Muny and walked up to look at the water spouting and falling, colored by stained glass fronting ancient spotlights in the foundation. There were lots of people lying about, some shockingly intimate. It was the era of "flower children," a time of ignorant behavior and strident rebellion, some of it too strident, too practiced. Maggie took his hand. She was tense; the weird behavior around them worried her.

"Is this what Europe is like?" she kept her voice down.

"Mm," Bakewell nodded, "People doing it all over the place." He enjoyed the question. His response made her laugh and put him on a roll. "Benches, beaches, sometimes standing up…against columns – famous marble columns! You should see the action at the Parthenon." He was loud, and she cringed as they made their way through the people on the grass.

"Let's get out of here and go have a drink," he said with disgust, pulling her away from the fountain. Maggie tripped, regained her balance in the deep grass and didn't resist. He said, "Coordinated," as he nearly dragged her away.

She asked him to drive her car, and when he ground the gears and jerked them to a start she made fun. They drove back to Clayton and stopped at a Steak & Shake on Brentwood Boulevard. All the Steak & Shakes had curb service then. When the carhop came Bakewell raised two fingers and ordered Cokes.

"I thought when you said drink, you might want to go to a bar somewhere and have a real drink."

"I don't think your old enough for that kind of drink."

"Thanks."

"I'm not being rude. Anyway, you should enjoy being your age. How old are you; I'm not breaking the law am I?"

"No. Do I look that young?"

"You look wonderful and you know it. You're beautiful, you know that too."

"I hear it all the time." Bakewell nodded without answering, and she quickly added, "I'm not serious. I know you think I'm stuck on myself, boys always do, but I'm really not… really."

"You're stuck on yourself," he said, returning the piercing eye contact.

"Well, it's hard not to be," she said mischievously, softening her look which could change from piercing and penetrating to sweet and tender, even vulnerable and encouraging.

"You're so beautiful; I thought my heart would stop when you touched my arm this evening."

"Are you always this honest?"

A car stopped in front and waited to be recognized. Maggie got out and went over and spoke briefly. When she returned he had moved to the other side, and when she got back in said, "It must be fatiguing."

"You get used to it" – more mischief. He felt cramped and awkward in the tiny car which was too low to the ground. Maggie recognized his predicament; other beaus had similar complaints. She waved and the curb attendant came and took their tray. She started the car, "We're outta here."

"Good, I've had enough *Teen Town*."

They picked up his car, and she told him to follow her home. Home was in upscale Clayton, most of Clayton was upscale, in a neighborhood with grand houses. When they got there she pulled into the driveway, left her car and came back and got into his and sat facing him on the edge of her seat. She tore a stick of gum and gave him half. Bakewell chewed slowly watching her, smelling her – the odor of her overwhelming in the enclosed car. She was an awesome package of scents. He couldn't get enough, luxuriated in the scent of her, waited for her, hoping for her, aware she had come back to him. He thought he would walk her to the massive front door; instead they were sitting in his car. He didn't know what was next, content to wait and see. There was more piercing eye contact. She was all confidence now, in her own environment, in charge, trying to overwhelm. He couldn't put a name to confidence, hadn't yet learned to appreciate it, but recognized its value without knowing why. When she didn't speak it put the ball back in his court, her expression – she used it often.

"You smell wonderful."

"Thanks."

"Your hair is… amazing."

"Meaning you like it, or amazing as in too much?"

"It's striking, beautiful, you know what I mean."

"You say beautiful a lot."

"It makes you easy to spot in a crowd. I saw you right away at the party."

"You think I'm stuck up, don't you?" He smiled without answering. "You think I'm stuck on myself," she said, nodding for emphasis.

"I think you're worried people might think you're stuck on yourself."

"Well, I'm not."

"I don't know what to think you are. You've surprised me twice: first at the funeral and again tonight. I think I'll wait and find out who you really are." She didn't respond, watched him closely instead, tried to make him uncomfortable. It usually worked; she had been mistreating boys most of her teenaged life. They stared at each other in the dark car. There was just enough light to see by.

Bakewell reconsidered, "No, I don't have to wait. I can tell you right now; I think you're sincere and honest and not afraid to show it, not afraid to take a chance."

"That was sweet." Maggie tossed her head each time the soft bangs brushed her eyebrow. She had perfect teeth, very white; they glistened wetly when she smiled.

"You were occupied all evening, mostly with preppy guys going off to famous universities; why did you pick me – sympathy?"

"No, sympathy's over. I know you're hurting, but I'm not spending time with you because I feel sorry for you."

"You had a lot of admirers tonight," Bakewell tossed the gum out the window. "Is it your style to play the field, or do you get serious with one man at a time?"

"I didn't know I had a style."

"Everyone has a style; they just don't want to admit it."

Maggie moved closer, threw her gum out the window behind him. "To answer your second question, I've never gone out with *a man* before; you might be the first. I'm not going to answer the first one, since you were putting me down." The first half of her answer had the effect intended, made his stomach flutter. He decided to take the easy way out.

"I'm not good at small talk. I wish I was more of a challenge for you."

"And you're very honest too. I noticed you were getting your share of attention at the party."

"Well, since we're being honest, I'd have to say…*honestly*…I'd never get tired of that kind of attention."

Maggie nodded as he spoke, decided to help him out, "Well, lots of girls were checking you out, Andy Bakewell. I was flattered to be the one you left with."

Bakewell thought he'd left with her and wanted to say so, but he was out of words again. His mind was running, fantasizing. He always had trouble thinking and talking at the same time. Maggie sensed his dilemma, had seen it often in her brief experience. She had managed the boys in her life well, knew it, loved the feeling and loved the power. She came toward him, and the scent of her was dizzying; made him lose track. When he opened his arms to put them around her she put her hand on his chest, shoving for emphasis – one more little assertion of control before they started. "Do you know how to dance?"

He nodded. Dancing, and almost anything else requiring coordination, came naturally to the Bakewell boys. He had learned to dance in grade school. "It's been awhile."

"You have to know how to dance. I'm not romancing another boy who can't dance."

He pulled her to him, choosing his words carefully, pronouncing them slowly, "I'm not a boy… and I can dance all right… and I would love to dance with you… but right now *all I want to do is kiss you."*

"Well Navy, we finally get our chance," she whispered through breath warm against his lips. "I've been wanting to kiss you for months."

It was a gentle kiss, simple, delicate; he didn't want to panic her. She liked the way they started; kisses gradually longer, more physical, eventually passionate. It was the greatest moment of Bakewell's life, and he was intricated instantly, id and ego, immersed in her, giving up and giving in all at once, no pretense of macho independence. He held her tightly to him, above him, trying to steady himself, feeling like he was going over backward. It didn't work. He was falling, a long way, falling and not knowing when he would land, or where. Margaret Leary was changing his life forever; without hesitation he looked forward to whatever she might bring as emotions joined them, swept them. In that first moment he was totally, undeniably committed.

Eventually he opened her blouse, pleased and surprised she didn't object, ready to quit at the first sign of outrage, determined if there was none. As he loosened her clothes and touched her she encouraged him with little movements and soft sounds, and he caressed her with a piteous gentility, coming from an unsuspected and tender reservoir deep inside, and Maggie, always sharply in control, intolerant of bumbling, youthful suitors, surprised by his boldness and by her own willingness, unsettled by the extravagance of his touch, determined to let him continue, happy for the darkness surrounding their intimacy. She had read the literature, watched the cautious films of their generation, had the typical, nervous curiosity, and wanted to be swept up like a romantic heroine. She was ready for someone mature, imagined or otherwise, glad to finally let go the restraint that had controlled her until then.

She put her mouth to his ear, trying to sound confident, even diffident. It didn't work. She knew it when she heard herself mouth the words, "The navy teaches this?" And when he nodded, she continued in the same panicky voice saying, "You've learned well," as if she'd had the experience to give a grade on passion. Bakewell barely heard the words as a riotous ardor campaigned through his brain; a chaos of emotion was suddenly interrupting his life and it would be months before he learned how big the plunge was, how far he would have to fall, and what it would feel like when he hit bottom. Instead he heard his chatty inner voice, the voice that plagued him always. He hated the voice but had no choice, had to listen. It was a critical voice, accusatory, derisive, often contemptuous, even of his successes. But the voice was encouraging him, assuaging his overactive conscience, stroking his ego as he stroked her lovely chest. The voice told him how fine he was, and what an adept lover he was becoming, so accomplished. It was a heady experience, the best night of his life, and the voice congratulated him all along the way.

Maggie asked a hundred questions between as many kisses, and he told her about places he'd been, the countries he'd seen and the cities he'd visited. He'd never talked so much, never been so descriptive and never stopped his hands in their quest to search her completely. She was more interested in New York than Beirut or Paris as he tried to keep up. Sometimes she interrupted with her mouth or her tongue. They spoke long into the night.

In the months that followed, her presence took him to unimagined heights. For the first time in his life he was full of himself, couldn't get enough of her, of them. His vanity suppressed his conscience, and his arrogance reached appalling heights, all the while encouraged by the inner voice. He was applauded by teammates who never tired of seeing her. She made him a sensation; his only redeeming quality was his refusal to discuss their intimacy.

Eventually, after too many burning nights, the heat of their relationship awaked Bakewell's Catholicism. What they shared wreaked havoc with his conscience. Her lack of experience in things sexual only increased his misgivings, but she was so fantastically appealing, it wasn't possible to control his need for her. The fascination of her and the vitality of their relationship so exaggerated him, he couldn't control himself as he took her through the preliminaries, always hoping for her, but afraid to take final advantage. He had put an artificial waypoint in their relationship, feared crossing it would cost him his soul, and his nights were filled with misgivings after they parted. His conscience worked overtime when they were apart. He fought the temptation for weeks, despite the comfort she displayed with whatever happened. Bakewell had never had sex with a woman less experienced than he was. He feared his remorse would be unrelenting if he made love to her, and he struggled mightily with this issue all the while fulminating with hormones.

In a tragicomedy of events, he became a regular at Saturday night confession. The year before he'd made friends with the Parish's new assistant, fresh from the seminary. As the junior man, the new priest had the late shift on Saturday evening, and Bakewell came late to confession on the Saturdays he wasn't with Maggie. Afterward they would cross Manchester for a beer and pizza at Caruso's. There were racial uprisings that year. Newark had exploded, more than twenty dead; later Detroit even worse, when whole city blocks burned and more than forty died. They spent their evenings talking the politics of equal rights, a concept new to them and to the nation. The priest was the first person to draw Bakewell's attention to the media's orchestration of the news, as they watched creditable people represent the media position, while detestable people always spoke for the other side.

It was a summer of contrasts: a world of violence and tender moments in his '55 Chevy; spiritual conversation with a holy man and obsession with a beautiful girl; a world filled with peaceful summer nights and youthful experiences, and a world filled with hatred and a jungle war. It was the fastest period of Bakewell's life, and time passed in days and whole weeks, instead of minutes and hours.

Maggie loved to drive the MG whenever possible, and Bakewell's mind would race with the little car as it crossed town, singing and whining as she shifted up gear and down, wondering what incredible location, what place she would take them literally and figuratively as they drove. If he made love to her, she would be his ultimate conquest and he never tired of the fantasy as he watched her manipulate the beautiful sports car. It never occurred to him she was doing the same thing, never entered his mind she might think of him as her "conquest."

If she was inexperienced in matters of sex, she was light years ahead of him in things social. She loved to mock him, enjoyed making a fool of him whenever he committed a social gaff. Older, he hated the reversal in roles but feared her derision, sharp-edged and scornful, knew he was outmatched in verbal combat. She referred to him as her "older man," and liked to describe him so when she talked with former boyfriends who called often to see if there was still a chance. Maggie hated Bakewell's fidelity. He was ready to make a lifetime commitment and she knew it; it was the only thing that gave her pause.

Late in August they finally managed to get to that glorious place where her virginity dwelt. Bakewell hadn't planned for it, and, thinking back months later, realized it probably hadn't been his doing. It was another soft summer night on a dock under a star filled sky. Their simple intimacy had graduated to a sobering lust that bordered on uncontrollable. When he realized she shared his frustration it created a wonderfully apprehensive high.

By then their friends had left for school and the ballgames, humid, dusty and mosquito ridden – Maggie grudgingly tolerated them – were over for the year. It was just the two of them most evenings. They had swum far out in the lake, using a small raft for relief, swimming for hours in the late afternoon sun. Back at the dock, the night was room temperature. Maggie wore a two-piece swimming suit, very modest. It was a simpler time. They were naked above the waist, the air warm against their skin. Perspiration scented her body with an odor more compelling than anything she'd ever worn. It set him on a course inevitable from that first night. They were too exposed on the dock and moved to a picnic shelter. Maggie had told him many times she didn't want to be in a car when it happened. It was the first time he had seen her chest bare and exposed in the moonlight; before she was always inside her blouse. They waited listening, making sure no one was around; took their time, kissing, touching, rocking, pulsating before finally deciding it was safe. Bakewell put their towels on the picnic table, as much for hygiene as for a softness. When he turned back to her, she was illuminated in the moonlight, enchantingly beautiful, irresistible, staring at him, confident in her nakedness. They looked at each other carefully without touching.

"You are so beautiful," he said breathlessly.

"Take your trunks off."

Bakewell did as instructed, was embarrassed, erect, trembling, wet.

"Oh my God," she said, frightening them both, "You're going to hurt me?"

"No..."

"How is it not going to hurt?"

Bakewell had been taking communal showers for years, "I'm not anything special, Maggie; most of us look pretty much the same."

"You're lying to me and it isn't a good time," she said tensely, giving way to her fears for the first time.

"I want you so much... I won't do anything that hurts you."

"It looks like it will hurt."

"You can stop me if it hurts."

"Somehow I doubt that." There was a harsh, nervous edge to her voice. "How will I be able to stop you once we get started?"

"You are so beautiful; I wouldn't do any thing to hurt you. I don't want to hurt you."

"I want to be comfortable, lying down. Not cramped up in a car seat," she said, changing the subject, her voice brittle with tension.

Bakewell indicating the bridal table, said, "We won't be cramped."

"I just hope it's safe." – The hard edge still present. She got up on the bench and took off the rest of her suit while he watched, hypnotized; the whiteness of her skin contrasted with her mysterious place. She sat on the towels, "Come and hold me."

He came immediately, reaching for her. "You are so beautiful. I want you desperately. I've never wanted anything so much."

"You're going to tell me you love me aren't you?"

"Desperately."

"I was afraid you might."

He wasn't listening. With what they were doing, what they were sharing, it never occurred to him she might not love him. She lay back on the table, and he came over her. They were libidinously wet in moments. He was right. It wasn't painful for her, but it was excruciating for him. He had been so desperate to have her, had been for so long, his gratification came long before she had time to stop concentrating on what was happening to her body and begin focusing on any pleasure he offered. He hadn't been aggressive, even slightly violent, determined to keep his ardor under control. When he felt the first awakenings in her it was too late. He had emptied himself and was humiliated when she realized he was finished.

"That was it?"

"I'm sorry, I couldn't control myself." He kept his face against her, ashamed to look at her.

"Gee."

"Are you cold?"

"Are you kidding?"

"Don't move. Please don't move. Stay with me."

"Stay with you?"

"Please, don't move. Just stay like this. Wait for me. Don't think about anything else but us."

He moved and she moved with him. He raised himself up and let the night air pass between them. When he couldn't hold himself off her any longer he lowered his chest to hers and pushed gently with his hips. She groaned, "How long will this take?"

"Not long if you keep groaning like that."

"I didn't groan."

"You made a noise."

"Did I?"

"Yes, make it again." He pushed gently, she groaned again. Time passed slowly. He feared she would make him get up. He was in a panic she would tell him to get off. The feeling of her was blissful.

"I'm all sticky."

"Don't think about it; just think about how it feels." He wanted her to focus on the pressure he applied. He kissed her neck and ears, did everything he could think of to keep her in the moment. After a while he started pushing again, slowly, always gently and she began to respond. He wasn't ready but knew he would be, knew his excitement would come more slowly the second time. Maggie was completely focused on what was happening to her body and him above it. Her noises began to match his movements and he was more grateful than he had ever been for anything he had ever received. When he felt himself finally aroused, he was so utterly grateful she had waited, so totally grateful for a second chance, so enormously grateful for the pleasure of her, he cried out. It was a mistake.

She never reached that place she needed to be, but she was gasping when they finished the second time. (It would take two additional weeks, the perfect moment and a little inebriation before she found fulfillment). As her breathing subsided she relaxed again. They were wet with perspiration and thankful for the towels beneath them. Then suddenly, she needed to be done with him, pushed at his chest and when he withdrew she groaned one more time.

"I love that noise you make," he said sheepishly.

"I didn't groan."

"I know. You make lovely noises."

"I don't make noises."

"Sounds then."

"Maybe. How was it? How was I?"

"You were a dream."

"Really? Tell me. Was I what you wanted?"

He handed her suit up, said, "Better."

"Tell me, I want to know."

"If you want I will kneel and worship."

"Was I better than a working girl?"

He knelt in front of the table. "I swear; you were better than anything, you were a dream."

When they were back in his car, driving north toward the city, Maggie resting her head on the seat next to him, watching his face illumined in the dash lights, said, "Will you tell your friends?"

"No."

"How many will you tell?"

"None. Nobody. Never!" He was stung by her questions, accused, even though she hadn't meant them as accusations. "I would never tell."

"Yes you will. Boys always tell."

"Never. And I'm not a boy."

She was quiet for a long time. Bakewell was uneasy, wishing for something inspirational. He wanted to comfort her, was feeling a lot of shame, even though he was still flushed with the pleasure of her. He feared her regret might match his shame. Instead she surprised him once more. "So that's how the baby boom came about, huh? That's how all of us got started?" She was being glib and he was put off, without an answer.

"Well, I guess I'm glad it happened. No…no I'm sure I'm glad it happened. Glad it happened with you."

"I'm glad it happened with me too," he said relieved. "It was very special."

Maggie grew more reflective as the car climbed the foothills back to St. Louis. Bakewell wondered if she meant to be so flippant or if she was secretly hurting. He worried she was filling with regret. There was one more surprise when she spoke again after a few more miles.

"Hell, I don't care if you tell. What's the big deal? I don't care. Tell if you want to. They'll all want to know. They probably thought we were doing it all along. You'll be the big man."

Bakewell remained silent, not wanting to profess his loyalty again. He didn't think he needed to declare his fidelity. He didn't know what to think.

She patted his leg. “It was nice. I’m glad you finally got around to it.”

“Around to it?”

“Yes.”

“I was ready months ago.”

“So was I. You’re a nice boy, Andy… I mean *man*. I’m glad you made love to me. I’m glad you were the one.”

The End of Something

Maggie had excellent taste in clothes, never meant to be flashy, even though her entrance into a classroom created a silent sensation. She was always well dressed – and well covered, very much in style. Physically, each of her features was imperfect in a minute way but, like a later, and famous creature of history, Princess Diana, she was a combination of imperfections, almost flawlessly blended, that created a complete package.

Although her clothes were modest, they were unable to hide the sensuality lying beneath. She rarely displayed skin; it wasn't in good taste then. She didn't have to really. In her expensive clothes, her firm, youthful chest appeared always on the verge of making a breakout, straining, almost yearning to escape the blouses, sweaters and shirts of the time. Thickly designed bras, stiffly ribbed, fought turbulently, to embrace her bosom; her graceful bottom coped with the same frustration. Bakewell flattered it with a favored expression, called it her "superior posterior."

That was right before softer fabrics made their appearance, were quickly adopted by the protest generation and became the raiment of rebellion. Softer fabric created *a natural look,* and although initially shocking, took hold rapidly. Women were allowed to display a natural sensuality, fleshy, that flattered and revealed figures that could withstand scrutiny. At the same time men's hair grew to remarkable, even revolting lengths, as they adopted, but wouldn't admit to, copying a culture from the 1950's: "The Beat Generation." It was all part of a trashy new culture corresponding with "Beatlemania," a culture of communal living, where the need for bathing became secondary, even with young women, which shocked and disgusted many, including Bakewell and his military contemporaries. Communal living, "dirty living," became the much-publicized downside of Beatlemania, and was featured on the covers of national magazines, competing with the strident fanaticism of the antiwar culture, both of which were heavily covered on the nightly newscasts and tediously over-reported.

Bakewell and his nineteen year old conquest had no interest in the antiwar culture, or the wretched communals, and avoided both on campus and off.

The upside was in cloth. Women previously thought of as hard and angular, (naïve young men actually grew up thinking women's breasts came to a point) were now soft, delicate, tantalizing and richly supple. The harsh, corseted, stifling designs that frustrated previous generations, gave way to the fashion of realism. Women were allowed to show what really lay beneath. A reality *PlayBoy* was quick to promote in a salacious cantibility that left nothing for imagining, and pubescent young men beheld the real thing, while sitting on johns with the other real thing in their hands, no longer imagining, during furtive, clandestine, restroom ejaculations.

Bakewell fell in love with the body and the bitch at the same time he came under the spell of Maggie Leary. The having and holding, the possession of the heretofore unpossessed, the taking and knowing of body and persona, left him bewildered, unbelieving of his richly corporeal fortune. It also left him sublimely unaware of the tentative nature of their relationship and unworried of losing the fantasy of her presence.

It took some adjusting for both of them: he with his sense of morality and awareness of sin, she with the idea of giving away so much to a paranormal presence she knew would have no tenure in her future. Bakewell worried about his soul, *but what the hell, he was young.* Still, he refused to fall asleep in a moving car, wanted to see death coming, maybe say a quick Act of Contrition? Maggie never gave a thought to the morality of it. Her problem was what to do when it was over. In truth, she thought of him only as a metaphor for men and their kind, and a measure for the one in her future. Bakewell was the perfect foil, the antithesis of the man she would marry. He played his role perfectly. He was a young and callow fellow, like the one in the song, the arrogant, egocentric rogue, trying to cover his inadequacies. He played the role hard, fearing she would find him out.

It fascinated her at first. Early on she was engrossed in him, and the outrageous way he would take every advantage, but she knew he wasn't getting away – no matter how much he startled her with his purpose – with anything she hadn't committed herself to before. Early on she enjoyed the narcissism of her own role.

But *bullshit will only take you so far* – a quote he would learn from Ned, and hear often in the years ahead. Eventually the seemingly reckless girl, the difficult girl with the tough exterior, became anxious and despondent over her fast life and her portrayal of *the beautifully abrasive lover.* She was tired of being the kept woman, though she knew she was not. It was too theatric. Maggie wasn't theatrical. Her parent's turbulent, episodic relationship had taught her pragmatism in the affairs of heart. She would become the ultimate pragmatist. And she was tiring of her arrogant GI. Their relationship was making her feel sordid, empty, worse, it left her feeling lonely.

She didn't understand him. The best part of him was still developing, and she was missing it, even as it took shape before her. In truth she wasn't looking for growth and improvement in her lover, was partially justified in thinking there was nothing underneath, nothing worthwhile. She never consoled herself with the idea she might have been taken advantage of. She had encouraged him, welcomed the whole affair. She could have easily held him in place, knew he would have waited. In the years that followed, she realized she had cheated them both. They might have discovered each other and found they liked what they found. She felt he took advantage of every opportunity their relationship provided. If she had wanted more from him, she could have told him so. She never asked. She created the lover in her life without wanting to find out who he really was or might have been. He was gentle, affectionate and supremely grateful, but he was lustful, infatuated with her body and with his growing technique. And sadly, there were times he made her feel like a shallow amusement. Her ardor, if it ever was, faded with the warm weather as summer turned to fall.

Bakewell could have done better by her, could have held himself responsible for her youth, cherished her innocence, kept her unsullied, uncorrupted. Instead, he liked the idea of having the delicious bitch at his side, showing her off at parties, later taking her away. In their haste to keep the physical nature of their relationship churning, neither was looking to discover anything else in the other. Bakewell missed the vulnerability she hid so well, while she never looked for anything in his character other than the obvious. His redeeming quality, his painfully honest profession of love not withstanding, was his honesty.

Before Bakewell understood what was going on, Maggie wanted to move on, and in the process, she reclaimed the "possession thing" that so engulfed him. If he thought of her as a possession, she would teach him about possessing. She conquered him as soon as she tried to put space between them, captured his heart, laid it bare, left it raw and exposed. She didn't want to upset him at first, didn't want to wound him; that would come later. She just wanted out, and without meaning to, showed him a part of himself he didn't know existed. When she finally informed him she was moving on, she touched his core, reached inside, yanked, very hard, and taught him what loss felt like.

By the time his conquest had given way to hers, it was too late. She wanted out, and he was desperate to keep her. In a reversal so swift it had him figuratively and emotionally on his knees, he frantically tried for a quick makeover. It made him seem ridiculous and predictably widened the gap. Her disinterest created a sudden and urgent sense of interest. But Act I was over. He was the spurned lover; it was on to Act II. They both referred to the second act as "Maggie's Rule."

She knew she had journeyed too far, and in an inexorable but reluctant way she still participated in the physical relationship, showed up at his apartment, albeit less frequently, but still lingered with surreptitious visits, especially when she was feeling discouraged. But Act II was different. What they shared left her incomplete, feeling tawdry and broken. The anger developed slowly, crept into the loving gradually, became evident, and, despite the longing she once felt for him, she began to dislike him while he was loving her. She was killing him with a sense of losing her each time they were together, and he began to hope for, even pray for (in a sick twist of irony) some kind of reconciliation. Eventually, sensing the rejection, and feeling her contempt set in, he responded in kind. That was early October, the "Maggie's Rule" period, when she began dosing out fewer favors, which left him yearning, incomplete, always hoping for more.

While the relationship became infrequent, the intimacies were curiously stronger, more vigorous and forceful, even aggressive, their rendezvous, copulations of contempt, where both tried to stab and wound the other with a ruthless physicality. Each wanted to leave the other scarred. For her, he wanted a feeling of being used; for him, she wanted a feeling of being forgotten. When it ended, Bakewell was not sure what she felt, but he would know the feeling of being forgotten for a long time.

When it was over Maggie knew she wouldn't get involved in another sexual relationship. She had made up her mind – the next man she slept with would support her for better or for worse, and she congratulated herself on choosing the right man. Bakewell had always been discreet and trustworthy, would never tell, even though she accused him of it often. A reputation was worth something in the 60's. Maggie was certain Bakewell wouldn't exploit her. She let it go on for another five weeks, not understanding why.

"Trudy, what day is it?" Bakewell said, coming through the door, following Ned's dictum, trying to put up a front, to keep morale up until the end came. "Let's keep up some kinda act 'til it's over," Ned had said. They had gotten pretty good at "carrying it off" during the lean times they'd navigated years before.

"It's Thursday, Andy and you got a call a few minutes ago. He wanted your cell number, no message, kind of a strange guy. Older...said it wasn't about work." Bakewell nodded absently, not really listening as he crossed the front office. He took the sheaf of papers from his mailbox and went down the hall to his office.

"You want coffee?"

"NO!"

He made several calls, returned a few, after twenty minutes he took the note she had given him. It was long distance, toll free. He wondered if it was a stockbroker or some good ole boy in Arizona wanting to sell him tools. Finally, putting the phone on speaker he dialed the number. The voice on the other end was a woman's, very professional, said "Corporate office." He was tempted to hang up. He hated to identify himself and hear the words, "thanks for returning my call" – a dead give away.

"This is Andy Bakewell. I'm returning…."

"Oh thank you, Mr. Bakewell. Please hold," she interrupted. He didn't wait long.

"Andy, how are you son?" the voice said, very warm, very pleasant. It was an older man. It meant nothing to him. "I was hoping you would call me back. You probably don't remember me, eh. No, no, I'm sure you don't remember. We met aboard ship, while you were anchored off Genoa. Quite a long while ago wasn't it?" Bakewell was sick, fear penetrating his gut, a cruel, icy invasion. He'd been dreading the call his entire life.

"You did a job for us, the results being quite beneficial for us both, wouldn't you say?"

"I remember."

"Yes. Well everything worked out well, didn't it? You were able to get through school; grades were a little disappointing at times, but all in all we were, I was, very proud of you. How have you been?"

"All right I guess," Bakewell struggled for words, reverted to a mentality and a form of speaking he had left far in the past, felt stupid, knew he sounded juvenile.

"Good, good," more warm friendliness, quiet charm, "I have watched you with some interest over the years, I confess. You have been a constant and pleasant surprise to me all these years, a real source of pleasure. I mean that sincerely."

"Thanks."

"We need another favor. It's a business proposition of course. A really handsome sum I might add. I think it would be of great benefit to us both. Just in the nick of time for you."

"Why me?"

"Because you have been so...dependable. Yes dependable. We have admired the way you keep a secret. We have always been in your debt for that. I should thank you on behalf of the entire organization."

"What organization is that?"

The voice chuckled. "Come now Andersen, don't disappoint; your greatest asset is your discretion. Don't offend me at this late date."

"I am very surprised to hear from you," Bakewell said cautiously. "I don't want to offend you people. I think you know that. I hope you know that by now," he added quickly.

"I know that," the voice said reassuringly. "Over the years you have been one of my greatest satisfactions. You can't know how refreshing it is to have known an honest man. It must come from that state of yours. Mr. Truman and Mr. Twain, right? People of that ilk? Such straightforward men, so dependable, not like these dreadful types who seek the limelight. Not typical of so very many capable men today: *the generation of degeneration*. It's really quite demoralizing to observe human nature nowadays."

"I'm wondering why you are calling me, sir?"

"Because we have another business deal to propose. I will be in St. Louis on Thursday and I want to meet with you. The Ritz Carlton, I think. For lunch?"

Bakewell's mind was sprinting; he knew he didn't want the old man to orchestrate the luncheon. "No," he blurted, "Amici's."

"Who's?"

"Amici's, it's in Kirkwood."

There was a slight pause. "Fine, let's say about eleven. I will see you then. It's been a real pleasure, Andy. I'm looking forward to seeing you in person after all these years." He hung up.

Bakewell knew others were listening. The old man never repeated the name of the restaurant or got the location. He remembered the old man's demeanor, was trying to remember his features. It was all coming back at once. He was always in a "cheerio" mood – everything so upbeat, so revoltingly nice. Bakewell's mind was going fast; his stomach in turmoil, but he wasn't physically ill, just filled with a cruel rush of anxiety. He was more afraid than he'd been in years.

The rest of his day was a shambles. He was even more forgetful, listless and indifferent to his real problems. He left early for the first time in months. Ned usually went home around three; Bakewell was home before Ned got back to the office. He tried to stay busy, to keep moving. He cut his grass and cleaned the kennel. He fertilized part of his yard, cut some low-hanging branches from his pines and bundled them up. Afterward he did something he rarely ever did: he went to Rick's and had a drink in the bar, staring at his image in the mirror while he thought. It had been thirty years since Bakewell had last spoken to the man. They had made a deal, he had made a deal – with the devil he often thought. The devil was back. He never stopped worrying this day might come. In time his senses dulled and the fear moved to the recesses of his mind. Just after Katherine's death he might have looked forward to the call, he'd been more self-destructive at the time, might have welcomed the dark threat. He had never stopped worrying he might hear from him, from them again.

On Thursday he went to the restaurant early, watching the rear entrance from the big church lot. The back entrance had a long, enclosed entry, like a handicap ramp, that lead to the bar. He was sure Snow would enter from that end. When it was time he walked up and went in, and before he could request a table the owner came forward with menus, like he was expecting him.

"You must be Mr. Bakewell; this way please." The man seated him in a lofted section of the restaurant, across from the bar. There was no way he could know his name. Bakewell hadn't been there since before Katherine died. There were only a few tables in the section overlooking the restaurant, and all the other tables were marked "reserved." They would be alone.

The old man came in as soon as Bakewell was seated. He was bent, and his hair was white now. Bakewell had done the math; he had to be eighty. When he had known him before, the old man was in the prime of middle age, his mustache and hair both dark. He was dressed just as Bakewell expected: Savile Row would have been an accurate guess. He was distinguished and authoritarian, without the edge authority gives most people. Bakewell always suspected he was from old money, from power. The old man approached with hand outstretched, a kind smile, genuine. Bakewell stood out of respect in spite of himself. They shook hands.

"Andy, my boy, it really is good to see you." The man sat down slowly, taking great care to position his chair. "What should we have? This is your place, obviously. It must be good?" He moved the chair in a little closer. "You should order for us. Shall we have a drink for old time's sake?" Bakewell ordered iced tea, feeling he needed to apologize, said he didn't drink during the day. The old man ordered a Manhattan when the bartender appeared on cue. He returned with their drinks and disappeared from behind the small bar, leaving them alone in the little room.

"I'll bet you are surprised to see me still alive, eh? Thought I might have gone on by now?" the old man smiled. "You don't look too happy to see me. You seem apprehensive, my boy."

"I'm apprehensive all right."

"Well don't be. I'm not here to push you. I have developed a real affection for you over the years. You probably doubt that." The question in his voice reflected on his face. Bakewell ignored both. The old man nodded and continued. "Each year as we evaluate our assets, your name comes up. You're surprised to hear that? Yes, we do a sort of review. So I've kept up with you all these years. You might think of me as your guardian angel."

"I wondered why I always had such great luck."

"Speaking of which, my ignorance is showing. It must be my age. Let me tell you how very sorry I am about your lovely wife. I mean that sincerely. I honestly felt like I knew her. I grieved for you." He put his hand on Bakewell's arm.

Bakewell thanked him. It seemed genuine, decided to go back to the part about his luck, saying, "You've fallen off the job lately."

"Yes. I'm sorry about your recent reversals, but I have been some help actually. You remember that rather large job back in 1988?"

Bakewell looked blankly.

"You know that very successful job? The customer paid you upon completion? Such a rare occurrence in this vicious world today. It was for nearly seven figures if I remember correctly."

"The car plant job?"

The old man nodded and sipped his drink, satisfied. Bakewell remembered the job like it was yesterday. He had gotten a call to drop everything and bid the huge project. There had been no other competition. It was a do-it-now-we-can't-wait proposition and they had made a huge profit in return for what they thought was a big gamble. As soon as it was finished they were paid in full, a never before and never since occurrence for such a sum. It was a dream-come-true job that put them over that year. Ned still talked about it.

They ordered tortellini. Bakewell told him it was the best; it had been one of Katherine's favorites. The old man stopped him there. Bakewell was relieved. He really didn't want anything in his stomach when he came to the point. He tried to relax but his whole being was voltaic. He wished he'd ordered a drink. He didn't need any more caffeine, he'd never been more alert. He wanted the old man to come to the point, but he took his time; Bakewell knew he would. They ate in silence, breaking bread together, literally. The bread was very good. And after they finished, they ordered coffee and the old man wiped the tablecloth with his napkin carefully from right to left. He was left-handed.

"Shall we talk business now?"

"Okay."

"Good. We want you to do another job for us. A shoot we'll call it. I think that's really a word that belongs to the photography business. It's good work and pays well."

"You've got to be kidding."

"No, I'm not much of a kidder."

"My God, Snow. Look at me. I'm an old man."

The old man blanched slightly at the use of the code name, recovered. "No. You are the perfect man for the job."

"You've got to be kidding."

"No. I told you, I'm not a kidder." The old man left that comment hang in the air. It had a menacing effect. "We want you to do something for us that you are perfect for, and we want to offer you this little opportunity, especially now, since you have the need, so to speak."

"I'm too old. The movies tell us the world's full of people like that. You need a professional."

"No, actually we need the most unlikely person on the face of the earth. You're that person Andy."

"I'm not your man."

"You are our man. You are perfect, son. The company likes to use people…like us…that are beyond suspicion. Why do you think they sent me? Who would think we could be having such a conversation here in this place?" added, "At our respective ages?"

"What company?" It was a question Bakewell had always wanted to ask, though he knew he would never know.

"You know I can't answer that. You don't want to know, anyway." There was caution in Snow's voice. Even at his late age the old man carried a manner Bakewell had to respect. He couldn't discount him because of his age, like he did with other older men. This man had scared him badly once. He was still scary, even at eighty.

"It's just plain crazy. You want me to…" Bakewell lowered his voice and leaned across the table, almost hissing his words, "Shoot someone?"

"On the contrary, not crazy at all; it will be like old times. Everything will be set up for you. We need someone with your skill to do this, someone impossible to suspect, someone beyond suspicion."

"There's no way."

"You answered your country's call a long time ago when you were needed. We want you to be our man again, one more time. We need your help."

"Come on, you leveraged me; it wasn't really voluntary."

"It was. You were a patriot."

"I was the dumb bunny." Bakewell's voice was full of sarcasm.

"Your country asked you to do a duty."

"My country scared the hell out of me, and offered me money too!" Bakewell kept his voice low but almost shouted the words. "And I doubt it ever was my country. Where's the patriotism?"

"Hazardous duty pay. You deserved it," the old man paused, resting his chin on the back of his folded hands. "It was your country by the way."

"Was the money to make sure? You knew you could intimidate me without the money?"

"I suspect that is why you're angry now, but no, we came to you because we thought you had the skill."

"I was afraid to tell you no. You knew that."

"You answered the call."

"I didn't know what I was doing."

"You agreed and you were needed."

"For the money."

"For patriotism."

"Tell the truth; you never thought I would get away?"

"I was rooting for you, honestly; but no, I never thought you would get away." He leaned back, resting his back in the straight chair. He looked directly into Bakewell's eyes. They were at a stand off, and Bakewell looked hard into the old man's eyes. "That's pretty honest isn't it?" Bakewell didn't answer. The old man looked tired. "I was very happy when you did get away. I hope you believe that."

"What are you doing here? You must be eighty."

"Close enough."

"Why are you getting dirty again?"

"Loyalty."

"Come on, after all these years? Where does loyalty end? When does it end?"

"It's hard to put a point on it. You just do your duty. Hope you're appreciated and the end justifies the means."

"I feel like I'm getting ready to die at my age. What does it feel like at yours?"

"Closer."

"Why me?"

"We've been over that."

"No. I mean why me back then?"

"You were unbridled; you had a history of being impulsive, but your service record showed you followed orders and stayed clean. We needed a follower, someone we could depend on. You had been inattentive in school and quite rebellious, with a history of trouble. We could have passed you off as a psychopath. Demented was the popular word then."

"You never expected me to get away?"

"We would have done something for your mother – you were nothing but a trial for her, you know. She would have gotten some help. We would have made you out a hero."

"Gee," Bakewell closed his eyes and lowered his head, fingers on his temples. When he looked at Snow again he was remembering the sour taste of fear, the terror of that day in Genoa. The pain showed in his face. He rolled his head back and forth, slowly stretching his neck each way. "I'm having a little trouble believing I could trust *your company* right now. You set me up once; why not again?"

"I never lied to you, son. I won't start now. I'm too old. The company will treat you well. You can count… *no, you can bank* on whatever agreement we make here today."

Bakewell shook his head. They sat in silence for several minutes, while the waitress refilled their cups and cleaned up the table. The old man ordered a crème Brule. After it came, he broke the top carefully, hesitated, looked at Bakewell, "Whatever made you go back?" Bakewell smiled, couldn't help it. It was only a small triumph, but it had saved his life. It was worth remembering. "You went the wrong direction. Who could have predicted you would walk back in?"

"I didn't have a lot of options. It was run, with everybody running after me, or wait and walk back in while they were all headed out."

"It was genius."

"It was a kid who'd been chased by the neighbor's dog."

"Seriously?" Snow's accent was clearer as he let his interest show.

"Nearly everyday."

"Tell me."

Bakewell was disarmed, despite the tension. He still remembered the simple event that had saved his life, and the memory came flooding back.

"We had a ballgame in the lot next to school. We all loved that game. It was nothing to have twenty kids there. We played baseball with a real hardball, whenever we could come up with one. We had this great field, with a backstop, made our own bases, had lots of room and no crabby neighbors to run us off. It was the big event every day of summer. Nobody wanted to miss a game. It was hundreds of yards around from my house to the field, twenty across the neighbor's yard. That's a big difference when you're thirteen."

The old man nodded, fascinated.

"There was this dog, a real scary dog. Sometimes the dog would be sleeping or interested in something. I'd wait and when he wasn't looking, I would jump the fence and go. He would take out after me snarling. Sometimes I think he was faking just to get me to cross. I'd hit the fence with my right arm low, left arm over the top and flip right on over. It was only about 40" high. I was pretty athletic." Bakewell moved his cup to the side. "One morning I pulled up with a hamstring, came to a one legged, hopping halt, hurting like hell. The dog was right on my heels. I stopped and turned around to face the music; the dog stopped too. I forced myself to stand and look at him. He didn't know what to do. After that I walked across the yard and turned around every time he came on. The first couple of times it was scary, after that easy. I walked slowly, letting the other guys see. Nobody else would go in that yard. Sometimes I would stop and cuss the dog, showing off for the older guys. They were all afraid. That dog bought me a lot of respect."

Warming to the subject and forgetting why they were meeting, Bakewell continued. "One time Mr. Faulke was cutting his grass by the fence and the dog bit him right in the back of his arm. Faulke was hell on wheels. We were all afraid of Mr. Faulke. Three of his kids played in the game. He was furious and went and got this rusty old potato spade and went over the fence after the dog. He tried to hit him half a dozen times, getting madder all the time. Each time he cornered him, the dog would skulk, low down, like he was defeated then make a dash when Mr. Faulke swung. He couldn't catch up to him. He would have killed the dog. It was Mr. Chiodini's dog. He was afraid of Faulke, I think. Mr. Chiodini never came out of the house. It went on for a long time. We were all watching from the ball field. After a while we were watching from the fence. Most of us were rooting for old man Faulke to kill the dog. I was secretly rooting for the dog."

"That's a wonderful story." The old man chuckled. "It has satisfied a question I've wanted to ask for years." He put his napkin down, chuckled again, as he cleared his throat. "Now I need to ask another. Actually I need a commitment, Andy."

"I'm not a killer."

"No, of course you aren't; a true military man never is. What you did for us was different. You know that. This is different. Your country will reward you greatly."

"I don't think my country's involved."

"You might be surprised. Your country has many assets, and they don't hesitate to use them."

"Then they should use one."

"It's not the company's style to use outside contractors, especially in cases like this." Snow looked him carefully in the eye, keeping his voice low as he spoke. "Those people are horribly expensive, seldom available when you need them, often quite difficult to locate, and there really aren't that many of them around, you know. Also they are often untrustworthy. You are perfect for this project, son. The company prefers more oblique methods. You should know that by now. They want the person they use to be so unlikely, so farfetched, no one would bother to look. If they could, they'd use a nun from a cloistered convent, seriously."

"I'm not interested." Bakewell tried to make his voice sound firm. "It's a sin to kill, you know."

"Yes. I understand you've become quite a Catholic."

"I was always a Catholic."

"That's good. A man needs God, especially late in life. However I'm instructed to tell you your conscience would never trouble you after you did your duty. That's about all I can say."

"I'm in the state of grace. I kind of like it that way."

"Mm. Yes, the state of grace. I'm familiar with the phrase."

"I don't want to get involved. I hope I'm not going to flunk next year's *review?"*

"No. That isn't a problem as long as you remain loyal."

"I thought it was more like self-preservation. I never thought of it as loyalty. How did I pass the first review? Was I in great jeopardy?"

"Yes." Snow paused, Bakewell wasn't sure if it was for effect. "As a matter of fact you were. I can honestly say I may have saved your life. You really saved your own life by being so discreet."

"I was scared for a long time. It still scares me."

"You had every right to be *scared."* The word sounded funny coming from Snow. It wasn't a word he would use normally, and it sounded strange when he pronounced it.

"And now you want me to get back in?"

"You're into your line of credit. You have trouble at work. You got raided a while back and it almost killed you – a shame really – just when you were doing so well. How are you doing now? Are things going better for you now?"

"Everything's fine."

"I wish for your sake it was true, but it isn't, is it Andy?" Bakewell didn't answer, let the question hang in the air. "We are prepared to pay a million dollars; that seems to be the magical sum in the world we live in today – all quite legal. You get a contract from one of those horrid little African nations that send out those dreadful letters asking you to front for them. Everybody gets millions; I presume you've seen the type?"

"Every year." There was such a letter in Bakewell's top drawer at the moment.

"Well, this one will be legitimate. It will be deposited in your company, where you need it. You will have to pay the taxes, but with the last few years you've had, you're entitled to some tax relief. The bottom line I'm told, after a full audit – which we will handle by the way – would be close to the original amount. You shouldn't have to pay more than a hundred thousand in taxes, possibly none at all."

"I don't think so; I'm still trying to get over the last one."

"Pity, you've been so trustworthy. I am curious about one thing. Did you ever tell anyone?"

"No."

"Not anyone, not even Katherine?"

"Especially not Katherine; murder isn't something you talk about, something you tell your wife about."

"I believe you. I've always believed in you. And you've never disappointed me." He took a long swallow of water. The old man drank a lot of water, wiped his mouth. "Well you have fine taste in restaurants."

"I guess I'm buying?"

"No. I believe they will remember you here after today. You have an account now. It's for taking the time to talk to us. Keep it under five hundred a year." He scooted his chair back. "I will go to the gentlemen's room and then leave. Please remain seated, and please don't follow me out."

"Don't worry."

The old man nodded his head again. "If you change your mind call this number. You just need to introduce yourself." He gave Bakewell a card. It had a single phone number, toll free, embossed on the card. Bakewell watched him shuffle off to the restroom. Later he came back by without speaking. He nodded from the area next to the bar as he put his coat on and he smiled in a fatherly way before taking leave.

After he was gone Bakewell waited for a long time, told the waitress not to clear the table. He ordered a Manhattan of his own and drank it slowly. When he felt it was safe, he took his handkerchief and lifted the water glass Snow had used, poured what was left into his own and wrapped it lightly in the handkerchief and put it in his pocket.

Confession

After leaving the restaurant Bakewell drove northwest through a residential neighborhood, reflecting. *Would they leave him alone now?* There was no reaching a conclusion, satisfactory or otherwise. *My god, it would have been an utterly ludicrous luncheon if it hadn't been so serious. An old man of eighty just asked me to shoot someone. Crazy. And who might it be? Who wouldn't be objectionable as a target for assassination?* Khadafy, some crazy Ayatollah? Most of the really bad guys were already dead. He knew a few contractors he would like to shoot, but that would be for amusement only, wouldn't pay anything. *Did he really say a million dollars?*

Talking to Snow had taken the lid off something rancid, and it was in the air he breathed. *The stench of regret?* There would always be regret… and remorse. Remorse was the undercurrent that ran in the gravelly bottom of his meandering life. He wanted to think of his life as a free stone stream, pure, clear. He had tried hard to clear it up over the years, but it always seemed to cloud, turn to a turgid runoff, particulates stirred, muddied by events beyond his control, only to clear again in the quiet seasons when the particles settled to wait for the next stretch of stormy weather.

They were never going to let him go; all these years later, a lifetime later, here they were again. He passed the rectory of St. Peters and slowed, thought for a moment, wanted someone to talk to, turned into the parking lot and sat quietly, brooding. *Am I really in the state of grace?* He was never sure anymore. He examined his conscience carefully, going over each of the commandments, skipping the ones that didn't apply, before he walked to the side door.

"Yes?" She was a pleasant looking woman about Bakewell's age.

"Is there a priest in?"

"Do you have an appointment?"

"No," he didn't elaborate.

"Can I help you?"

"Not unless you're a priest." Bakewell said testily

"Usually he does appointments."

"Like a doctor?" Bakewell was impatient. It wasn't the time for impatience and he realized it and switched gears, careful to stay quiet, not wanting to appear threatening. He let the pain and fatigue show on his face. She took measure of his mood.

"Come in," she said, indicating he wait in the foyer. She went through a 2nd door and closed it. The priest was late sixties, introduced himself as they shook hands, and asked Bakewell to follow him into a small office.

"Do you need Reconciliation?" the priest indicated a comfortable chair.

"Father, I always need the sacraments, especially Reconciliation."

The priest waited for him to start his confession, and Bakewell did so with the familiar lines, saying his last confession had been only a few months before. He also mentioned he was attempting to make the First Saturdays, something that had to be done five times consecutively; had been trying to make the First Saturdays most of his life, without success. The priest chuckled knowingly and Bakewell correctly guessed this one wasn't a bean counter. He hoped he had found the right man. He hadn't discussed what he was about to tell this man ever before, not once, not ever before in a face-to-face, open conversation.

"Most of my life I've been afraid, Father. Mark Twain had me in mind when he said 'the greatest deterrent to sin is fear.' It has always worked for me: fear of the Lord. It's the one gift of the Holy Spirit I managed to get in full measure."

"They call it Wonder & Awe in today's catechism," the priest said, "I prefer fear myself. Kids nowadays could use a little more fear. Respect might be a better word."

Bakewell nodded, picking up where he left off. He was prepared, prided himself in making good confessions. "Well, like most, I have lived a life full of arrogance. I have a lot of guilt about arrogance. I've behaved badly many times in my life." He shook his head in disgust, looking first at his hands then into the priest's eyes. "I was full of myself when I was young."

"Who wasn't," the priest said, encouraging him to get to the point.

"I don't know where to begin exactly. I could tell you I have deflowered several girls in my youth, Father. One in particular has been a real regret."

"Well, I hope you married the last one."

"The last one, yes, within the Sacrament," Bakewell nodded as he spoke. He was stalling, trying to hit a stride. "One of them probably would have deflowered me, but there was one…" he sighed. "I can't even remember her name. It's unbelievably discouraging to remember now. I hate not being able to remember her name..."

"Aren't we awfully far in the past for a man who has used the sacrament so recently?" The irritation showed. Priests had to listen to a lot of stories, sometimes life stories; they got cornered by lonely people. Bakewell knew people used the confessional for a soapbox, for therapy, or just an opportunity to talk to someone.

"I'm leading up to something. I'll hurry." The priest gave him a come-on gesture.

"I've never really cheated anybody, or stole anything. I'm not vicious and for some reason I don't really understand, I'm not vindictive. I never have a need to get even. I don't understand it. Anyway I think the greatest sin of my life is my lack of patience…."

"Part of the arrogance thing?"

Bakewell nodded.

"What you're telling me is sadly too common, Mr. Bakewell, but I…"

"Father I killed a man when I was only twenty."

The priest's eyes widened. "You were in the service?"

"Yes."

"Vietnam?"

"No."

"Korea?"

"No Father, I'm not old enough for Korea." The priest waited. "When I was in the navy I was recruited, more like approached, by a man who interviewed several of us separately; I think so anyway. I'm no longer sure. I guess I drew the short straw. The interview started off simple enough. *How are you? How do you like the service? What are you going to do with* your *life…?* He wasn't in the service; at least I don't think he was. He was dressed well, had a good education, seemed sophisticated, cultured. When he got closer to the point he told me it was for my country. Said he was appealing to my patriotism. He told me my country was asking me. Actually made it sound noble. I was young, didn't have a clue."

"You knew it was a sin to take a life?"

"Of course."

"You were raised Catholic? Catholic education?"

"Yes." The priest waited. "Father this man spoke to me in the captain's quarters, a civilian on a ship of war. He knew the commanding officer. There were twenty five hundred men onboard. When you're a kid, the captain of a ship is like God."

"The captain told you to kill someone on your ship?"

"No. I never saw the captain. We were in his quarters though, very impressive. I was scared. He said it was to be an excision. I didn't know what an excision was. He said it would be dangerous. 'Quite dangerous' was his phrase. He was kind of stiff-upper-lip-like, like a Limey."

"Limey, as in English, Limey?"

"English. Yes. He said they needed someone capable of making a long shot – someone skilled."

"You had this skill?"

"Maybe. I graded out pretty high on the firing range, but so did a lot of guys. There were others with the same skill."

"You agreed?"

"I was afraid not to. Do you know how much confidence you don't have at that age? They made it sound official. Said I would receive hazardous duty pay. I was half pumped up, half pissing in my pants."

"What happened next?"

"Once they had me 'on board,' they said I could count on the company's complete support…"

"What company?"

"I don't know. I never heard the expression *company,* until years later in a movie."

"The CIA?"

"Right. CIA. These guys weren't CIA. The CIA could have done this man their own way and nobody would have known."

The priest opened a drawer and took out a pack of unfiltered cigarettes, lit one with an old Zippo, polished from years of use. Bakewell couldn't remember the last time he's seen a Zippo.

"I agreed, and suddenly I was in quarantine. They told me not to shave. I ate better, got a few extra gedunks – you know, ice cream, candy stuff. They gave me a few private sessions about what to expect, what would happen, not much preparation really. Two days later they brought me some old civilian clothes, made me give up my skivvies. The clothes were poor, uncomfortable, sort of rough. I was used to clean. I was navy. They took my dog tags too."

"That doesn't sound right."

"No, it should have set off the alarms. It might have, I don't remember. I was scared. The clothes weren't smelly or dirty, just dingy looking. Anyway the next day they flew me to the beach in a helicopter."

"You had a helicopter on your ship?"

"Yes. I was on an aircraft carrier. Aboard ship we called the choppers 'Angels' because they flew mercy missions, moved sick people, recovered downed pilots, delivered the chaplain on Sunday, that kind of stuff. I had never been in one. I had only been on one plane in my life. I took the train to San Diego when I went to Boot Camp."

"So you got a ride to the beach in a helicopter?"

"Yes. Ashore. Anytime you go from ship to the shore you're 'hitting the beach.'"

"You 'hit the beach' in a helicopter, not literally," he said, trying to lighten things.

"Yes. It was midday. I wore an orange flying suit over the clothes they gave me. It took about ten minutes. Once ashore, we landed at this little place – it was like an installation or a compound – they drove me into Genoa."

"In Italy?"

"Yes. Genoa, Italy. I had been there once before. They took me to a square, into a building from the back, to a second story. It was an old building, masonry, like everything else there. We went down a hall to a room and they showed me a rifle. There was a wharf; they called it a quay, just the other side of the square. There were two men in the room, one of them left. The one that stayed with me had two pair of binoculars, big ones, like you see in the old war movies, very powerful. He gave me a pair and said to watch between the buildings. After a while, maybe twenty minutes, it could have been much longer, I lost all concept of time. A group of men came from the wharf. I think there were seven of them. One man in particular this guy singled out. He looked pretty much like the others, but this guy kept identifying him, asking me if I saw him. I saw him. Hell, he filled my binoculars. How could I not see him? This man handed me the rifle and said to watch him through the scope on the rifle, to get used to it, but not to shoot."

"How far away was he?"

"About two hundred yards at first, but he kept getting closer. When he was inside a hundred yards – that's when he had me switch to the rifle – he was most emphatic about not taking a head shot, said to shoot center chest, said the scope was zeroed dead on at 100 yards. He said to wait until he got closer. Then he left the room, saying he would go and make sure the escape route was safe. He said to give him a few seconds before I fired. He told me to leave the rifle in the room and run like hell after I shot him. He repeated, 'Don't take a head shot,' one more time. They had told me that many times on the ship. 'Shoot for his chest only.'"

The priest, growing more curious by the tale and Bakewell's gullibility, lit another cigarette. "So he left you there, and a minute later you shot this man and ran?"

"No. The jacket they gave me was tight. It bound under my arms when I raised the rifle to site through it. I took it off as soon as he left. It was a very thin, soft fabric. I'm not sure what. My mind was racing. I was scared, but I took the jacket and I wiped the rifle off very thoroughly. It only took a few seconds. My fingerprints were on the barrel and action. I cradled the stock under the fore end with the fabric. I used the end of the sleeve for my right hand. It just reached the trigger housing."

"What kind of gun was it?" The priest asked, leaning forward.

"A bolt action."

"What kind?"

"You know guns, Father?"

"When I was younger, yes. Bolt actions, an occasional autoloader. I was raised in Minnesota." He put his elbows on his knees and took a long pull on the Camel. "We hunted deer each year and very rarely a black bear. My father didn't want us to shoot the bears. I never understood why. They were a lot of trouble."

"Well," Bakewell also leaned in, "This was a Mannlicher…"

"Mannlicher-Schoenauer."

Bakewell nodded, "With a short barrel. I will always remember the stamping, German of course. It was very light, almost no recoil."

"A 6.5x53, I'll bet; a 1950 model." The priest said. "Did it have the full length stock?"

"You do know guns, Father. Yes, full length."

"European walnut. It had a cheek piece?"

"Yes."

"Double set triggers?"

"No, just one trigger."

"Butter knife bolt? Pistol grip?"

"Yeah, it had a flat bolt and pistol grip. I'm impressed Father. I think you're the first priest I ever talked guns with. You know a little bit about the Mannlicher."

"My uncle had this same gun. They were very popular with gentlemen hunters in the fifties, and my uncle was a wealthy man. He was my father's brother, very successful. He had quite a collection of firearms. I remember that one only weighed about six pounds. I always wanted to shoot it. The next year he came hunting with us he brought a custom stocked Model 70 Winchester. It was a beauty, but I'll always remember that little Mannlicher. I always regretted not getting a chance to fire it."

"Well Father, I wish I could say I never fired one."

"When did you finally shoot? How far was it?"

"Shortly after he left, it was maybe sixty yards, no more. My pulse was pounding. It was deafening in my ears. I was galvanic with fear and apprehension and intent. I guess it was adrenalin. I couldn't miss through the scope. I could count his buttons. Even if I had made a world class flinch, I doubt I would have missed." Bakewell was describing with his hands. "But I never flinched. Not until afterwards. I was full of flinches then. I'm sure I hit him center chest. The sound in that small room was tremendous.

"As soon as the gun went off, everything seemed to go a hundred miles an hour and in slow motion at the same time. I put the gun down quickly and went out the door and down the hall. When I was almost to the exit I got this strange feeling. I noticed the door was left slightly open. I didn't want to go through it. A crazy premonition came over me. I just knew the door was a bad choice. I went back past the room and down a dark staircase. At the bottom there was another door. I opened it. It opened into an alley. There was a small restaurant across the alley, a coffee shop with a side entry from the alley. I found a restroom just inside the door and went in there. There was a hole in the floor, a concrete hole with handles on the sidewalls. I think you held yourself and dropped your pants and went from the standing position."

The priest nodded knowingly. "I've spent much time in Europe."

"No one came in. After five minutes maybe, I walked out into the café and found a table. There was a siren; I'd heard it before in the rest room. It sounded like one of those Nazi jobs you always hear ringing in the movies. There was a lot of commotion; people were standing at the window when I came out of the john. Nobody noticed me when I sat down. When this thin old man, the waiter, finally noticed me, he came over and I grunted at the next table, pointing at what they were having. He probably thought I was just another young punk – Genoa was full of young punks. He brought me a thick espresso. The only time I ever drank the stuff. Terrible. I drank it and ate some kind of roll, not looking at anyone. When the next table left, I grabbed their paper and pretended to read it. I was scared. I stayed for at least two hours and ate several rolls. Drank this rancid black pitch and waited. The square was quiet when I came out."

"What did you do after that?" the priest considered another cigarette, reconsidered and put the pack back in the drawer. "They're old," he said, "very stale."

Bakewell nodded. He had smoked stale cigarettes many times in college. They hurt the back of his throat when they were stale.

"When I got closer to shore, fleet landing we called it, I took off the shirt and shoes and ran, turned myself in to the Shore Patrol. Told them I'd gotten jumped by a bunch of punks. They were really upset. Those guys could be tough. I don't know if they were madder at me, or the locals. There was a lot of animosity between us and the Italians at the time. Guys were always getting cut off from their group and beaten up, especially in Genoa."

"They took you onto the ship?"

"Out to the ship, in a liberty launch. We always anchored outside the breakwater. When I came aboard the OD, a young ensign, had a fit, wanted to throw me in the brig. There was a chief petty officer there. He was in control; he handled the OD. He told me to go to my compartment and clean up. He sent a Petty Officer from the Master at Arms Corps to escort me back. When I got to my compartment there were a couple of guys from my outfit there and another civilian. He was at my locker. He had my dog tags. The guys looked at me bug eyed. I asked him why he was at my locker, told him who I was. I was still very frightened. He was surprised to see me, asked how I was and regained his composure, said I should clean up. He left pretty quick after that, and I showered and shaved. One of my shipmates came into the head and told me the guy in the civvies had told them I was dead, told them he came to collect my things. The guys wanted to know what was going on, wanted to know where I had been for so long."

"You didn't tell them?"

"No. I wasn't talking. I mean, *I wasn't talking* – period. You could put an exclamation point in there too Father. When I got back to my bunk, I was told to pack my sea bag and report to the quarterdeck. By the time I got up there we were under way, headed out to sea. They fired up the TF, the Tango-Foxtrot. We all loved the TF. It was a small twin-engine job they launched from the deck the old fashioned way, without the catapult. It was a utility plane. I left on the TF, flew all the way to Naples. I was there overnight. The next day I flew all the way back to the states in a big transport – the first time I was ever on a jet. I had orders to report to Lakehurst, New

Jersey. We landed at McGuire."

"Tommy McGuire," the priest nodded. "He was a war ace, a fighter pilot, Medal of Honor winner out in the islands. My uncle served in the same outfit with him in New Guinea."

"That's amazing; my dad served out there too."

"Small world. That base was named after McGuire. He wanted to be the top American ace. Almost made it, died pursuing his dream somewhere out over the Solomons."

"Well, McGuire's only a short way from Lakehurst Navel Air Station. That's where I ended up." Bakewell paused and waited for the priest to speak.

"What do you think happened after you left?"

"Nothing. There was nothing in any newspapers or magazines that I could find."

The priest picked up a phone and made a call; a tray with two large glasses of water arrived. When the door closed he took a drink and said, "You've confessed this sin before, haven't you?"

"At least five times."

"When was the first time?"

"About a year after I got discharged. I was in no hurry to talk about it. I wasn't as concerned about my soul back then. I thought I was going to live forever. I never wanted to talk about it, not ever. Not even when I had too much to drink. I never spoke of it to a priest in my own parish. I never confessed it within a hundred miles of St. Louis, except once to an old Jesuit down at the College Church years later. Big mistake."

The priest almost laughed. He knew the Jesuits. "What did he tell you?"

"Told me to turn myself in to the authorities; give myself up to God's justice."

The priest shook his head.

"What authorities? I thought I was working for people with big time authority! Was I supposed to go back to Genoa and tell the police I was responsible for a shooting that never happened?"

"Why do you say it never happened?"

"Father I looked for years. I researched magazines, newspapers, spent hours in the libraries here and while I was at Mizzou. I even tried to learn Italian. I stared at old newspapers in the microfilm library until I was bleary-eyed, looking at headlines and photographs in papers I couldn't even read, hoping, maybe not hoping, I'd see a face or story that would explain what happened. Long after I was married with a family, during the off-season, I would spend winter days in the research sections of St. Louis University and Washington U. It was like it never happened, like a fantastic dream."

"Maybe it was a dream?"

"No. It was no dream. You don't have dreams about killing people. It happened just like I told you."

"When you got back to the states, what happened after that?"

"I got a call right after I checked in at Lakehurst, from this same guy, the civilian that recruited me, the second afternoon I was back. *They knew I was in the building*. He told me he was glad I was all right, glad that I'd made it home okay. He asked if I needed anything. I told him I didn't need anything. I wanted to be left alone."

"Maybe I'm being obtuse, but how did it make you feel, knowing they were watching you?"

"Scared. I was always scared. I had a lot of trouble sleeping. I was real nervous about leaving the base."

"What else did he say, or did you hang up?"

"No. You don't hang up on people like that. He told me to go into town. Tom's River, New Jersey, said to open a bank account. He said I had done a good thing, and I was entitled to hazardous duty pay."

"I've been to Tom's River. It's on the coast."

"Yes: marinas, yachts, fishing. It wasn't a bad place. I didn't want to go in there but I finally did. I stopped at the first bank I came to. I used five two-dollar bills to open the account. I still remember. We used to get paid in $2 bills – twice a month. I think it was around $46, plus room and board. Afterward I went straight back to the base.

"I hated life in the barracks even more than on the ship. There were arguments and fights all the time. You never had any privacy, but I'll tell you, I didn't mind sleeping with all those guys after I got back. I was glad for the company at night. Suddenly listening to so many guys rustling around in their bunks had an appeal."

"The bank account?"

"I'd never had one. A month later I got my first bank statement. There was a deposit for $5,000. Things quieted down for me. I was never reassigned or allowed to change quarters. I spent a long, boring year at Lakehurst, not a great place to be in winter. After I got out, actually I got what they called an *early out,* for college – I wasn't supposed to get discharged until September – I put in for an early out that summer, the end of July; two days later I had my discharge papers and was headed home."

"Did they contact you after that?"

"Never, and my bank balance was never lower than $5,000 until I graduated. I got used to the balance. It paid for books, tuition and fees for four years. They had just reinstated the GI Bill too, so I had another hundred bucks a month during the school months. They started shipping lots of Viet Nam guys home in body bags that year, so the GI Bill kicked back in. My brother came home in one of those bags in 1968. He never got any benefits."

Bakewell paused, trying to relax. "When I got home I kept my head down, had an older car, never wanted to draw attention to myself. I lived off campus before I was married, tried to keep a low profile. After I graduated, we took our wedding money and most of the balance and put it down on a house. The month after that I was overdrawn. It was only a few bucks but it was over. I always expected a little note or something."

"You wanted them to make a little gesture, signaling finality?"

"No, I didn't want them to signal anything."

"Nothing?"

"Huh, uh."

"If they weren't legitimate people, why did they pay off? Why did they let you go? It seems to me these people could easily have reneged on the deal."

"I don't know, principle maybe, maybe because I never talked. In their world I must have measured up. They seem to have this thing about honor and loyalty. I guess not talking was equated with loyalty."

"You have quite a story." The priest pushed the ashtray from the edge of the table. "I'm not certain how to respond. I guess I should ask you if you feel you have received God's forgiveness?"

"You tell me."

"No, no. I'm asking you? Do you believe this killing has been absolved?"

"I don't know," Bakewell sighed deeply.

"It's what your conscience is telling you…right now. How do you feel now that you've told this tale, confessed it once again? That's what is important. It's not up to me. I can't tell you how to feel. That's between you and God. "

Bakewell put his head in his hands, elbows on his knees and talked to the floor. "Father, I killed a man thirty years ago. I never knew who he was or why he was to be killed. I don't know if he was a good person or someone despicable. I don't know if he was in the state of grace when he died or if he even died for sure."

"That's true. You could have missed him. He could be a very old Italian today. How old was he?"

"He looked fortyish. I don't know if he was Italian. He could have been Greek, a Turk, eastern European maybe."

"You don't really know whether you took his life."

"I killed him. In my mind I killed him. God wouldn't care if I missed. You know that."

"No, God wouldn't care. You had the intent. That's all that matters. Now you have a need to be absolved again, a need to put this terrible thing behind you. How to make reparation is the question you're asking, I think."

Bakewell nodded. "I need to know if I can find absolution before I die."

"Absolution I can give you, if you are really sorry for this sin… if it was a sin. As an instrument of the Church, I can absolve you right now. Reparation is something else. It's between you and Almighty God. What has your life been like all these years?"

"Wonderful in many ways, although lately it's gone down hill. I lost my wife a while back. That has been very difficult."

"I'm sorry."

"I've had a lot of fear, and remorse too, over the years, but it has been offset by incredible good fortune with my marriage and my children. Originally it was just fear, but the fear gradually abated. Then remorse really kicked in…it took a while though. I guess I was out of school and raising at least two kids when I figured out no one was going to shoot me in the dark; that's when the remorse really set in. Remorse is a terrible thing to live with. I read recently that the greatest sin of all is to cause another to lose his soul. What if I took a man's life and he wasn't in the state of grace? It seems like the ultimate in capital punishment – spiritually."

"Yes, it would be a terrible sin. And it would be terrible to live with all these years. It certainly appears to have made you more compassionate. How much do you think it has changed your life?"

"I don't know. I was very arrogant as a young man. Maybe…I don't know, maybe its just time. Age. I've gotten a lot humbler over the years."

"It's not like you were on the front somewhere when you shot this man. You weren't involved in the fighting in the jungle with all those poor young men."

"No. They had plenty of reason to shoot."

"Yes," the priest was lost in thought. He stared at the paneling over Bakewell's head. There was a long silence before either man stirred. "I can't help wondering why they let you get away. They don't sound like military people."

"I've thought about that a lot. I think these people are really big bucks. They probably settle their disputes with dummies like me. If they ever did this sort of thing at all, my guess is they found somebody so improbable, so implausible – like me – inserted the guy in wherever; you know, offered enough money and put him in and afterward let them get whacked."

The priest sat back and pulled at his trousers, trying to get comfortable. They had been at it a long time. His look turned wry, "You think every time there's one of these crime of the century type killings, its them? Lee Harvey Oswald, James Earl Ray?"

"No. No. I wonder sometimes, but no, not with those guys, Father. Those were political. I don't think this was political. There was no story to tell. No news. With that sort of thing it's all news."

"Have there been other stories like yours? You've been watching for this sort of thing all your life haven't you?"

"All my life," Bakewell agreed. "I think maybe they're a Skull &

Bones outfit. You know, Council on Foreign Relations type? Maybe something like that."

"You've read about these organizations?"

"Yes and no. There isn't much to read."

"Have you heard of the Bilderberg Society?"

"I've heard of them, yes. But like I said; there isn't a lot of detail on those people."

"There is one such organization called the Tri-Lateral Commission – David Rockefeller is supposed to be one of them – they were purported to have written the charter for the League of Nations way back after the First World War. That would have been before Rockefeller's time."

"I read that somewhere, and I believe there is probably some truth to it. I think anything's possible when great wealth is involved. Who knows? Don't you think it possible, even probable, that an organization of phenomenally wealthy, influential people could have some kind of secret pact going, the idea being to make the world a better place, at least a better place for the practice of their kind of mega-commerce? I doubt they would be above money, if they are about money, but maybe they are motivated to serve some kind of a secret, omniscient purpose?"

The priest nodded, didn't answer.

"Hell, I don't really know, Father. I'm a simple guy. I went to Missouri, not Yale."

He smiled conspiratorially. "I went to Kenrick Seminary, myself."

"Yeah, for about seven years, and I'll bet you did some graduate stuff after that didn't you? You guys don't miss a chance to load up on education."

"I did, yes, in Rome, when I was young."

"You're a Canon Lawyer?"

The priest nodded.

"I don't know," Bakewell said, straightening up. He stretched and twisted his neck around. "I think the deal with them – if there even is a *them* – is to have a shooting like the one I was involved in happen, without happening, then there's no revenge."

"Unlike with the mobs?"

"Right."

"I think your right about that. When those people kill there has to be more killing, more avenging. They kill each other brutally, shockingly sometimes, to try to create fear. But if you kill in such a cavalier way I suspect there is no way to scare the other guy off. There's always someone more brutal."

"I agree Father. These people aren't brutal. I don't think so anyway."

"You've stepped across their invisible line today, haven't you?"

"By telling you about them? Yes, I have. This might be a singular day in my life; it hasn't gone well so far. This could be the day that moves me to the other side, talking about them. I never did that before, not even with my wife. I may be about to flunk my annual review."

"You think they have you bugged?"

"Don't make fun, Father. This isn't your normal confession. Keep this one strictly to yourself."

"All of my confessions are kept under the seal."

"I believe that, Father. I've always had confidence in the confessional, that's why I'm here."

"It's Andy, right?" Bakewell nodded. "Well Andy, we've been talking a long time and even though I don't know you." The priest paused and looked at him curiously, "I don't know you do I?"

"No Father."

"You look familiar."

"I don't think we've ever met."

"I feel like I might know you. In my business you meet a lot of people." He looked away and spoke to the lamp. "Clearly you've been living in a difficult situation, living a life of regret too. You're in a lot of pain, aren't you?"

"I think so. I used to equate pain with physical things. I'm learning the pain in my head is far worse than any kind of physical pain."

The priest nodded, "I believe this business has caused a lot of suffering in your life, created a long era of suffering for you."

"I was afraid for a long time. Fear is a different kind of pain, but it still hurts, hurts the brain anyway. If remorse is suffering, I've been suffering alright."

"Emotions are very confusing. Each is different. We tend to lump them together; the longer I'm at this, the more I understand how difficult it is to analyze emotions, to separate them."

"My wife died two years ago. I suffered a great deal. Watching her die was an emotion I learned to live with in time. Watching the pain her suffering caused my children was excruciating. I still can't deal with it. Sometimes I see it even now in their faces. It's unbearable."

"That pain is from vulnerability."

"You're not kidding."

"You can never learn not to be vulnerable."

"It's awful." Bakewell almost gave way to his emotions, got control before he started weeping. He hadn't wept at his wife's funeral or any other time during her illness. His voice started to shake. He always knew he needed to cry, but hoped for a more private time. When he lowered his head the priest put his hand on his shoulder and made it worse. He didn't want to give way, struggled to get himself under control. He hadn't really cried since Brenden died. He stared at the floor, gathering himself. There was a long silence before he finally slumped back against the wooden chair. Each man looked at the other intently, looked into the others eyes, one looking for help, the other wanting to help, both experiencing a dilemma, their moods alternating between sympathy and confusion.

"Each one of us gets his share of suffering," the priest said finally. "You know this already. Suffering plays a huge role in our lives. We have to have it. It has a three-fold purpose. First it tempers us like heated metal. It purifies us by controlling our ego, our vanity. We all are guilty of self-love. Suffering controls this tendency to be selfish. It also gives us more compassion, softens us up so to speak, sensitizes us to those around us.

"Lastly, it has a wonderful, redeeming value that allows us to make reparation to God, provided – and this is crucial – we learn to recognize it and accept it and offer it to God. This is where grace enters. Like Our Lord's Passion, we must offer our suffering for others." He put his hand up to give him absolution, paused. "Is there anything else?"

"No Father." Bakewell almost laughed, relieved for the swing in moods.

"Offer your suffering for this man you think you killed, Andy. Maybe through the grace obtained from your own misery you may be able to save his soul. Make an act of contrition."

Bakewell said the familiar prayer.

The priest raised his hand: "*God, the Father of mercies, through the death and resurrection of his Son, has reconciled the world to himself...* Bakewell heard the priest say the words of absolution slowly and, he thought, with special emphasis over his bowed head.... *And I absolve you from your sins, in the name of the Father, and of the Son, and of the Holy Spirit."*

"Amen," Bakewell said. The priest continued the familiar dismissal: *"May the Passion of our Lord Jesus Christ, the intercession of the Blessed Virgin Mary and of all the saints, whatever good you do and suffering you endure, heal your sins, help you to grow in holiness, and reward you with eternal life. Go in peace."*

"Thank you, Father."

The priest nodded they got up and walked to the door. He opened it, turned to Bakewell, indicating he go first. As Bakewell was stepping out into the sunlight, the priest stopped him. "What brought you here today, Andy? Why this day in particular?"

Bakewell hesitated, thought for a long moment, his creased forehead furrowed in thought. Finally he decided to answer truthfully. "They've contacted me again, Father."

The priest looked stunned, as if he was thinking the whole confession a farce. Bakewell nodded, understanding his dilemma and turned for his car.

Denny

With the exception of being hit by a few pitches, Bakewell hadn't been seriously hurt playing baseball. Football was another story. A fan of pro football long before it became the raging Sunday passion, he hurried home after eleven o'clock Mass to watch the Bears or the old Chicago Cardinals on the family television, a massive wooden box that housed a tiny 6" screen and gave off an indistinct black and white picture. Bakewell favored big, bruising rushers with names like Madson, Brown and Younger, but when tryouts began, he found the best rushing back in high school football – a guy who would go on to the University and later sign professionally – playing ahead of him and everybody else who had dreams of carrying the ball. In his junior year, Bakewell was a squarely built 165 pounds, nearly six feet tall with a Nordic bone structure that would eventually carry more. His powerful legs had grown him into one of the best runners in the district. He was the second fastest man on his team and the third fastest runner in the city, where he collected a handful of 3rd place medals and one 2nd in various relays and hundred-yard dashes over two spring track seasons.

Coach King developed an affection for Bakewell, liked his quiet, intense nature, liked his persistence and the way he played full out in the oppressive summer heat. He also liked the furious enthusiasm he brought to every practice, especially loved the belligerence and the pluck Bakewell demonstrated in those early practices. Bakewell was easy to coach and anxious to learn. He had a reputation for being a loner, but in sports he was a pure follower, a team guy, who loved being around the ball, hoping it might pop free, giving him his chance. There was no way the coach could play him in a backfield in front of the most sought after kid in the city, but he wasn't about to leave him on the bench as a seldom-needed backup. When he asked Bakewell to play defense, Bakewell refused. They came to an accord when Coach offered him the job of returning punts and kickoffs in exchange for his furious presence in the defensive backfield. Despite his speed, Bakewell lacked the flash and the instinct for open field running, but he held onto the ball and, keeping his half of the bargain, he hurled himself into the job of defending, played with abandon, was reckless, feverishly intense at game time, and had an instinct for knowing when to peel off his man and find the ball carrier on running plays.

One afternoon, using poorly focused 9mm film, Coach ran a play over and over for the entire team. "You don't see *this reckless kind of shit very often,*" he said, wrongly predicting that guys who played with Bakewell's wild élan seldom got hurt. The film session took place during one of Bakewell's many detentions, and, in his absence, several teammates took the opportunity to complain. "He practices like it's the final game of the season."

In the two years he played varsity football Bakewell broke his collarbone, cracked three ribs in two separate seasons and ended up separating his shoulder while favoring the cracked ribs in his final game. Before the injuries healed he was academically ineligible and on his way to a public school where he was expelled within weeks.

Bakewell's alter ego in the defensive backfield was Denny Murphy, from a family of pure Irish that bragged of three vocations in the family: an uncle, (priest) and a sister and an aunt (both nuns). Denny's people were from "Dog Town" and although the house was bedlam – seven kids, plus the usual gathering of cousins and after school tagalongs – it was a controlled bedlam that Mr. Murphy ruled with a kind, but iron hand.

Bakewell loved the Murphy's. Denny's parents entertained a stream of people in the kitchen and the old fashioned parlor of their three-storied house, where the beer flowed by the case most evenings. The Murphy's were St. James Catholics, half a mile too far to be walking distance from the high school but only a block and a half from the parish school and gym. Mrs. Murphy was in charge of all things not ecclesiastic, while Mr. Murphy headed up the scout troop and did everything he could "to keep St. Jimmy rolling," when his duties on the St. Louis police force allowed.

Where Bakewell had speed, Denny had plodding determination, and, what he lacked in speed he made up for in resolve and staying power. Denny couldn't run them down or hurl himself through the air with Bakewell's ability, but he stood his ground and handled what came to his side of the field. The coach never developed much affection for his thoroughbred running back whose autographed photos would adorn the school's walls for a generation, but he loved his duo of defensive backs, admired Murphy's tenacity the way he admired Bakewell's recklessness. He kept Denny in the backfield because he "had to find a place for the kid," and because "there was never enough speed to go around." Denny was a combination tight end/linebacker, and the only thing left to put back there with the "fast kid," who herded them to Murphy's side of the field, where Denny gathered them in with momentum stopping tackles, causing epic collisions, and, best of all – turnovers.

Denny brought the same bovine resolve to his studies, a resolve that kept him on the B Honor Roll each of his four years. He graduated from Benedictine College the year Bakewell got discharged, paid his tuition laboring for a concrete company each summer, and proudly joined his father on the police force upon graduation. He asked Bakewell, just home from the navy, to be his best man that fall. Murphy was one of Bakewell's few contacts with the old school. Bakewell reciprocated three years later when he married Katherine.

***

Denny answered the phone from his home in Dog Town where he and Helen lived not two blocks from his parents' home.

"Hey Murph, its Andy, got a minute?"

"Andy, son of a bitch," Denny said warmly then remembering how long it had been, how he had always had to call, switched moods. "Awe Andy, fuck. Where you been? You don't write – you don't call – you don't give a shit." There was more. "Damn it, Andy. Where you been? Where the fuck you been?"

Bakewell anticipated the irate reaction. "Busy. My ass's been in a crack lately."

"Bullshit!"

"I'm a rotten friend, Denny, but give me a break, I'm working sixty hours a week."

"Aw, fuck. How much time does it take to make a phone call?"

"I can't stay awake on the ride home most nights."

"You could pick up that *fruit* little telephone you carry everywhere and say, 'HELLOOO... HELLOOO DENNY... IT'S ME, ANDY-ARRO-FUCKING-GANCE BAKEWELL! YOUR OLD FRIEND!"

"You're right, I'm sorry."

"You are a rotten friend. You can't drop by the house? Helen's tried to make dinner for you a thousand times since Katherine..." Denny ran out of gas. "You arrogant son of a bitch, Andy..." He sounded like he was about to cry, and Bakewell wasn't sure if it was for Katherine or himself.

"I called because I need a favor. How much abuse do I have to take before I can ask my best friend for a favor?"

"I'm not your best friend. You wrote me off a long time ago."

"Denny."

There was another pause. "I'll do you a favor 'cause *I loved your wife...I loved your wife...*" Denny paused to get control, "...almost as much as I love my own, almost as much as I loved my high school buddy who dropped me for his yuppie-assed west county friends," there was a long pause, "But only if we meet for lunch or you come by the house. I'm not doing you any favors over the phone."

"Deal. I'll be by in thirty minutes."

"Tonight?"

"Yeah, am I welcome or do I have to have an appointment?" Denny was excessively, obsessively organized. In their early-married years he had refused to let people in the house if they dropped by uninvited, actually stood in the doorway and told them he wasn't expecting company, apologized and shut the door in their face, to the mortification of Helen who was known to take in strangers, listen patiently to Encyclopedia salesmen and refused to offend a telephone solicitor. In that one particular, Denny was the opposite of his father who never turned anyone from his door. Katherine told her husband the pandemonium that raged in Denny's childhood home had created his eccentricity.

There was a prolonged silence on Murphy's end before he said, "I don't know."

"You're such a *structured fuck,"* Bakewell almost shouted the words. "I get chewed out for not coming by and now I'm not welcome?"

"Come on by. I'll go wake Helen."

"It's eight-thirty!"

"Come on by. Have you had dinner yet? You want something to eat?"

"Sure." Bakewell knew letting Helen make something would be better than refusing and would lighten the tension. He hadn't called in years, including the year before Katherine died. Thirty minutes later and because he knew it would aggravate him, Bakewell came through the front door without knocking. There was a little boy on the floor and Bakewell started to scoop him up before checking himself, realizing they might not recognize him, or he them. *They aren't toddlers anymore*. He looked up at a young father.

"Hey, Mr. Bakewell," the boy said, "Long time."

Bakewell couldn't remember his name, instantly filled with guilt, tried to bluff his way, "How's young Mr. Murphy doing?"

"In here bro," Denny called from the kitchen.

"If you had a million dollars, Murphy, you would still spend your evenings at the kitchen table, just like your old man."

"You got that right."

Bakewell entered the bright kitchen. The room brought a smile to his face.

"Damn, Denny, I can still see your dad sitting in the kitchen, his waist bulging over a .38, teasing your mom about being *pigs-in-the-kitchen Irish* not *lace-curtain-Irish* while she spent the evening in an apron waiting on all of us."

Mrs. Murphy was always busy when Bakewell was a kid, moving from sink to pantry, getting something for someone. Denny's parents had the greatest marriage Bakewell had observed in his lifetime. They had taught a mess of neighborhood kids, including Bakewell how to run a marriage. The senior Murphy's had been devoted, deeply in love, and never afraid to let it shine through. Bakewell had patterned his relationship with Katherine after Mr. Murphy, had worshipped Katherine with the same devotion Mr. Murphy had shown his wife. Thinking out loud he said reverently, "Denny, your mom and dad could have been the poster couple for Marriage Encounter."

Denny nodded, pleased his old friend remembered. Bakewell had interrupted an elk-hunting trip and flown all the way from Salmon, Idaho to get back in time for Mrs. Murphy's funeral. Denny's dad had died of cancer a decade before. "Just being here makes me miss them."

"Thanks. You're no politician, but you're sincere. What's in the bag?"

"Got a favor to ask." Bakewell put the bag on the table, lowered the sides without reaching inside. "Can you run the prints on the glass and see what comes up?"

"What is this?"

"Just do it," he said, reaching out to shake Denny's big hand.

Denny held Bakewell's hand for a long time, wouldn't let go, testing him. Bakewell understood the game and kept shaking his hand, holding firm. There had never been a meeting, chance or otherwise the first thirty years of Denny's life when he hadn't subconsciously wondered if he could whip Bakewell. He was taller, had always been bigger, but memories of those neck-snapping, blood spurting tackles gave him pause. There was a pent up, creepy, secret something in Bakewell that worried Denny when they were boys. Still, he was always on the verge of fighting him, just to establish the pecking order, would have done it too, but Bakewell had those eyes – those damned crinkly, kind eyes – always creased at the sides, so candid and disarming. Throughout most of their youth Bakewell had been at war with the world of authority, filled with an animosity toward anything establishment, yet he marveled at the way Bakewell had always defused the tough guys with that laid back, nice guy charisma. *Nobody ever wanted to whip Bakewell the way they wanted to whip me*, Denny had told his wife. *If you picked a fight with Bakewell you ended up looking stupid, having to explain yourself to the other guys. It seemed disloyal to want to fight him.* Helen had smiled knowingly.

"How's the old bell-ringing, pad-popping, meanest son of a bitchin tackler in the world holding up?"

"I've had better years; how bout you?"

Denny finally let Bakewell's hand go and reached to his pocket for a pen and flipped the glass over with a practiced maneuver. He held it up to the light and viewed it through a pair of half-eyes. "More than one set of prints on here, bro."

The younger man came into the kitchen, carrying the toddler from the living room. Bakewell mercifully remembered his name. "How many does this make, Brian?"

"Three, Mr. Bakewell. This is little Denny here. Named him after this dumb Pollock," he grinned, indicating his father.

"Wow, that's high praise; I hope one of my kids will think to do that."

"Nobody's gonna name a kid 'yuppie-fuck'," Denny said, staring at the glass, enjoying the power of being right, placing blame. He had called Bakewell many times after they found out about Katherine, had called just to take his pulse, to get his emotional temperature. Denny and Helen had come by several times like everyone else, especially at the end when Helen's presence had been invaluable.

"Brian, get Andy some chicken out of the refrigerator. Put it on a plate with those peas and warm it in the microwave." Brian did as instructed.

Bakewell didn't protest. He was on fragile ground, and he was hungry, hadn't eaten since lunchtime. "So, what's the deal?"

"I'd just like to know who shows up. Not that many of us fingerprinted nowadays. Not like the old days when everybody got printed in boot camp." Bakewell addressed his words to Brian who nodded in silent awe. Like most of his generation, Brian had never served his country.

"Who we lookin for?"

"Rich guy from Boston maybe… someplace in New England."

"And?"

"I just want to know who he is, that's all."

"Huh uh, not buying – square with me if you want a favor."

"I knew him a long time ago," Bakewell sighed. "He comes around sometimes, usually a business proposition, wants me to do some work for him. Usually involves a lot of money. I would just like to know who he is, or if he's who he says he is. No big deal. If you can't help, I'll understand," Bakewell added, trying to turn the guilt trick.

"What's his name?"

"Don't know really."

"Bullshit, the guys gotta have a name."

"Calls himself Broughton," Bakewell lied. It was the first name that came to mind. Broughton had been the name stenciled on the helmet of the helicopter pilot that flew him to the beach that day in Genoa. Bakewell would never forget it. The bell rang on the microwave, and Brian took the plate and set it in front of Bakewell.

"Okay. Have a beer with me?"

"Sure, might have two, unless there's a limit on our friendship."

Denny got up ignoring him and went to the refrigerator and grabbed two long neck bottles. Bakewell held the bottle up for inspection, smiled, spoke almost reverently. "Busch Bavarian Beer, some things never change." He admired the bottle fondly.

"Not your brand?" It was sarcastic.

"Come on, Denny, remember we learned to drink this stuff together?"

Denny turned the bottle up and drank half of it in one long pull, the way his father had done years before. Bakewell looked around taking everything in. The kitchen was warm. He remembered it well. Everything was modest and well used, lots of things strewn about haphazardly: clean dishes drained in the sink, baby pictures stuck under magnets on the refrigerator, smear marks all over the door; patterns on the chairs, windows and wallpaper, all Colonial. The furniture was old and abused, but functional; seat cushions covered the hardwood chairs they sat on and some kind of soft material was under the checkered tablecloth that made it comfortable to rest his arms on. Helen's hand was everywhere. Much of the furniture had come from relatives, probably deceased, or bought at a value that couldn't be ignored.

The Murphys' lived carefully on what Denny made. Helen never worked a single day for a real salary after their marriage. The wedding had been at St. Raphael's – Helen was from "Hampton," a south city bastion like Dog Town. Bakewell remembered the night, had worried his way through the ceremony, concerned about what he would say when he gave the toast, afraid he would screw it up.

They lived on one salary, but food was plentiful and very good. Denny would never skimp when it came to food. Bakewell would have bet his negative net worth they had some kind of roast 3 times a week. They referred to it "poor house food" because it was most often cooked in a pot. Bakewell had been raised on the same fair, missed it still, now that he was feeding himself. He was disappointed when Denny said chicken, had secretly hoped for pot roast with lots of carrots.

They sat in the kitchen and talked for over an hour about the police force and Denny's pension. He wasn't far from early retirement. He was entitled. Denny had been wounded fifteen years before. Shot through the lung when he stood and displayed an unbelievable determination – in truth it had been a macho, careless heroism – that dropped one man and sent another out the back door of a small hotel lounge owned by the Lebanese mob, renowned for violence a generation before.

The Murphy's had bought a little cabin on the Gasconade River where they loved their family gatherings and the smallmouth fishing. It was humble and inexpensive, but had a lofted upstairs that could sleep ten kids, a place made for family, lots of it. Bakewell could see himself down there with Denny, arguing over who would fish from the front deck of the used boat Denny described – the one in the front would be bait-casting along the bank with a plug of Redman in his jaw. Bakewell had a gentle and artful touch with a fly rod, but always fished with hardware whenever Denny Murphy was along. Murphy had disparaged the gentle art of fly presentation as a snotty, pseudo-sport, practiced by the "limp wrested," called them "pussy willows". So Bakewell threw big, outrageous, clanky junk at the fish to keep him quiet.

Bakewell let his mind wander as Denny described their dream house on the river and the time they intended to spend there after he quit the force.

The highlight of the evening was Denny's beautifully crafted description of the Holy Father's visit in January and the fact that Denny, seasoned with experience and years of seniority, had gotten close to the Pope at the kid's Mass at the Kiel Center. His voice was softly reverent as he described the moment the aging Pontiff passed him in the hallway and patted his arm. It had been moving, Denny said, "Man, I'm telling you. It was something otherworldly to be touched by that man. I felt like I was in the presence of sanctity." And it was moving to hear a big man speak with such veneration. "It'll be with me the rest of my life. I'll never forget it," Denny said, looking away, affected, and they dropped the locker room language.

"I'd have given a month of my diminishing salary for the privilege," Bakewell said, adding, "But if there was ever a cop in my home town I would want guarding the Holy Father it would be you, Denny." He looked up at Brian. "You've got to be proud of your old man."

"Yes sir, I am."

Bakewell left the same time Brian did. As they went outside they ran into Helen coming across the front yard. She was coming from a meeting, and without asking, Bakewell knew it had something to do with helping someone else. After acknowledging her noisy grandson, Helen hugged Bakewell tightly, tearfully, pushed him back and looked into his eyes, hugged him again warmly. She kissed his cheek three different times before she let him go. Bakewell remembered the first time he had seen Helen. At the Red Carpet, a little nightclub in Gaslight Square with Denny, when "The Square" was running full steam. She was a cute kid, no more than twenty at the time and still had the same diminutive figure. Bakewell always wondered how people so mismatched physically managed to have sex, but scrupulously avoided the subject, fearing he would get either a flared-up, pissed-off reaction, or a lurid physical description.

Helen asked Bakewell about each of his kids, calling them by name. She asked about his grandkids too, made him give each one a name and description, shaking her head in agreement, nodding and smiling at the memories talking about his children rekindled. She begged him to come back into the house, but Denny, standing on the porch, sensing his fatigue, shouted, "He's been here long enough, let him go back to Yuppieville," in a voice so gruff it betrayed. Bakewell waved goodbye to his once best friend, promised Helen he would come by again, maybe bring one of his grandkids.

When he left, he took Manchester, not wanting to get on the interstate again. He left the window open and drove slowly, almost every block rekindling memories: places they had played, worked or simply bummed together when they were kids. He listened to the neighborhood sounds and smelled the smells of his youth and wished he had spent more time with the Murphy's. Katherine would have preferred it, he was sure. A dull ache filled him. He wasn't sure if it was his head or his heart. He was driving away from two people who had loved him and his family as much as any people he knew. He had walked away from them, abandoned their friendship years before.

In the halcyon days, the heyday of money making, he had abandoned the Murphy's for the revolting crowd that stood three deep at Annie Gunn's, smoking cigars, drinking expensive whiskey, talking simultaneously, nobody listening to anybody, the conversations always about how much they had, where they had been, how much their kid's private schools cost...

It made him sick to remember. He was suffocating with remorse, and with the pain of remembering the jerk he had become over the years, especially the years after they moved to West County. He had dropped Denny's friendship. They both knew it. Realizing now, he wondered how he could have done it, how he could have been so indifferent and so callow about something so worthwhile. They had a friendship that should have lasted a lifetime and he had terminated it in mid life. He had too many nights to remember too many inconsiderate things he had done. *Why – because you started to make money?*

When he and Ned finally started to rack up some real profits, Ned had been the same guy, kept the same friends, still had them. Bakewell thought he needed to make new ones. *Why?* He asked the question over and over on the drive home. *Why did you do it?*

The trip took thirty minutes; he could have made it in twenty on the interstate. As he turned into his neighborhood, he took the cell phone Denny loved to make fun of and called Amici's. He got a tired waitress who was probably waiting on a late diner, arranged for a gift certificate to be sent to the Murphy's, still remembering their address. He would never forget the address of their home on Floyd Avenue.

A Pinot Grigio Night

Bakewell's lady friends stayed away after the night in the pool. It gave him an opportunity to enjoy his daughter, who brought his grandchildren. Nancy, aware of her father's need for companionship, never came without checking first. Whenever one of her mother's friends answered the phone she would visit graciously, and ask them to tell her father she called. Nancy loved the attention they lavished on her father.

They had dubbed themselves the Predator Bitches, actually reveled in the name, and learned to speak of Katherine openly again, partly to console each other, partly in appreciation of his pain. They felt it themselves, deeply. They had known her longer, and missed her almost as much as Bakewell did. The weather was cooler and the meal moved from the pool deck to the patio at the back of the house.

Bakewell came home from work one Thursday and found them already there, a not uncommon thing, comfortable in the heavy wrought iron chairs. They pointed to the food and poured him a glass of wine and resumed the conversation.

"I need a damned career," Tee said. They were always more frustrated when they were sober. "I can't stand my part time job. My kids are all gone; I'm living in an empty nest."

"I know the feeling," Molly agreed.

"The feeling of being useless," Paula added. She moved her chair to make room. "Here, sit here next to me good looking. Make me feel useful." She threw off the last of her wine. Paula was in one of her wanton moods. Bakewell was glad he was off the hook now, hoped he was anyway, never really sure with Paula.

"So, what are our skills? What credentials do we have?" Paula filled her glass instead of her plate.

"I'm great at sex. I might need some practice. It's been a while."

"Me too, it's probably my only skill," Paula again.

"Well you could always be prostitutes," Molly said, much out of character.

"I got here just in time," Bakewell said. Molly filled his plate.

"Who is going to pay to have sex with a couple of saggy housewives?" Tee asked.

"Lots of people would pay I'm sure…"

"Sure, there must be *some* segment of our society that would be thrilled to benefit from our vast expertise." Paula said, sitting up quickly, spilling wine on her blouse.

"Maybe the VA hospital," Molly said. "You could go to the blind wing."

Bakewell choked on his first bite. They drank from a large bottle of

Pinot Grigio, Molly's treat. She brought it because Bakewell said he'd never acquire a taste for the sour Chardonnay they preferred. By the third glass, the conversation turned to the behavior of their children.

"The little brats all live in sin. They don't give a shit what people think."

"One of them is always shacking up. I can't stand it. They just don't care how it looks."

"I think we're just jealous," Molly said, still out of character.

"And these young women will sit right there in your home, smiling sweetly and you know they're screwing your baby boys brains out!" Tee's outburst was more in character.

"I have more of a problem with the boys." Paula said. "I look at this little jerk kissing up to me and know he's getting it on with my daughter. Where the hell's her father at a time like that?"

"Andy, what would you do if your daughter brought a young man home and you knew she was living with him?"

"Shoot him."

"I'm serious. What am I supposed to do? It makes me so uncomfortable."

"Molly, if Nancy lived with a boy she would have gone to great lengths to keep me from knowing. I think *she did* believe I would've killed him."

"I think Molly's right; we're all just jealous," Tee said. "We missed all the fun. Here I was protecting my virginity when I could have been sleeping around."

"You don't mean that Tee. Say you don't."

"Oh give me a break, Molly."

They moved on to the dicey subject of their own virginity and Bakewell was shocked – he thought they could no longer shock him – when Tee and Paula described in some detail the remarkable events that led to their loss of virginity. What amazed him even more was *to whom* they had lost it.

"It all started with dancing," Paula said.

"Yes!" Molly broke in, "The nuns told us slow dancing would lead to sin."

"I think it was more the fast dancing," Tee said. "You could really get dirty, put some moves on them with the faster stuff. Get them creaming in their jeans. Right, Andy?"

Bakewell raised an eye in acknowledgement, not sure what he was acknowledging.

"*Yeah baby, you could shake that thing*!" Paula said. "Tee might be right. I know Kenny was always horniest after we'd been to Sunset or out at Idlewild working up a sweat on the dance floor."

Bakewell did a lot of listening, ate quietly, tried to look preoccupied when they addressed him. They were starting to needle him about his silence. "Honey, if you don't pick it up we're going to have to kick you out of the club."

"Go ahead. I could use the peace and quiet."

"Oh no, sexy man, we'll still use your deck. We need to have a man around."

He decided to plunge in, knowing it would be a mistake. "Let me guess, Paula. When you and Kenny got home after Idlewild he tried to get in your pants?"

"*Yuck*! Get in your pants? *Men are so disgusting*. Whoever came up with that expression?" It was Molly's turn.

"Mm, let me think." Bakewell looked up at the night sky, "The first time I remember hearing that expression was when I was…maybe in…the fifth grade?"

"Well, it's Neanderthal," Molly said.

"Yeah, Andy, I'd like to get in your pants. How would you like it if I said that to you?"

"Well, if you had asked thirty years ago Tee, I think I might have been the one who deflowered you."

"Well I wouldn't have said it," she said with emphasis.

"Well, I was pretty simple. You would've been safe."

"Yeah right, we all knew about how simple you were. You were the rage."

"Get in your pants. Get in my pants. Wow. Let's all get in someone's pants. Isn't that a turn on?" Paula mocked.

Bakewell knew he should have kept quiet and said as much.

"Just keep trying." Molly smiled across the candlelight.

"Yeah, but try to raise it a notch; we're ladies, you know."

Bakewell wanted to say something about ladies, potty mouths, and the tilt of their conversation, but kept his counsel.

Tee brought a CD player and struggled to plug it in. "There's an outlet right there on the wall you dumb shit," Paula said, pointing to the outlet.

"Hits of the '60's," Tee crowed.

"Andy, you were a great dancer. Is that how you got into Katherine's pants?"

"I'm not going there, Tee. I'm here to listen. Kick me out of the club."

"No, no Andy boy, time to fess up. We all want to know about our best friend?"

"There is no way I'm going to tell you trashy women about the first time I made love to my wife."

"I like the sound of that: 'Trashy women.'" Tee said gleefully.

"Me too," Paula added, intent on pursuing the subject. "Come on big boy. How did you do it?"

"Fuck you Paula."

"Andy Bakewell, nice talk!" He never used bad language in front of them. "We just want a little information."

"You too, Tee."

"All right if you insist, but you other girls are gonna have to leave."

Only Molly was quiet, watching intently. She and Katherine had been closest. Bakewell knew what she was thinking, softened his look, lines cracking about his eyes, smiled at her, sharing an intimate moment, while the sound of *Moon River* came over the speakers. "She was a virgin, Molly," he spoke softly, reassuring Katherine's lovely friend, knowing she wanted reassurance. In that distant time, virginity and the sharing of it was supposed to be a tender, and hopefully, blessed moment. He and Molly still felt that way, despite the outrageous turn their conversations took. Bakewell thought Tee and Paula probably felt the same way, even though they would protest cynically.

"That song always makes me cry," Molly said, looking away.

"Everything makes you cry, Molly."

"She's right. You cry at TV commercials."

"Only Hallmark commercials, and once in a while a commercial at Christmas time."

The music changed to Dion's *"Run-around Sue."* Paula pulled at Bakewell's shirt, singing *Hey, hey, dum-diddy-a-diddy*. "Come on boy, you were always the best dancer."

"I can't; I forgot how."

"You can't forget! It's like riding a bike."

"Or having sex."

"Well, I just can't, I'm a widower."

Silence fell over all three women. They stared at him, momentarily surprised. It only lasted seconds before they burst into laughter and pointed at him derisively. "My God! He's using *the dead wife* excuse." Tee's eyes filled with tears and laughter.

"Andy, that is pretty low."

"Nobody loved to dance more than Katherine, Andy. She would want you to dance, not use her as an excuse."

"All right, give me a break." Bakewell got up, grabbed Paula and spun her very fast. Tee and Molly howled. Then they both got up and joined them. When the music changed, all three women lined up and sang *The Lion Sleeps Tonight*. They were off-key and awful. Bakewell sat back down, applauded dutifully. They knew every word. Later he danced with each of them, but only to the fast numbers. None of them wanted to be seen in his arms dancing to something slow or romantic.

***

Two nights later Bakewell was out at the pool with Nancy's children. Julie was up on the boulders and he held her hand while she made her way across the rocks, navigating from one flat spot to the next, crying delightedly at her success while the tri-colored puppy, kept a careful distance just above. The pool was covered; the heavy fabric stretched tightly below the boulders. After several trips Julie tired of the game and Bakewell put her down. As they made their way through the pine straw, Nancy bent and picked up a wine glass. Bakewell rolled his eyes.

"So, how are the girls lately?"

"Into dancing now, and doing sing-a-longs."

Nancy giggled. "I love your newfound gang, Dad." Going up the steps she stopped to remove an empty bottle from the neglected gardenia plant. "Left over, after 'teen town?'" Nancy raised her brow, her brown eyes widening. "What, Tuesday's Pinot Grigio night?"

Bakewell enjoyed her amusement, put his hand on her shoulder and pulled her to him affectionately and stared across the backyard lost in thought. Nancy looked up to her father, reading his thoughts, hugging him in return. When she pulled away, she wiped the corner of her eye. "They all loved Mom so much; I guess their affection just spilled over on you."

"I guess," he answered. "They do a fair amount of spilling."

"Mom always thought they would be vying for your affections after she was gone."

"They were…at first, but now…" he shrugged, "I guess I'm just one of the girls."

"We all love you, Dad." Nancy squeezed his arm and picked Julie up and held her close as she looked into her father's eyes. "Everybody loves you, Dad."

Bakewell returned the look, eyes creasing, filled with tenderness. There was trouble ahead. He would have to tell her soon, couldn't put it off much longer. He leaned over and kissed the top of Julie's head. His girls filled him with pride, made him think what a fine job Katherine had done. He and Nancy looked up to the October sky, and Bakewell silently thanked God for his daughter, asked God for deliverance. He didn't want to go on anymore. He was tired and wanted to quit. With so much life insurance it would be the perfect time to go. He was worth more dead than alive. If only he wasn't so afraid to die…. He wished he had Katherine's faith. He wished she were there to counsel him.

"So how was the trip?"

"Okay."

"Just okay?" Bakewell was always curious about Ned's outings.

Ned nodded to Dolly as she put his drink on the table. "Not as good as normally. We're one guy short now, you know, so it's not in kilter like before."

"Who's missing?"

"Horse."

They were in the usual place, in the back, where it was too dark to read the menu. Bakewell called it the aphotic zone. A word Ned had never tried. It didn't matter; the menu had been committed to memory.

"Horse!"

"Yeah. He's fell out of disfavor with them guys. I think it was over women."

"Women?"

"Yeah. Once he got rid of them coke bottles he thought he was God's gift. Started chasin skirts and hangin out. Couldn't answer the bell mornings for their tee times."

"He doesn't wear glasses anymore?"

"No. We all thought he'd be runnin little old ladies down at the bus stop, but apparently it worked out."

"He had laser surgery?"

"Yeah, he got that radiation carrot-totomy and ain't blind no more. It's a miracle I guess, what they can do with that radiation stuff."

"Radial keratotomy?"

"That's it. Got his eyes fixed by some nuk-u-lar physician."

"He and Beasley were inseparable."

"Not no more, Bease wants to drink and golf like the rest of us. He don't want be wearin out what's left of his reservoir, burnin the midnight candle, instead of restin himself for another day of ex-capades. Bease is pretty much in charge of the trips mostly, and he says Horse is out, so I guess he's out. Shame really, now the man can see his own golf ball and he wants to look elsewhere to be makin a score. He couldn't putt for shit through them coke bottles. Now he can see and he don't wanna play no more."

"I thought Horse was the entertainment."

"He was. Him and Bease was always cuttin up. It was hilarious; but ain't to be no more. Horse could make a mortician laugh, but with his newfound looks, he only is lookin elsewhere. Truthfully, I miss the guy, but he's on the wrong trail, and disfavor is disfavor. What a character though – shame."

Ned didn't care where they ate so Bakewell varied the luncheons.

More and more it was Rick's. Rick's was on the way home and it was raining; they were headed home afterwards. Ned suggested they "have one." "One" was a half glass of vodka on ice with four large olives skewered to a swizzle stick. Ned was in the mood to drink lunch more now that the end was near.

"Fuckin shame, really, but that's life I guess," Ned continued. "Be nice if the world coulda give us a break other than the ones we got. Be nice if we coulda retired like normal people and went home and played with our grand kids and maybe a little golf and fishin got done too."

"We got what we got, Ned; there's no point in complaining. To tell the truth I'm not all that crazy about this world." Bakewell put some money on the table to signal he'd had enough. He would nurse one drink while Ned had several. "There's got to be something out there besides fighting and feuding, money worries and dealing with all this lying and cheating we face everyday."

"You deserve more than this Andy. God's fuckin you over pretty good."

Bakewell held up his hand. "Ned, please. No sacrilege."

"Well, you know what I mean. It just don't seem fair you got so much trouble for all the trouble you went to for people that was in trouble all these years."

Bakewell was silent. He was very discouraged; he looked at Ned and shook his head. "It's the way it works out. Not everybody ends up like Job."

"Who's Job?"

"The Book of Job; comes right before the Book of Psalms."

"So who's Job?"

"Job had a bad time of it for years. God put all the bad luck in the world on him. He lost everything, but hung in there and never gave up faith. In the end God rewarded him with lots of stuff."

"What kind of stuff?"

"Sheep, camels, oxen, a thousand she-asses, the kind of stuff that represented wealth in the Bible."

"Well we spent most our lives together tryin to keep our asses out of cracks. I don't need no more asses, she or he, and we sure as fuck don't need no camels or oxes."

"Well God also blessed him with more children, sons and daughters. His daughters were supposed to be the most beautiful in all the land. Job lived for another 140 years after things worked out. He got time to enjoy life."

"Judas priests! More kids, more problems. One thing I know is, you've got kids, you got too many headaches. You ain't got enough money in the world for dealin with kids. Who the fuck wants to be a hunnert'n forty and have kids to deal with too? Fuck. What was God thinkin givin that old sunufabitch kids at that age?"

“Well that was how Job ended up.” Bakewell couldn’t restrain a smile.

“Sounds like God fucked over Job too, only he waited longer.”

No Way Out

It was another week of sleepless nights, just like the dark time before when he and Ned made their comeback. They had kissed rings, bowed before the bank's unhappy administration, genuflected before their largest creditors and got extended terms. It was the toughest period of their lives. Humiliated and intimidated, Bakewell turned to prayer, called on the Holy Spirit, asked Him to come to his aid and give him the resolve to keep going. He later said it was the Holy Spirit that allowed them to survive. Ned had called it "dumb luck," had attributed it to hard work, but Bakewell still remembered Ned's favorite expression at the time – *Please Jesus.* They paid off their debts, didn't leave anybody hanging, paid the interest too – three over prime with the doubters – became profitable again, never once considered bankruptcy or leaving somebody unpaid. The nightmare was back.

Tranquilizers put him to sleep, but had a 4-hour endurance that left him awake in the middle of the night. He'd learned the expression, "Three o'clock in the morning courage," long before he had to get reacquainted with the phenomenon a second time. Courage at three in the morning was hard to find. It was a dark time when everything crept up. Nothing had taxed his confidence and threatened his self-esteem like the impending bankruptcy of those years. That nightmare lasted fifteen terrible months. If just one creditor had called their debt, they would have gone "Blub , blub, blub," to quote Ned. But their reputation and the relationships they'd forged saved the day. They were asked to sign personal guarantees and did so unhesitatingly.

"Whatta we gonna do, bub?" Ned had asked.

"Put one foot in front of the other, come in each day, work as long and hard as we can and, if nobody calls our debt, do it all over again the next day."

Ned's willingness to trust his younger partner, together with his amazing ability to build relationships, got them through. They reinvigorated the company with a morale that produced efficiency and higher margins. Their reputation for profitability later made them the target for raiding, made their dissolution even more discouraging. Men they had hired at seventeen celebrated fortieth birthdays in their shop, then abandoned them for the competition. Fifty cents an hour induced most to walk from the two guys who had lent them money, attended their weddings, celebrated the births of their children, practically heard their confessions. Ned had been a surrogate father for some of the sadder cases. They'd put on Christmas parties, held picnics in the fall, anything to build a family atmosphere, build morale. They worked hard at it. In the end it meant nothing.

After one of his more inspirational speeches at years end, Bakewell was humbled when one of his guys, a veteran of twenty years said, "You're the smartest man I've ever known," and added, "You can count on me for the duration." Another, slightly under the influence, said, "Andy I'd walk over dead bodies for you." The first one left after the initial raid, owing Bakewell $200. The second lasted one more season before he jumped, saying he, "Needed to be with the other guys." Neither gave notice, just didn't show up for work, leaving the rest of the crew to take up the slack, adding to the demoralization, which later caused more defections. It was a grueling process strung out over a year. By the time it was over they had lost more than the work force. They lost sales and a lot of self esteem, along with $400 grand. They couldn't decide if the money or the defections hurt the most.

"It's like losin my own kids." Ned complained.

"Worse. It's like having your kids spit in your face."

After too many sleepless nights and too many days trying to squeeze profit from non-existent places, the strain began to show. Bakewell began to lose weight and as the good weather faded, his usually tanned face turned sallow. In early November, on a blustery, overcast day, Nancy came into his office and closed the door, fixing him with an intent stare, "What gives Dad?"

Her intelligent eyes searched her father's. He had developed a hacking cough and his immune system appeared to be maxed out as he cleared his throat. "It looks like were done. I'm going to have to shut down as soon as the weather runs out."

"We lost the lawsuit, didn't we?"

"Yes."

"Big time?"

"Big time, add it to the other mistakes, the disaster we've tried to ride out the last few years, it adds up to more than we can handle."

Fear showed in her face, "There's no way out?"

"No way out."

Nancy was silent for a few minutes. Bakewell couldn't think of anything to add. "So, when's the last paycheck?"

"Probably around Thanksgiving."

"That'll make for a great holiday." There were no tears. "What about Andy and the new baby? What about his family?"

"Everyone's looking for talent. With his education he should do fine." As an afterthought, Bakewell added, "He can always be an architect." Nancy nodded in resigned agreement. She loved her big brother, couldn't imagine a business life without him.

"Have you told him?"

"No."

"Why?"

"Because I need him right now."

"You can't lay him off right before winter, Dad."

"Winter's here, Nancy; why worry them now. I hate to worry you with it. Worrying doesn't help much does it?" She didn't answer. "We'll wait until the time comes. I'll give you both a severance to help you through the winter."

"Can you do that?"

"Why not? If I'm going down for everything I have, I might as well put another thirty or forty grand into the pot. It's the least I can do for my children." There were tears now. "Nancy, we were probably doomed after we got raided. I only kept it going for our people, and they left anyway. I should have shut down then; we were debt free."

"What will you do dad? Where have you got to go?"

"I don't know yet."

"Will you be able to keep the house?"

"No."

"Where will you go?"

"I'm thinking I might go into a monastery."

"Dad!"

"I'm serious." Bakewell moved to a chair, not wanting to be behind his desk when he talked to her. It wasn't an employer/employee conversation. "I'm beat up, worn out by the dreadful behavior. We used to compete on a higher plane. We didn't like each other in the old days anymore than we like the competition now, but it wasn't so vicious. Ned and I are a couple of dinosaurs; we're not in tune with the times, the current morality. We think we're supposed to like our people, take care of them, but they took off anyway…. Who knows anymore?" He leaned his head back against the wall. "They hurled themselves on the rocks. What did leaving us do for them? The bad guys are broke now, just like us, gone back to wherever. Everything here is ruined. Who profited from the whole fiasco?"

Nancy didn't have an answer, sat very still, looking very young and very vulnerable.

"Nobody has any loyalty anymore. They're like baseball players," Bakewell said, disgust dripping from his voice. "It's the *I gotta do what's best for my family* syndrome, some arrogant kid, walking for more money, forgetting what the team did for him, forgetting who gave him his chance." Bakewell got up and walked around the room. "That's probably what created this whole miserable era, that and not being required to serve your country anymore. There's just no loyalty in the world. The heroes of your generation are a bunch of 'me first' pukes. They should have had to go through boot camp, learn the buddy system, learn something about loyalty."

"Not all of them."

"Yeah, all of them."

"We kept some of them."

"They stayed because we gave them a raise, stayed and held a gun to our head. They'd leave in a heartbeat for one more nickel." He sat down again. "I hate this business. I'm washed up, and I'm worn out. All I want to do anymore is hide. The bills are piling up and we have no working capital. We'll stop making money any time now, then its over."

Nancy sat in his office for a long time. At one point she sighed quietly, said, "The poor man gets his ice in winter."

"Whatever that means."

Bakewell looked at his daughter, his heart breaking, pain in his eyes showing, pain deep in his chest, aching. He was defeated and hated for her to see it. There was no helping it; he couldn't help anything anymore. He was out of pretense. He had been her knight in armor, her daddy, the one who made it stop hurting, the one who made the bad people in her dreams go away. He was helpless and felt worse about letting her down than about what would happen to him. He had always been his own worst critic. He was a failed career – his worst nightmare had come true. *It's not how you start; it's how you finish.*

Bakewell's cell phone rang; he answered it reluctantly.

"Sorry bro, no can help."

"Why not?"

"Why not *please*." Bakewell waited. "There are three sets of prints on the glass. One belongs to a kid with so many "priors" it reads like a racing form, probably the bus boy. One belongs to a thirty something, got busted on a minor drug rap once, did a couple of overnights. She's okay. Her license was revoked about five years ago, but its okay now. The last set doesn't ring true. Something's not right."

"Meaning?" Bakewell welcomed the opportunity to focus on something else.

"Meaning something's not right. Those big computers do funny stuff sometimes. This one's in Washington, *The Big One*. Every once in a while we can get a favor from them. I tried, because *you have been such a wonderful friend*."

"And you know I would do it for you."

"Yeah, right. I don't know what it is, Andy, but my mole says he thinks the prints were on file once and were removed. 'The computer's acting funny' is the way he put it. It's almost unheard of to remove prints from the file. They've got em going back to Moses. They never remove them."

"Well thanks for the help, Denny."

"Andy, listen; let's get together and talk."

Bakewell watched his daughter get up to leave. "I can't do it today Denny; I've got too many problems. Let me call you."

"Andy, wait a minute. We need to talk, need to talk right away."

"Okay, I'll call you back. I've got fires to put out right now."

"Shit. You'll never call me. Listen, we need to talk real soon."

"Why?"

"Call me back quick, I'll meet you wherever; don't put me off, okay?"

"Okay, I'll call you."

"Please don't forget bro; we need to talk."

Papa Proust's

There was nothing to add after Bakewell hung up. Nancy looked at him gloomily. He didn't know if she was suffering for herself, for him or for them all. It didn't matter. She met his look and left. Bakewell sat at his desk looking at the mounting payables. He moved the paperwork around, a futile gesture, wondered what Murphy wanted that couldn't wait, looked at the number on his cell phone and dialed.

"Murphy."

"So, what's so important we need to talk?"

"Andy, good. Pick a place, and I'll meet you."

"Why the rush, what's going on?"

"Pick a place."

"Hell Denny, I don't care where we meet. It's the middle of the afternoon. We've both had lunch."

"You remember that little place down on the Hill on the north side of the highway? We used to go in there when we were kids?"

"Papa Proust's? I thought that place was gone years ago."

"That's it. I'll meet you there whenever you say."

"I can meet you right now. There isn't much going on…not much that's positive right now. When do you want to meet?"

"I'm fifteen minutes away."

"Okay, I'll be there. Denny, this isn't going to be heavy is it?"

Murphy hung up.

Papa Proust's was an old fashioned tavern, dating back to the Depression. When they were in high school they used to try and get served there. It only worked on certain days. After they were married he and Murphy would stop there for a quick drink on the way home. When he entered, it was dark inside. He looked around, waiting for his eyes to adjust. There were three guys at the bar. Night-shifters or non-shifters. Bakewell didn't think much of guys who sat in bars in the middle of the afternoon, thought again: *what the hell you're here, don't be too quick to judge*. He went across the linoleum and sat at a plastic table trimmed in chrome. The floor was uneven and he turned the chair and leaned it against the wall. The bartender ignored him. Within minutes Murphy came through the door, also pausing to adjust to the darkness. He looked at the bartender and raised two fingers before crossing to Bakewell. The bartender arrived with the two beers before Denny could get comfortable at the tilted table.

They shook hands quickly, no games this time. Denny put his big forearms on the table and leaned in. Bakewell was silent, observant, wondering. Denny waited for him to say something. When he didn't, Denny opened, "Okay Andy, what gives?"

"What do you mean?"

Denny frowned, upset.

"This isn't going to be heavy is it? You're not going to give me another lecture about friendship?"

"You're being sarcastic, but I'll take that as a compliment."

Bakewell leaned back in his chair, recalled better times. "You remember the way we used to come in here and brag about who got luckier at the altar? The way we used to brag about our little boys and tell each other how beautiful our little girls were?"

"I remember it all, Andy. Who'd a thought a couple of turkeys like us would have done so well in marriage?" Bakewell smiled and drank his beer. They sat quietly looking around, remembering. "How long's it been since you were here?" Bakewell shook his head. He didn't know. "I still stop by sometimes." Denny said, "It's not a regular stop, but it brings back memories of the old days." He took a long pull on his beer and raised his hand for the barkeep.

"The good old days," Bakewell raised his beer in toast.

"The days are still good, Andy. I know you're hurting, but you've got a great family and a good life left. Don't quit on it yet."

"Is this why we're meeting? I'm going to get psychoanalyzed?"

"No, you got Ned for that. How is that monster son of a bitch anyway?" Bakewell nodded affirmatively. "Ned's a good old boy. I've always liked him." Bakewell waited. Denny took his time getting to the point. Finished his beer and put it on the table. "Andy, something's going on with you. That guy you were checking on? He's important. They told me to go away in as few words as possible. The guy I was talking to? There was real caution in his voice. You never want to upset certain kinds of people. I think you're looking for trouble."

"Denny," Bakewell leaned into the conversation also, "How hard is it to change your identity?"

"What?" Murphy put his hands on the table, "Not hard, depending on what you're trying for. Why?" He leaned back again, stretching.

"You're a guy I can square with so I'm going to do it. I'm in trouble."

"Not with the law? Tell me not with the law Andy. You got problems with the IRS or something like that? Is that why you had me checking on this guy?"

"No, nothing like that, I've got some serious problems with money, that's all."

"You want to fake an identity?"

"Yes."

"Why?"

"Because I'm worth a lot more dead than alive and I just thought if the kids could collect on my insurance I could disappear and join a monastery somewhere far away."

"They got laws against that big time, Andy. Lots of people have tried to do dumb stuff like that. They would find out about it and prosecute you and you wouldn't get the money, only a lot of embarrassment. You would be front-page news too. It would be awful, forget about it."

"Well tell me how you do it anyway. I'm curious. Can it be done?"

"Not the way you're thinking, that's big time felony, and they watch for it… closely."

"I see it done on those TV shows about crime all the time."

"That's different. People are always disappearing. You can fake an ID and move to another place simple enough – if nobody's really looking for you. But if the FBI or somebody important's looking, they will find you in no time."

"Tell me how you do it."

"No. You might do something really stupid. You already got me stressed about this guy with the nonexistent fingerprints."

"Just tell me how they do it on TV. How can it be done?"

Murphy gave Bakewell a penetrating stare, part of the game, tried to make him look off, they had been doing it for years. Bakewell held his gaze.

"Aw shit, you'll find out anyway. I'll save you the time." He pushed the empty bottles away to make room for his hands. Denny talked with his hands. "For small time scammers, it's simple enough. You get a fake library card and some other identification stuff. You go to a records office and look up a birth certificate and make a copy of it. Later you pretend it's yours. Get a social security card from somebody else or make your own."

"How do you make a social security card?"

"All you need is a number. When's the last time somebody asked to see your social security card? It's probably buried in your wallet somewhere, stuck to the leather." Bakewell handed Murphy his social security card. "Nobody pays any attention to these things, even though they can kill you with a scam if they get your number. You put it on a copier and copy it and change the numbers or the name and copy it to another card and rough it up and leave it on the dash in the sunlight or someplace like that and let it age just like this one. Put a new number on it from the same era, somebody you know is already dead, better still, use his name. You'll need a little red ink. That's all. After that you open a bank account and get another driver's license and you're in business, just so long as nobody important is looking for you."

"It sounds too simple."

"It is. It's for small timers looking to get lost, but if somebody wants to find you they can. If you do something really stupid, like you just suggested, you're dead meat in no time."

"Thanks for the tip."

"Oh man, Andy. You got me real worried. Why don't you level with me?"

Bakewell didn't respond. Denny waited for him to talk, but suspected he was done. Silence between the two quiet men had always been comfortable. The sipped their beer and turned the bottles absently. They talked about life and family for another thirty minutes. It was good to catch up. Bakewell continued to discover how much he'd always liked Denny Murphy. Denny was Truman-like, elementary man, no deceit, straight forward, no bullshit; things were always black and white, with Denny. He didn't get crossed up with ambiguities. He lived in the daylight; there was no place for haze in Denny's world.

"Andy, I don't have any money, you know that, but what I've got is yours. How can I help you?"

"You can't Murph, and I wouldn't let you if you could. I'm going broke, and I just need to face up to it. I really don't mind that much. I just hate to take so many people down with me."

"Like who?"

"Like Ned and Nancy and her family, like my son Andy, and a few guys who stuck with me over the years."

"People get along all right after they go broke, Andy, especially people like you, people who have faith. Nancy's young, she'll bounce back. My guess is Ned's in good enough shape to live on social security and a penny ante job somewhere the fish bite."

"It's not that simple. We owe a lot of people. It's going to wipe us out, Ned, me, hurt Nancy badly. I've got a gal working for me that's got major problems with a daughter. I can only give them so much before I run out. I can't live with the idea of not paying somebody I owe, somebody that trusted me."

"I believe you. Despite all your arrogance, and your fucking social climbing, I always knew there was the same decent, honest son of a bitch I knew before, deep down in there." Denny pointed at Bakewell's chest. "I can't see you welshing on a debt."

"Unfortunately I can't see me doing it either; that's the problem."

There was a long silence. Murphy asked Bakewell if he wanted another beer. Bakewell declined. They reminisced for another few minutes, neither man was comfortable at the table, but neither wanted to be the one to leave first. Bakewell said finally, "Denny I appreciate your concern. You're a decent guy, a good guy, you know that."

"Took you long enough to say it."

"Come on. You and Helen are the two best people I've ever known."

Denny nodded, content. "Are we gonna get you back now because you need friends, because you're in trouble, or because you figured out you fucked up and left us for the Annie Gunn crowd?"

"You will never know how sad it makes me to think I left the two of you here in town to join the Annie Gunn crowd. All I can do now is apologize."

Denny nodded again, smiled gratefully. "I'll tell Helen you've rejoined the real world. She'll be delighted. And I'll also tell you this, she never gave up on you the way I did. She never said an unkind word about you all these years."

It was Bakewell's turn to smile. "That's a nice thing to hear. It makes me happier than finding a lost check. Helen is one of the truly great people in this world."

"So was Katherine, Andy. You did pretty good there. I grieve for you every time I think on it."

Bakewell hated to break it off. "I need to get going. I don't want you to feel obligated to worry about me."

"How'm I not gonna worry, Andy?"

"Well, keep me in your prayers, and I'll do the same. But don't burn a lot of emotional calories worrying over me, and tell Helen not to either. I'll live through it."

Denny studied Bakewell for a moment, "Listen, I'm afraid I'm going…I'm going – to quote our buddy Ned – I'm going to have to add to the burden of your load."

Bakewell frowned curiously.

"Andy, this guy you made inquiries on? You might have turned over some pretty big rocks, might have disturbed the stream too much. I'm not so sure, but maybe you're going to have your phone tapped. That's why I wanted to meet you here. If you are in some kind of other trouble, trouble you don't want to talk about, and it's big time, heavy trouble, watch out what you say over the phone."

Bakewell sighed deeply, shook his head in frustration, looked at Denny.

"You got a Nextel?" Denny asked. Bakewell nodded. "Nextel's are good. The snoops can't tap into them yet. They will soon enough, but as far as I know they are still secure. Use it to talk on if you have anything incriminating to say."

Algonquin

Bakewell reluctantly met Maggie for dinner in late October, this time at her club. Her father had been a member of Algonquin for many years. Maggie had been raised on the club's green landscape and around the pool. She loved the club and knew most of the old timers. It was easy for her to re-acclimate as a social member. They were glad to have her back. She didn't play golf or use any of the facilities, spent lots of money in the dining room, where she felt comfortable eating alone, played bridge with the ladies occasionally, and paid her dues each month. She no longer used the pool, though she had once reigned there, unrivaled, moving about the deck in a white bathing suit that the male members appreciated, especially the older generation. She had been the darling of the deck chair crowd.

They arrived separately, Maggie coming in from the west, Bakewell, westbound on his way from the office. She was waiting in the bar when he got there, surrounded by gray haired members in finely tailored clothes. She introduced him to her admirers and they had a first drink visiting there before moving on to enjoy the comfortable surroundings of the old dining room. Bakewell was reluctant to drink but felt obligated, not sure where the evening was headed. He was sure he would meet quite a few people he knew before the evening was over and wanted to be sober.

As a kid he had caddied at the club and told Maggie a story about caddying for an infamous member, a real life *Titanic Thompson*, candidly admitting he didn't know what he was doing as a caddy, while the guy needed a caddy of singular reputation. Bakewell had not been up to the task. The problem was none of the other caddies would work his bag and Bakewell managed to rattle the clubs in the middle of his backswing several times getting him off to a bad start.

"He was very profane and cursed in front of us tender-aged little boys. Most of the kids populating the caddy yard were less than fifteen and this guy made a habit of blaming everyone for his mistakes." Maggie was beaming as he told the story; her blue eyes sparkled liked the diamonds glittering from her ears. Bakewell warmed to the subject, sensing her appreciation. "After fanning a 9-iron out on Algonquin Lane on the 3rd hole, he threw the club in a moment of fury that scared us all. I think his playing partners were scared too.

"The golf club went down the street, bounced once way up in the air and hit the windshield of a car. It was in the days before shatterproof glass, and the club ended up on the front seat. It made a hell of a noise going through the window. I had to retrieve it from inside the car, and there were big shards of glass everywhere. The owner was working in his yard and saw me in the car and came over. He really wasn't that bad about it, just wondering what was going on, so I told him. He wanted *Titanic* to make amends but *ol'*

Titanic – the kids all used that sobriquet – he wanted to finish the round first, and they got into a furious argument."

"*Sobriquet*, I can't remember the last time I heard that word." Maggie said, teasing.

Bakewell dummied up, looked around the room sheepishly. As he fingered his drink she put her hand on his wrist. "Come on *touchy*, finish the story. I've a feeling there's a punch line." Bakewell looked at her guardedly. "Come on, tell me the story; it's not that easy to get you to talk, you know. I promise I won't interrupt."

"*Titanic* stormed off, *with his club,* and told the owner of the car he'd get back to him. The guy called the police." Bakewell stopped again.

"That's it? That's the whole story?"

"Pretty much." He sipped his drink.

"Come on, you're holding back. Tell me the rest of the story." Bakewell gazed at her; there was little trust between them, at least on his end. She always worried him. He wondered why he was there. "Please, Andy, tell me the rest. Use all the big words you want. I love to hear you talk." She was sincere.

He proceeded, carefully. "The police came in under the railroad where it spans the creek, where the creek flows across the fairway of the 5th hole. You know the place?"

"Yes. It's been years since I was out there, but I remember the place."

"There were two of them. They took the guy from the fifth green, arrested him. He was belligerent, unbelievably dismayed. I still remember the incredulous look on his face. It was funny the way they approached him."

"How?"

"Well, the older cop was a sergeant, I guess he was along for moral support; he made the younger one do the arresting, but the old cop kept touching his hand to the plastic grip of his pistol. No kidding! The guy finally gave up and went with them. They took him out under the railroad overpass."

"My God! Was it my father?"

"You thought it was your father? No, no. Your dad had more class. This guy was a big lard ass, who liked to intimidate people. I never understood why anyone ever played with him; anyway, I never got paid. I was a lousy caddy."

Maggie laughed at him in a familiar way he remembered from long ago, ending in a long humorous sigh that meant, but didn't say, "Oh Bakewell, you were always such a screw up."

"I hated the job. My mom insisted I go to work that summer, and it was the only place I could find. I think I lasted three weeks, and I always got paired in front or behind this same guy. He was part of the nine o'clock game. He wouldn't let me caddy in his foursome after that, though. God has a sense of humor, I guess."

Dinner came in carefully spaced intervals; there were more drinks, and wine with the meal. Bakewell hadn't intended on more than two drinks, but the atmosphere was quiet and chummy. Algonquin was the best private club when it came to atmosphere, a place conducive for drinking, relaxation and conducting business. He enjoyed himself carefully, actually liked being there with her. It was fun, reliving a part of his life so far in the past. She had always been a lot of fun when she was behaving, but she was dangerous and, despite the alcohol, he was restrained, cautious. She obviously orchestrated the entire evening. She knew all the members, or maybe it was the other way round; they all knew her or made a point of knowing her. She was mildly famous in the world of politics.

Bakewell knew many of the members. People stopped at their table all evening. They stayed very late; the place was nearly empty. Maggie could hold her liquor; they both knew it. He got quieter as the evening progressed, letting her chatter on, which she did with humor and skill. She was an excellent conversationalist, anecdotal. Her wonderful, confident charm had grown and matured in the big world she lived in now. She was quick, always ahead of him. He knew better than to match wits with her, so he kept up a steady stream of subtle compliments, trying to keep her off guard. She picked up on the ruse, let it go on for a long time, but toward the end of the evening she'd had enough and began to challenge him, skillfully switching gears, changing the subject.

"So who are your friends? Do you still see those old baseball players?"

"No, not much; I run into one occasionally."

"How do you spend your time, or maybe I should ask who you spend your time with? Is there a lady in your life, since Katherine?"

"No, I haven't been looking for a lady." Bakewell thought a moment, looked at Maggie, amusement showing.

"What? You're going to tell me you have someone aren't you." He continued to smile, wondering if he should breach the subject. "What, tell me?"

"Well, I have a little group, this peculiar little group of ladies – Katherine's friends. They come regularly." Maggie was unsure, looking for more, waiting. "They come for dinner, do a lot of drinking. It gets rowdy sometimes. They were all good friends of Katherine's, actually were a big help at the end. They still come by, and we have dinner. I listen mostly, while they bash their former husbands. Its funny most of the time, but to tell the truth, I think it's therapy for them, for us, for all of us I suppose."

"How often do you meet?"

"It varies; sometimes twice a week, sometimes more, sometimes less. They have a life and a schedule to keep, so it's not settled. Nancy refers to them as the Girls' Club; I'm an honorary member."

"They're not married?"

"No, all divorced. Katherine warned me about them before she died."

"Katherine must have known them well." He nodded, told her how supportive they had been. "I'll bet," she responded too quickly. He told her about the "predator bitches" label. Maggie laughed then. "They actually refer to themselves that way?"

"Prefer it."

"So you are surrounded by single women." He nodded. "Do any of them have designs on you?" She put her drink down quickly, held up one hand, "Don't answer that; I had no right to ask that question. It was tacky of me. I'm sorry."

"That's all right, I have no secrets."

"No, really, I'm happy you have so much company."

He offered a few stories about their get-togethers. Maggie wanted to move on, get past the subject. "So you have a plane?" she said, switching direction. "What started that?"

"I guess it was genetic."

"Genetic?"

"My dad was a pilot…during the war."

"I didn't know that. Your father was already gone when your brother died."

"Yes, my dad died in '52."

"How?"

"He was injured during the war, in a plane, shot up pretty bad. He actually went down more than once. He was shot down in the ocean near Bougainville first, then crashed in a place called New Georgia."

"Where?"

"In the Solomon Islands, in '43 or four. I'm not really sure. Brenden told me it was over the ocean again, but for some reason he managed to limp the plane to New Georgia. I vaguely remember him telling us he didn't want to ditch in the water because the plane was new; he wanted to get it to a runway. He ended up going down to New Georgia. I guess they had a runway. He didn't make it, crashed in the ocean, supposedly right at the end of the field, but they rescued him. The last time was the bad one, of course. He was shot down over New Guinea somewhere."

"He must have been a war hero, like your brother."

"Brenny thought so. He talked about him all the time."

"You never told me. Your dad was part of history."

"We're all part of history, Maggie, your dad at Anzio, my dad in the Solomons. Just wait long enough and somebody will memorialize us." She didn't respond, smiled, waiting for him to continue, determined for him to say more. "I guess my dad never really recovered. I only remember him as very crippled up."

She insisted he try a dessert he really didn't want. Maggie ordered a cognac for them both. They ate the raspberry dessert quietly. It was very good. Despite the fatigue of a gruesome week of angry collectors, and the numbing effect of the alcohol, his mind still continued to hum, ready for a quick shift in the soft mood. He was pretty far gone on the booze, but it only made him more cautious. He didn't want to stumble over his words, didn't want to make some gaff that might bring on her merciless wit. Like Katherine, she enjoyed making fun of him, but she could be ruthless. Katherine's humor was designed to tease him while at the same time adoring him. She never let anyone think anything else. Katherine had treasured him, and he had responded to her jests with an acquiescent shyness that made him even more lovable. With Maggie it was different, when she took her shots it was vindictive and brutal. It came from being up against two older brothers. Maggie had developed a thick skin in her youth. Bakewell didn't know anybody who had ever liked the Leary boys.

"Tell me about your brothers. I've never heard you speak of them."

"And you won't. My brothers were both perfect shits."

"How so?"

"In the usual shitty way. One of them found a lovely wife though, and they had one daughter before the divorce. I just adore her, but she is way off in Seattle and I rarely get to see her."

Maggie looked off across the room, remembering. He stared at her profile, which was fine. She looked back, saw him looking, "What?"

"I was just thinking how lovely you were when we were young."

"How lovely I was then? Thank you, Andy, such wonderful timing, such a perfectly timed thing to say, how lovely *I used to be.*"

"That's not what I meant. You're still beautiful; you know that. You hear it all the time."

Maggie smiled, not sure if she had taken offense. She could sense how tentative he was around her and was disappointed. She wanted him to relax. The alcohol hadn't worked the way she'd hoped. They watched each other in silence.

She was fun to be with, still carried herself with an intoxicating self-confidence. Bakewell enjoyed her, couldn't help it; she was infectious in her element. But he was still uncomfortable, even more so when one of her table-side admirers turned out to be somebody who had created adversity in his life. The place was crawling with architects and engineers – "stargazers," Ned called them. The stargazers had created more havoc in their business life than almost anyone else.

"Why can't you relax, Andy?"

Bakewell paused, another self-conscious smile crossing his face, "Maggie, spending time with you is like flying what we call *hard IFR* – it's very challenging, the simple surviving of it, very exciting, but it leaves you exhausted."

"Now I'm exhausting. Gee, I'm glad I spent so much money trying to get you drunk. You used to get sweeter when you drank, not meaner."

"It's a fine evening, and I'm having a fine time, in a fine place, with a fine woman. How's that?"

"You sure say fine a lot. You used to say beautiful."

"Maybe they both mean the same thing where you're concerned."

"Now that's a compliment I can live with. Drink your cognac."

"You drink it. I hate the stuff."

He had trouble forgetting their stormy past, remembered too many times when she had humiliated him, even though she seemed to have lost her mean edge. It was the alcohol he told himself. He was slowly becoming aware of how lonely she was, hadn't noticed it before. She seemed without place. Her loveliness was so comprehendible, even now, right there before him: to hear, to enjoy – but her loneliness…he hadn't expected loneliness. The way it was beginning to show surprised him. She didn't try to hide it.

"They don't dance here now, you know." He raised his eyes, meeting hers. "Do you remember how much we danced when we were young, how much fun we had on the dance floor?" Bakewell nodded. "You were such a lovely dancer, Andy, and such a lovely boy, so much fun to be with. I always loved to dance with you, loved to be with you."

"It was a long time ago, Maggie."

"You still remember. Tell me you still remember me."

"I remember. You were unforgettable."

"Thank you. That's a lovely thing to hear."

"Compliments are my specialty when I'm under the influence."

"And they're sincere. You stumble over them sometimes – *used to be so beautiful* – but I can hear sincerity in your voice."

"Used to be so lovely," he corrected.

"Are you under the influence?"

"Are you kidding?"

"No. Have we had too much to drink?"

"I'll say it again, are you kidding?"

"I hadn't really thought about it."

"I can't speak for you."

"I enjoy my drinking. I hope I'm not obnoxious."

"No. You do it well. Nobody would ever notice if you were under the influence."

"But you fear they might notice you?"

"I'm a contractor. We drink too much and everybody notices." Maggie smiled, dazzling the empty room. He thought for a moment, decided to proceed. "Maybe I'm just under the influence of you?"

"Wow, there you go again. Now that's a compliment."

"I forgot how pleasant it was to spend an evening in such a comfortable place, across from a woman who commands so much attention. You look very happy, surrounded by old friends, by so much attention. And I'll bet you don't get tired of it?"

"Did I just hear a voice from out of the past?"

"I think you might have."

"Thank you, and keep the compliments coming. Older women thrive on compliments you know."

"Maggie, I doubt you'll ever get old. I just can't picture it. I mean it."

"I know you do. You're sweeping me away by the way."

The comment brought him back. He knew he suffered from what his Girls' Club called "lack of companionship." He had the hormones, was growing more vulnerable because of them, but he hadn't expected to detect a softening in Maggie Walker's formidable character. It pulled hard against the current of his logic. He tried to keep a distance. He wouldn't step out on that limb again, the one she had sawed off so many times. He didn't care how long ago it happened. He would never forget; he didn't need her. He could find someone far less complicated if his needs got too far out of hand. The picture before him was tempting, but he would never be ready for her again. She was pure voltage and he knew absolutely nothing about her kind of electricity; she had taught him that years ago. Losing Katherine was pain enough; there would be no more complications in his life. It was reflection time, monastery time; he was past romance and their get-togethers were reckless for him and foolish for both of them. He became more guarded, even though the alcohol doggedly tried to numb his vigilance.

"So, you're still living in your home. No desire to sell it and move into something smaller?"

"No. My kids would be crushed. They love the house. Still like to get together there on weekends. They bring the little people. It's very pleasant, very homey. I love to have them. What father wouldn't?" It was a long sentence, and he heard his words starting to slur.

"I have thirty-five hundred square feet, not a soul in any other room. I don't know why I bought such a big place, but what the heck, I can afford it. It's sure not losing value."

"Well, Maggie if you can afford it *and I'm sure you can afford it,* why not?"

"I'm not ashamed of my money, Andy."

"Leary, you came wrapped in money." He didn't know why he said it, probably jealousy. Being broke was making him jealous of wealth.

"Bakewell, I didn't bring you here to be insulted. Do you really want to cross swords with me?" She was almost laughing at him.

"No, no," he said with emphasis, holding his hands up defensively. "No, I don't want to go there. I apologize. It was a jerky thing to say."

"Jerky. It was jerky. You were always jerky." She was chiding again with an old expression from the past, an olive branch he quickly seized.

"Let's go back to the compliments. I do those better when I'm drunk."

"You're not drunk."

"Yes, I am very drunk."

"I don't believe you. You're making too much sense."

"You wish I wasn't. It would make the compliments more meaningful." She looked squarely at him. She was good at it; always had been. He spoke defensively, "I appreciate your invitation tonight…both of them. Thank you for calling me too, for calling me first, Maggie."

"I called you because I knew you would never have called me." She held her glass between her fingertips her elbows resting on the tablecloth. "Why am I right in thinking you would never have called me, Andy?"

"I probably would have been afraid to…if I knew you were available." He emphasized *available.* "I don't get around much, socially anyway…not anymore."

"Don't get around much anymore…" she hummed from an old tune.

"I'm sure I would have thought…hell, I don't know what I would have thought. I probably would have thought you'd have told me to buzz off."

"I wouldn't have done that! Why would you think that?" She was hurt, hurt he would think she might reject him. "Andy, I just adore you as a man, as a husband and a father, even a grandfather now, although I can't picture it. You are just the best; everyone says so. Any time I mention you to someone who knows you I hear it again and again. Why can't you be comfortable with me tonight? And stop holding back. You look like you're about to jump. Relax. I'm not going to bite."

Bakewell nodded, didn't answer. "I promise," she added with a pouty face he'd seen countless times before. She leaned forward and put her hand on his arm reassuringly.

"It's a relief; you had the sharpest teeth." He sat up quickly. "No wait. I didn't mean that, either. I'm sorry. I need to *zip my mouth.* It's the booze." She waved across the room, and the waiter brought coffee. "Thank God," he said, "I couldn't have lasted one more round. It's a relief to know I might make it home."

"Hell, we can sleep in the car," she said vehemently. "The kind of money I spend here, they aren't going to evict me from the parking lot."

"Why can't I see you sleeping out in that parking lot in your fancy car?" he said, folding his hands, knitting his fingers together, back on firmer ground.

"Oh, you saw me on my back in a car more than once." She threw her head impudently. "I remember a few nights…" She intended to poke fun at him, to lighten the mood, her earrings flashed again in the candlelight as she tossed her head. Bakewell looked at the crumbs on the tablecloth, trying not to think of *those nights* or any like them. They troubled him now. He remembered Nancy at nineteen, absently wiped the condensation from his glass with one thumb. Maggie watched him closely. She let the erotic reference fall, leaned across the table conspiratorially, "I was looking for a gleam in your eye, not remorse."

He smiled apologetically, put his hands back on the table, fingers level, opened them, palms up, "I don't know how to respond. I remember it was a tender and romantic time, those nights in the car. I will always remember the tenderness and the affection. It is still clear. There was pure magic in those nights."

"Wow." Maggie looked like she had just gotten more mileage out of him than she ever expected. She shook her head. "You can say the loveliest things."

"But it was a lifetime ago. We each made other choices."

"And take them right back, so quickly I don't get a chance to really feel them before they're gone."

Bakewell was flooded with memories, surprised how easily it all came back. He didn't know if he should be ashamed, feel disloyal to Katherine, to her memory. He sipped the coffee, looked around self-consciously.

Maggie watched him closely. "Andy, what's happened to you? You used to be so full of confidence." She put her elbows on the table again, framing her cup and saucer. "What happened to the life, the attitude, the swagger you used to have? What did you do with your wonderful arrogance?"

He didn't answer, turned his head left and right, stretched. He was very tired. He looked at her again, into her deep blue eyes, wondered, needed more time, sighed, suspected the earrings she wore could solve a good percent of his financial problems. "Life's got me on the run right now, worn me down. I don't have much swagger left, and I've been trying to shed arrogance for years. Not too successfully, either."

It was very quiet in the big dining room. They were the last diners. Bakewell looked around, enjoying the peacefulness. Maggie watched him watch the room. Finally she spoke, another question. She smiled coyly, couldn't suppress it. "I've been wanting to ask someone like you, not you necessarily, but someone like you: what's it like to have sex with lots of kids in the house?"

"Surreptitious." He answered without hesitation, couldn't help smiling at her. "Almost like doing it in a car when you're not married." She waited, wanting elaboration, determined to make him say more. "Actually, Katherine liked to do it in the car, especially after the kids moved out. It was kind of her wacky period. We did it a lot in cars and boats, crazy places, once on a golf green one night down at the lake. I have to admit I loved it."

"Without children you get to do it anywhere you want. Joe liked the family room floor in front of the fireplace for a little while, but just when I started getting used to it he changed his mind; said it burnt his knees."

Bakewell nodded understandingly, remembered the sensation.

"Have you done well in business?" She asked, catching him off guard.

"No," he answered too quickly and with too much emphasis.

"What does that mean?"

"It means I've made too many mistakes and they've all come back to haunt me. I will probably die at my desk and I'm already burnt out. I don't want to think about it."

"You have nothing to retire on?"

"Huh, uh."

"What are you going to do?"

"I'm going to get up and leave if you feel sorry for me."

She looked at him closely, making fierce eye contact, the old Maggie. "I have about four and a half million in investments," she said, stirring her cup slowly without looking at it. "I own my house, everything I have, if I can help let me know."

"This is why we came in two cars. I can leave whenever…." he stopped himself in mid sentence and put up his hand. "Maggie, please. Don't do this. Don't make me walk out on you; I'm not sure I can walk right now."

"I'm sorry," she said; her remorse genuine. "Don't walk out on me, Andy. Really, I don't want you to leave. I'm enjoying you enormously. I forgot what a good listener you are, how much I've always liked you." She was contrite. "I wouldn't do anything to offend you. Really, I didn't mean to offend you."

"Well, I'm a little touchy about money right now." He put his napkin back on the table and smoothed it out. "It gets to be a big deal when you run out. I liked the sex talk better, let's get back to that." He grinned, inebriated, feeling ridiculous. There was silence while they collected their thoughts and the table was cleaned, both remembering.

"When exactly did you settle down? You were such a wild man. Was it a long time ago? And *when* did you get so humble?"

"Being broke will humble you. I settled down when I started changing diapers. Settled in would be more accurate. It has a humbling affect."

Maggie giggled. "I can't see you changing diapers. Most of my memories are of you playing baseball. Hitting and throwing that damned ball. You were very good. I loved to watch you play baseball you know. Did I ever tell you that?"

No. I remember how you used to bitch about the heat. I wasn't that good anyway."

"Did I? God, that's right. I remember the mosquitoes; they were the worst, but you played the hardball games in the afternoon. It was so unbearably hot. I never understood how you guys could you stand it in those wool uniforms?"

Bakewell remembered her sitting in the bleachers in a pair of shorts and a sleeveless blouse, wearing a stunning tan that contrasted with her stunning hair. Everybody on the team watched her. He suspected fantasizing infielders, not bad athletes, caused many of the errors. "Guys will make sacrifices when they're having fun."

"How can you afford a plane? Aren't they ghastly expensive?" It was on to another subject.

"I have partners who think I'm a better pilot than they are. They keep me around for comfort. I was their security blanket for a while. They're catching up though; they don't need me anymore. I'll probably sell my interest before the end of the year."

"How far can you go in it?"

"About four hours, that's all you can stand in a small plane."

"How far is that?"

"Maybe 700 miles."

"Is it old?"

"No, actually it's almost new."

"I have a place in Kiawah Island. How far is that?"

"It would be a long day. We would have to stop somewhere, maybe a place like Knoxville for lunch and then go on. Probably about six hours total."

"Mm. I have a place in Banff also."

"Up in Calgary? That's too far. I flew up there once. It's a 2 day flight."

"Well, I can make it in an afternoon. It's really lovely up there in July and August and, of course, during the skiing season."

"I was there in July; it snowed."

Maggie thought for a minute. "Are you a good pilot? Can you fly the way you used to play baseball?"

"I hope a lot better; I'd have been dead long ago if I couldn't."

"Well, maybe I would like to go for a ride in your plane sometime, but not to Kiawah."

"We could go somewhere close, just for lunch. Maybe we could fly down to the lake?"

"Let's plan a short ride when it's clear and we can see. I hope it won't be bumpy."

There was a small group in the bar and their revelry was the only sound left in the club. When they walked out to her car, Bakewell deliberately didn't take notice of the make, knowing it was expensive. They stood there in the lot under a light, and she reached up and put her hand behind his head and pulled him toward her.

"I'm not *that* inebriated, so don't misunderstand. I just wanted to give you this." She kissed his cheek and hugged him gently. It was pleasant.

"I had a nice evening. I owe you," he said.

"No you don't *owe me*. Let's do it again soon."

"Shall I follow you home?"

"No, it's way out of your way. Go home now and have a restful weekend. You look very tired; I'm worried about you."

"Do you think if you donate your body to science the medical students fool around with it?"

"I certainly hope so, Molly," Tee said, coming forward in her chair.

"That's terrible."

"Why not? Get one last little thrill? Especially with a younger man."

"God Tee, you are so bad."

"I don't think I would give my body to science," Molly resumed, "I bet they make fun of the bodies. Just think what they might say."

"Yeah. They'd say 'hey, get a load of the wrinkled up old lady with the perky little breasts'!" Paula pointed at Tee.

"That silicon never fails," Molly added, picking on her friend.

"Screw you, Paula. You've got a body full of silicon; without it you wouldn't have anything left. Everything else's been lipo-suctioned."

"Amen, Paula. You've got more incisions than anyone."

"You've spent a fortune in the body shops," Tee, relentless. "The only difference between you and Frankenstein is somebody got paid to hide the scars."

There was forced laughter all around. They were trying to lighten the mood. They had spent the afternoon at Katherine's grave, planting and manicuring. It always had the same affect.

"I think when I die I'm going to be cremated and have my ashes thrown on Mel Gibson," Paula said, looking for redirection.

"When I die *I want you all to promise me* you will throw my ashes in my husband's face," Molly being uncharacteristic again. Her husband's defection was the only thing that brought out any meanness in her otherwise delicate nature.

Bakewell was his quiet self, waiting to be called on, enjoying the sordid direction their sense of humor had taken. They had become an important part of his life, and he feared it was about to end once again. "The advent of Maggie Walker," was the way a friend had referred to it. Maggie had been right; the news was out after their stop at the Muny. He wondered when Girls' Club would get wind of their harmless rendezvous. He didn't have to wait long.

"Does anyone here remember Maggie Leary?" Tee fired the opening salvo.

"Who could forget her?" Paula said.

"Remember the old saying, 'Be leery of Leary'?" Tee phrased it acidly. "God, she was such a bitch. Did she ever have any friends?" Bakewell could feel her gaze on the side of his face, though she was off, across the table, in the dark. He kept quiet.

"She was too busy with her beaus, too stuck on herself."

"Yeah, and too busy spending money."

Bakewell sipped his wine.

"I thought she moved to Little Rock with that big shot lawyer who was so palsy with the Clintons."

"Well she's back in St. Louis again. Somebody I know saw her at the Muny."

Still silent.

"Actually she was escorted by our own best friend here, if rumor serves."

"Oh boy, here it comes." Bakewell straightened, putting the front legs of his chair back on the deck

"Andy, what do you see in her," Molly asked.

"Sex, stupid!" Tee shouted.

"Tee, give me a break." He leaned back in his chair again, looking up at the sky. It was already dark. Daylight savings was over. It was almost too cold to be outside. He feared they would give up and move on once the weather turned cold. They'd done it the year before. He wished they would keep coming this year. He knew he would miss them during the shut-in months.

"Andy, if its sex you're after you could have us." Paula said. She was staring over the top of her wine glass, another penetrating Paula stare, still full of mischief.

"Yes, Andy, you could have us."

"All at the same time!"

"That is disgusting, Tee!" Molly was upset by the comment.

"Yeah, a veritable smorgasbord," Paula added.

"That is completely disgusting. Andy, they are speaking for themselves."

"I know. They're trashy women, Molly. I know you wouldn't get in bed with more than one man at a time."

"Andy, I wouldn't get in bed with any man, unless…"

"Oh, bullshit, Molly. You'd be the first one in bed with him."

Molly looked at Tee, genuinely hurt.

"So what's the deal big boy? You going after her? Gonna go for the dough?" It was Paula again.

He held up his hands; it had become a habit. "It was just dinner Paula. I've had twenty with you girls for every one I've had with her."

"She always had everything she wanted," Tee said.

"But she never had children, did she Andy?" Molly sounded sympathetic. Bakewell shook his head.

"Exactly, the only thing she's ever had to think about was herself."

"And her mother; don't forget her crazy mother, Paula."

"Molly, I had a crazy mother. If I could trade my crazy mother for money and looks I would have gotten rid of the old bat long ago. And I wouldn't have had to take care of her either."

"Paula!"

"Well, what the fuck. Think about it. Men chasing you…"

"Men with money!"

"…Men with money chasing after you – panting around – wanting *to get in your pants!*" They had seized on the get-in-your-pants line.

"Clothes, money, cars, big homes…"

"Big *paid for* homes!"

"…and sex. Yeoww" Tee went on.

"I'm not chasing after her, she called me."

"Why?"

"I don't know."

"Well, did you get in her pants?"

"No. We went to dinner several times. She made fun of my truck the first time. We always part after dinner."

"She must be lonely," Molly said.

"I'm fucking lonely, Molly! Give me a break. Does she really know Tom Eagleton, Andy?"

Bakewell shrugged.

"How much money does she have, anyway?" Tee asked.

Bakewell could have shocked them with the exact figure. Instead he gave her a you're-asking-me look.

"She's loaded. She had money in high school. She only got richer in Little Rock."

"There's a rumor she knew Bill Clinton." Paula added.

"In the biblical sense?"

"What else? Didn't every woman know him in the biblical sense?"

"Gawd. Think about it. He probably tried to get in her pants. How would that look on the old resume? The President of the United States!"

"It sure would go a long way down at the VA hospital," Molly said.

"Andy," Tee said, suddenly sitting up. "You could be doing it with someone who *screwed the President of the United States*!"

"Whoa! Wait! Stop!" He held up his hands. "Listen to yourselves. Have you women ever stopped to listen to what you say?"

"Yes!" It was nearly a chorus. "Isn't it great? Where else can you re-live your life with your old buddies?"

"It's locker room talk; the good old carefree days, Andy!"

"It's like the high school locker room talk you always hear about. I never played sports so I never got into locker room talk until now." Molly said, "I like it. I think it's kind of fun."

"It's filth. You have no shame."

"It's the navy! The Sixth Fleet – isn't that where you were, with the

Sixth Fleet, Andy?"

"You girls are worse than the Sixth Fleet."

"And you get to talk filth, and do it with three lovely ladies, right here on your own deck!"

"I heard she buried two husbands," Molly said, resuming.

"God." Tee said, "Some women have all the luck."

"One is all I know about," Bakewell put his hands on the table, turned his wine glass.

"Well, *when they die* you get all of the sympathy and the kids get to look up to them."

"The kids get to have fond memories of the old man."

"And you get the fucking insurance money!" Tee nearly exploded. "How good is that?"

"Tee's right! Money, esteem *and you don't get dumped.*"

"I don't feel dumped, Molly. My God, the man went off with another man. How can you compete with that?"

"Get out of here," Bakewell said. There was a sudden expectant silence, also sudden excitement. They stared – new meat for conversation, surprised it hadn't come up before. When Bakewell didn't respond they continued to stare. They had a scoop, each one leaning in, brightening.

"Come on, Paula, Kenny was *Airborne."* They watched him, amused, no one speaking.

"What?" he said, exasperated.

"You didn't know?"

"Andy, are you kidding?"

"Know what?"

"He used to wear my underwear! The man was a fruitsie tootsie!"

"Aw bullshit," Bakewell said, moving in his chair uncomfortably, his foot bumped the gardenia plant by the rail – the one Nancy had kept alive all summer – nearly knocking it over. It was flourishing in the cooler weather. The candles were giving off just enough light. They could see each other across the table now; everybody was honed in, enjoying his discomfort.

It was chilly; the mood getting chillier for him. Bakewell got up in a huff and went inside. When he came back outside, he had an armload of faded cotton sweaters, all slightly shrunken in size XXL. He passed them out and each woman put one on, careful not to mess her hair.

"Andy, I thought you knew. I thought everybody in the world knew."

"I don't want to talk about it. I hate that kind of stuff." He sat back down. "Let's talk about something else. I would never believe that kind of talk about anyone."

"Well, it's true."

"I don't want to talk about it. I'm too simple to understand that shit. The older I get, the simpler I want to be. Don't talk about it."

"What ever happened to the jerky Mr. Know-it-all?"

"Yeah, the guy that swept Kath off her feet?"

"That's right, Andy. You were the mature older man in our lives." Paula was trying to go along, sensing his disappointment.

"You were really wild Andy," Molly said, warming to the subject. "We were all shocked when Katherine announced it was you."

"God, Andy. How old were you anyway? We were dating babies, and Katherine shows up with you."

"And takes you to the wedding rail!" Paula said. "How did that happen?"

"She just swept me off my feet," Bakewell said, happy for the change, still uncomfortable. They were staring at him, waiting for an answer. He looked at each one in turn before returning to the conversation. "We get older. We change. I'm an old man. I'm tired. Who here is the same person they were thirty years ago?"

"I think I'm still the same," Molly said quietly.

"I think maybe you are, Molly." Bakewell spoke the words gently, after waiting for some one else to speak first. When no one said anything, he spoke the words softly, like he was talking to a child, which he often thought of when he spoke to Molly. It was ironic. Molly was so well read, so much more intellectual, her simple demeanor belied her intellect. He knew there was more depth to her than the others, and he included himself in that group. She was his…he had trouble phrasing it sometimes…she was what Ned would have called, "One of them di-cot-o-mees."

"Molly, you're sweet and you can be so lovey-dovey simple, but you're still old like the rest of us, hon." Tee was back to brutality. It worked in a pinch, especially with older women, the same way it had worked with younger men. Usually it was brutality towards their husbands or men in general, but every once in a while they turned on each other. Bakewell suspected a subconscious need.

"Just because I'm older doesn't mean I've changed."

"Go look in the mirror, kiddo," Tee continued relentlessly.

"You know Tee, I think the reason you're so mean is your body is full of toxins."

"The only toxins running around in my body are the ones I've chosen to put there, Paula – vodka, wine, cigarettes and an occasional reefer – so keep your health food shit and you herbal enemas. I get my kicks the old fashioned way."

"I'm only saying the bad things we put in our bodies affect all aspects of our health, including our personality."

"That's what Prozac's for."

"Wait! Didn't he call us trashy women a while ago?"

"He says it all the time. Frankly, I like the sound of it. Andy, treat us like your locker room pals. Share the goods."

"Yes, Andy. Do come on. Tell us, are you getting the goods from her?"

Bakewell smiled in spite of himself. He loved them, loved their outrageous conversation. His only problem was deflecting it from himself. "What's for dessert? Since you girls got off those awful diet desserts I've gotten spoiled. Who brought what?"

"I want to get back to Leary. Andy, what's the deal? Are you going to try and get in her pants or not?"

"Paula, you make me lose all respect for you when you talk like that."

"I know. I love it, and I don't want your fucking respect. I just want to know what me and the locker room girls here can expect in the coming weeks. When are you getting together with her again, and, are you going to share with us?"

"I have no plans to get back together with her, and I sure don't have any plans to share my nonexistent sex life with anybody, especially *trashy women.*"

"There he goes again. How can we be trashy if you don't share with us? What have we got to talk about?"

"Yeah, Andy, nobody's getting in our pants."

"Andy," Molly said quietly, "You said *get back together with her*. Did you used to go out with her before you met Katherine?"

Bakewell was stumped. The conversation was going nowhere but downhill. He hesitated. It was a mistake.

"You were involved with her, I knew it!" Tee again. "Tell us before we scream!"

"Did you know her in the biblical sense?"

"She was only nineteen when I knew her back then."

"Did you know her in the biblical sense?"

"Did you get in her pants?" Paula was almost screaming. They were having a good time at his expense. It was the most fun they'd had with him all summer. They didn't want to lose the initiative.

"We were kids, Molly."

"So were Phil and I, but I let that son of a bitch get in my pants when I was only eighteen!"

Bakewell's face reddened. They had him on the spot and knew it, close in pursuit. He was silent and time passed. They'd watched his condition degrading steadily, knew something was wrong. When he remained silent they gradually left off, hated to give it up, but loved him too much to continue. The evening gradually wore down over cigarettes and coffee.

They cleaned up as always, made him sit tight while they did, loaded the dishwasher, and put things away. When they were leaving, Molly kissed Bakewell, hugged him. "I miss you so very much when winter comes, Andy."

Ned Grant was basically modest, had a wonderful humility despite his great heft and aggressive lean. His imposing tilt always gave the impression of threat, but he was pure kindness inside. He had a quiet respect and genuine admiration for his younger partner and was compliant, even submissive when Bakewell expressed a strong view.

Bakewell took Ned's counsel, always gave it careful consideration, but his judgment prevailed when final decisions were made. Ned never tried to intimidate Bakewell in all their years together, actually feared his wrath and often told his "buds," he liked being aligned with "a guy what's got some real balls that ain't afraid to go with his brain," told them, he liked, "bein around a college-smart guy like Andy."

In the beginning Ned had tried to do the talking. Bakewell had let him ramble, pointed out the inconsistencies in his arguments and articulated his own in as few words as possible. Bakewell could tell Ned he was wrong without ever saying so, and Ned soon learned to listen, although he complained many times, "It's like pullin teeth to get somethin outta ya when I'm needin somebody to unfuck my life."

Being the *intuitionative* person he was, Ned learned early on, if he needed Bakewell's advice on a personal matter he would have to circumscribe the situation, sip his drink, and wait for Bakewell's response. If none was forthcoming, he would ask additional questions, phrasing them obliquely, gradually work his way around the subject. Ned believed if Bakewell thought they were just talking, not about himself, Bakewell would be more willing to express an opinion. Ned called it "loosenin him up," claimed he was a master at "gettin guys un-loosened" – especially Bakewell. Ned claimed to be an amateur psychologist, said "I ain't too sure 'bout the amateur part."

His younger partner knew what he was up to, played the game as much for entertainment as for curiosity. Bakewell loved Ned Grant, and valued the time they spent together. Ned had the best sense of humor Bakewell had ever known. He crafted his amazing stories beautifully, despite tense changes and mutilated pronunciations. Ned was self-effacing when he told a story, and ninety percent of his stories were about situations he had gotten himself into over the years.

Ned was impulsive while Bakewell was cautious. Ned was in a perpetual hurry; Bakewell preferred to take his time. Ned would fly off; Bakewell would hold it in, even during the worst times. Ned was naturally friendly; Bakewell was composed, impassive. Ned was hopefully pessimistic, afraid to be optimistic, afraid to get too far "up" because he hated "them downs," but forever looking for the best in situations and people. Bakewell faked his sang-froid, pretended an equanimity that wasn't there, never had the confidence he was noted for. When Ned was happy everybody knew it; when

Bakewell was happy he smiled a little more. When Ned was hurting he was a hippo with a toothache; when Bakewell was hurting he was quiet, tended to look straight ahead, avoid eye contact, usually looked for a quiet place. Ned was naturally noisy, his size prohibited stealth; Bakewell was always quiet, liked being alone, especially in the outdoors. Ned made noise coming down the hallway; Bakewell moved about without being heard – and made everyone in the office nervous. He often approached wraith-like, spectral, from out of nowhere – a habit developed over a lifetime of still hunting and silent movement. When he entered Ned's office, Ned would invariably jump, startled, and protest Bakewell's apparitional presence with a hissed profanity.

Both men liked to read, and, like Ned, single now, without companionship on those nights when "Girls Club" wasn't in session, Bakewell became an even more voracious reader.

Ned read anything Bakewell put on his desk, which made Bakewell careful about his selections. Ned loved history, especially American, and he loved biographies. Over the years they traded books on both Adams & Roosevelts, Lincoln, Grant, Sherman, Hitler & Stalin, heroes, soldiers, statesmen, monsters, patriots...

***

Ned was on the verge of tears, would have done anything imaginable to ease the burden of Bakewell's load. His head ached from searching for a solution to the kid's problem.

"God took the joy of my life, the single greatest love I've known, the one thing I cared about most. He took my courage and broke my spirit, destroyed my life. I don't have anything left now. When somebody talks down to me or gets in my face, all I do is cave in. I just want to curl up in the fetal position. I don't have any *fight-back* left in me anymore. I'm out of guts and ashamed of myself."

Ned feared his partner might cry, never had seen him cloud up before, worried he might finally break down, not because it would have been embarrassing – Ned would never have been embarrassed by anything Bakewell did, was prepared to stand by him through anything, often said he would take a bullet for him – but because he was afraid of what might happen. He believed if Bakewell ever gave way to his tears, he might never stop. He had observed the way he kept himself in tight control, always reined up and holding in, never letting anyone but Ned himself in. Ned knew Bakewell never had these conversations with his children.

"I'm whipped, burnt out, totally defeated. I'm broke, washed up, ruined. I've got nothing left to offer this world and no reason to want to. I just want to quit. That morning at the cemetery, sitting there next to her casket… I just wanted to stop living. If there was a way I could have stopped breathing, I would have done it."

"Andy, come on. Don't do this to yerself. You're a fine man, a good purson. You got a life to live, a lot to live for, for peoples that's got a heart full of love fer you. Don't do this, bub."

Bakewell looked at Ned, then across the room. Dolly was watching them from a distance, pretending not to, seemed always to be watching them sitting back in the corner. She loved Ned and wanted to mother Bakewell. They were her favorite customers and she would have left the others and joined them at their table if asked. Bakewell pointed to Ned's drink when she looked his way again, made a long sigh and stretched. "I just want to give it up and find something else."

"I know, Andy, I know. Yer like General Lee on Traveler, comin into town, needin to surrender your sword like he done, and put it on the table and tell General Grant and the rest of the world you give up."

"General Lee had Appomattox Court House. I don't know where to go. I don't know where in the hell I can go. If I did I would do it. Where in the hell can I go, Ned? Where is the place where you go and say, 'here, take this damned sword and whatever the hell else you want from me and just let me give up?' Let me just *give the fuck up!*"

Ned shook his big head sadly; profanity from his partner was not good. He put his heavy hand on the younger man's arm, patted it gently. "I hate to see you like this. Yer too good a guy to be beatin yerself up. It ain't right, you bein like this. Treat yerself better, you deserve more."

There was no response. Bakewell was already feeling guilty about unloading on his partner. He never complained to anyone other than Ned, never felt justified when he did. He hated taking advantage of their friendship, felt disloyal to their partnership when he let his emotions get the best of him. Dolly brought the drink and Ned sipped and sighed and drummed the table, causing it to vibrate, while he searched for words.

"Of all the sweet, wonderful people and no-good motherfuckers I ever knowed in this world, there ain't never been nobody that could take a likkin and keep on tickin like you, bub, so don't go shortin out on me now." He paused for breath and looked around the room, like he was checking for spies. "You oughtta find some company. You need a friend besides me and all them other ones you got but don't wanna remember loves you." Ned became pensive, took another sip from his drink. Bakewell knew there would be more. "That's what you need right now more than anythin else. You need someone that's got more to offer than sympathy."

"I wouldn't know where to find what you're suggesting."

"Why don't you bang one of them gals that's always hangin around yer house at night?" Bakewell shook his head in disapproval. Ned wouldn't relent, was sure he had the cure. "What about that fine lookin lady Nancy's always talkin about? I bet she could get you up to goin again."

Bakewell grimaced, put his head in his hands and turned it back and forth. "What have I got to offer a woman like that? She's looking for love and happiness. She doesn't need a charity case."

"You wanna bet? I'll tell you somethin – I got real moments of see-ability about some things, as you already know – and this comes from my intuition-ative powers, so listen here to me now. Anyone's lookin to feel better about theirselves has only one thing to do, and that's find a way to make somebody else happy. Makin yerself available to others to do somethin for 'em is the quickest way to get rid of them blues."

"I'd be a rehab case for her, and I'm not going to let myself get into that kind of mess." Bakewell looked around the dark room, reflecting, looked at Ned. "As a matter of fact, I'm thinking about just what you're suggesting. I could go out to the missions and do something for somebody else. I might even make a difference for them, and cure myself..." He pushed his unfinished drink off to the side, "But first I have to cure this money affliction of ours, this economic disease we live with every day."

"You got a point there, but I'd call that gal and give her a twirl. What can it hurt?"

"I wouldn't know how to start."

"Well, I could give you some pretty simple advice there, bub. You offer her what she's probably lookin for and hasn't had in a while."

"Ned, come on! I wouldn't know how, even if I *was* looking, and I'm sure as hell not."

"Andy, Andy, listen to me. Its still six inches long, with a winesap apple hangin on the end..."

"Ned," Bakewell raised his hand in protest. "I don't want to have this conversation. Please, its going nowhere and neither am I. I just need to find a place where I can slowly unwind. I need a place where I can pray without worrying the IRS or the sheriff might show up with a subpoena."

"So, I'll see you after the tests?" Dr. Neville said, clapping him on the shoulder good-naturedly, completely out of character.

Bakewell had disliked Neville when they first met, had disliked him from the first minute. His full name was Colin Clive Neville, without any II's III's or IV's to indicate lineage. Bakewell thought the name affected, thought his parents might have been faking aristocracy, referred to it as *that name* when he described his new doctor to Katherine. Neville was arrogant, came to it naturally, arrogant in the John Houseman way: affected, pompous, superior, often condescending, talked down his nose or peered out over a pair of "half eyes" when he spoke.

Bakewell wasn't about to let him do any surgery, had no intention of becoming his patient, but Neville's enormous confidence asserted itself, kept Bakewell in his office long enough to hear him out.

Neville had plaques on every wall, professing a lifetime of acquired wisdom and accomplishment. He was originally from South Africa, but much in the acquisition of plaques occurred in England and Canada – one going so far as to declare him a "Fellow of the Royal Academy" of something Bakewell couldn't remember. He thought Neville had no bedside manner, had learned the hard way that bedside manner was the last thing one observed before going under the knife. He had no intention of ever going under any knife wielded by this pompous little proponent of Apartheid. He only went to see him at the insistence of two other specialists who did the doctoring but not the cutting. Neville excelled at the cutting.

Doctor Neville diagnosed Bakewell's problem after a brief examination. He had a terrible surgery in '88 under the heavy hands of one of Neville's protégés, whose name Neville refused to pronounce, a protégé held in lip-curling contempt. Amazingly, the end result of his first visit was a second surgery. To Bakewell's complete surprise, Neville showed up in pre-op with a bedside manner redefining compassion, which got Bakewell a hissed tongue-lashing from Katherine. Like everyone else, Neville was taken in by Katherine's down to earth charm, and they spent fifteen minutes chatting about high schools and colleges, while Bakewell drifted away under sedation. Under Neville's skilled hands the operation was so successful his recovery took only a week. The first operation had nearly killed him, left him recuperating for months.

"Could it be anything other than cancer?" Bakewell asked.

Neville shook his head slowly, gave him a sympathetic smile. "I'm afraid not."

"How can it come on so fast?" Neville shrugged, a feeble attempt at compassion. "Would it have made any difference if I'd come in sooner?"

"Some of my *esteemed colleagues* would tell you different," he said in his fascinating accent, with more lip curling contempt, "But I think you would only have learned about your condition sooner, and you would have felt like you do now, only sooner."

"I don't know how I feel right now." Neville nodded. Bakewell breathed deeply, shaking his head, sighed, exasperated. He was meeting his mortality. There was fear he knew, waiting just outside Neville's office. It was beginning to creep into the room and grip him already. "How in the hell do you get this kind of cancer? You told me it was rare."

"It's not so rare to die from liver cancer, but it usually metastasizes from another place. You get cancer in a different organ and it moves. It ends up in your liver and they call it liver cancer, but it's really colon cancer or some other cancer from somewhere else in the body. It just kills you when it gets to your liver. To get it in your liver first is unusual."

"How did I get it then?"

"It could be from several things. You said you had hepatitis when you were in the service?"

"That was Istanbul, Turkey, a lifetime ago."

"It would increase your chances. You could have gotten it from a fungus that attacks the liver, something we call *aflatoxins*."

"Where do you get aflatoxins?"

"Actually you can eat them without knowing it."

"When did I eat aflatoxins, for Pete's sake?"

"Probably not by choice. You may have ingested them without knowing it. They come from strange places, like very old peanuts or they form on grains that have been stored for a long time."

"Aflatoxins, liver cancer... Almost nobody gets liver cancer. I'm having a hell of a year." Neville didn't answer. Bakewell was out of character again. "My luck's been nonexistent the last few years. Now I'm the lucky guy who ingested aflatoxins?"

"I didn't say you ingested them. It's just a possibility."

"No, but I managed to pull the short straw."

Neville smiled, admired his "pluck." He knew Bakewell was afraid. He'd seen it too many times before.

"So how do I die?"

"Gradually, I'm afraid."

"Give me the 'how' part."

"Slowly probably, it could be quick. It depends on how fast it goes."

"I'm a numbers guy – how long?"

"Six months is the standard answer. I don't really know." Neville was frustrated. He wanted to be more specific, knew his patient wanted him to be more specific. "You could last six months, maybe longer, maybe less. We need to get the test results and see how it's doing."

"Give me the wicked scenario. Do I go heaving my guts out or wasting away, hooked up to some ghastly IV with ugly yellow junk dripping into my veins?"

Dr. Neville raised his hands, palms up.

"Am I going to be a disgusting wheel chair case, having some malcontented bruiser wheel me around some dreary-assed sick ward?"

Neville tilted his head back and to one side without answering.

"Is it debilitating? Is there a lot of blood? Am I in for long months of misery or do I get to lead a fairly normal life and gradually wind down the final couple of weeks?"

"I don't know."

"Doctor, please. Pretend like you're talking to yourself." Neville hesitated, was about to say something, reconsidered. "*Please*, pretend like you're thinking out loud, like you're talking to the front window of your Mercedes. Speculate, like it was you, not me."

Neville sighed and looked at his watch, then directly into Bakewell's eyes. The watch had an expensive band made from reptile hide. He took a deep breath. "Well, you can expect to lose weight gradually. You may turn yellow if there is a blockage. No blood. You're just going to… 'peter out', as you Americans like to say, toward the very end." Neville honestly wished he could give him more. "Go have the tests, we'll arrange treatments." He patted his arm sympathetically. It was the first time Bakewell had been in his office and not felt like he was being pushed down the line.

"The treatments will kill me before the hepa-something-or-other will."

"Hepatocellular carcinoma."

"And the treatment is radiation or some other ghastly process that makes my hair fall out? I gradually fade to yellow, look like an Asian communist before I go?"

"You might fade to yellow anyway, if there is a blockage. I want to warn you about that. It could happen." He paused. There was sympathy in his eyes. "Honestly, the treatment is discouraging and the results with radiation have been disappointing."

"Well hell, I'd rather die doing aerobatics…" Bakewell reconsidered, "But that's against my religion. We Catholics don't commit suicide you know." Bakewell was groping, "I could ramble on about different ways to kill myself – doing outside loops or tail drops. I've always been afraid of the really hard aerobatics." He had a need to talk that seldom came over him. "Once I thought I would die of a bullet in the back of the head."

Neville gave a curious look, had no idea what he was talking about, and didn't inquire. He reverted to his professional manner again, "I'm going to spare you the, *we all have to go sometime* speech, Mr. Bakewell. You've always been rather critical of my office manner..."

"That was before I got to know what a warm guy you are."

Neville smiled in spite of himself; it came from years of familiarity with the Bakewell's. They had known each other for a decade. Neville had treated Katherine. Bakewell sighed, "Well, I guess I get to do one final performance. My life's been one long…" he let his voice trail off, "My life has been a pretty bad performance up to this point. Now I'll have an opportunity to do something…unique for me…try to get it right for once." He slid off the examining table. "I'll show my children that I can die well." Neville watched, patiently. "My wife gave *the* Oscar winning performance, as you know…"

"I remember, an amazing woman, truly. She was one of my greatest disappointments, professionally. I try never to get involved with my patients, but I made an exception with your wife – lovely woman. Katherine?"

"Yes. Thank you." Bakewell nodded his appreciation. "So…I'll be measuring up to a higher standard." He reached for his coat, feeling fine, wondering how long it would take. He gave Neville a last look. "It's always fatal?"

"In the liver, yes, always fatal; go and have some more tests and we'll talk again."

"Don't tell me you'll look forward to seeing me."

"No. I won't look forward to that, Andy." Neville used his Christian name for only the second time in their relationship. The other time had been at Katherine's funeral.

Bakewell made his way out, noticing others in the waiting room. It wasn't often anyone had to wait in Neville's office, but there were two waiting; one man looked very unhappy. Bakewell wondered if he was dying too, wanted to bend down and whisper in his ear, say *I'm going to die.* He returned his magazine and left. Waiting for the elevator, he thought about what had transpired. *Half an hour ago I was feeling low, but didn't know. Now I'm dying. I'm going to die.* Fear *was* waiting right outside Neville's office. Physically he felt all right, wondered about his weight loss, but felt good enough. Now he was scared.

The next day was the 11th of November, Armistice Day – called Veterans Day now, after an expedient decree had reinvented the holiday – a calumny that desecrated the memory of millions who had suffered and died in The Great War. Armistice Day had always been special for the Bakewell's, who were fervently traditional about history and wars. The 11th would always be Armistice Day. It was a union holiday, so it created the unofficial "opening weekend" of the bird season, had often created special three-day weekends for Bakewell and his sons, weekends filled with bird dogs, tailgate lunches and treks to backcountry places where they found pockets of the greatest game bird in the world. The Bakewells believed quail, like bird-dogs, were one of God's special creations.

He called his office and told Trudy he wouldn't be coming back. He was going home to pick up his dogs and gear and head north, said he wouldn't be back before Monday.

"Everything OK boss?"

"Everything's fine. I'll call Ned and let him know. Let them know in the office. If somebody needs me, give them my cell number. I'll check it every couple of hours."

"Have fun!"

Ned was lukewarm to the idea. "You know, bub, we still got to make hay in the di-urinal part of the day. Every buck we make before the weather shuts us down is one we don't go down for when everythin else comes up at us in the end."

"I know, Ned. I'm working twelve hours a day just like you, running on fumes. Give me a break." There was a long silence, attempting to be upbeat he added, "Hey, I think I might have the answer to one of our problems."

"What's that," Ned said without enthusiasm.

"Wait 'til Monday. I've come up with something that will put some money back on the table." They both had half a million in "key man" life insurance. Ned could pay some heavy bills and might get out with something.

"We're gonna be secretive now? I thought we was buds, thought we shared everything."

"Talk to you Monday, Ned. Just look after things for a couple of days."

Bakewell took his girls and went north toward Hannibal and a wildlife area south of the river town he had hunted for years. Once a hundred miles free of the city, his thoughts found perspective. It happened every time. He and Ned both commented on the phenomenon. As he drove he let his thoughts drift back to better times.

For more than twenty years he'd enjoyed bird hunts with friends, most especially his sons. In the recent past one of the boys, usually Michael, would have scheduled the weekend, written it in on the family calendar where Katherine kept important dates. The note would have said, *Quail hunting with TOM,* been written in red ink more than likely. Or he might have gotten a call from the boys on his Friday night drive home: *where we going on opening weekend, Pop?* After the opening week it would have been a simple query: *what's on the weekend's agenda?* If an early morning trip was in the planning the boys would cut their Friday festivities short, so they could answer the bell Saturday morning. Eventually Andy went off to college and drifted away, went through the "girls are fun" phase, which preempted him from Saturday reveilles. With Michael there had never been any of the aberrational youthful behavior. Michael preferred weekends with *the old man* (TOM) more than chasing girls. It had been one of the more pleasant surprises of Bakewell's parenting life, and Katherine was quick to point it out whenever Michael was in hot water. After the boys were "gone," Bakewell learned to go alone, learned to enjoy the tranquility of life with only dogs. They didn't speak, expected nothing more than a chance at "fair chase," never disappointed him with their performance, and never had a prior engagement.

Quail hunting, quail looking really, after the last three pathetic years, was a solo business for Bakewell. "Just me and my girls," he said to the windshield. He let the dogs ride up front, one at a time, each leg of the trip. They were good company, listened, and never contradicted.

It was dark before they got to the wildlife area. Bakewell missed the turn and had to go back and find it in the dark. The old barn south of Peno Creek was gone, and the cover was even more overgrown. He let the dogs out to run briefly in the dark, knowing they wouldn't go far. Later he spent the night trying to sleep in the camper with three companions who couldn't settle down. It didn't matter; he couldn't sleep either. He got up and sat on the tailgate, wrapped in the down bag, listening to the night's sounds, trying to imagine what that *giant step* ahead would be like, wondering what happened, where you went after you stopped breathing. Bakewell was afraid. As a child he'd been taught to love God with his whole mind, heart and soul. After Katherine died, a calcification had grown around his heart; his mind had numbed with doubt; he wasn't sure where his soul was anymore.

Whippoorwills and tree frogs were still active. After a cold spell the weather had warmed again. A coyote called once then a bunch clamored briefly. Later a hoot owl started up and kept them sad company for hours.

It was reflection time – thoughts long forgotten, a generation gone now, tried to return, and he struggled with them the way he always struggled with his past:

I dwell in a lonely house I know
That vanished many a summer ago…?
I dwell with a strangely aching heart
In that vanished abode there far apart
On that disused and forgotten road
That… has… no dust-bath…?

He tried again:

The whippoorwill is coming to shout
And hush and cluck and flutter about;
I hear him begin far enough away…

He wasn't sure he'd gotten it right. Frost, a favorite once – once, long ago, when he still had a reliable memory – had clouded; his lyrics faded now, like too many other memories, into a radiation fog that always seemed to come at the calmest, clearest times, when remembering should have been easy.

In the morning he let the dogs run again just to take the edge off, to get rid of first-day-madness that typified every trip. The wildlife area was disappointing. Once a Valhalla, it was overgrown now and filled with turkeys. He gave up within an hour, disgusted that a place once so perfect had, *gone to turkeys*. The dogs came in reluctantly when he whistled. He packed them up and headed up to Hannibal, stopping for breakfast in the old river town.

Above Palmyra he turned west to place called Deer Ridge where he'd had great success over the years. Deer Ridge was huge – 7,000 acres. The trick to Deer Ridge was the walk. His favorite spot was in the grain fields down along the river, which took a half hour to reach. Not many hunters walked a half hour just to start. By the time they got down there, the dogs had settled into a pace and style that would have pleased the finest field-trialer. The big running setter was moving wide, flowing like windswept foam across the surf; his Brittany was right out in front where she belonged, hoping for anything the others missed. The little tri colored puppy was now a perfect medium range. She'd figured it out at the end of the first summer, now she had a range that put her between the other two. In all his dog-loving, bird-hunting life, Bakewell never had three dogs so perfectly matched.

God I love this stuff and the country and the creatures that make it possible.

Bakewell prayed when he hunted birds. Like with sheep way up high, it was a perfect time. He felt guilty praying when he chewed tobacco, so he would wait until the nicotine fix was in before the praying started. The tobacco chewing was something he learned during a tryout in Florida the winter before he enlisted. An old ballplayer named Hoyt Wilhelm gave him his first chew when he taught him to throw a knuckleball. He also gave him some good advice. "Don't try to make a career in this business unless you can control the knuckler kid, 'cause you don't have enough pop to your fastball, and you'll never be able to hit the kind of shit they throw you down here." Mr. Wilhelm had been right. Bakewell's next stop was the navy. Tobacco chewing was for fishing and hunting only. Unless he was doing one or the other he never thought about the stuff; baseball was long in the past.

The crops were still in the fields; the corn, stunted by the drought, was still over his head, milo at full seed, the heads so heavy they draped over and he could hear his dogs going through them. The biggest field was in soybeans, and the dogs knocked the beans from the dry stems as they rushed through. Bakewell stayed along the edge of the fields out of long respect for agriculture; there was no way to keep the dogs out. He hoped they would put something up as they crisscrossed the field, knew they would slow it down once they found birds. Things always got serious when one of them got a good whiff.

Hunting was serious. Bakewell never made it out to be anything else. He'd told Andy and Michael it was about killing; it was a blood sport. It was about killing and *dying* and dying was a serious thing, *a lot more serious now that it was getting closer.* Bakewell was developing a new appreciation for dying, seeing it from the other end.

There were no birds in the crops or anywhere around them. They worked the best cover in the ditches and between the fields, and later went down along the river bottom, hoping to raise some woodcock, when the cover started to favor timberdoodles, they ran into private property, trees lathered with purple paint, and were forced to give up. The "No Trespass" paint also prevented access to the river. When they turned back toward the road and the steeper country, his dogs started showing signs of stress. They hadn't had water in a long time. The river was far behind and water, which had never been a problem in the muddy bottomland, was suddenly a concern. The fall had been too dry. Bakewell was ready to turn back for the river when he heard the puppy splash above him on the uphill side of an erosion terrace. He went up and found her up to her neck cooling off.

"You're no dummy, little girl," he said, going down on one knee. He whistled the other dogs in and they got a long drink while he lectured them on the young pup's ability to sniff out the water, "Both of you bozos went right past this spot."

He hoped the birds were out in the thick crops where they couldn't find them, if not another great place had bit the dust. A huge flock of turkeys appeared about a quarter mile off in the cut stubble across the river. Bakewell shook his head in disgust; he hated wild turkeys: *the jackals and hyenas of North America.* In his childhood, before turkeys were re-introduced, the quail population had been tremendous, now the state was overrun with wild turkeys and the quail population continued to decline. He was glad the dogs hadn't scented the huge flock. It would have taken twenty minutes to get them back. The missing quail would mean nothing to him next year, but his sons, who had his love for upland birds, would need a place like Deer Ridge in the future.

They covered the big hill on the west side, refreshed and ready for another go. It lasted forty minutes before Bakewell gave up and headed back up the steep trail. He made a sandwich, put chips and a cup of ice in the front seat with a can of soda, loaded up and headed north.

His thoughts were confused, switching from the reality of his impending death to philosophical musings about all the wonderful times he had enjoyed in life. One minute he was stricken, the next he was talking to God about an eternity with Katherine. Gradually his mind wore down, the sharp edge of doom replaced with a blurred, hazy uneasiness, a cloudy fear. He knew his fear would intensify, had no illusions about his courage. He was afraid to die and prayed he would handle it with dignity.

He stopped at a place called Indian Hills, not quite as big as Deer Ridge, but with a better variety of terrain and twice the open acreage for birds. The bow hunters had taken the best campsites, but he found a place by the creek and put the dogs out again and headed east toward a cornfield. As soon as he stepped into the cover, the first woodcock flushed. He and the Brittany watched it go. *You're supposed to shoot dummy; they're in season too.*

The flood plain along the river was full of small saplings, so thick he had to hold his gun vertically in places to squeeze through. The cover was tough, but full of woodcock. In the first hundred yards he had six flushes. Eventually he was able to shoot, and the birds started dropping. It was difficult hunting. The dogs didn't want to hunt for dead birds, and finding the fluffy little timberdoodles on the leafy autumn ground without their help was impossible. Bakewell whistled them in after two went down without a retrieve and insisted they stop hunting and find the birds.

"We're not shooting anymore 'til we find the dead ones, so let's get our doggy acts together and *hunt dead.*"

He knelt down in the soft leaves and waited for each dog to report in. The big running setter was the last one to respond to the whistle. The dogs hated to quit the chase with so many live birds flushing around them, grudgingly gave up. Bakewell was the boss: the guy who provided room and board, health & welfare, retirement benefits too. With shoulders slumping, they glumly retraced the stale ground under his soft encouragement and eventually found the birds. Once Bakewell had the feathery game in hand they resumed the chase, bounding wildly through the dense cover, charging about enthusiastically, creating an air of hilarity. He had never seen them so exuberant, seen so much canine euphoria. At one point the puppy and her momma collided and the pup got the worst of it as she tumbled over backwards while her mother watched, then shook vigorously and ran off again to resume the chase.

That evening they enjoyed another camp out, dinner served from the tailgate. The dogs, worn down with exertion, stayed close to the truck, playing with a box turtle that attempted to cross the gravel lot. He was too big for their gentle mouths, and since they couldn't pick him up, they rolled him across the gravel lot until his brains were scrambled. Bakewell didn't think they would ever give it up. He fed and watered them an hour before putting them inside the camper shell, where he let them sleep outside their boxes again, mostly on top of him, as they cozied up to the down bag in the creekside chill. He slept well the second night, fatigued by the day's effort.

Most of the following day was spent in the open fields looking for quail – finding none. There were a few pheasants and the puppy raised two roosters at once on a small knoll above him. Bakewell and the young dog were both surprised; they watched the cackling birds fly off unharmed. He was amazed the roosters had let her get so close. He took one rooster that afternoon and that bird, along with a limit of woodcock, made his total bag for the trip.

The third day Bakewell went west across the state, driving for hours, looking at places he'd hunted years ago. The country was still there; hadn't changed much, but the quail were only a memory. He ended up at Lake Paho that night, letting the dogs run for two hours in wild indigo and the tall Indian grass without success. They camped out again, everybody settled in now, adjusted to the routine, as they enjoyed another tailgate dinner. Bakewell had been keeping a journal of hunting places for over twenty years. He wondered which of his sons would end up with the carefully annotated book, hoped it might become a treasured memento.

The journal was a product of many hunkers. Hunkering was an important part of hunting. Without the capacity for hunkering a man spent his time on public areas managed by the government. Bakewell learned early on that hunkering with a landowner was the key to having a place each year, and having little boys in tow, or a new puppy in training was almost a guarantee of successful communication. Without any little boys the tri-colored puppy was his contact now. She was a beautiful little thing, a great icebreaker, quickly became a favorite with the American farmer. She obeyed his soft commands, slept quietly during travel time, would gently nudge his elbow when it was time to stop.

He spent the last night in the pickup sipping a bottle of Rain vodka, a jar of anchovy-stuffed olives to vary the taste. The liquor depressed him and he worried about time wasted while inebriated. In the morning he realized his drinking days were over. It had been the same when Katherine had gotten bad, when he'd wanted to be lucid in case there was a sudden change in her condition. He wanted to be coherent from now on, see it coming, keep watch and worry his way through it, like he did with every unpleasant thing. He had to stay sharp; there was a really big event out there now, looming, just out of sight. The Civil War soldiers called the moment they went into battle, "meeting the elephant." If he was to meet the elephant, he wanted both eyes open, wanted to look it straight in the eye, see those enormous yellow tusks, wonder what they might signify. *No more boozing.*

After another day of frustrated looking, the discouragement of *missing quail* took its toll. He decided to head back. For four days his thoughts had been vacillating, his emotions spiking, keeping tempo with his pulse rate – fear trading places with periods of quiet reflection.

At one point, in an overgrown orchard among twisted, ancient fruit trees – their broken limbs and fractured trunks, like something out of a Disney cartoon – filling him with scary, thought-provoking uncertainty, and mayhems of misgiving under a gloomy low sky, his contemplation got the best of him and his thoughts turned to cold fear. Still later that afternoon, sitting under a giant oak, resolutely holding its drab foliage, waiting for the big running setter to check back in, the day brightened crisp and clear. He enjoyed a contemplative spell that allowed a look back over many happy years – years of beautiful infants, swarming little leaguers, pre-teens who listened, (even attentively), but mostly, (it had to be the hormone thing again), he remembered sex with a thirty-something who made his pulse race, made him shudder, convulse in paroxysms that left him believing it couldn't happen more than once, then happen again, a crescendo of fulfillment. *Forgive me for remembering, but Dear God you were good Lew, you were more than I deserved, better than I ever dared dream. You made me alive, exposed me to dendrites so alive with pleasure I didn't know possible... You revealed me to the fantastic pleasure – of us.*

There were quiet spaces in that last day when the serenity of remembering left him content, satisfied with the better parts. But just when he was most peaceful, he would come up again, interrupted with the remembering of that final act, the finishing every life had to do, and the worry would set in once more, be even more intense. He remembered another one of Frost's poems, but, frustratingly, only in part. Robert Frost would always be grouped there beside Byron and Donne in Bakewell's limited poetic library:

My Sorrow, when she's here with me,
Thinks these dark days…

Are beautiful as days can be;
She loves the bare the withered tree...
Her pleasure will not let me stay...
Not yesterday I learned to know
The love of bare November days
Before the coming of the snow,
But it were vain to tell her so,
And they are better for her praise.

Behind the wheel he worried and thought about the miserable luck of the last few years, unable to enjoy the back-road traveling. He traveled over ground he had discovered decades before, finding time once to interrupt his melancholy and stop at a place along a deeply rutted and hilly stretch of country where he made one last try, and where he actually found the setters solid on a small covey, a magazine shot, a photo of enchantment, the young dog on point, one foot curled under, her momma backing solidly, the feathers of her scimitar tail falling, nutant-like, perfect. Bakewell walked in and the birds exploded into a multi-directional commotion of motion. He wasn't carrying his shotgun, and when it was finished, called them in, praised them, and kenneled them for the last time, the older dogs each happily taking a place in the back of the truck, under the camper shell, enjoying the greenhouse effect.

There was something to be said for dying. It was causing a quiet to settle around him. He knew the insurance policy the company had would bring some huge relief, if they could just last that long. There was a second, larger policy that would go to the trust, to the kids. They would be able to live in houses without mortgages. The cancer gave him another kind of peace, gave him an out. It would take care of a lot of the worry that kept him awake nights. The trouble was he had to die to get the money, and *he might last six months*. There was no way to borrow against his death.

He had grown insensitive about emotional relationships. The calcification that settled around his heart had taken something away: the capacity to *miss*. The part that allowed him to *miss* people was missing. He no longer missed anyone. He still loved with true passion, worried about his kids and their families, but he didn't *miss* anyone the way he did before. It was abnormal, but his life was abnormal now. Nothing would ever be the same. He needed to be somewhere else, somewhere he could find peace and not die of his loneliness. He thought if he could do it, the kids could do it too. His children had other obligations and concerns now. They had gotten used to him being absent much of the time.

As he drove south toward the interstate he made his decision, and a sense of urgency overtook him. He needed to get to a phone. They headed for Macon, three worn out bird dogs, two snoozing comfortably in back under the camper shell, one limp puppy, sleeping soundly on the seat, her muzzle resting on his thigh.

As he drove, his processing slowed again, became deliberate. He focused on what he would say and how he would phrase it. It was a simple plan, discarded at first, later resisted, eventually a resigned fatalism set in. He followed the paved road to Chillicothe then east, as he thought and rethought the future. He was over the speed limit, noticed, set the cruise control.

He contemplated the "what-ifs" and the "how-to's" until his mind finally refused to focus any longer. The what-ifs were the easy part, the part that would just happen, be beyond his control. It was the how-to's that frightened him, the how he might *make it work afterward* part. When he got to Macon he pulled into a motel, looking for a phone in the lobby; a young woman pointed to one on the table, saying it was free, "As long as it ain't long distance and don't cost nuthin." He dialed the number, waited; didn't really think anyone would answer on the weekend, was surprised when the same woman's voice said, "Corporate Office."

"This is Andersen Bakewell," he started and again she interrupted him and asked him to stay on the line. She said it might take a minute. It took more than five. Bakewell waited with the young woman watching him from the counter.

"Andy, is that you?" The old man asked.

"Yes sir, I suppose it is," he said, resigned. He wanted his voice to sound withered, defeated; it didn't require much effort.

"Well good, that's grand, splendid, I was hoping to hear from you, and soon too, I might add." The old man had a style; he hadn't changed.

"I've been thinking about your offer."

"And?"

"I think we could make a deal."

"Excellent. I thought you would reconsider, certainly I hoped you would."

"Well here I am. You mentioned money at lunch a couple of weeks back."

"Yes. We do this sort of thing for the money, right?"

"Well, I don't need the practice, and I sure don't do it for the experience."

"One of your construction expressions isn't it?"

"It is, yes sir."

"The money was to be one million, less your tax liability?"

"Is the number negotiable?"

The old man chuckled softly into the phone, took his time, did it a second time before answering, "I believe *avarice and greed has reared its ugly head.*" It was a favorite expression of Bakewell's; he'd used it all his business life. It was eerie. *They know too much about me. Hell, they know everything about me*. He was going to have to be very careful. There would be no chance for luck this time. After a short pause the old man said. "What did you have in mind?"

"A million and a quarter," he answered without hesitation.

"Yes, you *have* become a businessman. Let's settle on a million and one hundred thousand."

"Only if you can put a hundred grand in an account for me alone."

"Mmm. Are you thinking about skipping out on us, Andy? That wouldn't be smart at all."

"No sir, I just think I might need a little running around cash."

"Well I suppose we can do that, but the tax ramifications will be your own. Don't look to us for any help with your individual problems with the Internal Revenue Service my boy."

"I understand sir. I'll have to pay the taxes."

"Mm," the old man repeated.

"Could I ask a question, sir?"

"Certainly."

"What's the time frame? Is there a target date…so to speak?" No pun was intended.

"Fairly soon. We will be getting our information out to you soon enough."

"Are we talking a week, a month?"

"Probably a few months. Our man's not in position yet. Is there some conflict? A wedding perhaps?"

"No sir, I was just trying to prepare myself. I want to be prepared."

"Good. I have always admired preparation. I don't think it's possible to over plan. There is nothing more important than to be ready when the time comes. I have a question for you?"

"Yes sir?"

"How is your health? Are you in good spirits? Annual physical find you in sound condition?"

They know I went to see Neville! Bakewell wanted to consider the question but knew better, had to answer fast. "Just the usual signs of old age, lots of aches and pains in the morning. My prostate's getting clogged up. I'll need a ream job one of these days." He doubted Neville would give up his medical information, but they might approach him on behalf of some super snoop organization. He wondered, worried.

The old man laughed gently again. "I understand that one's very painful. They tell me you shouldn't do it unless you absolutely have to."

"I'll take your advice, sir. I'm in no hurry."

"Would one more question be in order?"

"Yes sir."

"What made you change your mind?"

Bakewell hesitated, anticipating this one, knowing just how to answer, how long to wait before he sighed, sounding exasperated, reconciled. "It's hopeless. We'll never dig our way out without a miracle. You're going to have to be my guardian angel one more time."

The old man chuckled again, good-naturedly. "It's been my distinct pleasure to serve in that capacity. Would a wire transfer be all right? We can make one to your company, the other to your account?"

"Sure." Bakewell couldn't believe how casual the conversation was, reminded himself who he was talking to, said, "When?"

"Tomorrow. You need the money quickly don't you?"

"We need the money sure enough."

"Tomorrow then. I'm glad you have reconsidered Andy. I really am. Call me at this number if you have any concerns, otherwise we will be getting in touch with you, quite soon I might add." There was a brief pause before he continued, "And, by the way, you will be receiving some mailings, *sent to your office, special delivery*. You will have to be there to receive them, so let's have a plan right now. How about Tuesdays, between eight and nine? You will have to sign for each item."

"Okay, in my office every Tuesday between eight and nine."

"I'll let you get on with your weekend, then."

"Thank you, it's been eventful."

The old man hung up. Bakewell put the phone on the worn plastic coffee table and looked straight ahead; finally remembering the young lady at the counter, he turned to her. She was watching him closely.

She said, "Wow!"

Galleria

When he got home Bakewell turned the dogs loose in the yard with food and fresh water and spent what was left of the November daylight cleaning birds and shotgun on the deck. In the old days, he'd have cleaned everything in the kitchen where the light was better, and Katherine, never comfortable around firearms, despite a lifetime of exposure, would have told him to take them somewhere else. Michael and Andy would protest, fascinated by the weapons and a father, bigger than life, who knew so much about them. After they had been schooled in dogs, game and weapons – when they were big enough to go along, which meant not having to be carried back to the car – they would all come home together, excited with success, full of stories about their adventure. Bakewell would watch, amused, as Katherine got after them about bringing "dead things" into her kitchen. She would scold them about the condition of the dogs, who were always nicked up, displaying minor injuries as they rummaged about in search of treats.

He did the cleaning outside now, out of respect for her memory, while his dogs slept in sunnier spots out near the pines, each moving with the setting sun until there was no sunshine left. Then they came up on the deck, waiting for the opportunity to enter the house and find a familiar place to nap. Before going up to bed, Bakewell put them out in the heated kennel, not wanting their constant place-changing to wake him. He had enough to wake him during the night.

Sunday, after Mass, he spent the day raking, shaping pine straw under his trees. He went to Andy's house for dinner and, after a fine roast, spent a few minutes discussing the hunt and the dogs with his older son. Andy listened as his father described the way they worked as a team and so perfectly, despite the lack of game. His daughter-in-law fumed and glared at her husband from the kitchen. She was anti-gun, anti-hunt, anti-everything the two men had shared most of Andy's life, never tired of equivocating about the difference between domestic and wild meat. Mostly she equivocated with Bakewell. Andy kept a low profile whenever his wife and father were having "a gentle disagreement."

Karen was tall and willowy, very feminine, almost fragile, but Bakewell had learned early on of her formidability, avoided confrontations on whatever subject she chose. If he hadn't been so crazy about his new grandson he would have avoided her completely. He was reconciled to never having the same relationship he and Andy had shared for years. With Karen pregnant again Bakewell asked the obligatory questions about her condition, while he helped put the dishes away. Her answers were curt, almost irritated; her body language: *you-really-don't-want-to-know,* while Bakewell plugged along, clumsy and meager, sympathetically deficient, but determined to show concern, to try to make her smile and talk to him. After his grandson went to bed he excused himself and left.

He was strangely at peace and he slept well Sunday night; without the usual AM panic, actually overslept. When he came through the front door Monday, Trudy displayed amusement along with her pleasant greeting. "It's Monday, the 15th, boss, and it's after nine o'clock."

"I can still tell time."

"Yes sir, you can, and you sure don't need me to remind you how late you are this morning." When Bakewell mumbled under his breath, she said, "Excuse me," to his retreating figure. When he didn't answer she said. "A word of caution, Andy, Ned's been trying to get you. He sounds frantic, I might add."

"My battery's dead. I forgot to charge it."

When he sat down he flipped through the mail quickly, refused to open anything without first class postage, eliminating most of the stack. He checked the messages and turned to the computer, wasn't surprised to see the market was up. Trudy brought him a cup of coffee.

"What's that?"

"Don't give me any shit, Andy Bakewell. I brought you a cup of coffee. When guys show up *hours late* they're usually hung over and need a cup of coffee." She put the cup on his desk, took his Nextel and plugged it into the charger. He accepted the coffee and took time to take her in, complimented her on the hokey orange outfit she wore, got a smile for his trouble.

"You look like you got your ashes drug last night." Bakewell ignored her impudence and looked at the phone. Before he could reach it, it rang and Trudy grabbed it efficiently, gave her pleasant company greeting, handed it to him, raising her eyes in confirmation. "It's Ned."

"Hello."

"Andy, what's going on? Gallagher called me a little while ago from the bank. He said we got a wire transfer for a million dollars this morning."

"Sounds too good to be true."

"You know about this. What's goin on?"

"I guess all those no good SOB's who've cheated us over the years decided to pay…all at once."

"Don't jack me around, Andy! Don't fuck with me!" Ned shouted. "What's goin on?"

"Well it can only be good news, Ned."

"You know'd about this didn't you?"

"Yeah, I *know'd.*"

"What's goin on?"

"I got an inheritance from my uncle."

"Bullshit, you ain't got no uncle."

Bakewell tried to laugh, stopped when Ned lost it, waited for him to settle down. "Ned, I've got to get over to the Galleria. I overslept this morning, and I forgot we started that job today. I'm going over there now."

"I'll meet you there. When?"

"Ten minutes."

"I'm down in South County. It'll take me half an hour to get out there. Don't try no bullshit on me when I get there, Andy. I don't need this shit."

"Ned," Bakewell spaced his words carefully, "The worst thing that can happen would be for the money to be a mistake and they take it back. It's not against the law to receive money." Bakewell added, "It's not a mistake."

"Yeah? You remember that dipshit dame used to be on TV? She got money put in her account wasn't hers and she didn't report it? She spent it! She ended up goin to jail. I ain't goin to no jails." Ned was out of breath, his jowly expiations coming through the phone.

"No. You're not going to jail, Ned. You're going home." Bakewell hung up and looked at the monitor. The DOW was already up 173 points.

He took the interstate west to the jobsite. He could see the big excavator from the highway before he turned off. When he pulled into the huge parking lot he stopped next to some barricades and waved to the operator in the cab of the giant machine. The man finished loading a tandem. When the truck pulled away the operator idled the machine and got down from the cab and came over, beaming. "I was down at Dennises'," he said, mispronouncing the taxidermist's name the way they all did. "I saw a bighorn down there. He said it was the only one he had. I knew it had to be yours."

"What do you think; he'll go over 36 inches?"

"Shit, I guess. Denny said he was 42½ and 42¾. That's not dry, but it's awesome. I'll sure be glad to see them mounted. I'll bet he's close to a record when they do a dry measurement. He'll make the book, that's for sure."

"Well, they'll have to measure him at my house or maybe at Michael's. I'm not going to measure him once he's on the wall." The operator looked at Bakewell curiously, never quite sure how to read him. "He was a personal record for me, Jack. I don't care how he measures up green or dry. He was a dream hunt come true. I'm satisfied and I'm done."

"You're not going back? You could put in for Wyoming or Colorado next year."

"I always said I would only take one. I passed on a little guy years ago because I would have been ashamed to hang him on the wall. As a matter of fact I have this eerie feeling that little guy just might be the one I killed. But I'm done; I'm sticking to my word."

"Well, I'm glad you got him boss. I hope *I just get a shot* at one like him someday."

Bakewell shared the details of his hunt with the operator, one of the loyal ones; Bakewell could remember the day he first climbed nervously on a piece of equipment. While they were talking, Ned's truck showed up. He came right through the barricades, and when he got out of the truck he was all business. The operator had seen the look too many times, headed back to the machine. Ned came on full of purpose, a huge, intimidating bull of a man. Bakewell remained calm, almost amused.

"I want to know what's goin on, Andy?"

"I'm going to tell you."

"Fuckin A straight, you are. Give it to me without no bullshit."

"You're not going to like it, Ned."

"I already know that, and I don't even know what's gonna come out of your mouth next, but go on and spit it out so I can see where it lands."

Bakewell put his hand on Ned's huge bicep and steered him away from the excavation.

"Ned, I've got a million dollars in life insurance on myself, and the company's got another half million on me in "key man" insurance."

"And on me too, what's insurance got to do with it?"

"I made a deal with the devil, Ned. I'm going to sign my life insurance over to a guy in Chicago who does deals like this."

"What the fuck you talkin about?"

Bakewell took a deep breath, wondering what the words would sound like when he spoke them out loud, when he pronounced them for the first time, when he told his partner he was going to die. He'd practiced how he would phrase them on the way to work earlier, and most of the way home on Saturday. There was only one way to deal with Ned. He made eye contact, "Ned, I'm going to die…soon," shrugged self-consciously, "That's it. That's the deal." There was no answer from the bigger man. "It's not that big a deal, really."

"I don't get it...the fuck you talkin about, Andy." Ned hesitated momentarily, shuddered, almost lost his balance, reached for something to hold; there was nothing close by. He reeled around, disoriented. When he caught his balance he put one big hand to his mouth, and Bakewell thought he might throw up. He needed to continue, give Ned a chance to catch up.

"I endorse the policies to a guy in Chicago. The guy gets the proceeds, advances us a million against a million and a half for six months. He keeps two hundred grand. Think of him as a venture capitalist"

"More like a vulture capitalist. How you gonna die? How?"

"I've got cancer, I'm checking out in a few months, six at the most."

"Jesus."

"Yes, Jesus is involved, hopefully. It's his deal you might say."

"And he just dealt you the Ace of spa…" Ned broke off, choking, turned away. Bakewell knew he would. It wasn't something he wanted to watch. It was the reason he wanted to be away from the machinery. Ned was a shambles. They both knew the day would come; both thought it would be Ned to go first. He was a hundred pounds overweight, had high blood pressure, still smoked three packs a day. For Ned, exercise was drinking and fishing at the same time.

"I'm going to need a big favor. I'm going to have to ask you for a big favor now – a *big favor?*"

Ned's back was turned. Bakewell knew how he felt; he'd lived through it himself five days before. It wasn't as bad as it had been with Katherine.

"What the fuck is wrong with the world," Ned said, choking.

"It's not a fair place, not for people like us anyway."

Ned was a powerful man, but like hippos, rhinos and big crocs, he had a soft underbelly. Bakewell wished he could have come up with something better. The "Chicago guy" was weak, but he knew the magnitude of his pending death would stop any of Ned's questions, and he knew he would be able to count on his help and support. There was a bond that would hold them together to the end. He waited for him to get control. Ned turned back around. Bakewell said, "Ned, I need your help."

"What," was all he could choke out.

"You and my doctor are the only two people who know. I want to keep it that way for now. I don't want my kids or anybody, *ANYBODY* to know. Not until it gets closer."

"Where'd the money really come from, Andy?"

"You don't want to know. What difference does it make anyway; the money's good. It's ours. We will use it."

"It's yours. You gotta die to get it. It ain't mine."

"Right. It's mine and I can do whatever I want with it. Here's what I want to do, and right away, before I change my mind."

Ned looked at him closely, showing signs of recovery; talking money had an amazing effect on the contractor in him, forty years in the business.

"What?"

"We pay off the line and we get your name off everything you're personally liable for; you sell to me and go home. I don't mean not to come to work anymore. We need your help, but you're off the hook. You're just a consultant from here on out. I want you to help us wherever you can, but you won't be liable, won't even be an owner from here on out."

"It's too good to be true."

"Thanks."

"It ain't what I meant, you fuck!" Ned put his hand to his head again. "I didn't mean that, you know I didn't."

Bakewell smiled compassionately, wishing he could do something for the big man. "I know."

"Don't make me sound like no ungrateful fuck that don't care about his pard. I love you like you was my own brother; you know I do."

"Yeah, I know, and I guess I probably love you too, but don't tell anybody I said it." Bakewell smiled, feeling almost giddy, ridiculous, like he had just figured out the way to financial success. They were both going through a kind of emotional robotics. "It is too good to be true in many ways, especially for you. In many ways I'm happy for you. I've given it some thought the last few days. You said all you wanted was out. I'm going to get you out."

"Yeah, it's my dream come true, all right. It's too good to believe, only I'm gonna lose the one purson's the most important to me; what a deal that is."

"You're repeating yourself, *fuckhead*." Bakewell wanted to laugh. They were both in shock; neither knew what to say or think or how to act.

"I can't believe it. I can't believe you're gonna die on me."

"I'm just doing it to piss you off."

"I can't believe it."

"Believe it. Call our bean-counting lawyer and get with our accountant and tell them what's going on. Not about me though, don't tell them anything about me. Just tell them what we want to do with the company. Let's get it done, quick."

"What do I tell them about the money?"

"Nothing."

"Okay," Ned said dumbly, came forward. "Andy?"

"Get away from me. Don't go soft on me now." Bakewell backed away. "I need to keep moving. I can't stand around. I don't have much time left. I've got to get going." He was pantomiming Ned and his way of talking; he backed away farther. When Ned stopped coming on he said, "Ned, I might need a little extra time off too."

"Okay." Ned moved toward him again and reached out.

"I don't want any hugs," Bakewell held up his hands. "Get away from me. We'll look like a couple of fairies, hugging on a construction site; you're too ugly to hug anyway."

Ned started to break down again. He didn't know what to do with his enormous hands, kept holding them up, making little circular gestures, leaning in like he intended to do something, then rethinking it; stumped and hating it, hating the immobility that emotion seemed always to evoke, he…

"Ned, you're the best friend I ever had. You're the brother I lost in Viet Nam. You're the father I never had. When trouble comes – and I can't ever remember a time when we weren't in some kind of trouble, it's surrounded us most of our lives – you've been the only guy I could turn to or count on. Nobody's been any help to me in the hard times. You're it. I love you like a brother."

"I've had too damned many brothers and none of 'em was ever worth a shit. You're the only thing close to a brother to me, Andy."

"I know. I'm going back to the office to pay some bills now. Get with the professional people and let's get the deal done; let's get it done in record time. Don't let them bog us down with any technicalities."

He walked off. Ned stayed where he was. Bakewell stopped and talked to the foreman for a moment, going over the job, motioning with his hands before he drove away. Ned never moved. The foreman came over and asked if something was wrong.

"Get the fuck away from me," Ned said gruffly. He turned, started to walk away, paused, said, "fuck," called the abused man back over and patted him on the shoulder. "You do a hell of a job for me Charlie, you're a good man."

1st Mailing

On Monday of the following week, Bakewell called Nancy into his office and gave her the new plan of action. Bakewell said they had sold the property in Grover to explain the new found wealth. Later, he was sitting at his desk going over the accounts payable, enjoying it, when he heard the truck pull up. He paid no attention. The bank balance exceeded his accounts payable by a tidy six-figures, and the reality of having money again pleased him more than anything since the birth of his last grandchild. The information before him documented prosperity: the line of credit paid off, the long-term debt retired. Things looked normal again; the bank was happy. Ned correctly predicted the bank would be at the door, telling them they needed to borrow money, telling them they needed more debt. They had seen their creditors' darker side, remembered the looks when they were in trouble. Ned said he didn't want to talk to the bank, wasn't accepting theatre tickets, invitations to ball games, not even a free lunch.

"I don't give a shit if I never talk to another creditor, and that includes the time left before I die, and even that's gonna be too soon. I hope I never have to talk to one before eternity's over." Bakewell laughed for the first time in weeks, appreciating his partner, enjoying his *one-allowed-in-a-lifetime* status as friend, treasured the feeling. If dying would heal Ned, he thought it might be worth it.

"Andy, there's a delivery here and this man says you have to sign for it!" Trudy shouted down the hall. Bakewell liked shouting better than the annoying intercom. He no longer wanted the sounds of technology in his life, and he was in a mood to get his way, everyone had picked up on it. He didn't look whipped anymore, he'd stopped cringing when the phone rang, walked with confidence, his shoulders more erect, making eye contact with everyone. As soon as he came into the lobby he realized what was going on. It was Tuesday; Snow said to be there between 8 and 9 on Tuesdays. A curious feeling came over him, not fear, more like a tentative curiosity, like when he spotted a bad snake in time to avoid it, take time to stoop and take a closer look. He stepped inside what he thought of as the ring of danger and took the package.

"How ya doin today sir?"

"Pretty good," Bakewell said, "Where do I sign?"

The deliveryman handed him a metal case with a plastic top that accepted his signature from a strange pen. He signed. While Trudy made small talk with the driver about the rainy weather, he took the package and went outside and put it behind the seat of his pickup. Then he did an uncharacteristic thing – he locked his truck. He passed the driver on his way back to his office and got his jacket and told Trudy he was gone for the day.

"You're not going to wait for Ned? He said you two were going to lunch."

"He's too depressing to be around lately." Bakewell stopped at the door, adding, "Tell him something came up; we'll have lunch tomorrow."

"Where you off to boss?"

"I'm going to take my girls for a run in this wonderful weather."

Trudy nodded politely, told him to "have a great day." Bakewell hated the expression. "I'll have whatever kind of day I want to have."

"Sure you will, boss, and I hope it's great."

He stopped and got a cup of coffee and drank it in the parking lot, not wanting to get out in the rain, wanting to be alone while he handled the package, looking for a return address. There was none. It was a package within a package, inside a heavy packing, impregnated with some kind of lubricant. The smaller package contained a bolt from a bolt-action rifle. It was a Ruger; he recognized it immediately. He had two like it. One was the sheep hunting gun with the hand carved stock, the other a beautifully engraved .270 Hunt Turner had done years ago, putting his initials on the bottom of the trigger guard. It hung on his rack, but he no longer used it, saving it for his oldest son, who had the same initials. He intended to give the rifle to Andy one day. The sheep gun he would give to Michael, when the time came. *The time is almost here.* He turned the bolt over studying it. It was about seven inches long, slightly smaller than the one for his .243. He put it in the wrapping and placed it under the seat and drove home.

His yard was turning into a muddy swamp with three energized bird dogs racing around over their half acre. He called them in and put them in the kennel, hooked up his trailer, not wanting them in his pickup full of mud. They were likely to be muddier once they got done at the wildlife area. When he dropped the back door to the trailer and opened the yard gate they made a dash for the boxes. Everybody ended up in the same side, slamming into the heavy box before turning around, vibrating with anticipation. The trailer was separated into two separate boxes, filled with sweet smelling prairie grass.

"Which one of you bozos is going to move to the other side?" They looked apprehensive, expectant. He bent down and the setter came to him, slinking and humble, like she'd done something wrong. Bakewell praised her and put her in the other side and closed both doors.

As he was driving west on the interstate, coming up on Maggie Walker's exit, he took his phone and dialed her number. She answered the second ring, "I'm on the other line would you please hold, Andy? Promise me you won't hang up?"

Bakewell waited, when she came back asked, "What's Mrs. Walker up to today?"

"Andy Bakewell, as I live and breath. Hello, I wondered if I would hear from you."

"What are you doing for the next hour or two?"

"You think I'm that easy? You think you can call and I'll come right out?" Her voice filled with merriment, encouraging, "What did you have in mind?"

"Something wet, woodsie and outdoorsy. I thought you might want to come along."

She hesitated, "I need a little more information. Explain."

"I'm running my girls. We're going out to the wildlife area. We wanted to know if you'd consider joining us." He tried the soft sell. She wasn't a nature girl. "Actually I want you to meet three of my favorite girls. I can only promise mud, cold and wet, a lot of dreary weather. How's that sound?"

"I don't know how I can pass it up. What do I really have to do?"

"Wear something warm, and if you have such a thing as a pair of boots, bring them too."

"When?"

"Right now. I'll be there in five minutes."

"Let me think about it."

"I'm passing your exit now, make a decision?"

"You're such a shit."

"Come on."

"Come by and we'll talk about it."

He'd already made the turn. "I'll be there in...more like three minutes. If you don't want to go, you can come out in front and say, 'hello'."

"This is kind of quick, Bakewell."

"Maggie, tell the guy at the gate to let me in, and we can discuss it in front of your house. It's not often I share my girls with another woman."

When he got to her home he turned the truck around slowly in the cul de sac, careful not to run onto a manicured lawn. He opened the boxes and snapped a cord to each collar, tying them off at separate points, keeping them from getting crossed. It had stopped raining and Maggie came out front in a heavy sweater, looking very middle aged without makeup, looking like she had just enough time to brush her hair.

"Well," she said, coming to the trailer. She bent down and reached for the tri colored pup, soothing her with kind words. Her tail came up and she licked her hand and her face. "She's darling."

Bakewell looked on approvingly, while the puppy smothered her with affection. Maggie moved about, making obligatory visits, petting each one. The older setter didn't have the puppy's cuteness, but was lovable. She had a wonderfully soft coat and lots of humility, which belied her eye-popping style. The Brittany managed to incur his wrath for the thousandth time when she put one of her dirty paws on Maggie's sweater.

"It's okay, I don't mind."

"I do. She drives me crazy with her feet. She can't keep them on the ground. I don't have many rules, but one of them is keep all four on the ground."

"She's fine," Maggie said, petting the dog. "So where's the party?"

"Weldon Springs."

"The Busch Wildlife Area, I haven't been there in years."

"Come on. You'll love it. The roads are all gravel, so you can walk along, stay up out of the mud and enjoy the show."

"I'm not going to get caught in a rainstorm and look like a drowned rat?"

"No. I'll make sure you're warm and dry. We won't be that far from the truck. I'll buy lunch."

She agreed, went inside, saying, "I'll only be a minute." Bakewell put the dogs away and waited in the truck. It took twenty minutes. When she finally reappeared she was carefully arranged, wearing an expensive oilcloth slicker.

"You look like a member of the Dalton gang in that outfit."

"Don't make fun. It's required wardrobe in Banff. You know how the weather is up there." He opened the door for her, "I can't believe I'm going for a ride in a pick up truck."

"Get in and don't be such a stuck up bitch," he put his hand on her hip, none to subtly.

"You're asking for it Bakewell," she said, as he gave her a gentle push up into the cab. When he was seated next to her, he paused, smiled. Maggie said, "How do I look?"

"In a pick up?"

"Yes."

"Ridiculous." She straightened the long coat around her crossed legs and settled in. He watched in amusement. "Actually, and I know you don't want to hear it, but you look good over there, like you belong. There's hope for you yet, Margaret Leary."

"Drive."

It started to rain lightly on the way. They stopped at a deli at the corner of Highway 94 and got hot sandwiches, soda, and drove over to a big lake in the Wildlife Area and ate lunch in the truck, waiting for the rain to quit.

"My, my, does this take me back," she said, remembering lunches they had shared that first summer when she was still a teen and he an indolent baseball bum.

The rain stopped briefly. "Time to go," he said, taking a whistle hanging from the rear view mirror. He opened the trailer doors and the dogs shot out, churning the wet limestone. They walked down the road to the lake together. Bakewell liked to park on top of the hill, where he could keep an eye on the big running setter. Before they had gone twenty yards, the dogs were two hundred yards off, the setter hitting upon five Canada geese at the shoreline, so intent on the chase she tried to walk on the water the way the geese did as they half flew half ran out into the lake. On about the third bound the setter sank completely under and came up spouting, before turning back to shore. It made them laugh. All three dogs performed antics, trying to get to the geese. By the time the slower Brittany arrived, the geese were well out on the lake. She swam out after them, losing distance as she went.

"Will she be all right?" Maggie asked solicitously.

"She'd rather swim than point."

"What exactly is this pointing thing?"

Bakewell explained, "They chase about, know by instinct where to look and when they get a nose full of scent they get real birdy, quivering and very stealthy at the same time, then they just lock up solid and nothing moves them until the birds flush." He had a funny story about the way each had learned to point and hold game as a puppy.

"And you teach them how to do this?"

"No. They teach themselves. It's all in the breeding. They make lots of mistakes in the beginning before catching on, but eventually they learn to come to a full stop and make a solid point. It's something to see. Half the fun is watching them learn." He talked with his hands out of habit, describing. "They bump into the birds at first, but when they finally figure it out, well that's a special moment. It's worth all the trouble just to be there when they put it all together. It's magic really – being there, seeing the breeding take over. They're like athletes, the more they practice the better they get, but breeding is responsible for most of it; without the genes they'd just be doing parlor room tricks."

"How long have you been doing this?"

"We got our first birddog the year Andy was born. But my brother and I were raised with stories of bird dogs and quail hunting. My dad had a bird dog before the war. He told us stories of bird hunting when we were kids. It must have been something back then. I didn't remember much, but Brenny retold the stories while we were growing up. I wanted a bird dog out of respect for his memory."

"Your dad's or Brenny's?"

"Both, I guess, probably Brenden mostly. I loved him a lot more than I loved my father. I didn't really know my father."

"Brenny was a big part of your life, wasn't he?"

"A big part of my early life; he's been gone half my life."

"The world's a strange place, Andy. Here you are with a brother you loved, and I've had two brothers I wouldn't cross the street to visit. About the only good thing that came from my brothers is one darling niece. I just adore her. Other than that I could have lived my life without ever seeing them."

"She's the one out in Seattle?"

"Yes, I see her rarely, but we talk on the phone a lot, girl talk, you know. She's almost twenty-five."

The big setter came flying by at flank speed, her feet hitting the wet ground hard, throwing up gravel and mud, sounding like a small horse. She was gone in seconds down the north side of the dam.

"Yikes."

"She's a real goer, biggest running dog I've ever had. She's a field-trialer's dream."

"What's that mean?"

"The big time field-trialers hunt from horseback. They run their dogs in national events with judges and spotters and lots of folks on horses, watching. They want big running dogs. That one's about as big as you could hope for."

"And that's good? Big running?"

"It gets to be a pain. She runs so big she used to get lost. She's no problem now, but as a puppy I'd let her out of the car and not find her for a whole day. One time Katherine and I had to drive out to pick her up the day after we'd been running them. She was over twenty miles from where I let her out of the car. I keep a lot of identification on her, emergency phone numbers, name and address. If I didn't I would have lost her a dozen times."

"This cute little one with the three colors on her face; how is she?"

"Almost perfect! She's the closest thing to a natural I'll ever have. She does it all, and she picked it up on her own. All I ever did was take her out and put her down. They're all a joy to watch when they're little. We start them when they're really little. It can be comical. It's a lot like going to a Little League game, only dogs, not kids."

"I wouldn't know about Little Leagues."

He took her hand, helped her over a ditch, around a muddy place. Maggie held onto his hand afterward. "This is it," he said. "This is the Little Leagues. Pretend it's your kid and watch the tri colored girl."

Bakewell's Nextel rang; he shrugged at Maggie. "Duty calls." He took it from the holster on his hip. "Hello?"

"Andy? You got the package this morning I'm informed. Was it intact?"

"Yes sir," *back to reality.* He turned away from Maggie without thinking and walked off toward the truck.

"Good. The next one will be on another Tuesday just as we agreed. How are you?"

"Fine," Bakewell added, "How are you sir?"

"Well to tell the truth I've been better. It's my age you know."

"I'm sorry to hear that."

"Thank you. I will look forward to talking with you again. Is everything all right? Can I do anything for you? You got the money?"

"Yes sir, I did. Everything's all right. Thank you."

"I'll ring off then."

Bakewell turned and walked back to Maggie.

"That sounded important."

"Yeah, one of my big accounts; things are starting to go much better for me."

"I'm so glad to hear it. You seem more confident now; more relaxed than the last time I saw you."

"The last time you saw me I could hardly see. I don't know how I made it home."

They crossed the dam, walked another two hundred yards; Bakewell stopped, told Maggie to cover her ears, blew his whistle loudly. Two of the dogs turned and started back again.

"They do that to the whistle? And you're telling me you don't have to train them? They do that naturally?"

"They come when they're called or when I whistle, unless they get too far away. Some guys train them to come to hand signals. I don't go that far. My hands are usually full of shotguns and candy bars or twigs or flowers." He laughed self-consciously. "I like to collect stuff when I hunt, seeds and plants, catkins, buds, that sort of thing. I draw pictures of them in my notebook. Sometimes I ask a forester or a conservation agent what the stuff is."

"You're an artist too."

"No, no. I can barely draw. It's just a way to learn what gamebirds eat and what's out there. You usually get a good response from those people if you make an intelligent request, sometimes find a fellow hunter, sometimes make a friend. I have a lot of respect for anybody in the wildlife business. I've collected a notebook full of names and phone numbers over the years."

"Mmm, so you've become a botanist and a biologist – probably a vet too."

"No. Katherine was my vet. She knew what was wrong with them before I noticed anything might be wrong with them. She loved animals. She loved all kinds of animals. We stopped to save a box turtle crossing the street after Mass once. One of the dogs brought home a half dead squirrel one time, and we had to take it to one of those animal shelters. I'd have tossed it in the trash. One year she found a great horned owl at the farm and made me catch it and put it in a dog box and take it out to the Raptor Center. That was a challenge. Owls aren't grateful. Damned thing tried to bite me, tried to get those mean claws clamped on me." They fell silent and wandered along the dam. "Katherine wasn't too crazy about bird dogs."

"Why?"

"Well, that's not really true. She was good to them, but they're too big. Too much trouble too. She liked little, fluffy dogs."

He looked around for the big running setter, whistled again. Maggie wanted to know if she was lost. "No she'll turn up in a minute." As they walked down the dam the puppy got interested in a multiflora hedge, stopped in a classic setter point. "Look, I hoped that might happen. Isn't that the prettiest thing?"

Maggie watched, entranced by the quivering figure below them. "What happens next?"

"Well, you're supposed to go down there and walk in and when the bird flushes you shoot."

"Where's your gun?"

"Not here."

"This isn't the season?"

"Yes, it's the season, but not out here. Quail are protected here."

"What happens next?"

"She goes a little crazy when they flush, and, if you're really lucky you hit what you're shooting at. She sees the bird go down, finds it in the brush, fetches it, and gives it to you. Voila! You have a *made* bird dog."

"But you don't train her to do this?"

"You're getting into a gray area now, Maggie. The plot thickens when the retrieving starts."

He walked down to the dog on point. The Brittany came up behind. Maggie insisted on going with him. Bakewell hissed at the Brittany, whoa-ing her up as she tried to crowd in; she stopped and backed the puppy. He told Maggie to walk up behind the puppy. She started to, hesitated, looked back, apprehensive. Bakewell enjoyed seeing her on strange ground. He nodded for her to go on.

"If she's got quail, they will fly in every direction."

Maggie wasn't sure. "Should I be afraid?"

"No, it will be noisy. It might startle you, that's all."

She looked unsure; when she got close a covey of eight birds flushed from the winter cover and flew off in several directions. Maggie jumped back. Bakewell counted them out of habit. The dogs went wild after the flush. He called them back in and praised them for pointing and backing. They started up the steep slope, Bakewell holding Maggie's hand tightly, pulling her as they went. The big dog showed up when they were at the parking lot.

"Missed out jug head," he scolded, "Off seeing the world again, missing the show." The dogs got back in the trailer. They drove slowly through the wildlife area, watching for other game, before heading for St Louis. When they crossed the Missouri, he turned off at the Spirit of St. Louis exit, "One short detour."

They went to the hangars and he stopped, left the truck running, told Maggie to wait in the car. He opened the hangar and turned on the lights and motioned for her to come over. When she did, he helped her up into the cockpit. It was cold, the leather seats colder. Maggie got inside and he closed the doors and latched them. The cockpit warmed slightly. Bakewell flipped the master switch and the dash lit up. When he turned the electronics switch on, the radios came on and they could hear the ATIS report on the overhead speaker.

"Good Lord," Maggie said, taking in the myriad lights and dials. "How can you possibly know what all this means?"

"It's not difficult; it just takes a little training." He explained the controls, and when she showed interest he continued. Maggie pointed and he explained, touching the dials, programming the GPS to show them how far Denver, Calgary and Little Rock were. He programmed Gulf Shores, 530 miles from Spirit.

"How long does that take?" she was being a good sport. He noticed how cold she was.

"It takes three hours and you're freezing in here, being uncharacteristically kind, just to humor me. Let's go warm up."

"You're such a shit, Bakewell." Maggie went to the truck and waited while he closed the hangar. They stopped at Blaney's next to the terminal and sat by a window. A Gulfstream was loading on the ramp. The waitress called Bakewell by name. Maggie ordered a scotch and water. He looked at his watch; it was 4:30. He ordered a beer.

"Where have you been in that plane?"

"Everywhere."

"Where is everywhere?"

"Maine, Calgary, Florida, the desert, the Bahamas."

She asked how many years he had been flying, and he bored her with descriptions of planes he'd flown, interesting places he landed – a lake in Canada and several in Minnesota, a few sand bars in some of the bigger rivers, a grass strip in the Flathead Mountains. Maggie grew in appreciation of his flying career. She had a second drink.

"You were always an interesting guy, Bakewell. Not much has changed."

"No, I'm still just a dull working stiff."

"No, you were always interesting; there's just so much more now: wife, kids, hunting, fishing, business, bird dogs and flying… and time for the Little Leagues."

He looked out at the ramp. "Katherine put up with most of my interests. She let me do just about anything I wanted." Maggie's face was flushed from the winter air, her eyes glistening. "I did have one rule; I always took the kids with me whenever I could. Even Nancy went camping and fishing – and hunting – believe it or not. She went quite a few times."

"Katherine must have been a saint."

"More than anybody'll ever know."

"I'm happy for you, sad for you too. It must be very difficult to lose someone so special."

"You lost someone Maggie."

"No, not really. Joe wasn't special, Andy, successful maybe, but not special."

"That's a terrible thing to say, Maggie."

"It's more terrible that it's true."

They watched the activity on the ramp. It was quiet inside, not much activity in the dreary weather. They sat without talking, satisfied with the day, the part they had spent together. Finally Maggie raised her glass, "Here's to the man who's *had* everything," she tilted her head to the side, like she had done years before, tossing her hair, only her hair wasn't long enough anymore.

"And to the woman who *has* everything."

They touched glasses, making silent contact, watching each other, cheeks red from the cold, eyes moist from the winter wind, tender, aching, seeking tender, aching eyes in return, thoughts seeking thoughts, curious, speculative, content. They couldn't help wondering about the other, about the life each had lead and the misfortunes they'd suffered. They might have shared a life. They sipped their drinks.

Transaction

At Ned's direction, the company's lawyer drew up the necessary papers for the transfer of ownership. The company's accountant expressed concern about the price. They went over the details on the phone, eventually he agreed, but said he thought Ned was getting the better deal. Bakewell tried to explain he was underwriting – "No, that was the wrong word," a patient but irritated accountant explained – all the debt and getting Ned's name off of everything in exchange for his signature and his stock. The accountant eventually came round. The lawyer was another story. He was adamant, said he represented the company's interest only, said Ned needed legal counsel in order to get the deal done. The Friday before, shortly after Ned had met with them, and in Bakewell's absence, both lawyer and accountant took advantage of the opportunity to make their professional and individual protests, insisting Ned needed to be represented by council.

Ned had gotten riled. "I toll 'em both to do what I said and knock off the bullshit. But I held onto my tongue and kept my fucking counsel," he told Bakewell later. Bakewell nodded, congratulated Ned about getting better at keeping his counsel. "Andy, these guys are my friends and you are my pardner and my best friend; why can't they accept the single fact that we're gonna do this deal and we don't need any other motherfuckers involved? Geez, don't nobody trust nobody?" Ned put his huge palms to his forehead. "How'd the world get so fucked up?"

"Ned, they've known us for years. They want to protect us both. You can't blame them."

"Bullshit. Our lawyer talks about his conflict of interest. He's covering his own ass, not mine."

"No, you know that's not true."

"He don't want to fuck up, Andy. He's afraid my daughter will sue him if I die and she thinks I got screwed."

"Do you think you're getting a bad deal?"

"Gimme a fuckin break, yer gettin me off the hook for ever-thin; ain't nobody can touch me if we do the deal. How'm I gettin anythin but out? You're the one's stuck with all the bullshit, not me!"

"You can't really get away. We all still need you, Ned. Don't disappear on me."

"Where am I gonna go? What would I do? As soon as the weather shuts us down, if it ain't already, I'm goin fishin. I'll prolly spend a couple weeks down at the beach playin golf with my buds. After that I'll get tired of them fucks. I get tired of them morons after couple of days anyway; I'll be bored with it and want to get back." Bakewell nodded his approval. "I'm not cuttin and runnin on you Andy. You can count on me as long as my pulse's talkin to my brain; as long as I got a pulse you can count on me."

(Bakewell loved the lingo. "Nedspeak," Nancy called it. They'd all heard a thousand expressions over the years: "on me, like a chicken on a June bug," "treat me like a red-headed step child," were old standbys, dredged up when he was in a hurry. But the more creative stuff sounded like, "I was expectin a frontal charge with sabers drawn, but got a ditsy-palmed hand shake instead." Ned had coined more phrases and created more sayings than any man Bakewell had ever known. He told his children, if he'd started writing Ned's expressions down years ago he could have written a book, had a title in mind: *Yogi Berra in a Sport Coat.*

"Dad, Ned's more colorful than Yogi Berra, and a hell of a lot more creative," Nancy said.

Ned had an ability to craft a simile or a metaphor that was every writer's dream. Funniest of all, he forgot them as fast as they came to him. When the others repeated them back to him later, he'd laugh at the humor, not realizing he was enjoying his own wit.)

"I know I can." Bakewell said. "You're the key to getting them through next year. After that they'll have to make it on their own. But you've got to be around after I'm gone. It's gonna take a while, Ned."

Ned clouded up instantly. "Geez, I can't believe we're having this conversation. I thought it woulda been me."

"Don't go soft on me. I need you now more than ever before. I'll need you more when I'm dead than I do right now. You have to hang tough."

Ned looked at his plate, fell silent. Bakewell asked him how many people he had told.

"Nobody! You toll me not to tell nobody!" Ned looked hurt.

"I asked you not to tell anybody, but you only listen to me half the time."

"Well, we're haff pardners, so all's I got to do is listen haff the time. I never toll a soul, Andy. That's a fact."

"Not even your sister?" Ned had one sister he was close to. The rest of his family he wouldn't "give a bucket of warm spit for."

"No. Shit, no. I might as well tell Phelps County as tell her." Ned was uncomfortable. He would never get used to the weekly after-I'm-gone conversations. "Andy, how long's it gonna be before it shows? What've you got?"

"You in a hurry?"

"Aw, you son of a bitch, how can you say such a thing? Son of a bitch!" he put his paw on Bakewell's arm and patted it gently. "What's killing you, Andy? Does it bother you to talk about it? Does it hurt you? Are you in much pain?"

"Stupidity. I'm dying of stupidity. Neville says it's from all the dumb people I've been hanging around all my life."

"Well, he's got a point in there," Ned said, removing his paw, looking down at his plate. "We sure been surrounded by morons most of our lives together, all right. Why'd we get in this sorry-assed business anyway?"

"We've had this conversation before."

"Yeah, and it never changed a thing, has it? It's what we do. We chose this stupid business years ago, and our choice is stuck right up our asses." He looked across the room as a tray of glasses clattered and almost hit the floor.

"It's in my liver."

"Liver?"

"Yeah."

"That's a mortal organ? It always leads to fatality?"

"Always."

"Can't you take some treatments, put some of the neon stuff in your veins?"

"No. I mean… yes, I could get treatment, but I'm not going to. I don't want to go through that. I'll look like shit, and they'll all know. I don't want to go through it."

"Yeah. I understand."

"If I'm going…I want to go without everybody knowing. I don't want people I don't like, or people who never liked me, coming up and saying nice things to me, like they're sorry."

"Or give a shit," Ned said emphatically.

"Exactly."

"A buncha two-faced dicks comin round tellin you what a good guy they always thought you was."

"You know how to sympathize, Ned. You know how to make me feel like you wished you were in my shoes."

"I wisht I was in yer shoes, you fuck. I know I couldn't fill 'em as good as you, but I would try to make them fit me if I could."

"I wear a size ten. You probably wear a fifteen. You'd fill them all right."

"It ain't what I meant, dumb fuck."

"I know." Bakewell said, chuckling. "I want to do it like Truman and MacArthur. You remember when MacArthur died, the press wanted Truman to say something nice about him, wanted a mini eulogy, maybe. Instead Truman said he was an old man too, and he would die soon enough, and MacArthur was a son of a bitch when he was alive, and he was still a son of a bitch dead!"

"Truman said that," Ned responded, nodding. "I dis-rememebered it from a long time ago."

"He was honest. I need honesty. I've shit on a few people in my life and I'm sorry. I pray for lots of people I treated badly, but that's as far as I'm going. It's enough. I'm not a sympathetic person, so I don't think I have any right to sympathy now."

"Yeah, but I don't know bout that, Andy. You always said you wasn't *vindic-ative* neither and you ain't. I never seen you go after nobody in yer whole life, but you sure been fucked over by a lots of no good *vindacative-like* bastards in yer life. What's so wrong with lettin a few people know?"

"I just don't want to do it. I want to get through the holidays. Right now that's my one priority, my single biggest wish. It's what I pray for. After that I'm done. I've got to be gone by March anyway."

"Why?"

"You don't want to know."

"Why? You dealin with the devil again?"

"Something like that. If I'm still around in March, ask me, and I'll tell you."

They signed the papers in Bakewell's office two days later, the day before Thanksgiving. Ned thought it was a good omen. Their lawyer prepared the papers at Ned's direction, wouldn't talk to Bakewell, said he had a conflict of interest. He sent instructions along, but wasn't in attendance. Trudy notarized everything and their accountant, a life long friend, supervised the sale. No money was exchanged. The note on the building remained in the real estate partnership they had formed years before. Bakewell *was* the partnership now.

Changes were made in Bakewell's trust, leaving the company and the partnership to the Trust. When it was over, they went to lunch, like they'd been doing for years. Harvey didn't ask about the money, so Bakewell knew Ned had told him something about the "insurance deal." To confirm his suspicions Harvey's conversation was mostly about the past, the "old days," when they were young and "dumber than shit." Harvey loved his contractor clients.

"You like to get away from the pin stripe crowd and cuss with us lowlifes," Ned accused.

Harvey patted Bakewell's arm as they were getting up from the table and said, "You're something."

"What's that mean, Harvey?"

"Nothing, you're just something."

"Good or bad?"

"Come on," he said, putting his topcoat on; he put his arm around Bakewell, pulling him closer. They were the same size; Harvey had a wider reach, like a heavyweight.

"You told him?"

"Hey, he's our fuckin accountant, Andy. He's your friend."

"I've got lots of friends, you dumb cluck, but I don't want them to know!"

Ned looked embarrassed, Harvey pulled him in tighter. "Come on.

Don't be such a tough guy."

"Do you know how important this is? My kids don't even know. I wouldn't have told my Neanderthal partner here, if I didn't have too."

"I won't say anything. Not until you tell me it's okay…personally." As they walked across the parking lot Harvey asked, "Who's Maggie Walker?" Bakewell gave him a suspicious look. "Hey, come on. You're daughter said you found a nice lady to spend time with."

"An old friend from school," Bakewell sulked. He wasn't sure if he was irritated with Ned or secretly satisfied he had let Harvey in on the story.

"Wait a minute! Is this *the* Maggie Walker? Are you kidding me!"

"Who's Maggie Walker?" Ned asked.

"A rich bitch from West County. She was married to Joe Walker. He was a Clinton guy from way back." Harvey looked to Bakewell for concurrence. "She was like, the fucking queen bee of Little Rock, or something. Isn't she a real fucking bitch? I mean she's a knockout and all that, I've seen her picture, but I thought she was meaner than shit!"

"No, she's a little formidable. She can be a lot of fun – if you tread lightly."

"I heard she was a tough fucking act," Harvey said in his lowlife contractor mode, much too loud. It drew a scowling reaction from a woman getting into a car in the next space. "Do you really like her? I mean is she all right? She's really okay? Nice?"

"I knew her when we were in college."

"Amazing, fucking amazing, Maggie Walker!" Harvey said again. Bakewell smiled. He loved Harvey's approbation. "Does she know she's doing hospice work?"

"Aw, go fuck yourself, Harvey!" Bakewell said in a voice even louder. The woman got in her car and slammed her door. "This is why I don't want people to know. Now it's started."

"Andy, come on. It's me, you and Ned." Harvey loved Bakewell, had loved Katherine more. He and Katherine both had held Bakewell in mild contempt at times for his arrogance, a subject they'd shared for decades. Harvey appreciated more than anyone else, Bakewell's developing humility, loved him for it. He was an especially good person and Bakewell trusted him completely. "Swear to God," he added.

"You're Jewish, which God?"

"The same One you pray to, fuck! It'll be me, you and Ned."

"And Neville and his staff and who else?"

"Doctor Neville? I know this guy!"

"You know everybody, Harvey. This is a disaster."

"Andy, I promise; God as my witness," He nodded toward Ned. "I won't tell a soul."

Bakewell stormed off, pretending to be angrier than he was, maybe secretly relieved. He would have a lot of explaining at year's end, Harvey on the inside made it easier. He had no idea what would transpire in March when their taxes were due. He hoped Snow's people would be true to their word. He was putting a lot of faith in Snow. *What the hell, Snow sent the money didn't he. Where was the problem?*

Thanksgiving

When Maggie invited Bakewell to join her at her home for Thanksgiving he had demurred, but she assured him it would be just dinner for two, no politicos; the rich and famous all had family obligations. In a dimwitted, unthinking moment he accepted. When he told Nancy his plans, she was shocked.

"Daddy! It's Thanksgiving! You can't go to *her* house. We have a tradition! The whole family comes home to Mom's. It's our place."

She was right, of course; Thanksgiving was a lifetime of family memories and the kids had a right to be in their childhood home, just as they'd done all their lives. Nancy had gotten together with her sister-in-law and arranged for food to be prepared at their homes and brought to his, referred to as "their house." Preparations were made; dinner would be served there. In addition to his married children, Michael was due in the Tuesday before, and Bakewell's sister-in-law would be coming also. She was Katherine's only sibling. Plans for Turkey Day were complete.

"I'll bring the turkey, all the fixings, the jelly mold mom always made; Karen will bring the vegetables." Nancy was emphatic. "You're going to pop for dessert, which you can buy anywhere you like."

Bakewell got the same pitch from his daughter-in-law, who informed him in a confirming phone call minutes after, that she planned to bring much of the feast, "In order to continue your family's tradition," and, "Out of respect for Andy's mother." *Andy's mother...*

Humbled, he called Maggie Walker back and asked her to consider coming to his home instead. She also demurred, surprising him, explaining her reluctance to intrude on a family tradition. He knew how confidently she looked forward to any social challenge. Before she had sounded like she wanted to meet his kids, so he made an effort to convince her she would be welcome, explaining his problem, assured her she would enjoy the meal, the kids and the camaraderie, and took extra time explaining the entertainment that followed.

"It consists mostly of sitting about, watching grandbabies play on the floor. I admit it doesn't sound that great. I may be asking for too much here, Maggie. My children might not be that entertaining for you, but it will give you a chance to meet them."

"What about your *predator bitches*?"

"They have family of their own."

There was a brief question and answer session; Maggie was amused by his patriarchal tone, finally accepted. "It'll give me a chance to see you play *The Old Man*."

The best part of Thanksgiving for everyone would be seeing Michael again. The Bakewell children were very close. There were no inner family rivalries. Michael wasn't crazy about Karen, but he stroked her carefully, with a humor and aplomb Bakewell knew he could have only gotten from his mother. Michael left shortly after Easter to fish in the Bahamas, returned to Montana in the spring, where he guided on the Madison, and was within a few hours of the other blue ribbon streams. He was becoming a bona fide expert at reading water, handling a drift boat and understanding the complex entomology of fly fishing.

Michael and Andy had always been close; about the only thing that kept them apart was the woman in Andy's life, but Michael handled it well. Karen was tolerant of Michael, although she would no longer let her husband go off with his little brother, until that very Thanksgiving, when the boys pulled off a minor coup.

Karen and Nancy arrived at Bakewell's home at ten in the morning, giving him charge of his grandchildren while they prepared the feast. This was a minor problem. The morning of Thanksgiving Day was traditionally a quail hunt, followed by an afternoon feast. In the old days, Thanksgiving was followed by a three-day trip to northern Missouri, sometimes on up into Iowa for pheasants. Arriving Wednesday evening, Michael expressed an interest in bird hunting after a long season of fishing, despite his father's comments about diminishing quail numbers. Michael wasn't too concerned – he was, after all, a professional now, thought his new standing in the gaming community might turn the trick. Bakewell informed his younger son that Thursday morning was out; he had been called to a higher duty. Without missing a beat, the boy happily settled for his big brother, assuring his father he could talk his sister-in-law into a short hunt on Thanksgiving morning. They had hunted many times with the older dogs, handled them well; Bakewell had no qualms about letting them take the older dogs. It was hard to tell who was taking whom when the dogs entered the equation. They agreed to leave before first light in order to squeeze as much out of the day as possible. Bakewell heard them clinking about in his kitchen, making coffee and sandwiches about five in the morning.

"Good morning boys," he said, giving each child a hug. "How've you been son? It's been a while." Andy, shy as always, smiled and raised his eyes, a dead ringer for his father when it came to expressing emotion.

"Sorry to wake you dad."

"Sounded like it was planned. You boys have enough guns? You want to borrow the 20 gauges?"

"Yes sir," Michael quickly answered. Andy nodded, appreciatively.

Bakewell went out to his gunroom to retrieve the weapons. He cautioned them not to take his puppy, made doubly sure by walking out to the yard with them, retrieving her when they took the other two from the kennel. The tri-colored puppy, crushed at being left behind, wiggled and struggled to get free, unable to comprehend the shattering experience. She'd never been left behind, and voiced her distress loud enough to wake the neighbors. To quiet her Bakewell brought her into the house where she eventually settled down after he let her get up on the queen-sized bed he shared with Katherine's memory and a TV that often glowed in silence.

When his daughter-in-law showed up first, he was waiting, breakfast finished, for his second grandchild, who toddled out, Bakewell in tow, to play on the boulders surrounding the tightly covered pool. Nancy arrived minutes later, apologizing about a last minute baby emergency, and sent Julie out to join her cousin on the boulders where they cavorted. Bakewell handled Nancy's newly mobile enfant on the deck below, keeping a careful eye on the two who negotiated the boulders like little Billy goats.

"Are you all right out there?" Nancy called after forty exhausting minutes.

"I don't think they're ever going to give out. Can we bribe them with something other than exercise?"

"There's always food," Nancy said. It was almost noon. "Hey! You guys want some grilled cheese sandwiches?" The older two turned and looked at her briefly, went back to the endless climbing, making a procession around the boulders from deck to rocks to trampled plantings above, back to the fence where the dogs had worn a path, around to the deck again by the now dry waterfall. They finally gave out when Bakewell's sister-in-law showed up with her husband. Melanie was fond of Bakewell's grandchildren, showered them with gifts now that Katherine was no longer there to do the same. Her husband had retired from McDonnell Douglas and they had moved to Arizona, but returned for the major holidays.

Bakewell's sons returned around one o'clock, Nancy's husband had opted for eighteen holes of golf in the warm weather and showed up a few minutes later. They were all back outside with the dogs and the little people, Bloody Mary's in hand, when Andy whispered to his father, "Dad, there's a lady in the driveway by the gate."

Bakewell turned and waved to Maggie and went to greet her. He brought her out to the pool and introduced her to his sons, daughter-in-law and son-in-law, before Nancy came out with the baby and hugged Mrs. Walker. They had only met once before. Nancy took over, redoing the introductions with short descriptions of her husband's and brothers' shortcomings, and Maggie carefully shook everyone's hand, made a fuss over the grandchildren and later honed in on Michael, whom she decided needed to meet her niece. Like everyone else, Maggie teased Michael about not being married, to a chorus of agreement from the others. Michael, looking over Mrs. Walker admiringly, said he would sure like to meet her niece.

When they returned to the house for dinner, before Bakewell could give his annual, "This is my favorite holiday of the year" blessing, Michael preempted him with his own version. The kids had adopted their father's love of Thanksgiving as the best holiday of the year.

"It's a time when we get together to share a meal and enjoy family and friends for all the right reasons, *and* without the need to spend buckets of money on gifts," Michael said, quoting his father, before offering a short blessing and thanking God for their mother to the wet-eyed approbation of the others.

Nancy dutifully sided with her father about Thanksgiving, but pointed out her love of the Christmas Season and the joy her mother took in the season and the present-buying. She brought laughter to the meal when she repeated Katherine's description of Thanksgiving as a ho-hum, middle of the road, necessary prelude to Christmas, which Katherine had called *a time for over-eating a disgusting and hideously greasy bird.* Nancy mischievously referred to Thanksgiving as "opening day" for the Christmas Season and turned to Maggie and Karen and said, "My mother and I loved the day after the most. My dad took my brothers off every year to go and kill something, and we got to shop and eat healthy, and do whatever we wanted for three glorious days."

Bakewell, content, wondered at his misdirected willingness to accept Maggie Walker's invitation to attend a dinner for two on such a great American holiday.

Maggie spent a lot of time with Nancy, later when she thought she wasn't connecting with Karen, made an effort to win her over with flowing compliments about their "adorable little boy," and a barrage of questions about Karen's pending delivery. Andy and Michael baited their uncle into a long confrontational debate on religion, which Bakewell had come to enjoy, but steered clear of. They all ended up, as predicted, in the family room watching three little people jabber and share the wealth of toys Katherine had kept in the hall closet. The toys were in a big plastic container she put on wheels. They knew right where to find it, and rolled it down the hallway onto the family room carpet. Bakewell's sister-in-law brought additional gifts for the babies and was accused of rushing the season by her favorite niece.

The married kids finally gathered up the little people and left about seven. Bakewell's in laws had made plans to visit friends and left also, leaving Michael to visit with Maggie for a long time, while his father saw to the drinks and checked on his returned weapons, suspecting he wouldn't be missed. He was right. When he returned Michael said he had plans and would be home in time to get a night's sleep before they set out for Iowa.

"You were right Pop. The quail have gone somewhere. Let's do a pheasant trip instead."

"I'll see you in the morning," Bakewell said, and watched surprised, when Michael kissed Mrs. Walker's cheek before taking leave.

"'Maggie' please, Michael. And you call me about my niece."

"I'll be around until after Christmas, unless the old man kicks me out."

Bakewell made Maggie a scotch and water. They sat in the family room and Maggie commented on the décor, said what a wonderfully warm room it was. It made him uncomfortable, her asking so many questions about the past, about his married life. She complimented him on Nancy. "I just love her; and those two boys, where do they get the height?" Bakewell sons were taller than their squarely built father.

"Let's go somewhere?" He suggested.

"All right," she said, putting the drink down. "What have you in mind?"

"How about a quiet place for coffee? I forgot to offer anyone coffee earlier."

"Good, they were all so animated, so busy enjoying each other, such a joy to be with. I think coffee would have quieted the moment."

"Where would you like to go?"

"I'll go anyplace you suggest, but I'm driving. I'm not going anywhere in your pickup truck."

They ended up at Union Station, in the big lobby where a piano played quietly and the Christmas decorations were already up. Maggie laughed when Bakewell fumed about Christmas decorations that had been up since Halloween. They had laced coffee in the wonderfully warm and softly lit cocktail lounge – the mood uniquely sustained by heavily stuffed chairs on a carpeted floor that soaked up the noise of the marbled lobby and high entrance overhead.

"This is a lovely place. When did they redo it?"

"I can't remember truthfully. It's been a while though, too damned Christmassy."

"Here we go again; the family dispute with Christmas. I think it's lovely, so soft and atmospheric. I can't believe it was once a noisy train station. What a contrast. I remember being here once when I was little. It was very busy then."

"I caught a train right here for San Diego and boot camp years ago." They sat on a plush couch for two, a love seat, in front of a coffee table not far from the piano bar. Maggie continued relentlessly in her quest to know about his family, her determination heightened since she had met them now and could put a name to each face. Bakewell was beginning to see the obvious: she was lonely, wished for a family, had missed out on one with Joe Walker. It was too late to create one of her own and she was completely fascinated by his, and quite unembarrassed as she quizzed him, relishing the stories she had heard throughout the afternoon, especially the stories about "mom and dad."

It was a pleasant way to end a favorite day for Bakewell, and sure beat the somberness of the last two. *I'm talking to an attractive lady about my family and my children.* She made him feel satisfied with his life as he observed it from her perspective. Listening to Maggie's recap, quietly animated, full of curious bits of conversation from the day, he understood what he had, realized how special it was.

Maggie reached over and put her hand on top of his and squeezed it softly. "So, what's the deal with Karen?"

"Deal?"

"Uh huh."

"It shows?"

"Yep." She pronounced the word slowly, with emphasis: yeee-eph.

"I think she resents me. No, hell, I know she resents me. They met at school. She's very bright. She has a master's. She wanted Andy to go to law school and not come back to the business." He put his cup and saucer back on the table. "Andy likes the business, and I know he likes working with Nancy and the rest of us. He would be a fine architect, I'm sure. I doubt if he ever wanted to be a lawyer, but he apparently didn't want to tell her that. She settled on architecture grudgingly, but she's upset that he's working for a sewer contractor. She thinks he's wasting his time with us."

"Are you sure?"

"No, of course not. You never know what you're talking about when it comes to that sort of thing. I'm guessing. He does seem to like his job. He pours himself into it, but he's not the assertive type. Nancy will end up running the business eventually."

"And Karen will end up running Andy?"

"She's already doing that."

"Tell me about Michael."

"What would you like to know?"

"Everything. I'm interested in him…for my niece."

"He's a good boy. He's had his ups and downs but he's a good kid."

"He's a lovely boy."

"Well, I don't know about lovely; that's a woman's word. He's a pretty good kid."

"Was he Katherine's favorite? I bet he was."

"No. Not really. She loved both boys. They were each different, unique the way all kids are; she loved them each differently. I don't think she loved one more than the other. She had a quality. She could make them all feel like they were the center of her universe."

"That's a lovely way to put it."

"Yeah, I guess. She ended being the center of theirs, of ours. I guess we all knew it before she died. Maybe we just didn't realize it before she was gone; then it was too late."

There was a long silence as the waiter came and refilled their cups. They took only coffee the second round. The piano had stopped. It was quiet, only the sounds of the big empty room. The vaulted ceilings had a noise of their own, even in silence.

"Tell me something about Michael. Tell me some one thing that will help me know him better."

Bakewell looked up to the high ceiling and ran his hand through his hair. "He was very sensitive when he was a little guy. He loved his toys, loved his things; he was possessive about them. He kept a little inventory of his toys, especially his 'Joes.'" Bakewell explained about the little plastic GI Joe toys. "Michael kept his in a special box, carefully arranged after each session." Maggie listened with her eyes. They made silent little exclamations as he talked, encouraging him to say more. Bakewell continued, knowing he was being set up. It was too easy to talk about his children. "When he was about seven Katherine read him a novel. It took weeks."

"What was it?"

"To Kill A Mockingbird."

Maggie smiled; everyone from their generation had loved the story.

"It was summertime. I remember she read to him each evening out on the deck. Later toward the end of the book, we were down at the lake for a holiday. She read in the afternoons by the pool when he was bushed and again later in the evening after dinner. Nancy listened but not with Michael's enthusiasm. Michael knew every character and every role. Andy wasn't interested in that sort of thing. I was reading something else at the time, but followed along subconsciously. When she came to the part where Tom Robinson was found guilty, despite the wonderful defense Atticus had argued, Michael was shocked. He pitched a fit, was just outraged at the lack of justice. I remembered he cried. Katherine read Atticus Finch's explanation to the Finch children with great emphasis, adding little embellishments to soften the blow. Michael was disgusted with the verdict; he just couldn't cope; there was no explaining it to him. Then came the part where Tom runs from the law and they kill him and the sheriff comes to Atticus and tells of Tom's death. Michael erupted. He cried. He was beyond consolation, completely crushed, I watched Katherine try to mollify him. I watched closely. She grieved for Michael while Michael grieved for Tom Robinson. I know she regretted reading him the book, even though they couldn't have enjoyed anything more the entire summer up to that time."

"That is *so sad*. He was just a baby, wasn't he?"

"About seven, I don't think Katherine anticipated his reaction. She loved the book, thought he would appreciate it for a literary work, but he was too young to understand, beyond consolation. It caught her off guard when he lost control. He railed on about how unfair it was, storming about the deck in tears, he just about collapsed in grief. It took us the rest of the evening to get him under control. You would have thought one of the dogs had just died."

Maggie's face was pained, sympathetic.

"Katherine wanted to finish the book. Michael wouldn't hear of it.

The book disappeared, I don't know what he did with it, but we never saw it again."

They finished their coffee. Maggie talked about children in general, what a gift they were, how she missed not raising one, and how devoted she was to her niece and how much she had enjoyed his children. She told him she had never been exposed to a family atmosphere like "their day," said she had never had any aunts, uncles or cousins. "I realize how much I miss it all. How much I missed it all my life." There was a long pause. Bakewell was good at long pauses; she was tired, getting used to his failure to pick up his cue. The waiter came again; they'd had enough and asked for the bill.

"Andy, could we talk about you for a minute?"

"No."

"Please?"

"Is it going to be heavy?"

"No, don't be silly. I'm worried about you."

"I don't want to talk about anything heavy right now. I'm learning to enjoy you again Leary. Don't spoil it."

"What's happened to you?" She put her cup on the table, ignoring him, put her hand on his knee. "You seem so…lost, and so…I don't know, detached, like you're adrift. Why aren't you happier?'

"I'm having one of the best days of my recent life."

"No. Last month at the club, you seemed so…traumatized, like you were in pain almost. Yes, pain," she said empathically. "You just look so exhausted. What has life done to you to make you this way? So unhappy?"

"I'm not unhappy, Maggie. We've all had some bad luck, with Katherine, I mean. It was horrible for them all, my children. But everybody has bad luck. I'm a little bitter sometimes. I try not to be…but sometimes, it catches up. I'm getting better. A lot better, really."

"No. There's something more."

"I'm tired; it's been a long year."

"You're in some kind of trouble. I know it. What is it? What's troubling you so?"

"Maggie, I've got the world. Everything's breaking right for me now. Last month I was in trouble. Now I'm fine. Don't spoil this, okay?"

"You're not being honest with me," she sounded hurt. She picked up her cup, twisted it in the saucer. "What has changed you? You were so wild and impulsive once. That's what was so interesting about you, what I found so enticing about you. Now you've become so…settled, so…quiet…almost sad. And you seem so very vulnerable," she patted his knee. "It's what I find *most appealing* in you now." She tossed her head to the side, leaned in and smiled warmly. "*You're so damned vulnerable.*"

"Do you remember that night at that little drive in on Hampton? It was about this time of year...Cold…We were drinking hot chocolate. You were down about something." Maggie said she remembered it well. "I told you how beautiful you were, and I said something really dumb too. I remember, I told you *nobody would ever be ashamed to take you anywhere.* Do you remember? It was such a dizzy thing to say." He shook his head at the memory. Most of his memories about her had to do with regret, or worse, embarrassment, over something dumb he'd said or done. "Do you remember, me saying that?"

"Like it was yesterday," she beamed. "I've treasured that compliment all my life. I've always believed it was the nicest thing anybody ever said to me."

"It was a stupid gaff; it wasn't a decent compliment at all. I still regret saying it."

"No, no, please don't. It was lovely."

"Well, it was sincere. I remember you seemed so sad that night. I wanted to say something inspired. It probably sounded more like, 'hey baby, you're no dog,' but I meant well at the time."

"My mother – I was having a bad spell with her – we had clashed about something, and I was feeling terrible. She could be so unreasonable. She could destroy my self esteem."

He nodded, remembering. Sometimes Maggie would show up looking ragged, disturbed, appearing wasted. It never lasted long. There was an indomitability about her most of the time, one more part of her formidable character.

"It was a lovely thing to say."

"Really?"

"Yes. Sometimes when life gets me down – and it gets us all down doesn't it – I think about that night. You don't know how many times I've fallen back on that simple line. It was such a lovely thing to say, especially then, when I was searching for my confidence."

"You were always confidant, Maggie."

"No, Andy, it's not true."

"Well you make me glad I said it."

"Why do you mention it tonight?"

Bakewell looked around the huge room, motioning with his arm, "Because it is still so true."

He got up, excusing himself, went to the men's room. When he returned she was out in the lobby. They decided to walk, wandered around the refurbished train station, looking into shop windows, closed for the holiday, girded for the next day's onslaught. They strolled the hard marble floors, their steps echoing around them. They had valet parked; Bakewell had insisted on it. He gave the valet a couple of bucks when her expensive gold car pulled to the curb. Maggie wanted to drive. Bakewell was happy to let her. They toured Forest Park one more time. It was cold and dreary and, like all summer places, depressing in wintertime. Then they went through the Central West End, once a bleak place, going through a resurgence now, filled with trendy places.

When she dropped him off he said, “Can I follow you home?”

“No, don’t be silly.” She patted his hand. “You need to get some sleep if you’re going hunting with that long-legged, good looking boy.”

“I’m happy to follow you home. I should insist.”

“No, just bring him home safely. I want to fix him up with my niece.” She left him in the driveway, illuminated in the expensive headlights. They gave off a blue white color and were very bright.

2nd Mailing

Tuesday after Thanksgiving, Bakewell walked stiffly out to the shop area to visit with his mechanic, his mind refreshed, his body sore from three days of hunting. He and Michael had gone to Iowa where the setter had been a disaster on spooky pheasants, putting the wily birds to flight too far away. It had been annoying and would have infuriated him years before, a fact Michael was quick to point out. They'd both shown patience with the dog, appreciated her style, even enjoyed watching her go, admitting she was not the right dog for the trip.

"It wouldn't have been fair to leave her behind," he commented, during a frustrated moment when she was returning from one of her over-the-horizon expeditions, looking, "more sheepish than doggish," according to Michael.

The Brittany and the tri color pup had done well. They filled their limit each day. After one of the big dog's blunders – putting three roosters up simultaneously, hundreds of yards distant – Bakewell resorted to humor to mollify his frustration, joked, "One less pheasant I'll have to freeze, the way you're knocking them down." Michael beamed at the compliment, dropped in beside his father, putting his arm around his old man. "I know you're heading south for bonefish soon; you figure you can leave them in my freezer, right?"

"We'll have us a big feast for dinner Sunday, Pop," Michael said with mischief, "We'll get Karen to roast them up for us. Invite ourselves over to Andy's and watch the Rams whip up on somebody while she cooks."

"You're looking for trouble, son."

"Naw, she loves me Pop. You have to know how to handle her."

"What gives with the Rams? Who the hell is Kurt Warner?"

Michael laughed, "He hails from somewhere around here; he was an Iowa Barnstormer."

The setter redeemed herself later when they found her over the horizon and long missing on a solid point. She had nailed a little covey.

"What's this about?" Michael asked as they closed the distance.

"Don't know, but be ready. She's looks pretty sure of herself."

They both pulled a bird out of a pitiful little flush. It gave them second thoughts. "Dad, we should be feeding these birds, not shooting them," Michael reflected over the little quail the Brittany retrieved. "These birds are emaciated."

After that they stuck to pheasants. It was the first time they had limited out in Iowa in several years. Father and son spent their days filled with the dogs and birds and tailgate lunches made with Thanksgiving leftovers sent along by a loving daughter, renewed old friendships with farmers they had known since Michael was in grade school. They spent their evenings sipping a brew, watching the NFL wrap-ups on ESPN as the Rams continued to surprise, even awe the country with their phenomenal offense.

***

"The boom is cracked and needs welding," the mechanic was saying. He was one of the guys that had stuck with them in hard times. "It'll be the third time we've welded it."

"Look into buying a new one," Bakewell said matter of factly. "Maybe we should do a rental purchase?"

"Seriously?"

"Yeah, seriously. If this generation is gonna run with the business they're gonna need decent equipment."

"Andy, you got a minute?"

"Sure."

"There's a rumor, only a rumor now, don't get pissed off. Rumor Ned's sold his interest and maybe's gettin out."

"Ned's tired, Fred. He needs some peace of mind. I bought him some peace of mind. But you know he'll always be around. What the hell's he gonna do? Who would handle his accounts?"

"Some of the guys are worried about the future, especially without Ned around."

"We've had another good year. We're gonna be fine. Just hang with us and watch this younger generation. Go with them. Stop worrying."

"I heard we lost the lawsuit."

"Fred, the lawsuit was just one inning; there are always eight more. The rumors have somebody going out of business every year. Now it's us?"

Trudy came out for one of her frequent cigarettes, the delivery man right behind. She pointed him toward Bakewell, "Andy, you're going to have to sign for another one."

He patted the mechanic's arm, told him to stay the course, "Everything's going to be fine." He followed the driver back inside and signed for the package. It was heavy. He took it to the car and put it behind the seat. After signing checks at the counter in the lobby under Trudy's watchful gaze, he left, stopping at the super market for a salad and fountain coke and drove over to Tilles Park. The package contained three boxes of cartridges. There were forty rounds in each box, made of heavy cardboard, treated with paraffin. They were unmarked. He opened one and took a round from the box, Super X and stamped with .250 Savage. *A hundred and twenty rounds. They must want me to do some serious practicing.*

When he got home he opened his gunroom, sat at the reloading desk, and pulled a bullet from one cartridge, carefully pouring the powder onto a pan. He weighed it, callipered the bullet: it was a .243. It fascinated him, but made him uneasy. They knew he had a .243. The bullet was a 70-grained hollow point, with a boat tail. The powder, he couldn't identify, weighed in at 39.4 grains. He pulled down one of his manuals and looked up 6 millimeter, 70-grained bullets pushed by 39.4 grains. After much crosschecking, he found it in the Sierra Manual: *6MM International cartridge developed in the 1950's, a very accurate cartridge, a favorite of the bench rest fraternity*. He was able to interpolate the powder as H380. At that amount it would push the bullet at 3300 feet per second. *That's the fastest cartridge I've ever fired.* Checking the ballistic coefficient, he found it was .265, meaning it would hold together out a good way, but didn't have the punch a 30 caliber packed. He wondered why they were using such a small cartridge. An eerie feeling set in, *an explosive round, one that would detonate on contact*? He locked up the gunroom and stopped at Kirkwood Outfitters to see if Ruger made a 6MM International. They didn't. He began to wonder about the bolt still in his gunroom with the cartridges. He bet it had been retooled for the shoot and would be unidentifiable. At least they couldn't trace it back to him. He was looking for small consolations.

Ned Grant

Katherine Bakewell loved Ned Grant. She had loved him almost as long as she had known him, and she had known him for twenty-five years. He'd been her husband's partner and best friend, but she didn't love him because he was a faithful friend or a great partner. She loved him because he was Ned. Over the years Ned and the man she called her *One True Love* had had many minor disagreements. Often as not, she took Ned's side in their battles, which infuriated Bakewell.

Ned was a bit of a rounder, Bakewell once accurately described him as a philogynist: sly, secretive, never one to brag, but women found him interesting, especially "them middle-aged ones," "them got-the-horns types." Bakewell could no more understand it than he could Katherine's passion for taking Ned's side. Ned was overweight, out of shape, candidly admitted he hadn't seen his shoes in years – a joke about his robust waistline which had never stopped expanding. Ned had been separated, later divorced, and lived alone most of his life, with the exception of one arrangement that lasted less than a year. He had a daughter who worshiped him and called weekly, but she had found love and happiness in Wiscasset, Maine, had been only a phoned-in part of his life for twenty years. Ned spent as much time as he could in Maine and returned "at least twicet" each year; once in summer – no matter how busy they were – and once in winter, which he hated, "'Cause winters in Maine's colder'n a sperm whale's dick."

Ned had married young; was only eighteen years older than his daughter, who had married a man twice her age. Ned's grandchildren were the same age as Katherine Bakewell's children. It gave them one more thing in common.

Some of Ned's nightlife confounded Bakewell – one in particular mystified him more than all the others. He'd seen Ned at the bar with a fine looking woman the age of Ned's own daughter. The woman was obviously putting the make on him, so Bakewell stayed on the other side of Rick's with some flying buddies, trying not to be seen. The flyboys were drinking at a good clip, and Bakewell stayed late enough to watch his partner leave with the woman. The next morning Ned was late for work and one of his five-in-the-morning workers, said he had seen Ned about 4:30 that very morning, looking, "Pretty rough at the coffee shop.'" It was several years in the past, and Bakewell let it ride for a long time before he caught Ned off guard.

"So, what's the story with you and the bimbo from Southwestern Bell?"

"Aw get away from me," Ned said, "A Catholic boy like you askin me about a thing like that?"

"You're going to play dumb with your only partner?"

"I ain't playin dumb. I don't need to; I always been dumb, but not that dumb, you fuck."

Bakewell teased him about sharing, about his philogynous nature and let it drop. It had been snowing hard and they were finished for the day. Two drinks later Ned gave him a sheepish look.

"What's filogishness mean?"

"It means you're a rounder." Bakewell sensed he was about to open up. "Should I pursue this thing…about the Southwestern Bell belle…or leave it alone?"

"I'm gettin rounder that's fer sure. Naw, fuck. It ain't a big deal. I boinked her all right, but don't tell none of them morons at Rick's." Bakewell smiled, didn't pursue it. If Ned wanted to tell the story he would. He wouldn't badger him. It was enough to let him know he knew. The rest wasn't important. Ned wanted to share with his partner, since so much time had elapsed, said he was just a little nervous, "About yer religious convictions, was all." Bakewell nodded, giving him the go ahead.

"I gotta tell ya, bub, it give me plenty of pleasure, the fact that all them guys was tryin to make her, while I'd tried to steer clear of her. Apparently that turned the proverbial trick – bein Mr. Standoff and all. But them other guys was sure pissed."

"You didn't tell them what happened did you?"

"No. Didn't have to. They gave theirselves conniption fits tryin to figure it out. But they was pretty sure I done it. More I said I didn't, more they thought I did."

"So how did you finally win her over from the competition?"

"Them morons was never competition. They was all pantin around her all the time, like she was in heat. Women don't wanna put up with that shit. She got up close to me one evening and almost forced herself between my legs where I was sittin on my stool there in Rick's where I knowed you saw me fer sure. I told her she should be ashamed of herself, since she was always messin with the married men at work, and she told me that was what turned her onto me. 'Cause I was *morale*." Ned mispronounced the word all the time. "She'd been pesterin me fer about a whole year, and I was tryin to avoid her more and more and then that one night she got me off my guard with a bunch of Grey Gooses and the next thing I know I was done for."

Katherine often told her husband she understood why women found Ned appealing, called him "safe." Said, "Women like *safe* men."

"What the heck does *safe* mean?" Bakewell had asked, irritated.

"It means he won't hurt you, he's doesn't have a movie star complex about himself; he's sincere. But you don't have to make a commitment. He's not going to pursue you after it's over. He's just available and lovable."

At the time they also were sitting at Rick's in the cocktail lounge, having their Friday night drink, a habit usually preceding an early evening coupling. They often over imbibed – a word Ned loved – especially on

Fridays. Rick's was the place. And after a long week of construction, Bakewell was ready to unwind. Friday often became a semi-official date. After several drinks Katherine would rub her lover's leg under the table, flexing the muscle of her calf against his. He didn't need much encouraging. Afterwards, if the weather was warm, they would spend the rest of the evening on the deck, hoping somebody would drop by. They were seldom disappointed.

While they were having the "Ned conversation," Dolly came to pick up the empty glasses. She agreed with Katherine's assessment, used the "safe" word and had Bakewell rolling his eyes and shaking his head. "I just love him," Dolly added. "He's like a big old basset hound. I could just grab hold of those big droopy cheeks and give them a tug."

"A basset hound is sexy?"

"Loveable Andy, he's lovable; I'd go home with him in a minute, if I wasn't living with somebody."

"Good grief, Dolly, you're living with somebody?"

"That's exactly what Ned said to me, Andy! Only I got the complete lecture about my language and my blouses and a lot of other shit I didn't really need to hear!"

Katherine jumped in on Dolly's side. "They're both judgmental. Don't pay any attention to them." She patted Dolly's arm when she said it.

Dolly left, telling Bakewell to, "Fuck off."

***

Rick's was *safe* for Bakewell too; over the years he had been a regular with his wife and without, often stopping for a drink with Ned, or some of Ned's "buds." He always left early, refusing to have more than one drink, unless Katherine showed up. After her death he avoided Rick's. He'd only been there once in two years and was reluctant to meet Maggie Walker there. But Maggie had insisted, knowing it was close to his home, centrally located.

He got there about six. Ned was already there, looking much relieved, off the financial hook, and enjoying himself, despite the dreaded awareness he was about to lose his partner. He had been drinking more and more. It was Thursday, the night Ned's "buds" always gathered. As soon as Bakewell came through the door they called him over. He hadn't seen most of the guys in several years. Many had been at the wake; they were good guys, lots of fun, but Bakewell had avoided male companionship, especially in the evenings. He joined them for one drink, refused to sit, his back to the bar, watching the front door. The central figure in their group was a wonderfully generous guy with one of the new tech companies. He sold millions of what Ned called, "weird shit," some of it to very big companies. "Danny Boy," they called him. Danny was no dummy, had taken to hiring retired jocks, down on their luck, accurately guessing they could "press the flesh;" could tell stories about their playing days and sell his stuff. It worked.

According to Ned, "Danny's customers was always glad to schmooz with them former famous fucks." Explaining, "They all loved their jocks."

It made Danny rich and he ran a bar tab pushing $300 on Thursdays as a kind of week-in-review excuse to get his athlete/salesmen together. Ned was an adopted member, not because he ever hit .300, carried the ball or scored "one of them golds," but simply because he was Ned. Ned was always welcome, Thursdays or any other day. They had taken him on their outings all over the southwest, learning quickly he was in a class by himself when it came to schmoozing. Several of the big customers asked for Ned by name. One guy's wife had called Danny to get Ned's phone number, and when Danny inquired, she told him she wanted to personally thank Ned for helping her husband unwind, told Danny how her husband hadn't stopped talking about Ned since he got home. Danny used Ned whenever possible, called him, "my surrogate schmoozer."

"I don't get it," Ned told Bakewell. "Them guys like me more than they like them guys puttin up with the tab."

Ned was in the middle of the group when Bakewell joined them, came around the table and put his heavy arm around Bakewell and hugged him affectionately. "This is my pard, youse guys all know him. You should treat him real good. He's been down with his luck somewhat as you all only know so well, so don't fuckin mess with him or youse is gonna have to fuck with me in there too."

They laughed agreeably, hysterically actually, because they were drunk and because just about everything Ned said made them laugh. The revelry heated up as they took their shots in return. They called him "Hoss," because of his size. They also called him "The Sheriff." Ned was a natural leader.

Before he'd finished his drink Bakewell saw Maggie Walker come down the sidewalk through the tinted window, approaching the door. He whispered to Ned, said he had to go, had to meet her, nodding toward the door, tried to slip away when he was overheard by one of the guys who turned and spotted Maggie.

"Whoa, Andy, wait up; you ain't leavin 'til you introduce us." There was general and enthusiastic agreement.

"Watch all your fuckin mouths," Ned instructed. Bakewell waved to Maggie. She smiled brightly and walked to them. Before Bakewell could speak, one of the guys grabbed Maggie's arm and introduced himself and two of the others. Bakewell broke in next and introduced her to Ned, who took her hand and cupped it in his paw like he was going to kiss it, patted it instead and beamed at her. Maggie was clearly smitten as soon as he took her hand and spoke to her.

"If yer here to see my pardner you come to the right place. You don't need to know any of these others guys though. They're all morons, except for Danny here, who always picks up the tab."

Danny introduced himself over the laughter, shook Maggie's hand from across the table, and offered to buy her a drink. Bakewell cringed when she accepted, knew they would be staying. Ned put his arm around Maggie and pulled up one of the tall stools and asked her to sit down where they could all face her. Most evenings the newest addition was afforded a requisite and brief attention, asked how he was doing, what was going on. In Maggie's case it was different. She was the featured attraction, the evening's entertainment. Only the shyest guys remained quiet, the rest peppered her with questions. She recognized a couple of them, remembered one or more of their glory days. Several were as sharp as she was, and she fenced with them adroitly, to the amusement of the others. Ned enjoyed the repartee, but cautioned them to be on their best behavior because she was "The lady in my pardner's life;" said he wasn't, "Gonna stand for any ignorance of behavior."

When they finally left – two drinks for Maggie, Bakewell nursing his original – she was still talking over her shoulder as he steered her away.

"They're darling," she said as he seated her on the other side of the room, taking a chair to block her view.

"Yeah, darling; pay close attention to Ned; he called them morons." Bakewell chuckled as he spoke, enjoying himself and the attention Maggie had attracted.

"No, they were all darling. I love men – especially in groups, they're all safe then."

"That damned 'safe' word again." Bakewell told Maggie of his many conversations about Ned being safe.

"How long have you been partners?"

"Too long; I actually worked for him once when I got out of school."

"After you got out?"

"Yeah, the guys I went to work for thought I should learn the business from the ground up. So I started…on the ground…under it actually, with Ned… He was my first boss."

"He looks like he could boss people."

"He could. Still can. I don't know what they'll do without him."

"Is he going somewhere?"

"Yes, he's going home. He's worn out."

Bakewell ordered a second drink, Maggie had a third. They were there another forty minutes before Ned drifted over. Bakewell knew he eventually would. When he arrived he was weaving, towering over them. He looked down and smiled. Before Bakewell could invite him to join them, Maggie did.

"He can't stay very long."

"He can stay as long as he wants," Maggie contradicted.

Ned chuckled. Bakewell asked him how the trip to Gulf Shores had gone.

"Turra-bul. You can't believe what I'm going..." he pulled his chair in closer, "What I'm about to tell ya."

"I'll believe it," Bakewell said.

"It's Danny's sorry friend, you know, Carl."

Bakewell knew Carl. It couldn't be good.

"Carl's a real asshole. Excuse me," Ned said, turning to Maggie. "The guy's a moron from mars. He got us in a fight."

"Uh oh," Bakewell said, simultaneous with Maggie's "Oh my."

"Yeah. It was turra-bul. I shouldn't say it in front of a lady."

"Go ahead," Bakewell said, knowingly. Everything Ned did was interesting. Maggie leaned in toward Ned, a fellow conspirator.

"Well, we leave the course around dark the first night and me and Beasley are wantin to go back to the house and clean up, but Carl takes the bus down the beach instead of up it to our house. We ended up in a place with motorcycles and pool tables – the pits." Ned leaned into the table now too, crowding them with his big forearms. He used his hands to describe. "Let me give you a for instance, for example. The gal behind the bar had half her head shaved from front to back," Ned motioned, indicating a sort of Mohawk. "Her bald side had a tattoo on it, of a butterfly, on the side of her shaved head. I ain't shittin either. You gettin a feel fer this place?" he asked Maggie who nodded, wide-eyed, smiling expectantly.

"Yeah, so there's these three morons. They was bikers with shirts without sleeves, and armpits like crotches, real assholes. Excuse me," he patted Maggie's arm gently.

"They was playin pool. One of em had a shirt that didn't fit and I could see his navel, only it looked like a giant ass-hole." Ned made a circle with his thumbs and middle fingers. "And Carl and one of his ig-nert friends said they wanted to shoot some stick, trying to move these guys off the table sort of. Only they ain't gonna move are they?" Ned didn't wait for an answer. "Of course not, not for a couple of weenies like Carl and his sissy bud, so a fight breaks out and me and Beasley are tryin to stay out of it when one of 'em comes by us in a rush, and I grabbed at the guy and his shirt come off in my hand and when he turns, lookin real mad, Bease drops him with one punch in the mouth and there's blood all over and I'm holdin his shirt and feelin sorry for the guy, and Bease's already wishin he didn't hit him and we had gone back to the house instead of this pisshole of a place.

"Then one of them takes a swing at Carl and..." Ned paused to catch his breath, his face florid with exasperation. "...son of a bitch! Excuse me, honey." He patted Maggie's arm again. "He missed! He missed a chance to smack Carl one in the puss with a roundhouse!"

Ned's words were filled with disgust. He spread his hands wide, illustrating the miss. "I wisht he woulda smacked him one dead square, but he missed and Carl's moron friend breaks the fat end of a cue stick on the puncher's head and he goes kinda limp like, but doesn't quite fall down. The guy who owns the place starts shoutin about us all clearin out and Carl – probably feelin lucky, cause he got missed by that roundhouse – reaches in his pocket and pulls out a big wad, maybe $500 bucks, and says 'this is what we're gonna spend in here tonight, how much they got?' And the owner does a double take at the wad of dough and at his regulars and finally he says, 'Aw, well, Elmo, you and the other boys are gonna have to clear out. I can't have no more fightin in my place.'"

Ned mimed the owner in a drawly southern accent deep down in his throat and leaned back in his chair puffing with exertion, raising his hands to indicate the story was finished, but still full of regret about the guy missing Carl.

"Sounds like a typical outing with Carl." Bakewell said.

"So who is Carl?"

"A pig in the worst sense," Bakewell said, "Loud-mouthed, and so obnoxious, insulting and intimidating – when he can get away with it."

"Andy, that's awfully strong talk."

"I know; I apologize. The guy brings out the worst in me."

"He brings out the worst in ever-body. He used to be a good friend of Beasley's," Ned added.

Ned and Beasley were inseparable. Bakewell had encouraged Ned to go with Bease, as a twosome, had tried to tell them they would have a better time. They had done it on occasion. Whenever they did they had a great time. Bakewell didn't understand why they ever went as a group anymore, especially when Carl was along, but Ned said Bease loved a crowd.

Ned said he could only stay for a minute after the story, but proceeded to have two "Grey Gooses" with them and talked for an hour about what a great partner Andy was, how he loved him like a brother. He told stories about, "raisin Andy from when he was only just a pup." He told Maggie he worried about him. "You know he's always readin them Gospels. I guess they're really scriptures or somethin. But I can understand it now; especially now I can."

Bakewell almost jumped, asked another question about the trip, trying to divert him. Ned had a storehouse of memories, especially about his lifetime with Andy. He regaled Maggie with his stories, filled them with metaphors he conjured effortlessly. Maggie was completely taken in, loved the whole man, another admirer. Just before he left, Ned reached over and put his hand to the nape of Bakewell's neck and squeezed tightly. "This is my bud. He's the best son of a bitch in the whole world. He's the only brother I never had who wasn't worth a shit."

Bakewell said. “That’s a compliment.”

“I know,” Maggie smiled, eyes fixed on Ned.

When Ned prepared to leave they were ready to go also, and followed him out. His car was parked next to Maggie’s, a bright yellow Lincoln. Maggie commented on Bakewell’s pickup truck and Ned said, “He won’t never have a car that won’t carry bird dogs in it as good as it will carry people.” He took her hand again and patted it. “Shit, some of his bird dogs are as good lookin as people, better even than some of the dogs you see drivin ’round with better lookin people than they are theirselves.”

Ned continued to pat Maggie’s hand. “You know, you are one good lookin son of a bitch,” paused for a moment, added “I hope you and my pardner will be gettin together because you both deserve each other, and Andy here could use some better luck than he’s got lately.”

Ned drove off, leaving Maggie to unscramble the farewell while Bakewell watched, amused. When she looked at him he spread his hands, “Yogi Berra, in a sport coat; maybe a little more verbose?”

“I loved him.”

“I know. Everybody does.”

Obituary

Bakewell was driving cross-town on the Inner Belt, headed north. They had just contracted another job, and it was due to start soon, despite the cold weather. Nancy had asked him to meet with the general contractor to coordinate things, make sure everybody was on board and they got off to the right start. "No screw ups" was the company's byword now. Ned was no longer an owner, but was on a mission to "make it work."

Bakewell's radio chirped.

"Go ahead."

"You have another package, Andy. This one came "overnight". It looks important."

"I'll be in there after this meeting. Give me an hour."

"Right, you don't have to sign for this one, Mystery Man."

He drove back to the office just as the first snow began to fall. The office talk was about the coming storm. They were supposed to get six inches, a good snow in St. Louis. The package was on his desk, neatly wrapped. It looked official. Bakewell stared at it, almost dreading to open it. He'd learned to hate certain mailings. This one had the look. Trudy had been teasing him about his mysterious mailings, told the others, she thought he might be involved with a Columbian Cartel.

The address label was expensive looking, even worse, it was from a law firm, etched with a blizzard of names. He had no clue, lifted it once and found it heavier than expected. He secretly hoped it was some trick marketing device. Finally he opened it. Inside were two boxes. The first was larger than the second. He opened the smaller flat box. Inside was a roll of paper, heavy and expensive. On it was written:

Dear sir,

The enclosed box is hereby delivered to you per the instructions of the deceased as per the request of same. It is my duty to request that no additional correspondence is required from yourself, or to be directed to any member of the deceased family. I repeat: ***No further correspondence would be welcome, nor should any be forthcoming.***
Further it is requested that under no circumstance are you to contact any member of the deceased family by any means of communication, oral, written, Internet, etc. This being the deceased particular request and concern.

For the firm, I remain,

Paul McC. Armontraut

The signature was indecipherable. Inside the same box was a second letter in an envelope. Bakewell opened it with care and great reluctance, feared it might explode. It was a single piece of fine stationary. The letter was printed in a shaky hand.

My Dear Andy,

I hope you will find the enclosed of some help and some considerable relief. It had been in our possession, or rather I should say, my own possession for these past many years. I suppose it took the "boys" a good long while to finally let go of it and entrust it to me. Or maybe it was the fact that I finally reached a position within the organization, (thanks to people like yourself, who helped me so greatly and to whom I'm deeply indebted) by being a better judge of character than some of the "characters" I've had to deal with over the years. At any rate you are entitled to these items and they should give you some leverage if ever you are approached by us (maybe I should say "them") again.
I meant every word when I said you have always been such a happy circumstance in my life within the organization. One seldom meets an honorable man, and I fear you will find this particularly vexing with regard to my replacement. I urge you to keep a careful eye out for him when the time arrives. In the meanwhile you are safe until such time. I do not expect to have any further involvement after this month. I seem to have run out of time, as they say.
However, I have much influence within the organization when it comes to matters of money and accounting and taxes, so please believe me when I tell you that you will be safe in the future with the agreement we made. But I urge you, dear boy, to "watch your back" as they say in the movies when the time comes.

Good luck,
Ensley ("Snow")

Bakewell opened the second box. Inside the heavy cardboard was a large pair of binoculars. He felt a lump grow in his chest. The binoculars had troubled him all his life. They were probably the ones he had used that afternoon in Genoa. He had forgotten to remove his fingerprints from the glasses, hadn't wiped them clean. The last evidence tying him to the shooting was in his possession. He wondered how long the old man intended to keep them, wondered what might have happened if he hadn't sent them. The letter from the law firm was aged, had probably been written years before when Snow's will or trust, *whatever rich people used*, had been finalized. The handwritten letter was less than a month old. It had been an amazing few

months. He wondered how amazing the coming ones would be, how many of them he had left.
Two weeks later he received another letter, this one in an unmarked envelope, which he opened without curiosity, in the detached way he opened most of his mail. As he opened the envelope, a slip of paper floated to the floor, leaving the envelope empty. Bakewell bent down to retrieve it, read it there on the floor instead. It was an obituary notice from a newspaper with a photo of Snow in his late sixties? There was no date.

> Fortified with the sacraments, the late Charles Ensley Hamilton IV of Grosvenor, Pennsylvania. Dear father grandfather, great grandfather, brother, brother in law, uncle and cousin. Mr. Hamilton attended Yale University, BS '39 and Georgetown Law, LLD '47. He was on active duty in the North Atlantic during WWII serving in the Naval Reserve. Mr. Hamilton was a Phi Beta Kappa, member of the Rotarians, Opus Dei and active in the Archdiocese of Philadelphia for more than fifty years. He was a board member of the Art Museum and the Philharmonic. He received an honorary doctorate from Columbia University in 1966 upon completion of service with the Dept of Treasury. He retired from the banking and financial community in 1988.

3rd Mailing

Bakewell sat facing the television, the tri-colored pup next to him, the older setter behind the couch where he couldn't see her, but heard her tail thump when he spoke to her, the Brittany in front of the fireplace on a blanket. He let them in each evening, waiting until he'd finished eating, because they watched and begged, and he would end up feeding them something that shortened their lives. After what Katherine had called "the pandemonium of passage," when they first entered the house, nails scratching and sliding across the parquet floor, each dog checking every room in a race to get there first, things would settle down and they would settle in. Then it was mostly yawns and stretches the rest of the evening. They were good company and he kept them in the house until bedtime, when they would follow him out to the kennel where he gave them fresh water and latched the gate.

Lying across his thigh was a Ruger Red Label, a Model 77 bolt-action. It had a synthetic "all weather" stock. A "dead material," his friend John Hammond called it. John was his guru when it came to weapons, said wood was a living material that should be fitted to any firearm worth paying for, but, grudgingly admitted, "These goddamned plastic things made for a better shooting weapon if climate was a factor." Bakewell had a feeling climate would be a factor. The rifle was lighter by a few ounces, but felt cold to the touch and, like all things plastic, got colder when you wanted it to warm and warmer when you wanted it to cool. Bakewell hated anything man-made, loved wood, cotton and wool, things from natural products, disliked plastic, especially in his plane. Plastic saved 15% of the weight in a plane which was often the difference between take off and crash in the wilderness, so he grudgingly learned to accept plastic.

The rifle was interesting. It had been a .243 Winchester, but that caliber was stamped out and instead the barrel was stamped *6MM Int'l.* The bolt in his gunroom fit it perfectly as did the ammunition. He put his penlight inside the action, appreciating the work of a master gunsmith. The chamber had been re-bored for the cartridge shoulder to fit snugly into the receiver.

A note had come earlier in the day, with a postmark from Philadelphia, instructing him to take the key accompanying it to a storage locker on Lemay Ferry Road, where he found the number matching the narrow locker. He opened the door and found a box inside, leaning against the wall. He put it in the back of the truck, wiped his prints carefully from the door handle and took the lock with him. Later he opened the box and found the stock and barrel of the rifle taped, insulated, and wet with grease.

He was dozing through the evening's programming as he'd done for years, just as when Katherine controlled the remote. A story on the TV about a monastery in Europe somewhere prompted his memory. He called the long distance operator.

"What city, please?"

"Richardton."

"Go ahead."

"I would like the number for the Assumption Abbey, the Benedictine Monastery."

She came back with two numbers. He told her it didn't make any difference, was sure either would get him there. When she gave him the numbers, he dialed one and waited. It rang twice before being answered by a man who identified himself as Brother Donald.

"Brother, my name is Bannister. I was in Richardton a few years ago. I landed at your airstrip for a brief campout with my son. We were up there for a bird hunt. I'm sure you don't remember me, but…"

"The gentleman with the plane, yes, I remember. You had several dogs with you too."

"That's very good, brother. I didn't really think you would remember."

"Well, we maintain the airstrip here, you know." (He spoke like a North Dakotan – "shewer," "yep" and "you-betcha," – right out of the movies). "One of our brothers mows the grass and keeps it identifiable for folks like yourself. They tell me it's a little hard to pick out if you've never landed here before."

"You do a great job. I had no trouble finding it. It was dry that year, and it was a little bumpy, but I remember it was freshly mowed."

"What can I do for you?"

"Well, this is a little strange, but I was wondering what your policy is on guests? If someone drops in at the monastery, say to visit for a good while, are they welcome?"

"Oh yes. We have many visitors each year."

"We camped off your runway for two days back then, but I was thinking about a longer stay, maybe a few months if that wouldn't tax your hospitality. I'd be willing to pay for my room and board."

"Did you stay in the building when you flew in?"

"No Brother, my son and I were there to bird hunt. The Abbot was kind enough to allow us to land and camp out for a couple of days. We took communion each day and attended Sunday mass before we left. Unfortunately, North Dakota was fresh out of Huns that year, but we got our limit of sharptails before we went on to Montana."

"Well, I'm not a hunter. We sure have a lot of gophers though. Some of the brothers like to shoot them, for sure."

"Brother, I need a place to spend some time in late winter, maybe even later into the spring, a month or so. I lost my wife a while back, and I'm selling my business. After the deal is done, I'm pretty well finished up with life in the public world. I would like to look into the monastic life. I'm looking for a place that is remote. I've had enough big cities. I need a place that's more removed from the busy world. I would like a place where I can pray and enjoy the tranquility."

"I can have you talk to the Abbot or Brother Nathan, but neither one is here tonight. They are both over in Dickinson this evening."

"I'm handy and know a little about the construction business," Bakewell continued. "I might be able to add a little something, but I mostly want to blend in, hopefully go unnoticed."

"Why don't you leave your number and I'll have the Abbot call you when he gets back."

The cleric didn't want to discuss how Bakewell might fit in with life at the Abbey, sounded like he wanted to get back to whatever he was doing. Bakewell gave him his phone number.

Brother Donald signed off, "God bless you, Mr. Bannister."

***

It was Friday, December 10th. Maggie Walker was out of town, in the islands somewhere, ostensibly to renew her just perceptible but perfectly maintained suntan. Bakewell was surprised at how often he had thought of her since he'd gotten the bad news from Neville. *She's off looking for a man of wealth and sophistication, probably with a commensurate amount of free time, someone unencumbered by the need to make a living.*

He tried to amuse himself thinking of the next conquest in Maggie Walker's life, but truthfully, missed her phone calls. A million years ago he correctly presumed he'd been number 3 or 4, following a few cruelly smitten high school boys. Joe Walker he couldn't identify in the line up. Joe had won her fair and square. But he could never figure Joe. Had he been conqueror or conquered, or for that matter, did he care? It didn't make any difference. Bakewell knew there would be others. He found he enjoyed her company, albeit carefully, keeping a safe distance, walking softly. She still got lots of attention; men loved her or would love to love her, and it was fun to be seen with her, especially the way she'd started to hold onto him lately. He flushed with embarrassment at the thought of her holding his arm or taking his hand when they went anywhere. *Come on, Bakewell, stop daydreaming.*

He thought of her often now, wondered about their simple, carefully spaced get-togethers. He also wondered if Katherine was watching as he tried hard to constrain his venial meditations on Maggie's still fine anatomy. Testosterone was – and, he suspected, would always be, like vanity and arrogance – hard to rule, impossible to control completely. And he wondered when that part of his life would finally give out. All in all, he'd done a decent job, kept himself out of trouble, under control. There had been no regrettable peccadilloes, no stupid "impulses of behavior" as Ned liked to say. Still, he lapsed into vanity whenever she called.

The night at Rick's had created a maelstrom of speculation, and Ned kept him in tears with stories of what his "Buds, them stupid morons, was always sayin about you."

Ned was the first to ask. "Are you gettin in her knickers?" Bakewell answered honestly, and Ned had scolded, "Andy, you was a great husband and father fer all them years, now it's time fer you again. You need to get some. Yer still a young man for yer age. Use it if she wants you to." Ned always finished off with the little tutorial, "...It's still six inches long, with a Winesap apple hangin on the end."

Bakewell couldn't complain about his enforced solitude, had never lacked for invitations, had no one to blame for his lifestyle. He had preferred his nights alone, unless Michael was in town, but lately he was feeling lonely, was sure it had to do with the worrisome magnitude of events on the horizon. He couldn't ignore the fact that there was a possible shooting, unlikely but still possible, if his health didn't start to go soon. There was *that last part* too, when his health really started to go. It worried him more than anything his agreement with Snow might involve. He was getting moody and too somber, missed his relationship with the Girls' Club, missed their nasty talk. They had met one last time for an evening at Café Provencal just before Halloween, a farewell-until-spring-dinner.

The next morning he put on heavy down coveralls and took the 6MM and headed for the gun club, stopping on the way to fill a thermos with decaffeinated coffee, not wanting the jitters when he fired the gun. He got there before any of the others. They seldom got there before ten, especially when it was cold. He set up three different targets, laid out cartridges and spotting scope and set the thermos next to the bench where it substituted as a handwarmer, while he fired several rounds in the quiet, brutally cold air. Once he had it roughed-in, he hunkered down on the bench and fired it from the sand bags until he had it fine-tuned at a hundred yards. Finally he fired it "off hand" as he had been instructed to do. It was nearly without recoil and the bullet was so fast he held the gun right on, zeroed for a hundred yards. He began to pattern nicely inside five inches after a dozen rounds. The cartridge was a joy to shoot, but the stock was hard and cold and unpleasant against his cheek. Out at 200 yards the bullet had only 3" of drop. He could hit a pie plate with it between 50 and 200 yards by aiming dead center, enough to hit anything human. He wanted to be able to shoot the eraser off a pencil before the time came, a standard he held to whenever bench-resting.

Finally he leaned against the uprights so he could shoot the rifle with some support, knowing he would never be able to call his shot without some kind of support. He could probably find something to stabilize himself against almost anywhere in the world. He quit after forty rounds. When he checked the last target he saw a group of five within an inch and a half. *Not bad.* It wouldn't take much work over the next few weeks to get up to speed.

Christmas Eve

The phone rang while Bakewell was in the shower, and as he toweled off he checked the caller ID. It was Maggie. When he returned the call she answered on the first ring.

"Oh, Andy, good. I'm calling to ask a silly question." He waited. "I don't suppose you would consider spending Christmas out of town away from your children and those darling grandbabies, would you?"

"No."

"No, of course not. I don't know why I would have thought so; I'm sorry." She sounded flummoxed, out of character. "It's just that I have my home in Banff and it's so beautiful up there this time of year. I thought you might want to go up with me, I know you would love it. If it just wasn't such an important holiday I would try and talk you into it."

"You could probably talk me into anything, Maggie, but it is Christmas and I'd have to come home and face my kids; I'd never hear the end of it." He dropped the towel and reached for his shorts. "I'll confess I would sure like to see Banff in the wintertime."

"It's just lovely. Maybe we could go up after the holidays?"

"Maybe," he dropped the phone on the carpeted floor trying to get dressed. When he picked it up and explained she laughed, gave an imagined description of his predicament.

"Getting back to the holidays – are you determined to go up there for Christmas?"

"Well, if you're asking me to stay in town and spend another holiday with your children, I accept."

"No, I wasn't going to do that. I think I might have a date with another desperate divorcee."

"You are such a shit, Bakewell!" She said confidently, "But I know you too well. You would never hurt my feelings, not deliberately, anyway."

"Would you consider coming here for Christmas Eve and joining us on Christmas day?"

"I have no plans," she confessed, "Think I'll accept on both counts."

"I know a place where we can spend a quiet evening in a warm holiday atmosphere if you approve. I want you to come on Christmas day, and we'll have another Thanksgiving, only this time it'll be with presents."

She was amused with the Thanksgiving-being-the-better-holiday business, but refused to embrace it. Like Katherine, Maggie loved the shopping and gift giving; Bakewell suspected his children's children were about to be the recipients of her generosity. He could almost hear the sentiment through the phone, how much she missed not having a family to shop for at Christmastime. She had been estranged from her brothers and, although she said she spoke with the one brother's wife often, even more regularly with her niece, he doubted she had much company on Christmas. Bakewell wondered what it was like to enjoy Christmas with money in the bank before and after the holiday. *Well, you're about to find out rich guy.*

***

Maggie wouldn't let Bakewell pick her up, insisted on coming to his home so they could take her elegant car to the Ritz Carlton on Christmas Eve, where they ate yellowfin tuna with wasabi and pickled ginger and chased it with a stiff drink, soaking up the warm, festive atmosphere. The place was decorated beautifully; Maggie was decorated beautifully. Her lovely features framed again by a pair of glittering diamonds as she relaxed in a Queen Anne chair, legs crossed, her expensive clothes matching the season, matching the chair.

Maggie drove to the hotel, but made Bakewell drive home afterward. When they got to his house she came in and he set fire to the logs in the fireplace while she made them a drink. She took the couch, kicked off her shoes, and drank her scotch while Bakewell sipped beer from a can where they settled in the family room, the fire crackling nicely. Bakewell put an old movie favorite of Katherine's on the TV: *The Bishop's Wife* with Cary Grant and Loretta Young, and they commented on the wonderfully simple quality of life portrayed in the movie, and the wonderful old movies of their parents' generation. Eventually Maggie curled up on the couch while Bakewell reclined in his chair, both silent as Bakewell watched Maggie's attention turn from one object to another as she tried, surreptitiously, to study the room. He made her another drink during a manually imposed intermission.

"So where's that handsome boy of yours?"

"*Chillin* I think is the word they use now, out for the evening somewhere; he's dedicated to his craft, loves the wilderness, the hardship and the adversity of going without and pushing his luck, but he still revels in the comforts of home. He likes to regress whenever he returns to civilization."

Michael was living in his old room for the holiday season, running the dogs, bow hunting between bird-hunting forays, managing his time to allow for evenings down in Soulard, where he could hang with his many friends. He was much in demand since most of his friends were married and their wives constantly inveigled to find him a mate – an idea he steadfastly refused.

"Oh, I almost forgot the most important part," Maggie said, getting to her feet after the movie ended. She ran out to her car and came back with a gift and made him open it in front of the fireplace. They sat together on the hearth. He wasn't expecting a gift, never thought to buy her one, felt awkward, foolish really, once he realized his gaff. But embarrassing him was not her intention, and she was pleased with his reaction when he opened the box. It was a fine wool shirt, very expensive, perfect for the holidays. He told her he would wear it the following day and apologized in a mild stream of self-abuse for not thinking to get her anything.

Maggie enjoyed his predicament more than she would have enjoyed a gift. She had the upper hand once again, which reminded him of times he was trying to forget. Sitting there in front of the fireplace also called up memories for them both. They had spent several intimate evenings in her mother's home in front of the fireplace, although it had been summer at the time, without a fire, lacking the Christmas mood that surrounded them. Content with the lightness of the moment, no longer trying to engage him, she seemed to be soaking up the atmosphere, enjoying it unabashedly as they each stared at the scene in front of them. Nancy had somehow managed to decorate her mother's home with the many decorations Katherine had collected over the years and Maggie couldn't help but notice.

"I love your decorations. Do you have them done professionally?" she asked, teasing, recognizing a daughter's tender hand.

"I think its magic, really. I come home from work each night and there's a little more done and then one night... *it's all done."*

They sat in silence for a long time before he got up and put a CD on that filled the room with Christmas music. The mood was overpowering. Maggie unexpectedly got to her feet and said, "I think I should leave now." She turned and faced him as he stood up, surprised. She said she'd had a wonderful evening, thanked him, almost choking on her words. Bakewell was confused.

"It's all a bit overwhelming, really. I feel like I'm trespassing. This house is so full of your children, your past, your family and your wife. She must have been...so special, Andy." Maggie teared up; turning away she touched his arm, patted it softly. "I have to go."

Bakewell didn't know what to say, wanted to apologize but didn't know why he should. He had a sudden inspiration, "I shouldn't have brought you here, I just wasn't thinking."

"Are you kidding," she cried, then tried to laugh at herself. "This is the most perfect Christmas Eve I have ever known. Not even in my childhood did I feel the warmth and happiness I've experienced here tonight. It's just all so perfect. Too perfect! It's overwhelming. I'm repeating myself." She wiped the sides of her eyes with the heels her hands, trying not to smear her makeup. "I just wish it was mine. I'm so jealous."

Bakewell was about to speak. "No." She stopped him, patting his chest firmly. "You're a darling man, and I'm making a fool of myself. I'll come back tomorrow, and I'll be different; you'll like me then. Just tell me again what time I should be here." She reached for her coat. He helped her into it, and she was careful not to make any contact with him as she put it on. She walked out to the car in a hurry, and he followed, opened the door. Once inside she pointed at some wonderful gadget on the dash, and when he bent down to look inside, she kissed his cheek and thanked him for a lovely evening. She made a kind of shrugging/frustrated noise, saying, “Oh, I can’t believe myself,” sniffling loudly. She backed out of the driveway, leaving him standing in the blue white lights again. It was freezing cold.

Christmas

Christmas Day was a repeat of Thanksgiving, only, according to the Bakewell men, too much money had been spent. The girls tolerated the tired joke, maintained the festive atmosphere.

Two weeks before Christmas, Nancy had brought her family for an evening with her father, and she and Michael put up the tree, using ornaments Katherine had collected over the years – treasures from a lifetime of Christmases. Nancy and Michael repeated stories about each one as they trimmed the tree; the stories lovingly retold, standing on their own merit, while a satisfied and approving father listened and certified each one for his only son-in-law. It gave them an opportunity to remember and relive a past with a mother who had loved deeply, nearly to perfection. The night of the tree-trimming Bakewell was about to ask his daughter if she would mind, when she interrupted...

"Will Mrs. Walker be coming for Christmas Day?"

He told her she had been invited and wondered if it would be all right if she came for the gift unwrapping, to which they agreed, wisely as it turned out. Maggie arrived precisely at three, and brought each of them a thoughtful gift and spent some serious money on the grandbabies – outfits from a designer store. She asked Karen and Nancy repeatedly if the sizes were correct, which they were. Maggie had done her homework. Karen was still expecting and not happy about being late, but aware of the inconvenience her delivery would have been if she had had the baby just days before.

In a last ditch attempt to make forgotten-present amends, Bakewell called a friend from high school on Christmas morning, a guy who owed him a favor from years back. The friend was in the wholesale jewelry business and when he was coaching soccer a decade before Bakewell had given him a tractor to grade their church field with one weekend.

"Andy, my man, no problem," was Angelo's quick response. They met after Christmas Mass, and Bakewell bought an expensive gold necklace and matching earrings, which Angelo picked out and sold at less than half the price on the tag.

That afternoon, as the gift giving was coming to a chaotic end, the floor 12" deep in wrapping paper, Bakewell said, "Wait, one more present to unwrap before we're done," and, with unintended but perfect timing, gave Maggie the jewelry in front of the tree and in front of his family, pulling off a coup that impressed all. Maggie was stunned, said she adored the jewelry and replaced the earrings she wore with his gift, to everyone's approval. She accused Bakewell of teasing her the night before, saying he had the present all along, but Bakewell insisted on the truth, which made her even happier. She asked him to help her attach the necklace, which he did to the wide-eyed, beaming approval of his children. She almost teared up again after she heard the trouble he'd gone to. Bakewell, short on words, said, "I think it's time for a little Christmas cheer," and left the room to make drinks.

Later that evening, while they were standing together in the kitchen over a thirsty two year old with a fresh "tippy cup," Bakewell asked Maggie if she would consider flying down to the beach with him for a winter hiatus. Nancy overheard her father's invitation, her face registering surprise as she raised her eyes, nodding approbation to her oldest brother. Nancy cornered Maggie in the kitchen afterward and proceeded to tell her about the great times they all had at the beach, explaining places like Magnolia Springs and Fairhope.

Mrs. Walker insisted they all call her by her first name that evening, and Nancy went out of her way to encourage what she was beginning (in whispered tones), to refer to as "the advent of Maggie Walker." Said it couldn't have come at a better time, since it coincided with the season of Advent. When she saw the way her father and the woman in the gold jewelry enjoyed each other she sent a smiling endorsement to her self-conscious father.

New Deal

Bakewell couldn't get Snow out of his mind, after receiving the correspondence and the obituary, wondered how a man with so much education, so much influence, and so much stature, not to mention his apparent position in the hierarchy of the lay Church, could have been involved in a world that condoned violence and execution. He also wondered who would take the old man's place, or if someone else would even appear; wondered if he might be answering to a computer, or a voice that wished to avoid contact, any possibility of suspicion. If there was no one else to see in the flesh, he believed his chances of surviving would be enhanced. *Maybe he would be able to get away again?* But then he remembered Snow's cautionary words in the hand printed farewell note. For the moment it didn't really matter.

The answer came January 13th when his Nextel rang. Using the Nextel was no longer a surprise. He still remembered the guy who sold the system, his inference that his phones couldn't be monitored. Denny had corroborated that. The guy enjoyed saying, "It really hacked the FBI off." Snow had called him on his Nextel.

It was the Thursday before the Ram's playoff game with the Vikings, and thousands of out-of-towners were filing into the city. St. Louis had home field advantage for the first time in history. The incoming call was a local number. "Hello," Bakewell said, hoping it was a lead on another project; things had been going well.

"Bakewell, my name is Albrecht. We are going to be working together." The voice was surly. "No, that's not quite correct. You are going to be working for me from here on out, so we need to meet. I'm in this hick town of yours, ostensibly to see the football game; we need to meet before your team loses. The meeting is going to take place when I say, not when you can find the time to make it. Comprende?" He pronounced the Spanish word in three syllables.

"Okay," Bakewell said, trying to stay calm.

"Good, I will be getting back to you at this number. I don't want to hear any voice messages. I want to talk to you when I call. Make sure this phone has a fully charged battery at all times, so I don't have to listen to any voice messages. It will be our only source of communication. I hate voice messages. Com-pre-hende?"

"I understand."

"That's good. *You understand.* I'll get back to you when it's convenient for me."

"Can I ask how you know the Vikings will win? Or is that a company secret?"

"Never crack wise with me, dad. Write that down so you don't forget, okay? A guy your age forgets things. Never crack wise with me." The line went dead.

Bakewell's speed slowed, evoking the sound of a horn from behind. His thoughts came very slowly, as they always did when he was worried. *Not good...not dealing with Snow anymore. This one's not rooting for you... won't be rooting for you, for me, to get away...*He changed lanes and kept up with the traffic. *Am I going to get away...am I even going to try...will I be in shape to try...will I be in good enough shape do it at all?*

Too many questions without answers – he needed to think. He would need a get-away plan – *if I intend to get away.* It was going to require planning, knowledge, hopefully an opportunity for some research…and plenty of luck. *Damn, just when I started getting used to the idea of being a terminal millionaire.*

Well, what the hell. You know surviving is about as far fetched as the idea of them hiring you again...I hope it will be in the states. Some place I know, someplace I can get around. I know the continent fairly well, most of it. I'm weak in New England, but I can learn. Please let it be in the states...

He'd have to go underground after it happened. There was eighty grand in his account. He had gradually removed some, had it stashed in smaller bills. He intended to have all of it assigned and safe in joint accounts with Michael, Nancy and Andy. He also intended to have it spread around geographically. He wanted the deposits spread out. He would start with Michael who was due to leave for the bone fishing flats soon. That account would be set up in Omaha. There would be at least two others, one in Tulsa, maybe, and one in Indianapolis. While he was traveling he would try Denny's method of identity changing.

Arab Leader

The old Arab entered the limousine stiffly, said nothing to the driver as they left the dark interior of the compound and started out. The city was gray under dim lights, and the car had to weave from curb to curb to avoid the craters in the heavily pockmarked road, left from years of war. Like the rest of the country, subsisting on meager rations, suffering from a lack of medicine and virtually every other necessity, his people in need of the most basic staples, his country had groaned under the onslaught of high tech weaponry. It lay in near ruin now, without noise after dark, barely able to keep a pulse. The infrastructure had broken down long before; the remaining hydroelectric power couldn't keep up with demand during midday. Under the demand of illumination, it gave off only a measly glow, keeping vigil with the country's plight. At three in the morning the appearance of the capitol was dreary beyond description; at daybreak the sunlight exposed the carnage done to the landscape.

He was born 69 years earlier, the exact date not known, although his birthday had been celebrated madly by millions of countrymen for years – the celebrants now an ever-diminishing group of loyal followers. Sick with prostate cancer and under siege by many who had once ardently supported him, his tenure up; he had no options. It was time to run. He hadn't tried to delude himself or make the mistakes so many egomaniacal dictators made before him. He was a realist, and he was confronted with the reality of his physical recovery. There was no chance of maintaining control during his convalescence or of recovering control of the country afterward. Things were too unsettled.

His escape had been negotiated by carefully crafted agreements with two governments – one legal like his own, the other de facto – using *trusted agents* whose families had stayed behind, *recipients* of his paternalistic care.

He was born in Abu Kamal along the Euphrates River in what had once been Mesopotamia, the cradle of civilization. His homeland was actually part of the Ottoman Empire when his father had fought for the British and the Allies during the Great War of 1914-1918. That was the war against the hated Turks. His father had fought with the troops led by Faisal al-Hussein, under the leadership of the British General Edmund Allenby and a man named T. E. Lawrence – a subaltern who became famous and historically significant for his violent contribution. His father, also a violent man, fiercely loyal to the new King Faisal I, participated in the capture of Damascus, at a time when he considered himself a loyal Syrian. He had fought again, when his people revolted against both French and British control during the 1920's in what the Arabs perceived as a sellout by the Allies. Finally, once more realigned with the Allies, his father had fought one last time when World War II broke out in 1939. He was killed in the first action.

"Husni," as he was affectionately called by his brutal father, had immigrated south and later to the northeastern region near the Tigris. He joined the Party early on, while serving his compulsory military service, stayed on with the army in order to support a new family. He barely remembered his father, but his father's brutal nature, an inherited quality, had served him well for over thirty years. Although he was an atheist, he belonged to a small sect of Islam called Alawite, which also put him in a key minority that would eventually over take the country during one of the many revolutionary periods of unrest. In 1957 when the Eisenhower Doctrine created a massing of troops on the Syrian-Turkish border, with the intent of supporting Turkey in combating Communist aggression, he moved toward that region to fight the hated Turks, as his father had done before him. Then in 1958, when Nasser negotiated the establishment of the United Arab Republic, which consolidated Syria into one country with Egypt, over the violent objections of many extremist groups, he abandoned his homeland and moved further northeast. He moved "right" on the world map, but "left" toward Soviet influence and a new homeland, where he helped establish an independent state and endeared himself to the first King.

He managed to survive two purges in the military before resigning his commission and moving into the civilian dominated political arena. As attrition gradually took its toll, many comrades falling, as they failed to hold fast within the king's unstable government, during the many political "realignments", he rose through the Revolutionary Council. When he became President, his first act was the elimination of a monarchy he had once fervently supported. With that first purge came the elimination of virtually everyone of political influence who might have opposed him. He created a new Council of Ministers, which included immediate family members, and even more relatives. During the next thirty years he made his transition from an articulator of concessions, a man known for his ability to forge agreements, to a brutal, intransigent autocrat, where, eventually, he came to rely on violence and brutality exclusively to maintain his repressive grip.

His authority had never been challenged by any agency from outside, or from within, until he had declared one too many foolish wars with a neighboring country. His indiscretion had interrupted the flow of oil for more than five years, had cost the powerful and influential billions in trade, some of whom were his own countrymen. The last war, a gargantuan mistake, brought on by what *Time Magazine* had called, "the egomania of power," had cost him dearly in the support of his countrymen, and provoked months of repression to keep his government in place. If such a thing as a poll existed, his support among the people would have shrunk to less than 15% by the end of the last fruitless war.

Growing weaker each month, he knew his time had come, a challenge from within his own party was imminent. He decided to leave, after securing careful concessions from the de facto government of Bougainville, the Bougainville Revolutionary Army, known as the BRA in eastern Papua New Guinea. In exchange for 400 hectares of land along an isolated coast, he would secretly give the BRA money in carefully allotted installments. To cover his options, he negotiated a separate and equally secret agreement with the legal government for additional annual payments. Construction on his mansion/fortress was nearly complete; the last photos had demonstrated the facility was viable and well defended both electronically and with manpower. The manpower, supplied by the BRA, was in place and the perimeter was secure. He would have preferred to wait another six months, but several developments had made his departure urgent. His family, optionless, loyal to the end, and fearing for their safety, beseeched him to move quickly. He sent them ahead with several ministers – hostages – to be sent back once he was safely out of reach.

There was no caravan of police, no military vehicles when he left the city, only the single limousine. There was no traffic on the streets of the capitol either. In addition to the driver, there was one young army officer, unarmed – all were forbidden to carry a sidearm in his presence – although the old Arab had a small handgun in his side pocket. He wore a bullet proof vest and the simple uniform for which he was famous, and which resembled the uniform Fidel Castro had favored for years, this one a bland color that matched the color of the city and the mood of its citizens.

When they arrived at the airport the position lights on the small Citation were on, the strobe lights flashing. The limousine drove up to the aircraft and stopped not more than 10 meters from the wing. He left the car unescorted and unaided for the first time in thirty years, and passed a small entourage of elite officers, refusing to acknowledge them, in a pitiful attempt to be anonymous, and to the stunned surprise and frightened dismay of several young men standing close by. As soon as he entered the jet, the door was closed and the engines began to spool.

The tower cleared them for departure as soon as they turned at the last intersection. The plane proceeded onto the runway and began to roll. The old Arab sat in one of the cushioned seats on the right side and, as the plane climbed out over the city, told the young pilot, the only other person aboard, to turn right and circle the city as they climbed. In a solemn mood he looked down at the city, barely visible in the weak light, reflecting on the city's glittering years of greatness. During the early days of the monarchy, it had actually become a center of culture, entertaining thousands each year that made the trip some considered a mini Haj.

"Is it all right to go now, Monsieur le' President?" The pilot spoke in nervous French.

"Yes." The President said flatly.

The plane banked immediately and they headed southwest for

Damascus. The trip took less than an hour. When they landed, the plane was instructed to pull off at the first intersection, directed to a cargo area where another jet waited, also fully lit, with one engine running. The transfer took only minutes. There were others waiting next to the gleaming Gulfstream. When the President disembarked from the small Citation they all came to attention, waited to be greeted. He spoke to one uniformed man, before going up the stairs, slowly, trying to hold onto his dignity, trying to hold his stooped back erect. The man in uniform directed them to board the plane after the President, and they followed quickly, scrambling up the staircase in a barely controlled panic.

As soon as the Gulfstream was airborne it turned to the southeast. They flew for hours in darkness, later into the rising sun, stopping once for fuel in Sumatra, where no one left the plane, then on to a more eastward heading, until they finally landed at Rabaul on the island of New Britain in Papua New Guinea, just west of the Solomon Sea.

The President disembarked and entered another waiting car. The ride was only a few miles through what was left of "New Rabaul," the original city mostly destroyed by a volcano. This time his car was followed by an entourage of motley vehicles and drew the unwanted attention of the local population. They went directly to a small port where they embarked on a large yacht, lavishly appointed, belonging to a man who had entered into a multimillion-dollar contract to build a compound on the southwestern shore of the island of Bougainville, along what was known as the "weather coast."

The remaining trip across the sea took the rest of the day. The yacht cruised comfortably at 25 knots across 300 kilometers of calm water, the trip pleasant for most of the passengers. The President watched their departure from the enclosed bridge, went below as soon as they were underway. He was very seasick during the journey. He didn't speak to anyone until they landed at his own new dock in a small cove adjoining the compound not far from Empress Augusta Bay.

Albrecht

Bakewell was crossing town again; it was late in the day, cocktail hour, the snow blowing, when the phone rang. "Hello."

"*Mister* Bakewell." The surly voice had lately switched to sarcasm. Bakewell said hello a second time. "I'll be in town tomorrow. I want you to be at the Airport Hilton, room 203, at precisely four o'clock. Not four-oh-one. Room 203. Knock at the door. We'll have a short meeting."

"I won't have to knock. Just open the door and I'll be there. Room 203, four o'clock."

"I told you not to crack wise with me, dad." The phone went dead.

Miserable son of a bitch... The first meeting had been unnecessarily tense, Albrecht deliberately provocative, ridiculed Bakewell about his age, baited him, saying he didn't look violent, added, "Frankly, I'm disappointed. You're not what I expected."

The antithesis of Snow, Albrecht tried hard to project ruthlessness; it was overdone. Bakewell had seen the act too many times, known too many Albrechts over the years. They all hid behind the same façade. Albrecht was ill-willed, probably vicious, but the tough guy just wasn't there. Real tough guys seldom needed the act. Backstabbers and petty tyrants needed the act, seemed to have it in common, but a tough guy was just that and, more often than not, was honest and trustworthy.

After the first meeting Bakewell knew he couldn't trust Albrecht, and wondered how he could be so different from Snow. More important, how he managed to get into Snow's cultured world. He didn't fit their mold. *What are you talking about? You don't know anything about Snow's world.*

They had met outside the stadium, Albrecht enormous, looking like a woolly mammoth in an expensive topcoat and hat. In his shirtsleeves he looked to be 6'5", pushing 275 pounds, most of it in his lower end, pear-shaped and out of shape. He was a leaner, an intimidator, had a habit of putting his chin out and leaning in, was used to people leaning away when he did. Bakewell held his ground, barely. It wasn't the physical presence so much as the power he represented – *power over life and death?* Bakewell was afraid of Albrecht, knew he was supposed to be afraid of Albrecht. Being afraid of Albrecht was a smart thing to be.

During their unpleasant conversation Bakewell's attention drifted, he supposed somewhere in the world, there was a wife and little kids who called him daddy, even looked up to him. If he had a soft underbelly, like Ned and the other big carnivores Bakewell had known, it wasn't apparent. He was a mean son-of-a-bitch. Still, he couldn't intimidate with a stare, relied on the leaning, and his massive bulk, liked to crowd.

Too many Albrechts had filled Bakewell's business life, the type who would break a subcontractor and enjoy it – let him make a mistake and hang him out afterward. He and Ned had been at war with and hated the type. Bakewell remembered a conversation with Ned from years before, remembered it with discouragement: "Andy, let me tell you somethin I observed about people in my life. There's two parts to a man: he's got a personality – and that might be of a moron, or it might be of a brilliant guy, who's even smart – then there is the honor part. A fool-guy might be a straight-shooter, a guy with real honor in em; where's on the other hand, that smart guy with the brilliance in him might be the scum of the earth when it come to tellin the truth or bein square over money. Some guys are stupid and honest and other guys are smart, but ain't worth a shit."

The thought of having to pass a review that went before any board on which Albrecht had a membership troubled him. Bakewell wondered where he would be if he had worked for an Albrecht in Genoa. *Dead, stupid! Well, you won't have to worry so much about dying this time. There are some advantages to being a short-timer.*

The recklessness of Bakewell's youth was returning now that he was terminal. Albrecht's mirthless nature made him want to provoke the man. It was foolish and dangerous, but Bakewell was living the final months of his life, and they were looking to be dangerous months, no matter how he behaved. He suspected caution in his relationship with Albrecht might be a waste of time. There would be no building of loyalty in the relationship. He would be safe until the time came, would put up with the contempt and the abuse until it was time. When it was over, it wouldn't make any difference. In the meantime, he would put up with the crowding, the leaning, the getting in his space. He would put up with the leverage and the façade, see how it shook out. He never doubted Albrecht could say, "Shoot him," when the time came, could say it, and quietly return to his meal.

***

When Bakewell knocked, the surly voice called too loudly. As he opened the door, Albrecht was crossing the room, floor vibrations perceptible. He ignored Bakewell and sat down heavily on the couch, opened a small folder, removing several documents. "Your hour has come, dad." Bakewell looked on intractable, refusing to show emotion, even though his chest pounded and he feared it might make his shirt move. It didn't matter; showing fear would please and disarm Albrecht, might work in his favor. "It's time to put up. Sit down and I'll go through this for you quickly. Listen carefully; I don't like to repeat myself."

Bakewell sat, deliberately leaned back in the chair, trying to look relaxed. Albrecht gave him a photo of an island chain, said, "You're going to Bougainville. It's in the…"

"Solomon Islands. I know where it is."

"Apparently not; it's part of something called Papua New Guinea. So you don't really know where it is, do you, dad?"

"It's the northwestern most island in the Solomons, always has been. I don't care who's annexed it. It's part of the Solomons."

"Well, you better start caring who it belongs to. You might have to deal with their government. And it's not going to be the government of the Solomon Islands."

Bakewell looked at the map. Bougainville was part of Papua New Guinea.

"You will leave on the 21st, TWA to Los Angeles then on to Brisbane; Brisbane to Port Moresby. You get a layover there, just enough time to shit, shower and shave, then it's on to Bougainville by boat. We arrange the boat. We can't find a flight in or out of Bougainville right now. They seem to be having a civil war." Albrecht chuckled, closed the folder and leaned back satisfied, smiled for the first time as he watched the look of concern on Bakewell's face. He loved the leverage, the knowing. He watched Bakewell closely. "So you'll have to keep your head down. We don't want you getting involved in some chicken-little dispute with the natives. We don't want you to get your head blown off. Com-pre-hende?"

"When's it supposed to happen?"

"I told you, on the 21st."

"When does the action take place?"

Albrecht was put off, had missed the point of his question, started again. "My guess is shortly after you get there. We don't want you to get too acquainted with the country. Port Moresby is only a stopover before the islands. Keep your head down, hear? Learn to look like you belong. There are a lot of white people out there, I'm told, in New Guinea, mostly Australian. Fit in when you get to Port Moresby. I don't know what the drill is after that. I'm sure our people will fill you in. Have a nice trip."

"I may need more time."

"What do you mean, more time? I give the orders; you follow them, dad. Don't give me any ultimatums."

"If you want it done right you ought to think it over. Preparation is always the key. Snow emphasized that. You ought to be able to see that."

"You go when I say. Com-pre-hende? You don't have anything to say about it. You get paid to do what I tell you. It's our deal, not yours. You're just the guy on the right end of the scope. Com-pre-hende?"

They stared at each other. Employee versus bully, Bakewell ruminated on some of the bullies he had known. They weren't tough guys either. Ned was a tough guy. Ned could stare a cobra down at 12", didn't have to act tough to convince anybody. Albrecht was mean, but he was a lard ass, not a violent guy, what Ned called a, "me-first guy." Albrecht broke off eye contact and opened the folder again.

"Here's the target." He pushed a sealed envelope across the table, making Bakewell get up to retrieve it.

Bakewell's pulse was running when he took the envelope. He could hear it in his ears as he bent over the coffee table. He tried to act casual, like it was all old news. It didn't work. His voice was worried when he spoke.

"I get to see who the target is before the big moment? I thought you would put me back in some hotel room somewhere and say 'shoot.'" Albrecht kept quiet, enjoying the moment of truth, watching Bakewell closely as he opened the envelope and pulled out the photograph. Bakewell looked at Albrecht one more time before turning it over slowly. He stared at it, stupidly, for a long time. He had seen the same picture on the cover of *Time Magazine.*

"This is political," he said softly, dubiously.

"No. It's business. It's always business with them."

"No. This is political." He placed the photograph back in the envelope and put it back on the table, hoping his hands didn't shake, hoping it was a mistake, a cruel joke. He pushed the photo back across the table, rejecting it. "Snow said it was never political. It would always be business. This is political. It shrieks politics."

"No, it's *business!* This son of a bitch cost them billions. They want the money back. He took billions with him. He's giving their money away to the government over there, and to a bunch of revolutionary pukes, whoever they are, probably covering his ass with both his bloody hands. It won't work though." Albrecht got up from his cushioned seat, leaving his impression in the couch, and walked heavily across the room and made himself a drink from a tray: 100 proof Old Grand Dad. There was a large container of ice next to the bottle. Bakewell didn't move. When he finished making his drink, Albrecht turned back to face Bakewell. "They don't care about *Boogie-Ville* or New Guinea, or all those spades out there shooting each other up. They want to send a message. They want the money back. *It's business!*"

"It can't be done. There is no way to get close to this guy. He's a terrible man."

"Don't parry with me, dad. You're not in a position. Shut up!"

"I'll never get away with it. You'll never get away with it. Those people are vindictive as hell. There'll be a Holy War – a huge war of attrition. They'll never rest until he's avenged."

"Wrong again, dad. There won't be any fall out. They don't care about him over there. Nobody cares about this bum any longer. He's lost his clout. Once he left his country, he was done. He thinks he can buy protection…and loyalty. He probably could, if he was in trouble with anybody else, but he can't. Not with our guys. They want to send him a note. Think of yourself as the stamp."

"There is no way you could get me close to him. I can't shoot him from two miles away."

"We'll put you right in his face. Even you won't be able to miss."

"You might put me in his face somehow, but I would never be able to do it or to get away."

Albrecht came across the room, flushed, loving the leverage. "That's your problem. I really don't care, but I'll tell you what. *There will be no revenge.* So you'll be able to sleep comfy afterwards." He was almost standing over Bakewell when he added, "If you get away."

"Snow guaranteed my safety. He said it would all be taken care of."

"Then we'll take care of you. Don't worry about it."

"The guy's in the Middle East. He's untouchable. There's no way to get to him. It's impossible. It would be like taking a shot at Clinton. You've got the wrong guy. You'd need a professional for this one, and there's no professional out there dumb enough to try it."

"Wrong. He's skipped out. He's vulnerable as hell now, and we'll put you right in there, just like before. It's a no-brainer, even for someone with your limited skills." Albrecht left the room and went into the bathroom and started to run an electric razor. Bakewell never moved from the chair. When he came out he said with finality, "I'll be watching you from here on out. Think of it as a "tail," like you're being watched by the FBI." He held a towel in the hand he pointed with. "It might be the FBI. Don't do anything stupid. When the time comes, you'll be at the airport, an hour early. You'll be going through customs. That takes time, so you'll be an hour early for every flight. Your itinerary's in the gray envelope. Take it. Leave the rest. And leave now; beat it." He turned and went back into the bathroom.

Misgivings

Bakewell's head was spinning, his pulse pounding, but his hands were steady when he picked up the gray envelope. He walked out into another February day, wet, miserable and overcast and drove south on the Interstate. He didn't notice the weather, didn't notice the traffic, didn't really know what part of town he was in. He drove to Nancy's, dropped in unexpectedly, finding the family about to sit down to dinner. He had spent the day at his gun club before meeting Albrecht. Nancy asked him where he had been, saying she hadn't been able to get him on the phone or radio. Tom asked him to stay for dinner. He ate a small portion of the big meal and played with his grandchildren on the family room floor, focusing on his grandson whenever Julie's attention was diverted. He stayed late, waiting for his grandchildren to go to bed.

"They were so wound up with you here, Dad; they didn't know what to think."

Tom made them a drink and they sat and talked for a long time. It was warm and comfortable in their family room; the kids seemed to be very happy together. Eventually Bakewell got around to the joint account he'd set up, explaining some money would be transferred to a bank in Bismarck, North Dakota. He had decided to add one more bank to his inventory. He gave Nancy some additional papers to sign.

"Why, Bismarck of all places?"

"Because I intend to end my time not too far from there."

"Daddy!"

"Nancy, there's a place up there on the prairie where I would very much like to finish up my days. I'm going up there to check it out. It's a Benedictine monastery. I would like to have a few bucks in a bank close by, if I need some pin money."

"Twenty thousand dollars?"

"You get a better rate if you put a bigger chunk in," Bakewell said, trying to keep it light.

Nancy thought the idea was strange, but only shrugged, not wanting to argue over money. He was her father after all. She was more worried about his mental state. When he rose to leave she hugged him tightly. They stood in the hallway rocking back and forth for several minutes before she would let him go. Bakewell's heart was breaking; it was almost a repeat of Katherine's funeral. He tried to play the tough guy, the way he'd done with Ned and Harvey, but Nancy was different. His affection for her was lopsided. There was no explaining it. It wasn't really fair to her brothers, but they accepted it as a father/daughter thing. She was so thoughtful and protective, always trying to shield him from things, so solicitous about his life, so determined to make him happy. Holding her made his heart ache like it hadn't since the day of Katherine's death; the pain more than he thought he could endure. She was a wonderful daughter, and he desperately wanted to protect her from her pain, keep it away like he'd done when she was little, when he was her hero. He was still her hero, he just didn't realize it.

Snooping

With the death of his business following so closely the tragedy of his wife, Bakewell was traumatized, physically, emotionally and spiritually. He was shattered, needed a total rebuilding, a reconstruction of his damaged psyche. The pain of losing the business, compounded by the loss of Katherine left him damaged, missing, existing in part, unable to function any longer. The realization he was about to leave it all, became a catalyst for renewal, a spiritual and emotional sustenance that lifted him back to functionality. The sudden influx of money brought an awakening. He could pay his bills, move about in society again. More important, the knowledge he would be gone soon created a unique social leverage he'd never known. He knew, and they didn't. It was simple. He could behave, go out of his way to be decent to everyone, including the people he didn't like, the people who had never liked him. He had them at a disadvantage now. In any confrontation, he could be magnanimous if he chose, play the good cop to their bad act. Later, after he was gone, they would remember who had behaved worst. It was a weird satisfaction he lived with, and, at times, almost made him laugh.

He had one mission left before the time came to leave, and he had procrastinated, hoping the need for identity changes wouldn't be necessary. He picked up the phone again and punched in the number stored in *Memory* a few weeks before.

"Murphy."

"Denny I need another favor. How is my credit?"

"Your tank's empty. What is it? You still want to change your identity?"

"How did you guess?"

"I'm psychedelic." It was the Ned joke. Ned had thought it meant clairvoyant, and the first time he used it, it had brought down the house. They all substituted *psychedelic* now.

"Seriously, tell me again how to do it?"

"Do what? Change your identity?"

"Yes."

"Andy, what is this cops and robbers shit? Who're you doing business with, a fuckin Latin American drug lord?"

"I just want to know how to do it. Take me through it one more time?"

Jaded by longevity, the age of cynicism had crept up on them both, Denny responded, "You keeping off the phone? Using the Nextel for your nefarious purposes?"

"*Nefarious* is good Denny. I like nefarious."

"You aren't the only one who knows a big word. Where you wanna meet?"

"How bout that classy place with the linoleum floors?"

"Deal. Three o'clock."

Denny described the procedure again, advising caution all the way through. "I don't want to see your ugly puss on the front page of the *Post.*" Bakewell laughed at the humor, tried to throw him off, keep the conversation light, anxiously noting Denny's recap on identity changes, wanting to sound more zany than insane as he took his notes.

"You're a fucking amateur, Andy; you'll end up making a fool out of yourself. I've dealt with these dipshit amateurs all my life. Try not to make the big mistake every amateur always does."

"Tell me again."

"Don't try leaving a fake ID in place too long. A fake ID only lasts for a few months at most. You can't relocate yourself and your assets and not be found out. Sooner or later the ID washes out. I told you, if someone important – like that guy you had me checking on last year – is looking for you, your anonymity won't last two weeks, maybe not ten minutes if you cross a border or make flight."

"How many months if it's a simple wish to be left alone?"

"Three, four at the most, if done by an amateur, maybe a couple of tax seasons if done by the best. That's if you're on the run. But if nobody's looking for you, it might last a long time."

"So I go to a few towns and start with the bureau of vital statistics. Get a copy of a birth certificate of someone in the phone book, *which can be had for the asking?* – if a decent reason is supplied. Then I get a social security number. It sounds too easy."

"It ain't rocket science, but it won't work if you're in deep shit. Level with me?"

"The drop box sounds the hardest. They'll send on my credit cards – after I'm approved – just forward them to a drop box if I request it, even though I put an address on the application?"

"*They want you to have the credit card,* dipshit, *so you'll use it.* They'll worry about finding you for collection later. They get paid to issue you the card. They'll send your name down the line and let somebody else worry about collecting."

By the end of the month Bakewell had done the legwork, the fly work, bought a drop box in Tulsa, Omaha and Indianapolis, filled out credit card applications using his office address. On the second trip, he picked up a library card and bought new billfolds and filled out the information card in each and began to weather and age them. It took three separate days the first time, but on the return trip he was able to do Omaha and Tulsa in one day. The flying reinvigorated him, even when he was feeling run down. Flying always adrenalized him; it also left him exhausted the day after. He missed a lot of work in January.

He continued to pick Denny's brain over several long lunches. Denny knew he was being used, enjoyed the game the way he enjoyed playing their cat and mouse game in the backfield years before – the game to see if he could get to the guy before Bakewell did. In the good old days, because they had tended to run away from Bakewell, Denny got some great straight on shots at the ball carrier, still appreciated the memories. Denny enjoyed the new game too. The only part that jaded the program was his fear his friend was in real trouble. He'd done more inspector/detail work trying to find out what Bakewell was up to than he'd done on his last homicide case.

Their last lunch was in February on a sleety, crummy day, sitting in a wet and windy corner of a Kingshighway Avenue watering hole. By then Denny had learned more than he wanted to know, but still hadn't figured out what Bakewell was up to. Half way through the meal he stopped eating and gave Bakewell a recap on his recent investigations, which also included Bakewell's illness. Denny had gotten Dr. Neville to share nearly half an hour with him, got a curt and hostile briefing. He knew Bakewell's finances, had done an extensive search of banking records, personal and corporate. And he knew about his personal life – he hated checking on his personal life, or lack there of, but knew all about Maggie Walker, Ned's buyout, even his proposed traveling plans, which included the tickets Bakewell didn't yet know had been purchased in his name for the South Pacific. He gave Bakewell a full rundown on his health, his business fortunes and misfortunes, and his recently improved social life.

"At first I thought you were doing something stupid, like trying to avoid the inheritance tax, but after I did some checking I realized it was even dumber. You've accepted a big chunk of dough for God knows what, and you're obviously into some kind of deal with the people who sent the money. I have a bad feeling about it. I'm afraid it might be something related to the guy with the missing prints. If I thought you were going to be around for a long time I would knock some sense into you. I've been wanting to kick your sorry ass for decades, just to show you I could do it, but it doesn't look like you're up to it now. We'll have to wait until the next life for that.

"And," Denny lowered his voice, dropped the sarcastic tone, "It doesn't look like you have enough time to get into too much trouble." He finished a third big glass of iced tea and placed it on top of the $20 bill Bakewell had put on the table, pushing it across toward him. "You'll probably end up making an ass out of yourself somehow, but at least I don't have to worry about you doing time. I hate to visit people in the slammer. Those places make me want to soil myself."

"I thought I was broke until you so politely explained my current finances, you nosey-assed Mick. I ought to disown you for snooping, and kick your ass while I'm at it, just to show you, you can't handle me, but you're such an idealistic know-it-all, I'm going to give you absolution for being good-hearted and concerned."

"You're not broke. That I checked out first. Trouble almost always concerns money, so that's the first place anybody looks." He turned and waved for the check. "I thought you might be in some kind of financial jam. That's what makes people do stupid things. But, as we both know, you're loaded. Pay for lunch, rich guy."

Bakewell realized it looked to an outsider like he might have money. The only money he considered his own was in his account for the what-if games. The money in the company he never thought of as his. He couldn't see himself with money any longer, even when he tried. Bumping along, barely managing to get by ever since the raid, had left an indelible mark.

Denny had studied his friend closely during their recent lunches, watched his eyes whenever he answered a question. He decided to change the subject to throw him off. It was a favorite cop trick. "Have you told the kids yet?"

"NO!"

"Why not, for Pete's sake?"

"Because they're happier not knowing Denny. Pull your head out, and quit preaching to me."

"Andy, listen to me. They have a right to know."

"And I have a right to privacy, and I'm going to stick with it for a while."

"Judas, Andy, put yourself in their place; think about that. If your old man was dying and you didn't know it, if he lived the last 3 or 4 months of his life and he knew it and you didn't, all the things you would have said to him and all the things you *wouldn't* have said to him?"

"Give me a break, pal."

"Andy."

"Denny, don't talk to me about rights. Just please, respect my own – my right to privacy – and leave off with this. Let me handle it in my own way. It's my life and I've only got one to live."

"That's a quote."

"I know it's a quote."

"So who knows other than Ned? You had to tell Ned."

"I had to tell Ned, of course. It was lots of money."

"Yeah, let's talk about the money for a minute. Where did the money come from?"

"It's insurance money."

"Bullshit, you're not dead yet. You can't work that con."

"There's a guy in Chicago…he lends money against insurance policies, if you can prove to him you're going to check out in a reasonably short amount of time."

"Jesus, a guy in Chicago, Andy; give me a fuckin break!"

Bakewell refused to be drawn in further. He could hear the cop in Denny, trying to close in. Denny waited until the table was clear, started in again, "You know, I know you pulled that right out of your ass, I know you did – but son of a bitch – it's believable. There probably is a guy out there, some son of a bitch that would lend you money if he knew you were going to conk out pretty soon. Lord have mercy. It might even be true." Bakewell didn't respond. "I've been in a dirty business all of my life, and being a cop, you see the bottom half most of the time. And I've tried to stay reasonably clean, optimistic; I've stuck with the faith, the same one you've stuck with…"

"What else? We were raised that way. We're a couple of Baltimore catechists."

"Don't remind me. I don't need that shit right now. The truth is, the world's screwed up, not the whole world, just a little part of it, but that little part of it can wreck it for the rest of us. And there probably is some dark-minded, sick bastard out there that would lend you a hundred grand on a million dollar policy, or some weird shit like that, for some outrageous usury rate." Denny shook his head again. "Lord, you're giving me the creeps."

"You're not exactly cheering me up, Denny. You ask me if there's anything you can do for me, practically volunteer to lay down your life for me, give me your entire retirement, but you're not much on the hospice side."

"Yeah, well you can buy that kind of crap. I think it's about 25 bucks an hour. Get somebody to listen to you gurgle, sputter, clean up puke. Most of my time's spent in a tough world; I have to act tough."

"Yeah, I know. You've always been a tough guy. That's why you still want to kick my ass. Lord, look at us. We're on the high end of middle age, and still talking about fighting, like a couple of sixteen year olds."

"Okay, okay, never mind. Forget I said that. It was a dumb thing to say. I'm sorry I said that." Denny looked frustrated and uncomfortable. "I love ya, Andy. Does that make you feel better?" Denny honed in with his eyes, "I love ya Andy. I've always loved ya. There's something about you. You got this fucking quality. I look into those empty eyes of yours, those sorrowful fucking eyes of yours, and I've always worried about you. I see something in there. I don't know. I look into your eyes, and I feel like I'm standing in a funeral parlor. What the fuck is it with you? You're making me feel sorry for you; you're making me love you. Even when you were an arrogant fuck, you were still so damned exposed."

Bakewell leaned back in his chair; it was involuntary, trying to avoid the strange, abusive sympathy. He raised one hand in a defensive gesture. There was a long pause. Neither man was much of a talker. They were often comfortable together for long hours with minimal conversation, especially when they were younger.

"You know, I call you a dumb mick all the time, but it's not true. You're a pretty savvy guy. You see through most of the BS; you've always had my number. You're sympathetic in an insulting sort of way," Bakewell shook his head, suppressing a laugh, "So I'll confess…I love you too. I've always thought you were one of the two best friends I've ever had: you and Ned. There, I've said it." He looked Denny straight on. "Geez, look at me. We're both losing it. I love you Denny, I love you." He had to look away; there was too much emotion between them. Neither man spoke.

Bakewell broke the silence. "Look in on my kids once in a while. Let them know…I don't know…let them know you and Ned were the two guys I loved most in this world. It might mean something to them. I don't know. It might be kind of a figurative pat on the back. That's all I ask. Anything more is too much to ask. You've got your own kids and your own problems. Life is heavy enough. You don't need my problems. You don't need my kids, just a kind word, remember me to them. And maybe, if you get a chance, tell them about the better part of our youth."

There was another very long pause. They both wanted to move on, both had been moved by what had been said. Bakewell finally resumed, "Money help is a fine thing, Denny, and we each know people that have a lot, guys we went to school with. They enjoy giving it away, picking their spots, doing the right thing, but in the final analysis, it's the gesture, the little stuff. I guess what I'm saying is…it's the emotional stuff, not the material stuff that's got some real value."

The door opened one more time as the last of the lunch crowd departed, letting a cold blast of air into the drafty room. Denny told Bakewell to go ahead and amuse them both with "the secret identity stuff." It would give him something to do before he retired. He enjoyed playing detective one more time before he gave it up, especially now that it was out on the table and he didn't feel like he was sneaking around. He told Bakewell he was going to find out what he was up to before it happened.

"By the way, what do you need a passport for?"

"Travel."

"Travel where?"

"To leave the country. You need a passport to cross the border."

"Why a visa for Papua New Guinea? What's there?"

"The Franciscans, our missionary brothers."

"You're going out to the missions for a visit in your shape?"

"Port Moresby, in Papua New Guinea."

"I know where it is…although I didn't three days ago." Denny tapped the table with a large digit, smiled, making deep furrows in his doughy, heavily lined face. "The Franciscans, huh? I figured you for a Jesuit type, what with all the social climbing; figured you would be hobnobbing with Biondi down at his palace."

"No, I'm looking for humbler abodes. I don't need to glad hand the glad-handers. I've already done that…as you know."

"As I know. Let's talk about your illness. How bad is it? Your man Neville didn't want to tell me too much until I told him you might be a danger to yourself and might incriminate some *innocent others*."

"You jack-off. Where do you get off? Who's being arrogant now, Denny?"

Denny nodded. "I take your point; my heart's in the right place."

"Fuck you."

Murphy nodded. He knew Bakewell had a right to be upset. He'd been off base, but he couldn't stop. "Help me out Andy. Help me to help you. You know I will do anything you ask."

"Keep an eye on my kids after I'm gone, and I'll be grateful. And stop snooping. You're not smart enough to figure me out. And you don't owe me anything, so leave off."

Bakewell thought long about how he would break the news of his health to his children, speculated on how they would react to a second tragedy in their young lives, spent hours conjecturing what his death would do to each of them. In his meditations, he assumed Andy and Nancy would turn to their spouses to find the comfort they needed in the darkest part of their individual grief. Both children had married well, found stable relationships that would provide an important arbiter to their grief. Michael was another story. The boy was a loner like his father, spent days in the wilderness he'd been taught to love, was learning from his own personal experience now. Bakewell knew loneliness was fertilization for grief. Alone, Michael's suffering would be ungoverned and Bakewell worried what direction it might take. It would be hardest to break the news to Nancy, feminine emotion was always a greater challenge, but Michael would probably be impacted the most.

He thought about a family meeting, a regular get together on a Sunday evening, thought about making a general announcement, but he wasn't good at that sort of thing, feared facing their joint reaction. Another consideration was to tell them individually, but as soon as one learned the news the others would be informed immediately. They always turned to each other in a family crisis. Eventually he decided it would have to be Michael. A quiet, carefully orchestrated, conversation, gentle, simple and direct, leading up to the disclosure would soften the blow, and it would be just the two of them, alone, able to react without any outside distraction. They would have time afterwards to discuss the future and the impact his death would have on the things farther down the road. They would talk about the dissolution of his property, his few remaining toys, bird dogs, where the money from his share of the plane and the sale of the house would go, talk about any other details that came up. He would make each child a joint executor of his will.

Bakewell decided to give them two weeks notice before he left for the islands. He didn't want it to go on any longer than necessary, but wanted to be fair, give them some time to adjust. He would tell them his doctor said he had several months before his health really started to fail, say that he wanted to go out to the Pacific and visit the missions. As soon as that decision was made, he contacted the archdiocesan office, hoping to find the names of men and places out in the Pacific. When he received no response to his letter, he began his own search, soon learning the Marists' had a big presence in the Solomons in places like Bougainville, Guadalcanal and San Cristobal, which they called Makira. His first informative source was a priest at the Provincial House in San Francisco; soon he was emailing and faxing men on station on the other side of the world.

His only resource in Port Moresby were the Franciscans, and when he made contact with the seminary in Bomana, just outside the city, he got an offer of lodging and a volunteer to pick him up at the airport.

***

Michael wept openly when his father told him he was terminally ill. Later, he asked the obvious questions, questions that were logical, even sequential. Bakewell, speaking in a soft tone, answered each one, slowly assuring him in a firm, empathetic voice that there was no hope. He wanted to make sure it was final in Michael's mind, left no percentage for hope. It was important to make Michael understand. Bakewell hated doing it, but knew he had to make certain there was a finality in the boy's mind. Michael had lived the nightmare before; he was stronger now. Bakewell assured him he would be able to get through it, told him he was proud of him and proud of the strength he had observed in his character.

Michael sat very still, listening and nodding, in the large chair across the room next to the entertainment center. The chair faced the wrong way, had been a source of conflict between Bakewell and his wife. "Why would you have a chair next to the TV, looking out the family room windows," he'd asked, frustrated, during one of those ridiculous arguments where emotion won over logic.

"Because the TV's not always on," Katherine had answered calmly, as if explaining to the simple-minded, which only added to his frustration. "Just think of it as a space filler."

The chair, large and comfortable, should have been positioned in a place where it got more use. In the end, she had won of course, the chair had remained, un-sat in over the years, between the cabinets below the bookshelves, next to the entertainment center that dominated the wall. Michael sat in the unused chair, tried to remain calm, but appeared almost numb as his father quietly orchestrated the conversation. Never a talkative man, Bakewell had actually rehearsed how he would break the news to his son, going so far as to repeat his lines out loud, addressing himself in the rear view mirror. It was a technique he'd discovered years before, to overcome his fear of public speaking. As the magnitude of his news filled the paneled room, Michael had shown signs of doubt, which later turned to incredulity. Eventually he fell apart completely, under the lethal effect of his father's regimented, carefully delivered recitation.

Michael wept softly, slumped in the big chair, which for the first time Bakewell was content to see occupied, occupying the overlooked space in the corner of his favorite room. He made no effort to move, knowing any display of affection or emotion would only exacerbate the troubling reality his son was dealing with.

After long minutes of silence, punctuated by shoulder heaving sobs, Michael finally asked, "How long have you known about this Dad?"

"A couple of months."

Having no desire to take issue with his father, Michael was silent, looking at his dad through tear filled eyes, motionless, but overcome with emotion.

"I wanted to get through the holidays with you all one more time. I didn't want our last holiday together to be a big mess, filled with pain and regret." Bakewell took a sip of ancient whiskey he rarely ever drank, placed the icy tumbler on the end table. "Once, long ago, I lived through a time when I was so filled with regret I couldn't enjoy my life while I was living it. I didn't want to put the family in that situation."

He lowered the recliner under his legs and put his feet on the floor, sitting forward with his arms on his knees. "I didn't want it to be morbid. I wanted to have a great holiday together; the way it turned out it was a great holiday, at least for me."

"It was a great holiday for us all, Dad. That's the happiest I've seen us all together since the last Christmas with Mom."

Bakewell nodded, pleased with the assessment.

"Does Mrs. Walker know?"

"No, son; she doesn't need to know."

"Why?"

"Because she's not family and I'm not going to draw her in. I don't want her taking care of me. She already went through that with her husband."

"Who knows, Dad?"

"Ned, the doctor, Mr. Murphy, my accountant, and now you."

"Not Nancy?"

"Not yet."

"When are you going to tell them? Her?"

"I guess now. It's time. I might wait a little longer."

"Why?"

"I hate to bring any more pain into anybody's life. We've had enough pain in our family. You all have had more than your share the last few years, Michael."

"She needs to know, Dad."

"Are you glad you know?"

"No. I wish I didn't know, Dad. I wish it wasn't going to happen."

"I know. Another day without pain is another good day. Another day without causing pain might just be a better one."

Michael nodded; the tears began to run down his face again.

"You want something to drink?"

He shook his head and looked at his hands.

"I want you to go down and bonefish, son. Go and enjoy the time. It'll do us both good. You can't help me by being here." He got up and went into the kitchen and came back with a glass of ice water. The boy took it and sat there staring at the glass, feeling numb. "Go catch some fish and some sun. Get out of this miserable weather. It'll make you feel better. I promise I'll have Nancy call you in plenty of time. I don't want you around watching me waste away like you did with your mother. Once in a lifetime is enough. Besides," he said, sitting back down and reclining in his chair, "I'm thinking about doing some serious aerobatics again, now that there's not that much to lose. I'm thinking about learning an outside loop before I go."

"Gee, Dad, I don't know. Guys kill themselves doing an outside loop," Michael said, looking at his father again, making the eye contact he did so well. It was a learned habit now that he'd become a man. Michael nodded his head in recognition and closed his eyes. His father had a strange sense of humor, fit it in at peculiar times. They had spent a wonderfully exciting evening watching the Rams defeat Tampa Bay. A final seconds, one-armed touchdown catch had put them in the Super Bowl. Michael, like his father, had doubted the Rams would ever amount to much in St. Louis. And like his father, resented the way the NFL had held the city ransom, twice – first with the defection of the Cardinals, then making the taxpayers fund a second stadium. The city had also paid a bribe to the NFL, thinly veiled, before becoming eligible for one of their prized teams. Even the most diehard fan could see through the ruse, but they wanted a football team; it had worked out well, and to the league's consternation, the team had a miraculous season and trounced just about everyone with a record setting offense.

"You can watch the Super Bowl down there."

"No way, Pop. I'm going to be right here when we win the world championship."

"There's one other thing. I'm thinking about making a trip out to the missions. I want to go to the Solomons Islands. It's a long way, but there is a lot of history there and I would like to see some of it. Maybe combine a little history lesson with some missionary work. Your grandfather was there during the war. You've seen the scrapbook. I think I would like to see it."

"It's so far away, Dad; couldn't you find a closer place?

"It's where the history is. I really want to see it, Michael."

Passing Time

Bakewell spent hours at the range after the meeting with Albrecht, three days a week minimum, sometimes every weekday. He went in the morning when the place was deserted, not wanting to be interrupted or to show the rifle to anyone. He worked his way through the entire shipment of ammunition, reloaded another hundred and fifty cartridges, fired those and reloaded fifty more. Most of his shooting time was off-hand or leaning against one of the posts that held the large roof overhead. (He hoped he would be able to find something to lean against, a way somehow to brace himself on Bougainville when the time came). Off-hand shooting wasn't reliable with a light caliber weapon, since most of the rifle's weight was in the action and in the stock against the shoulder, not in the end of the barrel, causing it to wave about erratically, making a steady hold impossible. He finished each session firing from a sitting position, placing his down vest on the frozen ground for insulation, as he pinned his elbows inside his knees, and tried fruitlessly to dig his heels into the frozen ground to anchor himself in the tripod position. The tripod position was the least comfortable and least favored, but it was an effective way to fire accurately without a bench rest. There would be no bench rest in the islands and he spent little time firing from a bench, then only to verify the weapon was sighted properly.

Brenden had first taught him to fire a rifle. He had re-learned the techniques in the service, distinguishing himself in the process. Over the years had read many articles on body control – the way to regulate breathing, and the best and least favored ways to fire accurately without a bench rest. Some of the great shooters monitored their pulse rate and learned to fire between heartbeats. He could never master such a technique, but whenever he fired, he breathed slowly, once deeply, blew it away softly, gradually adding pressure to the trigger in order to "surprise fire" the weapon. Surprise firing was the universally accepted technique. He was a disciplined shot.

He often did calisthenics first to increase his breathing and elevate his pulse rate beforehand, just in case….His patterns grouped closely after a few days with the new rifle. It was a fast cartridge, but very light, and while it moved quickly, it was affected by wind on blustery days. Bakewell planned on a shot of 150 yards or less. There would be no wind in the jungle unless there was a storm. He knew nothing about storms in the fall of the year below the equator. If it was spring in St. Louis it would be autumn down under.

His patterns were getting very close, and he measured the targets after each session, sitting in the truck, heater blowing, cradling a metal cup of coffee while his fingers thawed. The patterns were all inside three inches. From the bench they were grouped so tightly the bullet holes touched.

He walked for hours each evening in a down jacket with a wool stocking cap pulled over his ears. It made him sleep better and took the bite out of the AM wake ups. He enjoyed many dinners with his children now; he was always welcome, even at Andy and Karen's home. Karen had developed a new appreciation for her soon-to-be-departed father-in-law, a genuine solicitous streak, and, along with the others, fed him healthy meals and self-consciously mothered him the way his lady friends had in the summers previous. In return, Bakewell spent hours doting on his three year old grandson, and made extra effort with the new baby who spent his evenings on a soft blanket on the floor of their family room, when he wasn't being held by his parents. Bakewell had discovered a new appreciation for his son-in-law, a gracious host, who never tired of his attendance, and made him feel welcome whenever he chose to stop by. On the nights he stayed home, he and Michael ate together between phone calls from Nancy and Andy, where table fare was less healthy; they reverted to steaks, chops, and heavy pasta, what they referred to as *guys' food.*

Maggie Walker re-emerged in late February, buoyant, chatty, full of curiosity: the single enigma left in his life. He didn't understand her interest, didn't really try, but he was always glad when she called. He suspected she was looking for another conquest, maybe even a mate this time. He teased her when she described her recent trips: a week long cruise she had taken with a mysterious party, in the Caribbean. She spoke enthusiastically about her cruise – several islands he'd heard about but never seen. There had been two weeks in Naples, "the real one," at a friend's hilltop villa, with a breathtaking view of the Mediterranean. She had been to Kiawah briefly, but the weather was windy; the blowing sand made walking the beach "a drudge." She had come home early.

"No Daddy Warbucks out there in the islands?"

"I don't need a Daddy Warbucks, Bakewell." She said tersely.

"Well, the search goes on." He was surprised by the harshness in his voice.

"Mm, I guess it does. So what has your life been like these past months?"

"Same old thing, monotonous." Again, there was suppressed aggression in his voice.

"Still grieving and celibate?"

"One of us has to be."

"Oh my God! Andy," she almost gasped. "I can't believe I said that. I am so sorry." Bakewell laughed. "I mean it. It was just an awful thing to say. I feel like such a shit. I am so sorry I said that."

"It was nothing," he said with a chuckle, warming to the sound of her voice.

"Forgive me. I don't know what got into me. I am sorry."

"It's okay. Don't be so humble."

"You know, I think it's catching," she said, seizing any opportunity to change the subject. "I am learning to love humility. It's actually very nice. I was hoping for more of it on my trips."

"Not to be?"

"No. You know there aren't that many nice men out there, and the ones that are, seem always to be with someone, usually someone just as nice."

"Well, it's not the university, Maggie. The action slows down."

"Tell me what you've been up to, and stop trying to insult me."

"Nothing very interesting." He had answered the kitchen phone again. It had a cord and he was tethered to the wall near the center island. He didn't have enough cord to reach the refrigerator.

"You've been hunting those little dogs to death in this cold weather, I'll bet. Is that darling little puppy all right?"

"Actually, that's been Michael's department. The season's over now, but he ran them more than I ever have. They all had a ball. He doesn't take the puppy. She's my company."

"I didn't think you needed company. You're so self-sufficient about your emotions."

"We all need company, Maggie. She and Julie are becoming fast friends."

"Tell me about that little darling." Bakewell filled Maggie in on a few grandchild stories, reluctant, but still overbearing in a grandfatherly way.

"If Michael's been doing the hunting what has Andy Bakewell senior been doing?" Maggie was persistent, determined to get some insight into his lifestyle, now that she'd been exposed to some of the finer parts.

"Well, I've been spending a lot of time with Julie; I guess she's the puppy's only competition. We take her to the park, and Julie makes conversation with the world. My children feed me when Michael's not around. I have a standing invitation most any night. It does give me a chance to play with the little people."

"How are Andy and Karen doing with the new baby?" Bakewell hemmed and hawed, typical of a grandfather not given to conversation, told her the child was too little to pick up, he didn't like to hold them at that age, would rather play with his grandson.

"I would love an invitation to go and see him," Maggie offered. Bakewell um-hummed and said it wouldn't be a problem. "I've been telling my niece about Michael. Let me know when he is ready."

"He's a man. He's ready. I'm wondering which one is going to travel all that way from Seattle to St. Louis though."

Maggie laughed dutifully, a soft, lovely sound. "It's good to talk to you again. I've been thinking about you a lot lately."

"Well, we ended up pulling the business out at the last minute. I'm no longer a charity case. Your money is safe."

She flared up instantly, "I don't want to talk about money, not now, not ever, and I want you to stop insulting me. I offered it when I thought you needed it because it was the right thing to do."

"You're right, I'm sorry I said it."

"Tell me something. If you found out I was a dreary old woman, living a dreary life in terrible financial need, wouldn't you have done the same thing?"

"Well, I'm old all right, but my life's really not that dreary…"

"You stop right now, Andy! You know what I was trying to say."

Bakewell backed off, heard the logic, more importantly, heard a pleading in her voice. He switched to tact. "You are right. You are a good friend for offering, and I'll never forget it either." He thought a little longer, added, "It's really nice to hear your voice again. Have I ever told you what a wonderful telephone personality you are?" It wasn't a bad effort.

"Now that's a little better. Actually it was very good. I was hoping we could be more than friends, but I'll take what I can get."

"Well, I'll say it again. It's nice to hear your voice, Maggie."

"You know you can hear my voice anytime you choose to call me." Bakewell was stumped once again. The thought of calling her never entered his mind, despite the fact that he thought of her often – whenever his head cleared and his mind wasn't preoccupied with firearms, travel arrangements and a crash course on the Pacific.

"By the way, when do I get my airplane ride?"

"Anytime you want to tempt fate."

"I've been talking about you around town. Several people at the club seem to know a lot about you. They tell me you are safe."

"Safe! That damned word again. *The Ned word.* Safe." Maggie laughed, Bakewell tried to keep her laughing, loving the sound of her voice. "Safe means you get lucky all the time."

"You weren't always safe; be content with the compliment." The conversation wandered: more about the world from which she had recently returned. "You know I checked my phone mail regularly, went so far as to leave a number where I could be reached."

If he had called, he would have heard the recording, with numbers and dates of where she would be in the world. She said she left the recording just to see if he would call. Bakewell stared at the ceiling, wondered how to react, what to say. She expected more. Michael sat across the kitchen, cleaning a shotgun, making amused faces under raised eyebrows, pretending to be occupied. They gradually wound down, Bakewell wasn't contributing much, and Maggie was out of ideas, but sounding like she wanted to keep him on the phone. She asked again about kids, grandkids, business, anything she could think of.

He talked, listened, milled about the kitchen, wishing he had a cordless phone. There was an old calendar hanging inside a cabinet door. He paced back and forth, indicating Michael find a different phone. Michael pretended not to notice. Bakewell took the three-year-old calendar and dropped it in the trash. It landed, partially folded with the month of February showing. On the page Katherine had highlighted Mardi Gras. Bakewell looked at the calendar again, at the dates staring from the waste can, and when Maggie finally wound down said, "Maggie, when is Ash Wednesday?"

"What?"

"Ash Wednesday. You know, Yom Kippur for Catholics."

"Andy, what *are* you talking about?"

"Have you ever been to Mardi Gras?"

"Once, in New Orleans, when I was younger, yuck."

"That's not Mardi Gras. I'm talking about Mardi Gras in Mobile?"

"No."

"It's got to be coming up." He waved for Michael to find a calendar. "How would you like to fly down to the shore and go to a Mardi Gras parade?"

There was a hesitation, just perceptible. She wanted to go, not necessarily to Mardi Gras, but go somewhere with him. *What the hell.* He took the plunge. "Come on Leary. I'll give you an airplane ride; promise not to get sick. I'll fly you down to the beach and take you to the best Mardi Gras parade in the world. You will love it. Have a go."

"Andy, I would love to go someplace with you, even in your plane, if it isn't too far, but I don't think I want to stand around in a dingy, windy, downtown part of some nasty city watching people misbehave. It's not the kind of thing I would enjoy, and it certainly doesn't sound like you."

He explained the Mardi Gras parades on the Eastern Shore of Mobile Bay, places like Spanish Fort, Daphne and Fairhope, told her they were family events where people came with their kids and grandkids and behavior wasn't a problem. He hadn't been to a Mardi Gras parade since the winter before Katherine got sick, and he suddenly wanted to go back again, wanted to see it all one more time.

"Mardi Gras down there is very tame and lots of fun. The only thing I could liken it to would be a Friday night game, like a high school football game. I think you would like it."

It didn't take much convincing; they quickly agreed to go down to the beach together, as soon as they could find the correct date and finalize arrangements. When he rang off Michael looked up.

"Dad, you're going off for a weekend with another woman? *Whoa,* what will people think?"

Bakewell watched his son closely, waiting for him to make eye contact again. "Listen son, this sort of thing – what you've just alluded to? It's frowned upon by my generation. I don't want you to get the wrong idea. And nobody's going to think anything at all because they won't know. Mrs.

Walker is a nice lady, she doesn't need any bad publicity and neither does your old man. Scandal is a terrible thing. The world's full of it, because too damned many people specialize in it. I know I can trust my son not to give scandal about a perfectly harmless event." Bakewell watched the boy as he pronounced his words. Michael, discomfited by his father's near accusation, agreed no one would hear it from him.

A History Lesson

"You know, I'm beginnin ta think Longstreet was under-appreciated. Them people done the writin after the war didn't know the guy, or what amount of contribution he done," Ned said. "They was all more concerned about Lee and Thomas Jackson. That Jackson, he got way over-told about." Ned had just finished a biography on James Longstreet. "You go down south and they got statues of Stonewall Jackson, but old General Longstreet, he don't get appreciated at all with them southern people."

Bakewell listened to Ned's take on history. They were both fans of the Civil War. Bakewell had read Shelby Foote's entire trilogy; Ned was gradually working his way through it. The books they read were always a source of conversation. Ned tended to do most of the talking when they ate lunch now, and lately, he'd been rattling on more than usual. Bakewell attributed it to a subconscious need, thought maybe Ned had a need to talk to him even more, knowing their time together was getting short.

The lunches were less frequent because of Bakewell's many visits to the gun club. The trip out and back, plus the time spent working with the rifle, took up half a day. He also spent a lot of time working out his itinerary, making plans, attempting to finalize some kind of strategy for getting to the islands before Albrecht's people intended, trying to schedule early visits, to Buka – and to Bougainville – which was the real challenge. There was no way to go by air to Bougainville. He would have to get to Buka somehow, and work out a visit by boat, if possible. It was a fascinating business, talking to people on the other side of the world. Bakewell had never crossed the equator. He knew nothing about Oceania or any part of the Pacific.

"Boy, Andy, in our heyday we was like them Blackfeet Indians, the ones that got the guns first from them trappers up in Hudson Bay."

"You mean from the Hudson Bay Company. The Hudson Bay is a long way from Montana."

There was a book in the men's room at the office on the Plains Indians. It was filled with short chapters, little vignettes that lasted about as long as a daily visit. Everybody in the office was growing in awareness of mountain men, fur trappers, and Plains Indians.

"Yeah, whatever; they got them guns and oncet they got em, they had the drop on ever-body. Kind of like us in our heyday. We never got the drop on nobody, but when we was makin all that money, I sure felt like we had it on em. It sure lifted my spirits though, when we was makin all that money." Ned took a sip and put his hands on the table, wide apart, and smiled. "Them was high times, Andy – high times with no misdemeanors."

Bakewell nodded, acquiescent, liked hearing Ned prattle on, realizing how much he would miss him. It made their lunches easier. He didn't have to answer so many questions about his health or his travel plans. His travel plans were the talk of the company. Nancy and Trudy had read the faxes that came from Port Moresby, Guadalcanal and Buka. Buka was a small island, almost contiguous with Bougainville, separated by a tiny straight called Buka Passage.

"Andy, you need to get with that woman again, the one with them soft eyes." They were on to another subject. Ned's conversation tended to bounce all over the place. "Women that got soft eyes, got soft hearts, and if they got soft hearts then they got a warm spot in em for the guys they're interested in, for the guys they got heartwarmin feelins for."

Bakewell nodded, raised his eyes, without agreeing. It was time to go.

"How're your plans gettin along fer gettin along out there with them Fathers you been writin to? Are they gonna put you up?"

"It's pretty sketchy right now, Ned. Let's not talk about it. I don't want anymore people knowing about my plans than necessary."

Bakewell had found a priest in Buka Town, and they had spoken one morning, during one of his 3AM vigils. When he realized the time out there in the islands was fifteen hours ahead of St. Louis, he took a chance and called. The priest was Belgian, a Marist, who had spent most of his life there. His English was good, but he seemed dubious about having an American visitor, doubted Bakewell's sincerity about visiting such a remote place.

Bakewell had his own doubts. During one of his conversations with a retired priest at the Provincial House in San Francisco he'd learned another priest somewhere in Bougainville had a similar visitor. The visitor was the priest's brother and the brother had been killed by the natives, whom they referred to now as indigenous people. The details were sketchy, but it had happened within the past year. Going to Bougainville would be more adventure than Bakewell had bargained for. It didn't make any difference now. He was going. It gave him another worry when the mental clock went off each morning.

The priest in Port Moresby had been contacted only by email and fax. He was a Franciscan. Bakewell hadn't yet spoken to the man, knew only that he ran the seminary there. The few times Bakewell had gotten through by phone, he had spoken to one of the seminarians.

Bakewell announced he was taking the plane to the beach on Friday afternoon and wouldn't be back until Tuesday. His daughter was happy to see him "up," but Ned mumbled as he went down the hallway, "Tryin to kill yourself in that little-piece-a-shit plane before you can die of yer own natural causes, and ruin all of our lives by yer absence from ours."

"Ned, please let him go. He needs to get away," Nancy said.

"Don't you start on me too, Nancy. It's bad enough all you girls back him. Trudy always, now you; he don't need anymore support than he's gettin already. Ever-body feelin sorry for his sorry ass, like I ain't."

A letter came, special delivery, later in the morning with instructions to ship the rifle to an address in Chicago. The letter was a surprise; the wording wasn't – it was blunt, almost offensive, vintage Albrecht. Bakewell put the weapon in the box it came in and mailed it the next day, following their instructions carefully. It was against the law to ship a firearm without a federal firearms' license. Shipping the weapon brought him back to reality. He hadn't seen Albrecht in weeks and life had almost settled into a normal routine. He considered his firing the weapon a daily exercise, a part of his routine. The gun club was also a great place to run the dogs, let them burn off energy.

Despite all that had happened in his life Bakewell never got over his love of firearms. Unlike a collector, he owned them to fire them. He hadn't shown the special rifle to anyone but his aging friend John Hammond, who looked it over carefully, pointed to the stamping and explained how the gun had been re-bored to accommodate the shoulder of the faster cartridge. John asked about the powder he was using and the weight of the bullet and the ballistic coefficient, whistling softly about the speed of the projectile. Bakewell didn't explain how it came to be in his possession.

***

He'd already made a date for dinner with Maggie Walker on Thursday evening, when Nancy asked him to look after Julie. He picked his granddaughter up in the late afternoon and he and Julie waited for Mrs. Walker in front of the house. The weather had warmed up again; the sun was just setting when Maggie arrived.

"Sorry I have another date," he said, indicating his granddaughter, "My little Juliet."

Maggie beamed, got out of the car and made a fuss over Julie, told her she was delighted she was coming with them. Bakewell put her in the back seat on the driver's side of the expensive car. Maggie carefully belted the child in. "Your grandfather can drive and we'll have a nice visit," she said.

When they started off Maggie spoke between the seats to Julie.

"Old Pop's gonna drive this crazy car?"

"Old Pop certainly is," Maggie responded. "And what's so crazy about this car?"

"It's just crazy," Julie said, pushing the button that controlled her window; the top of her head was below the glass. She was able to see only what was above the window. She patted the luxurious seat as she took in her surroundings. In one fist she held a silky fabric tightly. She liked to touch the fabric to her cheek and whenever she grew quiet she sucked her thumb.

"What have you got in your hand?" Maggie asked.

Julie looked at the wadded garment and said, "It's my softie."

"It's like an American Express card; she won't leave home without it."

Bakewell suggested they might want to go somewhere inexpensive and childproof, thinking Julie could be a problem, but Maggie wouldn't hear of it. "I've made a reservation and I love the restaurant, and they will just love having this little darling there." Julie was excited about dining out and chattered on about everything she could make out above her, which were mostly street signs and tree tops. Maggie kept her engaged in conversation during the ride, trying to win her over. She succeeded nicely.

"I'm spending the night at my Old Pop's house," Julie announced.

"Not tonight. You have nursery school tomorrow."

"Tomorrow night?"

"Maybe next Friday or Saturday, but not tonight."

"You could spend the night too," Julie said. Maggie smiled, didn't look at Bakewell, not sure how to respond. When she didn't pick up her end of the conversation, the child continued. "Sometimes, I forget my jammies, and I sleep in Old Pop's shirt. He doesn't wear jammies. He sleeps in his underwear."

Maggie looked at Bakewell, amused, said, "Yes, I can see him in his underwear."

"Can she spend the night Old Pop?"

"Well, I think I forgot to bring my jammies too." Maggie said.

"Old Pop is the boss of his house, so you can spend the night if he says so. He will give you a tee shirt, if you don't have your jammies."

Maggie looked to Bakewell again. "You're not going to help me out here, are you?"

Bakewell smiled, kept quiet.

"Do you want to spend the night with us?" Julie persisted.

"Let me think about it, darling. It sounds like a lot of fun."

"Do you wiggle? I wiggle a lot. Right, Old Pop."

"You're my little wiggler, that's for sure."

"If you kick the covers off, Old Pop will cover you back up." Julie pulled her thumb from her mouth each time she made a pronouncement then popped it back inside. "I kick the covers off all the time."

"She tends to sleep at odd angles, sometimes 90 degrees, so her feet are in your stomach."

"Does she fall out of bed?"

"Not so far. It's hard not to be aware of her when she moves around. I'm always pulling her back over to me during the night."

"Sounds charming; you're a snuggler?"

"She will make you a snuggler. She's very affectionate."

"Are you talking about me, Old Pop?"

"I am. You're my favorite subject."

Julie was pleased by her grandfather's answer. She was very excited. When they were seated in the expensive restaurant, she charmed the room with her chatty exclamations. The restaurant was elegant and Julie got lots of attention. She was very animated as she watched the other people in the dark dining room. They enjoyed a glass of wine. After fifteen minutes Julie quieted to the point where they could make conversation, and Bakewell took care to explain the flight to the beach: the feeling of being in the air in a small plane, the noise inside the cockpit, which would be minimal since they had noise attenuating headsets, the sensation of banking and changing altitudes and the sounds she could expect to hear as the wind hit the prop from different directions.

"It'll be fine," Maggie had said nervously, her eyes shining in the candlelight. She wore the simple gold earrings and necklace he'd given her at Christmas. Maggie usually had several drinks, but the challenge of his granddaughter held her attention. She said she feared she might commit some inadvertent gaff. "Parenting is not my forte," she explained, as she declined a second glass of wine.

She was obviously ill at ease. Bakewell wasn't sure if she was nervous about the flight, the challenge of the little gossip at the table with them, or about leaving town with him – any one of which might make her apprehensive. After dinner she ordered a cognac and they talked quietly. At one point Bakewell reassured her that the trip would be their secret. He wasn't going to tell anyone they would be together and suggested she shouldn't either, "We can't have a scandal, Maggie. St. Louis is a small town. I don't want to ruin your reputation."

"Andy, in this day and age I don't think people worry much about reputations." She took a sip of cognac, put the snifter back on the table and smiled. "But we'll carry it off like it's our private little affair."

"Well, I worry about your reputation. I would worry about any woman's reputation."

"In other words, I shouldn't be complimented you're worrying about mine?"

"You know that's not what I meant."

"I know. We'll be just fine. You'll be my private pilot, and it will be our secret. Besides everyone tells me you're a safe pilot, and I know you are *safe* by now."

"That safe word again."

"Well, people who are safe always get *lucky*, according to an acquaintance of mine." She had the same gleam in her eye as the night at Algonquin when she dropped the sensual line about her position in his car.

With time running short, Bakewell's focus was on the condition of his immortal soul. He had no plans to get involved with a woman, and absolutely no intention of having an affair with Maggie Walker. His main concern was being in the state of grace when he left for the Pacific. "I'm not looking to get lucky at this stage in my life Maggie."

"I *knew* you were going to say that Andy. You can rest assured; you also are *safe* with me."

Most of Julie's expensive dinner went uneaten, but she reveled in the fancy dessert Maggie had them make especially for her. The evening gradually wore down over polite conversation, and when Bakewell looked at his granddaughter, he saw her eyes had closed, and she was asleep in her chair. Maggie followed his look and said, "Oh my, I'm afraid she might fall out of her chair."

"Here, take her out to the car, and I'll pay the bill," he gave her the keys and lifted Julie up and gave her to Maggie, who was surprised at receiving her. She handled the baby like she was a live round. "It'll be all right. Just put her in the back seat, I'll be right behind you."

When he got to the car, Julie had roused as Maggie tried to snap her into her seat. She looked dazed and surprised to be with a stranger; Bakewell leaned in and reassured her they were on the way home. He and Maggie got in, and, as they were backing out Julie suddenly cried out, "Old Pop, Old Pop, I lost my softie!"

Bakewell stopped, knowing they were going nowhere without the child's silky little cloth. Maggie was instantly concerned, "Andy, wait here. It's probably under the table. She had it when we sat down." She got out of the car before he could protest and hurried back to the restaurant. They waited in the parking lot, Bakewell making small talk with his granddaughter, keeping her comforted until the "magic rag," as his son-in-law referred to it, reappeared.

When Maggie returned, she had the softie balled up in her hand, looking nonplussed. She got in the car quickly and said, "Go! Drive!"

"Was there a problem? Did you have trouble finding it?"

"Oh no! We found it right away, right where I expected it would be. Actually it had been found already. It was creating quite a stir."

Julie hadn't spoken, waiting for Maggie to give her the softie.

“So what was the problem?”

“Only this,” Maggie said, holding up the softie, spreading it out carefully for him to see. It was a pair of Nancy’s silk panties, more like a pair of bikini panties. “I’m not sure they believed me when I told them they weren’t mine.” Maggie started to laugh about the time Julie started to cry for her softie. She quickly gave the silk cloth to the child and soothed her with kind words. Julie balled the panties up in her fist and placed the soft cloth against her cheek and began to suck her thumb.

Maggie got the giggles and couldn’t stop. She thought it was hysterical and before they got to Nancy’s she was in tears.

“Just another childhood experience,” Bakewell mused.

“Well, it’s a little new to me. I’m beginning to see what I missed.”

“I should have gone back in there.”

“Oh no, I wouldn’t have missed the experience for anything. And thank you for bringing this little darling along. She made my evening.” Maggie was glowing from her brief maternal experience. When they got to Nancy’s house, she related the story with great amusement. Nancy looked mortified. “Nancy, please don’t be offended. I don’t mean to laugh at anything but the situation.”

“Sometimes, when she gets frantic for a softie, I just give her a pair of my panties. She loses them all over the house. Now she knows where to find them, and she just helps herself. I am so sorry I didn’t check to see what she had first.”

“I’m glad you didn’t. It was worth the experience. I haven’t laughed that hard in years.”

They got back to his home early, and when he suggested what she pack, she laughed, “By now I’m an accomplished light packer, Andy.”

“Well, weight will be no problem, so you can bring just about anything you want. I just want you to know it’s pretty informal down there.”

Fairhope

They landed at Gulf Shores late in the afternoon and unloaded the plane into a Crown Vic Bakewell kept at the airport. The weather was balmy as they drove west down the Beach Boulevard with the windows open. Bakewell showed Maggie around the house and put her upstairs in the lofted master bedroom and made them a drink, which they took out on the deck. It was a perfect evening and a welcome change of pace from the weather in St. Louis.

"The sun sets early this time of year, so we should get going if we're going to see the Eastern Shore in daylight," he suggested. They drove up to Fairhope for the parade, taking Alternate 98 to come into town from the south and miss the traffic that poured in from the east and north and reached the Eastern Shore at sunset, passing many beautiful homes on Mobile Bay. Between the houses they could see across the water, where the setting sun turned the horizon to gold then pink then gradually darkened in a quietly beautiful transition from day to night. It was one of the most memorable sunsets of Bakewell's life. When they got to Fairhope, they found a place to park above the pier, only a few blocks from town, and walked the rest of the way up Fairhope Avenue, under ancient oaks, dripping with moss, through a charming neighborhood Katherine had fallen in love with years before.

The temperature was perfect, warmer than any he'd experienced for Mardi Gras. Some years it was a blustery cold. One year it rained so much they had to cancel the parade. Temperatures in the 40's were the norm. It was closer to sixty, and as the wind gradually died it got warmer still. Maggie was captivated by the enchanting little town as they walked the streets under trees peppered with tiny white lights, passing shops filled with merchandise only a woman could appreciate. They found a strategic vantage point in front of the bookstore and Bakewell went in and bought a large Latte, which they shared, standing at the restraining cable on Section Street. As they drank the sweet coffee a crowd formed quickly and Maggie commented on the fortunate timing, adding, "You've done this before?" Bakewell nodded and she said, "Many times before?"

"Yes, many times before. This is what you might call a 'rite of winter.'"

"How many times before?" she wanted to know.

"Katherine loved Fairhope, and she loved this parade. At least the last ten years of my marriage we came here. Katherine had great taste in all things fun, but I've missed the last two years."

"Should I feel flattered you're sharing this with me?"

"Don't need to feel anything, please." He stopped a passing vendor and bought a lighted necklace for her. "I just hope you like it."

"It's certainly not like New Orleans. I've never seen such an eclectic mixture of people."

"Normal people," he corrected. No one ever misbehaved in Fairhope. The place had the atmosphere of a state fair. They were surrounded by grade-schoolers, teenyboppers, young couples, middle aged families, tattooed bikers, gray haired "snowbirds" wintering at the beach, and locals, dressed in elegant gowns and tuxedos in preparation for the Ball, following the parade. "This is a family parade. The greatest Mardi Gras parade in the world."

There was a young couple next to them with an infant in a large stroller loaded with gadgets and netting for storage. It was filled with everything they might need for an emergency.

"I had the feeling we were here because of Katherine," Maggie looked up and leaned back into him as she spoke.

"We're here because I thought you would like it," he said, putting his arm around her. "I wanted to include you in all of this." He pointed around them at the little town, electric with excitement. "Let you see it. I felt like I owed you."

"You don't owe me anything."

"Well, I wanted to enjoy it one more time. Enjoy it for me, with me."

"They must be here for good reason." She leaned back against him, letting him support her. Almost on cue, the parade music began at the end of the street. He explained what was about to happen. When the first float came into view, the crowd ahead of them started screaming. He shouted to her. "JUST REMEMBER TO KEEP YOUR HANDS UP HIGH!"

When the floats passed, the crowd around them began screaming and the "throws" rained down. He caught several beads, and put them over her head. After several floats had passed, Bakewell began to watch Maggie as she got caught up in the excitement. Her face glowed as she learned to yell and grab for the junk that filled the air. When the last float passed, the crowd flowed off to the east en masse.

"Where are they going?"

"Over to Fairhope Avenue to do it over again."

"They do it again?"

"They make a square. Three right turns and back down the street we came up." She looked up at him, eyes full of excitement, just as Katherine's had always been. "Do you want to do it again?"

"Yes," she said, fingering her beads.

He took her arm, and they walked to the intersection, struggling to get through the crowd. They stopped near the Old Bay Steamer. "Here. Let's stay back on the sidewalk under this balcony. They throw to the people up there on the balcony and a lot miss and land down here."

The floats came around a second time. There was just as much noise and crowd commotion as before. He was right about the "throws." They caught as many from their new vantage as before, including a stuffed animal

Maggie caught herself. She was jubilant. When the last marching band passed, the final float followed, then a fire engine, lights flashing, signaling the end.

"That was so much fun!" Maggie said.

He took the stuffed animal she showed him. "Wow, big time. Not many people catch such a prize."

"You're making fun."

"No, this is a genuine dollar throw. Most of the stuff costs pennies. You hit the big time."

She held onto the stuffed animal, and he took two of her beads and gave her several of his.

"Green, purple and gold; you have the official colors and three of each. You're legal; you're all set."

The parade had one more street to go. He took her to a little English pub around the corner on Church Street, got there right before the place filled up. Most of the tables were reserved, but they found one in an alcove, next to an old fashioned British phone booth. It was a tiny spot, not more than four feet square. When the owner came over, Bakewell asked if they could eat there.

"You know you can," she said, recognizing Bakewell. She gave him a curious look, said, "Gosh I haven't seen ya'all in a long time." She looked a Maggie, showing confusion, and back at Bakewell.

"My wife died two years ago, Lisa." This is my friend Maggie Walker."

"Oh my dear man," she said sadly. "I remember her so. She was just precious." She looked at Maggie when she spoke, asking if Maggie knew her.

"No, but I'm beginning to I wish I had," Maggie said.

Lisa put her hand on Bakewell's arm. "Oh you sweet, lovely man, I'm just so, so sorry." She squeezed his arm several times and Bakewell thanked her, appreciating her sincerity.

"You're really busy tonight", he said, indicating the commotion at the magnificent little bar. "Bring us a scotch and water and a Boddingtons when you can."

"Wow. She remembered you both."

"We started coming here the year Jim and Lisa opened; he's from England, she's from Mississippi. They met during the Gulf War. Don't be angry now," he said, holding up his hands to ward off her inquisitive look. "I love this little pub. I love this town. Hell, I love this part of the world, and I'm not reliving anything, Maggie. *You're not here in any surrogate capacity!*" He made a helpless gesture. "It's nothing morbid. I promise. I would have come without you, and I certainly would have come to this little place no matter who came along."

"I'm not about to be angry. It's a darling place, and I'm having a wonderful time. It's been perfect. So far," she added.

The drinks came and the place filled after the parade ended. It was bedlam. Service was impossible; the food came slowly. They couldn't flag their waitress so they gave up on a second drink and left more than enough money on the little table. Slipping out the side door, they walked back up to the intersection. As they turned to walk back down Fairhope Avenue they slowed, almost involuntarily, awed by the clear starlit night. The darkness over the Bay allowed the star-filled sky to explode above them. Without any wind, it was more like summer than late winter. The town was peaceful. The traffic had cleared. The only people left were the city workers, reeling in the restraining cable and putting the flowers back in the planter boxes.

Point Clear

They drove down Alternate 98 the same way they'd come up, Bakewell calling out familiar sights. When they passed the marina at Point Clear, Maggie commented on how beautiful it was. The pier lights were lit. He told her about the Point's storied past and turned into the main entrance at the Grand Hotel and stopped the car. "Look, it's still early. Would you like to have another drink?"

"More than anything," she said. "I'm having the most wonderful evening."

He parked far from the lobby, so they could enjoy walking the grounds. He took his jacket along for her. They walked slowly under huge live oaks loaded with moss. The warm weather had put the ornamentals in full white bloom. The camellias, nearly always in bloom, large enough to be trees, were carefully manicured, withered flowers trimmed and removed. He took her arm as they entered the Grand Hotel and led her past the central Hearth Room to the wonderful old cocktail lounge. Maggie ordered another scotch and he asked for a glass of Port. The waiter, a young man named Wesley, remembered Bakewell, and offered him a short selection.

"Are you that particular about port?" Maggie asked, amused.

"Not really. Just want to see if I can tell the difference between the better ones."

They sat by a large window and enjoyed a talented musician in a top hat who played piano, guitar and trumpet. He kept the music soft and low, with the occasional digression, paying homage to Jimmy Buffet. It wasn't crowded, and the plush carpet and low ceiling made it cozy and very quiet. Maggie asked him to dance and Bakewell apologized for not asking first as he took her hand. They danced to several numbers slowly on the little parquet floor. There were only two other couples. It was strange and very pleasant to hold Maggie again on a dance floor. The last time he'd danced with her she wasn't old enough to vote.

When they returned to their table, comfortable in the moment and on the deeply cushioned chairs, he looked out at the dark bay and tapped on the window, "Damn the torpedoes!" She looked at him curiously. "Right out there," he said. "That's where Farragut made his famous 'full speed ahead' speech."

"In Mobile Bay?"

"Just off Ft. Morgan. I will take you there tomorrow. We'll take the ferry over to Dauphin Island and go up to Bellingrath Gardens. As warm as it is, there'll be a quarter of a million azaleas in bloom."

They were quiet for a while, listening to the music, relaxing after all the Mardi Gras commotion. It was very pleasant. He asked her about Joe, feeling the trip had been too orchestrated, wanting to hear more about her life.

She talked for sometime, telling him things he had never heard, including a story about a deal gone bad Joe had been involved in right after Clinton came to office. Joe's business in Little Rock was common knowledge, but Bakewell was surprised by her story of intrigue, filled with people he had seen in the news, people Maggie referred to with bitterness. "He always wanted to be more successful, always, more and more. It got out of hand. The politicians were nearly an obsession toward the end." The conversation seemed to depress her, talking about her failed marriage and the disappointment of politics.

Changing moods, Maggie asked if they could go outside; smiling beautifully in the candlelight, she said she wasn't prepared, "To let go of the evening." He ordered another drink, asked Wesley if they could take them outside.

"For you its okay, Mr. Bakewell," Wesley said. "Just drop your glasses back here before you leave please."

Maggie insisted on paying, and left Wesley an excellent tip. She paid for everything in cash.

"Thank you for a lovely evening," she said, taking his arm as they stepped outside. They followed the uneven brick walkway to the water's edge and stopped by a low latticework, next to the putting green, under a sky filling with more stars every hour. They stared across the Bay at the lights of Mobile.

"You seem to have a lot of regrets, Maggie, I'm sorry it didn't work out with Joe."

"I have a bunch," she sighed." Oh, I don't mean about his death anymore. I just wish we hadn't divorced. He got sick almost as soon as it was official, and when he got really bad I ended up taking care of him anyway. He didn't have anybody else; his parents were too old. We needed to be divorced, but who knew he was going to die? *God*," she shuddered, "It all looked so sordid. If I had held on another year, it would have been over. I hated Little Rock. I had no friends there. Without kids I felt useless."

He put his arms around her and she gladly accepted his warmth, leaning back against him. It was meant more to comfort her than out of any physical affection, although he once had great affection for her. A new kind of affection had developed between them the last few months. He thought it was based on simple gratitude for friendship offered, and a mutual sympathy they found in each other. They stood there for a long time, sipping their drinks, watching the sky, listening to the water lap against the sea wall.

"What's ahead, Maggie?"

"What do you mean?"

"I don't know exactly. You know, what's ahead for you?"

"I don't know either. I have a wonderfully comfortable life now. I have plenty of money. I enjoy my friends. I go anywhere I want, do whatever I want. I love to travel." She put her hand over his forearm and held it and they rocked slowly in a silent dance, unconsciously swaying to the lapping sound of the water.

"You always had money," he teased, talking out toward the water, careful not to whisper in her ear. He was shy about touching her. It seemed strange and was always a forced effort when he put his arm around her. "Anytime anybody ever mentioned money, Maggie Leary's cute little face always appeared in my mind's eye."

She turned and pushed him away. "Whenever somebody said, *jerk*, Andy Bakewell's always appeared in mine." He was embarrassed and didn't respond. Maggie turned and backed into his warm embrace once more.

"Do you think you'll ever get married again?"

"I don't know. A girl doesn't usually get to ask. I'm old fashioned about that sort of thing." She looked up over her shoulder to him, added, "I don't see myself acting like all these little harlots on TV. I might change though." She tossed off the last of her drink. "You never know. I just might reach out one day and say, 'Hey big spender.'"

She knew all the words to the pop songs of their generation. He also noted, she had said, big spender. He still thought of himself as totally broke.

"Is there a big spender out there you've got your eye on?"

"Mm. There's someone I've got my eye on, how about you?" She turned to face him again, pushed at his chest with one finger seductively.

"I don't know," he said soberly. "Kids are all gone. Nancy's always encouraging me. I doubt if the boys would really care one way or another. They don't want much from me. I see them often enough. I love my grand babies as you've observed."

"You have great children and you had a wonderful marriage, Andy, and your grandchildren are perfect, of course."

"Of course."

"You did have a wonderful marriage. You've had a wonderful life. Really. You're a regular *George Bailey*." She turned and walked toward the railing, came back and stood in front of him very closely. "Who would have *thunk it*! Andersen Bakewell, the original Peck's bad boy," she stood on the tips of her toes and leaned into him, "High school dropout, for Pete's sake, then the navy, college, husband, father, citizen of the year, even." She raised one hand for emphasis. "The perfect catch! We all thought you were going to jail."

"You make me sound like the perfect schmuck."

"You are the perfect schmuck," she poked him again, "Every girl's dream."

"Guys want to be tough, macho. Our egos need that," he teased. "Nobody wants to be Mr. Schmuck."

"Is *cojones* the right word? Yeah. You have to have some *cojones* to be Mister Right in this world. You know that Andy Bakewell. Don't make yourself sound weak. I was married too, remember. It ain't easy, is it?" She was miming Ned. "A real marriage takes a lot of hard work. It takes a real man to love a woman faithfully, and it takes some humility too. You've developed this marvelous humility. It's so appealing in men now, especially at my age, especially after we grow up and get tired of the arrogant pricks."

"Whoa," he said, surprised. "That's a pretty strong word from such a proper lady." He was about to tease her more, reconsidered. Thinking about the past again, he said, "I was a prick," looking back out at the water again. "I was so conceited…so egotistical. It discourages me so. I think God hates arrogance most of all, and God knows, *I was arrogant.* I want to drop my head when I remember arrogance. It was like my shadow, my constant companion."

Maggie leaned back and looked up at him very amused. "And it's not just your humility; you've developed this *marvelous vulnerability. It's so damned appealing.*" She gestured as she spoke, holding her arms up.

They walked back inside, dropped the glasses at their table. Bakewell got his jacket. He hadn't taken valet service, but took a moment to talk with the guys there under the overhang. Bakewell had learned late in his life to talk to anyone who would make conversation with him. He spoke to maids and doormen, gardeners and attendants, desk clerks, waiters, anybody. Maggie refused his jacket, so he put it on and they walked slowly back to the car. She took his hand and swung it in an exaggerated, self-conscious way.

"So who have you got your eye on? Anybody I know, or is it one of your *big spender* friends from Little Rock." He was talking up to the live oaks above them, enjoyed teasing her, now that she'd lost some of her formidability.

Maggie stopped, turning abruptly, tilted her head up in the lamplight, formidability returning. "Are you really that obtuse, Bakewell, or is this just your stupid Gomer Pyle act?"

Caught off guard again, instantly embarrassed, the formidability confronting him one more time, her tone and her look putting him off, he tried to hide his embarrassment. She stared intently. Finally he said, "Okay, what act?"

"Are you that simple or don't you really know?" Her eyes glistened in the lamplight, and her face started to cloud. She recovered quickly.

Oh my God. I'm dying and she thinks I'm the one! It was suddenly too obvious. He realized the impossibility of their relationship, the mistake he'd made now, bringing her down to the beach. It had been a stupid impulse. He wanted to show off, try to impress her. He decided to act definitively, harshly. He looked into her eyes, but, taking in the hurt he saw there, he avoided her eyes and put his hands on her shoulders and shook her. "You can't be interested in me Maggie. I'm old, almost broke. Hell, I am broke. I'm an old, broken down failure of a guy with nothing to offer." He kept shaking her.

"Andy, really, get a life!"

"No, not me Maggie, please. I'm not a good person. Not the right one for you. Not now."

"Give me a break. You're a wonderful man. My God, you have a picture of the Sacred Heart in your car. There's a hand made cross, probably from Palm Sunday if I know you, on the dash of your airplane. You've got a prayer book in your bedroom here at your beach house.

"What were you doing in my bedroom?"

"Peeking, what do you think? Stop shaking me; you're making me dizzy. What do you mean you're not a good person?" Bakewell let go of her arms. She straightened his collar again and patted his chest reassuringly. "You have the love of family and friends. You've collected a ton of friends."

"I think they're mostly Katherine's friends."

"Don't be ridiculous! Your friends are all crazy about you. Anyone can see it. I see it and *I haven't known you for years*."

"Loving my family doesn't make me a good person, Maggie."

"*Don't you do this, you jerk*! Don't make me say you're a good person again"

"I thought you were feeling sorry for me." He took hold of her shoulders again tightly. "I thought we were feeling sorry for each other." He shook her, gently this time. "I brought you down here to show some gratitude, hoping you would love the beach, the parade, the town, thought I would treat you to some good food and sneak you home without a scandal."

"I've had just enough to drink," she said. "Now I'm getting pissed off." She pulled away and turned and walked around the car, "Unlock my door and get in the car!" When he got inside she was kneeling on the front seat. She pulled him over to the middle and came over him. "Listen, Catholic boy, you need me right now. And I need you. Let's do this for each other. I don't know about you, but…yes…yes, I do know about you, and you haven't had this in a long time." She had hold of his jacket, and she was jerking it for emphasis. "Have you looked lately? Men still want me as much as you did once. Wake up. You need this as much as I need it."

Bakewell was stunned. She was taking control again, like she had when they were young. He was unhinged, distracted by the smell of her, the proximity of her body above him, her thighs resting on his. He'd lost composure, was losing control of the orchestrated weekend he'd planned. He never intended to make a pass, had been treading lightly, treating her with deference, and despite the teasing, with respect – not to mention fear. Sometimes when he took her hand or they brushed close, he let his mind wander, but always came back to reality, laughing at himself in the process. He was cautious around her. He couldn't help it. She was more successful. Her life was in order. She was wealthy; he feared she might find him pitiful, suspected she already had, and hated it. When she grabbed hold of his coat and leaned in close, the smell of her warm breath, scented with scotch, and her hair and her perfume, the whole package was overwhelming, just like it had been years before. He felt like he was about to go into a spin, filled with a crazy apprehension, like something wild was about to happen. He was frightened and excited, alarmed and exhilarated. Maggie came onto him, ruthlessly.

"What if we crash on the way back?" he asked feebly, his head reeling.

"What are you talking about?"

"If we were to die afterwards…what then?"

"What! You think this would be a sin?" She pulled at his jacket harder. "Oh God! I'm such a fool. You make me feel like a harlot. Are you for real?" Her voice broke.

He put his hands to the sides of her chest, palms pressing against her ribs, thumbs just touching her breasts, feeling a passion from long ago. He knew what he wanted to do, suddenly wanted to do it very much, just as he had years ago, the way he wanted to do it that first night in front of her house when she was just nineteen.

She raised up, suddenly horrified. "Am I asking you to do something you can't?"

Bakewell laid his head back on the seat, looking up into her eyes; his own filling with amusement. Her question made him laugh, breaking the tension. "I may be over the hill, arthritic, losing memory and everything else. But when it comes to hormones, I'm blessed – no…hell...I'm cursed with hormones."

"Well it was a sin when we were kids, you idiot, and you didn't have a problem then. You took my virginity, Bakewell!" She hissed the words into his ear and shook him again. "So what's the problem now?"

There was a confused moment as they realized they had come full circle, were about to start over, momentous, filled with consequences. It made his stomach flutter. It had been years since that last evening in Columbia when they had bid farewell with sex so angry, so physical, almost vulgar, before she went off to Little Rock with Joe Walker. Here they were again, but now the emotion was back, just as it had been the very first night, when he felt like he was falling and didn't know why. The sensation of falling was back, only this time he knew he wouldn't be the one to hit bottom. He was afraid for her.

She bent down and they kissed, lips barely touching, barely parting. Then they kissed again, with just the slightest added contact. His hands moved softly around to her front, and she kissed him again, once more with real passion, then again and again, encouraging him. She kissed his ear, "Andy, let's sin again, together, and hope God will forgive two lonely people." There was a terrible urgency in her voice. It came from deep down inside, from her soul and it was filled with pathos. As his passion rose, she responded with more, always just a little ahead of him. The last time he had touched her she was just a girl, eight years younger than Nancy was now. Suddenly he wanted very much to touch her, and know her and remember her. She looked up as he kissed her throat and checked the windows. There was only one lamplight near the car.

"I can't take my blouse off," she whispered in his ear. "If someone comes by we'll get arrested." She started to giggle and managed to get out of her pants and helped him out of his and when she was above him again he reached inside her silky underwear and touched her very delicately. The feeling was exquisite for both of them, and she gasped in his ear. They made love in the front seat of the big car. It was an urgent lovemaking, intense and unrestrained, like something they had both been craving for years. When they were finished neither spoke for a long time. Bakewell continued to touch her tenderly.

Their clothes, the ones they were still wearing, were disheveled, others scattered about. When they finally straightened up and sorted them out, he got out of the car so he could tuck his shirt and put things away. She held the jacket to the overhead light when the door was opened. He came around the car, and when he got back inside she was nearly dressed. She put his jacket over her backwards and folded her arms tightly under it. He looked at her, and he looked through the windshield at the moss hanging down from the ancient live oak.

"Well," she said, her voice barely audible, "I knew what I was looking for, and I had some high hopes, but didn't know what to expect."

Bakewell didn't answer for a long time, looking straight ahead at the dripping moss; finally he said, "Wow," very quietly.

"Wow," she repeated, also quietly, repeated it again, giggled. "Wow. *That was really...wow."*

He leaned over and kissed her delicately but when he attempted to put his arm around her she said, "Don't move me," in a sharp tone.

He was confused, hurt by the sound of her voice.

"I'm full of semen," she said, "Your semen. Let's go."

Bakewell started the car and backed slowly out of the space, making a mental note of the tree's location. He would never forget the ancient oak there near the entrance to Point Clear. They went down 98 to Foley, taking the residential roads west and south of town, missing the traffic.

"Well, at least we don't have to worry about getting you pregnant." He said finally, sounding self-satisfied.

"How do you know?" she said in the same sharp tone. When she saw the worried look on his face, she laughed at him. After another mile they turned east and she sighed, a long exasperated sigh, leaning back against the seat, looking up at the ceiling. "Oh, dear God, I'm full of semen. Where was your semen when I needed it, Bakewell?"

Crossing the inland waterway, he asked if she needed anything. Sighing contentedly, Maggie said, "I can't think of anything." He stopped at Delchamps, said he needed to buy some bottled water. Katherine complained about the taste of the water at the beach. They always bought bottled water. He couldn't tell the difference. "Hurry," was all Maggie said.

When they got back to the beach house, she took the key and ran up the steps while he gathered up beads and coats. Later, after she changed, they went out on the deck and talked about the past again, avoiding the future. He found a bottle of Drambuie and poured a little into one glass and they sipped it out on the deck, listening to the sound track from *Out Of Africa.*

"Would you like to sleep upstairs? There's a skylight and it seems quite romantic."

"I remember," he said.

Maggie took his hand and they went upstairs. They took their time, very slowly and gently, without the terrible of urgency of before, in the big pedestal bed on the balcony, and Bakewell was careful and patient and made sure she had a full orgasm, before he took her in a final gasping act of emotion and lust that he never thought he would be capable of again in what remained of his lifetime.

***

They talked afterwards, until Maggie fell asleep beside him, breathing deeply from the alcohol. He laid in the dark, under a single sheet, gazed at the stars through the lofted window, and tried to pray, but it didn't work. He felt cut off now, knew he was no longer in the state of grace. It had been a long time since he had been cut off from grace. He thought for a long time before he fell asleep.

He woke about three and got out of bed quietly – Maggie curled around a pillow, her hair back, eyeliner mussed slightly, face just visible in the starlight. He went downstairs, out onto the deck and looked at the stars.

The sky below the continent was awesome as always on a clear night. He thought of his night up on the mountain in Montana, the contrast in the two places, something he did often. He loved to compare the distances and the variety of America, never got over the satisfaction of seeing as much of it as he could each year. He wondered if Katherine was watching. He was feeling guilty for the obvious reason and for other reasons he really didn't understand. He wanted to think it was a simple biological need, but it was more than that, unfathomable really. He wasn't sure if he resented the biological urge or considered it a gift. He'd been caught up in the moment, the need, the whole act. But it was more than just biological. Why had he wanted her a second time if it was simply testosterone? No, it was the woman upstairs in his bed.

He had enjoyed it fully, had lost himself and his self control because it was her. If it had been one of his lady friends, he would be overwhelmed with anger at his weakness. There were so many conflicting emotions: guilt, satisfaction, fear, an awakened need, shame for his weakness, but the strangest and strongest emotion was one of mystical confusion.

Maggie stepped out on the deck and came up quietly behind, putting her arms around his chest. “Everything okay?”

He nodded and looked out at the drill rigs in the gulf.

“Are we filled with guilt now?”

“No.”

“Andy, come to bed please. It’s lovely out here, but I’m cold and I want to be warm.”

They walked back inside, arms around each other, and went back up to bed.

Beach House

They slept late. The sun was far above the horizon, streaming through the beachfront windows when they came down to the small kitchen. Maggie made coffee and Bakewell made toast. They took it out to the deck and listened to the surf and watched the beach walkers moving along the water's edge.

"Are we having an attack of guilt after last night?" she asked quietly, staring out at the gulf.

"No, last night was spectacular." He told the truth about last night, added, "I didn't think I'd ever experience anything like last night again." The remark was heavy with emotion, too much emotion. He tried something lighter. "I can't believe how lucky I got. I thought that kind of stuff only happened to guys like Ned."

Maggie smiled but didn't speak. She walked to the railing and there was a long silence as they watched an old couple stop to investigate the detritus on the beach. He sat down in a deck chair and drank his coffee. Neither of them touched the plate of toast. She stood near the railing, sipping her coffee, holding the mug with both hands. She was wearing a pair of shorts, a baggy cotton sweater and a pair of fashionable basket weave strollers. He wondered at the color of her strollers. Mahogany he decided. She still had fine shapely calves, and he stared, thinking back to a time when she was younger than his daughter. Finally he said, "I'm sorry I took your virginity, Maggie."

"Oh, do shut up," she said disgustedly. She shivered slightly, "Just shut up, Andy. You're being an ass."

"Nancy was nineteen once. Raising her, I always worried she would succumb to some pompous jerk, full of himself, like I was back then."

"I take your point, but if you go wimpy on me now I'm going to get *really disgusted.* I might even leave."

"Please don't, I would feel terrible if you left." It was sincere. When she didn't respond he said, "Man, what would the fare be to St. Louis?" She ignored him.

They watched the water and listened to the pounding of the surf, sensing a change in the mood. They had been happy but distant before, both careful to respect the other, like strangers who had met and learned to like each other, but remain detached. They were different, seemed less friendly. There was tension between them now. He figured it was inevitable, had to be. He wanted to take the edge off.

"You've changed, Maggie. You aren't as tough as you used to be."

"Is that supposed to be a compliment, Andy?" she didn't wait for an answer. "I was never tough. It was an act."

"Well you seem different now. I think you have changed."

"I hope so. I was nineteen years old the last time we were intimate." Staring straight out at the Gulf, Maggie put her cup on the railing, took a breath, spoke slowly and softly toward the water. He could just make out her words. "You asked me last night what was ahead. I think we could be ahead. I've always been…a little bit in love…no, I think I've secretly loved you most of my life. There I've said it. Go ahead and gloat."

"How could I do that? You're so candid, so undisguised, I'd have to be the world's biggest jerk."

"You were always jerky." It was a favored attribution. Anytime she denounced him it was with *jerky,* unless she resorted to another favored attribution; she often called him a *perfect shit.*

"It's hard not to be overwhelmed by you right now."

"It would be easy to start again, to fall in love all over again, Andy."

He wasn't ready for the conversation, even though he sensed it coming. He wanted to lighten the moment, wanted to attempt humor, change the mood, thought about it. It wouldn't work, wasn't the time for humor. She was defenseless. He opted for silence, hoped the tension might pass even though he knew it wouldn't. His silence was exasperating.

"You are such a shit!" she said, turning about. "I don't know why I have pursued you like this." She took him in with a penetrating gaze. There was fury in her eyes. She may have mellowed, but she was formidable again, the old Maggie. "Have you taken a look at me?" He smiled at her, raised his eyes, wrinkling his brow. She misread the look.

"Don't you laugh at me, you…jerk!" she said, getting worked up. He pretended to be calm, but he was afraid of her, softer or not.

She looked back out to the beach, turned and confronted him. "I'm going to be even more direct, Andy. It was fun pursuing you. It was fun trying to court you for a time, an awfully long time, I might add. But I think I have succeeded now. I hope so anyway. I want you to pursue me. It's your turn. I need to be courted by the man I'm involved with. I need to be courted by *you*!" She stamped her foot for emphasis.

Bakewell went and got another cup of coffee and poured her one. When he came back out to the deck he took his seat in the corner. "What did you see in me back then?" he said, leaning back in the plastic chair.

"You know what I saw, Andy," she sighed "You were a bad boy, older. What most girls my age were looking for, only you were too stupid to know it. The boys I was dating were barely out of high school. You had been around the world, literally."

"Your mother hated me. The look on her face I recognized on my own twenty years later when Nancy started bringing them home."

Maggie finally smiled, satisfied, acknowledging his predicament. "I promised my mom I wouldn't get involved. I told her you were a passing fancy, I think. I told her you were just temporary. It was true. I knew I would never marry you." She paused and he didn't interrupt. "Who would have thought Joe would turn into a contemptible shit and you a darling, wonderful man."

"I'm hardly a wonderful man, but I always thought Joe was a shit. I didn't like him the first time I met him...if I ever met him." Bakewell couldn't remember being introduced to Joe Walker.

"He was very smart, and he had a wonderful confidence. I allowed myself to believe it was more than it was."

"He *was confident*, I'll give him that, so full of himself too. I hated to see you worshiping him."

"He was what I wanted. Anyway you had already had your share of me. You had no complaint coming."

Bakewell remembered it all: the sex, the pain, the rejection, and the loathing he lived with now. There were few girls he'd taken advantage of in his callous youth. Maggie hadn't been one of them. She had walked in with both eyes open. He had little guilt about her then or now. But he still remembered one other; the one who's name he couldn't remember. He held up his hand, cowering. "Don't please. I hate that part of me. Really. Don't do this."

She was beginning to buy into his remorse, finding it amusing, nearly laughed at his predicament, but changed her mood in a rush of emotion and looked away. "We were fine for a long time. Once he started to make money, he gave me everything I asked for. When he found out he couldn't have kids, he was filled with guilt. He gave me more of everything. After a while I didn't mind anymore. By then my girlfriends in St. Louis were getting fat, covered with puke from babies with tummy aches, and I had everything."

She stopped. When there was no more, Bakewell went and got them another cup of coffee neither wanted. Maggie took hers back to her corner of the deck. She was as far away from him as she could get when she resumed.

"He was okay for a long time, always attentive, affectionate. The sex was okay, in the beginning. Like everyone else we gradually learned how. When the babies weren't forthcoming, it was like he stopped trying. He had his needs of course, needed the sex well enough, but he started to ridicule himself, said he was firing blanks. I hated when he said that. The sex gradually tapered off as he got busier. He might have found someone else. I don't know. I didn't care, really. He thought he was wasting his time with me. Joe was into time management in a big way. He was always on the phone." She set the cup on the railing and put her hands beside it and leaned back.

"My memory of Joe will always be of him carrying the phone around, with a long extension cord. When he was excited he would get to the end and pull it out of the wall, cut himself off in mid sentence. I think we owned the first cordless phone in Little Rock. Joe used the phone like a carpenter used a hammer. Joe used the phone *like a hammer*." She tossed her head to the side, as if she still had her wonderful long hair. She still had the delicate bangs that brushed her high forehead. "He was always making a deal or conniving with someone over the phone, trying to make a deal, always talking about leverage, getting the leverage. Joe loved leverage. He said leverage was everything. When he had it, he used it ruthlessly. The only time I remember him being really upset was when he didn't have the leverage he needed to make something happen. Then he would smolder."

"I remember seeing him with his loud mouthed law school buddies." Bakewell interrupted. "They were so repulsively tight – same guys all the time, best table at the Heidelburg, descending en masse, practically running the Hofbrau House, schooled up like mullet at football games, always loud, always obnoxious."

"They all drank a lot."

"Who didn't?"

"When they were sober most of them were full of charm. They fawned all over me. I loved it."

"How did he get to Little Rock? I figured he was headed for the state capitol."

"One of his classmates, one of the nicest ones actually, his father had a practice in Little Rock. He begged Joe to come down and take a look. It was a textbook place, and they offered him the whole package. They were established. The place was old, storied with history, full of tradition." She'd been pulling on the arms of her sweater, stretching them out of shape. She pulled the sleeves down over her hands and put them back on the railing. "Everything was expensive. Joe's office was this amazing little paneled space, every young lawyer's dream. Later, they caught on with the Clintons, right at the beginning. They were always in the know with the Clintons.

"He took the job and you moved to Little Rock? Did he ask you if you wanted to go?"

"He promised me success. He said it was his big chance. What was I going to do? Anyway I needed to get away from my mother."

"So you moved to Little Rock to live the fairy tale?"

"You're being sarcastic. You already know I never found happiness there. Once he got in with the political types, I began to hate it. Things moved too fast."

"And you were hanging with the Clintons? Did you know them?"

"In the beginning; in his first few years as governor, we were invited to a lot of their functions. It was always crowded. I never got to know them well."

"He never made sexual advances?"

"He always remembered my name," she said, ignoring him. "He was actually quite charming. He always made time for me. He was very good at it, the schmoozing." She turned to look at him for emphasis, looked back at the water. "It wasn't them. It was their crowd. They were all so obsessed with succeeding, so consumed. I learned to hate the functions. Everybody was talking, trying to impress. Nobody was listening. They had no values, just objectives."

She was very upset. Bakewell was tempted to go over to her.

"Everybody had a career; men with wives, but looking for mates; women without values. I guess I looked just like them: men hitting on me, women hating me. The women who had children never seemed to want to talk to me about their kids. I would have liked that, even though I had none to talk about."

They were silent, Maggie walked back to the sliding door, fidgety, nervous, seeming embarrassed. He got up and put his arms around her and pulled her to him. She was still for a long time, not moving, finally let go, started to breathe again. She let herself fall back and accepted his arms around her, over her own. She leaned her head back against his shoulder.

"I've been selfish with you, Maggie. You've made all the effort. I didn't know how to react. I *didn't know you were after me,"* he teased, buffing her cheek for emphasis. "I didn't quite know what to do."

"You did pretty good," she said.

"Pretty well," he corrected.

"NO! You were *good* at it, not *well* at it. You were very tender and gentle, just the way I remembered you."

"I really wasn't expecting this. I want you to know that." He hugged her tightly and kissed her cheek.

"I meant what I said, Andy. It would be easy to get started all over again."

"I get this feeling we have started," he sighed, almost reluctantly, "Especially after last night." He turned her around to face him, held her away and looked into her eyes, "But I want you to believe I didn't expect this to happen. I just didn't think it out. It wasn't why I asked you to come down here."

She nodded, amused, but uncertain. She had lost her aplomb. He had never seen her like she was now. He wished he had more time. It *would* be easy to start over again. He was trying to let the thought in for the first time, trying to believe it. He never dreamed he would be involved with her again, had thought fatuously about her figure a few times, enjoyed her attention, but never let his thoughts go any farther. It was important that she understood he hadn't asked her along for sex. "I just didn't think it out. This isn't why I asked you to come down here."

"I know. If I thought you'd asked me to come for a nice little tryst – you know, for old times sake – I probably wouldn't have come." She added, "Probably," reached up and tried to button one of the never buttoned, buttoned down collars on his shirt. "But when I saw how vulnerable you've become, you were suddenly…irresistible." She took hold of his chin between her thumb and finger and tried to shake it roughly. "You really are a darling man, you know. Katherine did a great job training you."

Bakewell loved to fly over the beach and the Bay and talked Maggie into an aerial sightseeing tour. They made a circuit, flying east over Wolf Harbor and Pensacola, later very low along the beach, passing the house heading west to Fort Morgan. Maggie found the low flying exhilarating. They flew over to Dauphin Island, circling the oil rigs out in the gulf then flew diagonally back across Mobile Bay to Fairhope, where they circled several times, looking down at the scene of the previous night's parade, before going down the Eastern Shore, a few hundred feet above the water to Point Clear, crossing the estuary and Bon Secour, before returning to Edwards.

Back in the car, they stopped for cold drinks and drove west to Fort Morgan again, where they took the ferry to Dauphin Island. They stopped at the landing and split an oyster PoBoy before driving up to Bellingrath Gardens, where they wandered the grounds until a brief shower chased them back to the car. They returned to Gulf Shores via Mobile, crossing the Bay on I-10, taking the historic route through Daphne and Fairhope one last time. Just before Foley he detoured through Magnolia Springs, where the main street was canopied by enormous live oaks that left the roadway in shadow. They toured Bon Secour Bay, watched the shrimpers come in and they bought fresh fish. Their last stop of the day was at the giant mall south of Foley, and Maggie spent an hour in three different children's stores. By the time they got back to the beach house, it was dark. Bakewell made drinks; they changed to evening clothes and drove down the beach to a place called Mikee's, where they ate oysters on the half shell and fresh grouper.

Maggie had enjoyed the flying, the touring, especially the trip to Bellingrath, where the azaleas *were* in bloom. She enjoyed the food, the shopping and the side trips for local color. Her eyes were radiant and Bakewell, taken by her jubilant mood, drank more than he intended, while she made expressive and spirited conversation about how much fun they had experienced in such a short time. She thrived on his little attentions and the many efforts he made to entertain and amuse her. After dinner they drove down to the Florabama Lounge.

"I have to warn you about the Redneck Riviera," Bakewell said as they approached on the beach highway. "There is a divergent variety and flavor to our next stop. Some people think of it as the main attraction."

"I can't wait to see it."

The parking lot was only partially filled, Mercedes, Cadillacs, several old junkers, and half a dozen Harleys. The Florabama was tame for a Saturday night. Bakewell attributed it to the Mardi Gras parades. They found a seat in a dark corner where they drank beer from cans and listened to a talented guy sing a song called, "You Ain't Shit If You Can't Screw." It was a parody on the sex life of teenagers who lied about their sexual prowess, funny and entertaining. By the third stanza Maggie was singing along, her lovely features so out of place, bracketed by ears flashing diamonds that glittered in the dim light.

"Andy, look at that girl behind the bar." Bakewell looked. Half her head was shaved; there was a tattoo on the shaven side. "Is this the place Ned told us about?"

"None other; don't pick a fight with anyone in the pool room."

Maggie giggled. "Where's the pool room?"

"I'm not telling you, just to be safe."

"You think I'd start a brawl?"

"No, but somebody might start one over you."

"Tell me where it is. I want to see it."

"Behind that shed of a wall over there; you have to pass through it to go to the ladies room."

Maggie got up and left him for only a minute. When she returned she said, "I think I'll wait until we get home for the ladies room."

As a finale, the guitarist switched to a piece he hadn't written but greatly appreciated. It was by a group called, Outdoor John & A Sears Catalog. Everyone sang the refrain together:

You call me a dog when I'm gone,
And then when I do get home, with a hunnert dollar bill,
You say, daddy you been gone so long...

When they got back to the house, the sound system was playing an old piece from their youth. Maggie took his hand, looking up at him, her eyes refulgent as they tried to dance to the music.

"I never could keep time to this song," he said.

"You're doing fine."

"We'll just shuffle through it."

"You were always a great shuffler."

"I could fake it."

"No, you could do it," she said, humming the words in his ear. The next number was a wordless version of, "Time After Time," and they danced slowly, closely, Maggie clinging to him, Bakewell almost holding her off her feet, as she pressed against him. When the music ended, they stood looking at one another, Maggie's eyes shining wetly, causing Bakewell to lose track of time and place. She had that effect again and it couldn't have come at a better time, nor was it wasted on him. She knew it, loved knowing she was having that same effect on him once more, leaned in, up, expectantly, and he kissed her.

"Let's go upstairs," he said. She answered with a second kiss.

They took their time. Bakewell was patient and very gentle with her, amazed at the way she responded to his touch. He had tried to take his time when they were young, but her reaction then had been corporeal, rarely emotional. He had wanted tenderness, but she had been physical. He never was sure if she felt the tenderness he offered, even wanted it. Now it filled him with wonder, left him awed that anyone could want him so much, amazed him even more, that anyone could need him so much, or find him so necessary. It was unbelievable to be intimate and sensual once again, to rediscover someone who had been little more than a child when they first discovered each other. It was moving and incredible and unbelievably erotic, because her response and her pleasure were so undeniably genuine. When it was over, they were exhausted and lay silently, only an occasional slight movement of fingertips searching, appreciative, delicate.

The emotion between them stunned Bakewell, caught him completely off guard. He intended to be the giver, the possessor, the distant, in-control guy, not the receiver; he hadn't expected to be so consumed in or by another human being. The impact of her presence, her determination to make her very spirit penetrate him completely, pierce his fragile, aching psyche seized him, interned him and, just as suddenly, derailed him.

Sunday

"Are you all right?" Maggie said, coming out onto the deck. The winter sunlight was nearly blinding. Bakewell reclined, one leg on the plastic table, looking uneasy. He nodded, without speaking. Maggie started to touch him, changed her mind and walked to her familiar place next to the railing.

"I'm sorry, I'm really sorry it happened."

"It's all right; don't be. It was rather tender." She turned, watching him compassionately.

"I've never done that before. I've never cried in front of anybody before. I feel like…maybe, I took advantage of our relationship."

"I'd like to think we have a relationship," she said.

"Well it looks like we've got one now," he exhaled slowly. "I'm sorry…I didn't know I could do it, didn't know it was in me. I apologize."

"Please, Andy, don't apologize," she said. "I was glad it was me. I was glad I could be there. I just hope I helped you. It was very tender. I felt very touched. I felt sad for you. I could feel the sadness in you. You surprised me at first, but then I felt like I should be grateful that you chose me. I felt like…maybe I was the one that was supposed to be there, like you needed me." Bakewell didn't know what to say. "I think, and I don't want to take advantage either, but I think that you might need me. I certainly hope so. I would like…no I would love it very much, if I thought you needed me."

"Well, Maggie, I don't know quite what to say. I certainly needed you last night. I just didn't know it was going to happen. I didn't feel it coming. It just came on all of the sudden. And I haven't wept like that…I don't think I've wept like that, ever."

"I know, I could feel it, I could feel you in my arms."

"Well, it's not something you rehearse." Bakewell said, trying to be glib. "I don't know where it came from. It just seemed like everything kind of caught up with me at once. I've got a pretty full plate right now; I'm worried about too many things."

"What's worrying you, Andy? You said your financial problems had been resolved. You sold some property; things are going well now. Why can't you be happy? Why can't you look forward to the rest of your life?"

Bakewell sighed, looked away, shook his head, wished he could answer, wished he could tell her why he couldn't be happy. He wanted very much to tell her what was ahead, what was out there in the islands, what was out there waiting for him, if he ever got back from the islands – and he didn't think he ever would – but if he ever got back, what would be waiting: a hospital room and old folks home? Turning yellow*? Turning yellow, wouldn't that be something? She'd love to watch that.* He shook his head, wished he could confide in her. He had to move on and stop thinking about the future and live in the present with her. He owed her that much. He got up and went to the railing and put his hand on hers.

"Maggie, let me do something for you?"

"You've done a lot for me, Andy."

"No, I need to do something for you. Let me look after you. Let me be the patronizing, loving, wonderful friend that you need. I'd like to do that for you. I want to be your friend, and I want to knock myself out for you these next couple of days, okay?"

"Andy, I really don't want to be your friend, and I don't think we are friends, and I don't think we've ever been friends. It's just been one thing or the other for us. We've either been intimate or we have not. And right now I want to be intimate; I want to be close. I want to fall in love. I want to need and I want to be needed, and I want you to love me, and you don't have to knock yourself out for me. Just *be* with me."

***

They didn't go to mass and Bakewell wondered where they were heading and what he was doing – knew his actions were so far out of line, so outrageously questionable and so woefully inadequate regarding her with his future – but he simply couldn't combat the vitality, the wonderful verve they were discovering and sharing. He couldn't resist the compelling intimacy and affection they were rediscovering, so much in harmony, in such a perfect part of the world.

They spent most of the day outside on the deck, or walking the beach. It was partly cloudy, and there was a good breeze coming up out of the gulf. They walked for miles, stopping for breakfast on their way east toward Gulf Shores. After returning to the house, they changed to lighter clothes, took a bottle of water and started out toward the west. After about two miles, they sat on a sharp crest of beach, cut by the surf in the white sand, dangling their feet in the gentle swirl of the outgoing tide.

"Tell me something about your daughter," Maggie asked.

"What would you like to know?"

"I don't care. Tell me a story about raising her." Bakewell thought for a moment and she added, "Tell me a story about being a daddy, a story about a daddy and his little girl."

He looked out to sea, thought a moment. "When she was a little girl…"

"How little?"

"Maybe three or four…"

"Where does this story take place?"

He chuckled, "How 'bout on the living room couch?"

"Okay, I got the picture. Go on."

"…She liked to be read to. She was very bright, loved books, things educational, you know." Maggie nodded. "We had this little routine. Whenever we opened a book, I would read the author's name, say 'what does author mean?' and she would respond, 'the one that wrote the words.' Then I would say, 'illustrated by' and she would respond, 'the one that draw'd the pictures.' We went through this same routine with each book. Most of the books we'd read many times, so I would add parts that weren't in there. Sometimes I would really embellish. The book would be a silly little child's tale, and I would go off on a crazy tangent and say something like, 'and then the bad man came in and shot everybody to death with a machine gun.'"

"Good Lord!"

"Well, we were being silly and she knew it. Actually she loved the embellishing the most, once we had read the book a few times. I loved to teach her words too, ridiculous words, words she couldn't possibly understand, with lots of syllables."

"Tell me."

"Mm, crazy words, like…ostentatious, mellifluous – just to hear her pronounce them. I taught her embellish, of course; that was first, and whenever I went off on a tangent with the storyline she would slap the page with her little hand and look up at me and say, 'Daddy you're 'bellishing again.'"

Maggie nodded, smiled, amused, satisfied, looked out at the surf. The sun was out and it was blinding. She put her sunglasses back on. Bakewell's eyes were very dark; he seldom wore sunglasses. He said, "We're lucky it's been cloudy today."

"You're right. We'd both be fried by now."

"Not you, world traveler. You have a perpetual suntan."

"I try not to overdo it, but I like to have some sun. I can't seem to go for more than a month in the wintertime, without needing to go somewhere the sun shines. I think it has something to do with therapy. I feel healthier with a little tan. I guess someday I'll be a little old lady with sunspots all over me." He got up and offered his hand. She took it.

"Come on, little old lady, we have to start back. We're an hour away, the way you poke along." He put his arm around her. "I'll make you dinner tonight, and I'll try and get you drunk, and if I succeed, I'm gonna check out the lines of your suntan, maybe look for sunspots."

After showers and a change of clothes, they enjoyed the setting sun with cocktails in hand. Bakewell grilled the fish and Maggie made a salad and they ate dinner on the deck, illuminated by a hurricane lamp. They drank several bottles of Heineken, which Maggie called, "a fattening, but refreshing change of pace." When the meal was finished, they sat under the overcast sky in windbreakers, and talked for hours about the lives they had led. It was curious, some of the conversation bizarre, bordering on surreal, as they allowed themselves to ponder and wonder and drift to no purpose.

It was all so very pleasant and so unbelievably calming for Bakewell, whose life had been filled with so much tension. He drank far passed his self-enforced limit, all the while, his conscience pinched by the knowledge that what they discussed was not to be, could never be. The sky cleared briefly, and they watched the big dipper appear tangentially from Polaris. Bakewell pointed out the Pleiades, saying, "Look off to one side and they'll appear much clearer."

"I took astronomy, Andy. The Pleiades are simple; show me Orion if you want to impress me."

He couldn't do it, said, "The North Star is my specialty; after that I'm done."

She stood and leaned against him and pointed almost straight overhead, indicating Betelgeuse and Rigel. He pretended to see them, but wasn't sure, the stars billions of light years apart, their bodies on the deck so very close. It was different now. Before, he approached her tentatively and she him. Now when she wanted to touch him, she reached for him, and he was comfortable knowing he could put his arms around her, his hands on her, feel her revel in his touch. Bakewell couldn't get over the need she had for his intimacy, or the need he had for hers. He couldn't get enough of her, of the incredible pleasure of her, of the warmth and comfort he got from her. She was back in his heart, and she was welcome.

A third magical night emerged like the previous two, sensitive, delicate, in a serene, wordless and soothing mantle, Bakewell not believing he had that much to offer; and she, willing, more than willing, to accept whatever was left. He was amazed at the way she luxuriated in his affection, savored his touch, and responded to his tenderness. He had never known a woman with so much need for tenderness. It seemed to come up from the depth of some strange and deeply stored place, a place of untapped passion. She wanted him, there was no doubting it, and she was offering herself without hesitance, without regret, without holding back. She was living for him now, and he was awed by the realization that someone wanted him so desperately. Her happiness and her need frightened him.

Bakewell woke about the time the alcohol wore off, and went downstairs and took a glass of water out on the deck and drank it under the wet sky, pondering the uncertainty of the weeks ahead. If he had guilt the two nights before, it might have been about his failed fidelity, his disloyalty to Katherine. Upstairs, Maggie slept peacefully in the knowledge she had found her happiness at last, transported finally in time, to her space, ecstatic in her physical and emotional satiation, happy with life, with Bakewell, with her place, and with the future that awaited them. Now he realized his guilt had nothing to do with Katherine – Katherine was in a special place far away – his guilt was about what he was doing to Maggie. There was no way he could continue. The taking advantage part was the very worst part. The love she offered, and the look of pure adoration he saw in her eyes, was more than he could endure. He realized, under the wet sky, stars halo-like in the forming mist, that he would have to rid her of his presence, would have to harden his heart, turn his face from her, somehow make her see him for what he was, somehow reverse their direction completely.

There was no question; it had to be done, if he was to go out to the islands. And there was no turning back. He couldn't renege on the deal. The die was cast, the money was spent, the company had been saved, Ned was off the hook. When he made the deal, he had hoped his health would fail before the time came. He still felt fine. He got tired easier than he used to, but Maggie had energized him. He was going to be around and healthy enough when the time came. *It's already here.* There was only one choice for him, and that was to go back out, just as he had done so many years before, and let them insert him in the firing lane and find out from what direction the bullets would fly.

He lay down on the couch in the dark and tried to think of a way to make her understand they could never be, and do it without causing pain. It wasn't possible. The choice was only how to make her somehow reject him, or make her understand they were a mistake. How could they be a mistake after the past few days?

A Second Ending

Maggie found her love asleep on the couch, a glass still in his hand, the room warmed by the rising sun streaming through the sliding glass doors. She moved about quietly, and when the coffee was ready the smell woke him.

"How are you this morning?"

"Hung over," he said irritably.

"Mm, a little crabby too."

Bakewell left for the bathroom, and when he returned she observed a mood she didn't recognize, a mood she had never seen before. Bakewell was angry with himself: the excessive drinking, thoughtless behavior, dimwitted willingness to let her in, cavalier disregard for future consequences, all combined to infuriate him. He was always his own worst critic. He couldn't find enough words, enough accusations to ascribe to his behavior: detestable and despicable came to mind.

Maggie was looking for the shy, wonderfully amiable man she had been living with the last few days. Instead she observed a confused, irritable creature, stirring about, making an uncharacteristic commotion. Initially, Bakewell considered behaving badly, becoming moody and churlish, even practiced making faces while he shaved. But he couldn't do it, wouldn't be able to pull it off, and he didn't want to. He was completely without options. How could he break their relationship off? There would have to be another way, without cruelty. He didn't have to worry. It would be Maggie who solved the problem for him.

"Do you want something to eat?"

"No thanks."

"Did you come down for another drink or was it my snoring?"

"I just needed some water. I drank way too much."

"And decided you needed your privacy?"

He gave up the act, looked across the room and smiled at her. She looked lovely. "I couldn't sleep, wandered about for a while. I guess I fell asleep down here." She poured coffee for them. "I've never heard you snore, by the way."

Maggie smiled beautifully, grateful for a change in mood. "Can we walk down the beach for breakfast again?"

"Let me get dressed," he said without enthusiasm, wondering what direction that conversation would take, what direction he intended to make it take.

They started out to the east into the morning sun and the sound of softly lapping surf. They walked in silence for a long time. Maggie kept her hands plunged deep into her baggy shorts. There was a cool breeze from the east. It put an edge on the otherwise perfect morning. The sound of the low surf sucking at the shore below their feet added to the chilly mood. Maggie walked above him on the beach, away from the surf, and when the beach steepened, she bumped him several times as she lost her balance in the soft sand. The last time she bumped against him, he put his arm around her shoulder and squeezed gently. She cringed under his grasp, pulling her neck down between her shoulders. It was just perceptible. Bakewell looked at her quizzically. She furled her brow, curious and distant. He didn't understand, a question in his look, unasked.

They walked another fifty yards before she said, "I'm thinking we are a mistake, Andy."

He didn't answer, and she didn't pursue it, and they walked along the shore in silence, nodding occasionally to beach walkers going west. He wanted to respond, to get on to the main topic: the I'm-a-son-of-a-bitch-and-I've-got-to-leave-you speech, but couldn't find the words. They walked on for a long time, were half way back to town. The weather was warming again. The wind had dropped off and the sun was bright. It was going to be another magnificent day.

They needed to turn back, but were unwilling to make the decision, both knowing the turn back would signal the end of their weekend, a resumption of the "mistake" conversation. After another hundred yards Maggie stopped and picked up a circular shell, shook the sand from it, and held it up, inspecting it for chips. It was perfect.

"What's this?"

"I don't know, a whelk, maybe a murex?" Bakewell shrugged. It was only a simple cone. Maggie seemed satisfied with the answer. She put the shell in her pocket.

"I shouldn't have done what I did up at Point Clear," she finally said, sighing. "I forced myself on you, made you make love with me. I thought it was the right thing to do. I was wrong. It was a mistake." He started to protest, but she shook her head and went on, "You're full of guilt now. It's all over you. The way you look. The way you behave, walking the floor at night. You can't sleep."

"I've been walking the floor at night for years."

"Your heart's not in it, boy. You're not ready for me, or for anybody else." There was an embarrassed silence as they searched for words. Bakewell came up short once more. Maggie added, "I hope the *anybody else* part is true."

He looked into her deep blue eyes and they clouded, filled with emotion. He had to say it, had to do it, if for no other reason than for her sake. He hesitated before dropping the blow. "I'm still in love with…"

"You're still in love with your wife," she said, nodding emphatically. "You're not ready for another woman, not ready for me anyway."

"If I was ready for anyone, it would be you, Maggie."

"I believe that Andy. I want to believe that and I do. I wish it wasn't so, but there it is. I want you to call me if the time ever comes. I want to be the one…" she choked on the words, "The one that brings you back." She looked off over her shoulder at the horizon. "I'll understand if you don't call me. I won't hold it against you." She patted his chest for emphasis. "I don't want to anyway. Just remember me when you start to breathe life again. If you ever decide to rejoin us in this world, I want it to be me. Do you think you could do that? Could you put me in front of the line?"

He put his hands on her shoulders and squeezed. "I was wrong about you, Maggie. I take back all the mean thoughts I've harbored all these years," he said, trying to lighten the conversation. It didn't work. He shook her shoulders for effect instead. "You really are a good person, Maggie. You would be easy to…" Bakewell pulled her to him and hugged her tightly. "You're a keeper, Maggie." His voice was full of emotion, but it was controlled. This was his chance. The one she had handed him so unselfishly. She was letting him off the hook; he had to take the opportunity she offered, even though his heart was aching for her.

"Yes. Do think of me that way Andy." She looked up into his eyes. "I do so much want to be kept. I want to be kept by a man like you. *I want to be kept by you.*" She put her chin on his chest. The tears were flowing, an undisguised pleading in her voice. She nodded her head as she pronounced each word, like a small child, speaking to a parent. It tore at him. He gave her a tight, understanding, sympathetic smile with his eyes and pulled her against him again, so he wouldn't have to look into hers, held her tightly.

Bakewell couldn't break, not now. It was his chance to end it. It was already over. She had ended it.

When they finally separated, Maggie paused, eyes closed tightly, came back to him and pressed her cheek to his shoulder and gasped, "*Oh my dear God, Andy*. I've gone and fallen in love with you. Only this time you don't love me. I was afraid of this." She leaned into him, almost pushing him back into the surf. He didn't touch her, didn't encourage her this time, hoping the emotion would come to an end. "I'm not sure I ever stopped loving you. I wish I hadn't let you go. I had you once, and I let you get away."

"Come on Maggie, you make me sound like a prize. I'm not that much. I never was."

"You're the one that's a keeper," she sobbed.

He gave in to the urge and put his arms around her again. They rocked back and forth in the wet sand for a long time, holding each other, until the surf lapped up against his heels. Bakewell had an urge to suddenly give it all up, to make a run for it. *Go to Mexico? Someplace?* To ask her to hide with him on a beach in some secret place for the rest of his life, but it passed just as quickly. He knew he was yielding to his fears, to a brief panic. He didn't have time for panic, and he didn't have a life left to give her, and he had no right to take advantage of her. Even if he wanted to; he had no right to take her or keep her and use her, then leave her. She would be better off being done with him. She would be fine once she got back to her home and her things... And he didn't want her to watch him die.

When they returned to the beach house, Maggie insisted on making the breakfast they hadn't stopped for, mostly to prolong the morning. Afterward they cleaned together. It took a while because she insisted on overdoing it. Normally he would have called a cleaning service. Bakewell vacuumed each room; she told him he was getting pretty good at it. They made the beds together, while she teased him about his housekeeping skills through a steady stream of sniffles, bordering on outright weeping. She had never been a crier.

He tried to tease her about her tears, used a big word: lachrymose. She knew the word, had no retort, was too exposed, out of fight, empty; her tears coming regularly, without warning. She did her best to make light of her emotions, to talk through each tearful bout. She teased him about anything she could think of, resorted to mischief when she remembered the way he had kept his apartment in Columbia. She accused him of keeping her there too, but they knew better, even laughed about it, agreed it was "a thousand years ago." When the house was ready, a feeling of finality came over them, and a sense of urgency developed. It was time to get back to St. Louis. Bakewell called Flight Service and got the weather and filed a flight plan.

"We need to get back before sunset. There's some weather moving in this evening," he said.

At the airport, they returned the car and loaded the plane. After pre-flighting, they taxied out to get clearance. The plane had a wonderful sound system. He never used it. While he waited for Pensacola Approach to clear them, Maggie flipped through the compact discs listlessly, picked out a CD and showed it to him. It was the soundtrack from *Dances With Wolves*. He nodded as he read back his clearance, and she put it in the player. After liftoff they were vectored northwest out over Mobile Bay away from the navy traffic. Things settled down when Mobile turned them over to Houston Center. Bakewell turned the music up as they crossed the delta above Mobile and the sound of music filled their headsets. It was woodwinds, strings and drums, moving and dramatic, and when he reached to adjust the DME frequency, he noticed she gripped a tissue tightly. She was crying again, this time it was a real cry. She looked off in front of the wing so he couldn't see her face. It made him feel ruthless and cruel and inadequate once more. It had been like that with Katherine, whenever he made her cry.

The day was clear, and the weather was forecast VFR all the way to Memphis. Bakewell wanted to lose the emotion filling the cabin. It was suffocating. Mostly he wished for a way to make himself somehow repulsive to the woman seated next to him. In the end he opted to be himself and try and change the atmosphere by changing the mood. He cancelled their flight plan.

"Let's have some fun."

Maggie's face showed a childlike curiosity. In the airplane she was at his mercy, her eyes still red and wet. He lowered the nose, and they dropped down several thousand feet, the plane accelerating as they went. She inhaled suddenly, raising her shoulders as the plane descended. He gradually slowed their descent. When they were only a few hundred feet above the swampy, pine filled country, he leveled off and she gasped at the G force and grabbed his thigh and called his name. They streaked across the forests at 200 miles an hour and the noise of the plane scattered a small group of egrets below, their white bodies contrasting with the color of the green forests and the gray muck beneath. The music matched their speed, and Maggie enjoyed the adventure of low-level flying. They kept it up for miles. Bakewell made her take the yoke, and she rolled the wings and the plane flew a zigzag course. Eventually she pulled too hard and they climbed steeply enough to feel the force of a full G, and she shouted for him to take the yoke. Bakewell had been combating his troubles with aircraft adventure much of his life; it was exhilarating. Whenever he was discouraged he always turned to his plane. A temporary excitement replaced the troubled look on Maggie's fine profile.

When they were just south of Meridian, he put them back in the system, went up to altitude, and put the plane on autopilot. The conversation was mostly adlib, some about flying after Maggie's low level experience. She appreciated the ride home from a slightly more involved perspective. She told him she might decide to take up flying, adding, "It would be the first adventurous thing I've ever done in my life."

"Well, if you do, find a good-looking flight instructor; those guys are chronically broke." Bakewell regretted the words as soon as he spoke. It sounded condescending, demeaning. Maggie waited, let him suffer before she finally told him she just might do it.

"I might find a man I can keep, control him with my money, so he won't always be flying away."

They got quiet north of Memphis. The trip was boring once they were over the Missouri Bootheel, the scenery interrupted only by huge oxbows in the Mississippi below. They were lost in thought as they approached St. Louis, confused by the bleary-ing onslaught of emotions their time together had produced. Bakewell suspected they were too old for such emotions. Maggie was thinking the same thing. After landing, they drove back to town. He dropped her at her home, carried her luggage to the door. He didn't ask to come in, and she didn't offer. They looked at each other long and hard without speaking. He gave her an embarrassed wink and told her she was something special, regretted it immediately, knowing it sounded hollow and patronizing.

"The end to an *almost perfect* weekend," she said, taking her bag, after she opened the door.

"I thought it was perfect."

"Yeah, I bet."

He hesitated. There was one more thing he wanted to say, didn't know quite how to phrase it, blurted it out, "I hope you don't feel like you've been used." His voice shook, intensely sincere.

"No. I don't feel like I've been used, and I don't want you to think I've tried to use you either." She touched his cheek tenderly.

"I wish I could love you for the rest of my life."

"I wish you could too. I will probably love you for the rest of mine." Maggie tossed her head, tried to regroup, "Unless I find that flight instructor."

"He'll be the perfect guy; you'll see, full of obnoxious self-confidence, probably be like those arrogant law students you used to…"

She put her finger to his lips, quieting him. "I think I'll wait for my Schmuck," she said, pressing her fingers to his lips. "You won't forget your promise? You will call me? When the time is right?"

He met her unhappy gaze, lingered, taking a long, deep look within. Her eyes were clear again, framed by inflamed lids and delicate little lines, accented white, but looking so very fine, contrasting with the color of her softly tanned skin. He could get lost in her eyes, had gotten lost in them. It wasn't possible now. He touched her cheek, wanting to offer some affection, turned and walked out to the truck. Maggie went inside and closed her door.

It started to rain as he got into the truck. The rain had been out to the west the last hour of their flight; now it had arrived. Bakewell sat very still and listened to the light rain, spattering at first, changing to a delicate pinging on the roof, as it turned to a fine sleet in the cold air. They had timed the return trip perfectly.

He was worn out by conflicting emotions, knew Maggie was too. He had been trying to sort them for hours, was frightened by what had happened at the beach. There was an involuntary shuddering inside him; he felt sick. He was worried about his soul, and what his actions would mean in the eternity that awaited…soon. But at the moment, he worried more about what might happen to Maggie, how she would do after he was gone. He was tempted to go back and knock on her door, tell her about his deal with the devil, about his unbelievable travel plans, about the crazy thing he had committed to. It wouldn't work. He couldn't be responsible for her, no matter how much she might be willing. There was too much ahead and no time for any of it. He had given up on the idea of being responsible for her, knowing it was far out of the question. It filled him with still more guilt.

There was a single, brief instant, when he reconsidered, a fractional moment, the difference between staying and leaving, the kind of moment that affected so many of life's major decisions. He started the car, waited for the defroster to go to work. It took several minutes, more time for indecision, before he finally drove away.

Part Two

Going West

Bakewell left St. Louis two days later, so conflicted by the magnitude of his problems he trembled subconsciously. He was filled with a sense of dread, agonizing over children, grandchildren and the life he was leaving, sorry about the way it ended in deceit with Ned and Denny, and so many others, beyond remorse about the way he had left it with Maggie Walker, but determined to get going, to get ahead of Albrecht's people. If he would have any chance of surviving *out there* he had to assay his options first hand. There was only so much he could learn from books, maps and conversations. He had to find something, anything, any advantage, no matter how small. He also needed time to adapt to the equatorial heat and humidity, see the terrain and learn what he could about the biblical "creeping things of the earth" that were there. He already knew the freshwater streams were home to crocodiles.

His target was on Bougainville. There must be some kind of sanctuary, probably an installation of proportion, on the island the infamous and terrible man had chosen. He was probably already there. *Of course he's already there. Why would they be sending you if he wasn't already there?*

Although Bakewell was a numbers guy, he went with gut feelings often, had played a lot of hunches over the years. His ability to guess, "get a hunch on somethin," Ned liked to say, had been surprisingly accurate much of the time. If he had to put a number on it, he would have guessed his hunches had been about 80% correct. If he was right, he didn't think the Arab's hideout could be kept secret on Bougainville. An evil billionaire would have a hiding place ample enough to accommodate his lifestyle. Idi Amin had lived in luxury in Saudi Arabia for decades after his ruthless government collapsed. The Arab would surround himself with his administration – and *plenty of security*.

Bakewell subscribed to the simple dictum that *knowledge was power* all his business life. He tried to play out what was ahead in his mind, creating scenarios one after another. Without ever having been there, he knew no amount of planning was worth anything until he saw the island. He needed to study Bougainville, to see it, to feel it. He was determined to get there first, see what might develop, might eventuate, maybe come up with some kind of escape route, no matter how far fetched – in the event he was still alive after the shooting.

To get there first he had to deceive Albrecht and whatever "watchers" he employed. The tickets Albrecht had sent him were dated several weeks in the future. They were supposed to rendezvous right before departure. The last two weeks they would be watching him closely, in a heightened state of alert. He would get there, check in on location, tell them he was doing his preparation work, and await their arrival. It would upset them, but, hopefully make them appreciate him more in the bargain.

He would go underground in Port Moresby. They wouldn't be able to track him down out there. Once he was gone they had no choice.

He spent the late morning of his last day in America with his oldest son in a Clayton coffee shop, where they talked marriage, parenting and Katherine, over too many cups of sour tasting coffee. Katherine had been the center of their universe, Andy's, possibly, even more than the others, and Bakewell wanted some quiet time with his son before he left.

Andy had taken a job with an architectural firm, had relocated from the family business. It was a shock to them all at first, but Bakewell didn't want any of his kids in the business if they didn't want to be there. Nancy had assured him it was not a problem. Andy had taken on a lot of responsibility in a short time. Bakewell was sure the graying hair and somber mood were a combination of aging, raising children, his mother's death, and Bakewell's own deteriorating health. It all seemed to rob him of his remaining spark, the joi de vivre he'd inherited from Katherine. It was a difficult conversation, but they made the best of it by remembering good times, glossing over the bad parts. It was a macho, guys' conversation, filled with false disdain for emotion. And it rang hollow. It was not the conversation they intended to have, but neither man could find the words to put it in softer context. Andy had been closer to his mother. He and Bakewell had a strangely distant relationship over the years, even though they loved each other deeply. After Katherine's death their relationship had grown even more distant, his son preferring the solace he found in wife and small family, Bakewell having the sense to leave it alone. As they bid farewell at the curb Bakewell was moved when his boy, now inches taller, kissed his cheek and hugged him tightly there on the busy street in downtown Clayton.

"Be careful out there in the islands, Pop. Take the pills they gave you. Don't get yourself malarial…or worse." Bakewell nodded appreciatively. "You have all your shots?"

"Yep, all set, ready for the missions."

"I hope you find a safe place to stay. Karen pulled some stuff up on the internet that said they've been having a lot of trouble out there."

"Father told me."

"A civil war, Dad? Did you know they have a civil war going out there? Over ten thousand casualties!"

"I've done a little homework. Father says I'll be okay. Things have settled down now."

"It makes my stomach roll to think about it."

"Mine too. It's the missions, son. Somebody has to do it. Not me, don't misunderstand. I just want to see it." They separated on the busy street, and Bakewell watched his son walk back toward his new office. He hoped the boy would be happier in life, in his new profession, satisfied he had joined the other side, appeared to have found stability.

Earlier, Bakewell had called Michael and asked him to bring his backpack and travel bag to the center concourse at Lambert. Nancy would drop him off in his truck. He'd conspired to make it look like he was dropping Nancy off instead. Bakewell briefed his daughter on the drive to the airport, telling her what he thought she should do in the aftermath of his death, in case he took a turn for the worse while he was gone.

"You sound like you're not planning on coming back," Nancy said. She had been listening reluctantly, absently making notes, asking few questions.

Without much thought or anticipation, and never getting the timing right, Bakewell casually informed his daughter he didn't expect to return from the islands. Nancy came out of her dejection with a jolt.

"My God, Daddy! You can't just casually announce you're not coming back!" She was stunned, her anger turned quickly to unwanted tears, "Not while we're driving along having this stupid little chitchat about post mortems and emergencies!" She threw her notebook on the dash. There was a wordless pause; Bakewell couldn't think of anything to say. Nancy couldn't find the right words but didn't let it deter her. "Good grief! Damn it anyway! What are you thinking? We expect you to come home safely!"

"Nancy, I want to be as little trouble as possible. I think it would be easier if I just disappeared over the next few months to save you all the pain."

"Dad! There is such a thing as closure! That's why people have wakes – those macabre little ordeals you make fun of! *GOOD GOD!"* She looked out her window, confused, trying to hide her tears. She hated the fact that she cried. She lived in a tough contractor's world and hated her tears. The gloomy north county matched the mood in the car. A big airliner came down out of the overcast.

"We know how damned independent you are *but you can't just not return!* We want to be with you when the time comes."

Bakewell stared ahead at the slippery highway.

"Even *you* have learned to put your dogs down properly, to take a little time to bury them. We all get to say goodbye." She struggled on, "When I was four years old you shot Lucy out on some damned prairie and buried her. It took me weeks to get over knowing I was never going to see her again." She blew her nose, "And she was a dog!"

"That was a mistake. Lucy was a great old dog…"

"They're all sweet, and we all die a little when you lose one." She turned to him. "You're my father! You're not a fucking bird dog! We have a right to help you and be with you and do whatever we can when the time comes… if you're really going to leave us. You can't just *not come home*." The contractor was regrouping, getting a grip on detested emotions. Bakewell hated the contractor language. Another airliner came out of the overcast over the truck as they approached the airport. "I know what you're thinking. You assume we'll just get over it once you're gone. You think you can do whatever you want, but you can't, you just can't!"

Bakewell turned and followed the signs for the parking garage. "I'm sorry I upset you, I'll make every effort to get home if it's that important."

"Important! Dad, you're not even sick right now. You look fine. You're healthy. I never hear you complain. We're looking at our father and he looks perfectly fine to us. You can't get that sick that quick – not in a couple of weeks, and then just not come home!" Nancy pushed the tears from her cheeks. "Go on out and visit with the Fathers and help them build something or fix something if you want; do whatever makes you feel useful, then come home and tell us all about it. Let us love you and take care of you like we did with Mom. Please." The tears nearly stopped, she was almost under control again, upset, very animated, but getting control.

Humbled, feeling stupid once again, wondering if he would ever have a lucid thought around a woman, he pulled into a parking space. "All right, I'm sorry. You're right. It was a dumb idea."

"It was cruel, and it was ruthless."

"I know…you're right, I'll come home. I'll call or write when I get to Port Moresby. They have email."

Nancy slammed the door as she got out of the truck. Bakewell made a production of his exit from the truck, taking a large suitcase from the camper shell before taking his daughter's arm. The suitcase had a big pink ribbon around it with a large, gaudy pink bow. Nancy looked at the bow on the suitcase with curiosity but made no comment. They went inside and walked through the terminal and found Michael waiting at the metal detectors in the concourse. Bakewell put the big suitcase down next to Nancy, ignoring his own bags.

"Take care of your sister and my dogs and my grandbabies, Michael."

"Notice *dogs* came before grandbabies, Michael." Nancy's baleful look confused her brother, his comprehension of women only slightly keener than his father's. He was expecting emotion not anger. "What's going on?"

"He's decided he's not coming back," Nancy said, "Thought he would just go ahead and die and let them ship him home. Or were you going to be buried on an island somewhere?" Nancy was recovering her pluck, her voice dripped with sarcasm.

Bakewell turned to his son. "I've made another one of those *women mistakes."*

Michael nodded knowingly. "You said you would be back by April?"

"April? What April? What's April?"

"I told Michael I might want to stay until April."

"You just told me two weeks! You said you didn't think you had that much time. Now it's April?"

"Let me think on it. I'll call or write. You will both know what my plans are as soon as I've made them." Nancy stomped her foot in frustration, preparing to fire another salvo. He held up his hand defensively. "Please, let's have a peaceful good bye."

"You feeling okay, Pop?" Michael was nervous, put off by his sister's anger, always a little afraid of her. "You're doing all right now aren't you Pop? You look good."

"I'm good to go."

"Where's Andy?" Nancy asked.

"We met this morning for coffee. I left him in Clayton. We had a nice visit."

"You left him with the suits? Karen must be in heaven. Andy's with the suits and *the old man's* leaving town." There was no commenting; neither man wanted to fence with Nancy. "I'm sorry, I shouldn't have said that. I like Karen fine; she's a good person and she's good for Andy. It's just that I miss him."

"First stop's LA?" Michael asked, "The dirty city with beautiful women?"

"Not as bad as New York." It was an inside joke. They thought of themselves as mountain men, not city people, even though they'd spent most of their lives in the city.

"Ned is really pissed," Nancy said. "He said we should have locked you up."

"Where did he have in mind?"

"Nowhere, really, you know he doesn't think that far ahead. He said you'd probably make 'some kind of Rambo escape from any place where we could put you to keep you from flying the coop on one of yer impulses of behavior.'"

"I'm about out of impulses," Bakewell said, happy to have some humor.

"Where's your first night, Dad? Aren't you staying with the Franciscans somewhere?"

"Port Moresby. It's an all night flight. I have an hour layover in Brisbane, then Port Moresby," he said. "I'm staying with the Franciscans, at the seminary."

Nancy knew all about Port Moresby and the priest on Buka. She had heard her father talking with a man at the Provincial House in San Francisco. She also discussed her father's condition with her brothers daily, had the email addresses in Moresby and Buka and also one for the Marist Provincial on Guadalcanal.

Michael shook hands with his father. It was very formal, making Bakewell wonder how he could be so close to one son who shook his hand, so distant with another who hugged and kissed him. Nancy hugged him tightly, backed away and hit him on the arm saying, "All right, damn it. Go."

Bakewell put his baggage on the track. He had a Leatherman and showed it to the guard who regarded it absently and nodded. Bakewell zipped the tool into his pack and looked at his children, his stomach fluttering, almost nauseous. He doubted he would ever see them again. He had tried to do the best he could in the last few weeks, had given it all he had. It hadn't been much. It hadn't been enough, and he knew it.

"What gives with the girly suitcase?"

"It's for you to take home. Mrs. Walker bought some gifts for the kids in Gulf Shores."

"What are we supposed to do about her?"

"Does she know yet that you're off to the Pacific?" Michael asked.

Bakewell shook his head. "Why don't you treat her right if she calls? I think she would love to visit with you all. Michael, you could take her to dinner; make her feel young. You and Andy could make her an honorary grandmother, or something, Nancy."

"You don't have to advise us on how to treat Mrs. Walker, Dad. We know what to do if she calls. In fact, I will call her and keep her posted on what you're doing."

"It's not necessary to keep her posted on what I'm doing, but it would be wonderful if you would all treat her kindly. She likes you very much."

"You're the one that's not treating her right. I can't believe she doesn't know," Nancy shook her head, staring at her father intently.

"I'll call her," Michael said. "She's okay."

Nancy was out of anger, deflated, worried and unable to hide it. Bakewell put his arm around her again and pulled gently. She stood very still when he kissed her, finally gave in and kissed him and hugged him and started to cry again. "God, I can't believe you're leaving St. Louis and not telling her. I can't believe *you're leaving us*."

Bakewell was not a small man. He managed to get a window seat on the crowded flight to LA. When the plane loaded, he found himself crushed against the fuselage by an enormous woman from Iowa. She and her husband were headed for Hawaii. The pilot in him wanted to sit next to the window, watch things pass 30,000' below, while he kept track with a small hand held GPS. He'd bought an insert card for his destination in the South Pacific in addition to the card presently in the GPS. He was very claustrophobic with the woman's monstrous biceps sagging over the armrest, pressing against his own. He was miserably cramped and on the verge of panic. He closed his eyes, tried to practice self control. It took a long time to get control, but he managed to tough out the entire flight, by remaining almost motionless, opening his eyes from time to time to study the plane's location and airspeed on the GPS. Eventually he drifted into a defensive meditation, carefully reflecting on the last few months, and especially the last days he'd shared with Maggie.

He still remembered the nervous churning in his stomach the night she'd first called, identified herself with, "Andy, it's Maggie, please don't hang up," remembered how she had added, "and tell me instead you're happy to hear my voice," remembered how he had parroted the words in response, unable to come up with anything else, anything original. She had kept him engaged after that, so happy to be talking to him again and, truthfully, he to her, despite his reservations. His stomach had churned throughout the whole conversation, although he didn't understand why. He'd left her far in the past.

He remembered the night they went to dinner, the drive through Forest Park and the visit to the Muny, the way she bumped against him when they walked together, the way she still loved to tease him and quickly apologize afterward, afraid she might have offended him, remembered the long night at Algonquin, when they drank too much. That was the night she had actually come onto him, although he hadn't given it much credence at the time, and not for a long time after, thought she was *playing* him all over again. About the only thing he really noticed, now as he looked back over those long months, was the way she glowed whenever their eyes met. She had that dazzling glow that went with the smile and the eyes, that overwhelming joy that managed to radiate from what otherwise seemed to be an almost sad countenance. Why hadn't he figured it out from the first? Why was he so thick? *God, it's such a disadvantage being stupid. Why didn't I get some of the brains when they were being passed out? Even Ned had a better radar than me when it came time to figuring things out about women.*

He remembered their Thanksgiving together, when she had won over all the kids in a single afternoon, that night at the Ritz, when she had dazzled the room and practically glittered from the deep green Queen Anne chair she occupied (and nearly matched), remembered her odd behavior on Christmas Eve, when she got up and left early, and the way she had disappeared right after Christmas – for almost two months. What was that about? *Maybe she was trying to make you miss her, stupid, make some effort to keep the relationship going. What a dope you are!*

He was a dope, wondered if the problem would ever correct itself. *Well you're about out of time. If it's going to happen, it better happen soon. And how come I feel so good? Was Neville wrong with the diagnosis? How come I feel so damned healthy? Why couldn't I just go ahead and die, so I wouldn't have to go through all this anxiety, not to mention the danger! What am I going to find out there?*

They got into Los Angeles about six in the evening. The sun had already set, and the lady from Iowa and her equally massive husband, thanked him for being such a nice traveling companion, told him they were sorry they wouldn't be sharing the same flight to Hawaii. Bakewell outdid himself in wishing them bon voyage, relieved to be getting out of the seat. He was four hours early for his Quantas flight to Brisbane, and, after finding the international terminal, ate in a nice restaurant and began to keep a journal, more like a list of notes, questions. What about this? What about that? How long does it take to get from here to there? He studied his map of the islands with anticipation. He also kept a close eye on the empty reservation counter for Quantas. As soon as it opened, he approached a young man and asked about an aisle seat for the long flight.

It wasn't any problem, "No worry, mate," was the way the man phrased it. He got the seat in the aisle this time, *in the emergency exit aisle,* which afforded an additional 24" of blissful leg room. It would be like a deliverance after the flight from St. Louis. When he settled in, he luxuriated in the comfort of extra leg room. He would be spending the next eleven hours in his seat. The guy behind him was his size and already looked uncomfortable, jammed in a middle seat. As soon as they were airborne the giant plane turned out over the Pacific and left the lights of America behind.

America: *Oh beautiful far spacious skies...amber waves of grain...purple mountains' majesty...* He wondered why the mountains were purple – Julie pronounced the word, *popple.* The first adventurous men to cross America had described them as the "shining mountains," never said anything about being purple.

There were interruptions for food and beverages, all complementary, even the liquor, which came in quantity. He drank two glasses of wine with his first meal in hopes of anesthetizing his brain for the journey. He put his backpack under his feet, making a footstool that allowed him to stretch out and pulled the neck restrainers about his ears and fell asleep after the first hour.

Paraphrasing Lewis

Helen Murphy sent Bakewell a beautiful note, almost a letter, a few weeks after Katherine's death. She brought it by the house one afternoon when no one was home, left it on the dining room table. The Bakewell home was never locked. With the note was a little 4 volume set of C S Lewis. Two books, *The Problem of Pain* and *A Grief Observed* were of significance to Bakewell; he read them both within the month. Looking back almost three years later, he tried to remember the wisdom and the shocking accusations Lewis had hurled at his faith as he dealt with the loss of his wife.

Lewis was a confirmed bachelor, a university don, who lived a comfortable English life in the world of academia. Late in life he fell in love and found happiness with a woman who was already ill when they married. After bringing fulfillment to his solitary life, she died. In his grief, Lewis returned to writing, his outlet, unsure in the beginning, somehow attempting to assuage his grief. Bakewell had known the same emotions: the need for company, even though he seldom spoke to those about him; the distinction between fear and dread – and Bakewell was intimately familiar with both emotions. *Fear* – something he knew alone in the mountains, or when he couldn't pay his bills, (or maybe having dinner with Maggie Walker?) And *dread* – worse than fear, that *other* emotion. Dread is what he'd experienced most after Katherine's death. It was the same when he was confronted with the near death of his company. Dread is the knowledge that you awake in the world each new day, knowing the pain will return again, and with it, fear and the sense of loss and loneliness.

He was fascinated by Lewis's perception of God in his book on grief: when you're happy God is everywhere. He is in the people and places and things around you. God is in the flowers in the fields, in every aspect of life. What happened to God when Katherine died? Where was He then? According to Lewis, God disappeared in his grief too, when he needed Him the most. There was the fear of the future and the dread of each coming day in Bakewell's life after Katherine had died. The terrible knowing he would awake aware again of his loss. He could remember it still. *There's fear and dread in what's ahead in the islands too. What is ahead? What have you gotten yourself into with this madness? Your own death could have covered the losses! No, that wasn't really true. Not until it was too late. The bills had to be paid months ago. You couldn't have gone around promising people you would die for them so Ned and Nancy would have the money to pay them later.*

Lewis thought maybe his marriage had been perfected, reached what it had to be, and it was, in God's mind, time for his wife to move on to the next life. Once perfection was reached, it was finished here on earth. *Maybe that's why so many of the good people you've known are already dead.*

Bakewell shuddered. *The world's so screwed up: good people die, while the bums live on – seemingly forever. Ned's right about that. You live in a world surrounded by scoundrels, and you bury the really good people.*

Another of Lewis's questions concerned separation – did the dead feel separation? Did Katherine feel the pain of separation, the same pain he felt after her death? That searing, immobilizing pain he'd known? Was that same pain what he'd created in Maggie's life? There would be real pain there. Should he have told her? He shuddered again. There was no answering that question. If he told her he was going to the islands she would have wanted to go. If he told her why he was going to Bougainville, what would she have thought? Was the pain of separation some kind of purgatory in itself? Lewis had asked that question, but Bakewell had pondered it long before he read Lewis, had asked many of the questions Lewis asked. Maybe it was because Lewis was such a clear thinker, had the ability to put his finger right on the emotions and ask so many obvious questions: should you prolong unhappiness, feel guilty when your unhappiness gradually lessened, still ache for your loss, want to ache, play the tragic figure? Being tragic was necessary. Feeling the loss constantly was a necessary reminder, so he didn't try to escape the ache of losing her. Bakewell had experienced it all. Lewis just explained it to him.

Eventually he learned to live without her, realizing that wanting to bring her back was, in itself, the cruelest of acts. If she was in paradise why would she want to come back? Bakewell loved the incisive comparison Lewis had made between Stephen and Lazarus. Who had got the worst of that deal? Lewis asked. Stephen, the first martyr, after Christ's crucifixion, felt the pain of the stone throwers before he died, but had died only once. Lazarus had been raised from the dead – by Christ Himself! Lazarus had to die a second time. Lewis was brilliant; the literate world understood that. Bakewell couldn't kill Katherine a second time with his wants and his needs. The well-wishers had been right all along. She *was* in a better place. He just didn't want to hear it at the time, wanted her *in his place*, wanted her back, with him.

Like Shakespeare's coward, like every bereaved soul, he had died a thousand deaths, dealt with it, lived with it, until it gradually diminished. The little things left behind weren't for him. He learned that quickly. Her jewelry was for Nancy, other remembrances for the boys to keep. He needed nothing, not even photographs. They were flat, no longer satisfied, and couldn't bring her back. He had trouble seeing her face, just as Lewis had, could see the faces of too many others who meant nothing to him. But he could always hear her voice, would remember her voice always, could hear it in kinder moments, tender moments, frustrated moments, even angry moments.

Funny thing was, right now he could see Maggie Walker's face clearly, but had trouble remembering the sound of her voice, could see her sadness the night he left, her tragic face there on the beach under his gaze that last morning, and see her face shining with happiness in the restaurants where they celebrated the renewal of their relationship. He could still see her eyes watching his when he made love to her.

He slept deeply between brief interruptions on the long flight, dreamt actually, as he remembered thousands of little glimpses of his past life: Katherine, Maggie, Nancy, Michael, Andy and Ned, so many others, so many memories.

Sometime during the night, about four in the morning by his watch, somewhere near Figi, he didn't know the actual time, or even the day for that matter, he got up and visited with one of the crew in the kitchen area. The man had been everywhere and they had a long conversation about strange cities around the world. The steward told him of all the cities the crew visited, Johannesburg was the worst. "Jo-burg is the most dangerous city in the world. We only travel as a crew in Jo-burg, all twelve of us together." They talked about other dangerous places the world over. He asked Bakewell if he was going to New Zealand or Australia.

"Port Moresby. I'm taking a little side trip."

"Lordy, mate, that's a stretch. You must have a reason. Don't take a taxi in Moresby for sure. Have someone pick you up at the airport. And whatever you do don't be caught out after dark there."

***

They arrived in Auckland at six in the morning, the rising sun coming up from behind the plane, casting a small shadow far in the distance on the water as they circled to land. The stop was a surprise for Bakewell. He hadn't looked beyond the first page of his ticket, had no idea the stop was even planned. Everyone was required to disembark and he got off to stretch and wander about the airport in New Zealand. The stop lasted only an hour before the plane was cleaned, fueled and readied for the trip on to Brisbane.

Only half the passengers re-boarded, and he moved to the window seat for the last leg to Australia. They served another excellent meal and he enjoyed the food and fresh coffee, as he watched for the first sign of an entirely new continent to appear. The terminal in Auckland had been very clean; the airport at Brisbane was a model for airports the world over. He wandered about for half an hour, mostly watching the strange assortment of foreigners also wandering about. He exchanged some of his cash for Papua New Guinea dollars, a three for one exchange. The bills were made of plastic instead of paper and felt cheap and dirty. They were hard to wrinkle or fold.

By the time his flight departed Brisbane, he was ready to fly again, anxious to see the huge island of New Guinea. New Guinea was split in half now, along what appeared to be 142 degree of longitude. The east half was called Papua New Guinea, the western half, Irian Jaya. Irian Jaya was

Indonesian for New Guinea, and the name and line of demarcation between the countries confused Bakewell.

As they crossed over the top of Australia, continued on north over the ocean, he got a good look of the Great Barrier Reef. It was almost perfectly clear over northern Australia, but as soon as they were north of the Reef, clouds began to form in scattered to broken cumulus the rest of the trip northward.

Port Moresby

Crossing the Great Barrier Reef was fascinating. They were headed back north toward the equator and hot weather. Bakewell stayed glued to the window, observing other smaller reefs and tiny islands until the intermittent clouds covering the ocean below, billowed up around them, causing the plane to make heading changes to avoid the building thunderheads. Bakewell was very tired, but sleep wasn't possible as he continued on toward New Guinea and the Third World. *What had the guy meant about taxis in Port Moresby?* The flight took several hours.

Making the transition from modern airliner to Third World country was a shock, especially after going through the customs area, which was a quaint introduction to Papua New Guinea, with painted murals of happy people, displaying wide, flat-nosed, smiling faces caricaturized along a big wall. The cheerful room left a smile on his face as he passed nervously through to the quarantine area. The people in customs and quarantine were a serious looking bunch that forewarned of the reality ahead. Once through the last doorway and into the terminal, the reality was sudden. Bakewell was appalled by Port Moresby. His Discovery and Travel Channel viewings hadn't prepared him for what he saw. If there was such a thing as a fourth or fifth world, he was there. Not taking a cab or attempting to make it on his own in Moresby was good advice. He was relieved when a short, well-built man of Malay descent waved to get his attention. They shook hands warmly. Father Gerardo offered to take his shoulder bag, but Bakewell insisted on carrying his gear. The priest led him outside past all manner of unshod New Guineans, whose bare feet showed the ravages of a defenseless life – flat, splayed out, many missing toes.

"These folks don't go in much for shoes, do they Father?"

"They have no shoes, Andrew." Father Gerardo said, assuming Bakewell's given name. Bakewell let it go, taking in the landscape, going into shock at the same time. The hills and fields were dusty, arid, and smoke filled, spread out above the parking lot, which sat on a slight rise in the terrain.

"On your left, please." Father Gerardo said, indicating they drove from the right side of the car. Bakewell put his things in the van, and they drove away from the airport and the ocean and the clean air of the Pacific, into a squalid, unbelievably depressing scene of roads pocked with holes as wide as shell craters, where people squatted along cracked curbs and broken sidewalks. Buildings were either dilapidated, cracking block structures, or shacks thrown together with rotting plywood. After another turn to the south they approached a sea of humanity milling about in a large field.

"What is this, Father?" Bakewell managed to ask.

"It is market day."

"I have heard about the market. The Koki Market is in my travel report. It's supposed to be one of the places to visit here in Port Moresby."

"This is not that place. By the way do not go there; it isn't safe. There have been many incidents."

"Incidents?"

"Yes. It's not safe for you. This is not the Koki Market. Koki is by the sea, near Ela Beach. This is a different market. They come here to sell their vegetables." He pulled the shuddering van to the curb, where it rattled and vibrated over the rough running engine, leaving Bakewell only a yard from the onlookers who stared at him with malevolent faces and strangely vacant eyes. Slightly ahead was another ancient, dust-covered van. There were two men inside, making slow progress, little more than walking speed. On the side of the vehicle, barely readable under the thick dust *Police* had been stenciled. The men inside the vehicle looked like the people huddled in the market area. The market was just a field. There were a few posts that once supported some sort of roof or shelter, alone and askew, leaning crazily; forlorn reminders of better times, or signifying nothing at all. A few poles, supported warped, sloping plywood that offered little protection, the plywood hanging down at the corners, waiting for a strong wind to lift it off and send it sailing, Frisbee-like, wooden shrapnels capable of decapitation.

"They aren't much for clothes," Bakewell said, checking to see if he could find his voice. He was frightened by the angry and insolent look of the masses before him. His throat was dry and he wasn't sure he could talk without faltering. He was still in shock and his remark sounded rude. He hadn't meant it that way. Trying again he added, "My God Father, I've never seen so many people in so much need." The people were wearing shorts and tee shirts, mostly in dark shades, maroon or purple, or they were so dirty the color was unrecognizable. Almost all of them were barefoot. A few wore flip-flops in garish shades of red, lime green and international orange. Bakewell guessed the cheap sandals were a marginal indication of affluence.

"We have a lot of rascal activity here in Port Moresby." Fr. Gerardo said.

"Rascal activity?"

"Yes. It's what they call it when they break into our college, or when we are attacked. The police can't do much about it. We have been attacked three times in the past few months. The last time they shot two of our brothers."

The sinking feeling in Bakewell's stomach was changing to a churning fear. He couldn't ask the priest what happened to the two seminarians. His mind was racing. He was the only white man in any direction, surrounded by thousands of tribal people, hungry and wasted. He doubted they put much value on life, not the life he observed – they were starving and dying in the streets. He wanted to close his window despite the oppressive heat. After they left, Father Gerardo drove up a hill past the police academy, which offered some relief from the intimidating crowds below. Next to the police academy was a prison where he saw young men in prison rags working in the fields. Any lessening in the hostile environment passed. Bakewell noticed most of the prisoners were very young, probably in their teens. By the time these men were in their twenties they would be hardened criminals, smart enough to stay out of prison.

They drove up a long low hillside where the Bomana Cemetery appeared. The cemetery was listed in Bakewell's Weissmann's as a "must see." As he looked through the cracked, dusty windshield at the neatly cut grass in the historical cemetery, where so many Allied dead were buried, Father Gerardo interrupted his thoughts and said, "Do not go to the cemetery, Andrew. It's too dangerous. There have been many incidents."

Don't go to the cemetery. Don't go to Koki Market. What was Weissmann thinking? What am I doing here? What the hell am I going to do out here in this cruel, inhospitable place? He wanted to go back to the airport.

They came to a dirt road where clouds of dust billowed up, and Father Gerardo made a groaning sound, pointing to the dust. "It is good we came this way. If we had come the other way we would have been in all that dust. It is good we have taken the long way around."

"Why is there so much smoke everywhere, Father?"

"I don't know why they do it, but the people burn the grass."

"It stinks and it's a health hazard."

"Yes. Health isn't much of a consideration out here."

"How many in Port Moresby, Father?"

"About two hundred thousand. Most of them are out of work, at least a hundred thousand anyway. Every year more come in from the outside, always more are coming. They come to the city looking for prosperity, a better life. Life is very bleak for these people."

"I'll say." Bakewell was finding his voice again, wondering why the native people would leave their villages to become squatters, wondering why there was no pipeline of communication to alert them to what they were coming to, wondering where he would be spending the next few days himself. The smoke was terrible. There was no breeze. The smoke hung over the land.

The priest interrupted Bakewell's thoughts again, explaining they were coming to a place called the Central Theological Institute. He called it the CTI. They could see it in the distance. Father drove down the hill and turned onto the property. It was a large compound with many dormitories and a big library, the walls adorned with tall stick figure art. There were several aged chapels for the various denominations within the grounds. There was also a central church just above the library on the hilltop where all attended Mass on Sundays. There were signs along the roadway, delineating various orders: Dominicans, Marists, one for the Diocesan seminarians, even the

Jesuits – Bakewell wondered what the intellectual Jesuits were doing in such an inhospitable place. At nearly the end of the road, the Franciscan College was perched on a ridge top, surrounded by a heavy steel fence with razor wire on top. It was a prison in reverse, more like a modern fort, and just beyond the Franciscan College was a small Carmelite Monastery, where the road ended and the land became steep, overlooking a flat valley.

They turned into the tiny compound to a small courtyard, surrounded by block buildings with galvanized rain roofs like those on the Eastern Shore of Mobile Bay. When they got out of the van, Bakewell noticed a heavy lock dangling ominously from the gate latch.

Father called to several people, introducing Bakewell to the young men before showing him to his room. The room was large with a high ceiling; his bed was a hospital gurney, still on wheels, with a thin mattress. There was a set of carefully washed sheets neatly tucked, with a small blanket folded at the foot and two small pillows.

"It actually gets chilly late in the night," the priest said. He showed him a private bathroom. Bakewell put his pack on the large desk. "This will do very nicely Father, I hope I'm not putting someone out."

"Not at all, we are happy to have visitors. You will be a curiosity here among our seminarians. They will enjoy you very much. You are welcome to join us for vespers."

"What time is vespers?"

"Sikis," excuse me. "Six. You are also welcome to pray with us anytime."

"Thank you Father." Bakewell suspected he wouldn't miss any opportunity to pray.

"I will leave you now. You are very tired."

Bakewell looked at his watch. "It's about two in the morning in St. Louis. I've been traveling for more than thirty hours now."

The priest nodded knowingly and left. Bakewell evaluated his surroundings. There was a large closeted wardrobe and a substantial desk and chair. He guessed he was probably putting someone from the college out of a private room. The Spartan room, somber and depressing, would be a virtual palace to the population he had passed on the way up. He opened the valve on the shower and let the water run to see what color it was. It was only a leaky trickle, but clear. The floor was beyond cleaning with layers of black calcification that had probably been recently scrubbed. It looked worse that it was. Bakewell stripped down to his flip flops, not wanting his feet to touch the shower floor, stepped under the cool water, careful not to let it get in his mouth.

He took a long shower and changed to clean underwear and laid down on the gurney and slept for several hours, waking to a setting sun, surprised to learn it was just six in the evening. It could have been sunrise or sunset. He had no idea which direction he was facing. He walked down to the little chapel and found they were just starting. Inside the chapel were seven brothers arranged around the room. A center chair, facing the altar at the back of the small room was vacant. Bakewell correctly suspected it was for him. They took turns reading from prayer books, one of which a young man in traditional brown habit came and opened for him, carefully locating the pages to be used. All prayers were in English.

When vespers were over they dispersed quickly. Bakewell wandered out onto the ridge top, which he discovered faced west. He stood a few meters from one of the young seminarians who appeared lost in thought. Bakewell was lost in his own thoughts as he contemplated the scene before him and tried to remember the prayers they had recited. Below were barren fields, barely visible in the fading twilight with a backdrop of dark vegetation about a quarter mile off.

They were close to the equator, less than ten degrees south; Bakewell soon learned the days were nearly twelve hours long twelve months of the year: sunrise at six, sunset at six, with only a few minutes variation. It was peaceful, despite the hunger and need and suffering and pathetic plight of the people that lay only a few hundred yards off below them in the smoky haze. At first he thought it ironic, their situation, but quickly realized these men were here, living in relative comfort, to study theology and to learn to minister to the needs of the masses surrounding them. There was no irony, no conflict. This place they referred to as a college was little more than a series of outbuildings, but it was palatial to what awaited them after ordination. They would soon dedicate their lives to comforting, aiding and ministering to the needs of the same people breaking in at night, the same people who posed such a threat to their peace and their safety. *Well man, you've arrived. You're in the vineyard.* It was humbling.

He prayed and reflected as he stared off into the distance, squinting into the setting sun. His prayers were interrupted by thoughts of places from his past, where it snowed and rained and the weather was wet and cold, and he was absorbed, mesmerized by the contrast with this strange, arid, distant part of the world.

When it was time for dinner, a shy young man came and told him to join them. He met the seminarians as he moved about the dining area. They were very shy, careful not to approach him, with the exception of the young man he had spoken with on the phone the month before. He was called Theo, pronounced Tay-oh. Each seminarian gave Bakewell an embarrassed nod from a distance when they made eye contact. When addressed by the white man from America, they smiled broadly but had little to say. Bakewell heard the names of most of them that first evening and forgot most. Later, Father Jonas came in as the buffet opened and they lined up. Fr. Jonas was Irish, and despite years in the islands, still retained a heavy brogue. Bakewell learned from the friars that Jonas spent his days at the AIDS clinic, a bleak and depressing place in Gordons, a suburb of Port Moresby. Fr. Jonas was ten years older than Bakewell, but he was a powerful man, physically fit to a hardened condition. Shaking his hand felt like taking the grip of a piece of statuary and the man looked like he could handle himself. Bakewell felt a strange tension between himself and Fr. Jonas.

Later in the evening, Bakewell used the phone, to call America. It was yesterday in the morning in America. He spoke briefly with Nancy, assured her he was fine, told her to pass the word. The second call was to "Corporate Office." They patched him through to a stranger. Bakewell spoke definitively, notifying them of his plans, assured them he would be on location when the time came. There had been a tragedy the week before; a boat lost at sea. The man asked about the people that had disappeared in the boat, which had been headed for the Carterets, and Bakewell told him what little he knew. He left them no options, and no phone number at which he could be reached, although he suspected they might find some way to trace the phone call. He told them he would call back with a location where he could be reached when they arrived, said he intended to meet them on arrival. That was it.

In the days that followed Bakewell learned to put a name with each face, listened attentively, when they were together in the dining area where they spoke the wonderful pidgin language called Tok Pisin. It was the language of all of Papua New Guinea. They came from many places within the island country, where there were hundreds of dialects, Tok Pisin pulled the languages together, was the universal common tongue. Fr. Gerardo required them to speak English at gatherings, mealtimes, prayer service, or when they addressed the group, but they reverted to pidgin when they became animated and wanted to emphasize a point or describe something they couldn't keep up with in English. Fr. Gerardo smiled tolerantly at these times, raised an eye at the culprit, who would switch back and start over in English.

Bakewell asked Father if they couldn't all speak pidgin so he might learn to recognize some of the words. He was anxious to develop an understanding of Tok Pisin. He knew he would need every word in the complicated days ahead, knew his survival would be jeopardized even more without an understanding of the pidgin language. During these animated, humorous mealtimes Bakewell joined in, tried a few words, and laughed along with them, appreciating the need for laughter and lighter moments, surrounded as they were by such oppressive sadness.

He made arrangements to go into Port Moresby with a young seminarian from Rabaul. Rabaul was up in New Britain, and like Port Moresby, held a fascination for Bakewell. Rabaul was a place of the history books, a mysterious place he had read about, the infamous stronghold of the Japanese, during the fight for the Solomons. After the fall of Rabaul, Bakewell's father had been stationed there briefly.

During the early months of the Pacific War, the Japanese launched everything from Rabaul. For months they poured men and machinery down The Slot, a narrow watercourse amid the Solomons, to Henderson Field. Henderson was 600 miles to the southeast on Guadalcanal, became the first great flashpoint of the war. After the war, New Britain, like New Ireland, had been taken over by colonial administrators, but that was fifty years ago. It was now an island possession of Papua New Guinea, nearly a thousand miles north of Port Moresby.

Bakewell toured with the seminarian from Rabaul and together they explored Port Moresby, first the industrial area of Gordons on their way in, then the residential area of Oholo, upscale Waigani, overpopulated Ela Beach, where crowds swept over the dusty terrain just yards distant from the beautiful gulf. It appeared nobody ever got in the water, despite the fact the beach was magnificent. They passed Erima and Port Moresby Town, hitting the spots recommended by Weissmanns, but, at Father Gerardo's request, skipped the Koki Market and the Bomana cemetery. Later, despite the warnings, Bakewell went to the cemetery. His father had served with many men during the war and some of them were buried there. He would have felt cowardly, like he disgraced their memory if he hadn't gone.

They went to the botanical gardens one afternoon. The garden was famous for the largest collection of orchids in the world. There were over three thousand on display. They took a slow walk through a man made, carefully maintained tropical rain forest, which highlighted the garden, where Bakewell lingered, taking time to study the trees, foliage and especially the understory, observing as many features as he could, knowing he would need all the knowledge he could garner if he was to survive in the bush. Francis, the young seminarian, was noticeably curious about Bakewell's interest in the rain forest, and Bakewell jokingly told him he might want to camp out in the jungle sometime.

"Ah, Andy, you won't like it. It is too much bugs and crawly tings." The tribal people couldn't pronounce the "h" behind any "t."

"Tok Pisin, Francis, we must use the language of Tok Pisin."

Bakewell asked Francis endless questions, most of which began, "How do you say..." requiring translation. They finished the day in a rather dingy restaurant where they ate flimsy sandwiches and drank several bottles of purified water. Bakewell couldn't get enough water. The humidity in Moresby was less than 20 percent. On the second day of adventure they stopped at a large grocery store right at dusk. As they were crossing the parking lot, Francis assured him it would be all right. Bakewell watched the gentle young man cross the crowded lot amidst small gatherings of people bent on rapid inebriation. He would accompany the young man no matter how menacing it felt. *If you're willing to go in there I'm right behind you, kid.* The building was large, deep and low-ceilinged. Bakewell was immediately claustrophobic. He was also the only white man in the building. It was crowded with people, a nightmare of a place, like something he would have encountered in the deepest section of the worst American ghetto.

Wherever they moved, Bakewell was careful to make eye contact and nod at the dark faces, attempting to return each look. They bought about 50 dollars worth of groceries and paid for it in PNG currency: kina.

Bakewell insisted Francis pick everything, but when the young man started to go for staples only Bakewell said, "No man, let's get something special, something that is not available every day." They bought two cases of soda, several bars of chocolate, two gallons of ice cream, and as they were leaving, much to Bakewell's amusement, a bottle of scotch whiskey. Francis kept referring to it as "haat stuff," which Bakewell didn't understand until he saw him come out of the adjoining liquor store holding the hard stuff.

On the fifth day Fr. Gerardo drove him back out to the airport. Bakewell had made arrangements to fly out to Buka. Before he set off on his second adventure, Bakewell asked the priest for his blessing.

"You will do well, Andy. You are a man who makes friends easily, but I am happy to give you my blessing," Father Gerardo said, placing his hand on Bakewell's head, repeating the comforting words before he left for Buka.

Buka

The flight to Buka was just under two hours on an aging Fokker jet in need of paint, and in the service of Air Niugini, pronounced, "Air New Guinea." The obvious pronunciation had escaped Bakewell, to the great amusement of his new friend Francis. The flying was done by two aging Caucasians. Bakewell suspected the men had been forcefully retired in the civilized world. Now they plied their talents piloting an old plane across the Solomon Sea, where towering cumulus, emerging to thunderhead status in the saturated air, often assumed massive proportions and the power to smite the most powerful craft from the sky. They handled the tired plane with skill, putting it on the rough runway without mishap. The service had been good, the flight attendants pleasant and solicitous, and everything worked well but the toilet, which was unusable. The runway had recently been oiled, appeared to have been extended. Upon arrival Bakewell walked down a ladder like the one he'd climbed up from the ramp in Port Moresby.

The Third World again. Bakewell took in the terminal building and the greenery beyond. The wait was minimal. He was relieved. He had no desire to mill about in the PNG stronghold amidst a country of angry revolutionaries and kept to the nearby terminal, treated to a breeze that took the scorch out of the sun's midday rays while he studied his map of Buka and Bougainville.

Hendry Saris found him by the terminal building, which was undergoing expansion. Fr. Hendry was an email acquaintance of Fr. Gerardo's and had come by prior arrangement. He came a few minutes after the plane's arrival. Bakewell assumed he'd heard the plane coming in.

"Ah, Mr. Bakewell, you needn't have described yourself," he said.

"I can see that now, Father." With the exception of the man shaking his hand, Bakewell suspected he was the only other white man on Buka. He had foolishly described his appearance down to the backpack he carried. He gave Fr. Hendry the used GPS Fr. Gerardo had sent out to Buka, a gift from a "rich American," who had sent it at Fr. Hendry's request, and hopefully, "To prevent anymore lost-at-sea accidents.

The priest came from the mission called Hahela. Buka Town was called Sohano and looked like a small American ghetto transplanted to paradise. The trip through Buka Town revealed a hospital and post office and several stores, many of which were islander owned, to Fr. Saris' satisfaction. They passed a wharf where they could see across the Passage, to the island of Bougainville, a few hundred yards distant. The bigger island didn't look foreboding. From a distance it was another island paradise, smelling of flowers and fresh sea breeze, which cleared the air of human odors. There was a lot of coastal shipping and many barges were tied up against the wharf.

"The tensions have settled down a bit. I think you will be safe. We use *Tensions* for the ugliness between Papua New Guinea and the BRA. They are suspended by the ceasefire that is now in place."

Fr. Hendry was from Belgium. Once the sun went down he was happy for Bakewell's company. They spoke for several hours about Europe and America, his early calling to the priesthood and his desire to go out to the islands. They had a mutual friend in Fr. Springer at the Provincial House in San Francisco, where Bakewell had commenced his research, and first learned the names of the people he was meeting in the Solomons. Fr. Hendry was full of questions of his own, which Bakewell answered honestly, skirting the true purpose of his visit. His bedroom was different from the room he had at the seminary, with pleasant ventilation and a good screening, which the priest called "mosquito gauze." The mosquitoes were bad after dark, which came at six again. They were just five clicks below the equator, malaria a constant threat. Bakewell couldn't own enough bug spray, relied on the tablets Neville prescribed.

Fr. Hendry had duties to attend and left Bakewell free to wander about among a less menacing population of islanders, which he described as, "fine and gentle people."

Bougainvillians have dark visages – they are the darkest of all the Melanesian people – with burning black eyes that create fearful expressions, but changed to smiling, happy countenances when replying to a friendly word or gesture. Bakewell was relieved to see their faces brighten. They responded warmly to "the bigpela white man," when he went down to the wharf and attempted conversation with several men who had long, narrow, powered boats, which they called canoes. Bakewell spoke their happy language with limited success and to their great amusement. They mimicked his attempt to communicate in pidgin, were very animated, nodding with laughter. There were good-natured misunderstandings that got set right with enough words and gestures and after half an hour Bakewell felt comfortable among them. He knew an easy, comfortable relationship would be a prerequisite to any success on the mission ahead. Success was a word he'd been substituting for survival. His brief visit was designed to give him some small hope he might get along in the land of Tok Pisin. And he would get better at the language if he was immersed in it.

He enjoyed trying to speak Tok Pisin, but it bothered him to learn there was so much difference between certain words. Like all pidgin, Tok Pisin had developed over generations into another language. Time was *taim* and *yumi* meant you and me, *save* meant savvy and was pronounced the same, *wonem* for want and what, too much and how much were *tumas* and *hamas,* simple enough, but *long* meant everything imaginable, and occurred in most every sentence. *Lik lik* meant small, as in lik lik *sak (shark)*, *bigpela* meant large as in bigpela *puk puk,* which was crocodile, and there were many of those in the rivers. Bakewell warmed to learning the congenial language, but, despite his cheery reception, Bougainville was still a strange and eerie place just across the water.

***

Although he was by nature a loner, especially in the wilderness, it was obvious he couldn't make it unescorted on the huge island. He needed a guide. On the third day he found his man, Joel Nasali, a veteran of the fighting, wounded in '94, ironically the day before the first ceasefire. At the time he had been a policeman caught in a night ambush. Now at thirty-five, Joel had three bullet wounds and displayed an equal number of machete gashes on his closely shaven head. The wounds resembled fine dueling scars, badly misplaced, but very straight and deep. Joel was finished with the violence, had seen too much, had seen his family suffer too many deprivations, the sort of thing private citizens always suffer in the midst of a civil war. Joel's family had "gone bush" and survived on the traditional tribal foods for months during one period of the hostilities. It had been a difficult time. Most of the island people were used to the convenience of packaged goods that now invaded and littered the islands. It had been a great trial to live off the land. Bakewell wondered how his own countrymen would have fared, if forced to return to the diet of pre-settlement America.

Joel had gotten his warrior credentials the old fashioned way, he had earned them: violent skills acquired amidst real violence, not in a boot camp. He was a trained and hardened man who, although gentle and quiet, had experienced the real thing. Joel had practiced combat by trial, including hand-to-hand combat; had taken life and felt it ooze from the body he was forced to touch. Bakewell listened carefully to the descriptions extracted from this tall, unobtrusive man. Joel referred to all the actions he had been involved in as "incidents," and he had been involved in seven different incidents over the years. These brief conversations about action were the only time they communicated in English. Bakewell didn't want to miss any details. Joel was a shy man who had a habit of rubbing his large hand over his unusually small head and face, as if to shield it from the conversation. But through careful questioning, Joel had given his new white friend a thorough description.

They arranged to take his boat down the coast to a place twenty miles below Empress Augusta Bay. The entire trip would be over ninety miles on the "weather coast." Joel agreed to the trip, provided Bakewell accompany him another forty miles further to Kihili, where he could find overland passage on up to Buin. He had family business in Buin and it was a seldom made journey, sometimes years between trips. Buin was a stronghold of the Bougainville Revolutionary Army. The lowest end of the trip would put them at Moila Point, only 7 water miles from the Shortland Islands. The Shortlands were part of another country, the Solomon Islands, and from the Shortlands there was air service going on to Guadalcanal.

In his first week in PNG Bakewell had heard much of the weather coast. It was an adventure he could have lived without, but he had to make the trip, and he had to go by water. The trip was endless in the violent water; the sea took on proportions Bakewell thought would tax a naval destroyer, proportions so terrifying he would have cancelled out if he wasn't constantly aware of his pending death. His mortality steeled him during the worst moments, gave him an edge that allowed for taking greater risks. He told Joel candidly, he would never have attempted the trip without him and never intended to do it again. Joel nodded understandingly as they plowed on, periodically asking if he wanted to take a breather, always with the same, "Bikman, you poret or nogat?"

They made gradual progress southeast, spending their evenings fishing in the surf, avoiding rivers, crocodiles – some significantly large – cooking on the coast, wherever they found a comfortable place to beach the long powered canoe. The Solomon Sea was more like the North Atlantic than the tropical shoreline Bakewell had foolishly imagined. There were no gentle coasts, with quiet "rollers," typical of the soft tropical surf in Hawaii. Instead the water was immense and terrifying nearly every mile, and Bakewell was totally exhausted each night when they finally beached the boat for the last time. On the second day they passed a large compound that sat back away from the coast, barely visible through the foliage. There were several buildings, the place having the look of a fortress, although the jungle was rapidly reclaiming the view. Joel told him he didn't know when exactly the construction had started, but it had been going on for several years, and there had been a flurry of activity in the last months. They stayed out away from the coast. It was hard to see the coast and the buildings in the large swells, but they saw they were being observed by a group gathered on a new concrete pier. The men watching were not native people.

"Bikman, yu poret or nogat?" Joel said over and over again.

"Poret," Bakewell answered affirmatively. He was afraid, but knew they had to continue out away from the coast. They couldn't chance going closer in by the pier. The men on the pier were hard to make out. "Ha mani pela, Joel?" Bakewell asked.

"Sikis." Bakewell nodded. "Solwara long nabis i no save gutpela tumas." Joel didn't like this traveling on the weather coast either; Bakewell nodded and agreed it was dangerous in an expression that sounded like "oi," sometimes and "hoy," others.

Occasionally Joel would raise a white flag, letting it fly in plain view, "So they no shoot us."

There wasn't much talk between the two. Joel had his hands full trying to keep the boat on top the heaving sea. Both men understood the value of silence, neither made idle conversation, but as their time together passed, a mutual respect developed. Occasionally, when they did converse, Joel would speak English, which he spoke clearly. His employer would always respond, "Plis, olgeta taim yu man toktok long Tok Pisin." Encouraging him to stick to the language he was determined to learn military style, the crash-course-method always worked best for Bakewell.

On the third evening they made Kihili at sunset and spent the night in a shantytown. Bakewell would have preferred to sleep out on the coast, but Joel wanted to have the white man he was traveling with secreted away with former comrades. Bakewell knew better than to argue, making the best of a bad situation. He spent a long inhospitable evening, keeping to himself in impoverished accommodations.

They left the next morning at first light. Joel took him out where they could get a "loklok" across the straight to the Shortlands that were surrounded by many smaller islands. They could also see the much bigger island of Choiseul. Bakewell asked Joel "hamas" trouble it was to go across the border. "Veri dangerous for bikpela with white skin," but the island people from Choiseul and the Shortlands did it all the time. "It be quite different for a white man to make such a journey," Joel said. The international border was violated by the people of PNG and the Solomons with impunity because the violators were indigenous people. It would be different for a white man, "much veri dangerous."

There was an airport on Balalai, one of the smallest of the Shortland Islands, inside the Solomon chain. It was only a short canoe trip from the tip of Bougainville. If he succeeded in getting this far south on Bougainville, Bakewell wanted to cross over to a place no longer inside PNG. He believed he could get a flight there that would take him down southeast away from the trouble. Fr. Hendry had told him of several people that had made the very journey. Two Italians had traveled from Port Moresby to Buka and then all the way to Guadalcanal, before returning to Brisbane. *There was always a chance.*

They turned back to the northwest without ever getting more than five miles out into the sea. If anything, the water seemed calmer near the Shortlands. On the way back Bakewell was once more petrified by the power of the water, which swelled so high they often lost sight of the shore. When they did, he felt lost in the middle of the sea, was always relieved to catch site of the shore again. When he asked Joel if he had ever been in rougher seas, Joel confided he had made many long trips as a child with his father, saying they often went at night, in rougher weather, carrying large quantities of supplies, adding the canoe handled much better when heavily weighted with supplies. Bakewell suggested they stop along the beach and shovel in half a ton of sand before they ventured out the next time. They returned the way they'd gone down, allowing another view of the coast above and below the fortress.

Contrasting with the near catastrophic days on the water, they spent beautifully serene evenings, sleeping under netting and a canopy of vegetation where Joel selected trees devoid of mature coconuts, which dropped like cannon balls on the unsuspecting. The bush quieted the surf, allowed for whispered conversation, a relief from the shouting of the day. It also allowed them to listen to the peaceful sound of water meeting land and catch the breeze which moved the smaller leaves around them. The movement of air brought the smell of frangipani and other heavenly odors that woke Bakewell during the night. Originally he wanted to sleep on the coast where they could see the stars. The beach was soft and yielding and comfortable to recline on, reminding him of the gravel bars of his youth and so many peaceful nights on the streams of Missouri, but it held moisture which wet his bag and made for miserable three o'clock urinations amid a fog of insects.

Even in a tropical paradise, under skies filled with stars, cooled by ocean breezes scented with the odors of paradise, it was impossible to enjoy anything the nights provided, amid the ever present danger awaiting, and Bakewell was filled with apprehension, much like the marines of WWII had been a lifetime before, spending similar nights filled with trepidation before the next day's action. The stress of hours on the water left him ragged, exhausted mentally and sore physically, hoping for the relief of deep sleep, but it wasn't to be. There were always the fearful awakenings, during the long twelve hour nights, and they plagued him just as they had before.

On the second night going west they were protected by a small cape, Gazelle Harbor, where the water calmed. It was lowland and very wet in places, and there was no place to camp. Joel took them to a small village where there were only about thirty people, gentle and friendly who gave them food. They didn't need it, but Joel indicated they take gratefully. The people were afraid of the PNG and the BRA, but mostly feared the unknown. They were all smiles for Joel and the "Bikman white visitor." They weren't Joel's people but they knew many people in common. It was a pleasant place and a pleasant relief and when the weather turned bad after dark, they were invited in and slept comfortably under a thatched roof. When they left in the morning it was to hands waving and calls of encouragement from the beach.

When they finally returned to Buka, after seven days on the coast, Bakewell and Joel made a pact and shook hands at the dock where he surprised the former soldier with a gift of 2000 kina.

Bush Celebration

"This is my blood, which will be shed for you... and for the forgiveness of sins...Do this in remembrance of me." Fr. Hendry spoke the words as he held the small chalice up over the wooden table, and through the mystery of Divine Concomitance, both the bread and the wine he consecrated had miraculously become the body and blood of Christ – the mystery of the "Real Presence."

The priest said Mass in English, for Bakewell's benefit. Fr. Hendry traveled throughout Buka to say Mass and minister to his flock. The parishioners of the tiny Oceanic hamlet understood English. The Church called the daily service the *Holy Sacrifice of the Mass*, and it was being repeated at the same moment in thousands of churches that shared the same time zone from Tasmania to the Kamchatka Peninsula. It was half past eight in the morning on Buka, still yesterday in St. Louis. Bakewell took great comfort in knowing God was present in the little building, that he could find a place to practice his faith 11,000 miles from home.

There was an opening in the church without a door, and a narrow aisle led 20 feet down to the table in front. On each side were benches, crudely fashioned, eight feet long. The attendees knelt on the dirt floor during the consecration, overhead a thatched roof kept them dry. There were threads of fronds hanging from the thatched roof overhead, some long, dangling, others rolled into tight curls as they dried. The longer tentacle-like strands touched his head as he went forward with eleven other parishioners to receive the Eucharist. He returned to his place to pray silently for grace and for courage and inspiration. Subconsciously he hoped for some luck. The future was very gray, very dark in his mind and in his imagination.

They were at the top of Buka, about 25 miles from the passage in a direct line, looking out on the Pacific, but the road followed the coast and was a long day's travel on foot. Bakewell had asked to go along because he wanted to see the bush a second time and get another reading on the people and the reception they might afford a white man. Several times when they stopped, Hendry had let him introduce himself to the people in order to practice his limited language skill.

Travel was primitive on Buka. In Port Moresby there were enormous potholes in the street. On Buka there was mud, especially under the vegetation where sunlight was blocked by the jungle canopy. After showers and dinner at Hahala Mission, they enjoyed a quiet evening next to a hurricane lamp talking about their pasts. Bakewell was very interested in the world war now that he had come so far. He learned the names of several priests who had been stationed there when the Japanese invaded the islands.

***

Fr. Hendry didn't hide his concern about Bakewell's arduous trip down the coast, thought it was ill advised. More as a peace offering than out of any curiosity, Bakewell agreed to accompany him on his sojourn north to the top of the island. He hadn't meant to worry the man, and stayed two additional days on Buka, waiting for the plane that would take him back to Port Moresby. He spent the following day with Fr. Hendry explaining the vagaries of the complicated GPS. The rest of the time he spent in his room, discouraged by his exhaustion, listening to the surf and the sound of people enjoying a day off.

Fr. Hendry gave Bakewell his blessing before he departed Tuesday morning. Bakewell was extremely grateful for his hospitality and the information he had been able to gather through his good offices. He told Fr. Hendry he was off on another journey down the coast. This time he intended to take the north coast, going down the island via the quieter waters on the north side where the weather and the ocean were calmer and more hospitable, in order to visit Kieta, where they had just reopened to airline traffic between Bougainville and Port Moresby. The tentative peace was working. The priest asked him to reconsider. There had been too many needless deaths and far too much violence. Bakewell told him he felt invigorated, refreshed, despite his all too apparent condition and the man refused to take issue. Bakewell left the parish house and walked back to Buka Town. Later that afternoon Joel took him to the airport.

He took his seat on the Fokker jet at midday, getting a window seat again, from where he carefully noted the inhospitable jungle below, through openings in the ever-present cumulous layer, before departing the island chain to the south again for Port Moresby.

Bakewell got back to Port Moresby late in the afternoon and passed through customs amidst the raggedly dressed confusion. His passport was studied carefully before he passed on to quarantine, where he got a tough once-over from an angry-eyed woman with a gloomy, foreboding disposition. As soon as he made the lobby, he called Fr. Gerardo for a ride back out to the seminary grounds. While he waited, he went into a restroom and re-taped his passport to his abdomen, wishing he had shaved it before he left Buka.

Father Gerardo sent Father Jonas in his stead. Jonas arrived in his derelict little pickup, looking interrupted and, on the way back to the CTI, stopped to finish his workday at the clinic. Bakewell knew he was imposing on the man, and waited in a lobby, not wishing to see what might lay beyond. He was very tired from the week on the water, amazed at how the trip had jaded him, wondered how many days it would take to recover, if recovery was on the agenda. It was all he could do to stay awake while Jonas concluded another heroic day. When Jonas finally came back out, he looked preoccupied and just as tired as Bakewell, which was unusual. Jonas was a man of stamina, lean, powerful, took his health regimen seriously, working out each day, often concluding with miles around the dirt track below the college on an old fashioned balloon-tired bicycle.

They got in the little car and started for the CTI grounds where the Franciscan College sat high on the ridge at the rear of the property. It was dark, a bad time to be out in Port Moresby. They talked quietly to keep their minds occupied. Just before coming to Bomana, they slowed at a crossing in a bottom near a dry creek where people were milling about in the heavily damaged street. The small crowd stood on the better sections of pavement blocking the way.

"This is no good," Jonas said quietly. "I'm afraid they're rascals."

"Aw shit," was all Bakewell could manage.

Jonas slowed the car as the men in the street closed in, more appearing around the car from the darkness. They were quickly surrounded. There was no shouting, just a menacing low tone of conversation that Bakewell couldn't make out. A man little more than twenty looked in the window and spoke contemptibly to Jonas as the car came to a rolling stop.

"Sanap, Bikman!"

"What's up then? Wanem wan?" The priest said in a calming voice, heavy with Irish brogue. He stepped up out of the little truck.

"Opim dua!"

"Em i orait." Father said, continuing in the calm voice. "*Easy then, everybody*. Open your door and step out slowly Mr. Bakewell. Do what they say."

Bakewell stepped out into the night and the smoke and the stench of the trash in the street and tried not to look at the people around the car, but they were in his face as soon as he stood up. He put up his hands like a holdup victim and the man closest to him, who was younger than his own sons, nodded his assent at the submissive gesture. There was excitement in their voices, the talk was fast, many talking at once. Some of it was tribal tongue, but Bakewell was able to understand Fr. Jonas, who kept his voice level, speaking Tok Pisin pleasantly. He asked them what they wanted.

"Hamas moni yu gat?"

"Yumi gat amas moni, Andy? Give it to them please." His voice was almost singsong, very soft.

Bakewell looked at the young men around him. They were in tee shirts and shorts; no shoes. Mostly they wore rags. He reached into his pocket and pulled his last five hundred kina note from his pocket and gave it to the nearest man, who ripped it from his grasp. His wallet and credit cards were taped to the bottom of a metal cabinet drawer in his room at the college. Bakewell carried only his passport and cash when he left for Bougainville, hoping he wouldn't need anything else for the secret journey inside Papua New Guinea. They glared at him from every direction. He reached into his pockets very slowly and pulled them inside out. He had only the key for his room and a sweat stained handkerchief.

He was prepared to give them anything but the pack in the back seat of the truck, which held his sleeping bag and a mummy tent. There were very few things he really wanted to hold onto in the months before he died, what was in the backpack represented most. The thought of dying loomed closer now in the street. As soon as he remembered he was going to die, he remembered what was ahead on Bougainville and what was waiting after that… if he survived. It was all to do with death. He was in the state of grace, and, although it was a nasty place to hit the ground, was as ready as he would ever be. It might be quicker than a hospital room. He hoped he would be shot from the front, he didn't want to go down with a bullet in his spine, one that might leave him crippled in the street for hours.

"Yu gat ol wonem samting tu? Kisim i kam antap." The words were simple enough to follow. They wanted him to give them more. He smiled at the young man and shook his head. There was another man, older and taller, just behind the two in his face. He held a very battered gun. It was a pump shotgun. Bakewell had an idea.

"Is that a Remington?" he said in a friendly voice, "A Model 31?"

The man looked confused at first, recognized what was being asked, looked down at his gun with pride.

"A Model 31, is it?"

The man nodded.

"It is a fine gun. I own this veri gun myself," he said, rolling the "r" in "veri" very hard. Bakewell kept nodding his head in a friendly gesture. On the other side of the car there was much conversation, indecipherable. Jonas was speaking Tok Pisin, returning answer for question as fast as the rascals came at him. One man rummaged inside the car behind Bakewell, while others became interested in Bakewell's conversation. Then the backpack came out of the car and Bakewell moved toward the man with the gun who brought it up quickly, menacing him as they faced off.

"Iumi wanem mak deal?" Bakewell leaned toward the man with the gun, pointed to his pack. The man's eyes followed.

"What are you doing there?" Fr. Jonas asked. There was alarm in his voice for the first time.

"Father, it is important that I keep the backpack. Tell this man I want to bargain with him. I have more to offer him than he will get from the pack."

"It's not a good idea right now. Just let them have it please. You can get another." Jonas was back into the sing-song, devil-may-care rhythm of before.

"Not in time, Father. Tell him I want to bargain. Tell him the stuff in the pack is for cold weather. He doesn't need it out here. Say I will give him something he can better use out here."

"What would that be?" There was irritation in Jonas' voice.

"I don't know. Think of something. Whatever you come up with, I'll give my word on. I will send it to him. Get his address."

"His address! He's not giving you his address, man!" Fr. Jonas was indignant, incredulous. "More than likely he hasn't one, probably Port Moresby would do."

The crowd was intrigued by the sharp tone Jonas' voice. They tried to follow the priest's English. Bakewell was desperate to keep the pack. He continued to hold his hands up, but he leaned toward the older man again. "I nap yu tokim mi amas dis pak i is worth, savvy?" he mixed a little English in when he ran out of words.

"It isn't worth your life." Jonas said, losing patience. He spoke to the others, "This white man, he is not serious, just wants to keep the backpack."

"Father, tell them I am prepared to die for the pack. It is that important. It means nothing to them, but it is *big medicine* to me." There was a confusing moment as they digested Bakewell's statement.

"What kind of big medicine is it," the man with the gun asked. He spoke perfect English.

"My dead wife gave it to me. In it is my bed. She said I should never let it go. It was her final request before she died. She said whenever I was out in the wilderness, I should sleep in it and she would know I was warm and safe. It is for very cold weather. I can't give it up."

"Please don't go there, Andy. This isn't a good idea. Let them have what they want."

"Where is this wilderness?" the man with the gun said, moving in to look closer, not touching the pack.

"In the Rocky Mountains of the American west."

"Where?"

"Montana."

"I have heard of this Montana. It is a country?"

"A very beautiful country, like Papua New Guinea."

"I may want to go to Montana. I will need this pack then."

"The pack is big medicine; it contains a sleeping bag, veri special," again rolling the "r" awkwardly. "When I am in this sleeping bag, I can feel my wife around me. Her spirit is all around the bag. Her spirit talks to me when I sleep. Her spirit says she will take care of me. She says no one will ever sleep in this bag but me only." He tied the words together slowly, improvising as he went, emphasizing the word spirit each time.

"Andy, don't say anymore. You have made your point." There was encouragement in Jonas' voice, and there was concern in the man's face there in front of him holding the gun.

In an atmosphere of smoke and stench and furtive movements, in what seemed an eternity around the little pickup, the man with the shotgun finally moved, indicating the younger man put the backpack back in the truck. When the man with the pack protested the older one spoke harshly in a tribal tongue neither Jonas nor Bakewell understood. He turned to Bakewell.

"This car of the priest's…" he swung the gun barrel, "It is shit. It is falling apart. Tell him he can keep it. You may keep your pack, but you must take off the leather belt and the fancy shoes and give us also your shirt and your watch."

"Deal," Bakewell said with emphasis. "Give them your shirt and watch, Father. I will buy you a Rolex."

"We do not want anything of the priest's," the man with the gun said. "He is a good man. Tell him to get a better car so we can steal it later."

Bakewell removed belt, shoes and shirt. They disappeared quickly into the crowd.

"There is one other thing you should have," Bakewell said. He moved his hand toward the dashboard of the little truck. The man swung the gun, indicating he get it out. Bakewell reached in and took the ball cap he had been wearing for the past two weeks. "It is from Montana," he tried to give it to the man with the gun, who leaned away when he offered it.

"Does it have a spirit also?"

"No, it is a gift to show my appreciation to a man who is a good thief."

"Oh, Lord," Jonas said.

"Like the good thief who died with Jesus," Bakewell added quickly, offered the hat again. "He received much good medicine from God for his goodness to the Christ who died also next to him."

The man took the hat warily, held it up in the dim light of the burning grassfire nearby, said, "I will accept this gift. Go now. Take this priest of Christ and go."

Bakewell got into the little car wearing only his khaki shorts. Fr. Jonas got in also and tried to start the truck. It had died during the holdup, started after much cranking. Jonas was both furious and amazed at the proceedings.

When they were safely away, Bakewell leaned back and stared up at the ceiling, his nose nearly touching the roof of the little pickup. *I've used the dead wife excuse again, Lew; it worked.*

"Mr. Bakewell, that was reckless," Father Jonas hissed. "They don't usually become violent unless you refuse. You put us at risk. It was uncalled for, man, simply uncalled for."

"I know Father. I am sorry. I have to keep the pack. I am sorry I put you in danger."

"You put us both in danger! He might just have shot you when you leaned toward him so arrogantly."

"You are right," Bakewell sighed. He was exhausted. "But I don't think the gun was loaded."

"You've no way of knowing!"

"You're right. I would like to buy you a drink when we get back to the college, Father."

"We haven't made it yet. What else do you have to bargain with?"

They were passing the military cemetery in Bomana. Under the starlit sky the cemetery had the same serene quality of all military cemeteries, belying the terrible violence that created it. They had only few hundred yards to go.

"Don't stop for anyone else, will you, Father."

Fr. Jonas was silent, seething, frustrated; only his charity held him in check. He wanted to pull Bakewell out of the car and thrash him. In Bakewell's jaded condition they both knew he could do it. When they got back to the College, they were still flushed with adrenaline. They went to the kitchen together and found the "haat stuff" Francis bought on their tour of Port Moresby. Each man took a small jelly jar and poured a few ounces. Fr. Jonas offered his glass reluctantly when Bakewell held his up. They touched glasses in silence and moved to the soft couches next to the worn pool table and stared into the darkness and sipped scotch whiskey.

"What's your purpose out here man?" Jonas' voice was filled with disgust.

"I wonder," Bakewell answered, looking at the ceiling fan. "I ask myself that question often." He rested his head against the rough fabric and listened to the ceiling fan. "I wish I had the purpose in my life that you have in yours, Father. Sometimes I think I am a life without purpose."

"I don't think you've been candid with us. I think you are taking advantage of our hospitality."

"I think I am taking advantage also; but, I am very grateful for what you all have done for me."

"There is something not right about you man, something unsettling. Too many damned questions about Bougainville and learning the language. I fear your purpose among us might well be nefarious."

Nefarious? "You could be right, Father. I'll try not to upset anything. My time left here is very short now."

"Don't do anything that might embarrass us. Our people have great devotion and a wonderful simplicity, and they don't understand the way Americans think. You people are too full of deception. You have too much money, too much of everything. Don't betray their trust."

"I would do nothing to betray you…or them. I promise you that."

They finished their drinks in silence, later separated on the sidewalk, Fr. Jonas going across the compound to his room. Bakewell watched him go, almost envied him, despite the gravity of his work. He looked up at a waning gibbous moon, reflected for a full minute before he went to his room.

It was a very welcome room now, had taken on the appearance of a fine accommodation. He fell onto the wobbly gurney as the adrenaline finally gave way to a fatigue so oppressive it pushed him down into the thin mattress. He could feel the steel through the cloth. His mind, numbed by the long day, was still electric with so many thoughts of what had taken place on Buka and Bougainville. The word nefarious had set off other memories of Denny, children and home, and his other life that was gone, thousands of miles in the past. And there were memories of the big island, the violent island that looked so beautiful beneath the plane on departure. It would be waiting for his return.

It was impossible to sort out, all mixed together: ugliness, beauty, stench, fragrance, peace, shouting, tranquility and the supposed and proposed violence of his future visit. He was living a fiction, living a spy novel, and it was becoming an epic, a blearying stream of disconnected moments, movements. When he tried to focus on one event, too many others interrupted; but, there was a constant worrisome theme to his thoughts: he couldn't go back out there, put himself into a crazy, incomprehensibly dangerous situation, unless he could focus on one thing at a time. It all seemed to be coming at once.

He was elated to have survived with the pack, knew he had been lucky, so close to death, tried to think through it clearly again, but it didn't work. *Get your focus back! You're a dead man if you can't focus.*

Exhausted from boating on the violent coast, from the camping and living out of a pack in the bush, he was too tired to raise his head. *Please God, don't let them come for me early. I'm not ready. I need time to think. I need to prepare, and I need to recover. Please let me recover.* He stared at the ceiling and listened to the bougainvillea outside his window, brushing against the screen; smelled the indescribable frangipani. The fragrance helped him quiet down. He would remember the smell of frangipani for the rest of his life.

Gone Missing

The group in the small craft that had disappeared on their way to the Carterets contained six people who traveled without navigational aid. It was assumed they had encountered a storm and got lost when no report of their arrival was forthcoming from the Marist mission in the Carterets. After six days they were listed as lost at sea and presumed dead.

Several days later the authorities in PNG were notified and the consular in Madang was advised of the tragedy. The following morning the Consular office in Port Moresby notified the American embassy in Australia and the name of Andersen (NMI) Bakewell was added to the list. It was an ideal situation and Bakewell's employers conveniently re-arranged the dates of the accident to accommodate their "man on station."

"I'm afraid he's simply gone missing, sir," the legate said, his voice scratchy and intermittent. It wasn't a reliable connection, and he wished he had returned to the legation before calling. The ambassador's representative was quite put out and the phone briefing didn't go well.

"What do you mean he's gone missing, Ian. The man can't simply have gone missing. What the devil was he doing out there anyway?"

"Apparently he was out there on a do-gooder mission. You know, visiting with the missionaries or something. According to the Catholic priest out there, he went on some kind of suicide mission down the coast, made a miraculous return, and decided to try the other side. Said he was intent on seeing the lower island first. Trouble is he never arrived at the assigned destination. Apparently none of them seem to know of him in that area. He may have been corresponding with a group in Madang. Apparently he's been sending various wire transmissions about in that area." The legate used the word apparently three times attempting to explain. He was nervous. There hadn't been any deaths on his watch since he had returned to station after the cease fire. "The priest at Buka didn't seem to know anything about any involvement with that group going to the Carterets."

"Well it's damned inconvenient of him, Ian. I'll have to tell the ambassador, and I'm sure he'll want a full search. The works."

"There's really not much of that sort of thing up there, sir. Not many powered boats that can do much in the way of helping, just the usual canoes with outboards, maybe a few scow vessels for transporting freight about PNG."

The authorities in Brisbane looked into the loss of an American in the Solomons. No one bothered to check the sketchy airline reservations, and, after two days of misdirected and feeble inquiries, they phoned the embassy in Sidney, stating that Bakewell was indeed missing and presumed dead and followed it with an official facsimile transmission to that effect. The American government was notified and after an additional twelve hour delay, reluctantly informed the Bakewell family by hand delivered notification, which included a copy of the facsimile from Papua New Guinea, stating he was missing and presumed dead. The last line of the official correspondence ended:

> There is an overwhelming chance Mr. Bakewell did not survive the presumed storm and related capsizing of the craft, and due to the adverse winds and the current north of Buka Island the drift of any survivors would be to the northwest into a vast area of the Pacific. The likelihood of anyone surviving in the sea in this area for an extended period of time is very minimal. It has been twelve days since the accident occurred.

There was more, including the Ambassador's personal sympathies for their loss. Nancy was listed as official next of kin. She received the message at the office when no one answered the call at their home. Two weeks later they held a memorial service on a Tuesday evening. The church was nearly filled and each of the Bakewell children gave a short talk, resorting to funny stories about their father and their childhood. They wanted to keep it light and focus on the idea of a happy death and everlasting life, and the fact that their parents were reunited once more. Each child spoke of their father's devotion to their mother, his love of the outdoors and how much he had added to their lives. Nancy ended with a short description of his last weeks in America and his quest to visit the missionaries out in the Solomons.

After the service, Nancy invited Maggie Walker to her home for a short reunion with family members and friends, and later introduced Maggie as "the other lady in my father's life." It made Maggie uncomfortable, given the situation, but she was overwhelmingly grateful for Nancy's kindness and the generous way she was included by each of the Bakewell children. Maggie was desperate to be a part of their grieving, and just as desperate to have a place where she could share her own sense of loss.

Seclusion & Inclusion

The morning after their Mardi Gras weekend, Maggie Walker awakened slowly to a miserable, rainy dawn, after a night of thunderstorms, and spent most of the morning curled up in the middle of her king-sized bed, staring sideways at the silent television in the corner. When she came awake, she realized immediately where she was in her life. A piercing awareness of her dilemma, accompanied by a painful heartache penetrated in a sudden rush.

She had left St. Louis the previous week with great expectations, believed she would convince Andy Bakewell she was the one person in the world with whom he could rebuild his life. She planned to rebuild her own in the process, convince him to love her and trust her again. The joy and happiness she found in his company and his attention, had thrilled her beyond anything she dared imagine; and Maggie had imagined a lot.

She remembered – sometimes accused herself of imagining – the feel and the touch of him for such a very long time. She had lived a lifetime without him. He had been such a long time ago, but he'd been just as she remembered, even better; he had been just as she hoped. He was still socially clumsy, sometimes awkward in her presence (she was ready to love and enjoy him for it, as she knew Katherine must have). He was a good and decent man, and he was a kind and thoughtful lover, gentle beyond description. When he touched her, he made her feel like she was the single most important woman in the world, in his world. Maggie had reveled in the tenderness of his lovemaking. He was as much compassionate as passionate, and left her feeling loved, worshiped, adored, and completed. He made a pageant of lovemaking with her, displaying a deftness so convincing, she yearned to have him each time, when it was time.

That first time at Point Clear had been on impulse, her impulse. She had taken him by surprise she knew, just as she intended; but later, that second time…and the nights that followed….

He had fulfilled all her fantasies, filled each one with a sweetness that left her coupled and accompanied, in a sea, temperate and balmy, with his physical expressions, completely immersed in his attentions, and fulfilled with the passion of physical love. He had been her first lover. Now, she realized, he had been her only lover.

Waking was the worst part. She lay staring at the ceiling, thinking, remembering, tears running from her eyes occasionally, down fine, seamy lines across her temples, where they settled in her ears. When they dried they caused an itching sensation. She stayed that way, wondering, asking, over and over, how they could have been so happy, so satisfied together. Why? Why couldn't he love her? What kept him holding back, holding on to his past life, to his wife? Could the love he'd known been so powerful that nothing could get through to him? Was he imagining a woman that never existed? *No, that wasn't fair. He had a right to love his wife, and cherish her memory... You made your choice, Maggie, and, in the process, you made him make another.*

Maggie was no weeper, despite the fact she'd wept in front of him, and next to him most of their last morning together. She didn't care. She wanted him to know what she was feeling. It was too late in life for dating games. She set out to get him, thought she had succeeded, didn't care what he thought about her tears. But she hated herself for crying now, while she was alone, hated her weakness, *especially* when she was alone. She had a life to live and she had a style. She never forgot the night he asked about her style. Everybody has a style, he'd said. Her style was to live her life the only way she knew, to the fullest, to stay occupied, and enjoy the bounty she'd inherited and acquired.

She'd been an early riser. Now she stayed in bed until she couldn't stand the itching along her temples, and because she thought she'd suffocate from the simple needing of him. She made her way to the bathroom muzzy, miserable, and filled with regret. *God, you look awful. Get a grip woman, get a life. Get going!*

She would try again. Call him and ask him to take her to dinner. *Okay! Damn it! We'll be friends, if that's what he wants.* Friendship would put them in contact, keep them together, if only occasionally. He couldn't forget what they had shared. He would want her again. She was sure of it. *Not really, girl. Don't kid yourself. He's got more self control, more damned, bullheaded control than you've got. And, he's still in love with his wife! How do you compete with that?*

Maggie waited a full week before she called Bakewell's home. There was no answer and no answering machine. She called Nancy at work, and Nancy explained that both her father and Michael were gone. She and Andy were watching the house and looking after the pets.

"I don't think I follow. Gone where?"

Nancy sighed, hesitated. "Maggie, my father's gone out to the missions. I don't really know when he's coming home."

"Yee gads, Nancy. My God, where in the world, what missions? Mexico? Latin America?"

"No, he's gone all the way out to the Solomon Islands, someplace called Buka."

"They're in the South Pacific, the Solomon Islands."

"I know. Michael and I tried to talk him out of it."

"Why? Why wouldn't he want to go someplace close?"

"He told us he wanted to see the Solomons before he died. My grandfather was supposed to have been there during the war."

Nancy paused; Maggie couldn't find words to fill the space. She was spinning, disorientated. It was difficult for them both. Maggie took a shot. "Is he planning on dying soon?" She made it sound like a joke, made it sound like she was teasing Nancy's father, instead of talking to Nancy.

"Mrs. Walker…"

"Maggie."

"Maggie…how much have you and my dad talked lately? How much has he shared with you in the past few weeks?"

Maggie wanted desperately to tell Nancy what she and her father had shared at the beach – clearly not the sex; Nancy was an adult, she could put things together – but the joyful reawakening of their relationship, the happiness they had discovered in each other. Instead she said, "Not very much, I'm afraid. Is there something I'm missing?"

Nancy lowered her head, stared down at her desk. *Daddy! Damn it! How could you leave her like this?* She took her time, gathered herself, took a deep breath. "Mrs. Wal… Maggie, I am sorry to be the one to tell you this. I know how fond you are of my father, and I also know how fond my father is of you, but…"

"What is it, honey?"

"My father's sick. He said it is terminal. The doctor gave him a simple prognosis – it was for time remaining only, not for any kind of cure. I can't believe he didn't tell you."

Maggie was stunned; Nancy recognized her plight. "I am so sorry to be telling you this. I knew he didn't tell you he was going out to the islands. Michael and I both got all over him about that, but I thought you knew about his illness. I thought you knew he was sick."

Maggie's voice sounded distant, coming from some far away place. "I didn't know."

"I'm so angry with him right now, for the way he is treating you. I swear, if he makes it home alive, I am going to just kill him myself."

***

Maggie decided not to bounce back. *What the hell. Who are you trying to kid?* She would lay in bed awake in the mornings, and think about all that was not going to be, would never be. She was a wreck, looked a wreck, and didn't care. She moved through her apartment in her robe and bedclothes for hours, seldom left the house before noon. She ate most of her meals in her home, visited the club rarely. She would have become a complete recluse if it hadn't been for Michael. He returned home in mid March, to stay for another month, wanting to be at home, waiting for his father to get back. He called Maggie as soon as he got back, remembering his father's final admonition. *Take her to dinner, make her feel young.* He did his best.

And he succeeded. He had drawn her out and got her going again. The second time they went out to dinner, they stopped by Andy's home afterward, and Maggie visited with Karen and the new baby. By then Nancy had started calling her too, and they had lunch twice, before the news of Bakewell's death arrived. That sad night, after the memorial service, Maggie spent the evening at Nancy's home and, after the others left, Nancy persuaded her to spend the night. It wasn't hard. Maggie caved in; she didn't want to be anywhere else. Nancy put her in the spare bedroom and gave her a beautiful peignoir Tom had bought her for Christmas.

Maggie became a recurring visitor with the Bakewell children, another surviving relative, became a regular on Sunday evenings too, which they still celebrated at their parents' home. She played with the grandbabies, got very close to Karen, offered to help with any task suitable for a mother or mother-in-law. The kids all responded well, sensed her own grief, and shared with her generously. They all had each other, just the way it was when their mother had died. They were up to it one more time. There was no other way to be. The only difference was the satisfaction, comfort really, they found in sharing with Maggie Walker.

Convalescence

Over the next week Bakewell kept to himself, rising for Mass and breakfast, only to return to his room, zombie-like, sleeping late until the heat flushed him from the room. After he showered, he read and studied his maps in the dining hall, the coolest of the buildings. Occasionally he walked up to the main library, just to move about. He didn't need any exercise. He attended vespers each night and afterward visited with the seminarians during the evening meal. They were amused by his stories of America, loved his descriptions. He described steep hills with wildflowers, Midwestern prairies, rolling with wheat, farms with livestock, mountains without jungle foliage, which fascinated them, and the bayous above the gulf. He described the high prairies, told them about the game he had killed, fish he had caught. Most of the seminarians were from the "north," Lae or Madang, or the islands of New Britain and New Ireland, large cities like Rabaul. They came from better educated families familiar with the Franciscans, but had lived on the edge of civilization, near the bush where life was primitive. Their kinsmen still hunted with ancient weapons, dealt with crocodiles in the streams and more things poisonous than he could imagine.

The young men were interested in everything about America, especially rural Americans and their way of life. The seminarians were always happy, wonderfully entertaining, loved to laugh, especially at his miscues, as they attempted to teach him Tok Pisin. He filled his notebook with pages of words and phrases, anything he thought might be worthwhile. The notebook had hundreds of lines of translation by the end of the week.

After dinner they retired early. Bakewell was in sync with the twelve hours of daylight and dark that determined life close to the equator. He rested and was encouraged by how much stronger he felt after only a few days. Eating the simple, healthy foods, and sleeping twelve hours a day were rejuvenating, physically and mentally.

He was due to meet "his watchers," the evening of the 24th, their date of arrival according to the itinerary Albrecht had given him in St. Louis. He called to say where he would be staying, using the same number both Albrecht and Snow had used. He used the college phone. It was a tedious process, dialing the overseas operator, waiting, wishing to put the charge on his credit card. It would be one more substantiation of his whereabouts, so they would be certain he was there waiting. The message he left gave the name of a motel in Erima. He didn't want them sending someone after him at the seminary. He didn't want them bothering the Franciscans.

On his last day, Fr. Gerardo celebrated Mass at the little chapel in Bakewell's honor. Late that afternoon he spent time in the dining area saying goodbye. He could put a name with each face, which pleased the young men, and he could speak Tok Pisin with limited proficiency. It was time to go, to move on to the next phase. Bakewell asked them to pray for his safe passage. He had gotten closest to Francis and John, who continued to trade questions with him and who, always politely, offered correction to his mutilation of their language. Fr. Gerardo agreed to hear his confession and bless him before he departed.

They had a small party before he left, and he thanked each one individually for their help and concern.

He insisted on leaving before the evening meal, wanting it to look like he had been at the motel for some time when he was contacted. He felt certain it would be within hours of the flight's arrival. His ticket said it was due in at four. Francis gave him a ride into the city, not understanding why he wanted to stay at the motel, but too polite to ask. He left money for Fr. Gerardo and a note thanking him for the fine accommodations and transportation. He hadn't seen much of Fr. Jonas after their night on the road together. He left a brief note apologizing again, thanking him for interceding and for saving his life with his calm and masterful handling of the rascals. He said he would never forget any of them. It was an understatement.

There was a light knock and Bakewell, apprehensive in his strange surroundings, went to the door expectantly, opened it to find a man filling the doorway, his hand over the top of the doorframe.

"Mr. Bakewell?" he said in a friendly voice.

"Yes?"

"Hate to bother you, actually. I'm Powell." He put out a large hand.

The man in the doorway was his height, maybe 200 pounds. He was as formidable as any man Bakewell had ever met, had the muscular look of a professional, somebody from the Adventure Channel, the type seen wrestling pythons or fooling with a crocodile. He was light complexioned with thick reddish brown hair, very ruddy looking. Bakewell guessed he was late forties, but he had the dry, weathered complexion of light haired men. He smiled pleasantly, but his eyes gave him away. He had the cruelest eyes Bakewell had ever seen. His eyes made Bakewell want to look away. He forced himself to look Powell in the eye.

"Fellow named Albrecht sent me over. Not a very happy chap. Seems to think you should have been on the plane with him. Guess you've managed to piss him good." He gave Bakewell a friendly look and smiled through the hard eyes. "Supposed to have flown out here with him, eh? All the way from America? Don't envy anyone there. Spent two days with him myself, on and off. It's been an experience."

"Albrecht? Here in Moresby?"

"Yeah. Not happy about it either."

"I can't believe they sent Albrecht out here."

"Neither can he. Man's got a real blister on his butt. And he's not at all happy with the accommodations here in Moresby. Got completely soaked last evening. Likes his whiskey, he does. Hope he's not going to be trouble for us. You know?"

Bakewell's mind raced. Albrecht? *Was he a watcher?* He had always thought of him as a handler, more an arrangement guy, like Snow. He couldn't picture Albrecht in Port Moresby.

"Said we should all meet for dinner, if ya don't mind, eh? Can't say I'm looking forward to that, but since we're going to be working together for a while it might not be a bad idea?"

Bakewell nodded, wondering what Albrecht had done to get sent out to the islands. He didn't believe Albrecht was along as an observer. He didn't know a lot about who he was working for, and that included Albrecht, especially after this news. First it was Snow with his class and unsuspected compassion then Albrecht, the big pear shaped, baby soft, compassionless jerk with an attitude. He stared at the man in the doorway. *Pay attention to the little things, pay especially close attention to the little things. The big stuff will stick out, but watch for the little stuff and watch out for this dangerous man.*

"You want to come in?" Bakewell asked, indicating the small room behind.

"Sure," Powell said, brushing past. He made a brief inspection of the room and looked out the window. "Dry, isn't it? Guess you'll get used to it. Temperature's always on the tip of the scale up here. Be even worse in the islands." He turned and walked to the door. "Take your time; I've got an errand to run. I'll be down in the lot. I've got a car of sorts. Come when you can." He smiled again agreeably, the same hard eyes. "See you then."

Bakewell nodded, followed him across the bleak room and closed the door behind him. He took a shower in a small, dark, cubicle with poor lighting and little water pressure, thinking how a shower was once a luxury, now was an experience to be rushed through. He hadn't gotten to the motel any too soon, wondered what the facilities would be like in the islands. He took some comfort in the apparent fact that Powell was to be his escort for the coming adventure, knowing he might be a mad croc when the time came for him to be let loose, but might be an asset while traveling in Port Moresby, possibly to Bougainville.

When he got down to the parking lot, Powell was waiting against the car. It was almost dark, crowds were gathering close by, but appeared to give Powell room.

"You can't leave your things here in this place, man. Go and gather up your effects. We're heading for luxury and prosperity."

"What do you mean?"

"You're moving up to the top of the hill, Mr. Bakewell. Thought I'd let you clean up a bit while I ran some errands. Get your gear then. We'll be off right after."

Bakewell went and got his backpack, left without stopping to check out, and got in the car with Powell.

"You know you aren't supposed to be out after dark in this town." Bakewell said matter of factly.

"Right, but we're close in. Out in the suburbs, places like Bomana it gets real bad. Not closer in here. *No problem iumi*, as they say. Couple of formidable chaps like us. Are you armed?"

"No."

"Not a good thing, maybe. Maybe then again it is. You could get in a scrape and we'd never find you out here in a jail cell. People get lost out here regularly."

Bakewell didn't respond. There was nothing to say, and he had few questions about the city after his "tours" with Fr. Jonas and Francis. He was onto the language he overheard between white men mostly, but he wasn't sure how he would do with the natives. Although he loved the sound of the language, Tok Pisin was like a steady barrage of pellets, gradually losing sting. His marginal enlightenment just able to tolerate the pain of trying to decipher what was being said around him as he moved through the density of intimidating people, almost none of whom were his color. Closer in, as Powell had referred to it, he saw more white men. They all seemed to get along in English, most of the population of Moresby did.

"Where are we going?"

"Up the hill, Crown Plaza actually. Not a bad spot to view Moresby by night. Beats the street, as they say."

Powell drove skillfully through the traffic, familiar with the left side of the road and the right side steering wheel. It took fifteen minutes to get through the traffic and crowds of people milling about under the huge rain trees that lined the boulevards.

"So how did you come to be in Erima?"

"I tried Oholo. Tour book said that was the place, but there was nothing there. Then I tried Waigani, but everything was booked. There's not much here in Moresby is there? I milled around and ended up finding that place through a friend I met. It was close to the grocery store, and they sold liquor there."

Powell chuckled out loud. "See your point. Port Moresby has driven a lot of white men to the bottle. How did you make a friend so quickly?

"I went out to the Franciscan College and paid my respects. I have a friend near St. Louis who's a Franciscan; he put me onto them."

"How long have you been here then?"

"A few weeks."

Powell chuckled again. "Blighter Albrecht said you flew the coop, or missed the flight, or some such. He was upset about that. Can't imagine why you wouldn't want to spend hours flying across the Pacific with him, though. Such a fun chap."

When they pulled up in front of the Crown Plaza at one of the highest points in Port Moresby Town, a man offered to put the car in the garage. Powell agreed, telling Bakewell to get his gear. "Don't leave anything behind, mate."

They came through the front entrance and walked into another world as the glass doors slid open and presented a large, wide lobby with a marble floor. Across the lobby they went up a plush carpeted staircase and came to a balcony restaurant and bar, separated by a low, beautifully carved and stained serpentine railing that divided the two rooms. Powell went left to the bar and Bakewell followed. They took a comfortable table with cushioned cane chairs.

"What are you having then, Andy?"

Bakewell thought it over briefly, before he could answer Powell said, "Make it neat. You never know where the ice might have come from.

Supposed to be rain water, but you never know, eh."

Bakewell didn't want anything to drink. He asked about the beer and Powell shrugged like he wasn't sure. "I'll take an Absolut on the rocks."

"Think I'll just have the same, but in a chilled glass, mate." Powell addressed the bartender pleasantly. "No ice for either one of us, eh?"

The man bowed and went off. They were silent while the drinks were made. There were only three occupied tables, across the room by a temporary elevated bandstand. It was quiet for the cocktail hour. From where they sat, with the view of the harbor and Gulf of Papua, they could have been in San Francisco or Honolulu, overlooking a beautiful city. Powell read his thoughts. "Just like home from up here, eh. Almost livable in the dark, especially with the lights."

"How long have you been here?"

"Just today and yesterday, came in by private plane. Quite impressive too. Our friend Mr. Albrecht managed to bypass customs and quarantine."

"Was he carrying much?"

"Amen, lots of heavy packages, one curiously long. Thought the blighter might have a weapon he was secreting in, eh." It was worded in a harmless way, but it was a statement not a question, intended to let Bakewell know Powell knew they had a rifle.

The drinks came and Bakewell decided to try for a reading on Powell. "You're Australian?"

"New Zealand, actually."

"What do you do down there?" he asked and when he met the hard stare, added, "I've only been there once, just long enough to get off the plane. Nice airport though."

"Auckland then, was it?"

Bakewell nodded. He watched Powell lift his glass and peer through the mist before he took a sip. He told him it was "decent" vodka. Bakewell told him it was expensive in America. Powell countered, saying it was only $7 American out here. Not that much is it?"

"No. That's a third of the cost in the states." Bakewell decided to try again. "What are you doing up here, so far from New Zealand, in this terrible place?"

"I'm looking after you and your watcher, such as he is. Ah, here's the happy bloke now."

They both turned to see a pale looking Albrecht moving ponderously across the room toward them. He sat down heavily and looked at Bakewell contemptuously, turned to Powell. "I see you found him," he said, turning back to Bakewell, "Where've *you been, dad*?"

"Touring."

"What's that supposed to mean?"

"It means touring." Bakewell smiled when he spoke to Albrecht who looked out of place and less threatening so far from home. He was vulnerable now, like a great white, tumbling uncoordinated in the surf, too far from the open water where he could rule uncontested.

"Let's all try and make the best of this little vacation, shall we gentlemen?" Powell said amused at the exchange and at Albrecht's condition. "Feeling better now are we Mr. Albrecht. Won't try the water again, no matter how much you enjoy your ice?"

Albrecht ignored Powell, which Bakewell thought unwise, especially out here where Powell seemed to be in his element, where Powell appeared to be the only one who knew his was around such a dangerous part of the world. He decided to push Albrecht a little farther. It had an appeal he hadn't enjoyed before.

"He's still upset about the Rams and the Vikings," Bakewell said.

"Not to mention the fookin Super Bowl," Powell chimed in.

"If I want to talk football with you pop, I'll let you know."

"Now Mr. Albrecht, sir, you better listen up. Man's come from the home of the world champs. Might know a little something about American football."

Albrecht had another envelope. He put it on the table and made Bakewell reach for it again. Same routine, new location. "Here's something might be of interest to you, since you're in such a jolly mood."

Bakewell took the envelope and opened it under the watchful eyes of his employer and the mercenary. Inside was a copy of one page of the *St. Louis Post Dispatch*. It was the obituary page with the name of the paper, and the date clearly marked. Bakewell read his obituary carefully. It gave him a strangely detached feeling and brought on some unwanted emotion, which he carefully concealed from those watching. The heading read:

> St. Louis contractor listed as missing in the South Pacific.
> Andersen Bakewell of Des Peres reported missing while
> on a missionary related visit to the Solomon Islands.

The story went on to describe the loosely defined events of how he had disappeared northwest of Bougainville in a vast area of the Pacific, and made some kind remarks about his long association with his company and the construction industry in general. It was part of the agreement he had made with Snow back in November, and meant the insurance money would be a non issue once sufficient time had elapsed. Oddly Bakewell thought of Mark Twain's cryptic remark about the news of his death being greatly exaggerated. He didn't know what to think really. His mind moved from subject to subject, almost in slow motion, while his traveling companions watched. Albrecht most certainly knew what was in the envelope. He wondered if Powell knew. It didn't really matter what Powell knew.

The waiter came and brought a bottle of whiskey with him. It was

Maker's Mark. He poured some in a frosty glass, without the ice and Albrecht told him to leave the bottle on the highly polished table, which the waiter had anticipated. He bowed politely like everyone in service and left the bottle.

"This chap is one hell of a drinker," Powell said. "Polished off near half a bottle last night. I'm still in awe."

They watched Albrecht pour a stiff measure into the cold glass and take a long sip. A few silent minutes later, the bartender reappeared with a full liter bottle of water and held it, label up, for Powell's inspection. "Not me, show it to *bikman*." Powell pointed to Albrecht. The man showed the labeled ingredients to Albrecht, who looked at Powell for endorsement. "Seems all right to me." Powell turned to the barman and said, "Appreciate it mate. Just leave it here, then."

"Sir, I took the liberty of freezing some from another bottle in case you gentlemen decided it would be safe."

"Good man!" Powell beamed, "Bring it on then."

The barman returned with a large bowl of ice and they all helped themselves.

"This is more like it then. Just like the states, eh Andy? Got all the comforts. Blighter's working hard for a decent gratuity."

"They don't tip out here," Albrecht said sarcastically.

"We'll just have to make an exception then." Bakewell reached into his pocket and tossed a twenty kina note on the table and said, "I'm in. I haven't had ice in weeks," quickly regretting the offhand remark.

"By the way," Albrecht turned to Bakewell. "Where the hell have you been? What have you been doing in this cesspool for two weeks, and don't tell me you've been touring. No bullshit."

"Well you found me out then, did you," Bakewell mimed Powell's accent. Albrecht didn't answer. "If you really want the truth, I've been out to a place they call the Central Theological Institute. It sits up on a hill over near the Bomana Cemetery. I've been visiting the Franciscans. They have a college out there. I made what you might call an extended retreat. It's been a long time since I made a retreat. I needed to make up for a lot of misses over the years." He looked into Albrecht's eyes, smiling sardonically.

Albrecht turned to Powell. "The boat has been secured. We're set to go in the morning. I told them we'd be there at nine sharp. No New Guinea bullshit. Everyone's to be on time if they want to get the money I've offered. Everyone sleeps here tonight and we go together in the morning. No exceptions. I'll expect you to be here for breakfast in the morning Mr. Powell." He turned to Bakewell. "No exceptions."

"We'll need a van then for our gear. Three of us won't fit in one of these little taxis will we, not unless you're planning to walk on down to the wharf yourself, Mr. Albrecht, sir?"

"Get a van," Albrecht said. He poured another stiff drink and took most of the ice. Bakewell and Powell exchanged looks. It made Bakewell almost comfortable to look into Powell's eyes. They had a little pact going – temporarily – he knew the time would come when he would no longer be sympathizing with this secret man. Powell excused himself and went to see about their transportation. Afterward they went into the dining area and sat together and shared a meal. The food was a disappointment. Bakewell was expecting fare from the magnificent Gulf of Papua below them, something to go with the fine surroundings of the elegant room. He hoped for a giant crustacean with all the trimmings, but it was another disappointing meal.

They left right after breakfast, went out to a decrepit van, under the portico and loaded up. Albrecht sat in the front seat with a small black man with a wide flat nose. He drove them from Port Moresby Town out to the harbor without conversation. The sun was already up four hours and the heat was building. More fires had been set overnight, and the smoke hugged the ground tightly and drifted over the airless highway. A proud city government watered the delicate little candle trees, carefully spaced along the sidewalk, bordering the steeply sloping highway. They appeared to be holding their own in the harsh drought, trying to brighten the bleak landscape. With the windows open, the noise of the engine whining and the street sounds outside, Powell was able to take Bakewell into his confidence. He leaned over and muttered under his breath.

"Blighter put away another half bottle last night. Afraid he's spooked a bit, wouldn't leave the hotel at all, not once since we got out here. Only excuse I had to be rid of him mostly." He paused when they came to a stop and the noise quieted, resumed with the sounds of the traffic, "Not too sorry about that though. Be happy to get on the boat and get out of here."

"I won't be too sorry to get out of here myself. I've seen all I need of PNG and Moresby."

"Well, we'll still be in PNG up there."

"Really?" Bakewell wanted to come across as ill informed about Papua New Guinea, even more so about things up in Bougainville.

"Yeah. At least the air'll be clean again, and you can draw breath. Hope he knows what he's doing with this boat business. Says he paid top dollar. Not much around these parts to hire." He leaned back and looked out the window at the street scene, signaling the conspiracy was over for now.

When they got to the pier, Bakewell was surprised at the size of the boat. It was definitely a boat and not a ship. He doubted it weighed in at more than fifteen tons, wished it was bigger. It was newer than everything else in view. They found out later it belonged to a snorkeling and diving operation. The owner was out of the country, and they suspected it was being rented without his knowledge. The crew, which consisted of a young "captain" and one even younger deck hand, were probably freelancing.

"No matter, eh," was Powell's only comment. "We're not exactly representing the UN on our little jaunt are we?"

"As long as it stays right side up I don't care." Bakewell answered, anxious to be away from the dry, arid city of smoke and garbage.

They went below and did a quick inspection. "The head's usable and decent, and they have fresh water to wash with," Powell added, noting the large clear plastic tank near the shower.

"The galley is full of food. Good food at that," Bakewell commented over his shoulder, noticing the shellfish and several frozen snapper in the freezer. "Probably left over from the last diving expedition; might just have found the mother lode of groceries in this part of the world, Powell."

Powell agreed. They stowed their gear and helped Albrecht stow his. It was heavy. Albrecht wasn't very coordinated making the transition from dock to boat several times. They both worried he might fall between. When they pointed below, Albrecht followed their direction, went below, looked around, taking it all in. He quickly had them put his bags in the only private cabin and went topside.

"Looks like we're to be mates then, Andy," Powell said. "Hope you don't mind."

"Mr. Powell," Bakewell said in his best nautical imitation, "We'll probably spend the whole trip up there, I suspect." He pointed to the bridge and deck space beyond the windshield, where there was a comfortably cushioned area. "What the hell is your first name, sir?"

"Adrian." Powell almost scowled. "Hoped you wouldn't ask."

Bakewell doubted his first name was Adrian. He doubted his surname was Powell for that matter. They went topside and waited for Albrecht to give the cast off signal, which "captain and crew" watched for anxiously. The crew kept a sharp eye out all around, especially on Albrecht, during the loading and boarding operations, anxious to be underway. Albrecht tried to look imposing, stretched to his full height in a pair of deck shoes and a loose fitting purple shirt that went untucked. He told Powell to ask the captain how far it was to Bougainville.

"Em i long we long go long Bougainville?"

"I no long we. I mas sikis undred miles."

"About six hundred miles."

"How far in hours? In hours man, I don't give a damn how far it is in miles. How long on this damn boat?"

"Em i long we tu auas?"

"I mas tupela ten-na eightpela aua."

"He says it will take close to twenty eight hours." Bakewell understood. They had worked on numbers a lot at the seminary. Powell added, "Depending on weather and the current."

"A full day and then some?" Albrecht asked with a look of concern and added, "In this thing, on the open sea?" He looked confused. "Will we make it?"

"In this fookin bass boat, mate? We'll just be lucky to make the Coral Sea."

"Should we look for another boat?" Albrecht asked alarmed; his "crew" looked alarmed too, almost crestfallen.

"No. We should get on with it Mr. Albrecht, sir. We should make for the Solomon Sea and points north. Let's be on the bloody, fookin way, sir."

Powell gave a mock salute and turned to the captain and smiled grandly. He seemed a changed personality on the boat. There was a gay and upbeat air about him. His movements were quicker, more spontaneous. He displayed the athleticism of a powerful cat. He was the man Bakewell feared he might be, full of adventure, happy anticipation, like the part of his life he enjoyed the most was about to get underway, like his life was about to get underway again, in a gleaming nautical sports car. He turned to the captain and first mate: *Poro, yumi go het na mekim dispela wokabaut. Laip bilong yumi i save krangki na i no stret na sampela taim i save hat tumas. Yumi noken les sapos laip i hat, yumi go het na mekim wok!!*

Bakewell followed much, but not all of what Powell had said. Powell pronounced his pidgin like a white man and spoke slower than the natives. The drift he caught was a chorus of orders given spontaneously, joyfully, to infect the young crew and change the mood. It went something like: *Let's hit it then mate. Cast off and let's take this bloody ride. Life's a bloody challenge and some parts are more challenging than others, so let's do it man.*

The captain beamed with relief and nearly shouted to his mate, *"Klia long hap!"* It meant cast off. Bakewell had heard the expression often enough in Buka and Bougainville. The boat left the wharf and they moved out into the incredibly green water of the Gulf of Papua, all three white men wondering why a hundred thousand teeming masses in Port Moresby would choose to live in the squalid conditions of that desperate place rather than attempt to make some kind of life, out near the paradise of reef and shoal, point and lagoon – and the sparkling clean sea that surrounded the whole of Papua New Guinea.

***

The craft was sleek and moved well through the small swells in the sea. It would make good time if they didn't run into rough weather. But they each knew it would be a very difficult journey if the sea became heavy. They were a long way from Bougainville. Almost as soon as they got underway, Albrecht gave up his seat on the bridge and went below. There was plenty of bottled water, and Powell fetched two cold liters and handed one to Bakewell. "Too much vodka last night," he said, "Not as much as our friend Mr. Bourbon put away though." He took a big draft from the bottle. Bakewell sipped from his, wondering if it might become a precious commodity before the journey was over. Powell noticed his look and said "Iumi no worri, mate," pointed to the large plastic containers on the stern. "We have enough petrol to come about and make any island. As long as we're topside up we've no problem. We'll never be more than a five hour push from some bloomin island. We've got backup radios and portable GPS in addition to the ones aboard." He pointed to his canvas bag at the foot of the ladder in the lower compartment and repeated "no wori."

Late in the afternoon they made a pot of strong tea and drank it with milk and sugar. The captain was quiet, happy at the prospect of the money he was about to make. Powell quizzed him in pidgin and Bakewell listened, able to follow much of Powell's conversation. They learned the boat had been misappropriated as they thought. Bakewell kept his limited understanding of the language to himself, letting Powell explain they were at sea in what amounted to a stolen vessel. He was looking for any kind of leverage when Powell showed his dark side, anything that might give him an edge, like his comprehension of what the men said in pidgin. He listened carefully whenever the young captain spoke. He was more difficult to understand. Bakewell got most of what the white man said.

Four hours after the sun went down, they turned round the end of PNG, having gone nearly 300 miles and moved away from the mainland at Samara, which they could just make out through the moist air. It was time to go out into the real ocean. The air was fresh and clean and the breeze kept the temperature to a tolerable level and the boat did well as they swung northeast. Three hours later they passed east of D'Entrecasteaux. About an hour before sunrise they passed west of Muyua Island. Mr. Albrecht, as they were referring to him, came topside for brief inspections, looking hung over still. He drank large drafts of the bottled water, but took no food. Powell and Bakewell took turns preparing food, frying bacon and eggs and later steaming shellfish. The islanders never sliced pork belly, had no understanding of fried bacon. The Tolai crewmen enjoyed the "bacon" word, and savored the taste of fried bacon in shared and secret amusement.

On the first afternoon they spent much of their time outside on the open deck. Powell and Bakewell took turns napping most of the day. The sky was covered with a low cumulus that obscured the scorching sun. In the evening, after sunset Powell broiled fish in the butane oven until it was dry and flaky, squeezed lime over it and served it with coconut water laced with rum. Much later, under a clear, star filled night, sharing another pot of strong tea in the middle of the Solomon Sea, Powell became unusually conversable and told stories of his travels in the islands. He was acquainted with Bougainville and Buka both, "Not exactly my first choice, eh." He knew the whole of Papua New Guinea, the Solomons, Vanuatu, and most of Micronesia.

"You've spent most of your time in the islands, Powell?"

"Pretty much, mate." He answered agreeably.

"You're from New Zealand originally though?"

"That's right."

After several humorous stories about the bizarre behavior of white men in the islands, and a few more concerning women and his adventurous spirit as a younger man in places like Noumea ("now there's a place to have fun, mate"), Bakewell tried to press him about his business in the islands. They had just come in out of a short squall under the protective roof of the pilothouse and were standing behind the young skipper who was nearly somnolent in his chair after so much time at the helm.

"So what exactly have you been doing out here all these years Powell?'

"Harrying my bloody arse off, man."

"What exactly do you do?"

"Mostly, I've been working for the government. Was military for much of my time out here."

"Like guard duty, at an embassy, maybe?"

"Something like that, Andy." He pronounced Bakewell's name "Ahhnndee."

"Have you had a lot of training? Special Forces, that sort of thing?" Bakewell was starting to phrase his words like Powell.

"You could say that – lots of training."

"Did you do it for the government or maybe you got paid for it, what?"

"Paid for it? Like a bloody fookin mercenary, then? I'm a man of some principle you know. But I got paid a little hazardous time, here and there." Powell stopped talking, looked evenly at Bakewell. "Just fishin round a bit are we? Not exactly fishin though." The look on his face was pleasant, but couldn't mask the hard eyes, defied any further questioning. Bakewell had asked their captain what his tribal name was earlier and he answered Vilapaia. Powell turned to the drowsy pilot. "So John, what does Vilapaia mean in your native tongue?" Powell spoke to him in English for Bakewell's benefit.

The captain laughed. "It means, I don't know…in your language, sum ting maybe like, 'I'll go and take you there'?" He spoke with the same shyness they had come to expect from all New Guineans

"I like that," Powell said, patting him on the shoulder. "Maybe we change it a bit and call you something slightly different, like *you'll go and take us there…and get us fookin back too?"*

John smiled, nodded his head enthusiastically. "I don't know dis words, Mr. Adrian."

They were silent for a while. The conversation with John helped wake him up and made them both aware of his need for sleep. They agreed to put him below and take a turn at the wheel. When John went below, opening the cabin door, they heard Albrecht stirring around. Albrecht said he was "slightly hungry," and Powell shouted down the hatch, "Can I fix you some bacon and eggs, Mr. Albrecht, sir?" Albrecht let out an audible groan. John showed him where the bread and crackers were. Albrecht took them, thanked John and went back to his cabin.

"That's the first time the man's said *thank you* since I met him."

"Mi tink he go long seasick," Bakewell made a deliberately feeble attempt to speak pidgin.

"Maybe, the son of a bitch deserves to be seasick. A regular Captain Bleigh he is. Not much of an outdoorsman though. You speak Tok Pisin, Andy?"

"No. I just get amused listening to you two go at it is all. I do like the sound of it though. It's a happy language."

"Yeah? That's because whenever the blighters speak it to you they are happy to see you…and your money. Mind you don't want to hear them when they're having a spat though. Like we might find with this business up in Bougainville? Why the hell are we wanting to go up there anyway?"

Bakewell shrugged off the question.

"You've been out to the islands before?" Bakewell shook his head, indicating no. "Well the place has its charms. Mind the insects are terrible. Have you brought a balm? Malaria's not too bad in Moresby, but it's bloody hell out here."

Bakewell nodded he was prepared.

"You're from St. Louis, then? I take it not as important as your friend Mr. Albrecht? This is Albrecht's show is it? My job's to get you both in and out?" Bakewell continued to nod. "What's your business in Bougainville? Not many goin to Bougainville these days."

Bakewell looked off to port at the shimmering water in the predawn moonlight. Powell waited, unwilling to go on. Bakewell met his eyes in the reflection of the console lights. "Can't say; you'll have to ask the boss man."

"No love lost there, is there. He's got something on you, maybe?"

"You could put it that way."

"You're not much of a talker, Andy. Kind of a stoic bloke."

Bakewell nodded his head. It was the first time he had given Powell any encouragement. He wanted to keep him at a distance, but there was always something to learn from the man who talked the most. He almost found himself liking Powell. He was a man's man, but he couldn't let go of his fear. *Pay attention to the little stuff, eh?*

"Can't imagine why you would want to go. The cease-fire's just in place, you know. Doesn't mean some fifteen year-old won't pop one off on us. This isn't a place for a vacation. I guess you know that?"

Bakewell pretended confusion, "Will it be like Moresby?"

Powell nodded. "Maybe a little, but mind it's never safe during this tensions business; the war's been going for ten years, anything can happen. Just keep sharp.'" He checked the GPS and moved the wheel to port.

"I'll keep your advice forefront in my mind, Mr. Powell."

"This Albrecht fellow must be an important man, no? Plane was corporate all the way. He sure throws money around. Had to cure him of that back in Moresby. Out here they all figure we have a bundle. We don't need to prove it to them though, managed to get that fine plane offloaded without going through customs or quarantine." Powell raised his eyebrows for emphasis. "That's a bit of a stretch in PNG."

Bakewell was impressed; he had been through customs and quarantine twice and they were a tough looking crowd. The company's wide influence extended all the way to New Guinea. He hoped it extended to the Solomons, wondered if Snow had ever been to PNG, thought on it a while before deciding to get the conversation moving again.

"A priest I met at the college told me the wage was $50 dollars a fortnight. I think he meant American dollars. That's twelve hundred a year. I must have had a couple of years' wages in my pocket at the time." He braced himself against the bulkhead and held to the open porthole. "Most of these people have nothing. I understand why they steal. They're starving. I'd steal if I was starving, and I sure as hell would steal if my kids were starving. It's got nothing to do with morality, does it? It's about survival."

Powell nodded. He had heard the logic and the moralizing before. If a man lived in the Third World long enough he got used to the grinding poverty of the have-nots and the moralizing of the haves. He looked at the global positioning system glowing up from the lighted dash before him and corrected their heading again. They were in a current. The sea started to come up, a wind they couldn't feel beyond the glass freshening, causing some of the waves to cap. They both looked out to sea. It was almost daylight. They grew quiet as the boat began to rise up and slide down the swells, Bakewell asked Powell if he had any idea how much sea the boat could take. They could tell from its performance it didn't have much keel and they weren't making way like before. Their ground speed had fallen off 5 knots.

"Damned if I know. We'll be all right. These little crafts cross the water all the time. It will get us there. I'm more concerned about getting back right now, but we can ask the kid below if it gets too bad. He's probably made his life out here on the sea."

"If it gets too bad we won't have to ask him. He'll be up here with us, fatigued or not, we'll be able to see it on his face."

Powell nodded, reflecting on Bakewell's comment; he'd been doing his own observing. They cruised on in silence, holding fast to whatever was nearest as the sea threw them about. Powell looked across to the east.

"Usually the wind gets up about midday. Glad it's almost daylight. If it kicks up in the dark, without any starlight, we'd be blind and buggered. Couldn't see a big one."

Bakewell didn't answer. He had crossed the north Atlantic in a hurricane once, still remembered the sea coming over the carrier's bow. It caused the screws to come out of the water. He also remembered the destroyer escorts he'd been able to glimpse through one of the hatches they were forbidden to open. It took five guys to pull the hatch open. It was a terrifying sight, still made him shudder to remember.

"You're not going weak on me now are you Andy?"

"No, I was just remembering a bad storm I was in once."

"I don't want to hear about it."

They continued on for hours, changing positions, taking turns at the wheel, holding fast to whatever they could. It was exhausting. The wind died and the sea quieted right after noon. They spoke little after that, each man dozing off, neither wanting to leave the bridge as they took turns at the wheel. They drank the strong tea until there was nothing more the caffeine could do for either.

Around two the young captain returned to the bridge, looking sheepish about sleeping so long. Bakewell guessed he hadn't had much sleep before they left. He had probably been up most of the night secreting the boat away from its proper mooring.

"So, where are we headed now John?" Powell asked.

"Iumi go long place below Mamagota," he said.

Powell shook his head. "That's south of Empress Augusta Bay?"

John nodded his head.

"Right in the middle of the BRA, a jungley, vicious, godforsaken place…with a mean coast..." He let his thoughts trail off.

"Will we be on the weather coast?" Bakewell asked.

"It's all weather coast around Bougainville, 'til you get down near Buin and that's no bargain either. Buin is where the airport is, and there's plenty of BRA there. They control the place."

"How violent are they?"

"Depends. They have no beef with us. None that I know of anyway." He paused, letting his remark hang in the air, "But a lot of their forces are just kids from the villages. Half of them aren't old enough to drive in the civilized world. Just what is our business in Bougainville, Mr. Bakewell?"

"I have to refer you to Albrecht. You're a military man, Powell." He put his hand on Powell's shoulder, checking, finding hard muscle tone, what he expected. It was like touching granite. "You understand the need for a chain of command. Talk to the CO."

Powell nodded resolutely. They went back outside to the front deck and stretched out. They were very tired.

"Will we be able to see the Treasury Islands?" Bakewell asked, consulting his map, trying to shift gears.

"No, too far away; we could see the Shortlands, but it will be dark," we've lost too much time in the current. Powell stopped talking after that. He was brooding, uncommunicative; it made him even more sinister.

Just when I began to enjoy your company, Mr. Powell, admire your attitude surrounded by threatening weather and the unknown. Bakewell wished he and Powell were on the same side. He wished they were "mates."

Bougainville

They smelled the island before they saw it an hour after sunset. The captain and his silent mate were as relieved as their passengers when it finally hove into view across the starlit water below a clearing sky. At first sight, both Powell and Bakewell wondered aloud how a place so mystically beautiful, silhouetted in starlight and smelling like paradise, could be so troubled. The young captain watched his GPS closely as they approached the big island. He switched the depthfinder on and steered northwest, paralleling the coast, looking for a place to put in. The depthfinder put a glow across the pilothouse. They watched it paint the bottom, fascinated, as a reef slowly came into focus. The south coast was treacherous. It didn't have many reefs, which made the ones there even more dangerous. There was one in the very place he wanted to come ashore, appearing steep, close to the surface, made of jagged coral.

There was no conversation as they gathered closer in behind the young skipper in mute trance, staring at the moving map of the GPS, dialed in to its maximum resolution, and the depth finder, glowing above the console. The sea wasn't too rough, but the swells were large and capable of raising and lowering the boat suddenly, making it vulnerable to the jagged reef below. They really needed a cove with protected water, but that was up above Mamagota, Bakewell knew, in Empress Augusta Bay. When the engines slowed Albrecht came up and spoke to the captain, making it clear to Bakewell and Powell they had a specific destination, which appeared now as a fix almost dead ahead, hard to pinpoint as it bounced about on the screen. The boat heaved in the swells. Their only alternative was to go in guessing, hoping they didn't get trapped close in above the coral.

"Bloody coral could eviscerate a battleship," Powell said.

They cruised at a low rpm, the engine barely audible to its passengers, but Powell and Bakewell knew it could be heard a mile away along the shore.

Watching the GPS, Bakewell thought they were about twenty-five miles southeast of the "fortress."

After he reconnoitered the area with Joel, he had done his best to memorize the lower coast. He asked the captain to scroll out and give them a wider view of the island, which the young man did, but only for a moment, before bringing it back down to minimal resolution. Bakewell was sure about their position. The GPS showed a fix along the coast in lat/long, their landing site, and another to the northwest up the coast: the fortress. He couldn't recognize anything along the dark shoreline, and didn't want to volunteer any information. He waited and watched and listened to the muted conversation between a now recovered Albrecht and his young captain. Most of their conversation was whispered and intense, Albrecht grilling the rattled tribesman. Bakewell went back outside where he could watch the ominous coast. He was almost certain there was an inlet to the southeast, maybe thirty miles below the fortress, where he and Joel had also spent the night, now it was only a few miles southeast of them. It was protected from all but the worst weather and it was the most likely place to put in, far enough away from the fortress, maybe an hour by boat. When he realized they weren't looking for the protected area, he felt sure the obviously nervous captain of their commandeered vessel was unfamiliar with the place. There was comfort in knowing he might be more familiar with their locale than his shipmates.

Powell followed him outside, where they waited for captain and commander to make a decision. Powell was frustrated, becoming even more uneasy as the minutes passed. He didn't like placing his fate in the hands of people he didn't trust, said as much. He was full of contempt for Albrecht.

The island smelled beautiful, but it was foreboding in the dark, the shoreline impossibly black, nothing visible but the darkness.

"Don't know what the problem is," Powell said, indicating the cabin. "We've got enough technology to find a speck in a fish's eye!"

"We're doing our best," a nervous Albrecht murmured.

"*Wanem wan*?" Powell repeated to the captain in Tok Pisin.

"Mipela i paul liklik, Mr. Adrian. Em i orait."

"I give the orders now," Albrecht growled. "You'll confine your remarks to me, and keep it in plain English."

"Mr. Albrecht, sir," Bakewell intoned from the bridge in a hushed voice. "Why don't we just anchor out and take this potential for disaster out of the equation."

"I like that," Powell whispered harshly. "Man's a born sailor. Let's leave off with the search, and find a nice cove where we can anchor out. We can make a landing in the daylight."

A light appeared along the shore about half a mile down the coastline. Bakewell saw it the same time the young mate did. "Are we expected?" Bakewell asked Albrecht, while the mate pointed excitedly.

John increased his engines to make way in the swells. They went out and around to the light and came straight in toward the shore. When they were very near, they slowed to a crawl, watching the depth gauge again, waiting for a surge from the surf. There was no reef. The light came out into the water a few feet from the shoreline to meet them. It was an island man, extremely black. The shoreline was very steep, and the water was up to his waist before he came out five feet from the lapping edge. The force of the surf pushed the boat up onto the shore and John shut down the engines.

It was very difficult to move about in the boat, partially beached, tilted as it rocked from the force of the water behind, forcing it up further onto the beach. They all jumped off the bow, anxious to be on land again. As Albrecht attempted the short jump he lost his balance and cracked his tailbone on the sharp bow, making a loud noise as he hit, crying out. He pitched forward onto the soft, yielding beach, and rolled over onto his back. Nobody moved to help him, then, by common agreement, they all moved to him, unable to do anything for his pain, waiting for him to get a grip and catch his breath. When he finally rolled over, his teeth gritted tightly, he got up partly, kneeling. Bakewell felt the presence of other men around them. He couldn't see them, but knew they were gathering close by. Powell was also aware they were no longer alone. Albrecht raised himself up and got to his feet, wishing he had something to steady himself. They all backed away from him. He looked at the man with the flashlight, nodded in pain and exasperation.

"Bai yumi go nau?" The man spoke to no one in particular, calm but apprehensive.

"What do you think, Powell?" Albrecht spoke through gritted teeth.

"He wants to go. I think we are here to follow him. We've no other choice. We're in their hands, like it or not." Powell turned to the man with the flashlight. "Bai yumi go nau."

"Yes, yumi ken mekim nau." The black man said, nodding to Powell. He turned and walked away.

They followed him off the beach into the foliage on a narrow path, leaving mate and captain to struggle with the boat. They found a thatched hut about fifty yards from the beach. It wasn't elevated like the thatched huts Bakewell had seen before. They entered through an opening that appeared to be a ground level veranda, also covered with a thatched roof. There were several men under the low roof. They were nearly invisible in the corners of the veranda. There were benches against the hut itself and several wooden chairs, worn and greasy looking in the light of a kerosene lantern nearby.

The man with the flashlight indicated they should follow him inside the hut. Bakewell followed Powell inside, behind Albrecht. There were several beds, mats on roughly hewn boards. Each had a large mosquito gauze hanging overhead, tied in a bundle by a simple overhand knot. There was a table in the middle of the room with another lantern. Powell made conversation with the man who had met them, then moved on to another, older man who stood next to the table. All of the men in the room had a surreally quiet body language, a calmness that came to men who had been in action many times and knew when to relax. They were in their element and they were very dangerous. Bakewell felt like he was surrounded by crocodilians, waiting for a false move to incite them, feared they might end up in a deadly feeding frenzy. If he hadn't spent so much time with Joel, talking of the trouble and experiences the islander had had during his fighting time, he would have been even more frightened.

Powell moved with the same catlike grace he had shown when they arrived at the boat. All the men in the room followed him closely with their eyes. Bakewell noticed they watched him too. None of them looked at Albrecht. They listened as Albrecht talked to Powell and Powell translated, but their eyes never moved from Powell, or from himself. It was eerie; the single lantern on the table cast long shadows on the matted walls, illuminating their black eyes, intensifying the mood.

"Bai yumi stap hia long nait?" Powell asked the man in charge.

He nodded, "We will come for you in the morning and settle up. You won't leave until we have settled the bill." The man spoke deliberately, making sure each white man understood what he was saying.

"No problem." Powell tried to sound confident, even happy with the arrangements. Bakewell wasn't as sure.

The man nodded, indicating Albrecht and asked, "This is the one from America; the one with the gifts?"

"Yes. I suppose so. You have gifts for them Mr. Albrecht?"

"I brought along something to negotiate with..." Albrecht didn't finish the sentence. His voice was different. It didn't sound like any voice Bakewell had heard before.

The guerilla leader nodded a second time and spoke in English again for the benefit of all. "We will watch him the closest." There was irony in the comment. They weren't watching Albrecht at all. Bakewell wondered if Albrecht noticed. They all had heard the fear in his voice.

"He is no problem. He will make the deal. He is honest." Powell was adlibbing. Powell really didn't know why they were there.

"What about this man?" The leader asked, looking at Bakewell.

"Also honest – a veri good man." More rolling r's.

They seemed satisfied, walked back out to the shoreline following a badly limping Albrecht. When they got to the boat, Albrecht called up to the mate. He went and fetched a small box from below. He handed it to Albrecht carefully, leaning down from the bow as he did. Albrecht took it and opened it and gave it to the man in charge, who looked at it as the man with the flashlight came up and shined it on the box. It was full of gleaming brass cartridges. The Bougainvillian nodded, looked like he was about to change his mind, said, "It is very late". He took the box of cartridges, said they would return in the morning. They moved off about twenty yards into the bush and vanished.

"Bloody fookin hell," Powell hissed, after the BRA had disappeared. He was furious. "Ammunition? Are you crazy man?"

"It's worth more than money out here they told me."

"It's worth a fookin life. Maybe yours. Maybe ever fookin one's."

"Do you trust them?" Albrecht tried to stand up straight, but couldn't manage it.

"Look where you are man. Take a fookin look around. Does it feel like home?" Powell turned toward Bakewell. "If we were smart we would get in the boat and shove off."

"I doubt we would make it far," Bakewell said, his stomach churning. He hoped his voice didn't give him away. He wanted to be as calm as Powell.

He wanted respect now that the time had almost come for them to change sides.

"You would be right too," Powell scowled. "They would blow us out of the fookin water before we got a hundred yards out. The buggers don't look like much, but they've managed to hold off the PNG for ten years. Give em that." He shook his head in disgust. "Probably have a howitzer trained on the boat right now."

Bakewell looked at an obviously spooked Albrecht, taking no pleasure in the fact the man was in a lot of pain, and showing a lot of fear. He had lost his swagger. Bakewell turned and addressed him, mimicking the way Powell talked, "Well, Mr. Albrecht, sir, we're a long way from Saint Louie, eh? Made it at last, did we?

Albrecht didn't respond. He didn't make eye contact either.

"We might as well get a night's sleep," Powell said, turning back toward the path. "Get out of the mosquitoes and lie down. I've had enough tea and cakes. God knows what tomorrow will bring." He took a "torch" from his bag, flicked it on, and headed into the bush.

Before Albrecht could follow, Bakewell grabbed his arm and indicated the boat. He went aboard and retrieved his personal gear. When he came out with his pack, he asked Albrecht what they would need, or if they would need any of the gear he had brought along. Albrecht nodded and Bakewell went below and retrieved Albrecht's bag from the cabin and brought it to the bow without losing his balance on the tilted, rocking deck. He threw the bag and his own pack onto the beach and jumped back down.

***

They slept fitfully, falling asleep on mats under mosquito netting. After an hour and a half Albrecht was asleep, flat on his back, and began a deep sonorous breathing, his noises intervallic, painful groans coming when he moved. The mats were soft, made an agreeable bed and, despite Albrecht's breathing and groaning, Bakewell and Powell settled into the comfort the bedding offered. If they hadn't been in such menacing surroundings, waiting for the ominous reveille of the day to come, Bakewell could have luxuriated in comfort and the smell of flowers when a breeze stirred.

He wondered where the crew and the boat had gone, and just how the next few days would play out, trying to focus on what was to come, knowing it was to be soon, not exactly when.

"What happens tomorrow, mate?" Powell whispered, reading his thoughts. Bakewell suspected he wasn't concerned about being overheard by their fitful, injured leader.

Bakewell didn't answer.

"Andy, I think we're in a bit of a pickle here. My guess is you know why we're here and what comes next. I think we might need one another for more than companionship when this thing plays out. I offer a deal and you should think hard on it before you give me the 'chain of command' line. Level with me, and when the time comes, I'll be your mate. It's what I'm here for man." He paused, listened briefly to the silence, resumed, "Come clean with me now. You're a decent bloke. I can see it clear enough. I suspect you might be handy in a bad situation, but I think you're in over your head here. I don't know what he's got on you, but let's make a pact and look after one another for the next little bit? What say you mate?"

Bakewell pondered the question. He could almost hear Powell thinking a few feet away, wondered about this strange man with the persona of violence. The natives immediately picked up on that. They had watched him the closest during the meeting earlier. He understood now Powell was in the dark about their business, wondered how he would react when he found out he was in on an assassination. *Sure as hell will want more money than they'd offered, eh? Somehow I think you will get it too, Mr. Powell, sir.* He almost laughed out loud in the hut that seemed more like a tent. A tent filled with evil men? Was he an evil man? He wondered on that for a long time. *The tent of evil intent. It had a ring.*

Powell waited. He was a patient man. Most professionals were. It was probably the most important part of the job. Bakewell wanted to trust him, but knew better. What would it matter if he told him? Would he try to leave? Where would he go? Who would take him? He was in it up to his neck. Bakewell thought on it longer. Albrecht was dead to the world, in a lot of pain. He cleared his throat and listened to the sound of his voice. He wanted to hear it before he told him.

"Why did you come out Powell? What's in it for you?"

"It's a job, man. It's what I do. It pays good, and I do it well."

"You're a mercenary? I'm right about that? You get paid to risk your life…and sometime you take another's, right?"

"Yeah, you made me the first time, sure enough. I could see it plain. Now what's your business out here?"

Bakewell hesitated, decided to go ahead. "There's a bad man up the coast. He's done a lot of financial harm to Albrecht's people. Cost them billions." He rolled over on the mat to face Powell in the blackness. "He's here to hide out. They want to send him a message. Maybe the message is for his people. I don't really know. They don't explain it to people at my level. I just get paid to do it."

"You're a shooter?"

"Yeah."

"I never would have thought it man. You've a quiet nature," Powell added, "A gentle nature. I don't see it in you."

"It's what I do." Bakewell lied, hoping it might buy him some needed respect from Powell. He was confused as to whether Powell's awareness of his purpose would be helpful, or if it would be better to have Powell think he was an amateur. He would have preferred Powell underestimate him, given the choice, but that choice was gone. He wasn't sure just when he lost that opportunity, but it was gone. He knew it was gone, had recognized it earlier, when the natives paid him as much heed as they had paid Powell, overlooking Albrecht. He wished he *was* worthy of the respect they had shown him.

Show Time

The temperature cooled late in the night, but when the sun rose and began to light the jungle outside, the heat returned. Powell and Bakewell were awake, had been for some time when Albrecht finally came to a disagreeable awakening with a long moaning "aaaaagghh." It sounded like a man run through by a saber as it was withdrawn. As soon as he was awake he went from a thrashing, moaning unruliness to a sudden, complete stillness, remembering his surroundings.

"Not feeling too well, Mr. Albrecht? Only just?" Powell asked. There was no answer from Albrecht. He was weighing his options before resuming command. "Be worse tomorrow, eh. Then gradually subside, the pain will." Powell was enjoying himself. "My guess, it needs to be exercised. Keep moving, eh. Tough it out then."

"What time is it?" Albrecht asked quietly, trying not to move.

Bakewell sat up first, waited for Powell to rise. Powell came up off the mat and removed the mosquito gauze, pulling it up about him winding it in a knot expertly, leaving it as he found it the night before. Bakewell followed suit. Albrecht threw his to the side, tearing it as he tried to raise himself, gasped from the pain in his spine. There was no sympathy for the man, neither capable of sympathy anymore than Albrecht would have been. He tried to get to his feet. They watched to see if he could do it. His knees nearly buckled as he tried to straighten up. More out of logic than compassion, Bakewell reached down to his pack and took a small kit and pulled out a bottle of huge pills left over from an old surgery. He shook two out and gave them to Albrecht.

"What is it?"

"Hydrocodone. Take them both." He took a small bottle of water from his bag, and after taking a long swallow, offered it to Albrecht.

"Dope?"

"Dope." Bakewell nodded. "Take it. It won't affect you anymore than the pain might."

Albrecht hesitated.

"Take them man. Give yourself a fookin break, then. Better than listening to you moan all the bloody night."

Albrecht was in no position to refuse. It could have been poison, mattered little. He drank both pills down, using too much water. Bakewell took the bottle from him before he drank it all. It was the first overt act he made against Albrecht. He handed the bottle to Powell who finished it.

"So is today the day, Mr. Albrecht?" Powell asked; his voice cautious, edgy.

"Don't know," was all he could manage.

They followed him, limping badly out to the shaded veranda, where the breeze stirred slightly. It was pleasant. The boat was gone. They knew it would be. There was no place close by to anchor. There were coconuts on the ground everywhere. Wherever they were, they were far from a village, in a place of temporary habitation. The trees were loaded with coconuts. Cutnut trees were all about too, and full of fruit. Bakewell took a coconut from the ground. It would be drier and have more crunch than those on the trees, the ones the native people preferred. It was what he was used to in coconuts. He wished he had a machete. Powell reached up and took advantage of the cutnuts. They were full of fat. Bakewell found his knife in his pack and tried to hack his way through a coconut, making a mess of it.

They waited for nearly an hour, listening to the water crash and the sounds of the bush as the jungle came awake, then the guerillas were back, dark apparitions from the trees a few yards from the hut. They wore the traditional uniform: shorts and tee shirt, barefooted, only one wore flip-flops. They moved more conspicuously in the daylight and appeared less menacing. The man who had spoken English the night before approached Albrecht. He had a nasty scar that ran up his neck and across his jaw. He asked about the boat.

"It will be along soon." Albrecht said. He didn't seem quite as spooked as the night before. Bakewell wasn't quite as spooked either, but was nervous surrounded by men of such silent, intractable nature. Everything about them was formidable. They had been waging war for a decade and they hadn't lost; guerilla fighters par excellence. History had taught the world there was no beating a guerilla force. He suspected death was with them often, and wondered if a white man's death was more significant than an islander's, wondered which side they were on, knew it didn't make much difference. They would get along with the guerillas or they would die.

Before the islanders returned, he had gathered several coconuts and he asked one of the guerillas to open the coconut. The man took it and chopped the fiber from around it and split it expertly. With the very tip of the machete, he made the white fruit curl out of the shell and offered it. Bakewell took it, thanked the man and put it in his mouth, took a second piece and indicated he offer it to the others. It had a good effect on the group. There were smiles in evidence, everyone took some coconut. The boat's engines could be heard upwind. Minutes later it hove into view a quarter mile out. They watched as it relocated them with the GPS and came straight in like it had done the night before.

Albrecht, unable to move freely, but in less pain, indicated Bakewell go aboard and get the gifts. When he clambered aboard the rocking boat, Powell followed. They went to the cabin Albrecht had used as his personal domain and found several cases in one of his heavy canvas bags.

"Shit." Powell cried. "There's ten thousand fookin rounds here!"

Both men were familiar with ammunition. Each box contained fifty cartridges and they were two boxes long inside the case, two boxes wide, stacked five high, one thousand to the crate. There were at least ten thousand rounds. Neither man bothered to count them. They could do the math later. They took them out to the front of the boat.

The guerillas took the ammunition and disappeared into the bush again. The man who spoke English the night before was at the edge of the beach where the sand met the foliage, talking to Albrecht who appeared deep in conversation, listening mostly, staring at the ground, concentrating. Albrecht spoke briefly, then the man resumed talking, using his hands descriptively. They both looked up the coast, the map dangling in Albrecht's hand. Albrecht nodded finally, resolutely.

A premonition, growing, like a storm in the distance, heard but unseen, came over Bakewell, caused his stomach to roll. *Well, what the hell. You knew it was coming. It's what you're here for.*

Powell watched Bakewell, noted his reaction. The headman nodded one last time to Albrecht and backed into the bush and was gone. "I think the main event is about to take place," Powell said under his breath, leaning over the bow. Bakewell didn't speak. When they got down off the end of the boat Albrecht was almost there, struggling to walk erect, to straighten his spine, without success.

"We can shove off now," Albrecht pointed toward the cabin. "I'll need a hand." He waited at the bow. Powell called to John in pidgin and the young native brought a deck chair. It didn't look too strong. Albrecht took it and put it down onto the loose beach. When it was secure he stepped up on it, holding the bow, careful to keep his balance. He got aboard. Powell and Bakewell were left on the beach to push the boat off between swells in the surf. John started the engine and engaged the prop and when the boat came free, raced the motor enough to make way. Both men grabbed the rail and pulled themselves up.

"Couple of gymnasts we are, mate," Powell said edgily when they straightened up on the deck.

Albrecht spoke to no one in particular, saying, "We'll go up the beach slowly. We need to be in position around two o'clock their time."

"Then go down the beach away from the site and let's put in one more time," Bakewell said.

"Why?" Albrecht asked, unsure and honestly curious.

"I need to re-site the rifle. It's been through winter and summer in the last two weeks, probably up to 30,000 feet in pressure altitude, through a lot of humidity, temperature and atmosphere. I had it sighted perfectly. I'm not going to take the most dangerous shot of my life and have to jack five more in, trying to guess where it's shooting while the whole compound returns fire." It was a short speech, he had rehearsed it many times in the previous day and spoke it without missing a syllable, did it with such finality Albrecht didn't argue.

"Go down the beach a mile or so," Albrecht said to John.

"We'll think it over first," Powell interrupted. "The whole coast is theirs. You can't run that close without permission. Sometimes you need to fly a flag to keep from getting shot along this coast. Let's think this one out before we get blown out of the water."

"He's right," Bakewell said. He turned to the captain. "Go out away from the coast and go about five miles down and look for a small bay. We should be all right there."

Both white men looked at him. Bakewell took the rolled up map and flattened it. "Look at the map. We'll need calm water. There's a bay showing on the coast to the southeast."

Albrecht took the map from him and studied it. Powell watched Bakewell closely. The boat went out nearly a mile before turning southeast. The crew seemed more familiar with the coastline now, recognized hostile fire might come their way. When they got down to the small bay where Joel had encamped them the night of the rain, Bakewell was relieved to know he had the right location. Albrecht went below and brought up the long package, and unwrapped it, to the fascination of both crewmen and Powell. When the little rifle appeared from the last fold in the heavy blanket, it was intact with scope attached. Bakewell took it from him and took five cartridges from the box he offered. He filled the clip, left the chamber empty, and closed the bolt. Powell went and retrieved a pair of binoculars from the bridge anticipating what was about to take place.

The boat rocked steeply in the heavy water. Bakewell told the captain to put in on the inside of the hooked coastline where the surf was relatively quieter. When they came in to the beach, Bakewell jumped off the bow with the rifle in one hand and one of the water bottles in the other. He quickly lodged the bottle in the heavy detritus along the coast where the surf piled up anything loose during the stormy season. He trotted down the beach about twenty five yards, laid down in the sand and made a small mound, set the weapon on the packed sand, and fired the rifle into the bottle, then moved the power setting on the scope up to 9X and could see the bullet hole had almost eliminated the letter "o" on the label. He went down the beach another fifty yards and repeated the process again. The hole had nearly centered in the blue label, which was only 3" square. He went down the beach one more time, watching for activity from the village less than a thousand yards away. He regretted he would create a stir in the village, would create fear for the people who had befriended him and given him a dry place to sleep. He fired the rifle a third time, came jogging up the beach, picked up the bottle, and trotted back to the boat.

He handed the rifle up and Powell took it eagerly as Bakewell jumped aboard and signaled for them to pull back out in the sea. The engine was able to do the work in the calmer water. Powell had watched the bottle through the field glasses and identified each hit. He held the rifle in one hand and scrutinized the bottle, confirming the holes in the label. He handed it to Bakewell and looked over the small gun, opening the chamber and removing the last two cartridges

There wasn't much talk afterward. Each man concentrated on the coastline, watching for trouble. The tension lessened as they got under way and adjusted to the heaving water. The boat made steady progress well out and away from the coast. After twenty minutes Albrecht approached Bakewell in the pilothouse and asked about the weapon.

"No problem," was Bakewell's only reply. He wanted nothing from Albrecht. They would be changing sides soon. He had no need for small talk and he didn't offer more pain pills.

Powell approached after Albrecht moved away, said, "Got to give it to those plastic stocks. Never liked the feel of 'em though." Bakewell didn't answer, looked toward the bow, his mind on the "what ifs" and the "how tos." The next few hours would be about probables and improbables. He tried to imagine the improbables, tried to focus.

"You're a man of surprises, Andy." Powell clapped him on the shoulder. "This past day, one after another. Glad to have you on my team." There was no response. Powell thought it over, tried one more time, "Ever played rugby?"

"No." Bakewell flexed his fingers slowly, continued to look ahead. "American football, when I was a kid."

"Were you any good?"

"No, they wouldn't give me the ball."

Powell watched him closely, just before he went below, he said quietly. "You've got it now, mate. Don't drop it."

As they made their way up the coast, each man, as if by common agreement, took a turn in the galley, making his own fare. They were all hungry. When it was Bakewell's turn, he put some extra food in his pack, checked his gear one last time to make sure nothing was missing, went up on deck and put the pack under the console. Albrecht asked him if he was planning a trip, Bakewell said he wanted to have everything with him, "in case we get separated." He emphasized *separated*, reminded Albrecht of the last time he worked for them. "It gets pretty lonely once the shooting starts."

Powell and Albrecht were amused he might think they would leave him behind. It was the only thing that lightened the tension as they made their way up the coast. They watched the GPS over John's shoulder, each man holding onto something in the big swells now that the wind was behind them. John looked tense and apprehensive, was probably regretting his moonlighting excursion. He hadn't expected firearms.

Bakewell appreciated the difference traveling in a larger craft made. It was pleasant rising up and falling back in the bigger boat; before it had been a nightmare of heaves to the crest of giant swells, followed by traumatic sinkings, nearly inside the water around them. Even in the boat, the water was big. The Solomon Sea was an ocean, mighty, full of mischief and danger when the wind blew.

Albrecht turned to Bakewell and spoke carefully, distinctly, "We will put in a few miles up the coast. We will be a thousand yards from our objective. It's on the other side of a point sticking out in the water. We have a vantage point selected. It's been prearranged by our people and carefully noted on this map." He held a 7½' topo in his fleshy hand. "It's all been planned very thoroughly, based on information *obtained from inside.* They have no boats of consequence, nothing on the water capable of chase." He spoke to Bakewell, but each man listened like he was being given final instructions. Albrecht took a two-way from his pocket and indicated the other on the console. Powell fingered the mic. It crackled in Albrecht's hand, and Albrecht said, "Good" without looking at it, added one final caveat, "Mr. Bakewell and I will go ashore. No one else will leave the boat. I will call you in when it's time, and you will return and pick us up. Shut down your engines and drift offshore clear of any rollers. There should be no questions."

Mr. Bakewell? We're fast friends at last. You're trying to disarm me Mr. Albrecht? I don't think so. Bakewell looked over at the island. *Pay attention now. Watch for the little stuff. Watch Powell. Where's his weapon? Know what's going on behind you.* It was the same litany he'd used going after the ram six months before.

When they put in, Albrecht disembarked again, awkwardly, without hurting himself or his pride. It was a tough place to go ashore. Bakewell was surprised he could do it. He threw his own gear onto the beach, took the rifle and jumped free. He'd put five cartridges in the chamber. He had one buttoned in each shirt pocket and one in each side pocket of his shorts. He didn't really know why he had taken so many extras, felt sure he would only fire the rifle once, but not having enough ammunition was like not having enough runway. Albrecht had a bag thrown to him. They watched the boat back away, Powell stood in the bow, waved to Bakewell. Bakewell nodded in return. The boat turned and moved away. They were alone, the silence interrupted by the sound of the departing engine.

They moved quickly into the bush. Albrecht gave him an orientation on his map, after puzzling over it, turning it twice. Bakewell recognized their position relative to the target site instantly, was ahead of Albrecht. It gave him confidence as the man briefed him. He was very glad Powell hadn't come with them. Albrecht would be no problem. He feared Powell, especially on his own turf. Powell had told him he was at home in the bush. When they moved out, Bakewell took the lead, went fast, satisfied with Albrecht's laboring behind. After a hundred yards of uphill going, he stopped and waited for

Albrecht.

"I need to be right here on the map, right?" He took the map from Albrecht. Albrecht nodded out of breath. "I don't need a watcher. You can't go with me anyway. Follow me up to the top of this hill and wait. It'll give you a little vantage. Don't come any farther. You won't be able to see over the next ridge. He pointed at the lines on the topographic map. "This is steep. I'm not waiting for you. It says 'three o'clock' at this position on your map. We've got a lot of time, but I want to be there early. Wait on this hill and don't expose yourself."

They were together in the vegetation, Albrecht was disconcerted, leaned in, trying the bullying tactic once again. It only irritated Bakewell. It was his show now. He told Albrecht as much, leaning in for emphasis. "You're way out of your element here. Stay down and stay quiet. I don't want you shadowing me up there. I only want to shoot one man. You fuck this up and they return fire and you could get hit." He paused and said, "I may shoot you myself. You aren't exactly the nicest bloke I ever served with." Then, with a smile Bakewell couldn't resist, added, *"Dad."*

Albrecht nodded his assent, and Bakewell turned and took off, doubling his speed through the bush. He knew Albrecht would follow the trail he blazed and deliberately broke a lot of bush he could have avoided in order to leave a trail to the top of the ridge. Once over the top, he became selective, moving through the bush, breaking nothing, leaving no trail. There was a clear field of tall grass to the right. He dropped low, went across fast, and disappeared into the bush again before Albrecht could get to the top and locate him. There was thick jungle on the other side. He stopped inside the cover, rechecked his map, moved on up to the vantage point they had selected. It was at the edge of the bush, just inside the vegetation. He had a clear field of view outside the bush. Down the hill was an electronic fence and beyond it appeared to be an exercise yard, very long, rectangular. It had a footpath made of brick that led out to an observation point where a cupola stood overlooking the crashing surf. It provided a spectacular view of the ocean. Bakewell knew immediately why they had chosen the site for the fortress. It was a difficult approach from the water. They had built the heavy concrete pier and dock inside a small breakwater, and it would be easy to guard. He and Joel had seen it, barely visible in the heavy sea.

Bakewell thought the cupola would make a perfect place to spend time in contemplation, wondered if the old Arab had taken up a life of prayer. It was never too late. He hoped so as he settled in. He had done it many times before, waiting for larger game. Once in position he triangulated himself, butt and heels digging in, elbows against the inside of his knees, he swung the rifle back and forth as he looked for a spot to reference. It was less than a hundred yards to the fence, maybe twenty more to the path. The fence was obstructed from the walker's view by the heavy bush that had already reclaimed the area on both sides. He was barely able to see the steel fabric from above, razor wire shining bright in the intense tropical sun.

He used his pack to support his back and leaned against it and watched, taking in everything in his field of fire, estimating distances, waiting, imagining, thinking. *No dogs, no sentries, no movement. It's too perfect. What could be wrong? Where is Powell? Has he slipped in behind me? It's too perfect. It's a setup. Here I am again – set up.*

Bakewell opened his Leatherman, took one of the bullets from his pocket and examined it. It wasn't an explosive round. He thought about the same situation years before, much of it coming back now, amazingly distinct as he recalled those events. There had been little recoil from that weapon, little recoil could mean different things, balance, a flawless match in metal and stock, a shock absorbing perfection, achieved only in the most uniquely designed weapons. It could also mean a light load, a very light load. *Maybe the load fired in Genoa had been designed to hit without enough penetration to kill?* It was doubtful. He had hit the man center chest. *Still?*

With his site set up, he decided to move further back into the bush and hide himself, keeping his view of the path and the cul de sac at the end, next to the cupola. It wouldn't matter if they stayed on the path.

The adrenal ignition had worn off, his emotions quiet now. He had been stressed for over fifteen hours since they made land fall the night before. He hadn't slept well. Even though it was almost time, there was a let down. He knew there would be. He felt himself growing very tired, decided to rest, sure he had time. He would see them come down the path for a hundred yards before they got close enough. He would hear them long before they got close enough. He pumped a spray all about him to combat the insects and closed his eyes.

Forty-five minutes later – he'd checked his watch every five minutes before he fell asleep – he woke to the sound of voices coming toward him. They were very loud, almost like they were announcing themselves. Bakewell moved back to position, put the rifle to his shoulder and put the scope on them, moving across the field from left to right, one at a time. He settled on the Arab, his face recognizable still from the magazine cover. *People are a lot easier to shoot than animals, less caution, no instinct.* His mind came into focus as soon as he lifted the rifle, no sudden start, no anxiety. He was calm. It was eerie. He knew he would be calm, waited, knowing the calmness would leave him when he slid the tang forward, releasing the safety. He turned the scope to 6X. It was a favorite setting for this type of shot. When they were 100 yards off, he pulled the gun into his shoulder and adjusted the strap around his left bicep and forearm one last time. He was breathing very slowly. He could hear his heart pounding in his ears, but his movements were slow and deliberate.

The Arab was moving the slowest, setting the pace for the others. He looked beefy and out of shape, his shoulders draped, the sign of a heavy man, a sick man. Bakewell put the crosshair of the scope on his chest and followed him as he came, wondering where Powell was. It didn't matter now. *Concentrate.*

At what he estimated to be slightly less than a hundred yards he whispered quietly, exhaling, "For a million bucks. Here it is. One shot. One time. One…last…time." He pulled the trigger slowly, gradually increasing the pressure, holding to the tiny spot fixed in the crosshair, focusing. *Hold high. You want to miss high if you miss. You're not going to miss. It's show time.*

***

He came up out of the jungle running hard. As he approached the top, winded, drenched in the humidity, he spotted Albrecht waiting on the hillside in the opening where he left him. *Probably afraid to move.* Albrecht looked wide-eyed, frantic, kept giving him a "come on" wave. Bakewell raised his head, nodded in recognition, dropped back down, trying to speed his progress over the thick, tangled ground. He had been running hard, zigzagging in the tropical heat for five minutes and still hadn't covered the half-mile that separated them. Behind Albrecht was the open sea flashing and shining in the sunlight. Below Albrecht, over the hill, would be their boat. It wasn't out in the sea anywhere. Bakewell guessed it was already at the beach, on station, called in by Albrecht after he heard the shot. *Where was Powell?*

When he closed the distance to thirty yards he could see the boat. Powell was in the front, poling the bow as it bucked up and down in the surf.

"Hurry up," Albrecht hissed as he closed the gap. He indicated Bakewell give him the rifle, reaching out with both hands.

I'm almost done with violence and with anger too, but I sure don't like you, Mr. Albrecht. I don't want to kill you, sir, but I really don't care if it hurts.

When he was about three yards away he skipped once, bounced off his left foot, raising up to create momentum, and when he landed on his right he brought the rifle up, swinging the butt forward like he was offering it, holding the barrel in both hands. When Albrecht reached out for the rifle he was vulnerable. Bakewell pirouetted, coming round, bringing the rifle up and to his left just out of reach, made a one-eighty, and swung the rifle baseball style, right to left, and hit Albrecht in the face with the stock as hard as he could. The blow made a crunching sound as Albrecht's nose and the bones under his eyes caved in. He could actually feel the bones breaking through the stock, traveling up the barrel. He had practiced the maneuver in his mind, over and over, even gone through a dry run in the jungle several times. His biggest worry was the rifle would slip from his sweating hands, but that hadn't happened. He knew Albrecht would have to be leaning over. He was too big a man to hit in the face if he was standing erect. He hoped for a flat shot across his face and not one where the stock was turned on end, but the stock was slightly knife edged when he struck him. He didn't want to kill Albrecht. He just wanted him incapacitated long enough to disappear into the jungle, before the real killer got close. He knew the mercenary on the boat was the hit man. It was in his eyes plain enough.

Albrecht collapsed in a loud, sloppy commotion, sounding like a pile of wet snow sliding from a roof. He made only the slightest grunt, Bakewell checked him to make sure he was down to stay. Looking up, he spotted Powell, jumping off the boat. He knew Powell had seen him hit Albrecht, and he came running across the open beach very fast before disappearing into the bush below. Bakewell had enough time to disappear into the jungle before Powell could cut the distance. He checked Albrecht's pockets. He was heavy and hard to turn over, but Bakewell discovered a little Walther in his hip pocket. He took it and ran very fast, heading for the bush, down below the ridge and off to the right. Once inside the jungle, with the shading canopy overhead, he deliberately turned away from any kind of opening and ploughed through the dense vegetation, trying not to break his ankle in the labyrinth of root structure below, hoping he wouldn't disturb anything crawly down there. He didn't know if there were snakes in the islands like there were in PNG, but he knew there had to be something down there. He hated to put his feet in the nasty bottom growth. Bougainville had centipedes, and centipedes had a mean bite. He went about fifty yards before he stopped; his timing was nearly perfect. Almost as soon as he stopped, he heard Powell come crashing into the bush then the noise stopped. Bakewell waited, trying not to breathe, so out of breath he couldn't help himself. His breathing sounded like gasping, which it was, and much too loud; he hoped the foliage would dampen the sound. He kept his mouth open wide, inhaling the ever present insects, trying not to choke as he waved them away from his open mouth and gulped for oxygen.

There was a long delay then he heard the mercenary say "Shit!" loud enough to be heard through the vegetation. He stayed quiet, waited five long minutes, checking his watch, knowing Powell had to get away in the boat soon, but he didn't want to give himself up to a feint. Finally he heard another "Shit!" and actually got a glimpse of the man as he went out into the sunlight. He knew he had been right about Powell. He was a professional, had tried to get him to make some noise. If he had bought the feint, he would be dealing with him now on his own terms. He didn't think he was up to dealing with Powell at any time, especially in a jungle. He listened and heard nothing more. After about ten minutes, he made his way over to the jungle's edge quietly and very slowly. When he reached the edge, he sat down just inside the dense foliage amidst a swarm of biting things and waited.

He kept checking his watch. It was easy to lose track of time when things were racing. It was the second hottest time of his life. He wasn't nearly as disoriented as he expected to be. The insects were terrible and it was painful and exasperating to sit amidst them. Whatever repellent might have worked earlier, had dripped away. It had been thirty sweaty minutes since he had fired the rifle. He held it tightly in his hands still. After a few more minutes he heard a shot fired close by. It was small caliber. After another ten minutes, he heard the sound of the boat's motor across the top of the ridge, separating him from the ocean. He made a short dash up the hill, fearing he might be falling for another feint, but he had to know. When he got to the top he turned the rifle up to full power and looked through the scope. Powell was there on the boat with the two crewman and they were headed back out into the Solomon Sea, going down to the south the way they had come. He wondered where Albrecht was. Probably down in his room recovering. *I'll bet he is one pissed-off leader*. He didn't really care where Albrecht was; he only wanted to know Powell's location. He watched the boat as long as he dared, worrying about what was going on over at the compound. He had to get going.

After he retrieved his pack Bakewell sighed and turned back to the dreaded bush and started moving. When he had gone several hundred yards he stopped, opened the pack and pulled out a pocket GPS. It was the most expensive one he could find. He wondered if it would be adequate in a place like Bougainville; there was no choice. He punched in his *Present Position* and then tried to plot a course. After some confusion, checking his compass against the GPS and the damp map, he started to walk very deliberately to the northeast into the deepest part of the jungle.

Carrying the coveted pack and rifle reminded him of hunting in the mountains again. The difference was in the going – it was unbelievably difficult to blaze a trail in the bush without a machete, and it was unbearably humid. He wished he could have secreted a machete in his gear at some earlier time. He made only a hundred yards between stops. He kept up the pace for over two hours, constantly checking his GPS, wanting to be rid of the thickness of the bush, hoping to be out in an opening before night fell before it was time to make camp; all the while remembering the stories he had read about the Bougainville campaign of the Marine Raiders: the muck and the mud and how the terrifying fighting had taken place in quarters so close, men fought within yards of one another and died in miserable surroundings, perishing in a place so uninhabitable they had to be carried out to be buried. An hour before the sun set it got much darker, under a thin mist that gave way to a light drizzle, and the insects, a constant bother, became insufferable.

He crested a number of small rises, more than he could remember in the hours he kept at it. When he finally came to the top of one more he gave it up for the day and made camp, putting out his mummy tent and filling it with the soft down bag. He left most of his gear in the pack, and after undressing and coating himself with repellent to ward off the attack, he stood in the shade and fanned himself with a soaking tee shirt, trying to dry off. Finally he crawled inside the tent and laid down on the bag, zipping the tent flap overhead tightly. Once inside the protective cover he could listen to the swarms of would be attackers without the need to take further cover.

The tight tent, which had always provided warmth and comfort in the cold weather, seemed claustrophobic in the equatorial heat. He looked up at the fabric, just inches from his face and thought about what had happened over the previous twenty-four hours. It had been an incredible day, filled with challenge and with survival. He didn't think of it as adventure. Adventure carried the implication of romance; there was no romance in the jungle and even less in violence, and the apprehension and fear it created. It was one of the few days in his life he would be able to reconstruct from beginning to end.

He had been running on adrenaline, without fear and with little concern, now he was exhausted, his brain numb from the planning, his body from the exertion. Reality would return when he woke again, but he had peaked and was down-sliding fast. He had done well, had kept Powell off his back, had handled Albrecht with little effort. Albrecht had been a confusing concern since he learned of his presence back in Moresby, but the man's presence had diminished so dramatically, so far out of his element in the islands. He wondered why Powell had chosen to wait it out on the boat. He was almost sure he would have to deal with Powell afterward; thought he might find him behind after the shot, was almost positive he would feel his intervention. He wondered about Powell...and about the fortress. There was no return fire from the fortress, no response at all. It was almost like they expected what had happened to happen. There were no troops to protect such an infamous man, known for his paranoia about security.

What had he missed? There was nothing to do afterward, but disable Albrecht and shake Powell and go bush. The misery of traveling in the bush, not withstanding, it had been almost too easy. He couldn't have hoped for more.

He fell asleep quickly, only woke once during the night, just to roll over, too dehydrated to urinate. It was cool on the jungle floor. He opened the sleeping bag, and laid one side over him. In the morning he came awake to a heavy fog surrounding the tent. He made tea and poured in the thick honey. He drank the tea and ate several energy bars laying there, thinking about what was ahead. Unable to imagine much about what was to come, he let his mind wander. Where were his children and his grandchildren? What were they all doing? It was March 28th, according to Fr. Gerardo's watch, still the 27th in America. He was grateful for the gift of the watch.

March. He had learned to hate March. Katherine said it was his imagination, but he knew better. It was the month of bad news, the month of surprises, the month of big events – all bad. Just about every bad thing that had happened to him had happened in March. Both of his parents had died in March. Every financial debacle in his life seemed to occur in March. He didn't want to give up anymore time in life, but each year he told his children he would have willingly gone into a coma and skipped March, especially the last few. He wasn't completely serious, still he hated March.

When the fog lifted, he checked the GPS, switching it on and off, not sure how long the batteries would last. He had to continue northeast, more east than northeast in order to intersect the river. Eventually he would hit the river and find where it crossed the Buin road. He had little confidence in the GPS so far from home. In America it would be incredibly precise, but he was on the other side of the world. The river was the key. It intersected the road with a bridge or low water crossing south of Nagovisi. He broke camp and set out after the fog lifted enough to see twenty yards ahead. He couldn't see more than twenty yards in the bush anyway, so the fog was more of an emotional challenge than a navigational one. The going was just as bad as the afternoon before, and he was running down physically. He had to push on or die alone in the jungle. He was killing himself in small increments with each hour's exertion. He'd challenged himself many times in the wilderness over the years. This was a different wilderness; he was determined to make it, if only just one more time. He had always loved the challenge of surviving.

The traveling was the same as the day before, until the ground leveled when he neared the river. When he found it, he was too far south, used the river for reference and headed on a more northerly direction through the heavy foliage along the bank. He couldn't get too far from the bank or he would lose sight of the river. The river made no sound. He tripped so often he lost count, fell five separate times, landing with a wet thud on the soft ground. He laughed at the irony of falling so much. In the mountains a fall could have been disastrous; on the tangled floor it was just aggravating. He worried about crocodiles, knew the crocs would be small this far from the ocean, but a croc was vicious. He tried to watch for them, but in the thick vegetation it was nearly impossible.

About one o'clock, he stopped to eat and when he did, heard voices and the sound of a vehicle. After another fifty yards, the sounds of habitation were clearly distinguishable. When he was within sight of the road, he stopped and picked his way forward. Just where the road crossed the river, an old Toyota Hilex stood waiting. He stepped out on the dark worn earth. The roadway was clear and a man was resting on the bare ground on the other side of the car. He came off the ground with a start; a fellow conspirator, and helped Bakewell put his gear in the vehicle, took the rifle and dismantled it quickly, removing the action from the stock and placed it in the bottom of the trunk and covered it with Bakewell's pack, clearly spooked by the weapon.

When they got in the car he said, "Bikman, you kam long taim. Joel worri."

Bakewell only nodded, glad to be free of the thick bush. Joel described the excitement caused by a rumor about a "Bikman" who had been shot near the coast. It was only a rumor that had originated with someone making a delivery to "the compound." When Bakewell still didn't answer, the man of few words and fewer questions, came straight to the point. "Long wonem yu sutim dispela man?"

Bakewell didn't want to talk about shooting "dispela man." The more he told Joel the more danger Joel would be in. He was more interested in the BRA and their whereabouts. He wanted to know where the BRA were and how many. Joel said they were everywhere. They were deep inside the BRA's country.

"I think we can speak English now Joel," Bakewell said. "How far have we to go down this road?"

"I no long we," Joe started, switched to English, "A few hours only. We go on to Siwai and then to Buin. We have to wait outside Buin for night to come before we go to the city."

Bakewell nodded his assent. The road was terrible, full of huge holes, some twenty feet across. Fortunately none were more than six inches deep. The depressions were filled with dirty, gray colored water from a recent rain. When they arrived in Siwai, Bakewell got down low in the seat and covered his head with an old hat. He wrapped his towel around his neck up high against his ears to conceal most of his white skin. There weren't many people on the road; nearly all were walkers. They passed one old truck and an ancient van, both loaded down with passengers. Siwai was a non-event, and they were soon on the way to Buin, where they arrived after dark. A white man in Buin was rare and neither man wanted to draw attention. They went through Buin down to the water, where a canoe waited.

Bakewell told the guerilla to leave the rifle in the trunk. He removed the extra cartridges from his pockets and put them in the console between the seats. Joel locked the doors and they were in the boat and on their way in minutes. The trip across was twenty kilometers; they made it before ten that night. Joel had arranged a place for them to spend the night – a hut with dirt floors. They were alone during the short night. Bakewell slept deeply, trusting the guerilla with his life.

When he awoke in the morning, he was barely able to move. He wanted very much to take one of the hydrocodone pills, but toughed it out. They put back into the water and made Balalai before nine. When they reached the shore, Joel explained a white man could have come up by plane or boat from the southeast. Since no one had seen him on the trip down there was no reason to suspect he was anything other than another tourist in the islands. They were in the Solomons now. They went to the airfield, to a tiny shed where the ticket booth of Solomon Air was located. Joel negotiated the price south to Honiara. It was there on Guadalcanal that Henderson Field, now an international airport, had been established during the war. It would be another day before the plane came, so Joel found a guesthouse back out on the water, and they took lodging there. In the morning Joel said he had to leave. Bakewell had his ticket south to a safer place in the islands and needn't worry about his safety any longer.

Bakewell was grateful to the quiet, reliable man who had taken a serious chance on his behalf. He gave him five thousand kina.

"You have been good to me. Thank you."

"Bikman was no trouble," Joel looked around when he spoke, unable to speak straight on, always looking to the side. Bakewell wondered if it was from embarrassment, or an enforced habit, caused by a lifetime of trying to go unnoticed, head down, avoiding confrontation, trying to survive.

"It was a lot of trouble. I will be in your debt for the rest of my life. You are a good man." Bakewell shook his huge hand, held it firmly. "Always I will speak of the good man I met in Buka Town, but never will I tell anyone of our purpose."

The tall islander nodded vigorously. "That is good," seemed even more embarrassed, and put his left hand to his face as he shook Bakewell's hand for the last time. Bakewell continued to grasp his hand, overcome with gratitude. "You have done me a great service. My people will be grateful to Joel Nasale of Buka Island." The guerilla nodded. When Bakewell let go of his hand, he stood awkwardly, his small head bobbing up and down, then he backed away.

"God keep you safe," Bakewell bid farewell to the man as he turned and walked off. Joel raised his hand in recognition and went off at a graceful, long legged pace.

Bakewell waited in the guesthouse on another comfortable mat, on a man-made cot inside a mosquito netting, in a hut without any covering on the windows, listening to the sound of leaves scraping against the building. The soft breeze stirred the plants and the insects circling about them. The plane wouldn't come until afternoon, if it was on time. He found a shower outside in an elevated building. It had only a faucet overhead that allowed the captured rainwater on the roof to drop in a small stream. The water was warm and clean and the air hot in the sunlight overhead. It was cool and refreshing, and he spent ten minutes soaping and scrubbing under the flow. When he went to pay his bill, the woman of the guesthouse said it had been paid by, "the tall man from Bougainville."

Bakewell couldn't understand how the people could possibly tell one man from another. He had learned they could spot one islander as distinct from another instantly. Even in a country where all men were black, they were separate and distinct. Bougainvillians were a mercantile class in many ways. Later he would learn that down to the southeast, the Malaitans had a much lighter skin, many had blond hair, and they saw themselves as a super race, like the Aryans of another time.

There were hundreds of tribes in the islands and each island had a separate identity, with many tribes. Some tribes were large, numbering in the thousands; some were small, a few hundred or less. Sadly ethnic awareness created hatred and intolerance, *and* there was always "the tensions." They were about to explode.

At noon Bakewell walked over to the shed and waited for the plane to come. A dozen people came out of the bush to watch the plane land, a minor event in their lives. Bakewell heard the bush plane come in over the hills just above the treetops. Once clear the pilot cut the engines and the Twin-Otter decelerated rapidly, using most of the short runway. Only two men got off the plane. Bakewell was instructed to board after their luggage was removed.

The pilot kept the "off" engine running during the operation. Bakewell got on board and took a single seat next to the emergency exit where he could look out the window. The plane was nearly empty. The seats were small and cramped. He knew he would be claustrophobic if it were filled with people and determined not to give up his window seat. A young man got up and gave a quick emergency procedures review, using a tattered airline folder for reference, while the two young pilots, visible through the hatchway, spooled up the engines and turned at the end of the runway. They departed the opposite way they had landed in the windless afternoon and Bakewell bid farewell to Papua New Guinea.

Batuna

The plane took them southeast down the island chain for fifty miles. Without pressurization, they flew at 5000 feet and the view of the islands was breathtaking. After twenty minutes Vella Lavella came into view. They landed at Mbarakoma Airfield, took on three passengers and were airborne again in minutes. Bakewell saw a huge mountain on the next island. When he looked at his GPS it read exactly 7 degrees 00'00" South by 157 degrees 00'00" East. His fellow passengers dozed or stared disinterestedly out the small windows as they passed Kolombangara.

When they landed at Gizo there were many waiting to come aboard and they did so with a lot of pushing and scraping. Bakewell refused to give up his seat, wondering if he could deal with many more onboard. There were two seats on the right side of the plane, only one on his side. The passageway was narrow and the cabin roof so low people had to bend to make their way up the aisle. The tight quarters put off a foul odor; the only thing missing was the pigs and chickens of a 3rd world bus. Bakewell followed their progress carefully on his map, folding it as they flew southeast. They continued down to Vangunu Island where they landed next to a beautiful village, and the plane sloshed through large puddles on touchdown, the wheels throwing muddy water over the windows, adding to Bakewell's claustrophobic discomfort. When the plane came to a stop there was a crowd of more than fifty milling about in the knee-high grass.

Bakewell took his pack and climbed down and walked out on the grassy plain, breathing deeply. The odor of Vangunu was fantastically clean and refreshing. When it was time to depart for Guadalcanal he couldn't re-embark. The plane was packed with passengers for Honiara. His ticket was for Honiara, but the village, with its wonderful fragrance beckoned. He walked further away from the plane in the midst of a crowded confusion and observed the people gathered, watching, much like small town America had once watched the afternoon train come through. As the plane revved up and taxied away he spotted a tiny pikinini standing alone. Bakewell went to her and bent down and took her hand. She didn't speak English and the pidgin of the Solomons was different from that of PNG. He dropped to one knee, holding her hand delicately. He gave up the attempt to communicate and kissed her hand gallantly. The watching faces turned to broad smiles when he straightened up. His effort had the intended affect. He approached a man and asked if he spoke English.

"No sir," the man said sincerely. "But this man does. He is the assistant primary school teacher." He spoke his words carefully, pronouncing each word perfectly as he indicated the man a few yards away.

"You don't speak English?" Bakewell asked again, confused.

"No sir." The man was emphatic; he didn't speak English.

Amused, Bakewell looked to the man suggested, who came forward and bowed courteously, saying, "Good day sir," very politely.

Bakewell extended his hand. "It looks like I need an interpreter."

"Yes?"

"What is this place?"

"It is Batuna, sir."

"Where am I?"

"In Batuna. You are lost?"

"Not anymore. I am looking for a boat that I might purchase and use for some time. Is this possible?"

"I am afraid not, sir. A boat is very expensive ting. Not much are available here on Vangunu, sir."

"Is it possible to spend the night here?"

"Yes sir. We have a veri fine guesthouse. It is in the village." He also rolled the "r" in veri. "You would want to go there?"

"Yes."

"I will show you this guesthouse for guests."

Bakewell followed the man who was the assistant principal of the technical school, a man of some importance. They went through a grove of fine leafed pines, moving slightly in the soft breeze. Further on, they passed through a thick cane that was high over their heads, following a narrow, muddy pathway, avoiding the puddles. When they emerged from the stand of cane they came to one of the most idyllic places Bakewell had ever seen, a postcard come to life.

The guesthouse was on a steep, single hill rising, dramatic and unaccountable, above the water overlooking the Morovo Lagoon; the accommodation compliments of the Seventh Day Adventists who were gone, possibly in the field somewhere looking for souls? Bakewell didn't ask. Before going up the teacher showed him an unmarked store at the base of the hill where he bought food and several bottles of Vitro. Afterward, he spent a peaceful evening on the porch, overlooking the serene water, gently lapping the island, overcome by the scent of flowers wafting on a pleasant breeze.

The young man also brought a procession of visitors to meet *William*, "Who comes from America all the way here to Vangunu to see us." The sun set, and after several shy young people whom the teacher referred to proudly as "our pikinini," left, visitation came to a close. Bakewell had been the geography lesson for the day. He spent the night on the knob of a small, steep hill, in one of the most peaceful settings he had ever known. Bakewell had never needed peace more. Physically and mentally drained, he needed the opportunity to recover, unsure if he would bounce back this time. He was dead with exhaustion. *You've overdone it. You're a dying man. You've got to slow down.*

He slept inside the guesthouse behind windows well screened, without the need for mosquito netting. It was a sleep of the dead once more and lasted well into the long equatorial night. When he woke and relocated himself, he had another chance to put things in perspective and to focus on the future, and also time to pray, but prayer was no good. He'd read about great saints who had undergone periods of spiritual dryness in their prayer life. He was no saint, but his prayer life had never been drier.

He slept very late, waking to the sound of people below in the little harbor behind a man-made jetty of dead coral. When he came down from the guesthouse, the teacher reappeared; Bakewell suspected he had his spotters posted. He wanted to buy a boat, but after a short and futile attempt at negotiation, had to give up. He had offered as much as fifteen thousand Solomon Island dollars to no avail. The teacher told him he could find a canoe for hire if Bakewell wanted to tour the islands, and said he would arrange for such travel.

"If you must travel someplace else to visit, it can be arranged. There are many boats going and coming, but none are for sale." Bakewell agreed to book the first passage that would take him from the airport. He wanted to be away from the airport. On the following day two men from the north came to Batuna to do their banking. They were heading back that same afternoon and Bakewell agreed to go with them in exchange for "payment of the petrol, which is veri expensive."

Bakewell hated to leave Batuna. It was a perfect setting of soft breezes, beautiful little lagoons, and picturesque thatched huts on small promontories, surrounded by quiet protected water in the Morovo Lagoon; which he later learned, was the largest double reefed lagoon in the world. Morovo Lagoon was much trumpeted by the World Preservation Society. There was no lovelier place on earth.

His companions, Scotty who manned the small outboard and spoke little English, and a much bigger man named Frank Iputu, who sat behind Bakewell and provided an informative commentary whenever asked, were from the north end of Vangunu. Frank was twenty years Bakewell's junior, powerfully built and, as they went up the lagoon, Bakewell wondered in hazy fatigue if they might not cut his throat and dump him over for the sharks. He would be an easy mark in his condition. His fears were soon allayed. The men were pleasant and extremely polite. Frank made continuous conversation about America, questioning the purpose of his visit to Vangunu. Bakewell told him of his father's participation in the war and his misfortune in New Georgia. Like many islanders, Frank wanted to know why the war had been fought out in the islands and Bakewell explained the significance of Guadalcanal as an historic coincidence, saying that Henderson Field had been a flashpoint – a place where warring nations, recognizing the strategic importance of Guadalcanal, had met head on for the first time. He was unsure if either man understood, but they smiled and nodded politely.

They made several stops on the way north, first at Chea, where they bought fuel. Bakewell had no destination other than to be away from airports, as remote as possible. He would work his destination out as the trip progressed. It was tiring in the canoe with nothing to lean against and his back ached as he sat on an old wooden board that spanned the canoe's narrow beam. The boat leaked by the bow; seawater coming in through a rotted place each time they sank down in the light sea, washing down the length of the long canoe, passing under his feet and pack, which rested on another piece of rotting wood. When it reached the pilot, Scotty carefully baled the water with half a plastic milk carton, dumping it over the side.

They stopped at an island atoll, no more than a hundred yards across. It was called Warutu, and Bakewell met a man living on the island with a woman from Ontong Java who was the grandson of Harold Markham. Markham had once operated a plantation on New Georgia before evacuating, after the bombing of Pearl Harbor. His plantation home had been taken over and become the headquarters of the Coastwatcher Donald Kennedy, who managed to raise a small island force to combat the Japanese during most of 1942, before the Allies arrived and relieved him. Kennedy was a famous character with many of the older islanders. The man on the island said, "D. G. Kennedy, a fookin English colonialists, he was, eh," and told stories of Kennedy's propensity to take the rod to those who crossed him. The Warutu man said Kennedy was heavy-handed and ruthless; he didn't try to hide his contempt for Kennedy, even though the man had conducted a personal and very daring war against the Japanese, saving many downed pilots in the process, from his lonely outpost at Segi, which was now called Seghe.

They arrived at Michi, Frank's village, late in the afternoon, rounding a long, protective bend that led to a shallow flat of luminous green water. There were many pikinini swimming in the water, which shallowed over fine white sand where they tied the boat in several feet of water against some coral. The sand was gritty and mushy and made wadding difficult. Frank told Bakewell to remove his aging leather sandals before they were sucked off and lost.

The long trip in the scorching sun had taken a toll on Bakewell, and Frank Iputu recognized his failing state and politely offered accommodations for the night. Bakewell hesitated, but after visiting the village, decided to accept. He met Frank's children, some of his students and part of his extended family as they toured the scenic village. The school, a large rectangular building with a thatched roof, raised about four feet above the ground, and only a short walk from Frank's home, was perfect for a visiting stranger. Bakewell asked many questions about their village and its history, noticing how remote it was, how remote he was. Not knowing what he would find further up the island chain, he decided to stay in Michi, grateful for Frank's offer.

Using the identity of William Jennings, Bakewell stayed on at Michi, and in the days that followed, regained some needed energy. He slept much of the first few days, falling asleep to the gentle laughter of children each evening. He spent the cool mornings wandering the footpaths around the village, feeling blessed to be away from the trouble on Bougainville and PNG, thankful all was quiet at Michi. Rumors of the troubles further down toward Malaita and Guadalcanal had made there way up the chain.

He swam in the amazingly green water of the lagoon at midday, and later the children of Michi joined him when school was dismissed. He adopted their habit of splashing noisily whenever they saw a shark feeding. The sight of a shark in the water made Bakewell uneasy, but he learned to live with their presence, warily. He ate fruit and vegetables and spent most of his days alone. Frank instructed his people to leave the American to himself, and loaned Bakewell a small canoe which he paddled around the big lagoon, which was hundreds of yards wide and deep. He also went a few miles up and down the coastline, pacing himself, stopping to rest in the quiet water, napping along the beach on the way. In the evenings he pitched his small tent on the elevated veranda floor outside the school building to the amusement of the children and many of the villagers. The arrangement worked well; the sun came up hours before school started, giving him time to stow his gear before class began.

Michi was a place of solitude, the water calm and protected. The fishing was excellent, fresh fish always abundant. There was no electricity and none of the distractions that electricity provided, and by nine in the evening all was quiet. In addition to canoeing and walking the paths leading up to the higher elevations, Bakewell spent long afternoons napping or reading his ragged Bible. The book had taken a beating in his travels, gotten wet in Bougainville and again on the crossing to the Shortlands and was barely holding together. He'd found what he was searching for: leisure, apathy and intellectual emptiness, unless he chose to challenge himself with memories. Evenings with the Iputus were serene. Frank loved to practice his English and spoke it very clearly. Their conversation took place each night before Bakewell returned to his place on the schoolhouse veranda.

He read by kerosene lantern, and later watched the stellar display of the southern hemisphere, knowing nothing about the stars below the equator. Stargazing left him in awe of the mighty universe once more and his nights were serene, capped off by long deep sleeps; and, when he woke, aimless staring at the bright, cloudless starlit sky. When he dreamt, it was of things far in his past.

The gradual return of energy created another resurgence: he wondered if the hormonal thing would ever play out. He was dying and yet he still had the same yearnings that had plagued him years before. The brief interlude with Maggie Walker had brought him back to life in way not anticipated.

Bakewell wondered where she was, what she was doing, hoped she would find "A veri good man," as the islanders liked to say. In his dreams he saw the faces of his children and grandchildren often. With the exception of Katherine, he had no trouble remembering what anyone looked like. He hoped the news of his death had not caused too much pain, but knew better – he'd been there the last time. They knew he was dying, hopefully they thought he had chosen to speed the process by going off to the missions.

***

The summer following the year Maggie took up her pursuit of the law, Bakewell returned home to baseball and beer; playing with greater intensity; he got into several scraps on the field, banging into people he could have avoided. He hit the ball harder than ever before and cleared the levee six times in one week with homeruns that had only been incidental before. He was a contact hitter, a line drive hitter, but that summer he swung for the fences – and struck out a lot. They moved him to fourth in the lineup; before he had always batted third. Everything aggravated him, and his temper was so short his teammates began to razz him, nicknamed him PO, because he was always pissed off.

After the ball playing ended, Bakewell began a lifelong quest to spend as much time as possible sleeping under the stars. Brenden had been his only campmate. He remembered their float trips on the scenic streams of Missouri, the times they had talked long into the night about baseball and girls and the war heating up in Viet Nam. They also talked about their father and his wartime service. Brenden wanted to believe Charlie had been a hero. Bakewell was indifferent to the notion; he'd had enough of the service, and he didn't want to see his brother involved. But Brenden was one of those rare kids that didn't need the service for straightening out. He *was* straight, always squared away, always made a conscientious effort to do everything right. Brenny was never emotional, never got upset about things he couldn't control. Brenny loved the service and he had loved the idea of fighting for his country.

Bakewell's family buried their father's mother the following summer, right before school started. They hadn't seen much of her over the years. She was a very old lady by then, part of the "other side of the family." He returned to school right after Labor Day, but had to come home the following week to participate in her legal affairs. His grandmother had left them each $2,000. The next morning, before turning west for Columbia, he stopped at a little restaurant called The Trio, which sat precariously below the new highway, threatened by the inevitable progress of West County, and the construction of what would eventually become Interstate 64. The commotion work outside could be felt inside, and the building shook from the vibration of heavy earthmoving equipment.

The Trio was a hangout for "long hitters," a school term applied to the big drinkers bent on self-destruction, offering breakfast around the clock and, often as not, consumed in the early hours of the morning, a favored hangout of the just-turned-legal-drinking-age crowd. It was a 2½-hour drive to Columbia with only one decent place to eat 45 minutes further west, so Bakewell stopped to stoke up before the long, monotonous drive back to school. As he was waiting to pay he saw Katherine Durham enter the diner. He hadn't seen her in years and he was pleased to see how she had turned out. The last time he'd seen her she was a pre-teen with braces. What he saw that morning was a young woman with large, expressive eyes and a wonderful smile that commanded a smile in return from even the sourest disposition.

She came through the revolving door in a pair of Bermuda shorts and a soft V-necked sweater, sleeves pushed up to her elbows in the eighty-degree heat. Her muscled thighs and calves, darkly tanned, rippled right down to her browned toes, which showed through fashionable leather sandals. About the time Katherine entered, a tall, gangly man stood awkwardly, making odd gestures, raising and lower his head, bending from the waist, his face florid, and everyone watched his odd behavior, until a heavyset woman shouted, "Can't someone help this man?"

Without hesitation Katherine grabbed him from behind and put her hands together below his diaphragm and began jerking upward. He was well over six feet, Katherine much shorter and it was an awkward business, but she persisted while all watched the performance, trancelike, until the guy finally hacked up part of his meal, gasping for breath as he pulled himself from her grasp. When Katherine backed away Bakewell was shocked to see her soft sweater and sheer bra had been pushed up, and one of her finely sculpted breasts was exposed from the exertion. When she moved to straighten her sweater she discovered the reason for their attention was her dilemma and not the affirmation she might have hoped for, and she shrieked, horrified, covering her striking, youthful chest and bolted for the door.

Bakewell had watched, stunned like everyone else, and before he could move, she brushed passed, face crimson, humiliated, and ran out the door and vanished in a swirl of screeching tires.

He lived in a listless vacuum when he returned to school that fall, less angry, but indifferent about school, unsure what he wanted from it. His grades suffered and he returned to a life of carnal pleasure. There was a stream of coeds from Stephens College, half a block from his apartment, who provided amusement for the guys in the building. The "Steves" weren't looking for action as much as an opportunity to eat something other than cafeteria food. Bakewell, partially orphaned as a kid, could throw the basic stuff together and his thick, meaty stew was a hit with the young, impressionable girls, who showed a surprising willingness to give themselves to, "the vet in the apartment behind Tower Hall." Bakewell drew the line there. "Putting the make on these tender things," a neighbor across the hall compared to stealing from children. He was probably right, but Bakewell had no intention of finding out. It would only fill him with guilt; he was having enough trouble with his self-esteem.

For several months he took up with a local girl, up from poverty, who came with a resume of experience. "A townie," was what they called them. She was several years older, more than willing to bed down in his apartment, was creative and imaginative and accommodated him almost on demand. But it was a tepid relationship, and when one of his friends called her "tacky," the shallowness of his character showed and he dumped her without warning, and he was ruthless about it.

The townie found another boyfriend, a wrangler at the Stephens College stable with rodeo aspirations, and proceeded to tell the boyfriend about her interlude with Bakewell, elaborating to the extent that Bakewell had taken advantage of her. The boyfriend, a rural cowboy, nearly thirty and about his size, decided to teach Bakewell a lesson, coming by his apartment one night for an inebriated confrontation, intending to, "Give the punk a beating he wouldn't forget." But when Bakewell closed the gap and asked him if he really wanted to pay the price, the guy weaved a little, thought it over, and they ended up having a thirty minute conversation about what a great gal Ol' Shirley was. They shook hands before the cowboy climbed bowlegged back into his battered pickup and Bakewell sent him off, wishing him good luck on the rodeo circuit. After he left, Bakewell felt even worse about Shirley, wished he could call her and apologize, but knew it would only start things up again.

During the long school year he couldn't get the image of Katherine Durham out of his thoughts. A vision of her youthful chest was etched in his mind. He had known her since she was five years old and accused himself of being both pig and pervert as he reflected on the outrageous misfortune that had befallen her attempt to do a good deed. He was growing cynical, and the thought of such a thing happening to such a lovely creature made him madder each time he thought about it. He decided he would do something special for her when he got home, do it somehow without letting her know he had witnessed her humiliation. He was sure she hadn't seen him and was determined to keep her from knowing. He was also sure he would never forget the lovely contour and soft whiteness of her breast, exposed in stark contrast to the rest of her suntanned body.

Seghe

Frank Iputu leaned toward Bakewell as they were preparing the evening meal. Bakewell had been eating his dinner alone most evenings, cooking it on a campfire on the other side of the lagoon, enjoying fresh fish and an interesting variety of fruits and vegetables. The island people ate copious amounts of white rice with every meal which was filling but tasteless. Bakewell preferred to eat alone in order not to offend them, but Frank had asked him to join them for dinner. They were seated on the veranda of Frank's elevated hut, protected from the sun's rays by the drooping thatched roof, as it descended over the densely covered hills to the west. As they ate the children chattered in their tribal language. They all spoke the tribal language, except when they spoke to Bakewell; then they used the pidgin of the islands. Pidgin wasn't the universal language of the Solomons like Tok Pisin was in PNG. Most tribal people spoke their own language; pidgin was used rarely, between tribes when the difference in language was great.

"William," Frank said quietly, "There is news from across the water from Scotty." Bakewell nodded for him to continue. "A white man is in the Lagoon, asking about another white man who has this name of Bakewell." He paused, smiling into Bakewell's eyes, looking for cognition, before lowering his voice in a gesture of friendship. "Do you know this man, yes?"

Bakewell stirred the food on his plate and looked across the wide shallow bay, where the sun still illuminated the shimmering water. "Yes."

Frank nodded sympathetically. "I fear you might."

There was no way a white man could be looking for another white man without suspicion. After living amid so much tension, the islanders were quick to pick up on any potential for trouble. Both men were silent. Finally Bakewell asked, "Where is this man last seen?"

"Up about Gizo; a long way, yet not so long here in these islands."

They were both pensive; finally Bakewell spoke again. "Will he come in the dark do you think, Frank?"

"I don't think so. It is a long paddle. The motor can be heard. Maybe he comes from over there," Frank pointed beyond the peninsula toward the thick vegetation to the northwest, "Beach his boat and come through the bush to surprise, so the motor can't be heard from so far away."

"Do you know how many white men?"

"Only one I think." Frank's English was the best Bakewell had heard anywhere in the islands. The others never pronounced the "h" in think, making it sound like "tink." Frank pronounced it correctly. They were quiet for the rest of the meal. Later when Frank asked Bakewell if he would be leaving, Bakewell nodded, very discouraged. "If you would like to leave at night, without the sound of the motor, I could help you go myself."

"Let me think about it."

Frank seemed as preoccupied with his thoughts as Bakewell was. At one point, listening to the children, Frank looked over at his friend and smiled self-consciously, nodding at the playful and energetic noise, said, “Pikinini.” The children had become comfortable with the white man for whom their teacher had such respect. They no longer stared at him in awe, had returned to their extroverted, joyful nature.

“How long will it take to cross over without a motor?”

“Not long. Maybe two hours for us. You are a good man with the boat.”

“Would it be too much trouble to go in the middle of the night?”

“No trouble at all, William.”

Bakewell returned to the schoolhouse and unrolled his bag. He tried to sleep, but heard many noises coming from the bush. They were no longer comforting noises. He couldn’t sleep. When the time came, he put his pack together and met Frank on the beach. They left about three. It would give them three hours of darkness to make the seven mile row across the water to New Georgia. They used a traditional canoe. There weren’t many left now; most of the heavy dugouts were motor equipped. This one was sleek, with little draft, built for only a few paddlers. Bakewell put himself hard into the job of paddling; he didn’t want to be any more trouble than necessary. Frank pulled his paddle through the water effortlessly; no matter how much Bakewell tried to keep up, Frank was always right there, waiting behind him, telling him to take his time and not to overexert himself. Frank knew Bakewell was not well.

They passed an island with a steep hill that exposed many houses through the canopy of the bush. Metal roofs glinted in the moonlight. One was a very large building.

“What is that place?” Bakewell whispered.

“It is Patutiba. There is a mission there and a mission school. They also have a nice church.”

A little later the concrete pier at Seghe appeared in the moonlit darkness. It was cracked, badly spaulled around the edge, with rusty steel rebar showing when they got closer. Frank spoke very quietly, telling Bakewell there was a man with a guesthouse in Seghe, named Peter Lolo, adding, “He is a veri good man.” He assured Bakewell that Peter Lolo would be helpful and he could count on him. They brought the canoe in quietly next to the wharf. The rebar stuck out at vicious angles. Bakewell suspected it had been constructed by the Allies when they relieved Donald Kennedy of his coast watching duties.

He got out of the canoe stiffly and waded into the beach. It had been a long row and he was tired and sore and knew the soreness would be worse the next day. He bent down and held the canoe as Frank climbed up out of the boat onto the wharf. Frank looked around in the dark. He knew the place well.

"Over there is a store where you can buy some things to eat." It was a fairly large building, looming in the darkness; behind was the jungle, black and mysterious in the shadows. Bakewell looked around the wharf, a little daunted at the prospect of confronting new villagers and making new friends. There was a much smaller building off to the left of the wharf and several drums containing petrol. One had a small hand pump screwed into the top, visible in the moonlight.

Frank straightened up stretching, yawned once and said, "I will leave you now, William. It is better if I am not seen crossing the channel at daylight. Once passed the channel, I will look like an early fisherman of the day closer to my own village." He offered his hand and Bakewell took it, very grateful to the islander who had no reason to help him. He offered money, but Frank declined. "I hope you do well out here in this part of the islands. It is very beautiful up toward Tetepare. Tell Peter Lolo to take you there. It is quiet, and you might find a restful place." Then he added for the third time, "Peter Lolo is a veri good man."

Bakewell watched the islander climb back down to the canoe and back it out before getting in again. He turned it skillfully and began his voyage back across the channel while Bakewell watched, his spirits sinking as Frank pulled on the paddle and gradually disappeared in the darkness. He put his pack on the ground and sat, leaning against it. It was softer than the concrete pier. After a while he fell asleep. When he awoke the sun was coming up off to his right, warming his face. He hadn't shaved since they shoved off from Port Moresby. The beard gave his face some protection from the sun, but made him look older. He was surprised to look in the small mirror in his kit and see it was very gray. The last time he had attempted a beard it was more salt & pepper.

There was a noise, and he looked up to see a large woman regarding him curiously. She was standing in the morning light, shaded by the building. She didn't speak, turned instead and opened the door to the larger building and disappeared inside. Bakewell sat erect, feeling the pain in his back and arms and leaned forward, gaining leverage to stand. He stretched, trying to loosen his stiff and aching muscles, before picking up his pack. When he went down the pier to the building a sleepy young man appeared out of the bush on his left, walking slowly toward the store. He stopped when he saw Bakewell, appraising the white man.

"I am looking for a man named Peter Lolo, do you know this man?"

"Yes," was the single reply.

"Can you take me to this man Peter Lolo?"

"Yes," the boy said again. He walked past Bakewell and went into the store. When he came back out, he was drinking from a carton of something Bakewell couldn't identify. "I will take you to him now."

Bakewell followed the boy through the bush, and they soon came out onto a wide grassy plain. It ran off for a long distance. Bakewell stopped after they crossed fifty yards. "Is this the runway?"

"Yes."

"This is the runway built by the Americans?"

"Yes."

The ground was covered with a thick grass, which hid the coral underneath. The strip had been built by the Seabees, within ten days of the marines landing – one of the more remarkable construction accomplishments of the war. It had been built out of live coral. Bakewell knew the story well. Fighters landed on the twelfth day, while the machinery still graded and rolled parts of the runway. He was standing on the very site where his father had attempted to land his damaged plane. It gave him a surreal feeling. He wondered from which direction his father had approached the long field, and tried to visualize the old machines pushing out the coconut palms – the source of Markham's wealth, probably the work of a lifetime – leaving them to rot in the ditches, while the flat plantation land was prepared for squadrons of aircraft and an advancing stage of the Allied drive.

The boy continued across the runway toward a high stand of cane and grass. Bakewell followed. When they went through, following the narrow path, they came to a clearing where several huts stood in the early morning light, the water of the quiet lagoon lapping softly.

There was a man of about thirty, standing in the water, waist deep, moving a long fiberglass canoe about in a small, rectangular, manmade breakwater. When he looked up, the boy called to him in a tribal tongue. The man smiled broadly, showing red stained teeth from the addictive beetle nut most of the islanders chewed.

"You are come to Seghe for a vacation, yes?" the man said.

"Yes. To visit the islands I've read about in the history books and see their beauty."

The man's strong wide face continued to smile. He looked behind him and nodded at the beauty of the place of his birth then left his boat and came out of the water, sloshing across the worn coral in bare feet. It made Bakewell wince to see him cross the coral barefooted. They shook hands. Peter Lolo introduced himself and asked where Bakewell had come from.

"Kansas City; it's in America."

"I know of this place, Kansas City. I was in St. Louis once, and also in the state of Illinois. Do you know this Illinois?" Bakewell was stunned. "When I am in St. Louis, I see the Gateway Arch. It is amazing. Also Illinois is a beautiful green place. I stay there with friends for sometime."

Peter Lolo had been friends with a Peace Corps volunteer nearly a decade before, when he was in the islands doing his service. The volunteer took Peter home with him for a long visit when his time was up. The visit coincided with the 50th anniversary of the New Georgia campaign and

Solomon Island Veterans Association had held a big celebration in Springfield, Illinois while Peter was there. He had attended the event and had been asked to speak to the veterans.

"I am guest of honor for the old American war veterans. They ask me to tell them about this islands now."

Peter owned a guesthouse which stood a few meters away, separated from his home by a garden, carefully tended by his wife. The garden was filled with bougainvillea, ground orchids, hibiscus and separated into rows by a flowering plant called tatagala, which Bakewell learned was a form of cabbage. Peter offered Bakewell "A place of rest and two meals a day for thirty dollars." The Solomon dollar was worth 19 cents. He also confirmed there were no boats available to buy. "I have a small canoe you can use for the renting, but not to purchasing."

His guesthouse was also idyllic, with a soft elevated bed, covered with a clean mat and had a large mosquito gauze wrapped above. There was an outdoor latrine and a fine open-air wooden shower enclosure, made of wood, similar to the one he had used on Balalai, with a gravity fed faucet overhead that dropped rainwater from a narrow valve while the bather bathed in fresh water and sunlight from above. The following day they took Peter Lolo's canoe, powered by an outboard motor, and toured much of the famous lagoon area around Seghe. When they came back, they drove around the point occupied by Peter's home. It was a fantastic setting. Peter maneuvered them toward the wharf to get petrol. On the way, he asked Bakewell if he saw, "the Lightning." Confused, Bakewell looked over his shoulder for an approaching storm. The day was clear. Peter said, "There in the water below." It was an aircraft that had landed short of the field. They circled around and when it came into view Bakewell was able to see the twin fuselage of a P-38, known as a Lightning.

Made of aluminum, the aircraft sat on the bottom, perfectly preserved in the salt water. It was angled 90 degrees to the runway, appeared to have entered the water, just before turning final. Part of the empennage looked like it had been bitten by an enormous shark, showing jagged metal across the top of the "tail feathers." It was a shock and a fascination to look down into the water at the shiny piece of memorabilia. It brought a lump to his throat. Bakewell knew many planes littered the water around the airfields of the islands, still…

"I am sorry if I upset you, William." Peter said, observing his response. He kept the idling engine turned to circle around the aircraft, adding that the plane had been vandalized years before. "Men come from Australia and took the guns from the plane."

There were no cannons poking out from the noses of the twin fuselage. Bakewell recovered as he did the math, thinking about the corrosive effect the water would have had on the guns. The fuselage was perfect, and once located, perfectly clear in the water. They went over and purchased petrol at the wharf for the next day's journey.

***

The boat trip took them up the western side of the lagoon, passed many tiny atolls, some of which were the property of Peter's tribe. They were the Rhodo people, very small, only about 500 in all, but the property they owned in their part of the Pacific would have been worth millions, even billions closer to civilization. The beauty of the little islands dotting the lagoon was beyond describing, almost beyond comprehension. Peter's brother owned an island called Gatere, where they stopped for a drink – coconut water from fresh green coconuts Peter took from the top of a tree. He stripped the fiber and cut the tops expertly with his machete, and they drank the sweet, thirst quenching water, Bakewell had thought of as milk. Afterward, Peter split them and they ate the soft, mushy flesh, which the islanders preferred. They swam in the cool, refreshing water over white sand, in a calm sea without current, later stood in five feet of water near the edge of the steep beach. It was so quiet, only the slightest perceptible rise and fall lapped at their necks when they stood erect, the lapping caused by the enormous volume of water in the lagoon around them and not by any tidal action. There was land in every direction – Vangunu, New Georgia, bigger islands, little atolls, some only a thousand yards distant, other miles away.

Later Peter gave him a tour of extreme western end of the lagoon, passing his sister's guest house at Matikuri, which stood out over the water, thatched and bleached, against the green backdrop of rising jungle terrain. It was a picture of paradise. Peter's own share of paradise was called Kembekembe, and they floated past it slowly without getting out. At the extreme western end of the lagoon was the tiny atoll of Rujeje.

Bakewell stayed two nights with Peter Lolo in his guesthouse. On the third morning he asked, "Could a man stay on an island like Rujeje and live without being bothered, Peter?"

The islander peered at him, face bright with a broad smile, but there was a questioning in his eyes. He didn't understand Bakewell's question. "What do you mean, William?"

"Could a man stay out there on an island by himself?"

"The island, they belongs to another man. The man would ask him to leave."

"Is it possible to live on any island by yourself, without being bothered by anyone?"

"No. This islands are all belong to tribal peoples."

They were quiet, sat pensively on the veranda of the guesthouse, listening to the lapping water below the deck. Bakewell pursued his question again. “Could a man get permission to live out here on an island for a short time, say maybe, just for a short visit?”

Peter understood, told him it was possible to visit, adding, “It would be no problem.” He thought Bakewell had meant for a man to take residence on the island and said, “Some peoples come to spend an evening or more on the islands when the weather is good.”

They made an arrangement: Peter wouldn’t tell anyone where the white man was, would bring him fresh vegetables, fish and water every three days in exchange for $100 American dollars. Lastly, Peter would allow him the use of a small canoe and paddle for fishing and exploring. It was a very agreeable arrangement.

On that third day in New Georgia, Bakewell took his gear and, towing the small canoe, they went back out into the Morovo Lagoon, up to the tiny atoll of Rujeje. It was at the very end of the lagoon, where the mighty Solomon Sea pounded against the western side of the atoll in huge, terrifying rollers that poured in continuously, crashing against the coral coast. Tetepare could be seen far in the distance, out in the sea. There was a fine beach on the lee side, where the wind was calm and the water still and clear. Coarse white sand covered the beach and the bottom of the sea. There was a small lagoon on the north side where fish could be seen. On Rujeje, Bakewell again found safe haven.

Bakewell lived Robinson Crusoe-like on Rujeje, feasting on the fish Peter delivered and those he was able to catch, fire-roasting them and eating them with fresh vegetables and fruit. At first he substituted green coconuts for water, fearing he might run short if Peter Lolo didn't show, but Peter, always punctual, appeared with a friendly wave and broad smile on the appointed day and stayed long to visit and talk of America.

Alone on the atoll, Bakewell learned to handle the borrowed machete with skill and, after dark, gradually learned to handle the wobbly little canoe. He used his Leatherman for everything. The knife, a bulky device containing file, can opener, sawtooth blade, and an array of other handy tools, was the only accessory he brought on the long journey across the Pacific. Sometimes he ate fish raw. It resembled tuna. Brenny had taught him to eat fish raw long before – the only requisite being *fresh*. Fish pulled from the Pacific were minutes old when he butchered them. With a diet of fish, fruit and vegetables, his body responded once more and his energy level increased on the lean nutrition, and in the absence of toxins.

He read from Psalms & Proverbs extensively, and from the Book of Job, wondering if ever a time would come when he would find the peace and contentment Job finally found. He swam in the lagoon every day at midday, careful to avoid the early and late feeding times God's violent creatures favored, and only swam inside the breakwater the submerged reef provided on the north side of the island, where he could see the bottom for thirty feet in any direction. He would never learn the natives' indifference to "sak."

One afternoon, during one of Peter's stays, when they spoke of the *sak*, Peter laughingly confided, "William, a man who has never committed adultery, cannot be bitten by crocodile or shark." Laughing together over the indigenous maxim, Bakewell said, "I should be safe then from the sak, but nevertheless, I will watch for him. He is a scary fellow."

Puk puk, the crocodile was not on Rujeje. There was no fresh water, no creek. And although he never saw the "sak," Bakewell watched for his ominous dorsal each day as he contemplated the water for long periods. He read in the sunshine and in the midday shade, but mostly he dozed and thought of the past. At night he slept deeply again, and when it was time for the nightly vigil there was no urgency and little fear as he circled the island somnambulant, in shorts and badly worn sandals that were all but gone. He loved his leather sandals, had kept a pair for over thirty years, until Bass quit making them. This last pair, he decided, would die with him, out in the Pacific. "We're a pair of discontinued models," he said, worrying about their durability. "Just hold out a little longer, my feet can't take the coral like Peter Lolo's."

Bakewell spoke to anything that caught his eye, the water, the trees, even his hands and his feet. He kept to the beach at night, away from the vegetation and the insects that populated it, watching the starlight reflected on the calm water inside the reef. He wandered about Rujeje regularly. For drama, when the serenity of the island became monotonous, he would go around and watch the enormous rollers on the weather coast. But each night always ended with him lying on his back on the drier sand of Rujeje, different from the dark, wet sand of Bougainville, looking up at the stars.

As his strength returned he wondered how many times the cycle would repeat itself, before the end finally came. When he watched the stars his thoughts returned to the life he had left. There was nothing to do in the dark, no light for reading, time to think and remember and pray. He no longer had a plan, prayed often, spent hours looking at the stars, filling the southern hemisphere, wishing he had a book to identify the constellations.

***

When he returned home that Christmas, after *The Trio Event*, which was the way he thought of the morning in the restaurant where he discovered her, Bakewell determined he would do something about "little Katherine Durham." He always thought of her in the diminutive sense, even though she was now only six inches shorter than he was. In the back of his mind was a memory of her from years before where she had been on the sidewalk in front of her home, wearing what had once been called a pinafore? She must have been about five at the time, and he a surly youth of ten. But after that morning in the Trio, the memory of her perfectly formed breast got in the way of memories he had of her as a child.

Coming down Broadway, just before school let out for the Christmas holiday, Bakewell noticed a thick, cable-knit sweater in the front window of a store. It was a dark, forest green, perfect for Christmas. For the next three days he passed the same window, before deciding it would do. He was out of ideas and out of time. On that last morning of the term he also found a little gold cross and chain displayed in the bookstore window across from the University library. The chain was thin and delicate and he could imagine it around her neck, resting on her suntanned skin.

When he got home for Christmas he took the necklace and put it around the thick turtleneck, liking the way it contrasted with the dark green fabric, and carefully placed the open box on her front porch late the night before Christmas with a printed note:

> I saw what you did for that man in The Trio last summer
> and I wanted you to know it was a wonderful thing. I wanted
> you to know I thought you were a special person for what you
> did and I hope this makes up for your embarrassment.
> You should be proud of what you did. I want you to know I am.

It wasn't Shakespeare, but it was from the heart. He tried to write the note several times before he gave up and just wrote, his face coloring at the effort.

On Christmas morning he was kneeling across the church when he saw Katherine enter wearing the sweater, partially hidden under a red wool coat. He was there a week later on New Years when he spotted her from the same vantage as she took the same pew. When he returned to school his listlessness had faded along with his memories of Maggie Leary; their short lived association drifting to the recesses of his mind, getting a strong push from the healthy image of a well-intentioned, sadly humiliated Katherine, rushing from her misfired lifesaving attempt. The image gaining momentum every vacant moment that punctuated his long study sessions deep in the stacks of the University Library, where he put his academic life back in gear and attempted to salvage the fall semester. When the weather began to warm the stirrings within began to torment him until he was coming home virtually every weekend by Spring Break to take up his vantage in church. By then, if accused, he would have admitted he was practically stalking her.

Was it sympathy, the fact that she had grown up – and nature was outdoing itself one more time – or was it simply that an emotional gravity had hold of him? *You're like an orbiting neutron being pulled toward a nucleus of fetching attraction.* He resisted the pull for the rest of the school term, but when finals ended the day after Memorial Day, he made a quick exit and found himself crashing the gate of the Swim Club his first day back, where he watched Katherine teach a group of 4 year olds to swim in the morning, and where she put her long legs on display on the heavily beamed life guard stand, above splashing children each afternoon. The stand overlooked the shallow end of the big tank, catching the strong midday sun, which reflected from the silver lenses of her aviator style sunglasses.

She was picture perfect…but in the flesh, and he wandered by her guarding station several times on the days he was able to wrangle an invitation to the swim club. She returned his shy, tight grimace of a smile with her own white-teethed, time-stopping, joy-filled, all world smile each time. After awhile, she would take the sunglasses off so they made eye contact. The first time she gathered him in with those luminous brown eyes was so defining it froze him in the moment, and he looked away embarrassed. Katherine noticed the effect her suntanned anatomy had on him from the very first, and after three frustrating afternoons, brought things to a head when she showed up with three of her little swimmers in the shaded snack area. Bakewell had made no attempt at conversation, although he was aware of her presence, and she startled him when she dropped onto the bench in front of him, wearing a modest, black, one-piece bathing suit, taxed to the limit, trying to hide the final version of her now completely-packaged-and-ready-to-be-ogled-physique – a long-legged filly with perfect conformation.

“You’re Andy Bakewell.” He had looked up, trying not to show surprise. “You don’t remember me, do you?”

“Katherine?” It was a poor effort.

“Right,” she nodded, admiring the wet end of a Popsicle. “I didn’t think you would remember me.”

“I remember,” he mumbled.

“The last time I saw you, you were in your navy uniform.” It wasn’t true she had seen him every time he managed to get through the gate.

He remembered saying, “That was a long time ago,” and thinking, the last time I saw you, you were walking across the pool deck, and the time before that you were on the lifeguard stand, draping your gorgeous legs over the railing, and the time before that was last Sunday, when I stared at you from across the church.

“It was. I was a freshman in high school, and you were home on leave.”

He nodded, a bleak, almost apologetic smile, followed by a nervous look, thanked her for remembering him, and felt completely foolish. *Say something, you dumb cluck! Talk to her!*

He wondered what people would think, especially his classmates, if they saw him talking to little Katherine Durham, five years younger – he was going through his shallow period, a period he would spend the rest of his life regretting. She entertained her little people and they chattered away, calling her “Miss Katherine,” in an adoring way. They trailed after her like a knotted kite tail, when she moved around the pool. Most of the swim team under the age of ten trailed after her. Bakewell thought of her as the pied piper of little girls. Katherine finished the Popsicle, careful not to let it drip in the heat, while her pupils ate a junk food lunch, spilling soda on the table, and leaving a mess she carefully cleaned-up when they were finished. Eventually they wandered off and Katherine, making welcome contact with her large eyes resumed, “So, why are you hanging out at the swim club? I’ll bet you’re resting up for the next game?”

“You got me,” he said self-consciously.

“I see you a lot, playing ball in the evenings. You don’t look like you work; are you some kind of ball-playing bum?”

Bakewell laughed. He was definitely a ball-playing bum every summer, but Katherine wasn’t talking baseball; she was referring to the softball league, where she had seen him play twice a week after dark.

“What’s a nice Catholic girl like you doing following the beer leagues at Brentwood Park?” *Doing-following,* he winced as soon as the words were out of his mouth.

“We play down there too, in the middle diamond.” She seemed miffed that he didn’t know she was there to play, not to watch a beer-league game. He never paid attention to the girls’ league on diamond #2, assumed they were in high school.

"What position do you play," he asked.

"Shortstop." Bakewell was surprised. Katherine noticed. "You don't think I can field a ground ball?"

"I didn't say that."

"You looked it."

"I'm sorry."

"Me too; I'm behaving badly. I apologize." Before Bakewell could come up with anything else, Katherine got up quickly, said, "Duty calls." She walked off toward her little charges and Bakewell watched her go appreciating the fantastic view of her firm, flexing buttocks.

He began to follow her progress closely, hoping to see her after the games. It happened twice over the next week, and after one game they went with a group for pizza at the corner bar a few blocks away. She wasn't old enough to drink, and after the first night he decided he didn't need to drink either. The next week they were all there together after another game. Katherine remained after her friends left, and Bakewell lingered too. They ended up in the same booth as the group slowly condensed. When the last few left, it was just the two of them, and she looked across the table at him and said, "Andy, you know it might look like we are here on a date, just the two of us, by ourselves."

Bakewell nodded, liked hearing her say his name.

"So, what do you think?"

"About?" he acted dumb. It was easy.

"A date, stupid! We look like we're here on a date."

It made him wince, a kid five years younger, calling him stupid. He put his hands together and looked into her large eyes, then quickly down at the table.

"Are you praying?" she said mischievously, looking at his hands held together. He nodded, his throat constricting, and she persisted. "What are you praying for?"

"Mm…more hoping, than praying."

"For what?"

He took the plunge. He never regretted it. Not for the rest of her life.

"I was hoping…and praying too, I guess…" he looked up from the table, "That you might want to go out on a real date with me, Katherine."

She liked hearing him use her name. Her eyes widened and her smile broadened and continued to grow larger, eyes brighter, a moonflower at dusk, unfolding, coming to fruition. He admitted afterward, in a story told and retold to his children and friends – his hopes grew as her smile broadened. Then she dropped him with a straight-faced jibe that would become her trademark for the rest of their lives.

"Good Lord, I'm only nineteen years old. I don't want to be seen with a dirty GI at my age."

His jaw dropped, and he stared in disbelief. Katherine giggled, said she was kidding. He tried to recover, had given himself away completely, let his disappointment show. He would repeat the gaff too many times, and she would pull it off many, many times before he finally learned not to react. She put her hand on his, where they rested on the table. Neither spoke. She picked up his hand and put her hand inside of his, squeezed it with both of hers. The soft contact made him tremble inside, made his stomach flutter the way it did when he was about to give a speech at school. She caressed his hand, looked right into his eyes, her own completely sincere.

"I would love to go out with you, Andy Bakewell," she said softly, "You're my dreamboat. You've always been, ever since I saw you in your uniform." There was a light in her eyes as she spoke the words, and she lit a light deep inside of him – a light that would burn for rest of their lives. It was a moment of pure magic. Neither would ever forget the night, the place, the day of the week, or the date on which it occurred.

Bakewell and Katherine retold the story of that first night over and over. Their children loved the story, especially as they grew into their early teens, loved their mother's wit and their father's vulnerability. They could see that light in his eyes and in hers, loved the story of their parent's first night together and often asked them to retell it.

There was something unique and very special in their parents' relationship and each of the Bakewell children took a secret, unspoken joy in the way it radiated, not just in their eyes, but in the way they communicated. It was a nonverbal something that was always there, always glowing as their children watched them together over the years, always thrilled to see the warmth that radiated in their relationship. The light Katherine lit for Bakewell was the same light that went out the day she died, and each of his children watched the light die, saw the change in his eyes when her life ended and understood why he lost his enthusiasm for life, understood why he wanted to wind down and why he didn't put up much fight after she was gone.

The memory of Katherine left an ache in Bakewell's chest. Sometimes he thought the pain would stop his heart; sometimes he hoped it would. But the memories of their courtship still filled him with joy three decades later, especially as he sat on the beach of Rujeje, under the fantastic starlit sky. "Staka stars," the natives called the star-filled sky. He spent hours looking up at the stars, trying to imagine where she was, what she was doing.

***

Bakewell and Katherine had spent nearly every night together after that first evening when they were left to themselves. She quit her friends for a long time afterward and, remembering back, he knew it had been a real hardship for her to separate herself from them. She was a social creature who loved her friends. In time he would learn how much she treasured each one. Her friends had already become numerous at nineteen and would become uncountable in the years ahead. Part of the legion started to grow with her little pupils at the swim club, many of whom would grow into close friends in later years.

Bakewell found himself on the floor one night several years later, after baby Michael had pulled the gold chain from her neck, sending the small cross flying across the room, where it made a pinging sound as it hit the wall in her mother's home. They had moved furniture to help her search frantically for, "My favorite gold chain." She had it repaired the following week. She also wore the green sweater for years. On the night of their 10th Christmas together, they came home from her mother's house, where they spent Christmas Eve, and, after putting the children down, changed into comfortable clothes for the ritual of putting out the presents. They always dressed for Christmas Eve when they went to "the doctor's house," as Bakewell sarcastically referred to her parents' home, and, as he changed from coat and tie to a wool shirt, Katherine pulled the heavy knit sweater over her head.

"Are you ever going to get tired of that old thing?" he asked. She was in her stocking feet and seemed much shorter.

"It's one of my favorites, Andy. You know that."

"It's old, and it's out of style."

"Sweaters don't go out of style, not this kind," she said as she pulled the collar down around her graceful neck.

"Tell me again where it came from," he said. He had done it many times, enjoyed the knowing, the secrecy.

"I don't know. It just kind of showed up in my life once. I got it on Christmas. That's why I still like to wear it at Christmas time." He was filled with adoration as he watched her shake her long hair out of the turtleneck and she returned the look. Christmas was a magical time and their mood matched the moment. Katherine's eyes were wet with love and with the joy of Christmas. "It's special, you know that."

He turned away to hang up his coat, decided to come clean, making his voice sound gruff, "It ought to be. It cost me nearly twenty bucks." She was immobile, and he sensed it. When he turned and looked at her in the large walk-in closet, she was gathering him in intently, a flash in her eyes, shining under the bare light bulb overhead.

"It was you...*It was you.*" she nodded, eyes radiant. "It was you, wasn't it?" Seeing the effect of his words filled him with emotion as Katherine threw her arms around his neck. "My mom teased me about having a secret admirer. Once I read the letter I wondered if it might be you." They embraced for a long time. There were no tears. She held him tightly, arms pulling down hard around his neck as she nearly lifted herself off the floor. He still remembered the strength in her arms; the way his chest nearly exploded with love and an enormous feeling of gratitude. He would never forget that tight hug, had often thought about the strength in it when she was dying and she could barely lift her hand to brush his face.

Bakewell spent eight days on Rujeje, days filled with the wonderful monotony of idleness, of peace, interrupted by exercise, meals and visits from his island host. It seemed much longer. Each time Peter Lolo came with provisions they visited for long periods and Peter questioned his guest about anything that had to do with America.

"You keep the island most clean, William."

"Comes from an insistent wife, Peter."

"Yes, I am veri clean man myself, but my children are mostly not."

Standing up to their necks in the cool water on the east shoreline in the heat of the bright day they talked of Peter's fondly remembered trip to America. Peter never tired of telling Bakewell of his experiences.

After the Veterans anniversary get-together in Springfield, Peter had become a celebrity. They passed his name up the line, and, after Illinois he journeyed west to the mountains, touring the parks and up into Canada, before returning via the Great Lakes, always the guest of a veteran who was grateful for the opportunity to show a Solomon Islander his gratitude. On their last day together Peter told Bakewell an amazing story of a woman who had come out to the islands and spent time with him and his people. He brought her out to Rujeje to swim in the spot where they stood.

"She teld me she is important person in United States, in your parliament."

"Congress?"

"Yes, I am wrong sometimes about that. She is in your American Congress."

"She was a congresswoman, here in the Solomons?"

"No, not a Congress person, the other one."

"The Senate?"

"Yes!" Peter became excited. "She is a Senator in your Senate." Bakewell was amazed. "And, when I am in Washington, your capitol with some friends, they take me to the big, important building and I see this lady in the hallway and she say to me, 'I know you!' We have a big laugh."

"What was her name?"

"It was Nancy Kassabaum of your United States parliament, I mean Senate."

"Good Lord!" Bakewell was stunned once more. "You are a man of surprises." He thought about the senator from his neighboring state for a moment, remembering her history. "I think her father was Alf Landon, and I think he ran for President of the United States against Roosevelt. That was just a few years before the Second World War started!" Peter smiled, nodding his head enthusiastically. "He could have been the President during the fighting that raged down on Guadalcanal. That's amazing."

Peter left him with fresh provisions and Bakewell returned to his somnolent lifestyle on the atoll, reading, wandering, wondering, canoeing after dark. He stayed close to the atoll most of the time, but one night he let himself get too far out and got caught up in the rougher water of the weather coast and it pulled him back to his island atoll, where he got caught in the big rollers. The power of the water overwhelmed him and it took a long time in the small dugout before he could get clear again. Bakewell was sure he would be swamped as he struggled with the waves, and seeing the nearest land above the violent starlit water, he doubted he could make it to the shore if he had to swim. There was no life vest; the island people didn't use them. He'd never seen a life vest in any boat in the islands.

In the bright midday sun he could see the roofs of thatched huts bleached in the sunlight on the point at Matikuri. It was a half mile away and looked like a picture on a postcard. The huts were inviting and he was tempted to go over. The thatched roof reflecting in the midday sun was the roof of the guesthouse of Peter's sister, and Bakewell wished he could visit and see what was there, if only to break his monotony.

Waking

Both in his dreams and waking hours, during the long days and nights spent on Rujeje, Bakewell contemplated the last few weeks of Katherine's life. It was a time to come finally to grips, to make closure with her death, and her loss, and he allowed himself long, protracted periods, filled with painful memories, long closeted, to evaluate what had happened to them during those last bleak, exhausting weeks. Once the memories returned he was struck by the painful image of Katherine, by the physical tragedy of her. It wasn't the painful way of her passing – she was able to maintain a fervor and a devotion that never left any doubt – so much as the shock of her; and he remembered again showering with a skeletal creature, cleaning up, cleaning after, and the ghastly horror of knowing, seeing, feeling, helping, all the while substituting the memory of a once lovely creature, so beautiful and healthy and robust, filled with the joy of living, loving and being loved. *Dear God, how could someone die from causes that spring from the very place from where our babies came? That blessed place, a nest for a million microscopic vipers striking without relent, their poisons constant, pitiless, unmerciful, deadly.*

***

Just before his own marriage, Bakewell introduced Katherine to Denny Murphy's parents, where Katherine was a predictable hit. He had described their famous marriage at length, and as soon as the two of them settled into married life, theirs began to show the same signs of parallel devotion. Katherine was certain she had chosen the right mate, and despite the pessimism of school friends, they had gotten off to a wonderful start. In the years that followed the only issue that tried the relationship was a brief period when Bakewell became consumed with the making of money. Her altruistic nature not withstanding, Bakewell soon learned Katherine had a formidability that wasn't to be trifled with. Once they got passed his one aberrational period of monetary obsession they grew together in spirit and trust for the rest of their lives.

In the early years he'd been amazed by her in so many ways: her common sense, her perception, her inventiveness and many skills at raising and playing with children, her ability to cook an assortment of wonderful meals, her athleticism and so much more was but a small part of the total. She had been a natural as a mother; he kept pleasant memories of her pregnant figure, her shyness about it when they were alone, and later her determination to shed the pounds and get her muscle tone back. She had a ferocious determination when it came to objectives, and it was the sweet memories that allowed him to bear the pain of her final days and the awful circumstances preceding her death.

Fortunately they were spared the macabre ritual of feeding tubes and IV's, which she steadfastly refused in the final weeks, baring her pain quietly, the only real signs of it showing in soft whimpers when she moved in her sleep. Mostly she was content to be still and she spoke little. She had heard the raspy sound of her voice and confided she didn't like the sound. Bakewell attended her much of the time. They had a nurse, a patient woman who came late in the evening and spent the night. They watched television in the family room most evenings, while keeping vigil. Sometimes Bakewell dozed and when he woke, found her staring at him, her eyes tragically shadowed and deeply set, still held the youthful light as she tried to communicate. He knew she was mustering all of her strength to bring emotion from deep within. She was almost always too weak for conversation by then, would wink when he held her hand, patting it carefully.

Her wrists were just bones, protruding through pale flesh. Her strong, shapely arms formed a straight line from her elbows to her hands. She would raise a finger occasionally, place it on the back of his hand, tapping lightly. She didn't want any more shots, would twist slightly and turn her head in protest when they were offered. She wanted to be lucid when she was awake. She had learned long before to bear her sufferings without complaint, putting them in little compartments, where she could offer them, measuring and proportioning each one for someone else.

The last day of Katherine Bakewell's life ended at six in the evening. They had spoken of the last day, what it would bring, and what each hoped for at the end. Bakewell wanted a miraculous recovery, accompanied by the sound of trumpets and angels singing *GOD IS MERCIFUL!* Katherine answered with a weak smile, said she wanted to go peacefully. They all wanted her to go peacefully. And since she was nearly in control of that one detail, the odds, barring some ghastly medical calamity, were in her favor. In the end, the last few minutes of her life resembled a leaf falling quietly, touching down on clean, wet ground, there to absorb the dampness and slowly even out on the fresh earth, transformed finally, coming to end.

While Bakewell sat at one side, his sons close by, his only daughter holding her mother's hand, Katherine Bakewell stopped breathing and seemed to settle into the freshly laundered pillow. Dropping his head, Bakewell felt the floor dropping from under him, felt like he was falling, didn't want to ever stop falling, wanted it to go on forever. He knew what would happen when he hit bottom.

He didn't remember much afterward, until he forced himself to remember it all, in the middle of the Pacific Ocean, ten thousand miles and thirty-one months distant from that crushing day. The ritual of arrangements for funeral, for Mass, the ordeal of standing by at her wake, and later, at the gravesite, where he and his children called upon hidden reserves, caught up with him once more in unclouded detail under a contrasting canopy of black darkness and starry night.

***

Bakewell woke to the sound of the ever present sea crashing in the distance, the sound of the soft breeze in the leaves above him and to the smell of island flowers he hoped would never leave. He awoke with the sun as he had each day, always unsure at first of his surroundings, then gradually he would relax. But something had come in on the first light; something was different. There was another presence.

"Good morning, mate," Powell said, pressing his large palm to Bakewell's forehead, as he placed the weapon to his temple. "Let's not do anything too quickly, eh. Let me see both hands."

Bakewell, motionless in response, almost welcomed the sound of a white man's voice after so much seclusion, and when his hands came up out of the bag, Powell let him roll over, and they faced each other. "Come on out from under then. Try not to move too quickly. Let me see those hands all the way. I think Mr. Albrecht's little Walther might be in there someplace, maybe."

Bakewell crawled out of the mummy tent on his elbows, hands open. Powell kept the small handgun pointed toward him until he was clear of the tent.

"Turn around then," Powell waved with the gun and Bakewell turned slowly about in a complete circle. "All right, you can relax mate." Powell moved to the light tent, lifting it with one hand. The Walther fell to the ground and he pulled the tent away, discarding it behind, before picking up the weapon. "Had to make sure, knew you were 'carrying' as they say. Didn't want to find you pointing that nasty little piece at me, not after so much trouble finding you. Wanted to be friends again." He stood up and put the handgun in his pocket. "We need to have a nice talk."

Bakewell had raised his hands again, too many western movies in his childhood. He put them down when Powell put the gun away, confused. Was Powell testing him, wanting him to make a move, so he could dazzle him with his quick reflexes, his martial arts skill? Powell indicated they walk out to the beach away from the clutter of undergrowth, out into the not yet intense sun.

"You've been a bit of trouble, Andy; got to give you that. I've been keeping up with you, but only just. How did you manage to get out of PNG?"

Powell wore shorts and a short sleeve shirt with epaulets and double pockets, looking like he could be on safari. They sat on a palm log on the beach, facing away from the sun.

"So why didn't you put one in my ear and leave?"

"Shoot you! You think I'm out here for that; to get you?"

"Then what?"

"Your people sent me out to keep watch on you – one of your people, anyway."

"My people?"

"Aye."

"My people! Who sent you?"

"Don't know then? They sent me out to intercept you – one of your blokes – said he was obligated to look after you. Didn't trust this Albrecht fellow. Made it sound like he's been done a favor maybe...Someone high up in your organization?"

"Hamilton."

"Hamilton? Maybe. I don't know. Anyway this fellow sends me out to keep a look out for you. Supposed to make Albrecht think I'm part of the team."

"I thought you were part of the team."

"Did a good job then did I?"

Powell offered tea from a thermos. Later, when the heat was up, they moved inside again and Bakewell boiled water and they had fresh tea, eating by his tent site. Powell told him he had spent the night at a guesthouse to the east, said he saw Peter coming on the water, kept him in view until he was far down the lagoon. Afterward it was just a matter of approaching each of the small islands at daylight. Rujeje would have been his third choice, but at Matikuri he learned a white man had been seen in a canoe on his way to Rujeje. Powell had met Peter Lolo's sister. Bakewell could imagine Powell there, communicating like an islander. After breakfast they moved to a place among the overhanging bush along the south shore and resumed their odd, offhanded catching up.

"Albrecht was going to fix you himself, maybe," Powell said, pulling at a small branch overhead absently, looking off in the distance. There was a shimmering movement in the air above the water even though there was no breeze. "I doubt it though. Didn't seem the type really; not a killer. Probably going to give some rascal in Moresby money to do it. Bury you in some sad place, or drop you in the water outside the reef?"

"You said 'was going'? Is that in the past tense?"

"Past tense, eh? Yeah, past tense then."

Bakewell felt a stab of fear in his gut, stood and wiped the sand from his shorts and stepped into the sunlight, squinting at Powell. "So what happened to him?"

"He didn't make it."

"He didn't make it? What does that mean?"

"He's back there at Bougainville."

"I killed him?" Powell watched in amusement, without answering. "I know I hurt him with the whack I gave him, but I didn't think I killed him."

"Rest your mind then."

"I didn't kill him?"

Powell shook his head. "No, you didn't kill him, Andy."

"I heard a shot. It sounded like small arms to me. I took his gun but you had to have one?"

"I had one. Didn't mind really. Wasn't much left to do with him – out like he was. Put one in his ear, like you say. Hacked him up a bit. Made it look like the islanders did him."

"Shit!"

"Yeah, shit for sure, it was." Powell got to his feet and clapped the sand from his hands. "See now, we'll have to do things my way for a few days. Then you'll be your own man again. I'm supposed to get you back to civilization. Check you in like. Be your sitter as the English like to say. When you're on your way, I've done my job. I will report that you're okay."

The news of Albrecht's death created a cloud of problems. Bakewell never considered Albrecht might not return to his people – or that he himself could. The idea that Powell could be there to help him get home was even more remote than Albrecht's "not making it." He'd been so certain about Powell; he didn't know what to think. So much had changed in the time since he woke to Powell's presence. He was sure he was about to die; instead Powell was offering life. He was sure he would never leave the islands; instead, Powell offered safe passage – to America! He watched Powell closely, not able to trust, trying to look beyond. *Watch for the little stuff.* Was he really going back, or was Powell setting him up, so he would be no trouble until…what?

"You've done well out here, man. Made a lot of friends. None of these island fellows would give you out, Andy. Probably cost me an extra three days. You must have seemed as decent to them as you did to me. But you couldn't hide as long as you stayed out by the water. You would have had to 'go bush' like a coastwatcher, maybe. No way to hide out here for a white man. Might as well put a beacon on your head. If you leave the beach and go into the jungle, you disappear."

"I don't like the jungle," Bakewell said, "too closed in."

"Know what you mean. Buggy too, just a bit. I spent a month in the bloody bush once. Seemed like forever."

"Why didn't you come in after me up there?"

"On Bougainville? You *went bush* on me there, see."

"I thought you would follow."

"No, no. You had the rifle. I was afraid you might pop me off."

There was a long silence before Powell finally spoke, "There is a plane from Seghe to Honiara this afternoon, mate. We need to be back there before three. Never quite know if they'll be early or late."

"That's a five hour row. I can't do it."

"And don't care to myself. That's why they put motors on these canoes," Powell said with a smile. "Can't have you all knocked-up, can I? We'll just go back over to Matikuri, and those pleasant people will sugar us back to Seghe."

Bakewell smiled at the expressions. Knocked-up meant too tired to travel. Then in a sober moment he looked around the island, at the incredibly beautiful site surrounding it, down toward the dark green of Vangunu in the distance. The view was worthy of a travel poster. He hoped he would remember it, tried to memorize it. They went along the beach to the north side of the atoll, Bakewell leading, Powell following. "Take your time, Andy. No hurry, eh? No worry mate. We've got hours to make it to the guesthouse. After that we're only thirty minutes out." He moved up next to him; Bakewell watched him nervously. "But let's not miss our flight. I've had enough island holiday this year." Powell chuckled, tapped him on the shoulder. "Need a decent bath and the luxury of a hotel."

Powell started to walk away, "Come along then." They continued around to the weather coast where they found Powell's canoe in against a tangled mangrove. He wasn't surprised. If anyone could approach the island in the dark through the terrifying rollers it would be Powell. They walked the canoe out into knee deep water and pulled it along to the south shore before they paddled to Bakewell's campsite. Powell helped him pack and stow his gear. They retrieved his small canoe and tied it off to the bigger one before pushing off. Powell insisted Bakewell ride up front, "No fast tricks now, where I can just keep an eye on you, mate."

When they got to Matikuri they were taken back to Seghe in a large canoe, powered by outboard motor. Bakewell and Powell sat facing each other and Powell told him a story of another time in his violent life when he'd visited New Georgia during some island trouble. He'd been with the Commandos, a fact Bakewell was surprised to hear him finally admit.

The trip was less than 20 minutes under power, the green shoreline passing quickly to each side while the boat left a long V of turning water in its wake. When they got to Seghe, Peter Lolo was gone, and he and Powell spent a couple of hours on the veranda of the guesthouse, nodding in the afternoon heat, Bakewell hoping he would get to see Peter before he left. Peter's family provided a simple lunch. Bakewell settled his bill with Peter Lolo's wife and they collected their gear and walked across the wide grass runway to wait by the small ticket house. Fifteen minutes before the aircraft was due, a man came out of the jungle and opened the shed and sold tickets for the flight to Honiara. By the time the plane was heard, there were a dozen people there to greet arrivals or just watch the plane.

Just before they boarded Bakewell spoke to Peter's son Burness who was there to watch the midday excitement. "Tell your father, the man from America said he is *a veri good man.* I will remember him always for his friendship." The young boy smiled, but only with his eyes; he was very serious, so unlike his father with the smile. "When you see Frank Iputu, tell him also, I am indebted to him and he is *a veri good man."* He gave the boy an envelope for Frank Iputu.

The flight to Honiara was in and out of stormy weather. Upon arriving, there was just enough light to see the field, wet and gray in the mist, contrasting with the green of the jungle surrounding it. Bakewell watched from the port window as the plane turned downwind, passing the field before turning to land.

"Henderson Field?" Powell nodded. Bakewell was fascinated to see the place where the battle for Guadalcanal had raged for months during the summer and fall of 1942, while the world waited for news. The battle for Henderson field had come in waves, where a small contingent of marines, surrounded by thirty thousand Japanese troops managed, just barely, to repulse them in three full scale attacks and numerous smaller skirmishes. It was the first position Allied Forces held in the war for the Pacific. Bakewell had been reading about it for years.

Powell cursed when they got off the plane and crossed the wet pavement to the terminal. There was no Quantas aircraft on the tarmac. They had missed the last flight for Australia.

They took a taxi into Honiara. The capitol of the Solomon Islands' main boulevard was bustling with people and veering cars, a madhouse of humanity milling about on wide sidewalks under giant Bualo trees. The *tensions* were building. There would be a coup in a few months, with more death and much destruction to government buildings when the Malaitans came over…to take over.

They spent the night at the Mendana Hotel, "The only fookin civilized place in Honiara," according to Powell, where they dined outside on the patio in the dark – the air conditioning wasn't working. Later they walked over to the Point Cruz Yacht Club and enjoyed several drinks, and the starlit view across Iron Bottom Sound, where Savo Island appeared as only a large shadow.

With hours to kill the next morning Bakewell made a plea for some historical fact-finding and Powell agreed. They went up to the Memorial on the hilltop overlooking the city, where a fantastic view out over the sound to Savo and Tulagi awaited. There was an enormous bronze plaque depicting the battles that raged on land around the airfield and at sea, visible across the way. The plaque gave the names of the ships sunk – they renamed the water east of Savo "Iron Bottom Sound" because so many ships were on the ocean floor, some actually touching, like giant metallic pick-up sticks. It was a place of grave importance to history and to violence, heroism and death. Brenny would have loved it.

When they cleared customs they waited on Henderson's tarmac for Quantas to appear. The big airliner landed and taxied in and waited with the off engine running, the way the Twin Otters did out in the islands. Before boarding, they waited under a wooden overhang, protected from the drizzling rain, and Bakewell visited with an expatriate who had come out to the islands for a career in government service, and later made a second career – the British terminated his job after independence – working in the world of finance. He was going home to New Georgia, another place of history, returning from banking meetings in Honiara, the man familiar with the history of the islands, even had personal knowledge of some of the old coast watchers. Bakewell asked many questions before the Englishman's time for departure came, and he left to board a commuter flight headed up the island chain.

Bakewell's time in the islands held memories of sweet tranquility, but he was very surprised at the feeling of safety that came over him when he took his seat in the luxurious plane. The weeks since he left the states had been filled with monotony, excitement, apprehension and fear, mystery and intrigue. He hadn't realized how stressful life had been, until he felt it drain away inside the beautifully appointed plane, surrounded by so many comforts. He was back in the civilized world again. He drank an Australian beer, relaxed into the soft cushioned seat and quickly fell asleep.

Brisbane

"Hate to bother you mate," Powell said, as they prepared to land. "Been out-conscious for the whole sea crossing." Powell put his magazine away and raised his seat. "Almost home, then. Be living in civilization again." Powell sounded almost jubilant; Bakewell understood, but the drink had done him in; he was still groggy with sleep. They went through a very thorough customs and quarantine before taking the Airtrain into Brisbane on a bleak fall afternoon. It would be spring in America.

Powell checked them into the Carlton, where they took separate rooms, and Bakewell concluded, finally, he really was on his way home. Powell wouldn't let him out of his sight unless it was true. After another midday nap, Bakewell took a shower with water pressure – hot water pressure – and he let the water flow for a long time. The phone rang on the table next to the bed as he was toweling off.

"Are we up to a farewell dinner then, mate?"

"I hoped you'd ask," Bakewell replied. "Let's go to the best steak house in Brisbane, my treat."

"Actually, I'm in the mood for oysters."

"Oysters and steak then. *Only just. Eh*?" Bakewell mimed. Powell chuckled.

They met in the bar. The talk was genial, but Bakewell found it eerie talking with the man who said he had killed Albrecht, did it without remorse, remembering the casual way he said, "Hacked him up a bit."

They enjoyed drinks at a bar, below a looming television, which was *otherworldly* after such a long hiatus from the world's informational teat. Both men were enthusiastic, the mood brought on by the return to civilization. Bakewell drank carefully, minimally; unused to alcohol, still measuring Powell's mood, not wanting to underestimate him after so much caution. He had done well with Powell and he had the man's respect. *Just don't mess it up now.* Afterward they went into the hotel restaurant where Bakewell decided to pass on the steak, eating oysters and scallops, steering away from greasier fare, which had little appeal once available. At one point Powell laced his fingers together over his plate, elbows on the table, his powerful forearms much in evidence and looked closely at Bakewell.

"What did you do with the weapons?" Bakewell asked.

"Got rid of them."

"Just tossed them in the ocean?"

Powell nodded. "So what happens now? You go back to family and friends, or some fine lookin lady somewhere?" Bakewell didn't answer and Powell continued, "Resume living, and nobody knows about your mystery life?"

Bakewell shook his head.

"No? What then, eh? Just a bit curious."

"I don't really know. I haven't spent much time planning the last few weeks. It's been pretty much a day at a time."

"You don't want to go back, mate?" Powell *was* curious.

Bakewell shook his head. "No, I can't go back. I'm dead. It's Part of the deal." Powell waited, let him go on. "I'm not going to make it either, as you like to say. My time's about up."

"You're sick?" Bakewell nodded. "Aye," Powell said with genuine disgust. "Figured as much, I guess." He turned away to look for the waiter.

"I would like to go back," Bakewell said, thinking out loud. "I'd like to find a place where I can have uninterrupted peace. It was almost peaceful out on the island, but I never knew what the day would bring." He looked at Powell, returning his hard stare, able to look into his eyes without wanting to look away finally. Powell seemed kinder. "Never knew when some mercenary type might show up *and do me in, eh?"*

Powell smiled dutifully and moved his glass. "Did you kill him with the one shot? I only heard one, but it was hard to tell, so far away with the hills and vegetation and all."

"I didn't kill him."

"No way, mate!" Powell leaned in. "I saw you shoot that piece. You missed with that fine little weapon? Come on."

"No. I didn't miss. I winged him clean."

"Winged him? Clean? What the hell."

"I hit him up high, on the top of his shoulder – pretty sure anyway – just above the collarbone."

"How could you miss him with that fine little piece? You handled it like a bloody range instructor."

"I didn't miss him, I'm telling you. I hit him where I wanted to hit him. It was the best shot I could have made."

"You weren't supposed to kill him?"

"He's dying anyway. They wanted to scare him. The shot was a message, I think. They don't exactly explain it. My guess is, he gets the message then they negotiate. He has a lot of their money. They want the money." Bakewell added, "They want the money back and he knows he can't hide now. Not out there."

"Bly me, the fooker only gets a nick. We go through all the bullshit in Moresby – that cesspool of a place – and put up with Albrecht's shit, just to nick some raghead from the bloody fookin desert?" There was disgust in Powell's voice. He was visibly upset and not trying to control it. It was the first time Bakewell saw anything beside his calm, alls-well demeanor. "Fook it then." He leaned back in his chair. "I'll be pissed."

Bakewell ate meticulously, enjoying each portion of the meal, savoring each bite, like it was a movement in a symphony, also savoring the cleanliness, the crisp napkins and tablecloth. He felt like he'd been gone much longer. When they finished Powell ordered cognac, Bakewell went along, thinking he would give it one more chance, amused at Powell's frustration. Powell was a professional who thought finishing the Arab was a part of the exercise, that it needed doing. It had been the objective. Powell didn't like the idea of risking his life for something trivial like, "A winging." They sat in silence for a long time.

"How can you drink this stuff?" Bakewell asked, holding up his snifter.

"Cognac? It's fine." He held the glass up for inspection, looked down at his napkin, lying on the table. "How could you not shoot that son of a bitch, Andy? How could you not take him out? Do you know how many would have loved to have that chance?"

"You know who he is?"

"Yeah. It's been in the papers. The world knows where he is by now. It didn't take them long to get the word out, once the bugger ran."

"I never intended to kill him. That was the hardest part. Shooting at somebody, without a tripod, almost offhand from that distance, with the need to hit him and still miss just right." Bakewell looked at the dark liquid in his glass. "It was the best shot of my life. It was a tough shot…and I've made a few."

"How many men have you killed, man; killed and got paid for it, eh?" Bakewell returned the look without answering. "You're not a professional, are you?"

"I'm not killing anyone else, not ever again. I'm done. I took the deal. I fulfilled my contract." He looked straight into Powell's hard eyes. "I told a man I would do it, never intending to live long enough…but I did. So I lived up to the agreement. I needed the money. They owed me the money anyway. I have no guilt about the money. I would have had no guilt if I had died before I could live up to my end."

"The guy was a bum, a terrible man; a killer of women and children, old people. He was a fookin ethnic cleanser, for God's sake; a killer of babies, a raper of children. He was a pig." Powell's voice held even more disgust.

"I didn't think a professional cared about such things. Kill him, miss him, wing him, whatever. Why do you care how it was done?"

"It's the bloody principal man. He was no more than a terrorist. He just happened to be a head of state. He lived like a terrorist, holed up most of the time, fearing for his safety, for all the terrible shit he did. He was an animal."

"I'm not an intellectual guy, Powell; I'm not that deep. Hell, I don't really know what terrorist means. Is it noun or verb? Native Americans could have been terrorists once. Is it someone who ruins the lives of others for some misguided belief? Or maybe somebody who's fighting for what's his, or for what he thinks should be his? All I know is that it's always about killing people, wreaking havoc to ruin the peace. No I guess it's not a verb. They're supposed to describe action. But I'd have to think about that. Terrorism is always about action, isn't it?"

"Aw hell, it's just the principle. How many men would have loved to have your opportunity?" Powell shook his head again, totally disgusted. The waiter cleared the table and they sipped the fiery liquid. "So how much did you get?"

"Doesn't make any difference – it's spent. All gone." Except for the cash he still had, the money was committed; Bakewell smiled, satisfied the money was gone. He didn't need it.

"You're serious?"

"I'm serious…and poor as a church mouse, too." He nodded at Powell and at his predicament. *"How much did they pay you?"*

"Fifty grand…American."

"Not bad for a few weeks work. *Eh?*"

"I worked for this fellow once before, years ago. Secretive-like, very proper. Not a bad mate, really. He made you sound special, like he'd taken a liking to you, or something, maybe. Made it sound mysterious, as usual, only just. The last time it had been straight forward, in Africa, actually. Simple enough it was, back then. No shooting, no mess, the money was simpler too. Inflation. I remembered him. Sounded older maybe. Guess he was. The last time had been twenty years before. There were several others – Angola, if you must know."

"I didn't ask."

"Nevertheless, he was your mate, maybe? Thought you might have been related. Made it sound like he was asking a favor, instead of making a proposition. I was free enough, had the time. When he offered the fifty I took it. Told him I would do it, as long as it was before winter down here. I have to go up north when it gets warm. See some country I haven't seen in years."

"Don't tell me."

"Europe, if you must know. Eastern. Lot of trouble up there right now. Adriatic's lovely, the coast I mean. They've it all fooked up right now." Powell slipped a piece of paper across the table. "Your flight, tomorrow. Ten o'clock, then. Be an hour early. It might take a while; we take airport security serious out here."

"Thanks."

"You pay for the bloody dinner, poor or not." Powell was miffed, but he didn't look as dangerous as before. Bakewell trusted him at last, and was glad he could. He enjoyed the mercenary's dilemma. After he paid the check they left the restaurant; Powell refused to shake his hand, made the tough eye contact one more time and didn't say anything, just walked away. It was fine with Bakewell. He knew the hand he didn't shake had cut Albrecht's throat.

LAX

His return trip seemed much longer. Bakewell had been absorbed by the distractions of going west: the size of the massive plane, crossing the world's largest ocean, flying through an entire day – actually losing it across the Dateline – and the daunting proposition of what lay ahead in the vast Pacific. The knowledge that he was going to die didn't worry him as much as how he might die. He'd grown accustomed to the thought of dying. *Everyone's going to die; mine's just coming a little sooner.* His fear was he might give way to his fear, collapse in the face of adversity, that he might disappoint himself. He never deluded himself about courage, not after Genoa. If he'd displayed any, it was on impulse, when he didn't have time to think. His courage was the reactionary kind. Going across he knew his courage would be tested with a slow waiting and a not knowing. The not knowing would require patience, and patience was the hardest part, the hardest test of courage.

He worried whenever he wasn't distracted. Like arrogance, worry was a shadow, only this time it would be on the other side. He would be in the southern hemisphere. Could he grit it out, the waiting and worrying? *Maybe I can put it on autopilot, just go through the motions.* He tried to laugh at himself. It hadn't worked. Not measuring up, running at the last moment, caving in to fear – it was another worry. Physically he was running out of gas, his tank was less than half full. *Fatigue makes cowards of us all.* It was one of Ned's favorite Lombardi quotes.

How would it come – like the literary thief in the night, or suddenly, even dramatically, accompanied by violence? Violence was disorienting. It made thinking difficult. There was much to think about when he went west, and too much time to think about it.

Returning east had its own improbabilities. He still hadn't died. *What an inconvenience.* And there was a renewed reality: his family. How would he deal with them? Would he deal with them? *What will they think? How had they managed in the aftermath?* His death had already happened. He couldn't go back. It was that simple. No family, no Neds, no Denny Murphys, no grandbabies, and no Maggie Walker... He was about to land back in America. There would be no children at the gate, no greeters. There *could* be trouble waiting when he got off the plane – a new worry. If he could go underground things would be more agreeable, gentler. He wanted to get to the monastery in Richardton, wanted to find sanctuary.

Being alive is a pain. He speculated on his mortality. It was too long to still be around. The *Company* had put it all into motion, had finalized his life, had sent him on, across that terrifying threshold, if only figuratively, but it hadn't happened.

His cabin mates were mostly returnees from Down Under, initially happy, friendly people on their way home, but tired after long hours in the giant flying machine. Fatigue had faded to impatience and irritation. They would be glad to deplane. Bakewell could feel the weariness around him, felt it in his back and the cramping in his neck and legs too. Sitting in a narrow seat all night as the equator passed below, banking slowly to avoid huge tropical storms in the vast Pacific while lightning flashed, illuminating the cabin, left him drained, unable to identify the day or the date.

Bakewell was just as tired as he'd been when he got to Batuna or when he returned to Port Moresby from Buka. Those trips allowed a quiet sabbatical; sleeping on the aircraft had been fitful and interrupted, nothing like smelling Frangipani, looking at the vast southern hemisphere that had umbrella-ed his private atoll.

Los Angeles was crowded with travelers, some on their way out to the other side, where today was tomorrow. He was relieved to find his gear in the locker. There was no reason for it not to be, still, it had been one more concern. It was hot, mid-afternoon when he came into the sunlight. People slept in the grass on a small knoll, temporarily homeless – tired people, plane-exhausted people, needing a few hours. There were half a dozen sprawled next to the international terminal. Bakewell wanted to join them. Instead he took the courtesy van, wanting to get away from the airport; he got off at the last motel on the van's run.

His head ached and his mind was thick with fatigue. He fell into bed needing a shower, slept for twelve hours. When he woke, the dial staring from the bedside read 4:18. He wasn't sure what day or which 4:18 it was until he looked to the window. He lay there another 45 minutes, before going to the front office where he found a pot of rancid coffee and a sleepy Pakistani eyeing him contemptuously. He got a cup of juice from the complimentary bar and a stale donut and went back to bed and watched the Weather Channel, wanting to get a feel for what the weather was doing before switching to CNN to catch up on America.

Since Powell told him they were allies, the second best news he'd gotten was *April.* It was April. His long acrimony with March was over. He was sure he wouldn't survive March – the rotten month – the month of uncountable adversity. It was fitting he would die in March; he hadn't really cared. Before he left America he was sure he would finish life in the Pacific. The fact that he was going in March reinforced the certainty.

On his way out to the airport in Brisbane he'd read the top half of the last page of a folded newspaper lying on the next seat; other than that, he hadn't read anything but scripture.

The news on CNN was dreary. It was an election year and people were trying to get elected. The California version wanted whatever the voters wanted, wanted to be in harmony with their pending constituency.

They had a peculiar opinion about human life. Abortion was no big deal, but they were very upset about a life recently terminated for a violent crime, had conducted a midnight vigil in protest. They loved their animals, especially wildlife, had lately gotten on the bandwagon for mountain lions, even though mountain lions had taken to grabbing joggers from the hillside trails, caching their remains for future meals. The cats had been wandering into yards on scenic mountainsides too. The nature loving wealthy, who chose to perch their fabulous homes in such places, were upset about mountain lions, but the public still loved them. He wondered if a protesting victim, neck secured tightly by huge incisors, being drug off by a strong cat, was still opposed to hunting mountain lions? He thought of the big cat up in the Absarokas, silent, flexed, a powerful and proficient killer.

Californians were against guns too. Bakewell understood the thing about automatic weapons. Nobody needed to hunt with a machine gun, although re-enactors loved their vintage weapons, which now included a variety of WWII automatics. There would be confrontations over the automatics, but what was the problem with *shotguns?* And if they loved their animals, how did they feel about bird dogs, not to mention those big mean dogs the trackers used for hounding coyotes.

The news was a strange brew: down with power plants, especially nuclear, while LA glittered – and illuminated the front and backs of their properties, presumably to ward off criminals – since they didn't own guns. They were upset with pollution. Where did it go? They were against waste, but left it at the street each week, like the rest of the country, for somebody else to handle. Amazingly they seemed to favor cloning, euthanasia and fetal tissue research, while clamoring for a woman's right to abortion. He could hear Ned's take on California, "Dichotomies and oxy-morons all over the place."

Mostly they were for *rights*. Everybody running for office was for everything involving rights. Bakewell wondered, realized he was applying a double standard. His purpose in Bougainville hadn't been recreational. He was determined never to take issue with anybody on anything again. He was done with controversy, had grown accustomed to the stellar peace of his island nights. He just wanted to get out of California, wanted to see the stars again. He stared up at the bumpy ceiling plaster. April. My God. April. March is really over… He slept another five hours.

He ordered a huge breakfast, but couldn't eat it when it came. His meatless, fatless diet had redirected his culinary tastes; the thought of putting so much grease in his stomach now revolting. He picked at the food, eating the toast dry, loving the coffee. He drank four cups. He rented a car in the name of Joseph Olson, produced a Nebraska driver's license and credit card, addressed to Olson in Omaha. A map of Los Angeles came with the rental car and he headed northwest, without any direction. When he reached Lancaster he followed the signs to an outlying airport – Gen. William J. Fox. The FBO had a Mooney, a 201 that would do 160 knots at altitude in the cool mountain air. Bakewell hadn't flown a Mooney in years, but wanted something solid that would cross the mountains fast. More importantly, the plane had oxygen. In Olson's name, he produced an aging flight certificate that had him instrument rated, and single- and multi-engine endorsed. He also produced a logbook, his own, with an aged but different cover page. It contained many entries in dozens of aircraft, including float and bush planes. He found a young instructor who could check him out in the rental plane and they made arrangements for a few hours together after lunch.

"Olson," wandered around the place, checking out planes, enjoying the sights, sounds and smells of an airport once more. When his instructor came available they took the Mooney up. He demonstrated his ability to fly the plane, did all the required maneuvers, chatting with the young man, while hanging the plane on its prop. The Mooney had a few bad habits, but he stayed ahead of it as he talked his way through the checkout flight, telling the instructor stories of bush flying, float planes and places he'd been in North America in an almost giddy manner, so happy to be home in America, flying an airplane once more – *and he couldn't stop speaking English.* He was showing off, he knew; he wanted the kid's endorsement, and laid it on thick, going so far as to dive the plane, building speed before pulling it up and rolling it almost vertical in a wingover.

"What are you doing? This isn't an aerobatic aircraft!" The kid yelled.

"I'm not doing aerobatics," Bakewell replied calmly.

"We were upside down!"

"No, but close. It isn't an aerobatic maneuver, if you don't exceed the structural limits of the airplane."

"Bullshit! You had us upside down."

"This is a tough airplane. It likes to be compelled, like a spirited horse; it needs a firm hand, but if it understands who is boss it'll behave."

"You could have killed us!"

"How much aerobatic flying have you done?"

"None, I'm a straight and level pilot, a future airline captain."

"Have you had any *unusual attitude* training?"

"I will take my passengers where they want to go and get them there without any unusual attitudes."

"I'm sure you will make a fine airline captain, but learn more about bad situations. You might need some reference to fall back on someday."

"No sir, I'm not a cowboy. That shit went out with the last war."

Bakewell gave the plane back to the man after a third landing. Mooneys were tricky and the instructor, rattled, made a poor job of the landing. Afterward the kid signed him off, with an élan he couldn't quite fake. His hands shook as he made the entry. Bakewell wished him luck in his airline career and made arrangements to rent the Mooney for several days.

He could have driven the rental car (and left a trail), or bought a ticket on some dreadful bus or train (and done the same). He doubted he could sit still for that long ever again. There was no way he would fly commercially – that required a photo ID. And he wanted to fly an airplane one more time, fly it across the mountains (and he was almost sure, leave no trail). Traffic was rare in the sky, especially in the mountains, down low below the jet lanes.

He found a quick shop and filled a small cooler: sausage, cheese, apples, some chips and two liters of water. It was four in the afternoon when he departed Fox and programmed the GPS for Lemmon, South Dakota. About two hours out, lined up with Tonopah, Nevada, he decided to stop for the night. The airport was deserted and he slept well in his bag on the wing of the Mooney, getting a grand view of the dry-weather sky, sleeping intermittently, even enjoying the recurrent wakings. There was no panic, just a pleasant dozing. When he was awake, he watched the sky, enjoying the stellar display, the tent still packed in the airplane.

After fueling, he told the FBO operator he was headed for Oregon, but continued northeast after departing, enjoying a breakfast of apples, cheese and fresh water. He deviated around the higher elevations, staying below 10,000'. He wasn't in good enough shape to be up where the air was thin, and paced himself, swooping down through the valleys when the terrain allowed. He stopped in Fort Bridger for fuel and a short break, avoiding conversation, paid for the fuel in cash. Leaving FBR he went southwest and after about ten miles, turned northeast toward lower terrain and the Dakotas. Lemmon, South Dakota showed up mid afternoon Mountain Daylight Time. After landing he tied the plane down and went to the FBO.

He borrowed the courtesy car and went into town and checked into a motel. Back out at the airport he left a message on the bulletin board: "Anyone interested in ferrying a Mooney to Lancaster, California…" He gave the motel number, hoping he would find his man quickly, did a short hunker with the locals, weaving a tale about Joseph Olson from Omaha. When a ferry pilot didn't show, he called Lancaster to advise he would be out another few days, not to worry; he was having a fantastic tour of the Pacific Northwest.

His man showed the following Monday. He was late fifties, mechanical, but on the wrong end of a hard life. They agreed to take the Mooney for a test hop. The guy had lots of time, mostly in older twins, but was rusty and nearly lost the plane twice on landing. Once Bakewell was sure he could fly and navigate with the modern equipment onboard they went back to Lemmon and did a half dozen take offs and landings.

"So, you want it to go back to Lancaster in California?" Morris said, pronouncing it Cal-ee-fornya.

"I told them it would be back in a day or two."

"Why ain't you flying it back there yourself?"

Bakewell made a practiced sigh, "I lead a sort of vagabond life since my wife left me."

"How do you mean?"

"I move around a lot. The woman has tons of money, only married me for my looks. Once she got tired of me, she gave me half a mil and sent me packing."

"Damn, how'd you find a gal like that?"

"Wit and charm," Bakewell chuckled, low key, relaxed. He needed to fool the simple fellow, wanted to get the plane returned to Lancaster safely.

"Where's this woman now?"

"She spends a lot of time around Fox; that's where I would start."

"Maybe I'll look her up."

"I think you should."

"Where you goin?"

"New York."

"You rented a Mooney in Lancaster and now you don't want to go back. What's the deal?"

"Why don't you take it back to Lancaster and find out. She's got an experimental that'll do 250 knots, and a 185 that spends half its time on floats. You might have the time of your life. Just hang out at Foxy's; let everybody know you're looking to make Evelyn's acquaintance."

"Evelyn?"

"Uh huh, try not to be too obvious. You might get lucky."

"You really think she'll be there?"

"She comes and goes, but if she's around…"

Morry's eyes were full of anticipation; it was time to drop the hammer. "Listen up, now," Bakewell's eyes hardened like Adrian Powell's, as he looked into the other man's eyes. "You take your time, don't mess with weather, avoid trouble; once you get to Lancaster check the plane in; give them this envelope. It's for the time I've put on the plane and another ten hours you might fly, assuming you go sightseeing on the way back. Enjoy yourself. There's a big Money Order in there, made out to the FBO. Don't do anything stupid, like try and cash the money order."

"No, no, you can trust me," Morry said, leaning back as Bakewell leaned in. "You really think this Evelyn will be there?"

"Who knows? Enjoy yourself. Here's $500 for fuel. Don't piss it away and make me come looking for you. Your pilot's license's the same as your social security number. I used to be in law enforcement; don't do anything stupid. You don't want to lose your license, and you don't want to miss out on Lancaster, and you sure don't want me to come looking for you." He stared at the weaker man, handing him the money. "So take the plane on back and catch a commercial flight wherever. I really don't care once the plane's at Lancaster." Bakewell tried to intimidate the man, tried to create enough fear to assure himself there would be no problem. "Have a nice life, Morry, and when you get there ask that little oriental lady at Barnes Aviation to give you the envelope I left with her.

"You'll find enough money to fly you anywhere, with change to spare. That's the deal. It's a good deal, even if you strike out with Evelyn."

"Yeah, but what if there ain't no envelope there?"

"Morry, you're stupidity is discouraging. *I'm trusting you with a plane rented in my name."* Bakewell pronounced each word slowly, *"You've got money for your time and money for gas. You've got the money to pay for the rental. You can trust me for the rest. Don't get too curious. Nobody's interested in you or me, so don't make more out of this than necessary."* Bakewell made a long, deep sigh. "If you're worried about being set up, land the plane late at night and put the money in the drop box. They'll think it was me all along."

"You can trust me Joe. You got no problem there."

"Good, I know how to find you, if you let me down."

Morry took the money and the envelope and walked away wondering if his luck was about to change. He left for California that same afternoon. Bakewell watched until the plane was out of sight then he burnt his logbook inside a 55-gallon drum behind the FBO. When he destroyed his logbook his flying days were over. *All of my days are about over.* He was feeling run down again, it was happening more frequently, the intervals getting closer together, despite his excitement about being in America. When he looked at the charred embers of his flying career, he was surprised that it didn't discourage him more. He stared out at the vast prairie feeling strangely at peace.

Bakewell got a ride north to Dickinson, North Dakota the next day. He disliked traveling overland, but didn't want to risk landing so close to his destination. When he got there he found an eighteen-wheeler headed east and told the driver he was going to Michigan, offering to pay for gas, an unheard of offer over the road. The driver said the company paid for his gas, and he was only going to Fargo, but he'd be happy to have company. They left about six in the evening, spring sunlight still high behind them as they approached Richardton.

"Oh no," Bakewell said, sitting up.

"What's the matter?"

"I left one of my bags in Dickinson."

"Aw shit, man, all the way back there?"

"Yeah, pull over here and let me out. I'm going to have to go back."

The driver slowed the truck, "Look Joe, I'll turn around at the next interchange and take you back."

"No, no way. I know how much one of these rigs costs to run. I'll get another ride, don't worry about me."

"I was kinda happy for the company. I don't really mind."

"No. It's too much to ask. Just let me out here. I appreciate it though. You're a good guy to offer. I'll be fine."

The driver protested, offering to go back to Dickinson again. Bakewell refused. The big rig came to a dusty, noisy stop on the shoulder. Bakewell climbed down, saying he wouldn't have trouble getting another ride. "People out here on the prairie are good folks," he shouted. "Somebody will give me a ride. Thanks again."

The driver pulled back out on the highway. Bakewell watched him go, started walking west after crossing the median and didn't stop until the tractor-trailer was out of site. He removed the Joseph Olson identification from his wallet, tore it up and held it for the strong Dakota wind, letting it fly across the highway toward the greening fields to the south. From his pack he took another ID, this one from Tulsa and put it in his wallet. He looked across the highway toward Richardton and the twin spires of St. Mary's rising majestically.

"It's time to make peace with You, Oh Lord, my God." He quoted from the Psalms. *And I hope I've found the right place.* The Abbey roof was also visible in the distance. He started to walk north toward the buildings, remembering many of the Psalms he had read and re-read out on Rujeje.

Bakewell was very tired, feeling he had little purpose left in his life, desperately hoping to find peace and wind down. He would make reparation for his sins. He intended to spend his remaining days praying for his soul and for family and friends – and enemies too. *Pray for those who persecute and hate you.*

There were twenty minutes of daylight left when he approached the Abbey church and tried to enter. It was a big church. He remembered calling it a cathedral after their first visit. The doors were locked. He walked round to the east end of the buildings and found a monk, reading under a large weathered cedar.

"I'm looking for Brother Nathan."

The monk looked up, smiled pleasantly, indicated the glass doors at the corner of the building, lost in meditation. Bakewell went inside. There were two hallways: one heading north the other west, both empty. He walked west down a long corridor past the empty office, and came to a heavy steel door. On the other side was the church, and he stepped down into the darkness of the huge building. It was dimly lit, but he could see two monks praying in the front near the altar.

Bakewell remembered the church clearly. He and Andy attended Mass at St. Mary's, had taken time out from a hunting trip, rested the dogs while they went to Saturday evening Mass. He also remembered how devout Andy had seemed that evening, taking care to assist in the sacrament, showing great reverence. When they returned to St. Louis, Andy announced he was going to marry Karen Mendel. Bakewell and Katherine had only met the girl once at a parents' weekend. Karen was two generations removed from her faith, but the announcement had come as a shock, and sounded an emotional alarm with Bakewell, Michael and Nancy, until Katherine stepped in and told them what she thought, in a firm but persuasive voice. Katherine said Karen's religion was inconsequential. The ceremony had been hugely successful, gave Katherine another opportunity to plan and orchestrate. Karen adored Andy, was very bright and, most important, wanted to live in St. Louis.

Katherine won her over quickly, maybe it was the other way around. Later, Bakewell realized the relationship between Karen and Katherine had been a certainty. Katherine was committed to family harmony. It was smooth and peaceful sailing. Nancy too, had become friends with Karen long before the wedding. Only Michael kept any distance. Michael loved Andy, but was determined to keep Karen off balance, guessing. She was, after all, taking his big brother away.

Bakewell knelt down and waited for his thoughts to form, waited for the prayers to come. He hoped he was home at last. He was there to prepare, to prepare *to come home, maybe go home? Forever?* But his mind drifted and the prayers didn't come. One of the monks got up and left the church through a vestibule. He waited for the second monk, and when he finally got up from his pew and started to move in the same direction, Bakewell approached.

"I'm looking for Brother Nathan. Can you help me?"

The monk was young and well built, resembling Bakewell's sons in stature, nearly the same age.

"Follow me," he whispered and led him through another vaulted door, into a second corridor that paralleled the one he'd entered through. "I'm Brother James," he said rather loudly, extending his hand, now that they were no longer in church.

"Joe Bannister."

"Ah. We've been expecting you for some time now, Mr. Bannister. Can I call you Joe? We're on a first name basis here."

"Of course, Brother."

"We were looking for you last March."

"I've been delayed, several times actually. For a while there I wondered if I would ever make it." Bakewell had to walk fast to keep up with the long legged monk. They returned to the entry he'd come through and the young man left to find Brother Nathan.

Brother Nathan came down the stairs minutes later and shook Bakewell's hand warmly. "Ah, Joe, you are welcome. I'll show you your room." The room had a double bed, nightstand with lamp, desk and chair, best of all a rocking chair. Bakewell had loved rocking chairs all his life. (Katherine never cared for them, always sent them to the basement TV room within months of their arrival; from there they usually transitioned on, ended up at someone else's house. It was a simple disagreement without words, without rancor, that went uncontested for years).

"In here is your bathroom. You have your own shower. I hope you'll find it comfortable."

"It will be perfect," Bakewell said, dropping his backpack on the bed. "Thank you."

"We have morning prayer at six. You are welcome to pray with us. I'm afraid you've missed this evening's prayer."

Bakewell told him he intended to pray with them at all times, was looking forward to it. Brother Nathan left him, indicating the rules of the Monastery, typewritten on the door, and Bakewell said he would read them before turning in. Once alone in his new quarters fatigue overwhelmed him. He fell onto the bed and stared at the high ceiling for a long time. He couldn't raise himself to take a shower and fell into a deep sleep despite his strange surroundings.

***

The next few weeks passed quickly. He found himself in a routine of morning prayer, which consisted of readings, chants and much singing: Mass in the late morning, prayers again in the afternoon, and once more in the evening. They sat in assigned places each time. Fortunately, the newly ordained priest next to him had a strong voice and fine talent. He sang all the words from memory. Bakewell was able to get along next to the devout young man, who he complimented often about his voice on the way to meals. The priest always repaid the compliment by saying, “You do all right, for someone not familiar with our world.”

The food was ample, and there was a good variety of fruit and vegetables. Bakewell missed the fresh fruit of the islands, ate a lot of grain and roughage. Fish was available several times a week, but it was a disappointment after so many weeks of fresh fish from the sea.

In the evenings, he read from their extensive library, learned the Rule of St. Benedict. He also tried to compose a letter to his children, explaining where he had gone and what had happened to him. It was no good; nearly every line a lie. He couldn’t tell them the truth. His strength began to ebb. He could feel it now that he wasn’t putting himself through cycles of exertion and rest. A sense of urgency began to permeate him. How could he make peace with his family, tell them he was still alive and express his love for each one? Who would he send the letter to? It was impossible. He was in an impossible situation. *Did there have to be some type of closure, some act of finality? Why? Who would he be helping? You don’t want them to think you died in some unsatisfactory way on the other side of the world. You’re worried about yourself. They’ve already been through it. You’re dead man. Give it up. Think of them.*

He spent time out in the fields with Brother Placid, learning more about agriculture than he’d been able to pick up in the previous thirty years. Bakewell loved the farm, the equipment, the sounds and smells of diesel, grease and oil, and, most especially, the smell of cut grass and the out-of-doors. He cut the grass around the buildings occasionally; it was everyone’s favorite job. When they weren’t in prayer or reflection, he tried to stay outside, loved the ancient and enormous barn below the monastery, asked endless questions about animal husbandry. They had a herd of cows, a calving yard, and nine bulls in a separate pen. There were many outbuildings with hinges that needed repair, and the usual amount of farm chores any large livestock operation required.

Bakewell also spent time in the mechanic shop, working on farm equipment, helping with machine maintenance (it was the planting season and they maintained thousands of acres of cropland, predominantly in oats). One monk taught him how to weld and braise metal. He had owned the same equipment all his business life, but never had the time to learn to use it.

Mass was the highlight of each day; he looked forward to it. Confession was another story. He knew he needed to find a confessor, but telling someone he was a hit man, a government sniper, someone who shot people, or just a plain fugitive, would be putting a huge burden on whichever priest he selected. Eventually he chose to tell the former Abbot, who enjoyed his company, and vaguely remembered him for his airplane. Their conversations were almost daily, usually in his room after Compline or

Vespers. Father Robert always insisted Bakewell take the rocking chair.

He told the Abbot about places he had been over the years, and the Abbot told him stories of the people he had known. He was anecdotal, a good conversationalist. Conversation was something they both craved. Many of the monks were quiet and reserved. Conversation and reading were nearly the only forms of entertainment after dark in the Abbey. There was a television upstairs, but Bakewell never watched the TV.

Bakewell wondered, almost constantly in his new environment, what death would be like. It was getting closer, and he wondered if he would be able to look forward to it with the Abbot's confidence. It was during such a conversation that Bakewell finally slipped into the confessional mode. When the Abbot nodded his head, indicating he proceed, Bakewell started with, "I am sure you already know I have come here to the monastery for a reason, Father. I have a past."

"Yes, we all have a past, Joe." The Abbot nodded again, encouraging him to resume.

"I am terminally ill. I don't know how much longer I have, but I will get out of your way when the time comes, so you won't have that responsibility."

"We have had ill people here before."

"I'm sure. I don't have any desire to die here, don't want you people waiting on me around the clock. In fact I don't really have any idea how I'm going to do it yet. I'll think of something. I can always go home to my family when I get really bad."

"The choice will be yours. Will your family be happy to see you?"

"They'll be surprised."

"Is that good?"

"It will be…an event…if I go home. I hope to figure it out in the coming weeks. Anyway, I need to find forgiveness and get absolution, once again."

"Is absolution doable? Are you going to confess to something you have to make amends for, by returning to your previous life, maybe, before I can absolve you?"

"You're perceptive, Father. I guess that's why we've been having all these conversations? You're the guy chosen to find out about Joe Bannister? You *got the duty*, as we used to say in the navy?" Bakewell rocked nervously, thankful he was in the chair that moved for this rite of reconciliation.

"Not really. I've enjoyed our talks. You're a pretty good guy," Father chuckled. "You sure pray hard for a civilian."

"Well, here comes the hard part, stop me if I go too fast. It tends to get my pulse running at a high rpm." Bakewell cleared his throat, leaned in, "If it gets too wild you can slow me down with ecclesiastical questions." The priest smiled, nodded once again and Bakewell began with a quick recap of his dealing with the *Company*. He told him he didn't have too much concern about civil or legal problems, it was too late for that anyway, both in actions already committed and in time left to make amends. He described the first shooting in Genoa and then the trip to Bougainville and what happened after that. He was adamant and confident when he confessed that he never had any intention of taking another human life. The only real problem he grappled with out there in the Pacific, was whether he had the right to take a chance and try to hit his target without killing him. It was arrogant of him to think of himself as so talented with the weapon he could even take the shot. Besides, the act of shooting was sin enough in itself. He never deluded himself about that.

Bakewell admitted – he had decided long before – that he felt no obligation to those who hired him. Never expected to be around when the time came, so taking the money was as good as stealing it, no matter where it might come from. Still, if the time came, he was certain he could call his shot, or miss high, without any chance of killing him. Bakewell gave all the details, emphasizing his frame of mind throughout the entire episode, knowing it was crucial to his confession. Unlike a trial before the law, this was a hearing before God, and he had to be totally honest to be truly repentant. He admitted he had more concern about touching off an international incident, causing someone else to be hurt in the process, than he had about hurting the man he shot, all the while knowing there could be no holding back, and each time the Abbot queried him he answered frankly. He was ruthlessly honest with every answer, and was so thorough in his detailing of the tale the Abbot didn't need to ask many questions. The older man could see and feel his intention to make a good confession, could hear the candor in his voice. They talked for several hours about every question of faith and morals and, covering a lot of ground, they got off the subject several times. At one point the Abbot said, "Hey, there's a lot of people that would have liked it if you had killed that guy!"

When he had finished, the Abbot gave him absolution and told him he had made a good confession, said he was glad his sin wasn't something more grave. He told him there were many sins more serious than what they had discussed. If he was truly repentant he would find absolution. It made Bakewell wonder just how much a confessor like the former Abbott heard in a lifetime.

"You have one more very important detail to give me, you know."

"What is that, Father?"

"Your real name isn't Bannister is it?"

"No."

"I don't care if you choose not to tell me your real name. It's not important. But it is important that you confess, as yourself, and not be here in the confessional under any pretense. This isn't the time for you to be living a lie, even if it is necessary – for your safety, or for the peace and quiet of our life here in the Abbey."

"Father, my name is Bakewell. Andersen Bakewell. I've been using some IDs I created, rather poorly, I have to admit. I've used a couple of them since I left Bougainville. I didn't think they would let me out of there alive, that's why I *went under* so to speak. Out there they call it, going bush. It's not hard to get lost in the islands, believe me. If nobody is looking for you, you could get lost forever out there. But I'm no longer looking to get lost. I almost wish I could be found, in more than one way."

"I was lost and now I'm found?"

"Exactly, 'but now I see." I would like to be buried at home. It's crazy, but sometimes I think it's possible. They can take whatever parts of me they want to use on someone else when the time comes. I might even agree to give up some of my parts before I go, in order to provide them in usable order. I'm beginning to think I want to go home, as wild as that seems. I need to know my kids will be there to bury me when the time comes. I need their forgiveness and their compassion at the end."

"You will have their forgiveness, son. Do they call you Andy?" Bakewell nodded. "They have already forgiven you. It seems to me everything you have done, all this madness and chance taking, and the whole wild adventure was for their sake, wasn't it?"

"I don't really know. I can't answer that one Father. I would sure like to think so, but that may be a cop out."

The Abbot patted him on the arm. "Have you put us in any danger? Could there be an incident here at the Abbey that would embarrass us?"

"I really don't think so, but if I get the slightest suspicion, I will be out of here. I would never do anything to disturb the peace you have here. It's a wonderful place. I have learned to like it very much."

The former Abbot smiled knowingly. "Well, we will miss you, if you have to leave, Andy. You're an interesting fellow, and you have certainly stimulated my intellectual life these past weeks."

Leo

During his third week at the Abbey, Bakewell decided to walk into town and get a drink. He had lost any desire to get inebriated long before, just needed to walk, and Richardton was the only option left. He'd walked in every other direction, east, west, and up the vast, glaciated valleys and rolling hills to the north.

It was late evening when he went into town. Like all agricultural towns, Richardton was laid out north south/east west. He walked down 3rd Street to 2nd Avenue, avoiding the streets with deep-throated, barking dogs, and there were quite a few.

He stopped at the Elk Horn Cafe. It was the first time Bakewell had been in Richardton since his walk up to the Abbey the first day. He decided to sit at the bar, ordered a Rolling Rock, and wondered why: *must be the stimulus of being in a bar again.* He drank the beer, not enjoying the bitter taste, while the other three patrons looked at him. *This is no way to remain anonymous.* He finished quickly and left.

On the way back to the Abbey, he saw an electrical storm off to the north, approaching fast. He decided to job back to the dining area to watch the storm, and to see if he could still run, and for how long. The dining room was a large assembly area, with big windows across the entire room. The room was ground level, facing north, overlooking the valley below, where the ground fell away quickly, it seemed much higher, and allowed for a fantastic view. It was like going to a drive-in theater again. He watched the lightening flash and listened for the thunder that followed. It began to rain and soon became a tremendous downpour, filled with lightening flashes, booming thunder and rain driving hard against the large windows, and Bakewell realized how simple any craving for entertainment had become, how simple his life had become as he enjoyed the spectacular show.

He had learned the names of nearly every monk. Some were priests, others, simply Brothers, but each had professed vows or was preparing to. He spent most of his time with the livestock after the planting was done, fully adjusted to his life as an interloper in a spiritual community.

The week after his visit to the Elk Horn, Brother Gerard introduced him to a short, slightly built man, badly in need of a shave and a bath. He was shabbily dressed in a rumpled, overly large and badly weathered suit coat, which didn't match his baggy pants. His shirt was scruffy, one collar folded under the wrong way, leaving the other badly chafed and exposed between his weathered, heavily wrinkled neck and the lapel of the nasty coat. His pockets bulged with what they all suspected were his earthly goods. Brother Gerard confirmed this, saying Leo had showed up "With the sum total of his worldly possessions in his pockets."

The old man seemed indifferent to Bakewell, refused to make eye contact. Bakewell assumed his behavior was either out of ignorance or shame, or both. Three days later, while he was out, wandering the farm, amazed by the little blue crocuses that grew wild and covered the steep hillsides around the property, on a fantastic day, with a fresh breeze and the fantastic odors of the huge country, Bakewell spotted Leo, near the out buildings in the area below the barn south of the big lake. Adopting the Abbey's policy of, "No stranger within our gates," he decided to make the first effort with the little old man.

Leo was not interested in making Bakewell's acquaintance, was surly and uncommunicative, and rudely turned his back on him several times when Bakewell persisted. He also had a habit of touching his hands to his chest, then to his sagging, badly stretched, misshapen coat which reminded Bakewell of an old college don, searching for his pipe or some lost manuscript.

"You know, Leo, you can leave your belongings in your room. Nobody steals from anyone here. You don't need to carry them around with you all day."

Leo turned his back again, walked down toward the calving pasture without saying anything, leaving Bakewell to shrug and wonder. They were down next to the barn.

Half offended and half angry, watching the old man walk off, Bakewell had another premonition – one of his 80% hunches. It gave him a sick feeling. He waited, unwilling to turn his back on the old man, called out when he was far enough away. "Leo!" The old man turned about, looking irritated. "I'm going into the kitchen area, to clean up for Brother Placid, he's gone for the day."

Bakewell indicated the old barn. The kitchen was used for animal husbandry, made a big deal of going over to the barn, opened the door, and waved down to Leo. The barn was badly cracked and many of the roof shingles were missing. Light came through from above. It leaked in a storm. He was careful to leave the latch opened on the side door.

"Hey, Leo!" The old man trudged on down the hill. "I'll be in the tack room, cleaning up those old saddles if you decide you want to visit! Come on up and we'll talk!" Leo stopped shambling along and looked back, actually raised his hand in recognition.

Bakewell went inside to the kitchen through the heavy wooden door, which had been plated with aluminum to protect it from the constant abrasion of tool-carrying traffic. Once inside he put the wildflowers in a pan of water and left them in the sink. He took up a position behind the door, checked his watch, and hoped he was wrong. It was 10:31.

Eight minutes later he heard the barn door squeak. The barn siding was uninsulated, a single layer of wood. Once inside, Leo hesitated before he pushed the door open slightly to look into the empty kitchen. Bakewell knew the tack room door, aging with yellow paint, would be the point of Leo's focus. It was twelve feet across the room from where they were, separated by the opened kitchen door. Bakewell knew what was coming next, prayed he would be wrong. He saw the shaft of the silencer pass through the door first, leading the weapon into the room, preceding the old man. It was shaking visibly. Leo came in slowly, when he was sure he could grab the silencer, without chance of missing, Bakewell lunged, grabbing the cylinder and shoving the door with his left shoulder violently into the old man. The weapon came free as soon as the force of the door hit him. Bakewell was focused on the muzzle of the weapon, not on the old man, treated it like the viper it was. He pointed it toward the roof.

There wasn't much to Leo; he couldn't have weighed more than 130. He went sailing across the kitchen and hit the counter under Brother Placid's map of the Abbey property.

Bakewell came across the room after the old man, grabbed him, getting one arm around his neck, under his chin, and pulled violently upward, dragging him backward across the room. Leo's feet swung about wildly. They couldn't reach the floor. The old man's head was against his cheek. Bakewell could smell the stench in his hair. Leo tried to free himself; his arms flapped harmlessly.

Bakewell had no desire to hurt the old man, but he was angry, and there was only one way to handle the situation. He spoke into his ear, "Listen, you little puke. I could kill you right now; just one hard jerk on your skinny neck." Bakewell jerked his neck for emphasis, before sliding his arm down to pin the old man's arms to his sides. The old man gasped for air. Bakewell had cut off his air supply. He swung him and threw him, feet first, across the room. When he landed by the counter again, Leo tried to get under it, hoping to find some protection from his accuser. Bakewell was right on top of him.

"They sent you to kill me, didn't they? Then they would have killed you, you dumb ass." The old man covered his head with one arm, cowering.

Bakewell went back for the gun, picked it up, and looked at it in disgust. It was a Smith & Wesson automatic. The silencer was old, dented. "Do you know anything about how these things work?" Leo stared, wide-eyed at the ugly weapon.

"They're full of baffles, for baffling the sound. Understand? They are supposed to *silence it.* They're only good for a few shots, before the baffling wears out. After that the sound is the same, maybe louder. This is a piece of junk! Look at it! It's worn out!"

The old man looked at Bakewell instead, wondering what was next. "You're in deep shit here, Leo. You shoot me and the sound is terrific. Somebody calls the police, and you're a dead man." Bakewell shook his head. "You failed to get me, so you're a dead man, anyway. I might as well strangle you and sink you to the bottom of the lake out there. By the time you float up,

I'll be gone."

Leo watched Bakewell, eyes wide, cowering.

"Damn it! They set you up. You were never going to collect any money. Doesn't that make you mad? You have no obligation to them. You can run and get away clean or I can kill you now. What's your preference?"

"I didn't mean no harm!" The old man whimpered, the look in his eyes hysterical.

"Yeah? Well killing is always harmful." He yanked him out from under the counter; he would have to scare him badly. He poured himself into the task, and hurled the old man across the room where he hit the floor, rolling over against a heavy metal table. Bakewell came right after him again and dropped to one knee. "Listen, I'm a professional killer," he hissed his words for effect, leaning in threateningly. He pointed the gun at his head, held it close. Leo's nose had struck the counter, and he was bleeding. Bakewell moved the gun about, kept it in front of his eyes. Leo raised his arm again defensively, tried to move farther back under the table. Bakewell finally slid the clip out and ejected the cartridge in the chamber. It landed on the floor next to them.

"You know it's illegal to carry a side arm? *And these things are strictly verboten,"* he said, as he unscrewed the silencer. He held his hand up and signaled Leo to wait where he was, and then he reached into the tack room and got a small blanket and knelt back down on one knee. "Do you know why they sent you here to kill me?"

The old man shook his head, paralyzed with fear, with the knowledge the figure above him knew he had intended kill him.

"Have you ever killed anybody?" Leo shook his head, changed his mind, nodded his head, watching the expression on Bakewell's face, shook his head again. "What is it? Yes or no?"

The old man didn't know what to do.

"You killed someone once, didn't you?" Leo nodded. "Not in the service was it?" He shook his head. "Probably a long time ago, wasn't it? Maybe when you were a kid? When you were a dumb kid, I'll bet. You did time didn't you?"

Leo nodded.

"I've got a couple of ideas; let me think them out loud. We'll take them in order." Bakewell put on a performance for the cowering figure below him, put the clip back in the gun. He had to have him off the property right away. "How about I put this thing back on and shove it up your butt and fire it until its empty? Then I chain you to that big chunk of iron out in the yard and sink you to the bottom of the lake?"

Leo only whimpered.

"Or I could shoot your knee off, and we could tell Brother you somehow shot yourself accidentally and they could take you to the hospital?"

He tapped Leo's knee and waited for an answer, knowing none would be forthcoming. There was only a groan of fear. "No? Maybe not? It would hurt like hell and create an unwelcome stir here at the monastery." He pointed the gun at the old man again. "Why do I get the feeling the police would probably be looking for you if you showed up at a hospital?" Leo whined softly.

"Maybe today's your lucky day? Maybe today's my day off? I won't kill you today. Tomorrow's another story though. I think I'm going to kill you tomorrow. If you're here tomorrow, I'm going to kill you, understand? If I was you I'd get off this property quick." There was still no answer, but Leo nodded slightly.

"I want you to go up to the Abbey and tell Brother your heart is acting up. Tell him you need to get to Dickinson right away. They will probably drive you over. You know how generous these men are. That's what we'll do. You go tell them you have to get to Dickinson. When you get to Dickinson, I want you to head south and west. Don't ever get north of this place, not ever again. For that matter don't ever get east of it again, as long as you live. Understand? As far as you're concerned everything north of the Interstate and east of Utah is my territory. Never let me find you in my territory again, or I will kill you so slowly people will pay to watch."

The old man nodded; the possibility of survival becoming real. Bakewell helped him to his feet and told him to start for the Abbey. "Don't get out of my site until you're in the car heading west, understand? I'll be right behind you until you're in the car." He followed him outside, out of the glaciated valley up the steep hill to the Abbey. When they found Brother Nathan, Leo found his voice for the first time and spoke more words than anyone had heard from him since he arrived. He told the monk he needed to get to a hospital and get "My medicine quick," said he needed to get to Dickinson as soon as possible. He told the monk he was afraid he might be having another heart attack and needed to get his medicine. The words came in such rapid succession, neither Bakewell nor the monk could understand half of what he said, but the message was clear enough. Brother Nathan decided to recruit another monk, one of the men who did hospice work, to take Leo to Dickinson. He got one of the older priests to drive.

Bakewell stood next to Brother Nathan and watched them drive off the property toward the Interstate.

"To tell the truth, I'm happy to see him out of here," Brother Nathan said in relief. "Do you think he will be back, Joe?"

"I doubt it Brother. Once you filled him with enough food, he was bound to hit the road again."

The holy man nodded and went off to attend to other things. Bakewell took the weapon wrapped in the blanket under his arm to his room. When he got there he went to the bathroom and locked the door. It was a model 39 Smith & Wesson with a long heavily baffled silencer. The serial numbers on the automatic were intact. *I'll bet you're a weapon with a past, and a liability to anyone found with you.* The silencer was unmarked. He had seen such an item in the magazines. They were called Hush Puppies, and as silencers went, they were some of the most common available. He held the silencer up to the light. It was worn, as he expected. Bakewell doubted if it had much silencing ability. *If he had shot me with this damned thing it would probably have made one hell of a noise. They would have found him and turned him over to the police.* It was a setup, without any involvement on *their* part. Who would believe the old man's story?

With the gun's suspected past, Bakewell doubted if Leo would have found any sympathy before the law. It was a 9-millimeter and had a loud bark and heavy recoil. The total weight of both pieces was close to three pounds. *No wonder his pockets sagged.* There were six cartridges left in the clip, plus the one he had retrieved from the floor. Seven total. The gun held eight with one in the chamber. They probably gave him seven and told him to keep the chamber empty.

That evening at Compline, Bakewell prayed for Leo, asked God to forgive him for handling the man roughly, suspected he might have saved his life. He prayed for himself too. He was struck by two different passages from the liturgy at Compline. The first was from Psalm 17:

My foes encircle me with deadly intent
their hearts tight shut, their mouths speak proudly;
they advance against me, and they surround me.

The second, coming near the end of the prayer service from Psalm 133:

How good and how pleasant it is,
when people live in unity!

Bakewell was very discouraged when he returned to his room. He had been attempting another letter to his children, intended to finish the letter that night. It would have to wait. He tore the letter and his notes up carefully and put them in the wastebasket, before lying down. He stared at the ceiling for nearly an hour, thinking, wondering what might have been, weighing his options. His mind was focused again. There were no interruptions and no digressions, as he analyzed his situation.

He had a plan. It started to form as soon as Leo left. He would miss the peace of the monastery and the friendship of the monks, mostly the self-imposed solitude he found there. He would go north first, later turn west. After that he didn't know. It would depend on his health. He was down to one identity change, out of options, running out of time. He wanted to live his life out to the end, even if it meant dying in a hospital bed, hooked up to technology, a thought he had once abhorred. He wanted to be with his family again. He needed to contact them, to come in, to come home. They would be happy to see him, despite what he had done to them all.

Leaving

Bakewell waited long into the next day, nervously dreading what he would do, knowing the first few minutes would be the worst. He had no idea how to begin, other than to just begin. He would get through it. They would get through it. *Just do it.*

The old Abbot was right. He had one choice. He had to make contact. The impact of the call and the suddenness of his reappearing would create shock and pain, before it created joy and happiness. It would come like a thunderbolt. He worried all afternoon. They would all have a right to be shocked and confused, even more, to be disgusted. *If I'm going to die, why couldn't I just have died out in the islands and left it at that.* It made him want to swear; it also made him sick to his stomach. He told Fr. Robert how he felt, and Father sympathized, but he also chuckled and told Bakewell how much happiness would eventuate after the initial shock passed.

Hello Andy, I'm back. Yep, it's me, your old man. Tell your sister and brother I never really died; it was just a hoax. Right, a little boat lost at sea, but I wasn't on it, just a convenient coincidence. I let my watchers tell the world – fake my death for me. It was easy, a necessary little deception, but all a hoax. Actually it was quite necessary, since I never thought I would survive. It was supposed to be to everyone's advantage really. I meant well. Forgive me son, get over it quickly, don't be angry or surprised or hold it against me, you know your old man. He doesn't always get it right. He thinks he's doing the right thing. He means well, but forgets about the feelings of his family, forgets about the feelings people have for him. He didn't mean to cause pain...

Actually, that was pretty much the way it went. He'd been filled with dread when he dialed the number, voices screamed in his head. That chatty voice had been missing for a long time, but it was hurling abuse as he heard the phone ring. He really hoped making contact would make them happy, even for the short time he had left. He was hopelessly confused. But it wasn't about him after all; it was about his children. He made the call from the pay phone in town, next to the market. It was half past four in St. Louis when his oldest son answered.

Bakewell's throat was choked with emotion when he heard his son's voice. It went pretty much as he guessed. The boy was terribly confused, troubled and very wary. Not trusting the sound of his father's voice. "Dad?" Andy, had said, pronounced the word in two syllables, his voice tremulous, incredulous, and Bakewell could imagine his mind racing, imagining he was having that dream Bakewell had had so many times after Katherine died. The one where she calls and tells him she's all right. Everything is okay. He had begged for that moment, to hear her say it was all a mistake, she was still alive, still his.

That also was pretty much the way it went. Except Andy pointed out they had had a funeral service, a memorial service for him. Andy wasn't quite sure how they were going to deal with that. *You were killed in the islands; a boat disappeared out there somewhere north of someplace called Buka.*

Andy's voice had been so quiet, almost reverent, like he was talking with the dead. *There was a service, a note came from the State Department, said you were missing. They said you couldn't have survived.* Then his voice broke, and with it went Bakewell's own heart. He felt overwhelmingly sick, hearing the pain and concern in his son's voice. *How to make this right?* Andy had cried into the phone, so confused, disoriented. He choked as he spoke to his father. *Where are you dad? Are you really alive?*

Bakewell told him the truth, where he was. Told him how he felt, how the sickness was progressing, said he was feeling okay, for the moment. He was coming home soon, but not right now.

They had a formal inquest. It was very formal. They said you were traveling with some missionaries out to a place, some island place called Carterets." He became more coherent. "How did you survive in the ocean, Dad?"

Bakewell explained he was never in that boat, said he'd made a deal. They agreed to contact the legation, notify next of kin, and publish an obituary in the St. Louis paper. Make it official. *But why? Why would you do that? Why would they do that? The young man asked.*

It got very difficult after that, not the emotion so much as the logic. How to tell them what was really going on. "It's such a long story, son. You don't want to know, but I'll tell you about it when I see you. I am going to leave here in a few days. I will call you and let you know how I'm doing. I will call in the evening if I need to get hold of you, okay?"

Dad wait! You can't hang up, Dad. Dad! Wait! There was great urgency in his son's voice. And pain, Bakewell had caused the pain he heard coming through the phone. The pain in Andy's voice was alarming, filled him with shame, and a sense of urgency, an urgency to make amends. He was cursing himself as he listened to the disturbed voice, filled with relief, frustration, joy – and more suffering. Bakewell was sick with shame, with disgust. *You don't just die and then come back to life!*

Andy asked many questions. Bakewell couldn't answer any of them truthfully. They talked for a long time. He wanted to give the boy time to adjust. They both needed time. He tried to explain. It was hopeless. Each time he lied, he had to tell another lie, knew the story wasn't working. *You are lying to your own son. Tell him the truth! What difference does it make? Tell him everything. You have time. Talk to him. Tell him what has happened. Don't hold back. He's a man. He can deal with the truth. Tell him his father's a contract hit man, an assassin who misses on purpose. That won't work, but it can't be worse than pretending to die, calling him, telling him it's all a game!*

They talked for over an hour, agreed to sign off and talk again in a few days, give them each time to think. Andy would talk with his sister and brother. Bakewell would call them each when he could, maybe they would talk on a conference line. He didn't know how they would arrange that.

When he got back to the Abbey, Father Robert was waiting, full of compassion. He tried to convince Bakewell he had done the right thing.

"Why don't I feel like I've done the right thing, Father?"

The priest patted his arm, told him he was a fine man. God would handle the rest. "Give it to the Holy Spirit. Let Him walk you through. He will show you the way."

Bakewell was in a bad state, it wasn't the state of grace. He had been ashamed many times in his life; now shame had a new definition. Never once did he think out the part about the pain he might cause. He thought about the money, thought the need for it would be enough. Leaving them enough money would make up for his death. It had been short sighted. He wasn't ashamed about the money part, but how could he spend so much time thinking the money and the island part through, without giving a commensurate amount to the problem of family. *Because you can't explain killing for money to anyone! Not Ned, certainly not Denny, and not to your own children.* He sat in the big empty church, immobilized with shame for what he had done to his children. The others would just now be learning about his second coming.

***

Bakewell's emotions were scattered, fragmented. "Your mind is like a grenade, goin off all over the place," Ned used to say. One minute he wanted to return to his world, reconcile with family, with his partner, the next he wanted to disappear, run away, find some anchoritic place. He would explain his actions somehow, try to make them believe he had done everything for their sake. *It won't work.* He was jaded, filled with cynicism, his remorse again the unwanted companion. His mood swings went from full left to full right: first a tender need to refute arrogance, humble up, beg forgiveness, switching the other way, how to get away, where are you going, what are your intentions?

Despite the inner conflict, his inability to simplify his life, Bakewell focused on the immediate problem: safety. He was more aware of his surroundings, watched the comings and goings around the Abbey. He kept an eye on the front office, checked in with Father Richard to see who the visitors were, where they came from. Most were innocuous: two men from Bismarck who had been there before, a young high-schooler about to graduate from Miles City come to visit; and three elderly men who came together every year in May – all harmless, but there would be someone else, soon. This one might not be an amateur. There were plenty of Powell's out there. They knew how to shoot, cut, do an endless variety of bad things. He was anxious to leave, the peace of the Abbey a memory. Anxiety replaced peaceful reflection.

He spoke with his daughter the next afternoon. Later that same day he caught up with Michael, back in Ennis. Michael, steeled with the knowledge his father was alive, not caught unaware like his brother, kept his voice calm and they had a coherent conversation, unlike the one he'd had earlier with Nancy, who was nearly hysterical. The conversation with Michael was so matter of fact, it made Bakewell feel he was outside listening in. They talked for a long time before Michael's performance finally gave way, and he asked his father why he had done so many strange things. Talking with Michael had been pleasant until the questions came, and with them the searing guilt. After they hung up, Bakewell spent another hour in the church, staring at statues, altar, and so many painted windows, without seeing them, without being able to say a prayer. It was back to C S Lewis again: where was God when you needed Him?

He couldn't stay in Richardton. The Abbey wasn't guarded or even locked half the time, even if it was, it was nothing a skilled caller couldn't overcome. He packed and went to say good-bye to the former Abbot. They ended up talking much of the night, which suited both of them. Bakewell badly needed to talk to someone. He couldn't sleep anyway. The priest was sorry to hear he was leaving, but understood. Bakewell hadn't told anyone about Leo, but there were suspicions. They couldn't have trouble, couldn't have violence at the Abbey, and Bakewell had no intention of letting it happen. The Abbot wished he could be of help. He made Bakewell promise to call if he needed anything. After their conversation, Bakewell decided to try a different room, ended up tossing half the night in one of the other guest rooms. He left the building before daylight, before anyone was stirring in the halls, prior to morning prayers. He had food, water and about $15,000 in cash – plus the money in the bank in Bismarck.

And he had the automatic he'd taken from Leo. Having a gun created the possibility of violence and a quick death. He was so conflicted; he wasn't sure any longer about death. He wanted to live, but maybe dying quickly wasn't the most unpleasant option, if he could just *see it coming*. As he set out on the highway, he held to the slim hope of returning home before his time came.

He walked a long time, going west for Dickinson. There was an airport there. He hoped to find someone heading north who would welcome a fuel-sharing partner for the journey. Bakewell had friends in Glasgow, Montana. He could spend a few nights there. He told the former Abbot, in a moment of indiscretion, that he intended to go to Glasgow if he couldn't find a ride in Dickinson. Bakewell knew he could trust the Abbot, but his modus had been to tell everyone he was headed in a different direction. It took them three weeks to locate him in Richardton, or maybe it took them three weeks to find someone like Leo.

There had to be a faction that would want to get even for Albrecht. Albrecht was a vindictive bastard, but he had to have friends. Snow had warned him about Albrecht. There were probably others like him in the organization.

Bakewell got a ride eventually, made it to Dickinson. It was about seven in the morning when he found the airport. It was chancy on a weekday morning. There was limited air service at Dickinson. The military used the airport for helicopter operations. Nobody was headed north, nobody was even around. Bakewell milled around the airport for several hours, evaluating his dwindling options, before deciding to go on foot. He headed back to the highway, discouraged by the prospect of a long ride over the road. He hated the idea of traveling on land, knowing how easy it was to elude people traveling by small plane. The last time he flew to Calgary, he crossed the border and landed – simply phoned in and got a confirmation number, hadn't even needed a passport.

He would have settled for a crop duster, an ancient taildragger from a dusty barn somewhere, looked forward to it actually. Anything was more appealing than traveling overland. It looked like it might start to rain later. His spirits were going down with the barometric pressure. He started across the road toward the highway, as he did, two pheasants flushed from a hedgerow. Startled, Bakewell watched them go.

He heard first then saw, a large gray car coming down the highway toward the intersection, decelerating. He looked around. *You're wide open, uncovered.* He remembered Leo's gun, reached for it and chambered a round, slipped the safety off and on several times, as he watched the car make the turn toward him and begin to accelerate again. He felt the gun against his back, his thumb on the safety, prepared for the worst. A feeling of resignation came over him. *No, no more. You said you were done with this.*

He slipped the clip from the receiver and tossed it in the ditch and took the gun and threw it as far as he could, out into a greening field, watched it arc, end over end. "No more," he said out loud and with finality. He turned to face a big Lincoln Town Car. It slowed abruptly and skidded to a stop in front of him.

He saw her through the window first, couldn't believe it, was incredulous. When the door came open, Maggie burst from the rocking car. Bakewell was immobile. She came across the road, wild-eyed, stopped in front of him – and slapped his face as hard as she could – tears spurting from her eyes, as Bakewell's own teared from the blow. She stared up at him, hurt, furious. He didn't move when she hit him; his ear rang from the blow. She started to hit him again, he squinted, turned his head slightly, prepared to take a second blow; but she reconsidered, more tears, tried to speak, couldn't find her voice, choked, stood there staring, confused, outraged, hurt, never taking her eyes from his. Bakewell still didn't move, didn't say anything, stared back, feeling desperate, relieved, desperately relieved.

Maggie finally held her arms out, "Hold me, you son of a bitch!" He put his arms around her, wondering what he was doing, doing it on cue. He held her, and when he did, her arms dropped limply to her side. Then she wrenched free, and he thought she was going to hit him again. Instead, she threw her arms around his neck and hugged him so tightly it hurt. The release of emotion was tremendous. They were both overcome, clinging tightly, nearly losing their balance on the prairie road. Finally Bakewell spoke.

"We have to go, to get out of here. We might be seen."

"Seen by who?" she rasped. "What are you talking about?"

If she had found him so easily there might be others. "We need to go. Right now, we need to go, now."

"Maggie. Call me Maggie. Tell me you love me. Tell me you missed me. Tell me you missed me desperately, you miserable son of a bitch!"

"I love you; we need to get out of here." He took her arm and she followed numbly, as he led her around the big car and opened the passenger door. Before she got in, she turned and reached for him again, and he took her back and hugged her tightly. He let go of her and she looked into his eyes, tears filling her own, spilling down her face. When she was inside the car, she watched him as he went around, fearing he might disappear again.

"Where are we going?"

"I don't know. North, Canada, out of the country." He drove back into Dickinson. There was a long period of silence before he spoke again. There was much to be said, much that needed to be said. "These valleys were all formed by glaciers, scoured out during the ice age." He pointed north across the seat. She slapped his arm away.

"I don't want to talk about glaciers, you…ruthless…imbecile!"

Bakewell drove. After ten minutes, Maggie rested her head against the seat. She had been traveling for hours, her breathing sounded exhausted. There was a lot of tension in the car.

She needed to hear him say the words, needed more than just his presence again. She had lived through weeks of grief and dark depression, fearing she would never have anyone to love her, knowing she would never have anyone to love her. She had chosen him, left no room for anyone else, picked him out and put all her trust in their future together. He had played a false hand and cruelly, heartlessly, left her behind. She wanted some answers and some satisfaction for her suffering; she was entitled.

They went north on Highway 85 bordering the dramatic and starkly beautiful Badlands, and the Theodore Roosevelt Park on up to Williston. Thirty minutes later she said, "Your darling son, Andy, said you've been in the islands somewhere." Bakewell only nodded. "Nancy told me you went out to the Solomon Islands to visit some missionaries."

"Yes. I was in the Solomons."

"Why?"

"I can't tell you."

"You want to bet?" There was no uncertainty; her voice was suddenly filled with resolve, determined, putting him on notice. It was going to be difficult to deceive her. *I can't tell you?* It did sound lame. He would try to put off the inevitable, would lie to her, couldn't tell her the truth, but he didn't want to lie either. They crossed the Missouri below Williston, where it was wide and flat, more lake than river, and turned west for Montana.

Finally Maggie broke the silence. "Andy, you owe me one hell of an explanation – one hell of a *goddamned* explanation!"

"How did you find me?"

"I'm asking the questions! You just answer. Talk for a change. Exert yourself for me once, because you love me!" she was gaining momentum. "You don't ask questions! I'll ask the fucking questions! You'll answer my questions. I have a lot of questions!" Bakewell looked ahead grimly, she quieted, added, "Andy and Nancy told me. I was there to visit them the other night. To help them get through their ordeal. *THE TERRIBLE ORDEAL YOU PUT THEM THROUGH!"*

"Maggie, I'm so sorry. I haven't been thinking of anyone but myself. I should have put it all down on paper for each of you…"

"PAPER! PAPER?" She was nearly out of control, another first. "You've got a lot to explain. I don't want to hear any of your stupid, stupid lame excuses. *I should have put it down on paper! Good God*! How can you be so obtuse?" She tried to express her disgust with her hands, it was beyond her. She couldn't gesture with enough emphasis. "Tell me the truth! No more nonsense, you…you… *arrogant, pompous ass!"*

"I'm not sure where we are going, but it's going to be a long ride."

"You're damned right it is, and *you're going to talk to me* most of the way, and most of the time. I'll interrupt with questions only."

Bakewell looked straight ahead, feeling, smelling, loving the idea of her presence, of being next to her again, but worried, wondering where to start, what to say.

"You told me you were still in love with your wife."

"I'll always be in love with my wife."

"And so you should, but she is gone, and you have fallen in love with me…down there at the beach. I could tell. I could feel it. There was too much tenderness in your touch, too much gentleness. I could feel it. *I could just feel it.* It was in your arms, in your fingertips, on your lips. You fell in love with me. Didn't you?"

Bakewell wondered at his own silence as he drove on toward Montana.

"Tell me that you love me, Andy! Say it."

"I love you, Maggie."

She squeezed the tears from her eyes and looked out the window.

"I love you. You've made me love you despite everything. I've tried to put you out of my mind everyday since I left. I tried to forget you. I never once let myself think about you, if I could prevent it. And whenever I did, I tried to forget you again, right away, but it was no good."

"Why? Why would you want to forget me, forget us?"

"Because I didn't believe it would work, because…I didn't think we were capable of it."

As they drove, Maggie wept – alternating between moods of shocked, inconsolable grief, to joy and elation, switching to accusations about his arrogance, his callous disregard for her, his refusal to include her, back to vulnerable, susceptible moods of tearful, grateful relief. At those times she would come across the seat to rest her head on his shoulder, telling him how desperately she had grieved for him, and how empty she had felt. Telling him what life had been like after they got the news of his death.

He was supposed to do the talking, but for thirty miles she had to get her emotions out. "My God, Andy, there was a service…your children, your family, those little babies…" her voice broke. "The terrible, agonizing pain I felt for each of them. The loss I knew they were feeling. It was so awful..." her voice broke again. "It was so tender, so beautiful to see, to be there. Do you know how many people grieved for you? Your family, your friends, they were there, so many people. Poor, sweet Ned, he was just devastated. His shoulders were heaving while the kids were up there on the altar talking about you." She swept her hand across the car and laid her head back on the seat again. "I tried to comfort him. He was so alone...

"And you…you were in some lagoon, swimming in the ocean, lounging on a beach somewhere in paradise. Oh my God, Andy." Maggie broke down completely, was so distraught Bakewell thought her tears would tear his heart from his chest. She slumped back against the door, as far from him as she could get, exhausted.

They drove west into Montana, on for hours: Glasgow, across the

Milk River, onto Havre. It was his turn to talk. She refused to speak further, until he explained himself. He didn't give it a good effort. It was a suspicious chronology. He was vague and deceitful, fearing her reaction to the truth. By the time they reached Interstate 15, it was so contorted, and he had contradicted himself so many times, the story was pointless.

Maggie interrupted with, "That's not true," sometimes she would say, "You know there's no way I can believe that," once, "What in the hell are you talking about?"

When they reached the Blackfoot Reservation, it was early evening. They could see the Rockies and Glacier in the distance. Bakewell tried again, tried to piece together something about his need to see the Pacific, see the other side of the world, to go and see the missions. Much of it was believable, but most of it was inept, bumbling, even farcical. She interrupted each time the narrative got muddled or too obscure; her questions viciously incisive, causing him to stumble. Her voice was full of sarcasm, full of ridicule.

They stopped once for gas, right after Montana, but that had been hundreds of miles back. They needed to get out of the car. Maggie was limp against her door, far away from him physically and emotionally. And she had blown her nose so many times the box of tissues bought at the gas stop was half empty. Her nose was inflamed and her eyes were swollen. Her voice had changed too.

"Did you see the movie Patton?"

"A long time ago."

"Do you remember that scene in North Africa, right in the beginning, after the battle, where Patton views the carnage and kisses the wounded soldier on the head and confesses to his aide, that despite the horror of it all he loves it so much? He says something like, 'God forgive me, but I love it. My God I love it.'"

Maggie stared at him blankly.

"That's the way I feel about the mountains. I love them with that kind of passion. It consumes me, I love it so."

Maggie lit a cigarette, shook her head watching him. She had quit smoking years ago. She was a wreck of jangled nerves, conflicting emotions, trying to decipher him, wondering if he had gone mad. His story had been all over the place. He kept changing moods, versions. The whole tale was ridiculous. She was losing faith. She wanted desperately to love him, but was consumed by the hurt she felt, offended by his behavior: Port Moresby, wherever that was, Bougainville, some little island she'd never heard of, and a lagoon existence on something he kept calling an atoll. All of it ending in a monastery in North Dakota? She was afraid to ask herself why she had come after him. She was afraid of the very thought, the thought of wondering why she had come. She had put so much faith into their relationship.

She thought he would be contrite, deeply moved by her appearance, just as she had been stunned by the astonishing news that he was still alive – remembered the excitement she felt when she finally saw him, standing in the road. But, after the initial, all too brief affection, he hadn't shown the contrition she was looking for, had gone off on a mad tale about dying at a mission station in the Pacific, changing his mind, wanting to live out his life in a monastery.

"I've been on nearly every stream in Montana with my kids. We love the rivers, but it's the mountains, the knowledge of the wild things that are here, the purity of it that I love."

"No one's questioning your love of wild things, Andy." She wasn't interested in the mountains, wanted him to get to some point of clarity, and wondered if he was capable of it. "You haven't stopped rambling for hours, you're getting hoarse, and you're not making sense. I've never seen you like this. You're beginning to frighten me."

Bakewell stopped talking. Maggie smoked another cigarette in silence, staring at the empty prairie. Finally she said, "I'm exhausted."

"Do you want something to eat?"

"No. I want to rest. We have to get out of this car. I've been driving since Bismarck. How far is that?"

"I don't know, a long way."

"This may be the longest day of driving… this may be the longest day of my life," she said to the window. "I don't like to travel by car."

It wasn't so much a decision as an unspoken need. He pulled into a motel and went and registered. It was still daylight, but they couldn't have continued.

It was a strange, silent night. Maggie took a shower and got into one bed. When Bakewell came out of the bathroom her light was out. He sat on the edge of her bed, "NO," was all she said. He got into the other bed, waited for a long time before asking if he could get her anything, in the lightest whisper, more checking to see if she was awake.

"No," was the hurt reply. He listened to her suppressed tears, tried to think of a way to comfort her. Without something physical he was without options. They lay in separate beds, she sniffing, he listening to the hurt he had caused. Eventually they fell asleep – Maggie from crying, Bakewell from fencing, from holding back, and from a cancer that was finally, unmistakably, making its presence known.

Canada

He awoke to the sound of water running. Groggy, feeling exhausted still, Bakewell would have slept for hours, but Maggie's presence was compelling. No matter when she was in his life, she always had the ability to put him in motion. She opened the bathroom door, came out and dressed quickly, crossed the room and closed her bag with a crisp zip, and told him to get ready. By the time he had shaved and dressed, she was back in the room with coffee.

They turned north at Browning, and started up the east side of Glacier Park.

"Would you like to drive through Glacier?"

"No, we're not on holiday."

"Are you sure?"

"Another time. I'm not in the mood to go national-parking with you."

It was a clear day, but there were clouds above the mountain peaks, partially enshrouding them. It looked like it might be snowing up high. He tried again. "Looks like snow."

"Exactly. Snow is for winter. We're all tired of snow by this time of year, even up in Banff. I hope I don't see snow again before October."

They crossed the border at the Port of Piegan. Bakewell wanted to use the less traveled border crossing. They could have gone up I-15, earlier, above Shelby, made the trip much shorter, but that was a major port of entry. The crossing was uneventful. The guards asked about the nature of their visit. Maggie told them she owned a home in Banff. Bakewell offered to open the trunk. The border guards looked at the empty space in the big car, the absence of luggage. Maggie had one shoulder bag, Bakewell just his backpack. After producing their drivers' licenses and signing a form, they were on their way.

Canada flattened into a wide, rolling prairie. Bakewell loved prairies. The prairies of Canada were renowned for upland game. He wanted to give his mind a rest, let his thoughts drift. The prairie bored Maggie. She told him she had never driven into Canada before. She always flew to Calgary, before driving up into the mountains.

His thoughts wandered back to the airport, jumped to the present, back again. His mind still not yet adjusted to her. In the short time he had before the car got to him in Dickinson, he had made a decision. He was certain the car was for him, had decided to accept whatever it brought. In all his spiritual life, he had never been so prepared to die, even more than that night in Port Moresby with Father Jonas. And in all his life, he had never been so surprised to see anyone as much as when he recognized her through the windshield.

During their drive across Montana the day before, Maggie told him she had gone to spend the evening with his children, a family intervention night, she called it. She needed to share in their grief, to spend time with them. She had been making regular visits to see Nancy's little family. She had made a second arrangement with Andy and Karen. Michael had disappeared after the memorial service. She described him as strangely silent and preoccupied throughout the whole ordeal. With Karen, estranged from her family in Kansas City, and Andy parentless, Maggie had been welcomed, had been a favorite of both girls. Their time together after his death had taken on a primacy each relied on. Maggie spent hours with Karen and the new baby. She bought a car seat, took Julie with her on outings to the park, had taken her to lunch at her club. She'd had several dinners with Nancy and Tom at their home, and treated them to dinner twice at hers. Maggie had found the family she always lacked. A curious peace had descended over her when she was with Bakewell's family. Only family could help as she tried to put her life back together: his family. Her family?

Then Andy had stunned them all, had broken down, as he recapped the conversation he'd had with his resurrected father. She told Bakewell she knew as soon as they were directed into the living room, something wasn't right. Maggie described the scene, said she was carrying the new baby when they went in to sit down. Andy had gone straight home and told Karen, decided to wait another hour to tell the rest of them, said he felt God's intervention at the coincidence of their being together the same evening his father called to tell him he was alive. In a lighter moment, Andy confessed to almost running off the road, had to pull to the shoulder of the interstate to talk, and had feared for his life as the traffic rushed by. Later they called Michael to tell him the news. When Maggie learned where he was, she had chartered a plane to Bismarck, rented the car and driven the 85 miles to Richardton, most of it well over the speed limit.

"There was this sweet older man at the Abbey; he was the former Abbot. He told me you left on foot sometime after midnight the day I arrived. He also told me you were going west and there was an airport in Dickinson. Apparently you two talked about airplanes, among other things. He seemed to know a great deal about you. When I heard *airport*, I drove almost a hundred miles an hour to get there. I just had this premonition you would head for an airport to make travel arrangements. I was almost positive."

There was another long silence as they drove north. Finally, Maggie cleared her throat, lit a cigarette and looked at him. "Yesterday was a day of emotion. I gave you all the time in the world to explain yourself. You were dishonest. Your story was ridiculous. But now we are going to have some plain conversation, no, that's not right, not a conversation, more like an interrogation, and you're going to tell me very candidly what's been going on. There will be no more reticence on your part. No more Andy Bakewell." Maggie sighed, expelling smoke.

"Everyone loves Andy Bakewell, because he is such a quiet, shy, wonderful man. But today Andy Bakewell is going to talk to Maggie Walker, and he's going to explain himself. He's going to have a really good explanation for why he walked out on her, left her devastated, weeping, and miserable. You altered my life, and left me disgusted – no revolted – with myself for the way I behaved over you. And revulsion comes pretty close to the mark. So start talking and I will listen. Yesterday is done. Tell me your story. No more deceit, no more half truths, no more hesitance. It's your turn to talk."

It was agreed they would go on to Banff, after Calgary. Banff was perfect for the time being. She had a home there; he could hole up, try to figure out what was next. Hiding in Banff was a Godsend; what Bakewell would do with Maggie was something else. He had no idea what was ahead. He tried to imagine what the next few weeks would bring.

They were on the highway, back on level ground above the border, away from the mountains and rolling hills, the prairie set in all the way to the horizon, leaving a numbing sense of permanency.

"Everything you told me yesterday was nonsense. I know it and you know it, so let's start over. This time I want the truth. It is hours to Calgary, another ninety minutes to Banff. We have all the time in the world. Tell me where you've been, and what you were doing." Maggie sounded confident as she spoke, but before she could complete her words the emotion was back and her voice quavered. "No more lies. No more half-truths." She wiped a tear from her cheek with the heel of her palm. "I can feel them, the lies. I can hear them in your voice, and I hate it. You've done something terrible. You've faked your own death and disappeared. I want the truth. I don't care what it is, or if you think you need to spare me. I can deal with it, whatever it is, as long as it's true. Tell me the truth."

There had been an easing of tension during the silence earlier, accompanied by the mesmerizing effect of the vast prairie, but the tension was back. Bakewell hated the tension, knew if he told her the truth it would terrify her, and he doubted she could handle it, would even want to. He was silent for a long time. Maggie waited for him to begin.

"If you can't tell me everything, without anymore damned deceit, then we stop in Calgary, and I'm going back to St. Louis, or I'll go on to Banff without you. Something is terribly wrong here. Islands? Third World countries? Monasteries? Traveling on foot? It's Richard Kimball nonsense, Andy. What is going on?"

"Maggie, you really don't want to know. Please, trust me and trust my instincts about this. Let's put the whole thing behind us and start over again, right here, right now. We could be great friends, great help to each other. You could enjoy my kids, and they could enjoy you, and we could enjoy each other. Don't make me tell you something that will ruin whatever is left for us all. "

Maggie laughed bitterly. It was a terrible sound, pitiless and pitiful, desperate, and so gravely intense it frightened him. They were just below Claresholm. He pulled into a station for petrol. Maggie got out and slammed her door. She went across the street and got some food from a quick shop. When they continued north, she prepared his coffee, and handed him portions, one at a time, while she ate her own. When they were finished she put the trash in the bag, dusting her hands carefully over it, and sat back in her seat. She turned to face him, looked at him intently.

Feeling her penetrating look, he switched the radio on nervously, an FM station. It was playing a Dvorak piece, slow, threnodic; it wasn't pleasant music, but it matched their mood. Maggie turned the radio off.

"I know you're determined to know the details, Maggie. I just wish we could put this off for a while longer."

"No. It's time to tell me what has been going on. I think I have dissuaded you of my tough bitch reputation. You saw me at my worst down at the beach. You thought I wanted to diddle you for my own entertainment. You thought I would be off somewhere with someone else by now, but all that ended down there at your beach house." She put the cigarette out and sipped the last of her coffee. "I couldn't have been any more honest with you then, and I'm here now. I never dreamed, no I only dreamed about being with you again. Now it has happened, and I'm not sure I know you any longer, or even like you any longer. Please be honest with me."

Bakewell never dreamed he could have her again either, not after he left for the islands. When they got together at the beach, her honesty and her vulnerability had frightened him. He still remembered how terrified he was of falling in love a second time, but after their weekend….

The only thing he was sure of was that he didn't want to cause anymore suffering. Their farewell had been difficult, but not nearly as much for him; he went to the islands; he had so much to occupy his mind out there. He knew she had nothing but memories of their time together, and the mean way it had ended. It couldn't have been more unfair. But letting them get involved again, would only be trouble and another mean end for her.

Now that they *were* together again, he didn't want to lose her, and it wasn't fair…again. He could love her, knowing she would love him in return, probably more than he could even dream; then it would end again. His death might be slow and ugly – and tragic for her. People who watched the dying suffered more than the dyers themselves. He knew that too well. What was between them was simple and obvious. Only the truth separated them now. But the truth she was so determined to know could end their relationship. He had never shared the business in Genoa with Katherine; he didn't want to share this last episode with Maggie. If he told her it would drive her away. *What's wrong with that? It's what you're looking for.* But it wasn't. He wanted to have her back again. It was part of the arrogant, selfish thing to which he swore he would never return.

"I was wrong about having all the time in the world. I have a feeling this is a long story, and you don't have that much time before we get to Calgary. I'm getting out at Calgary. I've done all I am willing to do for this relationship. If you don't want me, you keep quiet. I'll get the message clear enough. If there's to be an *us,* you have to make it happen from here on out."

Bakewell sighed deeply, set the cruise control, put his feet on the floor. They were doing 120. The speed limit in Alberta was 110. He coasted down to the required speed. It was a magnificent day, a high cirrus sky above, widely scattered cumulus below, giving definition to the sky and the country. The visibility would let them see the mountains long before they got to them. He was looking forward to the mountains.

"All right, I'll tell you the whole story, and when we get to Calgary, you can get out, or I will. But I want to say, before that time comes, no matter what happens, Maggie, I will hate to lose you again."

"If you don't tell me the truth, I can guarantee you, you will lose me again. We've each managed to walk out on the other now. It might have taken thirty years, but we're all even. If the pain I caused you back in college was anything like the misery I've suffered these past months, then I deserved to suffer. But I'm done suffering alone. We will have to suffer together, or be happy together, from here on out."

"You know my history. I lost you years ago. I lost Katherine, lost my business. I've probably lost my own children, and I'm about out of time now too."

"We can discuss your health later. Right now I'm not sure I care whether you live or die. Just start."

"I don't know how to start. Let me think."

"You've thought enough. Don't take any more time."

"I need to clear my head."

"Just open your heart and your mind and *your mouth* and talk. Pretend you're in the confessional."

***

He told her about the day Snow approached him, and how he had gone to confession afterwards, and about the day in Genoa before he'd ever met her. He told her about the money, the shudder that went through him when the doctor told him he was going to die, and how almost immediately he began to think about Snow's offer, how it took the sting of death away and gave him something to focus on. It also gave him another chance to work things out financially for the business, his kids, and Ned. He told her how he knew he would never take another human life, but still, if he could get the money, could figure a way to get it disseminated before they could get it back, before he died, it just might work. How he couldn't believe they would give him the money in advance, and how they did it the very next day. It was all so incredible. It had to be Snow. The old man really had turned out to be his godfather. And he was able to get Ned off the hook. "I loved Ned almost as much as my own kids."

He told her how he thought he would be able to disappear after the "shoot" was over. How he wasn't supposed to live long enough to even be a shooter, and how he thought he could go through the motions without shooting, disappear, and how he never felt like he owed them anything anyway, because they had ruined a part of his life so long ago.

"They took my peace of mind with their contemptible disregard for my life. They never gave me a chance to live through it the first time in Genoa. I should have died years ago. If it hadn't been for the strange affection Snow had somehow developed for me over the years, I would have been dead before I graduated from college."

He thought Snow might have been a better person than he originally suspected. He was sure now, Snow had somehow contracted with Powell and despite Powell's wicked skills, he even believed the Hand of God might have been involved. Maybe it was divine providence. He would never be sure since there was a human life involved. Yet it had all evolved so simply, right there for the taking.

"I don't know what to think about Snow and Powell. I'll never be really sure. Why am I still alive after all this time? I was supposed to die long ago. That's the reason I decided to do the deal in the first place."

He told her he was sure he would die in March. He told her all about March; his endless quarrel with March. And when they got to Okotoks, Bakewell got to the part about Port Moresby and Buka.

"Buka?"

"Buka. There's been a civil war going on there, and in Bougainville, between the BRA and the PNG."

"What's BRA mean?"

"Bougainville Revolutionary Army. Not a friendly bunch. They've been slugging it out with the PNG for a decade."

"PNG?"

"Papua New Guinea. They are the regular army of the country, only the Bougainvillians don't think so. They think they are Solomon Islanders by birth and ethnicity. They feel their country is being pillaged by foreign companies. There is an enormous copper mine on Bougainville that has been mined for decades. Their wealth had been mined and shipped off, first by the Australians, later by whatever government they have been subject to. They think the copper belongs to them. And they are right, but that doesn't make them a good bunch."

Calgary

When they crested a hill south of Calgary and saw the city for the first time Bakewell slowed the car.

"That is a pretty sight."

"Calgary is a beautiful city," Maggie answered, and said no more.

He told her of the tremendous loss of life on Bougainville. Just as they entered the city limits, on a road called the Macleod Trail, he got to the part about the Arab, and Maggie gasped and put her hand to her mouth. Bakewell felt the alarms going off and wanted to stop. He was losing her, and he badly wanted to stop talking, or talk about anything else. He got his way. In front of them, in the middle of the street, stood a tall man in a red, all-weather coat, hatless, waving his arm for them to turn off onto a side street. Bakewell didn't know what was going on; any diversion was welcomed, if it would allow him to stop his narrative.

He didn't want to take a detour, or even slow down, afraid she would get out if he did, but when they turned off, there was another man dressed the same way, also hatless. Maggie cursed under her breath. "It's the Royal Mounted Police. You're getting a speeding ticket." They stopped at the curb.

"Sir, your license and registration please."

"How fast was I going?" Bakewell asked.

"Sir, you were doing sixty-nine in a fifty kilometer zone."

"Here, it's a rental car. I don't have the registration." Bakewell handed him his license.

"What year?" the Canadian policeman asked, interrupted himself, looking at the dash. "Oh wow, this is a new one." There were less than two thousand miles on the speedometer. He was gone briefly, returned with the ticket. "You have three options for paying the fine. They're outlined here." He handed Bakewell the ticket, adding. "I hope the rest of your day goes better."

Bakewell thanked him, apologized for his indiscretion. Maggie was silent, nearly holding her breath until they started up again. When he pulled away from the curb, Bakewell started to say something about the Canadian Mounties.

"What about the Arab!"

He sighed and continued his story to the accompaniment of little yelps, gasps and jittery sighs. Maggie moved about in her seat. He remembered how much she used to smoke when they were young, everybody did then, but he hadn't seen her smoke since their relationship had resumed. He thought she had quit like everyone else. She had smoked half a pack since Glacier. The pack rested on her purse on the seat between them. Each time he got to a part where a threat of violence came into play, Maggie would light up and inhale deeply and blow the smoke with force.

They neared the river. "Go under the bridge," she directed. It was a beautiful structure, spanning the Bow River, in the middle of downtown Calgary, a single lane, one way, underpass. He fitted the big car through carefully, coming out the other side into daylight again, and continued the story. "West on Memorial," she instructed, very animated, smoking, edgy. He told her about Albrecht, their unpleasant trip crossing the Solomon Sea to Bougainville, about the mercenary, Adrian Powell. "Cross over the river here," she said, her voice suppressing hysteria.

When he tried to describe the humidity and the mosquitoes she said, "No buggy details! We've both been to the tropics!"

He told her of his vantage point above the compound.

"Take the Bow Trail."

"Damn, it's confusing. Nothing is marked. How do these people find their way around?"

"Don't stop talking!" she yelled. "I don't know how much longer I can last." She looked straight ahead through the windshield, like she was focusing on something on the hood. They were getting out into the suburbs again, going west, away from the city. He continued the story, getting to the part about how he shot the old man. "I think I got him right on top of his shoulder, near his collarbone." Maggie groaned, long, anguished.

"I wanted to miss him high. Hit him right on the top. If I flinched, my shot could only go high. Only if I slipped, or lost my balance in the wet undergrowth, maybe fell forward, would I have hit him anywhere that might have been fatal. That would have been an accident. I wanted to tear flesh, but miss the bone."

"Oh, my God," it was more like a moan than a phrase. "Turn right. It will take you to TransCanada 1."

"Whoa," Bakewell said, as they got a spectacular view of the Bow River valley below the shelf of highway. The highway traversed the wide river below them for a long distance.

"Tell the story!"

"I'm sure I called my shot. I can't be positive. I had practiced until I could shoot an eraser off the end of a pencil, but that was from a bench rest. Shooting from out of the jungle, without any real support, was almost like shooting offhand. You really need something solid to lean against. Anything to lean against makes it simpler."

"Oh my God."

"Are you all right?"

"No, I'm not all right, damn it! Go on!"

"I don't want to upset you anymore than necessary."

"I'm already upset! Everything about you upsets me, and frightens me!" She made the same anguished sound again. It frightened him more than he was frightening her, made him anxious to hide inside his story.

"I saw the old man flail around. He fell backwards on the stone walk." Maggie couldn't suppress the noise, an audible intake of air. She held her elbows in her hands, clasping her arms, tightly, sitting straight up in the seat. He was losing her. He expected her to tell him to pull over, but he went on with the story, committed.

"If I had hit him in the collar bone, or anyplace lower down, he would have been writhing around on the ground. Instead, he jumped up, holding his left hand to his right shoulder. I'm almost positive I hit him where I was aiming." She made a soft whimpering sound.

They passed the Olympic village, where the ski jumping events had taken place. Bakewell paused and looked at the huge Nordic jump, built into the side of the hill. She didn't shriek this time, waited for him to continue.

"He came scrambling up off the ground, like I said. He was holding his shoulder like this," Bakewell said, explaining with his hands. "He turned to run back toward the buildings, while his people stood around confused; then after a moment, they all started to chase after him. The way some of them acted, I'm almost sure they were in on the whole business. I thought all hell would have broken loose when I fired the shot, but there was no shouting or pointing, no reaction like you would get if you took a shot at a president. There was no mad scramble to arms, no alarms, no barking dogs, just a bunch of out of shape guys, scurrying about, heading back toward the buildings."

"Oh my dear God," Maggie lit another cigarette.

"I did my job, fulfilled my contract to Snow's people. If they wanted him to get their message, he got it." Bakewell thought a moment, swallowed, composing his thoughts, "If I had broken his collarbone, I think he would have been bent over, running a lot more awkwardly, you know, with his head down. But he was running straight-backed, holding the top of his shoulder."

"What then? What came next?"

"We were supposed to go back to the boat. I was sure there would be a reception at the boat. I had to go the other way. I knew I never wanted to see Powell again, half expected to get hit from behind after I fired. If that didn't happen, I intended to move off toward the lagoon, go north away from the boat and the water. When I came back around to the hill overlooking the water where the boat was anchored, Albrecht was right there waiting for me. I hit him pretty hard. I felt the bones breaking in his face from the blow."

Maggie moaned, said something he couldn't make out, and hugged her elbows again.

The mountains came into view up ahead, under bright sunlight. The highway straightened and headed west. Bakewell reset the cruise control, kept his movements slow, trying not to spook her, still waiting for her to tell him to pull over. When she finally did, they were almost to the turn off for Kananaskis Country. Maggie needed to stop. They both needed to stop. Further on up the valley were heavy clouds, a mixture of gray and black and dark brown, billowing very high, enshrouding the mountains further to the southwest. It was still clear to the west and north when they stopped.

When she returned to the car, he was waiting with two fountain cokes. He'd already drunk half of his. His throat had been dry and scratchy. Bakewell had talked more in the past two days than he'd spoken in a month. Without the drink he couldn't have made enough saliva to spit.

As they crossed the Provincial Park line, east of the mountains, the weather turned dark. They entered the mountain valley and a combination of fog and mist rolled over them. The weather matched the mood in the car. Bakewell told her about Powell and Albrecht, about the conflict in personalities, as they drove in and out of light rain and fog. At one point, a partial clearing allowed them to see jagged mountain peaks. Bakewell was very glad to be in the mountains. He never thought he would be in mountains again. After the heat and humidity of the islands and the wonderful endlessness of the Dakotas, the mountains were more welcome than his own home. He felt like he was coming home.

Down in Montana they had barely touched the edge of Glacier. He never felt like he was in the mountains down there. It was more like looking at them from the side, than being in them. He finished his Pacific tale just as the weather cleared up again, his last line the part about not shaking Powell's hand and about Powell "hacking him up a bit."

The Canadian Rockies were breathtaking, and they both became quiet and reflective. Neither spoke for a very long time. Maggie seemed to be getting it together again. She wasn't as upset. After another fifteen miles, she told him to stop at a scenic pullout above the lake.

They got out and walked, neither speaking, nor wishing to start a conversation. They were talked out. It had been a long two days of conflict, talking, and silence, the tension non stop. Some of the conversation had nearly kept time with the engine rpms. It was bright and clear on the shelf overlooking the lake, but there was a wind and it was wet and chilly. Maggie shivered, returned to the car and he followed. They drove on northwest.

By the time they got to Canmore, the sky was clear, another stunning day. *Typical Banff weather*, Bakewell thought. Maggie directed him to take the exit to Canmore. They stopped where she indicated at the Fireside Inn. Maggie knew the man at the counter. He led them across the room to a table in front of a mirrored wall. The place was full of locals and early season hikers. The hikers were college-aged kids, sitting in a group, where they had condensed the tables in the corner. Many spoke French.

"I'm hungry. I've eaten nothing but junk food since St. Louis," Maggie said. Bakewell nodded; he wasn't that hungry.

Maggie looked at him then quickly away. She looked ravaged. His story had been a severe trial for her. He wished he could say or do something to make her better. They sipped coffee without speaking until the food came, not looking at each other. When he looked at her she looked away, but he could feel her eyes on him when he looked around the room – appraising, evaluating, and, he hoped, not judging. They ate in silence, occasionally their eyes met, looked away again without speaking. When the waitress came, he started to pay.

"No," Maggie said, taking some Canadian money from her bag. "The exchange rate is terrible. Wait until you have time to go to the bank and exchange money properly."

"Where did you get the currency?"

"You forget, I'm almost Canadian, I'm practically *a local* up here."

They went out to the street, looked into a few windows, going up toward the car. Canmore was a stepping off place for the climbing and rappelling crowd. The windows were filled with sporting and camping gear. They had no interest in the windows. She turned and walked off, leaving him on the sidewalk. He crossed the street, caught up to her and quickly unlocked the car. They drove on up the valley toward Banff.

"Can I ask you something?" Bakewell said, tilting the wheel and setting the cruise control. "I don't mean to upset you, just a question."

"You upset me with your stories. You can *ask* me anything. It's what you tell me that makes me shake inside." Maggie spoke to the side of his face, as he concentrated on the wet road ahead. "I'll never again know when you're going to tell me some ghastly thing that terrifies me." She took a long pull on another cigarette, blew the smoke up where it disappeared through the slit above the glass. "I understand now why you didn't want to tell me what you've been up too. I'll be afraid to ask you about anything ever again." She moved in her seat, got comfortable, "but I can't think of a question you could ask me that I would have any concern about answering."

"How much do you weigh?" Bakewell said. He didn't have a clue nor did he care about her weight.

"A hundred and thirty-seven pounds in my nightie."

"After us," he said, ignoring her candor. "Did you…I mean, after you left Joe, were there any others? Men, I mean. Have you taken others as lovers?"

"If you're worried about getting AIDS it's a little late cowboy."

"You know I'm not, I just wondered if you've had someone to share with. You don't have to answer," he stared ahead at the highway bathed in sunlight once more. "Actually I wish you wouldn't, that didn't come out the way I intended. It was a dumb thing to ask."

"Your specialty: dumb things. I hope it's not like AIDS, I'd hate to catch it." She took another drag, blew it out, thought for a moment, said, "I think I'll answer, since I suspect you really do regret asking. My answer might serve you right. Would it upset you if I told I'd been balling men all over the world for years?"

They were silent as he passed a large truck, the concrete pavement noisy going around, despite the insulation of the big car. Maggie blew a long breath, smokeless this time, thinking about what she was going to say. "No, I've taken no lovers," she paused, corrected herself. "Oh there were a few men." She moved in her seat again, brushed some ash from her coat and cleared her throat.

"Once, while we were in Little Rock, after the divorce – he was married of course – I think it was the first time for him. It was for me anyway. He was probably wondering what infidelity would be like." She continued, heartlessly she hoped, wanting to worry his hyper sense of morality. "He was very nervous, probably afraid of the consequences once we'd made the commitment. Anyway, he was anxious to finish before we really got started. I knew it would never happen with him again, even before we were done. He tried to hurry. I didn't help much." There was bitterness in Maggie's voice.

"Then later, the year after the divorce, I met an older man, much older. I went with him to Las Vegas for a few days. Sex wasn't a pre-requisite, but we tried it a few times." Another blast of smoke went through the gap. "I had two experiences on cruises that were meaningless. They were all very efficient and slightly inhibited. I have that affect, you know."

Bakewell didn't know, waited for her to make it clearer. She waited too, when he didn't speak she elucidated. "I'm a trophy date…was a trophy wife… Men want to be seen with me, want to have me. They're always wondering what it would be like to have me, wanting to get past the wondering. They want to know what I look like under my clothes. They want to see me in the buff, find me under the sheets, paw and gawk, and hurry to get finished, so they can know they've done me. They don't make demands. I've been hurried through sex most of my life. I think they just do it so they can feel pleased with themselves, think of me as a conquest."

"I'm sorry."

"Me too. You're the only one who ever took the time to love me, to make love to me and with me." She was getting emotional again, looked out her side of the car and grew quiet. Bakewell was confused. He tried to imagine Maggie as tragic, alone and in need. Before their weekend at the beach it would have been a stretch, but it was easier to see her as an unhappy figure now. He couldn't think of anything to say; she sensed his dilemma.

"Don't feel sorry for me. I hate that."

"I just want to understand you better. I'm not a sympathetic person."

"You're telling me."

"Don't be angry with me. It's not an emotion I know very well. I used to have it once, sympathy; I thought so anyway, but something happened. There's been a deadness inside me for a long time. It's hard for me to be sympathetic anymore."

"It's okay. Don't feel you need to be sympathetic. I hate sympathy. I was looking for attention, not sympathy," she sighed, thought about what she'd said, "Only now I'm not sure you're the one. Before, you were my dreamboat, my lost love and my perfect man, at least in my imagination. You were perfect before you became terrifying. You were humble, vulnerable and incredibly sensitive despite your obvious shortcoming."

"What's my obvious shortcoming?"

"You're dense! Thick! You don't get it; *you never seem to get it!"*

"I'm sorry."

"Don't be. It makes you more lovable." Maggie shrugged, revolted by her lapse into candor. "I wish I hadn't said that. You're a perfect shit, you know, a rotten, perfect shit."

He didn't respond. They were quiet again. Maggie lost in thought, Bakewell confused, wondering. He decided to try again. "That night you called me. The night you said hello and asked me not to hang up, do you remember?"

"Yes."

"I think that was the first night I began to think about feeling something for someone again. I had lost my ability to *miss*. When I was separated from people before, I couldn't find a way to miss them anymore. But that night I felt something. You made me nervous. You made me wonder if I could *miss* again. Do you understand; am I making sense?"

"I know what you're saying. It's about coming back to life after you've been dead. We've both experienced it. You made me experience it. Damn it! Why did you have to have this dark side? Now I don't know if I trust you, if I can ever believe in you again. I'm afraid you've gone and ruined us. I think I'm afraid of you."

"I would never do anything to hurt you."

"You hurt me all of the time! You've been hurting me for the last year. You pull me to you with that little boy kindness. You can be so sweet and sensitive and then you just walk away like I never existed and wait for me to call." She took the pack of cigarettes, started to take one then shook the pack at him accusingly. "You left the country without me. You died without even a goodbye, broke my heart, and when we all found out you were still alive, I had to be the one to come out here and find you!" She made a noise, disgusted, frustrated, moved in her seat, said, "Fuck," with emphasis.

"I'm sorry."

"That's the third time you've said I'm sorry; try something new. Use a few of those precious words from your grand vocabulary – the ones you hold onto like fresh-minted coins. Talk to me. Exert yourself for the woman you love desperately."

He stared ahead, hoping for inspiration, finding none, wishing he could come up with something. There was another long silence. They were getting close to Banff.

"Andy, you used to talk to me when you made love to me. You said beautiful things. No man ever talked to me that way, not when he made love to me or any other time. Do you need to be having an ejaculation to find your creativity? I've heard of men who think with their penises but…"

"Making love with you made sense to me. It's what I wanted, what I dreamed about before we did it. When the time came I wanted you to know how much I loved you. It was different, easy. I wanted you to know what I was feeling."

"It was lovely. I've never known anyone like you before or since. You said the loveliest things when we made love. I still remember them, each one, like it was yesterday."

"I didn't talk to you to impress you; I just wanted you to know. What I said had to come out. It was for me as much as for you, how much I loved you. It wasn't poetry or inspiration; it was just me trying to reach you."

"*It was poetry*. It was beautiful. And you reached me! You told me once in the preliminaries of ecstasy you hoped I felt the wonder and the pleasure of having you as much as you did of having me. It was poetry. You were my ecstasy. I just didn't know it at the time. I thought you were phase one, and phase two and all the others that followed would be even better. I didn't know I was experiencing the ultimate in love and being loved and possessed and that I would never know anything like you again for the rest of my life. My life was just beginning then. I thought you were part of the preliminaries, not the end all of my physical and emotional life!"

"I'm sorry. I wish you could have found better than me in your life. I can't see myself as the epitome of anyone's sex life."

"Not sex life! Love life! You turned out to be my dream – my end-all. I never found anyone like you after I left you."

They were beginning to reach and race with the moment. It was almost like having sex with words. Bakewell leveled the ground and pulled them back. "It was thirty years ago."

"It was yesterday," Maggie said, trying to hold onto the moment.

"It was a life time ago. It was the sixties."

"You shit! You remember it just the way I do. I'm not that forgettable. We weren't that forgettable."

He sighed. She was right, but he didn't want to go back. He had asked the question out of concern, wanted to find a way to reach out to her in her grief and confusion.

Maggie was back in her corner of the big front seat, against the door. She looked haggard. Her voice sounded strange after that emotional exchange. There was no more hostility, no belligerence. She looked exhausted, defeated. He didn't think she had any fight left. He was wrong.

They were approaching Cascade Mountain, became mesmerized by the unbelievably long, narrow waterfall that slid, dropped, and bounced off the rock face as it descended the mountain. He got off at the first exit for Banff. When they entered the city limits, a herd of elk was milling around in front of the sign on the shoulder of the road.

"Bienvenue a' Banff," Maggie read absently.

"Welcome to Banff," Bakewell stuck with the translation. "God, I forgot how much I liked it here. It's wonderful to see elk again."

"It is beautiful," she said in an absent, distracted way.

"It takes your breath, it's so beautiful. It's startling, easily one of the most beautiful places on earth."

She didn't respond. They drove slowly into town. Bakewell enjoyed the views to each side. Banff was tucked into a valley, between some of the most vertically dramatic and vicious looking geography in North America. He followed Banff Avenue straight through town, until they were at the city park, just short of the masonry bridge that would take them over the Bow River, up to the ancient and famous and spectacular Banff Springs Hotel, which could be seen perched in the forests ahead, like a medieval castle in Alpine Europe. Maggie told him to turn left. Her apartment was just a block from the river. He stopped the car across the street, following directions and got out and waited. She asked him to get her small bag, and he took it along with his pack and followed her across the street, up a short flight of stairs. She opened the door, and they entered a beautifully decorated, but very small apartment. When they were inside, she indicated with a nod he was to make himself at home. She took her bag from him and went down the short hall.

When she came back she said, “It’s been a stressful morning. I don’t think I’ve ever known one quite like it. I’m going to lie down. Make do for yourself. Look around, but don’t get too comfortable. I’m going to rest.” She looked at him bleakly, like he was a stranger. He understood. As she went back down the hall she spoke over her shoulder, “And try to compose my thoughts.”

Bakewell wasn’t sure if she intended to call the police or collapse in her room. He put his pack on a small table in the tiny kitchen, got a clean shirt and a pair of shorts, and went into the bathroom. He put his flip-flops back on. They were almost required wearing, after months in the islands and at the abbey. He settled in the living room, turned on Banff Radio and lay down on a large overstuffed couch, and listened to little vignettes about Banff and the Park that the station played round the clock.

After twenty minutes Bakewell was deep into an exhausted sleep, a turbulent collage of troubled memories, weird dreams that had him working constantly at cross-purposes. His dreaming made no sense; his subconscious was conflicted, flooded and bombarded. He was troubled about his children and what he had done to them, troubled by scenes of tragic people he'd seen in Moresby, their immense poverty, troubled by Maggie Walker and what he had done to her. His actions on Bougainville and what had happened to Albrecht filled him with doubt and with dread. They would continue to make him question what he had done for the rest of his life. Even in his dreams the confusion was there. After so many confessions and so much evaluating, he would never be sure about what was in the past. His dreams punished him – his grandchildren, his children, friends, even his dogs, had been left behind. He dreamt about the woman in the other room; he had left her behind too. His dreams were full of the islands – the heavy burden and heroic efforts the religious made, continued to make – full of so many wonderful people he had met in villages, people who had showed kindness and friendship, people who had helped him, had saved his life. He dreamt of holy men at the monastery, and he dreamt about his friends and what the implication of his actions might do to all of them, if his actions ever became public knowledge. His sleep ran downhill, like a steep stream, full of eddies, torrents, and backwaters, all mixed and muddled. He was so tired he couldn't roll over.

His dreams had lighter moments: funny words and phrases he had learned to speak and understand, of fabulous lagoons, and clean beaches and narrow rivers that drained into the sea. He also dreamt of dark, humid jungles, filled with biting things.

He was a long, far way down when there was a sharp rap on the door and a voice calling "Maggie?" The door opened and a woman came through. She was a large, attractive, woman, wearing an old, ill-fitting sweater. She stopped as soon as she saw Bakewell.

"Sybil?" Maggie said, coming into the room, her face swollen with sleep and tears.

"My God!" The woman said loudly. "You've found a live-in! And a gorgeous one at that."

Maggie looked to Bakewell, a look full of scorn. They both wished he wasn't there. Not Sybil. She came across the room toward him, indicating he stay put. He got up anyway, looking sheepish and interrupted, feeling foolish. He took her strong grip and shook her hand, "Andy Bakewell."

"I'm Sybil." She squeezed his hand. "I'm Maggie's best friend in the whole world. I'm sure she has already told you all about me."

She crossed the room where Maggie met her, and they embraced with great affection. There was hugging and patting, holding each other at arms' length, staring delightedly, and more hugging. They both talked at the same time, said the same things.

"How are you?"

"God, you look marvelous."

"It's *so* good to see you again."

They looked at him again and Sybil said, "I've found you out!" She turned to Maggie. "And it's about time too."

Maggie introduced them again, told Bakewell Sybil was her oldest and best friend in Banff. Sybil had a strong accent: British or Australian, he wasn't sure, but it was powerful.

"Actually love, I am her best friend, period. And that's anywhere she is in the world."

Maggie agreed, touched his pack, started to move it. It was heavy. Bakewell took it from her, and she indicated he leave them alone.

"There's a bathroom off the hallway if you need…."

He closed the door. As he did he heard them break into furious conversation, Sybil asking who he was, Maggie answering in a subdued, but unmistakably critical tone. Bakewell was groggy, dejected, needed more sleep. He laid down on the bed and listened to the muffled sound of their voices, the talk at first muted, louder after they stopped discussing him. There was laughter, lots of spontaneous conversation. He could have eavesdropped, instead he put a pillow over his ear to block their conversation and settled on the soft, deeply cushioned bed. It had a down comforter; he fell into another deep sleep.

***

Maggie knocked at the door. When he came out, she said they had been "invited out," if he felt up to it. He reentered the living room. Sybil was in the kitchen at the sink rinsing cups; she smiled at him. Bakewell learned she was from London, but had lived in many different places.

"Please do come out with us this evening, dear boy." She called him "dear boy," and "a lovely man," several times.

When she left there was an embarrassed moment, before Maggie asked, "Are you up now?" It sounded contemptuous.

"Sure."

"Well, I would like to take a walk. It's not raining. Up here rain can happen anytime, so now would be a good time to go."

He went back into the bathroom, rinsed his face and hands, gargled some water and got his jacket. They went out and walked into the afternoon sun toward the park, only two blocks away. There was an asphalt path that paralleled the south edge of the river, circled around the park and went on down under the bridge.

They walked separately. It was cool enough for a coat. Maggie's hands were plunged deep in her pockets; he kept his in his jacket. The ground was level; there was no bumping this time. As they passed a big wooden gazebo Bakewell said, "It looks like an old fashioned band stand."

"It serves a good purpose. The weather is fickle up here."

"You're not kidding. The last time I was here we had four seasons in one day, and that was in July."

Maggie made no further comment. Before they went another fifty yards, it started to sleet. The frozen water made a soft tinkling noise, like tiny pieces of chaff falling about them. Maggie continued on. When the sun came back out, it turned to a light rain and she changed her mind and went back to the gazebo. They hurried up the wide wooden staircase together and watched the river from the raised deck of the big wooden structure. The Bow was very wide for so high in the mountains. The valley flattened out north of Banff, slowing the current, giving the river an opportunity to spread. The dark water moved peacefully as it passed the park and went under the bridge. From there it turned again, and began a descent down to the falls. As it gained momentum, the Bow turned into a cascade, then a roaring, massive falls, just above where it intersected with the Spray. The Spray flowed quietly in from the south, adding its volume to the Bow, creating a really big river downstream.

The park was filled with young people milling about, sleeping on the ground under thin plastics and eating at the many picnic tables that dotted the grounds. It was the end of the school term, the beginning of the hiking season. The packers were moving in with the advent of climbing weather. After the rain stopped, they returned to the path again, idling along, both lost in thought, worried about the pending conversations they knew they would have, and the reason and logic each would try. Maggie still couldn't understand how he could have left her, didn't care about what his life had been like in the previous months. She was shocked and astounded at what he had been doing, but more than the craziness, the violence, and chance-taking, she was dumbfounded that he would have even considered pretending to die – *and allow the world, his own family, and the people he had left behind to believe it had happened!*

They followed the path down to the bridge, went under, on down toward the falls. When they were about two hundred yards below the bridge they came upon a single elk, standing on the path, feeding on the fresh new grass that sprouted in the rich soil of the mountaine, the soil from which Banff had sprouted a century before.

"I don't want to get closer," Maggie said, pulling up.

"Good for you," he said, happy she recognized the danger. Too many tourists pushed the animals with their curiosity and paid a heavy price.

They watched the elk feed. Each time the cow raised up chewing, she flared her nostrils and laid her ears back, dark eyes looking fierce. She was dangerous, her cloven hooves capable of serious harm.

"Isn't she lovely," Maggie said, forgetting herself in the moment.

"She looks lonely, but I'll bet she isn't. Elk at calving time can populate spontaneously, especially when they're disturbed."

Bakewell was sure she had company, even though they couldn't see any other elk through the dense conifers flanking the path. He remembered the woman next to him; she could be dangerous too. He turned to her, taking her arm, making her face him.

"I thought you would get out in Calgary, or ask me to."

Maggie didn't answer, looked right through him. He still had a lot to answer for. She looked at the river, bathed in the glancing sunlight again. It was very clear when the sun was out, turned dark and foreboding when the sky clouded up. Her moods were like the river's, changing from dark to bright, and back again.

"Did you call the police and tell them you have an international fugitive in your home?" Maggie refused to be drawn into conversation, or even let him conduct a conversation, could see no humor in his comment. "Am I supposed to think I'm welcome to stay, to go to dinner with you and your friend? Should I stay in your apartment this evening? Or should I go?"

"Condominium."

"Why are we here Maggie, together in this paradise?"

"I'm working on that."

"I'm at a real disadvantage."

"Good. *Suffer a little,* for me, for all of us, while I try and work things out."

He'd given it a try, was out of ideas. They headed back to her home without further conversation, beating the next rainfall by seconds. It was raining very hard by the time they had their coats off. Maggie gave him bath towels from the closet, put her coat back on, deciding to go to the market. He asked to go along, and she didn't object. She had an umbrella by the door. It was very big, with a maple leaf logo on top. They went out into a pouring rain.

There were several markets in Banff; Maggie chose the one closest, saying she liked to walk everywhere she could, said she hated to use her car unless it was necessary. She used as few words as possible, her voice strained, filled with contempt and anger and frustration. He worried he might be hearing the strain of fear in her voice too. She stayed just close enough to him to be under the protection of the umbrella. There was no other talk.

When they got to the market, she bought some perishables and food for lunch. It amounted to two small bags. When they were back outside again, the rain had stopped. They each carried a bag of groceries back to her home. When they got there, she made tea with milk and sugar, put it in a serving set and placed it on the table in the tiny kitchen.

"Call the leasing company and tell them where the car is. Their statement is in the car. Tell them they can pick it up here in Banff, or I can have it delivered to Calgary, or, if they're upset about it, tell them I will buy the car."

Maggie took her cup and returned to the master bedroom. Bakewell called the rental company. Then he called his son and told him he was with Mrs. Walker. He had to explain how they had gotten together again, said he would check in on a regular basis, apologized one more time, very sincere, very repentant. Young Andy told him he was getting used to having a father again, albeit a mystery man, and asked when they could expect to see him.

Later, Bakewell read the Calgary newspaper, and thought seriously about leaving. At seven Maggie came into the living room; she used the phone and made arrangements to have her car brought around. She went back to her room and after another ten minutes came back into the living room, dressed very attractively. Her face was freshly made up. She looked very beautiful. Bakewell had the good sense to tell her so. She sat down in the big overstuffed chair, making a point to face him. She looked directly at him, knowing it would be more difficult for him.

"I want you to make me a drink," she said, crossing her legs. She put her reading glasses on and reached for a book on the table. *Selected Work of Earle Birney*. Bakewell had looked through it earlier. Birney was a poet who had grown up in Banff. She opened it and waited. He went to the kitchen, dutifully made her a scotch, cut a peel from a lemon. When he started to top it with tap water, he asked. "Do you use any special kind of water?"

"Not up here."

"I put a twist in it," he said, bending down to her. She smelled wonderful. He told her so.

"Thank you."

He gave her the drink and sat back on the couch waiting, suspecting another inquisition, not sure what decision she had come to. She took a sip from her drink, put it down on the table and looked at him over the top of her glasses, trying to make him as uncomfortable as possible. He gave a sheepish smile, trying to encourage her.

"I want you to be nice to Sybil. She is an especially good friend. I don't know what I would do here without her."

He spread his hands, indicating she continue; there was no more. "That's it? Be nice to Sybil?"

"That's it. Be nice to Sybil."

"How long are we going to be like this?"

"Like what?"

"How long are we going to be strangers like this? How long with the monastic existence? The enforced silence."

"You're the monastery boy."

"Right, I'm used to it." He crossed the small living room and spoke over his shoulder, going to her kitchen. "Kind of liked it actually," turned back to her, "But it's a little strained up here. This isn't a church, although I feel an *Almighty Presence*."

"What was life like out in the islands all by yourself every day?" she asked, sounding like she couldn't have cared less.

"Every day was Saturday, except Sunday; I prayed a little more on Sundays."

"And what was life like at the monastery. You must have fit right in with your affinity for prayer."

"Everyday was like Sunday, except Sunday. You didn't have to work on Sunday." He took a Heineken from the refrigerator, not really wanting it. "Tell me what your life has been like. Have you been traveling?"

"I've been spending a lot of time with your children."

"Tell me about my children. Please. How is my little granddaughter doing? How tall is Ben? I'll bet he's ready to run by now. What does my new little grandson look like?"

Maggie put the book back on the table. "They have all been absolutely wonderful to each other. They gathered themselves after your death, pulled together beautifully. You must have suspected that part. How else could you have been so unconcerned about them?"

"I was concerned about them. I was just preoccupied for a while."

"They couldn't have been kinder to *that bitch* Maggie Walker. I have never felt so included, nor have I ever been more grateful. Karen's a special joy for me. We've had so many afternoons together." Bakewell waited, eager to learn more of his family. Maggie filled him in with brief descriptions of everyone in St. Louis.

"How is Michael?"

"I can't say. He became my beau for a few weeks before he learned of your death." Bakewell hung his head; it was no act. "He was so wonderfully considerate. He picked me up, insisted on driving his own car, took me to nice restaurants, insisted on paying." Maggie smiled at the memory of Michael.

"He gets it from his mother. They all do."

"Clearly." Maggie looked at her watch. "It's almost time to go. We'll have dinner and talk with Sybil. It will be a lovely dinner." She took a drink of Scotch, sighed, "Please don't tell her any stories."

"Like what?"

"I don't know. You can be very worrying. Don't worry her."

"What am I going to say? You think I'm going to tell her I shot somebody?" Maggie ignored him. "I could tell her about the fun I've been having in the South Pacific. The wonderful outing I had up on Bougainville."

Maggie wasn't smiling.

When they went up to Sybil's apartment, Maggie tapped lightly on the door. It opened immediately. Sybil came out, throwing a wrap around her shoulders. Bakewell tried to assist her. They walked to dinner. It was a special occasion, so they went to the Tuscany in the Mount Royal. They didn't have a reservation. It looked like a place that required a reservation, but the young lady doing the seating greeted them warmly, recognized Sybil right away and said, "Mrs. Walker, it's been a long time."

Bakewell was impressed with everything. It was a beautiful restaurant, in a spectacular setting in the mountains. The furniture, curtains and art work on the walls gave it an air of elegance.

The conversation was animated. Sybil was Maggie's match at the fine art of conversation. Both were quick, and they parried and matched wits, remembering their past together. They teased one another, also made many oblique references to Sybil's life before Banff. Bakewell got the impression Sybil also had "a past." He was typically quiet most of the evening, appreciating the clever, fast moving banter, listened attentively, tried to remain outside, although Sybil drew him in repeatedly with her questions.

Bakewell answered candidly, under Maggie's anxious gaze. Sybil's questions were what, where, when and how. She was sorry to learn of his wife's death, and when he spoke of Katherine briefly, she put her hand on his arm and patted it. The evening was a success. The women shared a bottle of Australian wine, while he sipped a heavy ale. It was relaxed, pleasant. After so much travel and so much atonement, so many weeks of expiation and simple doing-without, he enjoyed the fine food and surroundings. He was extremely grateful to be included in their evening, the evening they resumed what was obviously a special friendship. At one point he got a nod of approval from Maggie, as he was asking Sybil about her life and travels.

Sybil had been most everywhere and was outrageously candid in her assessment of people, especially men, most especially the men of the Mediterranean. She talked a long time about Greece and Yugoslavia. She was blunt about anything that had to do with men, and repeatedly inferred Maggie needed a man in her life again. As they worked their way through the wine she made a point of phrasing it, suggested Bakewell might want to "Get on with it." Bakewell was embarrassed, looked to Maggie for direction. Maggie ignored him.

They walked back to their complex slowly, looking at whatever interested them in the display windows, neither woman missed an opportunity to make comments as they went. It was only six blocks and they were back by nine-thirty. It was almost dark.

Maggie and Sybil had been fun together. Sybil had clearly made her evening, but Maggie was hurting. Throughout dinner there was no enthusiasm for him from her side of the table. The conversation she participated in was with Sybil. She had carried herself off well, but part of her was missing. With Sybil, she was witty, sly and infectious, displaying the part that dazzled. With Bakewell she was missing. He and Sybil worked their way around it, although Bakewell didn't contribute much. Sybil tried to carry it off for Maggie, to pick her up and pull her into the *Andy* part of the conversation. Her presence alone would have been enough, if she were anyone else. But she was Maggie; Maggie brought a presence. Regarding Bakewell, the humor, the wit, the impish behavior wasn't happening. She was aching with the strain of him. Her zest for socializing, passion for discussion, her zeal for witty exchanges, dropped off when the conversation turned to him.

Before her disaster – and that was the way she was beginning to see her relationship with Bakewell – Maggie had always focused on the simple pursuit of happiness, had pursued it most especially whenever the two of them were together. Bakewell watched her all evening, aware, and perceptive for a change. Maggie had lost her confidence. He had taken her confidence when he disappeared. It had been too much. Ever since she showed up in Dickinson, she had the look of a survivor. He remembered the feeling, had lived through it once, long ago at the University, but hated to see it in her now.

Once he wondered what it would be like to have the upper hand in their relationship. It was here now; he didn't like it. He had excluded her from what he thought would be the last part of his life. Now that he had returned, he realized he had disappointed her more than he could ever make up for. There would never be enough time. He wished he had left some kind of note, some little expression, a gentle thought, wished he hadn't gone off without a word. She was right; he had abandoned her.

***

It hadn't really been that hard for him in the first weeks, with the travel and the change of life, the amazing change in his life. At first it had been easy not to think of anyone else, especially during the wilder times. But out on Rujeje, after he had finally stopped running, after Peter Lolo left him to himself with time to reflect, it all came back. He tried to think of his past life with his wife, think about all the things that had happened to him during those years of near perfection. He *had* thought of Katherine, had tried to substitute their history to avoid his current history, but Katherine was no longer real. Katherine was in paradise.

The memory of their weekend at the beach quickly returned. Once there was time to remember, it found him out there under a full moon, on a bright beach next to a crashing surf, warmed by a tropical breeze. Despite his intention to shut her out, thoughts of their time together seeped back in. Maggie was real, was inexorable, a clear mental picture. There was no haziness, no mist when he remembered the two of them together. And he remembered it clearly: the parade, her eyes dazzled by the magic of the evening, adding a magic of her own, the wetness of those blue eyes each morning on the deck, the luster and sparkle they displayed for only him in the afternoons walking the beach, later in the evenings…

Her apparition back in Dickinson had arrested him. He was already intoxicated by the memory of her before Dickinson. No matter how he tried to combat her memory, he knew it was no good. She got in the way whenever he tried to pray down in Richardton. The remorse and worry he lived with over his family sat heavily on a sagging shelf in the back of his consciousness. His guilt, suppressed for so long, had surfaced and was terrible. It brought on a combination of emotions, and there was that other thing, his physical need, his weakness, that haunted him all over again. Still, he hated himself for his weakness. She was going to get hurt all over again if he didn't leave right away. He knew he wasn't going to leave right away, not if she let him stay.

After Powell found him, got him back to Brisbane, and he knew he would be coming home, he thought of her constantly. The simple biological influence, the hormones she had recreated. His need was back and hard at work once the Pacific madness stopped. When she showed up in North Dakota and he held her, he felt a terrific rush. When he got into the car and the scent of her hit him again, the whole package, he was full of thoughts, wants, needs – running in every direction.

He felt relief, anxiety, fear, temptation, lust, couldn't begin to categorize them. He was in the state of grace, *and he wanted to die in the state of grace,* more than he wanted anything in his life, but *he wanted her too*. She was a presence, a temptation, but also a joy he had tasted briefly in February. How long ago was that? Was it really May?

Despite all the reparation he had done to obtain grace, he knew the moment he held her, smelled her, touched her, he wanted her. He was powerless, didn't want to run anymore. She was a gift: more, she was an avalanche of long suppressed feelings, a passion that swept him away with terrifying force. Even though he could see it coming, he would do nothing to avoid it.

***

They bid Sybil goodnight, watched her go up to her door and close it behind, waving and blowing Maggie a soft kiss on the way. Bakewell opened the door, and they went in to Maggie's apartment. He locked the door, turned, wondering, waiting for her to go to her room again. Instead she went to the big overstuffed chair and sat down.

"Did you go to confession after you left off with me…after our little trip to the beach?"

Bakewell looked at her, wishing for another direction in the conversation. Maggie waited for an answer, stolid, determined to make him tell her what he was feeling, despite her fatigue. She would interrogate his obtuse makeup one more time before this longest day ended, would have some more answers. He would have to rise to the occasion; she was determined to suffer whatever grief the conversation might bring.

He suspected she wanted to purge herself of the humiliation she seemed to feel so deeply. She was obviously regretting him, regretting them. His life was full of regrets, he was used to regret, wanted no more, wanted no more pain for her or for them.

"Well?"

"Maggie…"

"Did you?"

"Yes."

"I'll bet it was as soon as we got back to St. Louis, wasn't it, had to get rid of *the sin of me*?"

"Maggie, please."

"Come on Catholic, tell me how I absolve myself. I really don't want to confess you."

"You don't need absolution. You didn't do anything wrong."

"What? You think you're the only one who can sin? Only you can live with regret?"

"I never regretted you. I regretted what I did to you."

"Gee, there's some consolation."

"Please…you're accusing yourself, and I don't know why. I don't understand what you think you have done."

"Well, for starters, I've made one hell of a fool of myself, shacking up with an old lover from out of my past, thinking he might still care, thinking we might still have something together."

"Why do you think that…that you have somehow been foolish?"

"Somehow! Did you say somehow?"

"You're such a good person; you don't have anything to be ashamed of…."

"You want to bet? Words can't describe what a fool I've made of myself. Never in my whole life have I ever felt the fool until you left me. You've managed to take me down to another level. You've introduced me to self abuse."

"Don't do this. You brought all you could to our relationship. I just couldn't accept it. And I didn't know how to tell you, or how to act, so I did what I always do – nothing – and it caused you even more pain."

"I need to get rid of you forever. I've thought about nothing but you for so very long and…it was all a mistake. I was looking for the wrong thing…no, I was looking for the right thing, I just picked the wrong person."

"I wish you wouldn't hurt yourself like this. I'm not worth it and you…"

"You're not worth it? *You're not worth it!* You've got that right, congratulations!"

Bakewell was out of words, wanting badly to find the right ones. He felt trapped, wanted to be somewhere he could pace.

"It's time for expiation – time for me to purge you forever from my life. I've got to move on and find someone worthy of me and, clearly, it isn't you. I know that now. I've been wasting my time, and I'm too old to be making foolish mistakes with men. I've already made two in my lifetime, and they both have been very painful. I can't do this anymore."

He wanted to make her happy, make her feel good again. He desperately wanted to make her feel good about herself, but everything he could think to say sounded like pity. She didn't want pity.

"So when did you get to confession?"

"Not right away."

"I'll bet you called the rectory that very night, after you left me feeling absolutely horrid on that miserable, rotten, rainy night. You couldn't have picked a better night to dump me."

"No, I didn't go that night or the next day, and please don't say I dumped you."

She lit another cigarette, and blew the smoke angrily. "Really? Weren't you afraid of dying?"

"I'm always afraid of dying."

"Well get over it; there's no angry God waiting on you. He's got bigger fish to fry."

"A scary metaphor."

"I mean it. You dwell too much on your *damned soul*. God has real villains to deal with. Get off it with your big ego! You're chump change, as Ned would say, just chump change for a God with more important things to do."

"*Damned soul*, you know how to hit the notes."

"If you make fun of me Andy, I swear, I'll burn your glib face with this cigarette." Bakewell believed her, shut up. "So tell me when you managed to expunge the sin of me from you holy soul."

He sighed. "It took some time. I didn't think I was ready to go looking for forgiveness."

"Should that flatter me?"

When he didn't respond she waited. It was her time to wait, to hope for more. Subconsciously, she wanted him to somehow turn the whole subject of them around, wondered if it was possible. They seemed to be getting farther apart the longer they were together. She wanted him to find the magic to cure her pain, or maybe make it worse, not sure she cared. But she wanted him to talk, wanted to hear him talk to her.

Bakewell sighed, sensing her need and his obligation, "I wasn't sure I might not call again."

She laughed harshly, couldn't help it. "Me? Lecherous woman! The devil's own instrument...*seeking the ruination of your soul?"*

"Come on."

"No. I'm not coming on; I need an answer."

"I thought maybe we might get together again. I didn't want to be a hypocrite."

"Just thought you might call me again, ask for a little more…guilt?"

"Please? This isn't good for us."

"Us now! There's an *us*?"

"Maggie."

"No, Andy. Tell me what exactly were you thinking?"

"I was confused. I didn't know what I was thinking. I was sick about the way we left it down there at the beach. I wasn't honest with you; I let you think the problem was Katherine. I couldn't draw you in any further. I wanted to be away from you. Not take advantage of a situation that was hurting you. But I wasn't sure, wasn't sure I might not give in to the idea of calling you."

"Thought you might want one for the road?"

"No. I thought I might want to change my mind about you, about us."

"Gee. And then you went off…went off and forgot to let me know you were never coming back." She got emotional, hated it, paused, trying to get control, "But it's reassuring to know you were confused about me… before you walked out of my life forever. What a guy."

"If you're trying to hurt me you're succeeding."

"Hurt? We could all tell you a little something about hurt." She looked across the room at him, disgusted, on the verge of tears. "Well it's something anyway. I can still hurt you. Where did you go to confession?"

"You mean what priest? Did I mention your name?" Bakewell resorted to sarcasm. He hated sarcasm.

"Don't be a smart ass."

He looked at her, tenderly; it worked. She was silent, eyes flaming with anger, with grief, with pain – he hated to see the pain – but she was quiet again. They were silent, tired, totally exhausted; neither wanted to continue, but both had more to say. She needed more than a tender look, more than the tenderness his body language expressed. He owed her more than he was giving.

"I went to confession in Port Moresby, at the Franciscan Seminary."

"Was that before you took up the sword? Before you became an avenging angel?"

"Yes." He shook his head slowly; her anger was fatiguing.

"You made a *transoceanic flight,* and you weren't in the state of grace. Wasn't that kind of risky?" she got up from her place on the couch.

"Most of my life, after the beach weekend…actually, starting with the beach weekend, has been kind of risky." He followed her about the room with his eyes, nervously.

"Let me make sure I understand this. Did confession come before you went out to that island, wherever, and tried to shoot somebody, or after?"

"Before."

"Interesting," she was pacing now. There wasn't much room for pacing, and she was forced to turn about quickly, adding to her frustration. "How could you seek absolution, knowing you were going to kill a man?"

"I knew I wasn't going to kill him. I didn't think so, anyway. It wasn't a problem."

"You thought you would clear your conscience, and then, maybe decide to kill him later, and in the meanwhile you would be in the clear, morally speaking of course?"

"Nothing in my life gave me the impression I was in the clear when I was out there. I didn't think I would ever come home until I woke up in Los Angeles in the middle of the night."

He walked across the small living room. There was a crystal decanter with small glasses on the table. He poured some. "Don't drink that." He looked at her curiously. "It's leaded glass. It's been in there a long time. It will poison you." Bakewell tasted it anyway. It was the port and it was good. "Go ahead, poison yourself."

He wanted to end to the stress, wanted to get to a softer part, wishing he knew how to make the transition, wanted to comfort her, was surprised how much he wanted to comfort her. He was also surprised how she could bring out that other part in him, the angry part; the part he was never going back to. Maggie was silent, unyielding. It surprised him to feel anger again, surprised him he could still be capable of it. It felt strange; he didn't like the feeling, wanted to be forever done with anger.

"Maggie, I knew I wasn't going to kill him. I knew if I did it would be a mistake. My intention was to do just what I did."

"And that's okay? Let's see now. It's all right to shoot at somebody if you don't want to kill them. It's okay to think you are so good with a damned gun, you can shoot at people and miss! And God won't take offense? To be so arrogantly confident *with your talent for killing or not killing,* that you can just go ahead and God won't mind. Is that it?"

"No, that's not it. You know that's not it."

"My, haven't we regressed. Mr. Humility, back to Mr. Arrogant, suddenly back where he started from, re-inventing his morality as he goes along?"

"This isn't good. It's not like you and it's agonizing…for both of us."

"I want to understand. I want to know what made you go out there and do what you did, made you take such a crazy chance, and not think about the consequences. And by the way, I don't care about your *damned soul* right now."

"I was pretty sure of the consequences."

"That's not true. You said you thought you were never coming home."

He didn't answer, struggled to think his way through, wishing for inspiration. He knew what he wanted her to believe, and it was the truth, but he was not sure how to phrase it, how to make her believe. She walked over to the settee and poured herself some of the port, looked at him accusingly. "We die together." She threw it off.

Bakewell decided to try again, make a real speech: "When I went out there, I wanted to immerse myself in the places I would be getting around in, the places I would have to survive in, and to decide if I could fulfill my commitment to them. I didn't feel like I owed them anything, but I did take the money, and I was trying to sort it out. I went out there to look it over, maybe work out some kind of plan where I might imagine myself surviving, it might give me hope." He put the glass down. "I needed something that might give me hope." Maggie watched him, unmoved. "Have you ever lost hope? Do you know what it feels like to be out of hope?" His voice cracked and he paused to catch his breath.

"But I'll tell you this; I didn't expect to find the people I found out there – the goodness and the friendship they showed me. I thought of the whole place as a mysterious part of the world, where they all preyed on each other. I thought they wouldn't be like real people, and how I behaved wouldn't make any difference. But it wasn't like that. The place was crawling with saints, and with the good people they were ministering to – people who'd been victimized by decades of war and exploitation and violence, people who just wanted a peaceful life. They were like us, just poorer, but good people, trying to make a life in a bad situation. They were victims just like those people in the Middle East that monster had been mistreating for decades, and looking at them, understanding his exploitation, made taking a shot at that guy a lot easier."

Maggie grew impatient. His explanation was taking the wrong direction. "I know it's terribly selfish of me, inserting myself into this Third World business with saints and all, but I haven't been there, so I don't know about them, and what interests me, is me. Where do I come into this narrative? Do I even have a part? Were you really going to forget about me, us, and what happened at the beach? Were you going to actually go off and die without ever saying another word?"

Bakewell didn't know what to say, just nodded. It was a mistake.

"You rotten, perfect shit! You son of a bitch, Bakewell! You rotten, unfeeling, hateful, insensitive, ruthless…"

He made a move toward her. It was a mistake. There was fire in her eyes. She was about to go berserk. When she looked at a heavy decorative piece on the end table, he stopped and waited for her anger to subside. Just as quickly she clouded up, and he knew the words were coming before she spoke them, could feel them coming and didn't want her to say them.

"I want you out of my life forever. I want you out of here and out of my life forever, do you hear? You don't deserve me."

"You called me arrogant before. Where do I have the right to come back to you, to pull you into my life and the mess it's been? I can't justify calling you up and saying 'I'm back in the country, let's have an affair.'" He turned and put himself between her and the table with the potential projectile. "I'm getting ready to die. I don't want you holding my bedpan."

Maggie was unmoved, hostile and needing a lot more.

"Do you think I could do that to you? Do you really think I could make that call; ask you to pick up where we left off? When I left you I told you…you told me…hell, we agreed, I was still in love with my wife..."

"That wasn't your decision to make! I had the right to reject you or want you. You had no right to assume anything. If you cared for me you had an obligation to tell me and not write me off, like it was for my own good. You don't make decisions about what's good for me. You have no right."

"I felt like it was selfish for me to…I don't know…I felt like it wasn't right…"

"I felt, I thought, I wanted, I, I, me, me. You're such a self-righteous shit. I don't know why I drove all this way to see you. I should have written you off."

"I can't argue with that."

Maggie's disgust showed. "That's more of the same self-righteous nonsense I've been listening to since North Dakota."

He wanted to touch her and thought she wanted him to touch her, but it was impossible to reach for her, the gap between them was an abyss.

"Could we make some tea?"

She turned and went into the kitchen and he followed. It was a small space, barely room for two people to move in. He came up behind her at the sink as she filled the teapot. He decided to give up on words. He put his hands on her shoulders. She shrugged slightly but let them stay. He kept his touch very light. "Can I tell you I thought about you and what happened to us and I anguished just thinking about all the misery I knew I brought into your life after I left?"

"You brought a lot of misery to more than just me. You hurt a lot of people with your…with your callow disregard for us all." She spoke very quietly, fearing her words might do too much damage, determined to say them anyway. The water continued to run. He rubbed her shoulders. She turned the water off; the teapot was running over. When she moved to the stove he let her go, and when she had the water on, she sat down at the small table across from him, unavailable. He couldn't cross that small gap, forced to look directly at her, through a gloomy, wretched fog, wet with shame. He'd never felt so ashamed, wanted to put his head down on the table.

"I'm drowning in shame, you, my kids, everyone, especially you, here in this room with me now." It was honest, could have been better, but certain kinds of words were beyond him. He wished he could touch her, if he could get across to her somehow. Maggie knew it, stayed where she was, looked at him, accusing and angry, very angry, but not wanting to damage him too much. Still…

"By the way, I know you must have been terribly worried about *my soul too,* and I'm sure it was just an oversight. You probably just forgot to ask, but I also went to confession; face-to-face, the modern way, with my pastor. Sometimes I think maybe I just go for consultation and advice. I seldom have anything juicy to confess. Monsignor was very considerate. Sometimes I think he's the only real friend I have to talk to, the only one to tell my troubles to, anyway." She got up from the table to tend to the boiling pot. "No, that's not quite right. I have befriended your daughter and Karen also, you remember, your daughter-in-law, Karen?"

He nodded, dismayed by her sarcasm. Maggie was too complex, too advanced to stoop to sarcasm. Sarcasm was for lightweights, simple minds.

"But they wouldn't be the ones to discuss my affairs with, would they – especially not given the earthy nature of our recent past."

"You've been talking to Karen?"

"You look surprised."

"How is that going? I can't see the two of you being friends." He was surprised to hear Karen's name. She was a welcome new direction in the conversation.

"Actually she's lovely. Very intellectual – deep; you already know that. She's also sensitive, and she's a good listener. Even more important, she's a good sharer. She hasn't anyone other than Nancy, and I don't think they're that close. They're good to each other, but not really close. I think she's fond of me. I hope so anyway."

Bakewell couldn't help smiling, satisfied with the obvious turn, nodded for her to continue. Whenever Karen came into a conversation his mind went defensive, and totally blank. Karen had been the last great enigma of his parenting life. He never had a rational thought where she was concerned.

Maggie poured tea as he held his cup to her, worrying she might decide to pour it onto his outstretched hand, her anger still very apparent though suppressed, less volatile, just beneath the surface, lurking.

She returned to her little sanctuary, knowing he wouldn't cross the tiny gap, still an abyss. She might be vulnerable with him behind her, but there was no crossing over when she faced him. She put her cup down and sighed. "A lot's happened today…and yesterday. I'm very tired. In a moment I'm going to go to my room. I need to think. You look exhausted. You can sleep in the guest room. Put your things wherever. We'll talk later." Bakewell listened to her pronounce her words carefully, wishing he could somehow make things right.

When she got up from the table, he made sure there was space for her to pass without any contact. She went down the hall and closed the door, and he heard the cruel sound of the lock turning.

Confidants

Bakewell woke to the sound of Maggie in the kitchen. He showered quickly and came into the room. They sat in the little alcove kitchen at a table designed for no more than three. He suspected the house had been purchased for Maggie to live in alone. She later admitted as much. It was cozy; her home nicely decorated. Most of the furnishings were for the winter season. There were comforters and large pillows all over the place. The furniture was large, overstuffed, heavy and comfortable.

"I've made something to eat."

"Thank you. It looks good."

"Healthy things for a recuperating man. Are you feeling better? Last night you looked like you wanted to die."

"When I think about things, I think maybe I might want to die."

"Well, eat something first."

She was still in armor, ready, managing to look very feminine, but he recognized the adversary across the miniature kitchen, still bellicose. She let him enjoy his food, poured him a cup of coffee.

"What did Katherine think of this mysterious life you led before you were married?"

"I never told her about it."

"You never told Katherine any of this ghastly business? Not in all the years you were together?"

"Never."

"Never?"

"No. I never spoke of it with her, with anyone… I told a few Catholic priests over the years, but that was in the confessional. They didn't know who I was, and I never heard any doors open when I left. I didn't give my name, rank or serial number."

"You never told Katherine?"

"No Maggie, I never told Katherine."

She was at the sink speaking to the window. "So, aside from your penitential obligation, I'm the only person you've ever confided this amazing, mystery life of yours to?"

Bakewell got up and poured more coffee. He was drinking it black the way she did. She knew he preferred it with cream. When he sat down she got some cream for him. He mixed his coffee and took a sip, smiled, hoping for a new start; it was a new day.

Maggie made her own breakfast and set it on the table.

"If you can find some comfort in the fact that you are the only person in my life that I've shared my dark side with, take it," he said, talking and chewing at the same time.

"I'm just surprised you didn't share it with Katherine."

Bakewell wasn't crazy about the direction of the conversation, but it was better than what had gone before. "There was no way I would share it with her. I didn't want her to know any such thing about me. What if it got out? What would my children think of me? I didn't want anybody to know such a thing about me. I don't want you to know it, Maggie."

Maggie was thoughtful, sitting across from him. His reluctance to tell his story to his wife, or to anyone else, was *almost* surprising. She thought she knew him well, knew he was reticent, but this kind of reticence redefined taciturnity. How could anyone so normal have such a secret existence and never speak of it with anyone...? *There was something to be said for the confessional.*

"Taciturnity," Maggie said quietly, thinking out loud.

"I like taciturnity. It's right up there with stentorian and tangential. It's a mouthful, but it's a good word." She ignored him and drank her coffee, indicated his food, only partially consumed. He was getting to be a picky eater.

"Maggie, for what it's worth, I don't think you should share my story with anyone." He tried to put his hand on her arm. She moved it away.

"It's not something I would care to repeat, or even remember for that matter."

"Well promise me you won't share it with anyone else."

She raised her eyes. "Are you serious, Andy?"

"Yes, promise me."

"Good Lord. I promise." She shook her head. "You've only shared this business with one person in your life, and that's me, and now you think I'm going to tell the world."

"That's not what I meant."

"Well it sounded like it. Let's move on. What's this talk about you being ill? The kids told me you were terminally ill, said you had something awful. I'm not sure they even knew."

"I didn't give them many details. I just told them that it was terminal, and I wanted to go out to the islands, and they agreed."

"Agreed! How much choice did they have? You told them you were going, and you went, without telling anybody but your sons and your daughter – five minutes before you departed!"

"Please, no more anger. Let's not be angry for a little while."

"So what do you have? What's killing you? Why don't you have any time left? You look pretty good to me right now. No, that's not true; I'm sorry I said that. Actually, I'm so disgusted with you right this minute, you look almost repulsive to me."

It made him chuckle. "Well, I know I'm not much…"

"Don't start with me. Don't start. I don't want to hear that routine anymore. I hate that self-deprecation thing of yours. Tell me what is wrong with you."

"I think I have liver cancer. Dr. Neville says I have it; he said it was incurable."

Maggie thought about what he'd just said. It took the edge off her anger, which had been diminishing all night, and all morning. She had gotten up early, while he slept late. It wasn't like him to sleep late; he was a contractor after all. "Are you well enough to go for a walk?"

"Yes."

"Get your coat; it's chilly outside. The radio said five degrees."

"I hope that's Celsius."

They walked around the city park again, down the river to the end of the path. She made him climb up a short, steep incline that put them on the road above the falls, still determined to punish him. They walked down to where they could see the river dump its tremendous load in an awesome display. It was much warmer when they got back to her home, and they left their coats and walked into Banff. After wandering the streets for another hour, they went back to her apartment again. Bakewell laid down on the couch and soon fell asleep. When he woke, he was alone for the rest of the afternoon. There was a note. Maggie had gone with Sybil.

They returned at five. Sybil came in and talked with Bakewell briefly, said she had things to do that night, but before she left she filled the room with exuberance and commotion.

"Walk me into town tonight and we'll have a drink," Maggie said. "We'll go somewhere simple."

Bakewell showered and dressed in the only decent clothes he had. As they were leaving, Maggie said, "I need to buy you some clothes. Why didn't I think of it earlier today?"

He had no answer for the question. But her mood had changed. *One little step at a time.*

There was a lofted bar at the corner of Banff and Buffalo Street, with a view of the park and the bridge and the Old Hotel in the distance. They took a table by the window, listened to a group of noisy Japanese at the next table. Banff was always crawling with tourists, and half of them were Japanese.

They enjoyed the crazy antics of the ravens in the thick trees that forested the city park across the street. Maggie drank her scotch quickly, had a second; Bakewell nursed one. When she suggested they go home, he quickly agreed, and when they were back in the apartment again, Maggie told him to make her another drink.

She took the big chair next to the coffee table, looking strangely content after so much hostility. She got comfortable, crossed her attractive legs, almost smiled. He felt compelled to start the conversation.

"I'd like to treat."

She thought the sentence wasn't complete, waited for him to finish.

When he didn't, she said, "Treat me? To what?"

"I'd like to make peace somehow. Could we not have any more questioning? Any question you could possibly want to ask, it seems to me, would be redundant by now."

"You want to make a treaty with me?"

"Yes."

"Like an interruption to hostilities, like warring nations?"

"Yes."

"Sue for peace?" Maggie was enjoying the line of questions.

"Maggie, this isn't a war, or even a fight. You're attacking and I'm defending. I'm out of fight. I can't fight with you, but I do want peace, or at least a cessation to hostilities. Hell, I'm more like a prisoner of war than a combatant – undergoing an interrogation, to use your word."

She almost smiled, listening to his analogy. She was still looking for, listening for, some *magic*, knew he was capable of it. She wanted to keep pitching, see if he might hit one out, a homerun. She was hoping for the grand slam that ended the game, turned out the lights, sent the crowd home and sent her down the hallway to wait for him to come knocking. *War and home runs, such ridiculous analogies.* She wanted to hear the words that would allow him to enter her life again, take them back to the sweet precinct of their interrupted love affair.

"All right, no more interrogations," she said, almost resigned now.

"Thank you."

"What would you like to do? I'm not a bit ready for bed."

"Well, that takes care of that."

"Are you seriously thinking I'd let you in my bed?"

Bakewell smiled sheepishly, waited.

"Amazing. You have some nerve, Andy – putting us all through this torment, this horror, and then thinking I might want to bed you again, like nothing's happened?"

"You're right. I'm sorry. I shouldn't have presumed. It's all been too much."

He looked around the room, uncomfortable, feeling closed in. Bakewell was a lounger. If he wasn't rocking, he needed to be leaning back, legs crossed, taking up space. He wasn't lounging, his arms rested on his knees, his hands twisting nervously. He looked penitent and unsure of himself. "I need to make some plans," he said. "I need something short term, where I know I can bed down each night."

"And you're asking if that might be here?" He nodded. "I have the extra room. You've already spent the night there. Are you asking to pay rent?"

"I have quite a lot of money with me, actually. I could leave it with you, when the time comes. Or I can get someplace up in the hills. There are some nice places up on the bench above town. I stayed up there a few years back. The views are amazing."

The thought of him leaving frightened her, but she enjoyed his ridiculous, fabricated predicament. She was glad she had him on the defensive, but afraid he might really leave. She wished they could move on to intimacy. When she didn't reply, he became typically uncomfortable. He was used to silence, preferred it she knew, but he hated silence when it confronted him head on. She gave him a penetrating stare, deliberately making him miserable. The time for confrontation was coming to an end. It had to come to an end. She could only hate herself so much. She knew she could never hate him. Most of her fury had been directed at herself, for her weakness. He had exposed her to a part of herself she didn't recognize, a part she detested. He had just gotten in the way by resurfacing.

She picked up the Earle Birney book and paged through it absently. Bakewell finally leaned back, rested his head on the back of the couch. Maggie read one of Birney's poems; when she looked up he was asleep again. She watched him for a long time, feeling disappointed. Eventually she gave up and went quietly to her room.

Sybil

The third morning, Sybil came down for breakfast. She brought rolls that smelled of cinnamon and apples. Bakewell enjoyed them, thanked her and complimented her repeatedly.

Sybil loved conversation, wouldn't go near the "horrid telly," and her affection for Maggie was apparent in everything she did and said. Maggie loved to listen to her talk. Bakewell understood why. Her conversation was lively, spirited, also worldly and absorbing. She had a wonderful variety of little expressions and, in addition to being an amazing storyteller, she was fascinated with everything either one of them said. Sybil encouraged conversation, and, like all good conversationalists, she was an active listener, knew when to ask without interrupting. She had been everywhere and spoke with authority on an enormous range of subjects, the most interesting of which were her previous lives.

At first Bakewell thought she was kidding, "Having me on," as she liked to say, but soon learned otherwise, learned to recognize and appreciate he was being treated to something unique. He and Maggie were fascinated by her remarkable stories, which started that morning.

"Syb, tell Andy where all you've been in your lives," Maggie encouraged.

Bakewell looked curiously at Sybil. "You've been traveling?" he asked.

"Not in the way you might think. I've been no place but here for years."

"Go on," Maggie said. "He's such a cynic. I want to see what his reaction will be. Tell him."

Sybil was reluctant, but Maggie kept after her. She told Bakewell she had lived many times in other lives, thought she had lived in many different centuries. Maggie asked, "Have you been anywhere interesting lately?"

Sybil said, "Egypt."

Bakewell had always been fascinated by Egypt. He was an admirer of Sadat, whose biography he had read two years before, during a week of inconsolable loneliness. He listened up. When he asked if she knew anything about Sadat, Maggie interrupted, holding one hand up, "What century?"

"About fifteen hundred BC," Sybil answered, "During the reign of the co-regents."

"Really?" Maggie was serious and genuinely interested.

Bakewell suppressed a smile.

"Thutmose III, I think. He coexisted with the pharaoh's daughter Hatshepsut, who was his stepmother if you can imagine! They ran Egypt for years. I was a chamber maid to one of her friends, but III removed her from most everything after her death."

Bakewell watched Sybil closely, eyes widening. When he found Maggie's eye, she gave him a look so menacing, if it was armed it would have killed him. He didn't interrupt. Maggie quizzed her friend gently. Sybil answered honestly, wherever she could, but got bogged down in details, which added to Bakewell's amusement. After that third morning Sybil became a regular part of their life. They had frequent discussions about her past. Sometimes it took a while to draw her out. Bakewell learned to listen sympathetically, as Maggie always did. Once he understood she was so intensely certain of her previous lives, he asked questions, which were honestly curious and not intended to discredit. In addition to Egypt, she said she had lived in Reykjavik, and died there during a smallpox epidemic in 1708. She served in the American Civil War – as a man – a common soldier from South Carolina, which she described as "a loathsome, malarial swamp of a place."

The Civil War business fascinated Maggie, since she had a home in South Carolina. Maggie loved Charleston, but Sybil had a mental block about the place, had refused to fly to Charleston and visit Maggie many times. Her most disturbing life had been in the early part of the century when she lived in Bukovina, Romania during The Great War and where, she said with a shudder, she believed she'd been an evil person who had something to do with medicine.

Sybil believed everyone lived many times, and each life had exit points at which the soul could either exit the body or decide to stay. She was completely serious, and the calm detachment she used to describe different events from the past *was* believable, even compelling. It left Bakewell fascinated, without criticism, which Maggie proclaimed "A singular departure." Sybil also believed everyone had obligations to their past lives and often lived again, served time, in order to make up for what they had done. Bakewell had likened it to "a sort of purgatory here on earth," which Maggie roundly criticized, accusing him of forcing his Catholicism, but Sybil defended him sympathetically.

"No, no, Maggie. You mustn't criticize Andy. He's a right to his opinion, and he's a love."

Maggie and Bakewell also began to make conversation, escorted and encouraged, at Sybil's softly incanted behest. Sybil was didactic and felt a need to involve herself in their obvious quarrel.

"Saying, 'I'm sorry' and 'you were right,' is the ultimate form of humility. It is so becoming in others," Sybil said. "It is what I've always admired most about you, Maggie dear. You have a wonderful ability to give yourself up and accept. You've always had a way with those wonderful words."

Maggie beamed at the compliment. Bakewell wondered if Sybil had the right person in mind. He still remembered the formidable young woman who had grown up to be such a formidable older one. He couldn't identify the person Sybil was extolling with enthusiasm.

"They are *so blissfully significant.* Really, they are momentous, those two words," Sybil looked directly at Bakewell, said *"I'm sorry,"* nodded, and skillfully switched to the vernacular. "Big words kid," she said with emphasis. "Those words are big. Really big." She patted Bakewell's arm.

Bakewell wasn't sure if he was learning to see Maggie in a different light, or maybe being taught to see her in a new light. *Maybe Sybil was a Merlin?*

He watched Maggie closely when she listened to Sybil talk. Maggie *was* different now, was vulnerable, and it *was big,* which gave him further pause and a still greater worry.

Sybil had a storehouse of expressions they both enjoyed. She called their daily visits "chinwags" and used words like "blighter," and phrases like "in two sticks!" and mixed "shan't have it!" into the conversation regularly, especially when Maggie was having "a low time." On the last day of the first week in Banff, over another gallon of tea, Sybil turned to Bakewell, cup in hand, eying him intently. "You've been in the islands somewhere, haven't you?"

Bakewell returned the look without answering, wondering. "Why do you say that, Sybil?"

"I don't really know. What were you doing there?"

"I was visiting a priest friend, several of them actually. Missionaries."

"He wasn't really a friend."

"He was, a fine man too. I would like to think of him as my friend."

"I get the feeling you were there for a…something not good… maybe you were there for a wicked purpose." She spread her hands briefly, apologizing, indicating it wasn't important to her. "It's only a feeling. If you don't want to own up, we'll let it go."

"Let's talk about something else, Syb," Maggie said.

"Maggie, I'm worried about you both. There's something in the air. I love you both, as you already know, but something's not right in your being here. Are you in some kind of trouble?" she asked, turning again to Bakewell.

"Just chasing after Maggie; it seems to be my only occupation."

"More like I've been chasing after you," Maggie replied, taking something from the oven. "I chased him halfway across the continent last week."

"Well, let's change the subject then. You've apparently found each other, and I'm just wild for the both of you." Sybil's tone was sincere, full of uncertainty, but Bakewell could feel the warmth underneath.

"Thanks Syb," Maggie said, patting her arm.

"You are such a lamb," Sybil said in return, but searching Bakewell's eyes.

Reconnection

It was early evening. They had just returned to the apartment after spending part of the afternoon at an espresso shop, sending and receiving emails to and from his family. The nearness of her there in front of the computer, the slight contact of shoulders and arms, touching accidentally, as they sent and read messages from St. Louis, had incited a riot of awareness in Bakewell. He had a compelling need to touch, to feel, to have her again. He closed the door and crossed the room as Maggie was taking off her coat, turned her to him, catching her off guard to prevent any demurral. He leaned down, and kissed her cheek. She was very still. He kissed her again. She didn't resist, just said, "Please stop." He felt like she had put a knife in his heart.

That old feeling of humiliation from so long ago came rushing back. He felt foolish and unbelievably disappointed. He straightened up and looked into her deep blue eyes. They were just as blue as that first night when he had kissed her thirty years ago.

"Please. Forgive me. Forgive me for all the unhappiness I've caused, and for the suffering I've caused you to observe in my children. I'm sorry about all of it. I will get out of your life. I can still do it. I think I can still do it."

"Why don't we sit down," she said offhandedly, "You can make me a drink." She took the overstuffed chair next to the table again.

Bakewell made the drink, brought it to her and sat down tentatively.

"What'll I do with just a photograph to tell my troubles to?"

"I think I should leave Maggie, no matter how much I might want to stay. It isn't fair. You were right about wanting me out of your life forever."

"When I'm alone, with only dreams of you, that won't come true, what'll I do?"

"Are you quoting from a song?" he asked, catching on.

She smiled. She had listened to the song for hours when she thought she had lost him forever, could remember all the words, and all the painful moods that went with them. She smiled at him again. She was almost out of anger, still "pissed off" – an expression she had taken to over the past days – but her querulous tank was about empty.

Bakewell loved to see her smile, hadn't seen her smile since February.

"So, what am I to do?"

"I can't answer that," he admitted.

"Try."

"I have a need for you right now. I've had a need for you for a long time. I just didn't recognize it. But…"

"Please don't fuck this up."

"You have learned some new words since February."

"I've learned a lot of things since you saw me last. It's what I will do with this knowledge, this heightened awareness, that's got me confused."

"I have nothing to offer, not money, not security, not even time, but I love you."

Was that the magic she was listening for?

"I'm sorry I hurt you, Maggie. I don't have enough vocabulary to tell you how sorry I am."

"Andy, you've got more vocabulary than anyone I know. You just need to use it."

"I can't leave without telling you how I feel. I wouldn't care if you diddled me and dumped me, the way you think I tried to do you. I am just as vulnerable as you pretend to be, and I am in need of you. I don't think I have ever needed anyone as much as I need you right now."

There. It's what you came for. "Do you think I'm pretending?" she kept picking her glass up, putting it back down without drinking it.

"I don't know. I don't think so, but thinking hasn't been my strong suit lately."

"Where do we go from here?"

"I don't know. I don't have much time left. It's up to you."

"You're such a shit; I knew you would hand this decision to me."

"I want to tell you how I feel. I don't want to miss the chance again."

"Andy, I came all this way to find that you've already planned your life, and your plans include leaving me again?"

"All that I've got left is yours, if you want it."

Did the grand slam just leave the park?.

"It's not much of a deal, is it?"

"No," he agreed sadly.

"So the ball is in my court, again?"

He nodded.

Would it be worth it, the pain, another ending? Woman, who are you kidding!

She put the drink down again, looked at the table then at him. "Tell me if you think I'm getting a good deal."

He shook his head. It wasn't a good deal for her. He knew it and she knew it.

"Tell me I'm getting a good deal."

"I can't."

"Say it. Say, Maggie we belong together, if even for a little while. Say, 'we will be happy together for whatever time we have left.'"

"I will do anything that makes you happy for whatever time we have left. It's not a good deal and you know it's not."

Maggie got up and took her glass into the kitchen. He was right behind her, but he didn't touch her. When she turned around they were inches apart.

"I want to touch you so desperately; I feel like that young kid you gave your virginity to so long ago. But it is so terribly unfair of me to want to do that."

There were tears suddenly, streaming down her cheeks. She said, "Oh my God, Andy."

Bakewell interpreted her mood finally, even his rusty radar able to recognize the submissiveness. They were back on the beach above the Gulf again. He truly believed he had no right to touch her, didn't believe he deserved her. All he could manage was, "Forgive me."

"Oh dear God, I've…I'm not in control," she said, added, "I'm almost never in control around you anymore. I think I liked it better in the old days when I had the control." She started to reach up and put her arms around his neck, changed her mind, put her forehead on his chest. He kissed the top of her head. "No, that's not true; I don't want to be in control," her voice was very low, speaking to the floor. It sounded far away.

"I don't know what to do."

"I know. It's the damned vulnerability! The damned kindness! Where does it come from?" she looked up at him again. "How can such a perfect shit of a man have so much sweetness and goodness and kindness and still be the most awful, cruel man in the whole world."

She turned her head to the side and he put his hand to her cheek, turned it back to him and kissed her again with infinite tenderness, barely making contact with her lips.

"What do you want me to do? I don't want to take advantage of you when you're like this."

"Do please shut up with your taking advantage, just do shut up." She put her hands to the side of her head, pressing at her temples, shook her head to clear it, looked up at him again, eyes full of tears, very beautiful. "Oh dear God, what to do." She clapped her hands together without making any sound, fingers touching, like she was praying, held them there, squeezed them together, unable to move away from him. She decided to quit fencing. It was too ridiculous.

He sensed her willingness. It was a crazy, foolish thing for him to do, if he really cared about what was to happen to her; but he put his arms around her and held her so tightly her shoulders caved together, elbows touching. He kept it up, trying to squeeze the love from her.

She gasped. Spoke to the collar of his shirt, "I can't breathe." When he relaxed his arms, her head dropped backward. Looking up at him, she opened wet eyes. He kissed her again, trying to be gentle, but unable to hide his passion. She tried to respond but wasn't up to it, almost limp. He picked her up, and she made a soft sound, a combination of reluctance and submission, hesitance and anticipation. It was all he needed – his mind made up again, just like that night thirty years before. He was going to take advantage once again, only this time he knew he was taking advantage, no matter what the inner voice said. It was a much different voice now, so many years later, a voice of conscience, still critical, judgmental, but it had taken a moral turn over the years, had become the voice of reason, of propriety, and it was not happy with what he was doing. He didn't care. She was what he wanted, more than anything else. He would sin again, fall from grace.

He put her down on the soft downy bed. She looked up at him, seemed very young again as he touched her buttons. She closed her eyes and waited, waited for him to open her up. When he had, he leaned forward and softly kissed her chest.

"You're still so lovely. I was wrong, so stupid to say what I said that night at Algonquin – you were beautiful when you were young and you're still beautiful."

Maggie put her arm over her eyes and didn't move. Bakewell looked at her exposed chest as he pulled her shoes off and her expensive slacks. When she realized she still had short pull ups covering her feet she sat up and reached for them self-consciously.

"Let me do it, please," he said soothingly. She leaned back, looked at him again then covered her eyes a second time. She was still a trophy and knew it, didn't care if he took her naked body in the way she had taken in his that first night when she told him to take his trunks off. He undressed quietly and while he did, she raised her arm and watched him.

It was incredibly erotic, her lying there watching him get out of his clothes. She knew it. When he approached her she slid over to make room for him. He reached for her and she turned her head to him and it began almost suddenly, an implosion. They were like gravity for one another, crashing bodies falling through space, and the lovemaking was a near crash too. It became stressful and aggressive as they twisted and turned, pushed and shoved. She forced him to be rough with her, even though he wanted it to be delicate and tender. They both had waited a long time since February, waited through a lot of uncertainty. He didn't understand why it had to be so forceful. When it was over he lay next to her and looked up at the moonlit room.

"What was that all about?"

"I don't know. I think I was trying to punish you, maybe punish myself too. We've both been such fools."

"You are full of anger, Maggie. It's my fault."

"It sure as hell is your fault!" She pulled a sheet over her naked body, angry again. I have made a fool of myself over a man, a little boy I once knew – and got dumped in the process! And here I am, the perfect fool for allowing it to happen in the first place, allowing it to happen all over again."

He stayed in the room until she fell asleep went down the hallway and slept in the other bedroom.

Giving & Taking

Over the next day and a half, conversation became agreeable again, even when Sybil wasn't present. It started with little things, like what they would eat and when they would go for the walk. The walk became mandatory after the first afternoon. Sybil's visits were regular but impromptu, and they both came to anticipate them happily. One afternoon they returned from a walk on the hillside above the falls, making a dash the last fifty meters to beat a sudden cloud burst. They came through the door out of breath and excited. Maggie put her coat away and came back into the living room and watched him as he started to fix tea. When he looked up she was staring at him. There had been no more lovemaking and very little affection, other than the requisite kindnesses. He looked at her, making firm eye contact. She seemed to be getting her confidence back. He was seeing signs of the formidable girl from his past.

She had something to say; he could see it in her eyes, refused to look away. It hadn't been easy to make eye contact for either of them until after the physical reunion. He'd been filled with guilt, didn't think he had the right. She had avoided looking at him for a different reason. But there was a gritty, resolute look in her eye now. She indicated they sit in the kitchen at the small table. When they were seated, he waited. She put her elbows on the table and folded her hands under her chin in that familiar way she'd done so many times before.

Her look was penetrating. He hoped it was concern and not anger; it certainly wasn't fear. It was a new look. He'd not seen it before. It was appraising, measuring, almost the way she looked at him that night at Algonquin, but different. That look had been curious, this one was more… He wasn't sure what she was thinking, felt no need to talk, happy to wait, revert to his stoic nature. She was still an exhausting proposition. He got up to retrieve the teapot.

"You know," she started, "Other than being the most outrageously arrogant…callow…selfish…inconsiderate jerk in the entire world," she paused for effect.

"I get the picture," he said, holding up one hand.

Maggie took the cup and saucer he handed her. "…You really have been motivated…in many ways…in the right way. You know?"

Bakewell didn't respond.

"Your intentions have been mostly for others, not much for yourself. Maybe you're not quite such a complete, pompous…selfish shit after all. You know?"

"You're beginning to talk like Ned, but I do love it when you try to sweet talk me."

"I love Ned." She continued, determined. "Really, all of this, this outrageous traveling, the craziness of it – missionaries and monasteries – it's all been about trying to do the right thing for your family and for Ned."

Bakewell smiled without speaking.

"Am I wrong?"

"I don't know." He almost laughed. "I'm not in a position to judge myself. I haven't been able to put it in perspective yet."

"Well, let's put it in perspective! Everything you have done has been for someone else. What have you gained by all this madness?"

He didn't answer. She persisted, "What have you got out of the whole deal, the whole *ordeal*?"

"Well, I've got about fifteen grand in my pocket, and I've sure seen a lot of the world."

"Don't joke with me," she warned, continued her rationale, admonished him several times for his insensitive behavior, but returned each time, re-developing her logic, weaving a tale of two eccentrics, changing sides as she did a chronology of the previous months.

"This is beginning to sound a little like praise. You're not trying to compliment me are you?"

"No, Andy. You're a moron, but your intentions seem always to be good, despite your dimwitted logic. But then you never really were exactly brilliant."

"Ned again. Was that a compliment?"

"You better stop making fun of me." He held up his hands. "I want to understand you. I want to make sure I'm not going to make a fool of myself all over again. I want to define this madman I'm living with." She put her hands in her hair, fingers spread, from the inside next to her ears, pushed it up and out, making her hair flow back. It was slightly wet from the rain.

"No, Maggie. You haven't made a mistake. Your intentions have been good too. You only have to ask yourself if everything you have done was for the right guy."

"*And that's the question!* Have I been chasing the right man, or some idiot who's lost his mind?"

He spread his hands and raised his eyebrows, giving her the creasy-eyed look once more. It had become an habitual response since they got to Banff. Maggie waited. He got up from the table and moved toward the stove and turned to face her. "I'm in a bad spot here. Am I supposed to tell you, you did the right thing – chasing after me? Am I supposed to hurt your feelings, tell you that *that fool* you keep talking about is a waste of time? Either way it's about ego. I don't have much ego left."

"Tell me you love me and you're glad I chased you across the country. Tell me you're happy I did it, that you were so terribly glad to see me back there in Dickinson, your heart nearly burst with joy."

"My heart's bursting with joy right now."

"Why do I have to put the words in your mouth?"

"You don't. I've said them before; I struggle with them, I know, but that's because I'm still a little bit afraid of you."

"You're afraid of me?"

He nodded, helplessly.

"You're the one who shoots people!" her voice hissed with false intensity. "Who should be afraid of who here?"

"I don't want anybody to be afraid of me. Not ever again, in anyway. I just want peace. I would love to hold onto this quiet we've found here too. After all my time, running in the islands, and hiding in the monastery, I've learned how important peace is. How much I like it. How much I like the simple *quiet* of peace." He paused. "I like us being together here. I love having you near, being with you. I love you."

"Come here," she said and they put their arms around each other again, her anger finally gone. There was tenderness and caring and humility as they exposed themselves to each other, a mutual giving in to the vulnerability that comes from deep within, from the simple wanting to love and be loved and to let go. She was what he wanted, and he was finally, irrevocably what she had come after.

"I've wanted this ever since that first night last June. You must have realized it. It's what I've wanted ever since I saw you again, ever since we had a chance to talk once more, and I was able to see you hadn't changed, not in all these years."

Bakewell kissed her, hugged her. The confusion about the future and what would happen to her was always right there confronting him, but, for the moment, he was only focusing on now.

"Andy, tell me we've gotten beyond the hard part," she spoke into his ear while he held her against him. "Tell me you forgive me for what I did so long ago, and I will forgive you for what you've done to me. Give us a chance again, for happiness. Trust me and I will love you forever."

"I trust you and I want you, but I don't want to take advantage. I'm nobody any woman should be looking for. I don't know why you're so nutty about me," he tried to laugh, "But I'm grateful."

"After all these years, I want to get back into your life again. I don't care for how long it might be."

"I want you to be happy, Maggie. I'm not sure I can make you happy. I don't have enough time left." His protest was meek at best; he held her tightly as he spoke.

"I get to make that choice. Don't do my thinking for me."

She had been so tightly strung, but her control had spun off, come undone. She was unsure, afraid, maybe losing her fear, all opportunity now, so obtainable. He had never seen her so helpless, not even at the beach when they were feeling their way through the renewal. Back there she had worried he might change his mind at any time. He had changed his mind. But she was ready to give herself without hesitation, done with analyzing, with evaluating, no longer cared about what he had done, and Bakewell didn't care if it was wrong. He would be selfish. He wasn't going to analyze it either, didn't want to think about it. It was dizzying – but the inner voice was back, telling him it was a mean, selfish thing he was doing. He pushed her back gently and put his arms around her shoulders, gathering her physically, emotionally.

Maggie spoke into his shirt front. "You win."

"I don't want to win."

"You've already won. I can't help myself anymore." She looked up at him. "You have taken everything I have. I'm so unconnected I can't function anymore."

He wiped her tears with the side of his thumbs. "You're hurting and you're confused."

"Yes."

"This isn't fair."

"It's the way I am." She was crying again.

"You're too vulnerable."

"I can't help it. I can't hide it any longer. I can't deal with it anymore. You've just got to love me, fill me up with your love. Take it from that reservoir you have for Katherine, and let me have some of it. Katherine doesn't need it."

Bakewell remembered something he had read years before:

You give but little when you give of your possessions.

It is when you give of yourself that you truly give.

In her case it was true, but it wasn't true in his. He was rationalizing and he hated rationalization. He wasn't giving her anything. He was taking.

Maggie bought a computer and they set it up together. Once it was up and running she logged onto the internet. “What shall we call ourselves?” she asked.

“How about ‘up and running?’”

“I like that, Andy, very creative. What shall we use for a password?”

“Fugitives?” Maggie smiled conspiratorially. “Don’t forget you can’t leave any spaces between the words.”

“I know, I know. I’m not a computer dummy,” she said, typing and focusing like a first time user, her face determined, a child-like pride showing in the new experience.

He stood behind her, reached under her arms, and put his hands on her chest affectionately as he kissed her neck. She wriggled but didn’t protest, loved the physical affection she had come to expect, loved any affection he offered. He couldn’t keep his hands off her and showed no restraint when it became apparent there would be no protest.

Maggie spent the afternoon emailing Nancy and Karen, requesting an address for Michael, and, when Bakewell was not there looking over her shoulder – began her research on liver cancer.

The computer was a needed addition. Bakewell sent emails out to Port Moresby and contacted his friends at the Franciscan seminary. He sent an email to the priest on Buka, who was dumbfounded to learn he was still alive. He wished he could somehow contact the men who had helped him on Buka, Bougainville, Vangunu and New Georgia. He did his own research on secret societies: Skull & Bones, Bilderberg and the Trilateral Commission, but it was fruitless. There was nothing but window dressing, a lot of literary nonsense by people who tried to pass themselves off as knowledgeable.

The computer also provided them each with some private time to get lost in their own pursuits. One of Maggie’s pursuits was to contact several lawyer friends about her lover’s secret life without being too specific. She queried them about the legal ramifications of dying and coming back to life, about being liable for an international incident that never happened. There was nothing to learn about his time in the islands, no news about any shooting on Bougainville. The more she pursued it, the more confident she became of his rehabilitation. She was sure, with her list of contacts in government, she could find someone who would plead his case if there was a case, if there were any legal complexities. If no one knew where he’d been, or what he’d done… *what had he done?*

They walked into Banff each day and spent hours along the river. One afternoon a young kid dressed in black stumbled into them with a glazed look. When Maggie spoke her friendly hello, he asked for money. She gave him ten dollars. Bakewell shook his head, called it a waste.

Later, after staying out late one evening with Sybil, both women drinking too much – Bakewell chiding them about being the designated deliverer since they seldom took a car anywhere – they ran into the same kid in the same dirty black clothes, this time sitting on the cold ground, back against a wall. He was wet and miserable and obviously stoned. Maggie helped him up and gave him fifty dollars and told him to find a place to get warm and clean up.

"That was a waste," Bakewell said, as they left him behind with his lode of good fortune.

"Be quiet," was all Maggie said. Sybil didn't say anything.

"I guess the first $10 did so much good, you decided he needed more."

"He's someone's little boy. Somewhere there is a mother in this world, worrying herself sick over him."

Bakewell looked at Sybil, smiled, said, "How're you going to argue with that kind of logic?"

Sybil called Maggie a lamb. She used the expression constantly, said, "Maggie love, you'll run out of money before he ever comes around." Sybil had a cynical, acerbic side. The kid looked wasted, totally beyond redemption.

"He looks to be about Michael's age, wouldn't you say Andy?"

"Yep, about Michael's age Maggie. If he were Michael, Michael's old man would be grateful too."

Maggie had looked self-satisfied after the exchange and made a point of seeking the kid out after that evening, went so far as to tell Sybil to keep an eye out for him, told Sybil she would reimburse her.

"I've got my own sums, love. I'm not a ward, you know." Sybil had nodded at Bakewell, said, "I guess Maggie's given us a project, Andy. What do you call it in America?"

"A rehab case, Sybil, same as everywhere else."

It had been a long day. When they got back to the apartment Bakewell crashed. He was running down fast now. Maggie went straight to the computer and continued her research in earnest. They were doing liver transplants at Washington University, right there in St. Louis, and she was going to find out what was involved.

***

They were in the bedroom again, lying together, peaceful, remembering. It was a time for honesty; most of their time together now was a time for honesty and Maggie had gratuitously asked Bakewell why he loved her when she was young.

"When you were young I loved you because you were beautiful, and I was shallow and full of myself, like that young & callow fellow in the song."

"Did you love me before you had me?"

"I don't really remember when I fell in love with you, but having you would have cinched it, if I wasn't already crazy in love with you."

"That's a lovely thing to hear."

"You were so…unapproachable, and you seemed so…untouchable, so unattainable. I couldn't believe I might possess you."

"Well, *I certainly disposed you of that notion*! And quickly I might add," she suppressed her laughter. Maggie had taken to disparaging herself, seemed to enjoy mocking herself in his presence, whenever they discussed their youth.

"And I thank you for that," he said, "Thank you from the bottom of my heartless, cruel heart." Bakewell couldn't suppress his own amusement.

"Wasn't I awful, such a hussy? You must have thought me dreadfully forward and easy."

Bakewell laughed. "Hussy. That sounds like one of my mother's old words."

"Tramp then. I was so forward with you, so permissive. I still can't believe the way I carried on."

"The way we carried on."

"If I hadn't come to your brother's funeral or hadn't approached you that night at the party, what would you have done?"

"Probably nothing."

"You mean you wouldn't have ever asked me out?"

"I doubt it."

"Now I do feel like a hussy. If it wasn't for me you would never have had to confess all those sins.

"I was totally crazy about you."

"I remember."

"I probably would have mustered up the courage to speak to you, but believe me, without your encouragement I would never have made a pass at you that night."

"And thanks for that – more guilt. Do you want to know the worst part?"

"I didn't think of any of it as a worst part, not until it was over. I thought it was the best thing that ever happened to me up to that time."

"Until you met Katherine?"

"Until I met Katherine."

"Well, here's the worst part. I didn't think you were worthy of me. My God, can you imagine?"

"I don't think I was ever worthy of you, Maggie. I still don't."

"Oh God, don't say that. You were a lovely boy." Bakewell studied her discomfort. "I must have been so terribly vain. Can you ever forgive me?"

He took her hand, and she withdrew it. He took it back again and held it, and she didn't resist. "I have been very blessed in my life. I've had the incredible privilege of loving the two most desirable women I have ever known.

"And you love me now? Say you love me now, Andy."

"I love you Maggie."

"Why?"

Bakewell paused, thinking about the words he would speak, knowing she would be hanging on every clumsy phrase. "The first time I loved you… I had a need for you. It was unquenchable."

"And now?"

"Now I love you because *you* have a need for me."

"Are we talking… do you pity me?" Her voice sounded worried.

"No, not pity. You have a need now, for me, a need you didn't have long ago. It makes you so beautifully vulnerable and that makes you so desirable. Knowing you need me makes me have to love you, makes me want to love you even more, want to cherish you."

She rolled against him, burying her face and whispered, "You go so long without saying anything. You don't say much for such a long, long time, and then you say so much in such a short time."

Another Proposal

"Maggie we need to have a serious talk about the future."

"Oh my God."

"I love being here with you…"

"Please, I don't think I can do this again. Don't break my heart."

"I'm not going to leave you unless you tell me to go, but we need to talk about what's ahead."

"Wait, let me fasten my seatbelt." She made a silly gesture, raised her hips and straightened out in the bed.

"I love you. You know that. I didn't think it would happen a second time, but it has, and I am so glad it has. I am so grateful for you. I love you deeply, but I can't go on like this." He raised up on one elbow. "I'm going to die, getting ready to die, and pretty soon too. I know you don't like to talk about it, but I have to tell you, this life of sin is not the way to prepare. I need grace. I need grace more than I ever needed grace before. I need forgiveness, and I need to make peace with God. It's so important to me. It's the final jump off. All my life I have believed in an afterlife. I always prayed about it, prayed for it. My mind's been dwelling on it almost constantly since last fall, especially when I was out in the islands, or when I was alone. I need to find God again and ask for forgiveness and for mercy. It's time for me to seek reconciliation."

"No." She shook her head like a child, her face clouding up. "It was awful without you. I don't want to lose you again." She turned and looked at the ceiling, pensive. There was no further talk for a long time, just simple touching, fingertips exploring, caressing, tentatively, searching. Finally Maggie turned to him.

"Andy, let's get married."

It was his turn to stare up at the ceiling, looking at the familiar shadows made by the streetlight. "You're crazy."

"No. Please. Let's get married. We can do it. Right here in Banff. We can have a life together. There is still the future." She sat up, pulling her pajama top around her. She turned and looked down at him. There was so much emotion in her eyes, her gaze was winnowing. It was humbling. When she was like that her mood froze any desire to tease.

"After you talked to Nancy today, I called her back. The kids haven't gotten your life insurance yet. You can show up and tell the world you're back. It isn't against the law to get lost in a far away place and return after everyone thinks your dead!" She was kneeling in front of him in the bed, the bottom button of her pajama blouse still undone, revealing part of her lovely chest as she spread her arms for emphasis. "Please, please, think about the future. Don't give up. You don't have to die. There is a way. You just have to take it."

He stared at her kindly. Wishing it was true, not believing.

"What's holding you back? Why won't you consider it? It's right there for the taking!"

"There was an obituary. There was a memorial service. They've all grieved for me."

"They know you're alive now. Everybody knows by now. They know you're up here with me. They all know I'm involved. Walk back in Andy! Choose life!"

"There's no way Maggie. They think I killed Albrecht. It's gone wrong. It's not like the last time. One of their people has been killed. This time is different. Powell's killing Albrecht has queered the deal. Albrecht was a vindictive guy. My guess is the new administration is the same way. They would never let me walk now. They'll never let me go. I just want to die before they get to me. It's my only hope now and I'm tired."

"I know people in Washington who could help. I know a lot of people who would help you. Tom Eagleton's been a friend for years. He would make inquiries about you. They would listen if he asked. He would do it for me. I know he would. All I have to do is ask. I would even call Bill Clinton if you wanted. I would do it for you. I would do anything for you!"

"It'll never work, Maggie. Nobody's going to believe my story. Even if they did, I have committed a crime with international consequences. I've attempted murder. They think I'm an assassin."

"No. There's been no crime, no story, nobody even knows but those men that were there and the ones that put you up to it. Let me try. Please."

He shook his head. "It's hopeless. I'm an international crazy. They're probably looking for me all over the place right now. I'm probably putting you in danger. Think about that," he nodded emphatically. "I may have put you in danger just by associating with you."

"Andy, please. You're trying to scare me and you're succeeding."

He sat up quickly. "I don't want you to be afraid. I shouldn't have said that. With these people it's not about revenge. They do one guy at a time. They're after me, not my family or my girlfriend."

"I'm not your girlfriend."

"It's the way you would appear to them."

"Let's get back to your blessed soul and solve that problem first. Then we will solve your health problem. I have some good news for you there, by the way." Bakewell looked curious "It's about your liver. They are doing liver transplants now. They take a piece of another person's liver and replace yours and it actually begins to grow. Eventually it's just like another liver again."

"Who told you that?"

"I got it off the internet. It's all very experimental, but they are doing it." She looked self satisfied, added, "I called someone who knew someone who had had the procedure."

"Someone who knew someone," he almost teased, but she was so serious, so concerned. He spoke to the ceiling again. "It seems so farfetched." Bakewell was pensive. *Liver transplants? Why didn't Neville tell me? Maybe because you haven't been to his office since last year?*

Maggie shook him out of his reverie. "Andy?" He looked to her again. She was beginning to look like his savior. Each time he bottomed out she seemed to bring him back to life again. "Please, marry me."

"Maggie..."

"Please. Do you want me to get down and beg? I will do it."

"No. I don't want you to do that. My time's up; I don't think I have much longer. By the time they get the transplant thing perfected, I'll be long gone. Just let me walk out of here."

"No, no," she pleaded. "Why are you like this? Do you want to die?"

"No."

"Then listen to me. I can save you; I know I can. You can't leave me again. But if you insist on dying, at least let me keep you and have you until then. Please."

"I don't want to hurt you anymore. You're a beautiful girl. You're a beautiful person." He smiled, eyes tender, shook his head, wanting to comfort her. He had promised himself he would never hurt her again, but their sex life was a total barricade to his spiritual life. He hadn't been to Mass since he left the monastery. He searched for words, resorted to humor. "Where did you come from anyway? Are you sure you're Maggie Leary?"

"Let me help you! Please."

"The only thing you can do for me is let me go. I have to go to confession and make my peace."

"With who?"

"With God. You know that."

"God doesn't care if we are here together, Andy."

"Remember your Catechism."

"Listen to me. *We can get married.* If God wants us to live in the state of grace, and I believe in that just as much as you do, as any old fashioned Catholic does, then he wants us to get married. Marry me." She jumped up from the bed. "Here, I'll get down on my knees and propose to you!"

He grabbed her arms, pulling her back to him and held her tightly so she couldn't move.

"Marry me you arrogant fuck."

"Oh man! And where did that word come from?" He groaned, rolled his head back and forth, pretending to suffer, looked at the ceiling. "What have I gotten you into?"

When he let her go, she sat up, reached down and pulled at his shoulders. She couldn't lift him so she pushed him down into the bed several times, trying to shake him, but he was too heavy. "Come on. What do you have to lose? Marry me."

"You called me arrogant."

"Yes, and I'll do it again," she cried happily. "Come down off it and get a life. Stop being an arrogant prick. How many times do I have to ask you?"

"Listen to the words you use!" He said, trying to change the subject, not sure he really wanted to.

"You deserved it. You are behaving like a contemptible, selfish, arrogant jerk. *'Oh, Maggie, I'm sick. I'm going to die.'* Who isn't? I may die before you. Get off it and marry me, and make me happy, and do something that isn't selfish before you go!"

"Do you know how many times you've called me arrogant and selfish? Do you know how many times a day I accuse myself of the same thing?"

"I don't care."

"Do you know what I put myself through every single day? You know how to make me hurt, girl."

"Tough. Get over it."

"It hurts."

"Not as much as you hurt me. Do you know how much the thought of having you and losing you hurts me? You can't hurt me again, Andy. You just can't." She pouted and beat gently on his chest. "You can't hurt me anymore, Bakewell. I'm sorry I walked out on you. It was the dumbest thing I ever did. It ruined my life and made yours one of blissful happiness. I'm the reason you had a wonderful family, with a wonderful wife, with great kids, and beautiful grand babies and friends and everything, and…oh, I don't know what I'm saying...I ended up giving up everything that really mattered when I gave you up."

He stared up into the sad, pouting face she made and smiled. "I never thought of it in that way."

"Think about it. Without me you would never have had what you had. I could have reeled you in and kept you for myself."

"There *was* an upside to getting dumped by a beautiful, sexy bitch, wasn't there?"

"Andy Bakewell, please marry me. Show me some gratitude for what I did for you."

"What you did for me?"

"Yes. Please marry me… within the week."

"Week?"

"Yes."

"Where?"

"Right here in Banff, at St. Mary's. And do it right away! Tomorrow!"

Could they really get married? Was there enough time? Was it fair, nurse to a dying man then a widow? He was quiet for a while and so was she. Finally he said, "Tom Eagleton?"

"Tom Eagleton."

"Isn't he a Democrat?"

"He was a great American. He is a wonderful man. He has been a true friend to me. Don't make me apologize for my friends."

"I don't know…a democrat?"

"You're being contemptible again. And you're being so arrogant. Arrogant, arrogant, arrogant…" She stopped talking and began to mouth the word, coming over him looking down at him below her in the bed.

"Don't call me arrogant…" He put his hands up in self-defense. He was beginning to believe in her, wanted to believe in her, wanted to have an option. "Would he really talk to you?"

"Of course he would. He would do anything to help a friend. He's helped lots of people."

He frowned. "What the hell, ask him if you want."

She got up and went into the other room and came back with her big traveling bag. She flopped it down on the bed and got her leather bound book, full of notes, dates, names and addresses. Maggie was forever making notes. She was very organized. She quickly found what she was looking for and picked up the phone. It took a minute.

"Tom? It's Maggie. I am *so sorry* to call you at this hour, but I need to talk to you urgently. I have a huge favor to ask, and I need you to say yes before you even hear it." She waited and listened to the senator at the other end. "Thank you, Tom, *thank you so much.* I knew you would help me and believe me *it is important*. It will take some time to explain. We might even need a conference line." She listened again. Then she said, "First thing in the morning. And please, bring that fellow who's involved in international situations in your firm. You're not going to believe the story you will hear." She talked with him for several more minutes, asked about his health and his family's. "Tell Barb I said hello, and bless you Tom." She hung up the phone and dived back on top of him.

"He said he would try. I knew he would. I'm going to save you. I'm going to make you go back and get a liver and love me for the rest of your life." She was trying to shake him, pulling the cloth of his tee shirt, almost tearing it, overjoyed. Bakewell was beginning to feel some hope too.

St. Marys

Maggie took him to St. Mary's on Tuesday, right after the daily mass, introduced him to Fr. Vincent. They spoke for some time about Banff and their relationship and the priest's vocation. He was from Calgary and had spent most of his life in the rural parishes of Alberta. He'd known Maggie for over a decade, told Bakewell she had been generous many times, helped the parish through periods of genuine need. Maggie waved him off and got quickly to the point, explaining they were both widowed, had known each other "forever", had a "fervent desire" to marry as soon as possible. The priest was cordial, interested and sympathetic to their need. He was enthusiastic for Maggie, but dubious about the timing.

Bakewell left them and wandered about the small church. He could hear the sound of Maggie's voice but not her words echoing across the vaulted building. He knew she would persist, and he suspected she would use his illness as an excuse to put them on the fast track. He didn't want to hear her plead. He knew how effective she could be when she was determined and he wanted to give her privacy while she was about it. When he reached the front door, he heard them lower their voices and he was sure she was giving Fr. Vincent the "Only got a short time to live" part. He was glad he'd walked away; he was still getting used to the idea she wanted to marry him.

Afterward they walked uptown. On the way, she stopped and made him follow her into a store, insisted on buying him a down vest. He put it on, mumbling about being a "kept man," but enjoyed the additional warmth. It was better than the thin plastic jacket he had worn when they were in Fairhope.

"My jacket is full of the scent of you. I'm going to have it framed and hung; it brings back such memories."

"You'll get used to this one. It's warmer. We'll fill it with memories, and I'll make sure it is scented for you," she said. She patted him on the chest seductively, leaned in and kissed his cheek. She was always a wonderful mixture of scents. Sometimes the scent of her was like an explosion in his brain. They walked up Banff Avenue together, weaving through tourists filling the sidewalks.

"So what can Father do for us? Did you tell him you were pregnant; it was an emergency?" Maggie only smiled, looked satisfied as she held his arm. "Can he put us on the fast track?"

"He's going to call the bishop, see what he can do."

"Does he know we're living in sin?"

"He didn't ask."

"Weren't you embarrassed to talk to him about marriage with me standing right there and him knowing we were shacked up?" Maggie laughed derisively. "Well?"

"Oh Andy, nobody shacks up anymore."

"What do they call it then?"

"Living together, stupid, what do you think?"

"I think it's a phony way of saying shacking-up."

"You need to read more tabloids. They're right there at the check out counter. Everybody's doing it, nowadays."

"If everybody was murdering everybody would it become socially acceptable? Does the sheer volume of sin make it acceptable?"

"It's only ten-thirty, but if you don't shut up you're going to drive me to drink."

"I'm going to marry a woman who's bought into the contemporary morality. What will my children think?"

Maggie stopped short, looked at him wide-eyed, shocked. "What are your children going to think? We haven't even discussed it with them, asked them, or invited them for that matter. They will think I'm a horrid woman."

It was his turn to be amused. They were stopped on the sidewalk, forcing people to give way. "Let's send them an email and tell them to gather together at somebody's house, and we'll call them when they are all together and tell them you're forcing their old man to make an honest woman out of you."

Maggie didn't look too confident; the new proposition was unsettling. She was concerned about appearances, more so about the proper protocol. She said as much.

"Let's see now. You're worried about protocol and not about them knowing you're shacking up with their old man?"

"Oh do shut up and try to focus on the right things."

Bakewell hooted, people turned to look; he took her arm again and pulled her along. "Come on, let's send an email. I am going to have some explaining to do, I'll tell you that. I'm glad they aren't going through the mating rites any longer. I am going to look like one hell of a phony."

"I'm more worried about how I look right now, about what they will think of the idea of having me marry their father. I hope there won't be an objection."

Epiphany

It was the week after the night Maggie called Eagleton. She had been on the phone for a long time, extracting promises from what sounded like a variety of professional people who were now apparently familiar with his situation. When Maggie finally got off the phone, Sybil showed up and insisted they go for another walk. They ended up at boutique where the women had first discovered the wonderful quiviuk wool.

Sybil took Bakewell's arm and led him outside, leaving Maggie at the boutique, where she was being fitted for a special outfit made of the fine musk ox wool she and Sybil had been excessing about, using words only women were allowed to use. Maggie wouldn't say what the new outfit was for, and Bakewell hadn't asked. She had a fantastic wardrobe as it was; he doubted she would ever wear all the clothes in her closet, especially not in his lifetime. He and Sybil walked up Banff Avenue toward the river together. Sybil appeared irritated at Bakewell's indifference to the surprise that awaited when the new outfit was ready.

When they got to the park she indicated they cross the street with a nod of her head. He took her arm and they crossed. They stopped at one of the large picnic tables in the park to rest. Sybil had taken Maggie's cue, rested him every few blocks, whether he wanted to stop or not. Bakewell sat on the top of the table, and Sybil took a seat on the large precast bench. There were the usual gang of tourists gawking and milling about, but the only wildlife on display were a few squirrels, a jay, one curious camprobber and the daily convocation of ravens who amused and irritated with their aggressive antics.

"You've many kids, Andy? I think you said three?"

"Three."

"They are all married off now, on their own?"

"Two married, one a bachelor. Not quite confirmed."

"Give him time. He's probably searching for himself."

"I guess. He might be searching for something else, but let's not go there."

"Sex?"

Bakewell shrugged. He didn't want to discuss his son's sex life. He didn't want to think about his son's sex life. Twenty years before he and Katherine had prayed the boy might have a vocation to the priesthood. Now it was not likely.

"He would be the middle child?"

"No, he's the youngest."

Sybil raised her head and furled her brow. "Sometimes the youngest is the most trouble."

"He's no trouble. Very sure of himself actually. He's a good kid. They're all great kids."

"Maggie was the youngest, you know."

"I remember."

"You knew her when she was very young?"

"I did. I've known her since she was a teen."

"Teen? Oh, of course, a teenager. Yes, she told me. She said you knew her in the biblical sense.'

"God," Bakewell put his hand to his forehead, looked under his palm to the ground. "This stuff never does end, does it?" His voice exasperated.

"You're sorry you made love to her?"

"Yes...No…Maybe. Yes, yes I'm sure."

"Sure you're sorry?"

"I guess. I don't know Sybil. I have a daughter. She was nineteen once. I worried about her. I still worry."

Sybil studied him, her head held very high, raising her brow, looked him over carefully, nodded. "It's good to see a man with remorse. You're a pleasant exception to the norm, you know."

Bakewell said, "I guess" again, not really sure what to say, added, "Is there a norm?"

"What was she like at nineteen?"

"Beautiful."

"She's always been a beautiful person."

"Not a beautiful person, but beautiful. Full of self-confidence. She was 'a beaut.'"

"A beaut?"

"Amazing, full of life, joy, daring, ready to take a plunge. She was a piece of work. The boys were all crazy about her."

"And you were the lucky one?"

"Go figure. She could have had anybody." He shook his head. It still made him wonder, even now. He admitted as much; it had never been a secret. He never deluded himself about Maggie Leary, not even now.

"Well, she hasn't had much joy in her life."

"She's fooled a lot of people then."

"Really."

"She's been the envy of too many…the envy of a hell of a lot of beleaguered women in my lifetime. I'm sure they would trade places with her in a minute."

"I hate to hear that. She's been unhappy for a so long. Her life has been such a huge disappointment." Sybil opened her bag and took a cigarette from a paper box. Bakewell didn't recognize the brand. She lit the cigarette and blew smoke over her shoulder. "I hate to think she has been envied. It implies she's held in contempt. No one who knows her the way I do would want anyone to dislike her. It bothers me that she might be held in low regard by other women," she added, "Jealous women."

"I didn't know she was unhappy."

"Wake up dear boy."

"She's had quite a life. Always been in the fast lane as long as I've known her…or known of her," he added.

"You knew her family?"

He nodded. The ravens were going at it in the trees above them, making their scratchy-clacky sound. Fully fed, they had taken their place high up in the conifers, noisily talking back and forth, trading places every few minutes, never satisfied. They did it every afternoon.

"What were they like, her parents; Maggie's parents?"

"Her parents were divorced. Her father was successful, in business anyway. They had money. I only met him a few times."

"Her brothers?"

"I didn't know them to talk to, only on sight."

"You didn't like them?"

"No." A magpie landed next to the heavy picnic table looking for crumbs. The sun disappeared again above the clouds, and it was cooler. It would warm quickly when the sun appeared again. They both wore down vests.

"They were about my age, but they lived in a different world, in the county club circle. St. Louis had a lot of old, family type clubs; it wasn't like today. People built their lives around the clubs if they could afford one. They spent their time at the pool or the tennis courts during the summers. I never saw them. I was a dirt lot kid with an oily baseball glove. If I went swimming, it was in a river or a creek, not a swimming pool, certainly not at a club." Bakewell laughed. "I've got more time free falling with a parachute than in a country club."

"Tell me about her mother."

"She was legendary."

"In what way?"

"In the extreme way. She was always off on a flight of fancy somewhere, only she only had one wing."

"Oh my."

"Yes, she tended to crash a lot," Bakewell said, finishing the metaphor, "Sometimes in public. She was an embarrassment. I think she was too much of a cross for Maggie, but that's hard to tell. Maggie never seemed to let much bother her. She wasn't a sufferer, you know. She was too busy dazzling. She dazzled us all."

"I wondered. She doesn't talk about her much. Hasn't over the years. You know, I've known Maggie for twenty years."

"I didn't know that."

"I met her here in Banff way back, after she bought her flat. She came here often. Always alone, never brought a beau. I think her world had started to crumble by then." Bakewell shook his head. He had no words for Sybil. She continued. "I think not being able to have children just about ruined her. She wanted desperately to be a mum. I think she wanted to raise a child the right way, maybe to make up for her own childhood. Without that opportunity she lost her chance at redemption. I think it must have meant everything to her."

"I didn't know her then; I lost track of her. I had my own troubles," he said lamely. He didn't know what he was supposed to say. Finally he said, "Well she has certainly lived a life a lot of women would have traded for…"

"Don't say that Andy. Please. Show her some compassion."

"I'm not trying to be insensitive, Sybil."

"Good. She's had too much pain. Her husband wouldn't consider adopting. I think that was the final blow. She's never been dependent. No drugs or booze. Never even seen her daffy with drink. She's had nothing to waste herself on."

"She drinks me under the table."

"That's different. She can hold her own, but she's never been one to get smashed or lock herself up like some do. She's actually quite strong."

"You're telling me."

"Don't be caustic, dear. She's also quite vulnerable. I've watched her for years and I've watched for the signs. She keeps to herself, shares very little. Walks for miles. I don't mean she's a hiker. She wouldn't spend a night up on one of these ghastly mountains; she's not a grubby packer, you know."

Bakewell couldn't help laughing at Sybil's unintentional wit. He couldn't see Maggie packing up in the mountains either.

"But she walks everywhere and she talks to everyone. I think it's how she holds on really, the talking. She talks to everyone she meets, and she's adopted every young priest the Catholics have sent up here.

"I didn't know she practiced her faith," he confessed.

"My God! She spends hours walking them, wearing them down. She takes these younger ones to dinner, always up to the Springs or some wonderfully upscale place. When she was younger it was the older fellows, now it's the young ones. Never saw her with one her own age though. I've learned more about your damned faith over dinners and desserts than your little ones get from their catechisms. Half the time we dine out we've a holy man with us."

Bakewell was beginning to understand Fr. Vincent's willingness to put them on the fast track. Sybil leaned in and put her hands over Bakewell's, taking them in hers. "Andy love, please don't hurt her. She adores you. She talks of nothing else. She's gone absolutely daft for you, for your family. I know more about your children and your grandchildren than I care to, but I confess she makes them sound lovely."

"You asked me how many kids I had five minutes ago…"

"I lied. She's described them in detail. I know too much about them. I think they took her in awhile back, while you were off somewhere."

Bakewell smiled. He could see her with Nancy and Karen. Knew they would have taken her in. Maggie had told him so. He had been worried, under pressure then, hadn't paid enough attention to her description of his memorial service and what happened afterwards, was too worried about what was in front of them. Now he could visualize it, all of them getting together after his funeral, holding onto one another, looking for consolation. There were tears in Sybil's eyes. She squeezed his hands tightly.

"I know there's something up with you. You've been bad. You're a bad boy somehow, but you are a good man too. I can feel it." She squeezed his hands tighter. "Please Andy, return her love and give yourself to her. Do this one thing that will give her happiness at last. Please give her some happiness before it's all done. Don't hurt her. Please." She let go of his hands, but kept looking into his eyes, a pleading look that was not like her.

"I don't want to hurt anyone. I just want to wind down peacefully. I want to do the right thing by… I want to do the right thing for everybody."

"For Maggie, not for everybody. For Maggie." The tears were coming now. Sybil was about to break. "She is so vulnerable now. She isn't strong. Don't do anything to hurt her. I'm begging you dear man."

Bakewell spotted Maggie at the corner, nodded in her direction. Sybil turned, wiping her eyes, as they watched her approach. Maggie's countenance had given way to joy, her eyes, her smile, the way she walked, the sound of her voice calling to them. She was an expression of happiness as she came toward them.

"Is that what you're looking for?" Bakewell asked Sybil.

Sybil turned away, trying to compose herself, losing it all over again. She got up, patted his arm. "I'm a complete havoc; tell her I'm off and make it convincing. I don't want to see her when I'm like this."

Bakewell stood also, started to put his arm around her, she pushed away.

"I hope you deserve her, dear boy." She went off across the park toward the bookstore.

When Maggie got closer she called after Sybil, who only raised her arm in recognition.

"Have you done something to upset her?" Maggie's face had changed to concern for her friend.

"No, I think maybe you have," Bakewell said. He watched Sybil's retreating figure. "I think maybe your happiness has brought a contagion that's more than she can bear."

Maggie looked confused as she took Bakewell's arm. They made the requisite ambit around the park slowly, arm in arm. It was a spectacular day in May in Banff.

Intimacies

Maggie Leary had always been a trophy: a trophy date, a trophy affair and a trophy wife, just as she had described herself to him on that long, unpleasant drive into Banff. She fulfilled her physical responsibility to her husband, allowing him his pleasure, much as she had done with Bakewell a lifetime before, when sex had been a curiosity, an exciting and dangerous sidebar to her vaunted and envied social life. She had delighted in the stimulating newness of it, despite the precarious, defenseless position involved. She often worried as she gave herself up, feeling susceptible, often helpless, especially when she was unable to turn the table and hand off the vulnerability thing, or when he managed to set her off and make her really want him. Bakewell had been surprisingly competent, had managed her well in her youth. He'd been ardent, he'd been capable, but most of all he'd been honest. His honest passion for her had caught her off guard, convinced her to let go. He had brought her to fulfillment many times.

Maggie never quite got over feeling exposed during sex, was never able to completely trust her mate, not even Joe Walker. When the act was over, she never lost the opportunity to turn the table on the slathering would be wooer in her bed. Now she was willing and receptive. Before she thought she fulfilled *their* expectations, sometimes even found some of the fulfillment she needed to dilute the loneliness and take the sting out of the empty and missing emotional life that escorted her through her own.

It worked well enough. Men loved to possess her, if only briefly. She was a "stunning piece of ass" for any suitor looking for that sort of thing, no matter how short lived. And that was the problem. The result of a long and dissatisfying love life was passivity. Maggie was submissively inactive in the art of love. The lovemaking she resumed with Bakewell began enthusiastically, but with the same passivity. She chose to be appreciated and stimulated; in return she gave herself up to the man above her. But with Bakewell it had always been different; it started again that first night in Point Clear. She had seldom been satisfied, orgasms were unique and decades apart. Bakewell was determined to make her happy in bed, wanted to satisfy her physically and fulfill her emotionally when their sex life resumed. He wasn't used to sex without gratification for both partners. It had been a way of life with Katherine. He had seldom known a need for simple gratification on his own. He most always refused to copulate with Katherine and she with him any other way. Maggie wasn't going to be an exception.

She wanted him desperately, even surprised him with a series of shockingly impassioned nights where she begged him to take her ruthlessly. Bakewell understood the psychology and had little desire to worry her body or her fragile psyche and go where he and his wife had been. As a result he was not overly creative, often tangential, during their lovemaking. It was about making her happy and enjoying her in the process. It was simple, straightforward, passionate sex, and it was good.

After the wedding, her love for him was so complete, so devoted, so unrestrained and so honest; he began to feel he was cheating her. She loved him desperately, to the point of understanding and respecting his concern with the past. She told him constantly not to worry about what might happen in the end, even told him she would give him back to Katherine in the next life. She just wanted the last part of him. It made her too vulnerable, and he worried what her existence might be like after he was gone. In response she told him she had everything she had ever wanted and no matter what happened in the future she would change nothing, never trade "their time" no matter how much the future might hurt.

He tried not to think about it when they were separated, but it created a sad anxiety in him. He thought about her constantly just as he had dwelled on all the problems of his life. In the past, if he had a serious problem he thought of nothing else until it was resolved. Truman could decide to drop the atomic bomb, then get a good night's sleep. Bakewell could ruin a good night's sleep worrying about a $400 problem that awaited the following day.

This was a different problem, not about conflict and resolution, but about where he wanted to take their physical relationship. Before the wedding, he thought he might bring a controlled reserve to the lovemaking, keep it within bounds. But his wish to maintain his resolve, to never allow himself to get lost in another woman, to never let another woman possess him again, fell away like the talus under his feet on the hillsides they hiked almost daily above the Bow.

Once he made the decision to love her, to fall in love with her again, his desire to have her physically took a turn he hadn't expected.

***

Maggie sat back against the headboard, arm across her forehead, dazed, amazed, satiated, sighing; she spoke tentatively, "I've never done that before."

"I know," he said, not wanting to make contact with her sensitive blue eyes. Maggie trained her gaze to the side of his face, asked. "What got us started?"

"I think its called lust."

"I've never wanted to do it before." She looked away, across the moonlit room.

"I believe you."

"I've read about it of course. It's in all the books."

He nodded without answering. She could intuit his nod, had learned to feel it when she wasn't looking at him. They were silent a moment longer.

He wanted to say more, had trouble getting started. "I shouldn't have done it. I feel I've forced you."

"Yes, maybe." She spoke to the space across the bedroom. They could just make out the lacey curtains billowing in the night air. It had been very warm all day.

"I'm sorry."

She touched his cheek with the back of her fingers, gently rubbing his rough jaw. Then she rolled to him, "I'm such a fraud," she sighed with disgust. She put her arm back across her chest, her nipples still enlarged. "I liked it."

He put his head back against the headboard next to hers, looking straight ahead.

"Did you like it?"

"Of course, it was my idea."

"Was I responsive enough for you?"

"Let's not talk about it."

"Answer me."

"Yes."

"I mean, I wasn't quite sure what I was to do."

"I shouldn't have made you."

"I'm glad you did. It's just that I didn't know quite what to do."

"Don't talk about it."

"Why?" She peered at him curiously.

"It makes me feel…it fills me with guilt I guess."

"Please don't say that. I'm prepared to share you most always, just not now. Please."

"It's not what I meant. Not about Katherine, if that's what you're thinking."

"Then what?"

"It makes me feel…opportunistic."

She rolled against him, putting her hand on his shoulder. "It's supposed to be natural, at least according to the books I've read."

"A man should always feel guilt when it's over. He's taking advantage. I always felt guilty, like I was imposing."

"I don't want to know about your previous love life, your sex life with Katherine, or any of your bimbos before her." She was silent for a minute, added, "I have my own selfishness. I want to have this little business with you in the privacy of my own memory. I don't want to think of you that way with anyone else right now."

Bakewell had the presence to remain silent. It was a tender moment, a special time for her. He knew words would only spoil it: his words.

"I want you to hold me."

He put his arms around her, and they were quiet.

Three In The Morning

It turned cold over the weekend. Another storm front was passing through. It happened all the time up high. There were ice fields around Banff, permanent glaciers of nearly flat ice that melted little, even in August. They hauled tourists up to them in huge tracked conveyances, some with handicapped access, so people could get out and walk around. Bakewell never had any desire to do it. The Canadian Rockies were a harsh place, even in summer, with a fickle, often cruel climate that caught warm weather climbers unprepared. There were deaths in the mountains every year.

He woke at the usual time. It wasn't as bad as the old days. His fears now were about the future, the stepping off time, and what that first step would be like. He could feel his body failing. His time was coming, but there wasn't the urgency that had characterized those times before, during his business life. It was a time of reflection, a time of quiet concern that lacked the terror and the urgency of the past. He got out of bed quietly, trying not to wake Maggie, and went into the kitchen for a drink of water. They had split a bottle of wine earlier. Wine always dehydrated him and added necessity to *the waking hour*.

There was movement outside the window, a shadowy figure? It was gone quickly. A car passed outside. He watched through the window. It was the RCMP, a local police vehicle. After it passed, Bakewell saw the shadowy figure move again, coming out of the darkness. It was the kid in the black clothes. He was limping. *Probably frost bite.* Bakewell cringed, watched him move slowly down the street, shook his head, thanked God it wasn't somebody's kid he knew. The figure made halting progress. It discouraged Bakewell to watch him go. It was very cold outside, very warm in the kitchen. It made him shudder.

He had an idea and went quickly down the hall and got dressed and went to the closet. Maggie had bought him a nice pair of mukluks, and he slipped into them and reached up for his backpack. He pulled it down quietly and went through it quickly, checking to make sure what was inside. Then he went out into the biting cold, regretted it immediately when the first blast of icy air struck. The figure was over the rise in the street, heading west he suspected, but out of sight. Bakewell moved quickly up the street, silent in the soft shoes. He spotted the kid as he crested the hill and closed the gap without making any noise. It pleased him he could catch up to the cautious figure ahead without being detected. When he closed the gap, he reached forward and tapped the young addict on the back. He jumped and turned at the same time, lost his balance and started to fall. Bakewell caught his arm.

"Whoa, bud. Hold on now. I've got something for you."

The kid straightened up, looking frightened. He tried to back away but Bakewell held his arm. "Here. A gift for you."

Another vacant look. Bakewell tapped the rolled up bag secured to the top of the pack. "It's a sleeping bag. It's down. You open it up, and fluff it up, and get inside." He held the pack out to the young man who said nothing.

"Take it."

The kid watched him without speaking.

"Take the bag off the pack, fluff it up when you unroll it. Don't get inside it with your clothes on. Take them off first. Don't get it wet. It's no good if it gets wet." He showed him the pack and the sleeping bag again. "Go down under the bridge, out of the weather and unroll it. It will keep you warm if you take care of it, *and you don't get it wet.* You understand? Take your clothes off before you get inside. Leave them out on the ground and they will dry no matter how cold it is. The climate up here is very dry. Your clothes will dry out overnight if you put them out in the wind. Understand?"

The kid was less cowered, still not sure.

"It has saved my life many times. Go down under the bridge tonight and warm up. Tomorrow find yourself a place up in the hills where you won't be found by the police; make yourself a small campsite. Make sure you keep the bag dry. Do you understand? You have to take care of it and keep it dry or it's no good."

The kid nodded without speaking.

"In the morning turn it inside out and let it cool. Then wrap it tight and put it inside the plastic bag and keep it dry, okay?" Another nod, a slight sign of recognition. "You better get going before the Mounties come round again."

The young man nodded one last time. Bakewell indicated he get going. He limped off past the bookstore toward the bridge. Bakewell watched him go, returned home at a fast trot. He was freezing. *You need long underwear to be out in this weather.* When he got back inside he put his coat and boots away and went back into the bedroom and tried to get in bed without waking Maggie.

"Where have you been?" she sounded sleepy, but concerned.

"I've been thinking."

"I heard the front door open. Where did you go?"

"For a walk."

"Andy, it's freezing outside, what were you doing?"

"Nothing, go back to sleep."

"I thought you were leaving me."

"Is that why you came running to the front door when I left?" he loved to tease her about her insecurities. By now his fealty was a sworn and betrothed fact.

She touched him and said, "You're cold. Why did you have to go outside?"

"I did your friend a favor."

"I'm so sleepy..." she groaned. "I don't know what you're talking about."

"Go back to sleep. We'll talk about it in the morning."

Maggie was quiet for a minute. He though she had gone back to sleep. Then she said, "What were you thinking about?"

"My wife," he said, tenderly.

"Mm," she pulled the covers over her shoulder. After a moment she turned back again, said, "Which wife?"

"Both of you."

She made another soft sound, sighing contentedly, patted his leg with her warm hand and fell back asleep. Bakewell thought for a moment. *You've burned your logbook and now your pack and bag are gone. You're about done.* He was surprised at his contentment.

Banff Transition

After the wedding, a time of joy and contentment settled in, while Maggie tried to recapture wasted years, and, to their amazement, they found they could discover the life they hadn't known.

Despite Maggie's determination, Bakewell doubted they could find much happiness in the time remaining. When it happened, neither dared put it into words, fearing their happiness would evaporate like Banff's early morning mists. Their sojourn passed in blissfully pleasant routines, filled with clean, simple appreciations. They enjoyed each other and each hour, and passed each one in an enchanted minimalism. It was a routine Bakewell had yearned for.

First wife. It brought a strange sensation. He thought of it constantly, even verbalized it once. First wife, *second husband* – the thought affected them both in a confusing, yet similar way. Maggie was his second wife; Katherine was his first wife. He used the expression only once in her presence. Maggie didn't seem to mind. Maggie loved their lifestyle, a lifestyle she had craved ever since Little Rock. She told him it was what she wanted and hoped for, once she realized the life she had was never going to be the one expected.

Maggie talked constantly about returning to St. Louis, to his children and grandchildren. She wanted his family almost as much as she wanted him, and teased him about it daily, telling him she couldn't decide which she wanted more. She also corresponded with Karen and Nancy daily via the internet. There was an equal number of phone calls. They were scheduled to return to St. Louis before month's end.

Each day was a treasure of simple tasks performed, seldom separately. Maggie said she was prepared to bathe with him just so he wouldn't be out of her sight. Bakewell laughed gratefully, said she would get tired of washing his back, but he would never tire of washing her front. Everything they did together was described by warmth, satisfaction and a near mystical acquiescence.

Mass was a part of the daily routine. It was idyllic to be reunited in the sacraments: to be in the state of grace together, in spirit literally, and in a place of stupendous beauty and immense structure, surrounded by the drama of mountains and ice fields, protected in a gentle valley, between the awesome peaks and sharp spines towering over, fearsome, spectacular near vertical walls of dark granite that contrasted with the whiteness of the snow caps and the lush green valleys.

Bakewell learned to enjoy the tourists almost as much as the pleasant residents. Even the pushy Japanese, with their militaristic aggression no longer troubled him. They looked at everything differently, him for the first time, seeing it clear and unsullied as they saw life fresh and new. They noticed things they had never noticed before – the odd way people talked without making eye contact, and the intense way they used body language. They tried not to miss anything, took turns pointing things out, bringing a fresh perspective. They did things quietly, soaking it all up, drinking it all in. It was fascinating and it was exhilarating.

At other times they ignored everything, saw only each other, always in front of the ever present, stunningly embroidered feast of colors, accents, sounds and alpine smells that were Banff.

They toured the valleys and steep mountainsides, stopping the car at fantastic pullouts, where they viewed bighorn, mule deer and elk, even a giant moose one evening, down in the wet green valley – spacing out each day with leisurely walks on the gentler trails.

They hired an alpine guide, a young woman who became a particular favorite because of her familiarity with the countryside around Banff. She gave a running commentary on the plants and animals, which Bakewell encouraged. She talked about everything they came in contact with, much of which Bakewell had discovered before she was born, but couldn't properly identify. She was a medical student from Calgary, who had studied biology and zoology extensively, before deciding to try medical school. Her name was Mary, and she had a phenomenal knowledgeable of the ecosystems of the mountaine and the sub-alpine. Her descriptions were often anecdotal, filled with little experiences about the flora and fauna. Mary could extemporize, with witty stories about tourists, regularly accusing Bakewell of such status by innuendo. Bakewell protested. They were most emphatically not tourists, he said, which made her accuse more. But she was subtle. Her stories melted his aggressive nature, which still surfaced at times, no matter how hard he tried to keep it in check. She kept him coming back for more, never tired of his endless questions.

Mary added a happy diversion that brought space and fresh air to the *passion* that was now *the Bakewells*.

"Mary, where have you been all my life," he asked. "You're the perfect hunting companion. You know the answers to all the questions I've been asking for the last thirty years: grass, trees, flowers and wildlife too. You know the country, and love and respect it without being a tree hugger." Mary soaked up the praise, like young people do when they have impressed the ones who've gone before.

"And you are a hunter too, a veritable killer. You could be a bloomin member of the NRA, to quote a former acquaintance of mine."

"Mary wasn't here thirty years ago, Andy."

"Damn shame," he'd muttered, trying to catch his breath as he brought up the rear. "Wish you could have known me in my youth, Mary. We could have had some times up on the prairie with my bird dogs." They stopped to look across the valley at the breathtaking view of Banff, and the old hotel, nestled up into the steep valley above the city.

"Mary, don't listen to him," Maggie said, hugging his arm, trying to steady him, without being obvious. "You should know this old geezer's son, though. You two were made for each other."

Bakewell had to agree, nodding out of breath. "Talk her into coming home with us and becoming my daughter-in-law. I could use one."

"You already have one, and she's quite lovely." Maggie smiled, extending a secret meaning to Mary, in the process.

"Well I want an outdoor girl this time."

On days when they were out on their own, they saw other hunters, four-legged ones, sharing the wilderness with too much humanity, not too happy about it either, trying to be surreptitious, trying to make a living in the wild. Foxes and coyotes were everywhere, even to the untrained eye. Once a good sized grizzly, lustrously brown and glistening wet from a recent creek crossing, went by at less than a hundred yards, heading downhill into a dark drainage, where he crossed a steep chasm and disappeared. They waited for him to reemerge but never caught sight of him again. Maggie persuaded her husband to leave, fearing the bear might circle around.

With the car just a few feet away and the door standing open, he came up behind her as she got in, growled and grabbed her. Maggie wheeled about, her elbow catching him painfully just below the eye. He squinted, eye tearing and tightly shut, not moving as she cried out and made over him with a stream of apologies. He knew it was his fault and tried not to make a big deal out of it, but she was horribly sorry and insisted on ministering to his swelling eye. When they were in the car, going down the mountain, she continued to apologize. Bakewell knew she felt badly and not only because of his eye. He was losing weight steadily, weighed less than 180. The last time he weighed less than 180 he wasn't old enough to vote.

His run down condition made him a target for her sympathy. It was a role he was unaccustomed to, and he didn't want to make the adjustment late in life. He thought of himself as her protector even though she babied him at every opportunity. She waited on him to the point of servitude. He didn't like the reversal, wanted to make all the effort now. It was about charity. It was a new time in his life, a time when he needed to be the one making the sacrifices, but she beat him to every opportunity. It frustrated him to the point of wanting to be upset with her, but that wasn't an option either. She had her own need, had no opportunity in her life to do little motherly acts. He understood, tried to make her understand he had a need too, but she was incorrigibly attentive.

***

There was a downside: his life had been filled with regrets. Now that it had slowed down, it gave him time to reflect, dwell on the past, and he didn't like many of the parts he remembered. He had done some good in his life, could actually remember being generous, but most of his memories were about mistakes, moments he wished he could change. He remembered so many unconscious, thoughtless times, especially with Katherine, during the early years of their marriage. And he remembered making mistakes with his children, memories that swept over him, almost brought him to his knees. Sometimes, caught off guard, he'd emit groans of remorse while they discussed something that stirred an old memory.

Maggie would inquire and, just to torture himself, maybe to expiate his guilt, he would describe an event in detail. She would respond by putting her hand on his, often with a gentle admonition, "Andy, why do you punish yourself so? You are a good person. Everyone loves you. Everyone thinks you were a good man, knows you *are* a good man."

During one of their extended conversations about memories and remorse, Maggie became too effusive in her attempt to defend him and he interrupted, said, "Maggie, remember…I shoot people." She had grown quiet then, waiting for them to be served and left alone at the table.

"Andy, how could you do that?" He raised his eyebrows, smiled softly, out of habit. "How could you shoot someone, knowing how wrong it was? How could you square it with your conscience?"

"Square it?" he chided. "I like dis words 'square it' merri," he said, rolling the r's like an islander. Merri was the island word for woman. She waited, without responding. He looked at her kind face, softer now, softer than it ever had been. It was a gentle face, full of trust, thoughtful, compassionate, tender, but questioning. She waited for his answer.

"I never thought I would have to shoot him. I took the money with a clear conscience. I felt like they owed me. I know that sounds like I'm rationalizing, and I do hate people who rationalize, but think about it. They ruined a big part of my life with their indifference for mine…"

"I don't want to talk about the money. I don't care about money. How could you shoot that man?"

"I figured I would be dead before the time ever came. I never had any intention of shooting him."

"Andy, you shot him. You told me you shot him."

"I spent a lot of time rehearsing for that day. I promised myself I wouldn't shoot unless I could call my shot. I'm pretty decent with that kind of weapon. I promised myself I wouldn't squeeze unless I was certain I could just nick him."

"Andy, you shot the man. You could have missed. You could have killed him accidentally. How could you shoot at him thinking you would miss? It's so arrogant of you to think that."

The *arrogant* word again. It made him fret visibly. Would it ever leave him alone? He mumbled it just loud enough to be heard.

"Okay. Forget arrogant. Just answer me, how could you shoot him, knowing it was a mortal sin?"

He looked down at the tablecloth then out the 2nd floor window. It was a beautiful clear day outside, and the streets were crowded below. He wiped the tablecloth with his hand.

"When I first got out there I was filled with a desire to just "go under," to make the rest of my life pass in quiet contemplation. I really thought I could be happy in a monastery. I wanted to spend the last part of my life praying for forgiveness. I don't know if I could have made it work. But when I got to Moresby and I saw all the deprivation, saw those sad people in that part of the world; I realized this man had caused misery and deprivation in his own country. People lived in misery under his regime. He was at fault for all their suffering. They lived through horrendous periods, and I had read the stories of torture and all the outrages he had inflicted on his people, even the ones that were supposed to be close to him." He paused, looked into her eyes. The look she returned needed an answer, the right answer; he steeled himself and continued.

"When I had him through the scope, I almost wished I could kill him. He was such an evil man. I think subconsciously I hoped the scope might be off just a little – maybe just enough to kill him. I don't know for sure what I was thinking, but I remember thinking *you deserve to die you son of a bitch.* I was in a position to do something thousands of people would have done in an instant. I've often thought it was lucky for him that I had been so conscientious with the practicing. Lucky for him I had nothing better to do than to go out and shoot for weeks at a time in all kinds of weather. Lucky for him it was me and not one of a thousand others whose life he had ruined. There are a lot of people in this world that would have loved it if I had hit him between the eyes."

There was another long pause. Their eyes locked once more. He saw compassion in her eyes again. He wanted to see compassion, but he wanted there to be no mistake between them either. "I'll tell you this, Maggie. It's too late for me to live any more lies. If I had killed him, I don't think I would have felt much sorrow. He deserved to die…like a dog…if any man ever did. He was a merciless brute." Bakewell looked away for a moment then returned her gaze and spoke with a boyish candor. "But I sure would have worried about his soul, because I don't think there is anyway that guy could have been in the state of grace, and I would have had to live with the knowledge that I killed him and I killed his soul too."

Secrets

They were in the master bedroom, lying together staring up at the skylight, which was covered with another snow that let just a little of the starlit sky through. Outside all sound was muffled by snow falling in the windless night. The silence was almost complete, interrupted occasionally by the crunching of passing tires. It was three o'clock in the morning again, a time to wake up and feel Maggie lying warm beside him. The hour at last had lost its sting.

"Are you awake?" She asked, breaking the reverent silence.

"No."

"Be serious. Can I tell you something?"

"This isn't going to be heavy is it?"

"Yes. Well, not heavy exactly. More like…emotional maybe?"

"Wait, let me fasten my seatbelt," he said. He took in a deep breath, pretended to buckle up and leaned back into the pillow, exaggerating the effort, like an astronaut preparing for liftoff. They both did it often, especially when one thought the other was about to crack the fragile enchantment of their now perfect, crystalline lives. "Okay…go ahead."

She giggled quietly, not wanting to break the mood, put her head on his shoulder, her soft, wonderfully fragrant hair and her warmth and her touch, filled him with a satisfaction so complete, it was almost beyond comprehending.

She put her hand on his chest and patted softly. "I want you to know how jealous I have been of you these last few years. I have been very envious of you and everything you have." She continued to pat his chest as she spoke, "I just wanted to admit that to you so you would know." She raised again and looked at him, the light soft, natural from the skylight. "I wanted to admit that to you, so there would be no secrets between us."

"Whew."

"What did you think I was going to say?" she shifted emotional gears, her voice tentative, self-conscious.

"I thought you were going to tell me you found someone else, that this whole marriage thing had been a mistake. I thought you were going to dump me again."

"Be serious," she came over the top of him, looking into his eyes, which she could barely make out in the dim light. He couldn't see hers at all. "I wanted to tell you how much I love you, and how sorry I am that we never made a life together."

"Well now," he sighed, cautious, but wanting to sound sincere. "That's covering a lot of ground." He spoke slowly, thinking about what he was saying. "I would have to reject a lot of wonderful…of wonderful things that have happened to me to say I'm sorry we didn't make a life together."

"You know that's not what I'm looking for," she said, kissing him delicately. "I just mean I wanted you to know I know I made a mistake, made the wrong choice a long time ago."

She laid her head back against his chest, and they were silent. After a long time, more checking to see if she was awake than asking, he stroked her hair, pulling it away from her eye and forehead and asked if she wanted to make love again, adding, "Now that we're legal."

"No," she pouted. "I just want you to hold me. I'm worried about you, and I don't want you to do anything that might hurt you now, now that I have you all to myself."

"I wasn't thinking of doing anything dangerous…maybe just a little selfish."

"Will you go back and get some treatment? I know you could find a transplant. One of your children would surely be the right match. I know any one of them would give you any part of their own if it would save you. They are so full of love for each other and for you. I know they would do it."

"They get it from their mother."

She was silent. He loved the way she could talk about his life and his children and Katherine without resentment. He knew she had the capacity to share him with his family and his past and his memories. He was trying to offer her some equal trade, but couldn't find a way. She had been right about getting married; he was totally in love with her now for what she was and for what she had become. He never thought there was a chance he would ever meet anyone with Katherine's ability to love and to give so much and ask for so little.

Her friend Father Vincent had pulled it off, gotten the Church through the red tape and made it happen quickly. Bakewell liked Fr. Vincent. He was a doer, an action guy, someone who could cut through the BS, get around the bureaucrats. When they first talked, Bakewell had mistaken him for a bean counter. The priest was also a fine homilist and added much to the celebration of daily Mass. They went to Mass every day.

Bakewell would do anything for Maggie now. He realized how vulnerable she had become, more than he believed possible. When Fr. Vincent had asked her to repeat her vows after him, she had spoken each word into Bakewell's eyes, her voice full of conviction and emotion that came from deep within. The sound of her voice had been so very serious neither Bakewell nor Fr. Vincent had spoken for a moment afterward, both touched by her sincerity, by the intensity of her profession.

She had held nothing back when she professed her love for him at their wedding. She had unburdened herself of everything, let it all go, and he realized in doing so, she had obtained a purity of spirit he couldn't match. Her devotion to him had given her a freedom she had never known. If exposure and helplessness was the price she had to pay, she intended to pay it, mortgage everything to pay it. She had brought every emotion to the table, hadn't left anything behind. She told him how completely happy she was every day, how she only wanted to share in his life for whatever forever was theirs. She said it so often, with such complete candor, such conviction, it was humbling and he felt overmatched. Overwhelming him had become her passion.

Once long ago their relationship had been a game for her. Now it was for real. He couldn't get enough of her, even though he couldn't match her ardor. In a sense their love had become a competition, only this time, like the last time, she had already won before he could get started. It was game, set, and match before he had an opportunity to make a first serve and, just as it had been with Katherine, Bakewell felt overmatched and outclassed. He felt like he was looking at a surreal scoreboard of tenderness, and the score was 6-love, 6-love all the way across the board.

Later that Friday evening after the wedding, over a candlelit dinner at the Tuscany, Maggie told him she had only one wish for the future, for him to go home and get well. They talked more of small liver transplants, and she explained what she understood of putting a piece of someone else's liver inside a sick person. How the new transplants were growing normally. Bakewell didn't believe it, but he wasn't about to argue with her over anything, especially something that had to do with their happiness and his longevity.

He told her that night he would go back to St. Louis in a voice he didn't recognize, filled with so much emotion it caught in his throat. He couldn't make his upper lip move properly to form the words. He struggled to speak. He said he wanted to live very much, that he had found something he wanted to live for very much. He knew he had always had a great deal to live for, but living was just becoming a reality again.

They fell asleep that night with happy thoughts for the future, and, once more she won, by quickly falling into a quiet sleep before him, her breathing, graceful and rhythmic as her fingers raised and tapped his chest occasionally in a reflexive, contented and sometimes metrical cadence. He stared up at the skylight and felt her breath on his chest, deep and contented and wondered how he could possibly have been given two women so extraordinary in one lifetime. It was the same way they fell asleep each night, always with happy thoughts about the future. He promised himself he would never complain about anything ever again, since he had been given a second chance, a second tremendous gift. He'd come a long way from the South Pacific.

***

In the morning he sat in the alcove kitchen. Breakfast was finished, and Maggie stood at the sink putting things in a strainer after he insisted on washing them. He told her often if he was to be a "kept man" he was going to earn his keep. She refused to acknowledge his little sarcasms about being dependent, but loved the idea of taking care of him. Bakewell was at the table with a cup of coffee.

"I think I might want to share something with you Maggie. Something I've never shared with anyone before."

"Oh my God, Andy," she gasped. "I'm not sure I want you to," she put her hand to her throat. "You're not going to tell me another *ghastly something,* are you?"

"No. This is pretty mild really. I just thought I would share something with you because you have been so honest with me." He looked at her tenderly, the lines around his eyes cracking. (Maggie told him she had fallen in love with his kind, smiling eyes, long before she knew him, how she had often thought of them through the years, especially during the loneliest times). The soft creases aging them now, accentuated them.

"I don't know if I can handle any sharing. You're so full of... surprises...except your surprises are the kind that make me stop breathing."

"It's not important. I don't want to upset you."

She sat down at the table in front of him. "I'm kind of fragile and feeling more than a little vulnerable after some of your recent revelations." Her voice quavered. She put her hand to her throat again and waited.

"No. It's nothing like that. I don't really have to share it with anybody. I've managed to live with it most of my adult life. We can forget it if you like."

"No. Come on," she indicated, with a backward lean. "Let me hear it." She looked uncertain, tentative, continued clutching her gown to her throat.

"Nancy's not my daughter, Maggie."

She looked at him with relieved interest, her eyes widening, her face flushed with embarrassment. She didn't say anything.

"I mean...she is my daughter. She's my daughter, all right. I wouldn't trade her for anything. I've been her dad all her life, and she's priceless to me. But I'm not her biological father."

"I don't understand, Andy."

"No. It's not easy to understand."

He got up and walked over to the counter and poured more coffee in his cup, added some to hers when she offered it. "It happened in the early years obviously. Katherine and I had one of those fights young people have. I couldn't tell you what it was about, so you can imagine how unimportant it was, but it put a huge strain on our relationship." He looked almost apologetically at her. "You know, the kind you have when you're going through that early time in a marriage. The first few years are a time of adjusting. Nothing's easy then. We would have these meaningless arguments.

It was my fault. I was on a fast track, making money and growing a company, thought it was what my family needed. I think she felt taken for granted."

Maggie watched him expectantly.

"Maybe it was just the timing. I don't know. Anyway, we stopped speaking, only this time it lasted for weeks. I was very involved in my job and not paying nearly enough attention to what was going on at home. We stopped having sex too. Then late in the summer she came to me one evening. We were down at the Lake with friends, at a very romantic place we had all gone together and rented as a group. She hardly ever drank back then, but this one night she got tipsy and started to put the make on me, like you girls do when you want to get your way. I was still feeling churlish about the whole thing, but I was dying to have sex with her again, and it didn't take more than a "come on" look to get us back in bed together. Two weeks later she told me we were going to have another baby."

"How could you know?"

"I could do the math. She was already pregnant when we made love that night. We hadn't had sex for weeks before and counting backwards put conception weeks before we got back together."

"I don't believe it."

Bakewell shrugged. It didn't make any difference if she believed it. He had told her something he hadn't ever told anyone else. He was sharing an intimacy. He wanted to share it with her. He knew he would never share it with anyone again. He hadn't told anyone in over a quarter of a century. He hadn't ever told anyone. He stopped talking and sat down and started to read the Canadian paper. Maggie left the room and came back a little later, dressed for the day. She had been in an elegant dressing gown before. She sat down in front of him at the table and took his hands in hers.

"Andy, why did you tell me about Nancy?" She was beaming in the newly found confidence he had shared with her.

"It just seemed appropriate after last night; I thought you should know." He hesitated a moment before adding, "I have to deal with this issue if a liver donor is involved."

She watched his face closely, hers filled with emotion, with a tender trusting love that radiated from her eyes, from her whole countenance. It made him uncomfortable. When she finally spoke, she asked, "What did you do? What did Katherine say when you confronted her?"

"I never confronted her."

"Why not? It's not like it wasn't a big deal."

"It wasn't a big deal." He looked directly into her eyes when he spoke then, averting them, back to the paper, unable to keep up the intensity of the moment.

Maggie continued to watch him. When he didn't respond she said,

"Amazing." She squeezed his hands with both of hers, waiting for more.

"I knew…and I think Katherine knew I knew, but we never discussed it," he said, looking back into her eyes. "I didn't want anyone else to know. I sure wasn't going to walk out on her and Andy and a new baby. I just went along."

She gasped in disbelief. He wasn't sure if it was a good thing or bad, added quickly. "She was deliriously happy with a little girl. So was I. We were a family again. Our sex life picked up a lot after she announced she was pregnant. I know she felt guilty. We just went on." He shrugged.

Maggie put her hands together and rested her chin on them and smiled. "You are amazing. There's a new chapter every time I think I've finally heard the last."

"Don't get me wrong. I worried that the real father would show up. I hoped he wouldn't. I don't think I could have put up with that. Some arrogant jerk telling me he had sex with my wife. But it never happened and we just went on."

Maggie's eyes filled with tears. They spilled over down her cheeks. She wiped her face with both hands, sniffed once.

"Don't give me more credit than those tears indicate. I loved Nancy as much as I could love any child of my own. She was a perfect little girl, lovely to raise, wonderful to observe over the years. I will admit I looked for resemblances in her that might favor one of *my friends*. I looked for a long time. But there was never anything to see except this wonderful little girl, growing up in front of us, making us proud, charming us with her personality. Nancy always had a presence. I never felt like anything other than her father all my life."

"Didn't you wonder?"

"Maybe, maybe a little. Maybe a lot at different times, but you can lose your mind doing that. I never really persisted with it." He shrugged. again.

They sat there in the kitchen for a few minutes, Bakewell already dressed. Maggie left, went and got her coat and came back with his. She handed it to him, said it was eight degrees outside. They kept the temperature in Celsius, which Banff radio announced several times each hour.

"I'm calling the doctor. We're going to get you a liver. I'm not letting you die on me now. You're too good to be true Andy Bakewell."

With tears in her eyes she straightened his collar. She window shopped while they walked, usually ended up buying something for someone in the family, their family now. Walking was a ritual, Maggie hugging his arm closely, making him stop in a coffee shop, deli, anyplace where she could make him sit down. The walks were as important to him as they were to her. They believed the crisp mountain air was good for them both.

The Old Hotel

You must remember this, a kiss is still a kiss, a sigh is just a sigh...

They were in the Bistro, a second floor restaurant of the old Springs Hotel, over a small table with a heavy, starched tablecloth, finishing a dinner of pasta and delicately thin veal, celebrating. It was the 3rd anniversary of their wedding three Fridays before. “One more week of perfect happiness,” she’d said, raising her glass. Maggie enjoyed a cognac while Bakewell swirled the last of his red wine in a huge wine glass. It was after ten; the sun had finally gone down minutes before. In the corner a large man spoke and sang his way through an old classic in a deep baritone, an ancient piano, glittering with polish, kept him company.

And when two lovers woo, they still say, “I love you,” on that you can rely...

Earlier they’d walked up to the ancient, castle-like buildings, stopping first at the bookstore across from the park to avoid a shower. They walked everywhere so when it rained, and it rained almost every day, they would put in somewhere and wait for the weather to clear, watching the huge dark clouds pass over the valley, obscuring the jagged peaks and ridges, moving on like giant sailing vessels from another century on an endless broad reach. The bookstore had become a favored retreat a few blocks from Maggie’s home. After crossing the bridge they walked up into the forested foothills past the tennis courts, taking advantage of the perfect spring evening, keeping a safe distance from several elk grazing on the lush grass near the courts in the last hours of sunlight.

Moonlight and love songs never out of date, hearts full of passion, jealousy and hate...

“I do love this song so,” Maggie said, stroking his hand. “Such lovely, wonderful words. Hoagie Carmichael?”

Bakewell shrugged and tilted his head. “I don’t think so.” Maggie had a musical background, played the piano once. Bakewell’s background was baseball, roughhouse and heavy equipment. The damage to his hands would have prevented him from ever attempting the piano, but he loved the old songs, loved the classy lyrics just as much. They both had good taste in music, despite his shortcomings.

It’s still the same old story, a fight for love and glory, a case of do or die...

“I think Hoagie might have sang it.” He said finally.

"Yes, I think you're right. I don't think he wrote it."

The world will always welcome lovers, as time goes by.

Maggie continued to stroke the back of his hand with her fingertips. There was a tinkling of silverware and china in the background. "How are you Andy, my darling?" The waiter had cleared the last of their dishes. She was radiant; a rapture had set in after the wedding, was still present.

"Pensive, Maggie, pensive."

Her face, overflowing with tenderness, quickly changed; tiny worry lines appeared next to her mouth and around her deep blue eyes. Bakewell gave her an appreciative smile and looked at the dark remains of his glass. She didn't pursue it, and he didn't add more. They were quiet again. They were often quiet together. Conversation was always worthwhile between them. Occasionally there would be light humor, sometimes they bantered, but more often when they talked to each other the conversation was meaningful. They seldom talked about frivolous things; there was never a waste of words.

Maggie waited, dreading the subject, but knowing they needed to talk about it. She put her hand back on top of his. "I think the correct expression is 'a penny for your thoughts?'"

Bakewell was quiet for another minute, avoided looking at her before continuing. He loved to look into her eyes, but it wasn't the time for eye contact. "I was thinking about dying," he said. "More worrying than thinking, I guess." He pronounced his words very slowly, addressing them to the tablecloth. He straightened up looked at the hurt in her eyes. The subject of his health was put on hold after the wedding, like the fact that they were happy together would somehow cure him. But the time had come. He was still failing, and they both knew it.

"Oh Andy, please," she said passionately. "Why do you torture yourself so?" She had expected his answer, remembering the words from the second reading at Mass that morning. It was St. Paul's letter to Timothy – a farewell epistle, in which he had spoken of fighting the good fight, finishing the race, acquitting himself and being at peace, ready to meet God. Maggie had winced inwardly when the words were read, able to absorb his thoughts as he sat next to her listening to the words of the Church's first great orator. St. Paul had been the first itinerant preacher, a man who heeded the call and took the message to the people. His epistles were still read at nearly every Mass.

"I just feel like…I'm about out of time. I worry about the end." He knew he\ was reaching; she had become his last hope. She had been his last hope for some time, and he needed her confidence, her words were always reassuring. It was a cheap bid for sympathy, but he was frightened.

"You worry about the wrong thing. Try worrying about the rest of your life and the rest of us."

He looked again at the dark wine in his glass. "You're right, I know. I should be thinking of all of you." He looked into her lovely eyes. The candlelight flicked in their wetness. "This one's a big worry, though: the biggest one of all." He tried to smile back across the table. There were lines of pain around his eyes.

He was thinner and she had taken to teasing him about his shape as his weight dropped. It showed from his face to his feet. She'd teased him about his forearms and thighs being "sculpted." Said he looked like a Michelangelo sketch, complimented him on his leaning torso, but she knew the weight loss was ominous. He was losing his color too, despite her relentlessly exposing them to a daily bath of mountain sunlight. She detected a yellowing of his skin, was careful not to talk of it, until he finally told her he thought he had a blockage. The doctor had warned him it might happen.

Maggie was hugely relieved they were returning to St. Louis the very next day. They would drive down to Calgary in the morning, catch the mid afternoon flight, which would put them in St. Louis the next evening. The arrangements were made. The kids would be at his home for a long overdue homecoming. The following morning he would check into the hospital for the first round of tests. Michael and Andy had worked out some kind of arrangement. Bakewell suspected "a contest of wills." Michael had told Maggie, in what she described as a near exuberant moment, that he had drawn the "lucky straw." He would be the donor.

"Andy, didn't you listen to the gospel Sunday?" she asked, sounding incredulous. "Jesus was seeking consolation when He asked Martha who she thought He was. She told him she believed He was the Son of God and He answered 'he who believes in me, believes in the Father and he who believes in the Father *will...have...ever-lasting...life.*'"

Bakewell looked at his wife, his expression filled with doubt.

"You believe in the Father. You have faith. You've received the sacraments faithfully all your life, received reconciliation; you've done your penance. You're married in the Church – no more *illicit sex outside of marriage!*" She hissed the last, in a low voice, raising her eyebrows for emphasis, smiling impishly. He was silent. "You receive the Eucharist every day. Andy, *you're in the state of grace*!"

"I'm sorry," he said dubiously. "You know I struggle. I guess I always will." He shrugged. He'd been doing it throughout the conversation. "I just don't feel like I've fought the good fight, you know?"

"No. I don't know. I don't understand?"

"I just don't feel like I've finished the race. No, that's not right. I've finished all right. I just feel like I left a lot out, and there isn't time to make up for it."

"Have faith; it's enough. You'll be ready to go when the time comes.

But I'm not letting you go. You have a long time left. Trust me." She dabbed her eyes with the huge white napkin. "Trust, have trust. When it happens you will be ready."

"Just hold my nose and jump?" he chided. It didn't work.

Taking his cue, she raised herself up and put her shoulders back against the chair. Her posture was always excellent, but when she straightened up fully, her breasts filled the beautiful quiviuk sweater, stirring a need in him, taking his mind off his fearful dilemma. She pretended to be strapping herself in. "When the time comes you just take a deep breath, and you fasten your seat belt, as Ned likes to say, and 'you just blast off!'" She raised her hands wide for emphasis. "We all have to do it. Nobody gets to stay behind, you know. Have faith." She appeared to raise up even straighter and smiled as her arms went up. "You just do it. Don't worry about it."

Bakewell returned the smile, couldn't help it. She was infectious. She was a joy to talk to, to be with, even when talking about death. But he was still frightened. It showed, and he knew it showed, and he didn't try to hide it.

"How can you doubt?" she said, coming back down, her voice lower. "It's your faith. You've practiced it all of your life. It's what you believed and lived all this time. When the time comes you will be ready."

"I wish I could believe that, Kaa...," his voice trailing off; he looked away across the room.

"Maggie."

"What?"

"Maggie. You started to call me Katherine."

He slumped in his chair.

"Don't be sorry. It's sort of a compliment." She looked at her place then straight into his eyes with an intensity he had grown accustomed to, appreciated beyond telling. She was his rock. "I love you so, Andy."

He shook his head, disgusted and troubled by his carelessness, his never ending preoccupation with himself.

Maggie was amused by his predicament. It was so much lighter than the other. "Don't worry about it, Joe." She said, leaning in over the table.

"Somehow I don't think that makes us even."

"Want to bet? I'll get even with you tonight. I'll scream Joe's name when you make me have another one of those wonderful...those wonderful events you create in my life. You'll see."

"I will look forward to that," he said sincerely, amazed by the love and affection she poured out to him. She was incredible and he was incredibly lucky to have her.

"Thank you." She sat back and looked at him smugly. "Do you want to leave now and have terrific sex with me or do you want to continue this morbid conversation about your inevitable trip to hell?"

"No more conversation." He shook his head, feeling desperately sorry, desperately in love with her.

"Then let's leave now and walk back under a beautiful starlit sky and think how lucky we are."

Bakewell paid and they left the big room, taking time to wander slowly through the old building and look once more out the huge windows at the fantastic views beyond, views just perceptible in the long shadows cast by the moon and bright stars overhead. When they came out the front entrance, he took her hand and kissed it affectionately for everyone to see. They were surrounded by the usual gaggle of activity in front of the giant hotel. They began a leisurely walk back down the hillside past the lighted courts where a few inveterate players made ball-bouncing, shoe-squeaking sounds that were quickly soaked up by the forest.

Maggie had redone her hair for the wedding; she looked radiant under the lamplight. Her eyes sparkled; her face was full of joy. She swung his hand in an exaggerated fashion. She wore the same basket weave strollers she had worn at the beach and she was in the rich, nearly white quiviuk outfit she had worn the night of their wedding. The necklace he had given her at Christmas dangled over the high, loose turtleneck and the earrings flashed occasionally in the lamplight. Her face was filled with happiness, her mood so gay it caused an ache in his chest. He was totally in love with her, totally in love with the idea of being in love again.

"You are my strength and my energy. As long as I have you, I have a future."

"Andy, no more talk of dying. I've listened you out on the subject for the last time. I know you're scared and I understand – even if I don't understand why you worry for your soul. But I'm not letting you die. When we get home you will get cured by a wonderful doctor. He will be some kind of medical genius. And he will send wildly extravagant bills for his doctorly skills. And you will fuss and complain about the damned money, and when you're well again, you will probably fuss and complain about the way I keep house and cook your food, and about my drinking, and later I'll get really old and have to watch you, to make sure you're faithful. But we will be just deliriously happy together until the day I die, and I won't ever, ever, ever let you be afraid to be happy again."

Bakewell was content, walking next to her, holding her warm hand, thumbing her wedding ring gently. The mood had passed. It always did. He was thinking about what they would do when they got home. She was sexy and sensuous again. He was thinking about that too. The alcohol always had that effect early in the evening, and they usually ended up in bed at just the right time. It was in total contrast to the way it was when he was younger. Then the timing was never right. They were running late this night but the timing was always perfect in Banff.

"You think I would cheat?"

"Well, I chose you because of your track record, but I'll keep a sharp eye out when I start to droop."

"That was it, huh? Fidelity won the day? It wasn't my social skills?"

They had stopped under one of Banff's street lamps in a pleasant residential section. She leaned her head back in an exaggerated way and nodded with great emphasis. She was pleasantly inebriated. "That was it, pal. Fi-del-i-tee. I don't think I could bear the thought of loving a man who cheated on me." They started to walk again and she added, "You know I never once cheated on Joe. Not once. Even when we stopped being intimate. And I had lots of offers."

"Not once?"

She bit her lower lip, smiled. "Well, maybe just once," she laughed and began to swing his hand again in a wide arc. "But it was a President, after all. It was my patriotic duty."

They continued a few more steps before he stopped her, faced her squarely. He didn't ask. He didn't have to. He just looked into her face, which was like looking into her soul, and she burst into laughter and turned and dragged him along down the street after her. He pulled her to a second stop, but it wasn't easy. He didn't have the strength he once had, and she had the momentum.

"You are kidding. Right?"

"I'm kidding," she said. She threw her arms around his neck and hugged him and kissed him hard on the mouth and then backed away and punched him gently in the stomach. They resumed the walk. After a few more steps she spoke quietly under her breath, "But *you'll* never know for sure, big boy."

They were silent. He pondered her words. She added, again very quietly "and I'll never reassure you, *'on that you can rely.'*" She looked up at the trees and tried to whistle the melody of *As Time Goes Bye.* She couldn't whistle and he laughed at her attempt. Maggie was amused too, satisfied now with the conversation. She began humming another tune. She was better at humming. Bakewell listened, joined her. They did a complete refrain.

"What is the name of that song?"

He thought about it, began to sing the words quietly, she joined him.

Won't you tell him please to put on some speed, follow my lead, oh how I need...

"Someone To Watch Over Me?"

"That was too easy, but still *very good.* I didn't know you knew the words, Andy."

They continued on for another block before he said, "You know, you don't owe me any reassurance, Maggie. You don't owe me anything."

"*YOU GOT THAT RIGHT*, Mister," she said enunciating each word. "I *don't* owe you. And you do owe me – big time. So from here on out, I am the boss of this marriage and you do what I say."

"I can make that deal without hesitation," he added, with his own emphasis. "Maggie, I *never want to make another decision as long as I live."*

"You got it!"

He was having trouble keeping up with her. In her ebullience she walked faster. She noticed, and slowed as they came to the bridge, falling in step with him, not wanting to bring attention to his jading condition, and not wanting the evening to end. They strolled across the lighted bridge span. It was a beautiful structure, made with native stones. It had wide sidewalks that allowed flocks of tourists to ford the Bow on foot. They walked on down to her intersection without speaking. When they got to the traffic light she turned to him.

"Andy, I know you're tired and I want you to be honest with me," she straightened his collar, patted his chest affectionately. "I want you to tell me if you're too worn out to go on. Just tell me if you are. But I would love to walk around the park and down along the river one last time. We could come around under the bridge to the little dead-end street, and take the path we always take up from the river to get home." She looked up at him, eyes bright in the lamplight, a pleading in her sweet face. "We can do it tomorrow if you want, but I don't want to wear you out with a walk on such a long day of travel. Please tell me if it is too much."

He put his arms around her and hugged her gently. He knew she couldn't get enough of his affection. "We'll make one last walk around this mildewy old park, but you have to promise me something, boss. Promise me you will bring me back up here next year on this very day – when I am well, and bitching and complaining about everything – and we will do it all over again?" Her eyes sparkled along with her earrings, which glittered in the lamplight. "I want to eat the same dinner, on the same night. We'll even stay at the old hotel. It'll be my treat. We'll use my AARP discount."

She took his arm and hugged it to her cheek. She pushed it upward as she hugged it, more holding him up than holding onto him. They went down Buffalo Street on the north side of the park and found the old asphalt path, wrinkled by years of tree roots and traffic, turned on down to the river. After a hundred yards she asked. "Andy, do you think your children will welcome me into your home?"

"No, they don't like you. They will be filled with resentment." She chuckled deep down in her throat, but was uncertain, despite his weak humor. "Don't be dopey," he teased. "*Will your children welcome me, Andy?* No, Maggie. They will call you terrible names and close the door in your face, like Denny Murphy used to do."

"I know Denny Murphy! I know him. I met him at your funeral. He was at your funeral, Andy. He gave Nancy a big hug, and she introduced us; he gave me a hug. He was a darling man."

"He just wanted to feel you up. That's how big guys do it, with big hugs." Bakewell looked at her.

"He was big, all right."

"Really, Denny hugged you?" She nodded. "Denny Murphy is the finest man alive; he and Ned Grant. You're making me want to live again, you know, if only to see the look on those two big dumb faces. Boy there will be some stuff hitting the fan when I see them."

"I think they like me."

"Who wouldn't?"

"I'm talking about your children. I think they will welcome us into their lives – even you – the father that ditched us all."

"You're more right than wrong there. I have some explaining to do. I hope they let me get well first. I'm not up to it right now."

"They will be thrilled to see you again. You'll see. What are you going to tell them?"

"Anything but the truth."

She hugged his arm tighter. "Do you think that's smart?"

"No."

"Then what will you tell them?"

"I don't know. Maybe you could make something up while I'm recuperating, while Michael and I are both recuperating. God, I hate to think what that kid is going to be going through for me, if they decide to cut us both open."

"Are you kidding? They were lined up to donate. They think of it as a privilege. The one who does the donating is the lucky one. Michael will be the envy of his brother and sister the rest of his life."

"Yeah well, you've heard me say it before; he gets it from his mother."

"Oh, don't I know," she said, looking off toward the moonlit mountains. "We all know his father never amounted to much," she added impishly, finishing her thought then looked back across the river at the current moving the dark water under the lights. "He's going to hell you know."

Bakewell chuckled despite himself. There was a patch of cumulus clouds about to cross over the peaks again, moving fast. Bakewell shuddered to think what the wind chill up there would be. It was so pleasant in Banff. They continued on along the dark river. There was a residential area just across the way, a few hundred yards off. The lights of the homes reflected on the water.

As they approached the bridge span, the area underneath was dimly lit by the street lamps, mostly in shadows now. It was getting dark. It was also getting wet, condensation beginning to form in the cooling air. When they came up to the span, a figure roused from the boulders in the shadows. It was the kid Bakewell had given his sleeping bag to, probably still sleeping there in among the boulders under the span. The kid tried to stand, stumbled, fell down to the path below, making a loud, head-cracking sound.

"Oh Andy!" Maggie said, letting go of him. She rushed forward, leaving Bakewell in trail.

As the kid struggled to get up, Maggie bent down to help him. Bakewell heard the sharp crack of a revolver, came forward instinctively, catching Maggie with his right arm as he slammed into the assassin with his left shoulder. The impact sent the puny kid sprawling across the gravel path, the weapon clattered on the wet stones.

Bakewell pulled Maggie toward him; she had gone totally limp. He curled his arm around her, cradling her neck as her head fell back inertly. There was no expression; her face had gone completely slack, the light gone out of her eyes. In the middle of her chest a dark stain was spreading out into the wool sweater.

"Maggie?" Bakewell asked stunned, not wanting to comprehend the magnitude of what had happened to the lifeless form he held in his arms. He gasped her name a second time, just once, barely audible then threw his head back, looked up at the lamplight above, turned his head about violently, not wanting to recognize, mindlessly seeking anything that might give some relief.

He lowered her from him, looked again, hoping it wasn't true, her beautiful sweater, off white, so bright in the light, filling rapidly, the blood flowing from her, soaking the wool. He pulled her back to him tightly, knowing she was gone, knowing when he felt the blood and heard the terrible sucking noise coming from her chest, she was gone. Her loss so sudden, so unexpected, it sucked the life from him, the suddenness of it. A moment before she was his joy, his life. Now she was his agony, warm and soft and so tender, bleeding in his arms, gone, forever gone in an instant. The pain pulled a deep groan up from within him. He couldn't scream for help, couldn't ask God for a quick fix, knew it was futile, had no words to call out – out of air, sucked dry, the tragedy of her limp body in his arms. He lifted her to him and squeezed her tightly, as tightly as he ever had, ever could, trying to deal with the shattering hurt. He lowered her back away from him again to see if it had really happened. Her head fell back and her earrings sparkled in the lamplight and he groaned again, deep, aching, pulled her close again there under the bridge, kneeling.

***

There was movement to his left. He saw the kid, dazed, trying to get up. He wasn't feeling any pain, wasn't feeling anything, looked confused and frightened. He was obviously unaccustomed to violence, shocked by what had happened, but too stoned to feel anything, even remorse. He made a move, just perceptible. Bakewell saw the gun on the pavement next to him. The kid froze. Bakewell tried to focus on the gun through the miasma of his grief.

The kid's eyes were glazed over; it was obvious even in the dim light. He was motionless. Bakewell looked at the gun again, short, snub-nosed, hammerless – one of the ugliest, most offensive weapons ever made. He looked at the kid again, at the gun, put his foot against the weapon, careful not to lower Maggie to the ground, balancing on foot and knee and against the warm, lifeless body of his wife. He shoved the handgun hard and it went scraping across the wet pavement toward the kid, tumbling over once. The kid didn't move.

"Pick it up! Do it! Pick it up!" He nodded toward the gun. The kid moved slowly. "Pick it up! Hurry! You don't have much time."

The wasted young man moved across the pavement sideways, like a wounded crab, looked at Bakewell again before he picked up the gun. Bakewell nodded, motioned for him to come on.

"Do it!" he hissed. "Get over here!"

The kid came forward slowly.

"Here! Behind me!" Bakewell shouted.

When the kid came over behind him, he said, "In the back of the head. Don't miss! In the back of my head!"

A look of recognition came into his eyes. He was about to commit another murder, unsure if he wanted to, unsure if he had done the first one. He lifted the gun. He was left-handed.

"After you leave, go down the river... Throw the gun out in the river! Don't go back to anything you ever knew. Never go back where they can find you. And forget about the money. They aren't going to give it to you anyway."

Bakewell returned his cheek to Maggie's, pressing it against hers, still warm, his chest as wet as hers now.

"In the back of the head," he said to the wet pavement, squeezing Maggie tightly to him. "Do it!" He kissed her cheek and her forehead, closed his eyes and pressed her close one last time and waited.